Reed College Library

D0951419

THE BEST TALES OF
Hoffmann

Kapellmeister Kreisler

THE BEST TALES OF

Hoffmann

BY E.T.A. HOFFMANN

Edited with an Introduction by
E. F. BLEILER

Dover Publications, Inc., New York

This Dover edition, first published in 1967, is a
new selection of ten stories by E. T. A. Hoffmann.
The material has been reprinted without abridg-
ment.

Translations used are those of Major Alexander
Ewing ("Automata," "Nutcracker and the King of
Mice," "Tobias Martin, Master Cooper, and His
Men," "The Mines of Falun," "The King's Be-
trothed"); J. T. Bealby ("The Sand-Man," "Rath
Krespel," "Signor Formica"); Alfred Packer ("A
New Year's Eve Adventure"); and Thomas Carlyle
("The Golden Flower Pot").

These stories were selected and edited by E. F.
Bleiler.

Illustrations in the text are drawings by E. T. A.
Hoffmann, reproduced from W. Steffen and Hans von
Müller, *Handzeichnungen E. T. A. Hoffmanns in
Faksimiledruck*, Berlin, 1925 (Plates 10, 24, 25, 35).

International Standard Book Number: 0-486-21793-0

Library of Congress Catalog Card Number: 67-18740

Manufactured in the United States of America
Dover Publications, Inc.
31 East 2nd Street, Mineola, N.Y. 11501

INTRODUCTION

I

Toward the end of September, 1814, a literary supper was being held in one of the best restaurants in Berlin. Julius Hitzig, a Berlin publisher who was something of a patron of the arts, was host, and among the guests were Ludwig Tieck, Adelbert von Chamisso, Baron Friedrich de la Motte Fouqué, and Philipp Veit. The first three men practically composed the literary wing of the Late Romantic movement in Germany, while Veit was an important painter. Also present was a small wiry man with large, deep-set eyes, sharp features and short bristly hair. He was introduced to the company as a Doctor Scholz of Rathenau. The mobile features of his deeply lined face were in perpetual motion, so that he gave the illusion of being a succession of men rather than one individual. His hands and feet, too, shared this activity, and the simile may have occurred to the others at the banquet that he was like a stick puppet in his movements. Equally restless was his conversation: bon mots, witticisms, flights of fantasy emerged in a tumble as the wine began to flow.

Conversation was not the only entertainment, however, for the twin Marcuse sisters arose and sang arias and duets from the opera *Undine*, a recently finished work that had not yet been performed. It was fitting music, since the opera was based on Fouqué's novel *Undine*, which had been set to music by E. T. A. Hoffmann. After the music was over, however, the high point of the banquet came. Hitzig arose, and attracting attention, said, "Friends, Kapellmeister Johannes Kreisler is here among us!" He signalled to "Doctor Scholz" who was then revealed as the foremost Romantic music critic, Ernst Theodor Amadeus Hoffmann.

Johannes Kreisler was a magic name to this group. For the past few years a series of brilliant articles about music had appeared in the journals, written under the transparent device of papers by an imaginary violinist and conductor, Kreisler. "Kreisler" was not only an excellent writer; he was also a remarkably perceptive critic who was highly skilled in musical technicalities, profound in his interpretations, and (as it proved later) almost always right in his judgments.   Kreisler ranged more widely over music than had any previous German critic, and he was the first to establish new standards to fit the new cultural era.   He did not write in terms of absolute rules derived from 18th-century France; he considered the individual needs of the work and the listener's emotional response. Unfortunately, the story went, Kreisler's nervous constitution was so delicate and so finely balanced that he was perpetually on the edge of breakdown; indeed, at times he did break down.   This disability, the story continued, was not wholly unfortunate, for it was the cause of the almost pathological sensitivity that made Kreisler such a novel, perceptive critic.

It soon became known that Kapellmeister Kreisler was the creation and in some ways the reflection of one E. T. A. Hoffmann, a former member of the Prussian civil service, who had been a casualty of the Napoleonic Wars, and was now trying to make a living as a composer.   And although the guests at Hitzig's party did not know it, they were welcoming to Berlin a man who was soon to become the foremost Late Romantic writer and one of the world's greatest storytellers.

Ernst Theodor Wilhelm Hoffmann had been born in Königsberg, East Prussia, in 1776.   A member of a family with strong legal connections, he had attended the University of Königsberg to study law.   At this time Kant was still living and teaching at the university, and his thought permeated the entire school.   While Hoffmann did not formally take courses from Kant, it still seems certain that he attended occasional lectures.   More interesting to him than law or philosophy, however, were the arts, and Hoffmann pursued with equal diligence and intensity music, painting and literature.   He graduated with a very high standing in 1795, and a few months later, in midsummer, passed the first examinations for the Prussian civil service.

It might have seemed that a pleasant, profitable life lay ahead of Hoffmann, for he was personable, remarkably social, hard-working, and one of the most gifted and versatile men of his generation, but there was a certain instability in his mental constitution that persistently overturned his abilities and brought him into trouble.   In his later life he drank much too heavily; at this period, in 1796, an affair with a married cousin made it necessary for him to leave town.   This established a recurrent pattern: hard work, achievement, trouble, exile or flight, and a new start.

Hoffmann's first period of exile lasted nearly four years, and was spent at Glogau, a small Baltic town, where he served as a judicial aide, worked hard at his music (finishing his first opera, *Die Maske*), assisted in a local dramatic society, and continued in his civil service examinations. He received marks of exceptional excellence in his third series for the post of Assessor.

In 1800 he was transferred to Posen, which was at the time an administrative center in Prussian Poland. Here he found congenial company, and continued his music and painting. He wrote a cantata, which was performed, and did a dramatic version of Goethe's *Scherz, List und Rache*. For two years this uneventful life continued, until Hoffmann created a new crisis for himself. The military and civilian authorities in Posen were not on the best terms, and clash after clash had taken place between the two organizations, who had divided authority. Hoffmann took part in this feuding, and was indiscreet enough to caricature the commanding general as a drummerboy beating a teapot with a spoon. The military were outraged and complained to Berlin, and Hoffmann, who was now a candidate for promotion, came close to degradation. His superiors finally relented: he was simply transferred out of the comforts of Posen to a muddy village in Central Poland named Plock.

From the end of 1802 to April, 1804, Hoffmann and his new wife, Maria Röhrer, vegetated in the wilderness. The only good thing that could be said about Plock was that it gave Hoffmann time to work undisturbed at his music and to begin to write critical articles.

In April, 1804, a new factor entered Hoffmann's life: his intimate childhood friend Theodor von Hippel, who had inherited great wealth, a title in the Holy Roman Empire, and by marriage had acquired political influence. Although Hippel, what with the wars and political upheavals, eventually lost much of his wealth and power, he always retained enough to intervene in future instances of Hoffmann's indiscretion and temper any punishment. In this instance Hippel finally managed to have Hoffmann transferred out of Plock to Warsaw, which was a center of intense cultural activity. Here Hoffmann soon became a prominent figure in the musical world. He founded an orchestra and conducted the works of Gluck, Mozart, and Beethoven. From 1805 and Warsaw comes his first piece of important music: the incidental pieces to his friend Zacharias Werner's *Kreuz an der Ostsee*. Hoffmann's score, with its wild, braying trombones and rumbling drums, has been called the first really Romantic music.

Napoleon, however, destroyed this pleasant period. By the middle of 1806 the French had defeated the Prussians and taken Warsaw. French administrators took over from the Prussians, and Prussian officialdom was out of work. Just before the French arrived, it is true, the Prussian officials had seized the treasury and divided it among themselves in lieu of salary, but the amount of money each received did not last very long, especially for Hoffmann.

Hoffmann now tried to make his living as a professional musician in Warsaw, and composed prolifically. His first symphony, the E major, was popular for a time, while his chamber music, sonatas and other compositions, many of which are now lost, also circulated considerably. Life was very difficult, however, and Hoffmann was seriously considering moving to Vienna when the French authorities began to be worried about subversive activities. They demanded that all the former Prussian officials take an oath of allegiance. Penalty for refusal was deportation within a week. Hoffmann refused to take the oath, and in June, 1807, he was deported to Berlin, while his wife and infant daughter remained in Warsaw.

Such financial difficulties as he had experienced in Warsaw were mild compared to his plight in Berlin, where he really came close to death. At one time only the help of his friend Hippel saved him from starvation. To make matters worse, a pestilence broke out in Poland, in which his daughter died. Day-to-day chores, including musical hackwork, set painting for the stage and similar odd jobs, kept him and his wife (who had joined him) alive until the spring of 1808, when he was offered the position of theatre musical director in Bamberg in Southern Germany.

Bamberg, to the Romanticists of the day, like Nuremberg, was a sort of semisacred shrine, for it had been one of the stimuli a generation earlier which had set off the Romantic movement. Two of the most important Romantic writers, Ludwig Tieck and Wilhelm Wackenroder, when young men, had left their northern homes and had wandered on foot like pilgrims through the countryside to the medieval towns of South Germany. These towns, with their Medieval and Renaissance survivals, quiet somnolescence, and religious pageantry were still practically terra incognita to the Enlightenment culture that pervaded other parts of Germany. Not that others had not been there; simply that for the first time Nuremberg and Bamberg were interpreted as remnants of a very pleasant, very colorful way of life rather than as barbarism unredempt. Out of Tieck's and Wackenroder's experiences emerged much of the strong medieval tinge that pervaded so much early 19th-century German literature.

For Hoffmann, too, Bamberg proved to be a mind-opening experience, although he never shared the enthusiasm for the Middle Ages or the nationalistic extravagances that at times beset his contemporaries. His experiences with the local theatre, however, were not all pleasant, for the orchestra and the personnel seem to have been inefficient and riddled with politics. A change in the management improved the theatre, and Hoffmann soon showed himself to be a remarkably imaginative director and producer. In addition to preparing musical settings for the plays he produced, he was instrumental in staging Shakespeare and Calderón, as well as the German classics.

Until April, 1813, Bamberg remained the center of Hoffmann's activities. He continued writing music beyond his duties at the theatre, including the opera *Undine*, which was his most important musical work. It was based on a highly romantic nouvelle of a water nymph who died for love, written by Hoffmann's future friend, Baron de la Motte Fouqué. Hoffmann also began to devote himself more and more to writing. During his unhappy Berlin period he had established contact with the *Allgemeine musikalische Zeitung*, issued by the great musical publishing house Breitkopf and Härtel, and he began to contribute articles regularly. "Ritter Gluck," his first successful attempt at fiction, appeared there in 1809, as did his famous Kreisler papers. This series, which consisted of musical criticism mixed with fictional elements, became enormously popular, though not very profitable for Hoffmann financially. He also wrote about one hundred long reviews and translated a book from French. Hoffmann was always hard-working, no matter what his manner of relaxing.

During his off-duty moments Hoffmann scintillated with his boon companions in the Rose Tavern, and was soon recognized as the "drink master" of the town. (It is said that when he left Bamberg his wine bill at the Rose was enormous.) Here he spent his social evenings, and also many of his days for he wrote his music and prose at one of the inn tables.

Yet the Bamberg period was not entirely happy. He was physically ill much of the time, and often depressed, at times almost to the brink of collapse. In Bamberg, too, occurred one of the peculiar crises that kept disturbing his life. Since the death of his child he and his wife had been growing apart, for his wife's gifts

were domestic rather than intellectual.   He became infatuated with
a 16-year-old girl named Julia Marc, to whom he was giving music
lessons.   She was apparently a superb musician as well as a handsome, charming and intelligent girl.   Julia seems to have liked
Hoffmann, although there are no indications that the acquaintance
between her and the middle-aged musician ever became a physical
affair.   Her family were worried about the situation, however,
and managed to marry her off to a merchant from another town.
Hoffmann never saw her again after her marriage in 1812, and he
felt her loss bitterly.   He now began to seek about for ways to leave
Bamberg.

   In April, 1813, Hoffmann and his wife set out for Dresden, where
he had been offered the position of musical director in the theatre.
The Napoleonic Wars broke out again, and Hoffmann found himself trapped in Dresden without the work he had been promised.
After great difficulty the Hoffmanns were passed through the opposing armies to Leipzig, where Hoffmann joined the theatrical
company.   For something like a year and a half he alternated
between Leipzig and Dresden, according to the schedule of his
company, and the location of the troops of the various nations.
During this period Hoffmann watched the battles at close range, for
he seems to have been physically fearless.   He was once wounded
while exposing himself recklessly.   He also conducted his operatic
troupe, was on intimate terms with an Italian company with whom
he shared the billing (and from whom he probably absorbed much of
the Italian operatic spirit that permeates his work) and quarreled
with his superiors in the opera house.

   During this Dresden–Leipzig period, Hoffmann's literary work
assumed more and more importance, while music receded into the
background.   His last major piece of music was the so-called
Battle Symphony, in which he tried to relate musically his own
experiences at the Battle of Dresden.   His first published book
appeared in separate volumes during this period: *Fantasiestücke in
Callots Manier*.   It was published by a wine merchant named Kunz.
It is a characteristic note that Hoffmann sold his rights not for
money, but for a cellar of wine.

   During 1813 and 1814 Hoffmann's best work alternated with some
of his poorest.   "The Golden Flower Pot" ("Der goldne Topf"),
which almost all critics now consider his best work, was followed by
"Ignaz Denner," which many consider his worst.

   The final period of Hoffmann's brief life began in the fall of
1814, when his deus ex machina, Baron Hippel, rescued him once

again. Hoffmann was recalled to Berlin; his sins were forgiven him; and he was given a meagre entry into official life. He was authorized to work at the Kammergericht (the Prussian Supreme Court), but without pay. It seems to have been understood that if he proved satisfactory, he would eventually receive a formal, paid appointment. In May, 1816, Hoffmann received his permanent appointment, and since his seniority dated from 1802, when he had first received his certificate, he soon became the chairman of the court. It would seem that Hoffmann should now be out of financial trouble, what with such an appointment, but his mode of life kept him heavily in debt. His literary work made the difference between occasional solvency and duns.

During this Berlin period, from 1814 until his death in 1822, Hoffmann continued to produce criticism and fiction. Much of his work appeared in periodicals, although two major books appeared during this period. *Die Serapionsbrüder* (*The Serapion Brethren*) was a collection of stories, connected by narrators and critics who represent Hoffmann himself (in different projections) and his friends. It appeared in separate volumes from 1819 to 1821, and contains much of his best work. *Die Elixiere des Teufels* (*The Devil's Elixir*), his most ambitious novel, appeared in 1816. It is an enigmatic blend of M. G. Lewis's *Monk* and Romantic theories of personality fragmentation and individuation. In his musical career, his opera *Undine* was finally performed in August, 1816, and was entirely successful, although a fire destroyed the costumes and sets and even part of the score, so that it could not be performed any longer. Hoffmann hoped to rewrite the music and redesign the sets, but did not live long enough to do so.

Despite his appetite for drink and good companionship, Hoffmann was a first-rate administrator and judge, well versed in the law, very conscientious and just. This conscience was to cause him, indirectly, his next crisis. Hoffmann had been appointed by the King of Prussia to a commission to investigate subversive activities after the end of the Napoleonic adventure. Under subversion were included political liberalism, French sympathies, support of Napoleon, local nationalism and many other areas of thought and action. Hoffmann, who was unpolitical and not a nationalist, still took the "Voltairean" position that others had rights to their opinions; he refused to take part in a witchhunt. The King thereupon formed a second committee of investigation, with powers and duties that overlapped with the first. The two committees collided almost immediately.

The immediate source of Hoffmann's approaching downfall was the case of "Father" Jahn, the founder of the Turnverein movement, which combined gymnastics with violent nationalism. Hoffmann's committee investigated Jahn and discharged him as innocent. The second commission, however, immediately placed Jahn under arrest again, thereby creating an impossible legal situation. Hoffmann, who disliked Jahn and his movement, felt that injustice was being done, and undertook to interrogate the second commission. The situation became so tense that the King was forced to intervene. What with the publicity that the incident had received, the King was forced to support Hoffmann's group, no matter what his own wishes may have been.

Hoffmann won this battle, but lost on a larger field. Just as he had made enemies in Poland by drawing cartoons of the military authorities, he now very foolishly satirized his principal opponent in *Meister Floh*, a novel he was then working on. He was even indiscreet enough to boast of his action. *Meister Floh* was being printed in Frankfurt, which was then a different country, so that diplomatic representations went back and forth between Prussia and Frankfurt as the Prussians worked to have the book suppressed. Hoffmann tried to save the situation by proposing alterations, but his attempt was taken as an admission that his work was improper. He was then cited for trial for unbecoming behavior.

Hoffmann now seemed lost, but his friend Hippel intervened once again. Since Hoffmann was by now quite far along the path of the sickness which was to prove mortal, the process was a perfunctory discussion in Hoffmann's own house. Hoffmann escaped with an official reprimand, a serious enough punishment, but as circumstances turned out he did not live long enough to receive it.

Hoffmann's health had started to break down before 1820. He had long had digestive difficulties—which were not helped by heavy drinking and overwork—and his liver became more and more troublesome. By the end of 1821 he was quite seriously ill, and to his liver degeneration was added a neural disorder which is not diagnosable with any precision, but seems to have been tabes dorsalis. Paralysis set in early in 1822, beginning with his legs, then his hands, and finally much of his body. His finances approached bankruptcy, and he found it necessary to continue working up to his deathbed. He dictated the last portions of *Meister Floh*, worked upon further stories and, optimistic to the end, was planning new series of reminiscences by the Tomcat Murr and Kreisler.

He died on June 25, 1822, not long after dictating "Die Genesung" ("Recovery").

II

Music was Hoffmann's first love and his true love. He tried to make a living as a composer, but was forced to take up literature as a livelihood. Yet even in his later life, when his income was assured with fiction, he invoked music in his stories whenever possible. He delighted in writing about the lives of musicians, in comparing the music of his day with that of the past, and in analyzing the dynamics of musical creation and performance. In honor of Mozart he changed his middle name from Wilhelm to Amadeus.

His unique mixture of literary and musical gifts made him the foremost music critic of the day. He had an almost unerring ear for the best in music, and his papers containing the analyses and estimations of his character and mouthpiece Kreisler were eagerly read and discussed all over Germany. He was one of the first to recognize the merits of J. S. Bach, and one of the first critics to support Beethoven intelligently, for which he received a very laudatory letter from Beethoven. He also anticipated the critical work of both Carl Maria von Weber and Robert Schumann. Schumann acknowledged his debt by calling one of his piano works *Kreisleriana*.

As a composer, however, Hoffmann was more productive and less successful than as a critic. His known works include some ten operas; incidental music to more than a dozen plays; much vocal music, including two masses, several cantatas and many motets; a considerable amount of piano and chamber music; two symphonies, and quite a bit of miscellaneous work. No one really knows how much music he wrote, for most of it was never published and has been destroyed or lost.

Hoffmann was not a great composer, according to E. Istel and Hans Ehinger, two musicologists who have studied his work thoroughly. He was an excellent technician whose work somehow lacked the fire and spontaneity and brilliance of his prose—in other words those characteristics that made him a world figure in literature. It has been said that his music sounded much like Mozart's (with a little Beethoven and Cherubini added), but without Mozart's genius. Hoffmann was also unfortunate in maturing late. At about the time that he achieved a relatively personal style, he was forced to abandon music as a serious mode of life. Yet at times Hoffmann apparently did reach a high level. His opera *Undine* was revived occasionally in Germany before World War II, and it is said to have been a capable work, on the whole very pleasing.

Even if Hoffmann was not a great composer, his music was extremely important historically, for he was the first Romantic composer. It has been said that Weber and Schumann and even Wagner stand on his shoulders musically. Hoffmann may have been the first to write an opera on Germanic folklore; he certainly anticipated Weber. He was perhaps the first to create unusual program sound effects, as in his incidental music to Zacharias Werner's *Kreuz an der Ostsee*, where braying instruments imitated the crashing waves and conveyed in this vivid manner the spirit of the pagan Lithuanians. In his use of new harmonies and progressions he is said to have anticipated Wagner, who was acquainted with both his music and prose. Unfortunately, none of Hoffmann's music ever seems to have been recorded, so that we must remain content with accounts and evaluations of it at first remove.

Paradoxically, despite the death of practically all his own music, Hoffmann still remains very much alive in music, for his stories have been a fruitful source for operas.

The best-known of the operas derived from Hoffmann is, of course, *Les contes d'Hoffmann* by Jacques Offenbach. Offenbach's last work and his first true opera, it uses a libretto by two veteran French dramatists, Jules Barbier and Michel Carré, who based their work on French translations of Hoffmann. In Offenbach's opera Hoffmann himself is the hero and he narrates his experiences in love, thereby integrating several stories into a single biographical plot. The first episode, the adventure of the dancing doll, is adapted from "The Sand-Man"; the second, the famous Venetian episode with the barcarolle, from "A New Year's Eve Adventure"; the third, the story of the singer Antonia, from "Rath Krespel." Other stories contribute less important elements: the ballad which Hoffmann sings about Kleinzach of Eisenach is based on the story "Klein Zaches genannt Zinnober"; the name Pitichinaccio comes from "Signor Formica"; the Miracle Doctor who kills Antonia is a combination of traits from "Signor Formica" and other stories.

Before writing *Les contes d'Hoffmann*, however, Offenbach had set another story by Hoffmann to music, a light opera called *Le Roi Carotte*, libretto by Sardou. It was a political satire on Napoleon III, based on incidents from "The King's Betrothed" and "Klein Zaches." Some forty years after Offenbach's death (1919) a third

Offenbach–Hoffmann opera was created by Julius Stern and Alfred Zamara, who adapted music from Offenbach's *Corsaire Noir* and minor works to a libretto based on Hoffmann's "Das Fräulein von Scuderi." The resulting pastiche was titled *Der Goldschmied von Toledo*.

Other operas based on Hoffmann's work include *Die Brautwahl* by Ferruccio Busoni (performed 1912); *Prinzessin Brambilla* by Walter Braunfels (performed 1909); *Der goldne Topf* by Wilhelm Petersen (performed 1940); *La Poupée de Nuremberg* by Adolphe Adam (performed 1852); *La Poupée* by Edmond Audran (1896-7); *Nussknacker und Mausekönig* by Carl Reinecke; and Paul Hindemith's *Cardillac* (first version, 1926), which is based on "Das Fräulein von Scuderi."

In the ballet, too, Hoffmann's work has been important. Delibes's *Coppélia ou la Fille aux yeux d'émail* is based on the dancing doll in "The Sand-Man." Tchaikovsky's *Nutcracker (Casse-Noisette)*, based on Hoffmann's "Nutcracker and the King of Mice," is familiar to all. In this case Tchaikovsky worked with Alexandre Dumas père's translation and adaptation of Hoffmann's story rather than with the original.

It is as a writer of fiction, however, that Hoffmann stands as a figure of first importance. His stature was recognized at an early date outside Germany, and not too long after his death his work was extensively translated into French, in which language it spread widely through Europe. Russian literature was especially influenced by Hoffmann, with all the major figures in the later 19th century heavily indebted to him. Dostoievsky, for example, frankly admitted his debt, particularly in psychological matters. In the English-speaking world, however, Hoffmann has been less fortunate. Although certain major authors like Scott, Carlyle, Poe, and Hawthorne have known his work, translations into English have been few, poor, and difficult to obtain.

Some of Hoffmann's fiction was written hastily, under time pressures, to pay for expensive wines, to settle tavern bills, or, as a last resort, to pay living expenses. As a result he wrote potboilers, stories that lack the Hoffmann touch and might have been written by one or another of the minor fiction writers of the day. An odd point about these stories is not that they date from a period of immaturity, as might have been guessed if their dates were not known, but that they are sandwiched in among his best work.

Hoffmann's best work, however, is sui generis. There are few writers who can match him where the principle of Serapionism is

concerned—the technique of presenting the supernatural convincingly. He can arouse momentary conviction and acceptance for even
the most outrageous fantasy, leading the reader, as in "The Golden
Flower Pot," from the prosaic Biedermeier streets of Dresden into the
wildest wonderland achieved in literature up to his time. The
greatness of his achievement here can be seen by comparing his work
with the Romantic short stories that preceded it. Hoffmann is
also a very subtle writer, with a remarkable ability to merge levels
of explanation, blending literalistic fantasy with allegory, symbolism,
philosophy, and the psychology of the day. The result is a very
personal amalgam which is worlds removed from the crudities of
The Horrid Mysteries and similar Gothic material that stimulated
him when he was young. And yet he is often elusive and tricky,
and the reader may often discover that he has not always fathomed
Hoffmann's true meaning at first reading.

Technically, Hoffmann at his best was very strong. Characterization was one of his fortes, and strange personality after personality
emerged from his pen. No matter what their origin—whether very
deliberate embodiments of contemporary psychological theories, or
fragments of himself, or caricatures of his friends, or whatever
else—they carry conviction. Experimental forms in which stories
are told from the point of view of the "wrong" character, where
letters alternate with editorial reflections, where essays on musicology
interrupt the narrative, where characters split and combine, where
his characters reflect back on Hoffmann's works—all of these are
handled masterfully. Hoffmann usually remains in control and
does not lose his individuality or become swallowed in confusion as
so often happened to his Gothic prototypes.

In imagination, too, Hoffmann has few peers. The little touches
of fantasy—like the remarkable ambassador from the Vegetable
King in "The King's Betrothed," the magical battle between the
Archivarius and the witch in "The Golden Flower Pot," the
sorcerous duel of the microscopists in *Meister Floh*, the theatrical
world of 17th-century Rome in "Signor Formica"—these are
among the parts of Hoffmann's work which will always be cherished.

Yet Hoffmann does have faults, despite his many excellences.
He is sometimes too sentimental, particularly when he is writing
under the influence of Jean Paul Richter. This sentimentality,
however, is an isolated phenomenon, and seldom affects the hard
brilliance of his work. His experiments with form, in addition,
occasionally do not come off. At times he seems to have arrived at
the end of a story with no clear idea of how to close it convincingly.

In such cases he gives the impression of having cleared the stage as rapidly as he could, with some impatience. His personality sometimes obtrudes into his work, and he is not always a well-balanced writer. Much of his thought, if stripped below the narrative level, and, sometimes, placed in his life situation, is not pleasant. Goethe, who could admire aspects of "The Golden Flower Pot," applied to Hoffmann's work as a whole the 19th-century equivalent of "sick, sick, sick."

Still, if Hoffmann lacks the serenity and balance of a Goethe, and is an excited and exciting man, his very lack of balance often creates a drive and motion in his work that Goethe's sometimes lacks. Hoffmann is seldom dull. One of his strongest assets is his tremendous nervous energy and narrative drive; he must surely be one of the most rapid authors in all literature. His motion is breath-taking.

In the opinion of many modern scholars Hoffmann's work represents not only the last chronological work of the German Romantic period, but also its culmination. As Professor Ralph Tymms has pointed out, Hoffmann channelled the Romantic impulse, particularly the supernaturalism which was its heart, into a final bed from which it could not break. For Novalis the supernatural was numinous, poetic, and ethical; for the Schlegels it was philosophical and critical; for Tieck it was self-laughter; for the minor writers, it was emotion—thrills and longing; and for Hoffmann it was science. Once the misty ideas of the anti-Enlightenment were themselves organized into the clarity and logic of a legal brief, and the supernatural became merely a division of abnormal or depth psychology, the creative impulse could go no farther.

III

Most critics agree that "The Golden Flower Pot" ("Der goldne Topf") is Hoffmann's best story. Hoffmann himself considered it such, and while working on it, he wrote, "God grant me to finish the story as I have begun it. I have never done anything better; everything else is still and lifeless compared to it." Nowhere else has Hoffmann been so successful in blending the real and the fantastic as in this story, in which the powers of the supernatural world run rampant through Dresden.

"The Golden Flower Pot" first appeared in 1814 in *Fantasiestücke in Callots Manier*, Hoffmann's first collection of stories, and was revised slightly in 1819 for the second edition of the book. It is his

E. F. Bleiler

first major literary work, and it marks his unheralded emergence as an author of world stature after he had written only a few critical essays and semifictional musical critiques.

It is a many-leveled story, and as might be expected, a great amount of time has been spent in trying to interpret Hoffmann's intentions. Two opposing general interpretations have been the most favored: (1) that it is an optimistic story about the emergence of a poet, and (2) that it is a basically pessimistic story in which the sad problems of the poet are treated with irony. The proponents of optimism claim that this story mirrors Hoffmann's excitement and joy at his decision to turn to literature instead of to music for his livelihood. According to the pessimists, however, Hoffmann states that a poet must abandon the life of this world, marry a dream girl of his own projection, neglect all worldly advantages—and where shall he go? To Atlantis, the mythical kingdom that does not exist and never did exist. At present the pessimistic interpretation seems the stronger, especially since the text incorporates a letter which Hoffmann first wrote to accompany the story. In this letter he stated his discouragement at the turn that events had taken.

A modern reader, perhaps more than Hoffmann's contemporaries, is likely to find difficulty in isolating and evaluating the various levels of interpretation that lie within "The Golden Flower Pot." On the most superficial level, it can be read simply as a fantastic thriller, in which the supernatural emerges and invades the world of everyday life, just as supernaturalism within a pseudohistorical setting did in the Gothic novels that Hoffmann delighted in reading. Some of Hoffmann's minor fiction, indeed, is written on this level, but it is very unlikely that "The Golden Flower Pot" is to be taken this way.

Beyond the external events of magic in Dresden and the emergence of the elemental world of the Renaissance Rosicrucians, for example, there lie several themes that appear in much of Hoffmann's other work: that loss of faith or denial of revelation can be destructive; that there is a connection between madness and the suffering world; and that art and life do not mingle, but must be separated.

Individuation, in the modern psychological sense, offers one of the most plausible symbolic interpretations of "The Golden Flower Pot." This amounts to a statement (in fantastic terms) of character growth. It is thus the story of the awakening of poetic sensibility in Anselmus, and of the upheaval which the new developments cause in Anselmus's personality. According to this interpretation the incidents in the story are simply fictionalized metaphors. The old apple woman, Liese, is simply fear, and Anselmus's hesitation before the doorknocker which assumes her shape is simply a metaphoric way of saying that Anselmus became frightened and did not enter. Serpentina would stand for Poesy; the strange experiences in the boat and around the punchbowl are simply ironic ways of stating that all parties had had too much to drink and that alcohol evoked the demonic forces within each. The enclosure of Anselmus in a glass bottle simply describes the paralysis which occurs when faith and hope have been lost. According to this interpretation the entire story of "The Golden Flower Pot" is the projection of Anselmus's mind. His emergent sense of ecstasy colors and transforms everything he beholds, and the daily life of a staid, bourgeois early 19th-century city is seen as a mad scramble of occult powers, half-insane super-humans, strange perils and remarkable benisons as Anselmus becomes a poet.

Yet beyond this there are other possible levels of interpretation. It has been noticed that the characters and ideas of "The Golden Flower Pot" are arranged in two series, each with one pole in the world of reality and another in the world of fantasy. Indeed, there is even a sort of identity between the two forms: Serpentina with Veronica, Anselmus with the Registrator Heerbrand, Archivarius Lindhorst with Conrector Paulmann, and so on. According to this interpretation, Anselmus is simply a projection of the Registrator which disappears in the world of fantasy, while the Registrator, giving up his dreams, marries Veronica. She, in turn, recognizes that she cannot possess the Anselmus complex but must be content with the Registrator-turned-Geheimrat.

Both of these interpretations may seem to be far-fetched interpretation for its own sake, but the fact remains that some justification exists for them or comparable unriddlings. Hoffmann's work is permeated with the concept of personality fragments coming to separate identity and acting as characters. To quote one example which is beyond dispute, in Hoffmann's remarkable novel *The Devil's Elixir (Die Elixiere des Teufels)* the identities of two of the characters, the Monk Medardus and the Graf Viktorin, are so merged and interchanged that the characters themselves do not know where one begins and the other ends.

The heart of "The Golden Flower Pot" is the märchen, or literary myth, that the Archivarius begins in the tavern; it is concluded by a strange glossologia from an Oriental manuscript that Anselmus is copying. The archphilistine of the story calls this märchen

"Oriental bombast," but as the Archivarius replies, it is not only true but important. It recapitulates the central thought of "The Golden Flower Pot" sub specie aeternitatis, stripped of the accidentals of time, space, and personality.

The central idea of this märchen is the birth of poetry, expressed in terms of cosmic symbols drawn from the Naturphilosophie. It tells of the divine spark (phosphorus was the chemical symbol for the nervous fluid or intelligence in some of the systems of the day) which awakens and fertilizes a vegetative life. This in terms of mounting triads (a concept borrowed from the philosophical systems of the day) must die to give birth to a higher principle.

Lindhorst's märchen is thus a combination of several elements: a pseudobiblical creation statement; an allegory in which details have special meaning, although it is not always clear now what each point means; a fanciful statement of the human situation; and perhaps an ironic spoofing of some of the philosophical systems of the day. Hoffmann, although he was greatly interested in the outgrowths of Schelling's philosophy and accepted much of it, could be expected to retain a pawky incredulity at certain aspects of it. But perhaps analysis should not be pushed too far; it may be enough to say that this is a numinous statement of life, in which both profound and trivial concepts are fused.

German literature at the end of the 18th century frequently made use of märchen, or literary myths. These often appeared as symbolic kernels or germs within the larger context of a story, offering in a frankly poetic and mythical form the point offered more or less realistically in the full story. The märchen was thus a microcosm within a macrocosm.

This form and its use were not Hoffmann's invention. Goethe had written an independent allegorical story called "Das Märchen," which aroused a great deal of criticism among the Romantics, and Wackenroder had incorporated the fairytale of the Naked Saint in his *Herzensergiessungen eines kunstliebenden Klosterbruders.* Novalis, who represents the high point of the Early Romantic School in Germany, had incorporated two such märchen in his unfinished novel *Heinrich von Ofterdingen.* Novalis characterized the märchen as being "like a dream vision . . . beyond logic . . . an assembly of wonderful things and happenings . . . a [pregnant] chaos." This description fits his own work and Hoffmann's when it is remembered that chaos to the Romantics did not mean an empty waste as it usually does for us, but an infinitely rich, undifferentiated, undiversified "plasma," out of which universes could be formed.

All in all, it seems unlikely that there ever will be complete agreement about all the details of "The Golden Flower Pot." Perhaps Hoffmann himself was not entirely clear about his intentions. It would lie more within the realm of the Romantic movement to leave things in a tantalizing mist than to strip them of illusion. The symbol should be permitted to unroll and expand as it will. In any case, the modern reader can exercise his own judgment in deciding what really happened to Anselmus.

"Automata" ("Die Automate") first appeared as a whole in the *Zeitung für die elegante Welt* in 1814, although it was written between parts of "The Golden Flower Pot." It falls into two parts: the untitled Ghost Story in the foreword, and secondly, the experiences of Ferdinand with an automaton called the Talking Turk. There are also other elements in the story, notably an essay on the mechanical creation of music, new musical instruments and man's relation to music; Hoffmann is said to have included this material so that he could sell the story to a music journal.

The Ghost Story is built on two supernatural motives, one of which has had considerable importance in the history of the supernatural story. This is the motive of the White Lady, in which someone impersonates a ghost and receives supernatural punishment for his rashness. M. G. Lewis based his narrative of the Bleeding Nun in *The Monk* on this idea; it is the subject of one of the *Ingoldsby Legends*; and in more recent times Ambrose Bierce, E. F. Benson, W. W. Jacobs, H. Russell Wakefield and others have made effective use of it. In most instances, however, the story has been developed beyond Hoffmann's narrative, which remains at best sketchy. The second element in the Ghost Story is an attempt to defeat fate by distorting the time sense. It is related to an important literary form of the day, the so-called Fate Novel, the central idea of which was an attempt (usually unsuccessful) to dodge an inevitable fate.

In the second part of "Automata" much space is devoted to one of Hoffmann's idées fixes, the automaton or robot. The story reveals Hoffmann's own strong feelings when he describes the horror he feels at the possibility of mistaking an automaton for a human being. (This concept later became even more important in the episode of the dancing doll in "The Sand-Man.") For us much of the emotional power of Hoffmann's story may be lost since the late 18th-century and early 19th-century automata are now mostly destroyed or inoperative. We can have no real idea of their remarkable performances nor can we regain their emotional impact, since robots and mechanized intelligence have become part of our daily life. During Hoffmann's lifetime, however, Maelzel's chess player (which was a fraud) aroused a sensation in Europe, while Vaucanson's mechanical duck (a remarkable mechanism that would grace any era) and his speaking head and similar marvels of mechanics were held to be almost miraculous. The historical works of Chapuis and Droz can hint to the modern reader something of the wonder which these figures inspired. In Hoffmann they aroused a multiple reaction: admiration for their skill, horror at their inhumanness, and perhaps fear.

"Automata" remains a mystery story in the narrower acceptance of the form, for no convincing explanation can be given for the mysterious events that befall Ferdinand. Hoffmann's "explanation" of the functioning of the Turk involves clairvoyance, which is awakened through the mechanical medium of the Turk. This strange theory, which Hoffmann does not propound in the clearest way, is not his own, but was advanced by several early 19th-century psychologists to account for paranormal phenomena. It is connected with theories of animal magnetism derived ultimately from F. A. Mesmer on one side and from philosophical mysticism on the other. Even beyond the phenomena of the Talking Turk, however, are Ferdinand's adventures in Poland, which simply cannot be explained rationally.

"A New Year's Eve Adventure" ("Die Abenteuer der Silvester-Nacht") was written late in 1814 and was published in 1816 in Hoffmann's first collection of stories, *Fantasiestücke in Callots Manier*. It demonstrates a literary device that is very common in Hoffmann's work: the narration of two or more stories, which at first seem different, but upon closer examination prove to be the same story told on different levels. The two levels usually consist of the level of daily life and the level of fantasy, which are so intermingled that the reader sometimes is not sure of boundaries.

Just as the student Anselmus in "The Golden Flower Pot" lives two lives (one in the realm of poetry and the other around the Biedermeier establishment of Conrector Paulmann), the Travelling Enthusiast or Roving Romanticist of "A New Year's Eve Adventure" and Erasmus Spikher are polarities of the same personality and situation. One is set in humdrum Berlin, the other in the counterpole of Italy, which often appears in Hoffmann's work as a synonym for luxury and decadence. Whether Hoffmann was completely successful in telling his story in this way is open to dispute; at worst he tells two repetitive stories, at best his method offers a strange parallelism and fusion of experience. The mundane narrator confines the fantasy of Spikher and is in turn enriched by it.

Personal elements from Hoffmann's life are evident in this story. It was not too long after his unhappy association with Julia Marc in Bamberg that Hoffmann wrote "A New Year's Eve Adventure," and when he read it to his circle of friends in Berlin, as was his custom with new work, they must have recognized the reflection of Hoffmann's personal affairs in the story. Hoffmann pictures Julia in two facets, on the one hand a cold opportunist who did not even have vision enough to recognize the quality of her admirer and on the other hand as a witch of Satan.

Another element of Hoffmann's personal life appears here in the presence of the famous Peter Schlemihl, the character created by his close friend Adelbert von Chamisso. The story of Peter Schlemihl, who sold his shadow to the Devil, was one of the most famous and most popular stories of the day, and Hoffmann obviously admired it greatly. Many of the details of the episode in the Bierkeller acquire new depth if the reader is acquainted with Chamisso's story. Just what Peter Schlemihl lost, however, is no clearer in Hoffmann's story than it was in Chamisso's. For Chamisso, interpretations of Schlemihl's plight have ranged from poverty to statelessness, from loss of virility to the inability to form human associations. What Hoffmann considered the "shadow" is also mysterious; indeed, he evaded the question. Erasmus Spikher's lost reflection, on the other hand, is rather clearly identified with an alter ego, a dream-self, the ability to dream, a personality focus that is associated with dreams and passions. This story would then be another statement about the separateness of art and life.

The mechanisms that evoke the world of fantasy in "A New Year's Eve Adventure" are quite different from those in "The Golden Flower Pot." While it was the poetic impulse that awakened the ecstatic experience in Anselmus, in the Travelling Enthusiast/Spikher the impulse was alcohol. For Hoffmann there were several such doors to the supramundane world, and the type of door could condition the transcendent experience which was attained. In this theory Hoffmann simply stated in fictional terms what several of the psychologists and natural philosophers of the day said in more or less technical terminology. For such theorists the human autonomous nervous system, to which they assigned a center in the solar plexus, was an organ of experience which far transcended the sense organs of the conscious mind. This nervous system was the seat of a secondary, unconscious personality, which by its very essence was in intimate contact with all Nature. Normally, this Dream Self was silent, submerged by the clatter of the conscious mind, but in sleep, in religious ecstasy, in drug states, and in insanity it sent its energy up to the cortex, where it could be perceived. If this energy were controlled by the higher spiritual faculties of man, the result could be a great aesthetic impulse, or prophecy; if it were uncontrolled, it could be the distorted mumblings of the clairvoyant, or the unhappy visions of the addict. It is the lesser voice which inspires Spikher.

In the fall of 1816 Hoffmann finished "Nutcracker and the King of Mice" ("Nussknacker und Mausekönig"), which first appeared in a Christmas collection of children's stories entitled *Kindermärchen von C.W. Contessa, Friedrich Baron de la Motte Fouqué und E. T. A. Hoffmann*. The story was based in part on his own life situation: the family among whom the adventure takes place were modelled after the Hitzigs, friends of Hoffmann's Polish and early Berlin days. The two children in the story, Fritz and Marie, represent Hitzig's children. Hoffmann himself served as a prototype for Grandfather Drosselmeier, for he had built a cardboard castle for the Hitzig children the previous year, just as Drosselmeier does in the story. It might be noted that the same combinations of whimsy, aberration, ineffectuality, insight and ecstasy enter the character of Drosselmeier as enter the other masks of Hoffmann.

In "Nutcracker and the King of Mice" a märchen or literary fairytale serves as the "unconscious focus" of the story. It indicates the inner relationships in the ideal world that created the present story situation, together with possibilities for future resolution. In this case, however, the märchen is not a literary myth, as in "The Golden Flower Pot" or *The Master Flea*. It is basically a children's story, in which medieval Nuremberg receives one of its first glorifications. The concept linking this myth with the relationships Drosselmeier–Hoffmann and Stahlbaum–Hitzig is that a child is closer to the primal innocence (as in Wordsworth's "trailing clouds of glory") than an adult, and can enter and savor realms of experience or beyond-experience that even an adult with insight cannot enter. Dreams can become real only for children.

Hoffmann himself did not regard "Nutcracker and the King of Mice" as an entirely successful story, and apparently his friends agreed with this opinion. In the critical parts of *Die Serapionsbrüder* two of Hoffmann's characters, Lothar (a sceptic, modelled in part on Fouqué) and Ottmar (perhaps modelled on Hitzig), discuss the story. They conclude that the mixture of children's elements with elements that only an adult would appreciate is not completely acceptable. Hoffmann would have been better advised, it is stated, to have written either a children's story or a symbolic narrative for adults, not both. In a later story, "The Stranger Child" ("Das fremde Kind"), which was written for the Christmas annual of the following year, Hoffmann adhered more closely to a children's level. Despite this formal improvement the story itself lacks the vitality of "Nutcracker and the King of Mice," which has long been a favorite, both in itself and in its various musical and dramatic adaptations.

"The Sand-Man" ("Der Sandmann"), which appeared in *Nachtstücke*, Volume I (1816–1817), is one of Hoffmann's most bewildering stories. His contemporaries were inclined to read many personal references into it, and Hoffmann's friend Fouqué considered himself reflected in the personality of Nathanael.

There are many problems involved in "The Sand-Man." The first and greatest, of course, is the meaning of the story. Are Nathanael's adventures to be taken literally or symbolically? Is Hoffmann again using his old device of treating mental projections as personalities? Do the characters in the story exist, or are they fragments of personalities, or are both conditions true?

Psychiatrically oriented readers have considered Nathanael to be mad, and have dismissed the story of Coppelius/Coppola as a projection, as the influence of a traumatic childhood experience on an unstable young man. The story is thus interpreted as a figurative statement of growing mental illness, in other words, the emergence of insanity. Everything that Nathanael sees is distorted by this peculiar defect of his "vision," and his life is a succession of wild misinterpretations.

Other readers, however, have taken the position that Hoffmann intended the story to be primarily a fate drama, in which the central idea is that man is powerless against an external fate that moves in on him. According to this interpretation Nathanael was saved from death once by his father, once by Clara and her brother, but must succumb on the third occasion. Nathanael may go mad at the end, but his previous experiences are objective. Coppelius/Coppola really exists; he is the Enemy.

It would be pointless to select one of these interpretations and reject the other, since Hoffmann offered clues to support both. In all probability he had both interpretations in mind when he wrote the story, and was deliberately creating a mystery. A unifying factor can possibly be found in the saying, "Things are as we see them."

Many strange threads run through this story. One is the motive of the eye. Over and over Hoffmann brings the physical organ and its function (or malfunction) into the story: the eyes that appear during the experiment that Nathanael watches, Coppelius's threat to destroy Nathanael's eyes, the distorted vision of Nathanael when he assigns life to Olimpia, the destruction of the dancing doll's eyes, and the manifestations at the end of the story when Nathanael goes mad. Indeed, even the names Coppola and Clara are important: "coppola" means eye-socket in Italian, while the significance of Clara is obvious. Allied to the motive of eyes is the nature of the "experiments" performed by Coppelius and Nathanael's father. They are usually interpreted as alchemy or perhaps magic, but we cannot be sure of this. To Hoffmann's contemporaries this incident may simply have been a fanciful way of suggesting coining. Certainly the furnaces and cauldrons are all to be connected with casting.

"Rath Krespel" first appeared as an untitled story in the *Frauentaschenbuch für das Jahr 1818*, where it was prefaced by a long letter of dedication to Fouqué. It was revised a little when it was included in *Die Serapionsbrüder*.

One source of the story was Johann Bernhard Crespel (1747–1815), an eccentric German official who was a friend of the Goethe family and is mentioned in a letter from Goethe's mother to the poet. Crespel apparently designed his own clothing to fit his moods, and at one time designed and built a house in the same way as Hoffmann's Rath Krespel. How Hoffmann learned about Crespel is not known, although it has been speculated by H. W. Hewett-Thayer in his excellent *Hoffmann, Author of the Tales* that Hoffmann may have heard of him through Brentano. This, however, is only part of the personality of Krespel. It is generally conceded that an element of Hoffmann's own personality has been added to that of the historical Crespel. Hoffmann's Krespel is not really mad, but is very much like Hoffmann himself. He is really a man without a skin—as, indeed, Hoffmann describes him. Krespel's sensitivity is so great that daily life would be impossible for him if he could not take refuge in semi-madness to abreact his unconscious processes. Ultimately, he is really horribly sane.

Hoffmann's musical life is also reflected in this story, particularly in the clash of the Italian and German musical cultures of the day. Such a clash of musics is often described in Hoffmann's work. "The Interrupted Cadence" ("Die Fermate"), for example, describes a tempestuous affair between an Italian soprano and a German composer, who discover that there is no real possibility of understanding between them. Hoffmann himself shared such a tension between his admiration for the German tradition of Bach and Mozart on one hand, and his delight in Italian opera. It may be significant to Hoffmann's point of view that in "Rath Krespel" the ideal combination of power and beauty, Antonia, cannot survive; she bears within herself germs of destruction.

"Rath Krespel" is one of the most tragic of Hoffmann's stories, since it involves not only death, but the destruction of an art and the misery of sane insanity. Equally sinister is the equation of Antonia and the strange violin, and the life-bond between them. It would be curious to know if the name Antonia had any special significance for Hoffmann, what with Antonio Stradivari.

"Tobias Martin, Master Cooper and His Men" ("Meister Martin der Küfner und seine Gesellen") first appeared in the *Taschenbuch zum geselligen Vergnügen auf das Jahr 1819*, and was reprinted with some alterations in the second volume of *Die Serapionsbrüder* (1819). Like another of Hoffmann's stories, "Doge und Dogaressa," it is essentially a program piece written to explain a painting by a now nearly forgotten Romantic artist, Karl Wilhelm Kolbe. "Tobias Martin" was suggested by a very large oil entitled "Die Böttcherwerkstatt," which shows a group of coopers in antique costume working in an open shed. Hoffmann's story creates the background against which this picture situation arose, and also carries the situation through to a resolution. Hoffmann thereby transmuted an academic painting into one of the most entertaining stories in early 19th-century German literature.

The source for Hoffmann's information about medieval Nuremberg and the meistersingers and early guilds was Johann Christoph Wagenseil's *De sacri romani imperii libera civitate Noribergensi Commentatio*, or *Chronicle of Nuremberg*, which later became more famous as the source for Wagner's *Die Meistersinger*. This same book also served as the source for Hoffmann's well-known story about a homicidal maniac motivated by aesthetic impulses, "Das Fräulein von Scuderi," which has been variously translated under the titles "Mademoiselle de Scuderi," "Cardillac the Jeweller," "Cardillac," and so forth.

In "Tobias Martin, Master Cooper," as in most of his historical nouvelles, Hoffmann used a straight-line mode of narration which contrasts greatly with the involved avant-garde development of his fantasies, what with their double narratives, symbolic cores and fragmentations of personality. Yet even here there are unusual features. Another author might have told the story more strongly from the point of view of Friedrich, and might have pushed Meister Martin, the title figure, more into the background. Another artist might have treated Martin's "growth" and his interpretation of the mysterious prophecy a little less ambiguously. At times it almost seems as if the story cannot be permitted to end until all of the major characters have learned that they must be honest with themselves.

"Meister Martin" has long been a favorite, and around the turn of the present century it was usually regarded as Hoffmann's best story. It has since fallen in esteem, while the fantasies have risen. To me it seems unfortunate that Hoffmann confined himself to writing "program fiction" simply to elucidate a mediocre painting. If the story had been independently written, it might be stronger in central situation and less sentimental. Nevertheless, the basic personalities of the story emerge with charm and clarity, and Hoffmann evokes the personality of Nuremberg so attractively that the story has served as the suggestion for much other work, chief of which is Richard Wagner's *Die Meistersinger*.

"The Mines of Falun" ("Die Bergwerke zu Falun") first appeared in 1819 in *Die Serapionsbrüder*. In a critical afterword to the story one of Hoffmann's spokesmen tells where the idea came from: an anecdote in G. H. Schubert's *Ansichten von der Nachtseite der Naturwissenschaften*, one of the most influential books of the day. According to Schubert, when miners opened a new tunnel in the great Swedish mine complex at Falun, they found the perfectly preserved body of a man dressed in archaic garments. Hoffmann was one of many writers who seized upon this incident as the kernel for a story, and the basic idea became as important for the early 19th century as the motive of the Frozen Pirate was at the turn of the 19th and 20th centuries.

Hoffmann's story is written against a background that is strikingly romantic in its concepts and associations. Starting with Novalis (Count Friedrich von Hardenberg), prophet of German Romanticism, the miner as such took on a peculiar significance in German literature. He was not considered to be an exploited toiler or a laborer in a particularly dirty and dangerous mode of work. He became a quasisupernatural being who knew the intimate secrets of nature, of creation, and of the fructifying force that was believed to create the minerals. His knowledge passed beyond that of ordinary men, and he had a touch of the divine or demonic about him. Novalis in his *Heinrich von Ofterdingen* says of miners and mining, "Possessors of a much-envied happiness in learning nature's hidden mysteries, and communing in solitude with the rocks, her mighty sons. . . . It is enough for the miner to know the hiding places of the metallic powers and to bring them forth to light; but their brilliance does not raise thoughts of covetousness in his pure heart. Untouched by this dangerous madness, he delights more in their marvellous formations, the strangeness of their origin, and the nooks in which they are hidden. . . . His business cuts him off from the usual life of man, and prevents his sinking into dull indifference as to the deep supernatural tie which binds man to heaven. He keeps his native simplicity, and sees in all around its inherent beauty and marvel. . . . In these obscure depths there grows the deepest faith in his heavenly Father, whose hand guides and preserves him in countless dangers. . . . He must have been a godlike man who first taught the noble craft of mining, and traced in the rocks so striking an image of life." Novalis's comments are not simply a literary device; there are also elements here of the ancient magic associated with metals and minerals (as Mircea Eliade has discussed them in his *Forge and the Crucible*) which persisted strongly up through the Renaissance.

For Hoffmann, the miner owes allegiance to a supernatural power personified as the Metal Queen. The heart of the story is Elis's rejection of the metal revelation. Once again the artist (as in many other stories by Hoffmann) must choose between loss of his supernatural aims and the death of the domestic man. The agent of Elis's death, the demonic Torbern, is really a creature out of Germanic literary folklore. Many of the Numbernip (Rübezahl) stories by Fouqué, for example, discuss folkloristic demons as erratically malevolent beings who are associated with the chthonic powers and serve both to lead and mislead man.

"Signor Formica," or "Salvator Rosa," first appeared in late 1819 in the *Taschenbuch zum geselligen Vergnügen auf das Jahr* 1820, and was reprinted with minor changes in the fourth volume of *Die Serapionsbrüder*. It was subtitled a "novella," and probably was written with the work of the Italian Renaissance novelists in mind. One of the critics in *Die Serapionsbrüder*, however, criticized it as resembling Boccaccio more in the beatings its characters received than in much else. Another facet of Hoffmann defended the story mildly by pointing out that both Cervantes and Boccaccio did not hesitate to propel their stories by physical violence.

For "Signor Formica," which in many ways is one of Hoffmann's most interesting stories, Hoffmann drew upon the life of the great 17th-century Italian painter Salvator Rosa. At the time that Hoffmann wrote, Rosa stood high critically. The early Romantic revival of the late 18th century found him congenial. His well-known *terribilità*; his devastating energy; his highly felt painting technique and subject matter, in which the forces of nature seemed to be the real subjects, with but a few scattered humans as symbolic punctuation; and his general evocation of untamable, dynamic violence—all aroused enthusiasm. Rosa's life was reasonably well known in Hoffmann's day, and Hoffmann made a thorough study of French, Italian, and German sources. To get local color and to create the atmosphere of Italy, Hoffmann read extensively in travel accounts, particularly the reminiscences of Karl Philipp Moritz, an 18th-century German traveller. Hoffmann also collected Italian prints and maps, which he hung on the walls of his rooms, for inspiration, just as his character Peregrinus Tyss in *Meister Floh* does for China. Hoffmann, of course, was saturated in Italian musical life, and for this needed no special sources.

Basically "Signor Formica" is accurate—with occasional liberties—although the personality of Antonio Scacciati and the incidents of his courtship are fictitious. Salvator Rosa did leave Naples a few steps ahead of the police because of his share in Masaniello's insurrection; he did act as a member of a commedia dell' arte group in Rome; and he did later found an accademia in Florence. Like Hoffmann himself the historical Rosa was a virtuoso in many media: painting, literature, music, and the stage. Today, however, he is a nearly forgotten member of a branch of Baroque painting.

One of the most curious aspects of "Signor Formica" lies in its use of the double or doppelgänger. Originally, the doppelgänger was an element of Germanic folklore. It amounted to seeing one's own ghost, an exact double of oneself: this meeting was usually an omen of death. (In origin this idea would seem to go back to the primitive idea of multiple souls and soul-loss as a cause of death.) Around the end of the 18th century the doppelgänger became an important element in German fiction. The sinister elements were often suppressed and in their place came an intellectual interest in seeing oneself. The most curious incident involving a doppelgänger came from the life of Goethe: the great poet believed that on several occasions he had seen his own doppelgänger.

For Hoffmann the doppelgänger had a special significance. It was not simply a mysterious, supernatural double; instead it was associated with the strange phenomena of the mind, with personality fragments, with multiple personalities (a phenomenon which interested early 19th-century psychologists) and with emergence of an unconscious mind. In story technique this meant that a personality complex could assume spontaneous, autonomous life and become a character itself. From a converse point of view, two persons who were physically nearly identical might fuse, to form a single personality, or to create an impermanent, rotating personality which shifts from pole to pole of identity. This is the case in *The Devil's Elixir* where two persons in a doppelgänger relationship to one another contaminate each other. At times this concept of the doppelgänger (as in Jean Paul's *Doppelgänger* and Goethe's *Wahlverwandschaft*) can become attenuated enough to drop the idea of likeness or identity, and to indicate inner relationships, like "elective affinities" in the chemistry of the day. This results in a horizontal concept of kinship as opposed to a vertical one. The strongest bonds of relationship are between persons who are similar rather than those of vertical blood descent. Persons in a doppelgänger relationship are *sympathetic* (in the derivational sense of the word) to one another's experiences. A later stage of this idea, familiar to us from Dumas' novel, is the motive of the "Corsican brothers"—identical twins, perhaps separated Siamese twins, who both feel pain if one is injured, no matter how far apart they may be.

In "Salvator Rosa" Hoffmann makes use of the doppelgänger motive in a novel way. The idea is now completely secularized and stripped of its supernatural associations, and as stage imposture it serves to resolve the story. The confrontation of a lecherous old miser with his double twice dissolves the frame of difficulties that beset Antonio and Salvator Rosa.

All in all, Hoffmann's story is successful in evoking the atmosphere of baroque Italy, with its violence, egotism, saturation in the pictorial arts, and devotion to music. It is probably not an exaggeration to say that in this respect "Salvator Rosa" is the most successful historical novel that had yet appeared in Europe. Where Hoffmann may have lagged somewhat in literary technique (as compared with, say, Goethe), he was ahead in the intuitive apprehension of alien times and places which was so characteristic of the German Romantics from Herder on. As a result, his picture of 17th-century Italy carries conviction. In other respects, however, the novel suffers a little from Gothic survivals. The concept of the hero as one "der nie als Held des Stückes, sondern nur als Vermittler" forces Antonio Scacciati to have a passive role, while Salvator Rosa, the demonic activist, initiates and creates. The point would seem to be that the artist can succeed in his work and his love-life only with the assistance of a daimon. To a modern reader, this peculiar plot device may make the story seem less a true nouvelle than a narrative, but the fact that "Salvator Rosa" is written to an unfamiliar aesthetic need not impair our pleasure in reading it.

"The King's Betrothed" ("Die Königsbraut") was written especially for the last volume of *Die Serapionsbrüder* (1821). Each volume of the collection ends with a fantastic story, and "The King's Betrothed" concludes Volume IV and the set on a note of fantasy. It is very heavily ironic in tone, and it satirizes several contemporary phenomena: bad poets, particularly the sickly sentimental poets of a school parallel to the English Della Cruscans; ineffectual, ivory-tower mystical philosophers and philosophy; and stories describing erotic relationships between mortals and supernatural beings. Of such stories Fouqué's *Undine* is the most famous.

The subject matter of "The King's Betrothed" has been taken from Renaissance and Enlightenment books on occultism and magic, an area in which Hoffmann was well-read. The doctrine of Paracelsus and others in this tradition was that the natural forces were the product of ideal substances, which were personified as supernatural beings, usually called elementals because of their relationship to the Aristotelian elements: salamanders as the spirits or essence of fire; undines for water; sylphs for the air; and gnomes for the earth. Slightly variant classifications may be found in the several sources. Hoffmann found the precise origins of his system and many of the ludicrous historical details about human-elemental relationships in one of the early books associated with the Renaissance Rosicrucian movement, *Le Comte de Gabalis*, an eccentric novel by the Abbé Montfaucon de Villars. Yet beyond this occult background is Hoffmann's probable intention of showing a personality (Aennchen) who has submerged herself in the vegetative life so deeply that it emerges separately and tries to swallow her.

In this edition all ten stories have been edited slightly: a few errors and mistranslations have been corrected and a few omissions rectified. I have also tried to restore something of the briskness and modernity that is to be found in Hoffmann's German text. It is somewhat unfortunate that most of Hoffmann's translators were Victorians, who unconsciously equated the archaic and the fantastic. Whereas Hoffmann's German is usually simple, modern in vocabulary and contemporary in feeling, his translators all too often have rendered him into an English that is complex, curious, and sometimes tedious.   This may seem to be an academic point, but this recasting of Hoffmann by his translators has resulted in the loss of three of his greatest gifts: nervous energy, hard clarity of expression, and narrative flow.   In German Hoffmann is one of the most rapid authors; in English, he often seems to be slow.

I have tried to correct this situation somewhat by removing the "thees" and "thous" and other archaisms that tend to retard the story flow, and by simplifying some of the involved constructions, which are often more intricate than the German itself.   All this, of course, involves another problem—the degree to which one can edit another man's work and still leave it his.

Thomas Carlyle, whose version of "Der goldne Topf" is included, has been a special problem.   In many ways his translation is a work of genius, and yet it is also at times a bad translation.   His Scottish dialect and linguistic willfulness are not only disturbing in themselves, but seem to have corrupted many of the later translators. The problem here was to remove as much of the Scottishness and eccentricity as damaged Hoffmann, and yet not destroy Carlyle. Perhaps this cannot be done.

This present volume, it would seem to me, is best considered an interim edition, prepared to satisfy a need until something better emerges.   Hoffmann deserves to be retranslated into modern English in a manner that retains his strengths.

E. F. BLEILER

New York
1966

CONTENTS

ILLUSTRATIONS

All illustrations in the text are drawings by E. T. A. Hoffmann.

THE BEST TALES OF
Hoffmann

THE GOLDEN FLOWER POT

On Ascension Day, about three o'clock in the afternoon in Dresden, a young man dashed through the Schwarzthor, or Black Gate, and ran right into a basket of apples and cookies which an old and very ugly woman had set out for sale. The crash was prodigious; what wasn't squashed or broken was scattered, and hordes of street urchins delightedly divided the booty which this quick gentleman had provided for them. At the fearful shrieking which the old hag began, her fellow vendors, leaving their cake and brandy tables, surrounded the young man, and with plebian violence scolded and stormed at him. For shame and vexation he uttered no word, but merely held out his small and by no means particularly well-filled purse, which the old woman eagerly seized and stuck into her pocket.

The hostile ring of bystanders now broke; but as the young man started off, the hag called after him, "Ay, run, run your way, Devil's Bird! You'll end up in the crystal! The crystal!" The screeching harsh voice of the woman had something unearthly in it: so that the promenaders paused in amazement, and the laughter, which at first had been universal, instantly died away. The Student Anselmus, for the young man was no other, even though he did not in the least understand these singular phrases, felt himself seized with a certain involuntary horror; and he quickened his steps still more, until he was almost running, to escape the curious looks of the multitude, all of whom were staring at him. As he made his way through the crowd of well-dressed people, he heard them muttering on all sides: "Poor young fellow! Ha! What a vicious old witch!" The mysterious words of the old woman, oddly enough, had given this ludicrous adventure a sort of sinister turn; and the youth, previously unobserved, was now regarded with a certain sympathy. The ladies, because of his fine figure and handsome face, which the glow of inward anger rendered still more expressive, forgave him his awkwardness, as well as the dress he wore, though it was at variance with all fashion. His pike-gray frock was shaped as if the tailor had known the modern style only by hearsay; and his well-kept black satin trousers gave him a certain pedagogic air, to which his gait and manner did not at all correspond.

The Student had almost reached the end of the alley which leads out to the Linkische Bath; but his breath could no longer stand such a pace. From running, he took to walking; but he still hardly dared to lift an eye from the ground, for he still saw apples and cookies dancing around him, and every kind look from this or that pretty girl seemed to him to be only a continuation of the mocking laughter at the Schwarzthor.

In this mood he reached the entrance of the Bath: groups of holiday people, one after the other, were moving in. Music of wind instruments resounded from the place, and the din of merry guests was growing louder and louder. The poor Student Anselmus was almost ready to weep; since Ascension Day had always been a family festival for him, he had hoped to participate in the felicities of the Linkische paradise; indeed, he had intended even to go to the length of a half portion of coffee with rum and a whole bottle of double beer, and he had put more money in his purse than was entirely convenient or advisable. And now, by accidentally kicking the apple-and-cookie basket, he had lost all the money he had with him. Of coffee, of double or single beer, of music, of looking at the pretty girls—in a word, of all his fancied enjoyments there was now nothing more to be said. He glided slowly past; and at last turned down the Elbe road, which at that time happened to be quite empty.

Beneath an elder-tree, which had grown out through the wall, he found a kind green resting place: here he sat down, and filled a pipe from the Sanitätsknaster, or health-tobacco-box, of which his friend the Conrector Paulmann had lately made him a present. Close before him rolled and chafed the gold-dyed waves of the fair Elbe: on the other side rose lordly Dresden, stretching, bold and proud, its light towers into the airy sky; farther off, the Elbe bent itself down towards flowery meads and fresh springing woods; and in the dim distance, a range of azure peaks gave notice of remote Bohemia. But, heedless of this, the Student Anselmus, looking gloomily before him, blew forth smoky clouds into the air. His chagrin at length became audible, and he said, "In truth, I am born to losses and crosses for all my life! That, as a boy, I could never guess the right way at Odds and Evens; that my bread and butter always fell on the buttered side—but I won't even mention these sorrows. But now that I've become a student, in spite of Satan, isn't it a frightful fate that I'm still as bumbling as ever? Can I put on a new coat without getting grease on it the first day, or without tearing a cursed hole in it on some nail or other? Can I ever bow to a Councillor or a lady without pitching the hat out of my hands, or even slipping on the smooth pavement, and taking an embarrassing fall? When I was in Halle, didn't I have to pay three or four groschen every market day for broken crockery—the Devil putting it into my head to dash straight forward like a lemming? Have I ever got to my college, or any other place that I had an appointment to, at the right time? Did it ever matter if I set out a half hour early, and planted myself at the door, with the knocker in my hand? Just as the clock is going to strike, souse! Some devil empties a wash basin down on me, or I run into some fellow coming out, and get myself engaged in endless quarrels until the time is clean gone.

"Ah, well. Where are you fled now, you blissful dreams of coming fortune, when I proudly thought that I might even reach the height of Geheimrat? And hasn't my evil star estranged me from my best patrons? I had heard, for instance, that the Councillor, to whom I have a letter of introduction, cannot stand hair cut close; with an immensity of trouble the barber managed to fasten a little queue to the back of my head; but at my first bow his unblessed knot comes loose, and a little dog which had been snuffing around me frisks off to the Geheimrat with the queue in its mouth. I spring after it in terror, and stumble against the table, where he has been working while at breakfast; and cups, plates, ink-glass, sandbox crash to the floor and a flood of chocolate and ink covers the report he has just been writing. 'Is the Devil in this man?' bellows the furious Privy Councillor, and he shoves me out of the room.

"What did it matter when Conrector Paulmann gave me hopes of copywork: will the malignant fate, which pursues me everywhere, permit it? Today even! Think of it! I intended to celebrate Ascension Day with cheerfulness of soul. I was going to stretch a point for once. I might have gone, as well as anyone else, into the Linkische Bath, and called out proudly, 'Marqueur, a bottle of double beer; best sort, if you please.' I might have sat till far in the evening; and moreover close by this or that fine party of well-dressed ladies. I know it, I feel it! Heart would have come into me, I should have been quite another man; nay, I might have carried it so far, that when one of them asked, 'What time is it?' or 'What is it they are playing?' I would have started up with light grace, and without overturning my glass, or stumbling over the bench, but with a graceful bow, moving a step and a half forward, I would have answered, 'Give me leave, mademoiselle! it is the overture of the *Donauweibchen*'; or, 'It is just going to strike six.' Could any mortal in the world have taken it ill of me? No! I say; the girls would have looked over, smiling so roguishly; as they always do when I pluck up heart to show them that I too understand the light tone of society, and know how ladies should be spoken to. And now the Devil himself leads me into that cursed apple-basket, and now I must sit moping in solitude, with nothing but a poor pipe of——" Here the Student Anselmus was interrupted in his soliloquy by a strange rustling and whisking, which rose close by him in the grass, but soon glided up into the twigs and leaves of the elder-tree that stretched out over his head. It was as if the evening wind were shaking the leaves, as if little birds were twittering among the branches, moving their little wings in capricious flutter to and fro. Then he heard a whispering and lisping, and it seemed as if the blossoms were sounding like little crystal bells. Anselmus listened and listened. Ere long, the whispering, and lisping, and tinkling, he himself knew not how, grew to faint and half-scattered words:

"'Twixt this way, 'twixt that; 'twixt branches, 'twixt blossoms, come shoot, come twist and twirl we! Sisterkin, sisterkin! up to the shine; up, down, through and through, quick! Sunrays yellow; evening wind whispering; dewdrops pattering; blossoms all singing: sing we with branches and blossoms! Stars soon glitter; must down: 'twixt this way, 'twixt that, come shoot, come twist, come twirl we, sisterkin!"

And so it went along, in confused and confusing speech. The Student Anselmus thought: "Well, it is only the evening wind, which tonight truly is whispering distinctly enough." But at that moment there sounded over his head, as it were, a triple harmony of clear crystal bells: he looked up, and perceived three little snakes, glittering with green and gold, twisted around the branches, and stretching out their heads to the evening sun. Then, again, began a whispering and twittering in the same words as before, and the little snakes went gliding and caressing up and down through the twigs; and while they moved so rapidly, it was as if the elder-bush were scattering a thousand glittering emeralds through the dark leaves.

"It is the evening sun sporting in the elder-bush," thought the Student Anselmus; but the bells sounded again; and Anselmus observed that one snake held out its little head to him. Through all his limbs there went a shock like electricity; he quivered in his

The Student Anselmus and Conrector Paulmann (detail from illustration following page 230).

inmost heart: he kept gazing up, and a pair of glorious dark-blue eyes were looking at him with unspeakable longing; and an unknown feeling of highest blessedness and deepest sorrow nearly rent his heart asunder. And as he looked, and still looked, full of warm desire, into those kind eyes, the crystal bells sounded louder in harmonious accord, and the glittering emeralds fell down and encircled him, flickering round him in a thousand sparkles and sporting in resplendent threads of gold. The elder-bush moved and spoke: "You lay in my shadow; my perfume flowed around you, but you understood it not. The perfume is my speech, when love kindles it." The evening wind came gliding past, and said: "I played round your temples, but you understood me not. That breath is my speech, when love kindles it." The sunbeam broke through the clouds, and the sheen of it burned, as in words: "I overflowed you, with glowing gold, but you understood me not. That glow is my speech, when love kindles it."

And, still deeper and deeper sank in the view of those glorious eyes, his longing grew keener, his desire more warm. And all rose and moved around him, as if awakening to glad life. Flowers and blossoms shed their odours round him, and their odour was like the lordly singing of a thousand softest voices, and what they sang was borne, like an echo, on the golden evening clouds, as they flitted away, into far-off lands. But as the last sunbeam abruptly sank behind the hills, and the twilight threw its veil over the scene, there came a hoarse deep voice, as from a great distance:

"Hey! hey! what chattering and jingling is that up there? Hey! hey! who catches me the ray behind the hills? Sunned enough, sung enough. Hey! hey! through bush and grass, through grass and stream. Hey! hey! Come dow-w-n, dow-w-w-n!"

So the voice faded away, as in murmurs of a distant thunder; but the crystal bells broke off in sharp discords. All became mute; and the Student Anselmus observed how the three snakes, glittering and sparkling, glided through the grass towards the river; rustling and hustling, they rushed into the Elbe; and over the waves where they vanished, there crackled up a green flame, which, gleaming forward obliquely, vanished in the direction of the city.

SECOND VIGIL

"The gentleman is ill?" said a decent burgher's wife, who, returning from a walk with her family, had paused here, and, with crossed arms, was looking at the mad pranks of the Student Anselmus. Anselmus had clasped the trunk of the elder-tree, and was calling incessantly up to the branches and leaves: "O glitter and shine once more, dear gold snakes: let me hear your little bell-voices once more! Look on me once more, kind eyes; O once, or I must die in pain and warm longing!" And with this, he was sighing and sobbing from the bottom of his heart most pitifully; and in his eagerness and impatience, shaking the elder-tree to and fro; which, however, instead of any reply, rustled quite stupidly and unintelligibly with its leaves; and so rather seemed, as it were, to make sport of the Student Anselmus and his sorrows.

"The gentleman is ill!" said the burgher's wife; and Anselmus felt as if someone had shaken him out of a deep dream, or poured ice-cold water on him, to awaken him without loss of time. He now first saw clearly where he was, and recollected what a strange apparition had assaulted him, nay, so beguiled his senses, as to make him break forth into loud talk with himself. In astonishment, he gazed at the woman, and at last snatching up his hat, which had fallen to the ground in his transport, was about to make off in all speed. The burgher himself had come forward in the meanwhile, and, setting down the child from his arm on the grass, had been leaning on his staff, and with amazement listening and looking at the Student. He now picked up the pipe and tobacco-box which the Student had let fall, and, holding them out to him, said: "Don't take on so dreadfully, my worthy sir, or alarm people in the dark, when nothing is the matter, after all, but a drop or two of christian liquor: go home, like a good fellow, and sleep it off."

The Student Anselmus felt exceedingly ashamed; he uttered nothing but a most lamentable Ah!

"Pooh! Pooh!" said the burgher, "never mind it a jot; such a thing will happen to the best; on good old Ascension Day a man may readily enough forget himself in his joy, and gulp down a thought too much. A clergyman himself is no worse for it: I presume, my worthy sir, you are a *Candidatus*. But, with your leave, sir, I shall fill my pipe with your tobacco; mine was used up a little while ago."

This last sentence the burgher uttered while the Student Anselmus was about to put away his pipe and box; and now the burgher slowly and deliberately cleaned his pipe, and began as slowly to fill it. Several burgher girls had come up: these were speaking secretly with the woman and each other, and tittering as they looked at Anselmus. The Student felt as if he were standing on prickly thorns, and burning needles. No sooner had he got back his pipe and tobacco-box, than he darted off as fast as he could.

All the strange things he had seen were clean gone from his memory; he simply recollected having babbled all sorts of foolish stuff beneath the elder-tree. This was the more frightful to him, as he entertained an inward horror against all soliloquists. It is Satan that chatters out of them, said his Rector; and Anselmus had honestly believed him. But to be regarded as a *Candidatus Theologiæ*, overtaken with drink on Ascension Day! The thought was intolerable.

Running on with these mad vexations, he was just about turning up Poplar Alley, by the Kosel garden, when a voice behind him called out: "Herr Anselmus! Herr Anselmus! for the love of Heaven, where are you running in such a hurry?" The Student paused, as if rooted to the ground; for he was convinced that now some new accident would befall him. The voice rose again: "Herr Anselmus, come back: we are waiting for you here at the water!" And now the Student perceived that it was his friend Conrector Paulmann's voice: he went back to the Elbe, and found the Conrector, with his two daughters, as well as Registrator Heerbrand, all about to step into their gondola. Conrector Paulmann invited the Student to go with them across the Elbe, and then to pass the evening at his house in the suburb of Pirna. The Student Anselmus very gladly accepted this proposal, thinking thereby to escape the malignant destiny which had ruled over him all day.

Now, as they were crossing the river, it chanced that on the farther bank in Anton's Garden, some fireworks were just going off. Sputtering and hissing, the rockets went aloft, and their blazing stars flew to pieces in the air, scattering a thousand vague shoots and flashes around them. The Student Anselmus was sitting by the steersman, sunk in deep thought, but when he noticed in the water the reflection of these darting and wavering sparks and flames, he felt as if it were the little golden snakes that were sporting in the flood. All the wonders that he had seen at the elder-tree again started forth into his heart and thoughts; and again that unspeakable longing, that glowing desire, laid hold of him here, which had agitated his bosom before in painful spasms of rapture.

"Ah! is it you again, my little golden snakes? Sing now, O sing! In your song let the kind, dear, dark-blue eyes again appear to me—Ah! are you under the waves, then?"

So cried the Student Anselmus, and at the same time made a violent movement, as if he was about to plunge into the river.

"Is the Devil in you, sir?" exclaimed the steersman, and clutched him by the lapels. The girls, who were sitting by him, shrieked in terror, and fled to the other side of the gondola. Registrator Heerbrand whispered something in Conrector Paulmann's ear, to which the latter answered at considerable length, but in so low a tone that Anselmus could distinguish nothing but the words: "Such attacks more than once?—Never heard of it." Directly after this, Conrector Paulmann also rose, and then sat down, with a certain earnest, grave, official mien beside the Student Anselmus, taking his hand and saying: "How are you, Herr Anselmus?"

The Student Anselmus was almost losing his wits, for in his mind there was a mad contradiction, which he strove in vain to reconcile. He now saw plainly that what he had taken for the gleaming of the golden snakes was nothing but the reflection of the fireworks in Anton's Garden: but a feeling unexperienced till now, he himself did not know whether it was rapture or pain, cramped his breast together; and when the steersman struck through the water with his helm, so that the waves, curling as in anger, gurgled and chafed, he heard in their din a soft whispering: "Anselmus! Anselmus! do you see how we still skim along before you? Sisterkin looks at you again: believe, believe, believe in us!" And he thought he saw in the reflected light three green-glowing streaks: but then, when he gazed, full of fond sadness, into the water, to see whether those gentle eyes would not look up to him again, he perceived too well that the shine proceeded only from the windows in the neighbouring houses. He was sitting mute in his place, and inwardly battling with himself, when Conrector Paulmann repeated, with still greater emphasis: "How are you, Herr Anselmus?"

With the most rueful tone, Anselmus replied: "Ah! Herr Conrector, if you knew what strange things I have been dreaming, quite awake, with open eyes, just now, under an elder-tree at the wall of Linke's Garden, you would not take it amiss of me that I am a little absent, or so."

"Ey, ey, Herr Anselmus!" interrupted Conrector Paulmann, "I have always taken you for a solid young man: but to dream, to dream with your eyes wide open, and then, all at once, to start up and try to jump into the water! This, begging your pardon, is what only fools or madmen would do."

The Student Anselmus was deeply affected by his friend's hard saying; then Veronica, Paulmann's eldest daughter, a most pretty blooming girl of sixteen, addressed her father: "But, dear father, something singular must have befallen Herr Anselmus; and perhaps he only thinks he was awake, while he may have really been asleep, and so all manner of wild stuff has come into his head, and is still lying in his thoughts."

"And, dearest Mademoiselle! Worthy Conrector!" cried Registrator Heerbrand, "may one not, even when awake, sometimes sink into a sort of dream state? I myself have had such fits. One afternoon, for instance, during coffee, in a sort of brown study like this, in the special season of corporeal and spiritual digestion, the place where a lost *Act* was lying occurred to me, as if by inspiration; and last night, no farther gone, there came a glorious large Latin paper tripping out before my open eyes, in the very same way."

"Ah! most honoured Registrator," answered Conrector Paulmann, "you have always had a tendency to the *Poetica*; and thus one falls into fantasies and romantic humours."

The Student Anselmus, however, was particularly gratified that in this most troublous situation, while in danger of being considered drunk or crazy, anyone should take his part; and though it was already pretty dark, he thought he noticed, for the first time, that Veronica had really very fine dark blue eyes, and this too without remembering the strange pair which he had looked at in the elder-bush. Actually, the adventure under the elder-bush had once more entirely vanished from the thoughts of the Student Anselmus; he felt himself at ease and light of heart; nay, in the capriciousness of joy, he carried it so far, that he offered a helping hand to his fair advocate Veronica, as she was stepping from the gondola; and without more ado, as she put her arm in his, escorted her home with so much dexterity and good luck that he only missed his footing once, and this being the only wet spot in the whole road, only spattered Veronica's white gown a very little by the incident.

Conrector Paulmann did not fail to observe this happy change in the Student Anselmus; he resumed his liking for him and begged forgiveness for the hard words which he had let fall before. "Yes," added he, "we have many examples to show that certain phantasms may rise before a man, and pester and plague him not a little; but this is bodily disease, and leeches are good for it, if applied to the right part, as a certain learned physician, now deceased, has directed." The Student Anselmus did not know whether he had been drunk, crazy, or sick; but in any case the leeches seemed entirely superfluous, as these supposed phantasms had utterly vanished, and the Student himself was growing happier and happier the more he prospered in serving the pretty Veronica with all sorts of dainty attentions.

As usual, after the frugal meal, there came music; the Student Anselmus had to take his seat before the harpsichord, and Veronica accompanied his playing with her pure clear voice: "Dear Mademoiselle," said Registrator Heerbrand, "you have a voice like a crystal bell!"

"That she has not!" ejaculated the Student Anselmus, he scarcely knew how. "Crystal bells in elder-trees sound strangely! strangely!" continued the Student Anselmus, murmuring half aloud.

Veronica laid her hand on his shoulder, and asked: "What are you saying now, Herr Anselmus?"

Instantly Anselmus recovered his cheerfulness, and began playing. Conrector Paulmann gave him a grim look; but Registrator Heerbrand laid a music leaf on the rack, and sang with ravishing grace one of Bandmaster Graun's bravura airs. The Student Anselmus accompanied this, and much more; and a fantasy duet, which Veronica and he now fingered, and Conrector Paulmann had himself composed, again brought everyone into the gayest humour.

It was now pretty late, and Registrator Heerbrand was taking up his hat and stick, when Conrector Paulmann went up to him with a mysterious air, and said: "Hem!—Would not you, honoured Registrator, mention to the good Herr Anselmus himself—Hem! what we were speaking of before?"

"With all the pleasure in the world," said Registrator Heerbrand, and having placed himself in the circle, began, without farther preamble, as follows:

"In this city is a strange remarkable man; people say he follows all manner of secret sciences. But as there are no such sciences, I take him rather for an antiquary, and along with this for an experimental chemist. I mean no other than our Privy Archivarius Lindhorst. He lives, as you know, by himself, in his old isolated house; and when he is away from his office, he is to be found in his library or in his chemical laboratory, to which, however, he admits no stranger. Besides many curious books, he possesses a number of manuscripts, partly Arabic, Coptic, and some of them in strange characters, which do not belong to any known tongue. These he wishes to have copied properly, and for this purpose he requires a man who can draw with the pen, and so transfer these marks to parchment, in Indian ink, with the highest exactness and fidelity. The work is to be carried on in a separate chamber of his house, under his own supervision; and besides free board during the time of business, he will pay his copyist a speziesthaler, or specie-dollar, daily, and promises a handsome present when the copying is rightly finished. The hours of work are from twelve to six. From three to four, you take rest and dinner.

"Herr Archivarius Lindhorst having in vain tried one or two young people for copying these manuscripts, has at last applied to me to find him an expert calligrapher, and so I have been thinking of you, my dear Anselmus, for I know that you both write very neatly and draw with the pen to great perfection. Now, if in these bad times, and till your future establishment, you would like to earn a speziesthaler every day, and a present over and above your salary, you can go tomorrow precisely at noon, and call upon the Archivarius, whose house no doubt you know. But be on your guard against blots! If such a thing falls on your copy, you must begin it again; if it falls on the original, the Archivarius will think nothing of throwing you out the window, for he is a hot-tempered man."

The Student Anselmus was filled with joy at Registrator Heerbrand's proposal; for not only could the Student write well and draw well with the pen, but this copying with laborious calligraphic pains was a thing he delighted in more than anything else. So he thanked his patron in the most grateful terms, and promised not to fail at noon tomorrow.

All night the Student Anselmus saw nothing but clear speziesthalers, and heard nothing but their lovely clink. Who could blame the poor youth, cheated of so many hopes by capricious destiny, obliged to take counsel about every farthing, and to forego so many joys which a young heart requires! Early in the morning he brought out his black-lead pencils, his crowquills, his Indian ink; for better materials, thought he, the Archivarius can find nowhere. Above all, he gathered together and arranged his calligraphic masterpieces and his drawings, to show them to the Archivarius, as proof of his ability to do what was desired. Everything went well with the Student; a peculiar happy star seemed to be presiding over him; his neckcloth sat right at the very first trial; no stitches burst; no loop gave way in his black silk stockings; his hat did not once fall to the dust after he had trimmed it. In a word, precisely at half-past eleven, the Student Anselmus, in his pike-gray frock and black satin lower habiliments, with a roll of calligraphic specimens and pen-drawings in his pocket, was standing in the Schlossgasse, or Castle Alley, in Conradi's shop, and drinking one—two glasses of the best stomachic liqueur; for here, thought he, slapping his pocket, which was still empty, for here speziesthalers will soon be chinking.

Notwithstanding the distance of the solitary street where the Archivarius Lindhorst's ancient residence lay, the Student Anselmus was at the front door before the stroke of twelve.   He stood there, and was looking at the large fine bronze knocker; but now when, as the last stroke tingled through the air with a loud clang from the steeple clock of the Kreuzkirche, or Church of the Cross, he lifted his hand to grasp this same knocker, the metal visage twisted itself, with a horrid rolling of its blue-gleaming eyes, into a grinning smile. Alas, it was the Applewoman of the Schwarzthor!   The pointed teeth gnashed together in the loose jaws, and in their chattering through the skinny lips, there was a growl as of "You fool, fool, fool!—Wait, wait!—Why did you run!—Fool!"   Horror-struck, the Student Anselmus flew back; he clutched at the door-post, but his hand caught the bell-rope, and pulled it, and in piercing discords it rang stronger and stronger, and through the whole empty house the echo repeated, as in mockery: "To the crystal, fall!" An unearthly terror seized the Student Anselmus, and quivered through all his limbs.   The bell-rope lengthened downwards, and became a gigantic, transparent, white serpent, which encircled and crushed him, and girded him straiter and straiter in its coils, till his brittle paralyzed limbs went crashing in pieces and the blood spouted from his veins, penetrating into the transparent body of the serpent and dyeing it red.   "Kill me!   Kill me!" he wanted to cry, in his horrible agony; but the cry was only a stifled gurgle in his throat.   The serpent lifted its head, and laid its long peaked tongue of glowing brass on the breast of Anselmus; then a fierce pang suddenly cut asunder the artery of life, and thought fled away from him.   On returning to his senses, he was lying on his own poor truckle-bed; Conrector Paulmann was standing before him, and saying: "For Heaven's sake, what mad stuff is this, dear Herr Anselmus?"

THIRD VIGIL

"The Spirit looked upon the water, and the water moved itself, and chafed in foaming billows, and plunged thundering down into the abysses, which opened their black throats and greedily swallowed it.   Like triumphant conquerors, the granite rocks lifted their cleft peaky crowns, protecting the valley, till the sun took it into his paternal bosom, and clasping it with his beams as with glowing arms, cherished it and warmed it.   Then a thousand germs, which had been sleeping under the desert sand, awoke from their deep slumber, and stretched out their little leaves and stalks towards the sun their father's face; and like smiling infants in green cradles, the flowrets rested in their buds and blossoms, till they too, awakened by their father, decked themselves in lights, which their father, to please them, tinted in a thousand varied hues.

"But in the midst of the valley was a black hill, which heaved up and down like the breast of man when warm longing swells it. From the abysses mounted steaming vapours, which rolled themselves together into huge masses, striving malignantly to hide the father's face: but he called the storm to him, which rushed there, and scattered them away; and when the pure sunbeam rested again on the bleak hill, there started from it, in the excess of its rapture, a glorious Fire-lily, opening its fair leaves like gentle lips to receive the kiss of its father.

"And now came a gleaming splendour into the valley; it was the youth Phosphorus; the Lily saw him, and begged, being seized with warm longing love: 'Be mine for ever, fair youth! For I love you, and must die if you forsake me!' Then spoke the youth Phosphorus: 'I will be yours, fair flower; but then, like a naughty child, you will leave father and mother; you will know your playmates no longer, will strive to be greater and stronger than all that now rejoices with you as your equal. The longing which now beneficently warms your whole being will be scattered into a thousand rays and torture and vex you, for sense will bring forth senses; and the highest rapture, which the spark I cast into you kindles, will be the hopeless pain wherein you shall perish, to spring up anew in foreign shape. This spark is thought!'

"'Ah!' mourned the Lily, 'can I not be yours in this glow, as it now burns in me; not still be yours? Can I love you more than now; could I look on you as now, if you were to annihilate me?' Then the youth Phosphorus kissed the Lily; and as if penetrated with light, it mounted up in flame, out of which issued a foreign being, that hastily flying from the valley, roved forth into endless space, no longer heeding its old playmates, or the youth it had loved. This youth mourned for his lost beloved; for he too loved her, it was love to the fair Lily that had brought him to the lone valley; and the granite rocks bent down their heads in participation of his grief.

"But one of these opened its bosom, and there came a black-winged dragon flying out of it, who said: 'My brethren, the Metals are sleeping in there; but I am always brisk and waking, and will help you.' Dashing forth on its black pinions, the dragon at last caught the being which had sprung from the Lily; bore it to the hill, and encircled it with his wing; then was it the Lily again; but thought, which continued with it, tore asunder its heart; and its love for the youth Phosphorus was a cutting pain, before which, as if breathed on by poisonous vapours, the flowrets which had once rejoiced in the fair Lily's presence, faded and died.

"The youth Phosphorus put on a glittering coat of mail, sporting with the light in a thousand hues, and did battle with the dragon, who struck the cuirass with his black wing, till it rung and sounded; and at this loud clang the flowrets again came to life, and like variegated birds fluttered round the dragon, whose force departed; and who, thus being vanquished, hid himself in the depths of the earth. The Lily was freed; the youth Phosphorus clasped her, full of warm longing, of heavenly love; and in triumphant chorus, the flowers, the birds, nay, even the high granite rocks, did reverence to her as the Queen of the Valley."

"By your leave, worthy Herr Archivarius, this is Oriental bombast," said Registrator Heerbrand: "and we beg very much you would rather, as you often do, give us something of your own most remarkable life, of your travelling adventures, for instance; above all, something true."

"What the deuce, then?" answered Archivarius Lindhorst. "True? This very thing I have been telling is the truest I could dish out for you, my friends, and belongs to my life too, in a certain sense. For I come from that very valley; and the Fire-lily, which at last ruled as queen there, was my great-great-great-great-grandmother; and so, properly speaking, I am a prince myself." All burst into a peal of laughter. "Ay, laugh your fill," continued Archivarius Lindhorst. "To you this matter, which I have related, certainly in the most brief and meagre way, may seem senseless and mad; yet, notwithstanding this, it is meant for anything but incoherent, or even allegorical, and it is, in one word, literally true. Had I known, however, that the glorious love story, to which I owe my existence, would have pleased you so little, I might have given you a little of the news my brother brought me on his visit yesterday."

"What, what is this? Have you a brother, then, Herr Archivarius? Where is he? Where does he live? In his Majesty's service too? Or perhaps a private scholar?" cried the company from all quarters.

"No!" replied the Archivarius, quite cool, composedly taking a pinch of snuff, "he has joined the bad side; he has gone over to the Dragons."

"What do you mean, dear Herr Archivarius?" cried Registrator Heerbrand: "Over to the Dragons?"—"Over to the Dragons?" resounded like an echo from all hands.

"Yes, over to the Dragons," continued Archivarius Lindhorst: "it was sheer desperation, I believe. You know, gentlemen, my father died a short while ago; it is but three hundred and eighty-five years ago at most, and I am still in mourning for it. He had left me, his favourite son, a fine onyx; this onyx, rightly or wrongly, my brother would have: we quarrelled about it, over my father's corpse; in such unseemly manner that the good man started up, out of all patience, and threw my wicked brother downstairs. This stuck in our brother's stomach, and so without loss of time he went over to the Dragons. At present, he lives in a cypress wood, not far from Tunis: he has a famous magical carbuncle to watch there, which a dog of necromancer, who has set up a summerhouse in Lapland, has an eye to; so my poor brother only gets away for a quarter of an hour or so, when the necromancer happens to be out looking after the salamander bed in his garden, and then he tells me in all haste what good news there is about the Springs of the Nile."

For the second time, the company burst out into a peal of laughter: but the Student Anselmus began to feel quite dreary in heart; and he could scarcely look in Archivarius Lindhorst's parched countenance, and fixed earnest eyes, without shuddering internally in a way which he could not himself understand. Moreover, in the harsh and strangely metallic sound of Archivarius Lindhorst's voice there was something mysteriously piercing for the Student Anselmus, and he felt his very bones and marrow tingling as the Archivarius spoke.

The special object for which Registrator Heerbrand had taken him into the coffee house, seemed at present not attainable. After that accident at Archivarius Lindhorst's door, the Student Anselmus had withstood all inducements to risk a second visit: for, according to his own heart-felt conviction, it was only chance that had saved him, if not from death, at least from the danger of insanity. Conrector Paulmann had happened to be passing through the street at the time when Anselmus was lying quite senseless at the door, and an old woman, who had laid her cookie-and-apple basket aside, was busied about him. Conrector Paulmann had forthwith called a chair, and so had him carried home. "Think what you will of me," said the Student Anselmus, "consider me a fool or not: I say, the cursed visage of that witch at the Schwarzthor grinned on me from the doorknocker. What happened after I would rather not speak of: but if I had recovered from my faint and seen that infernal Apple-wife beside me (for the old woman whom you talk of was no other), I should that instant have been struck by apoplexy, or have run stark mad."

All persuasions, all sensible arguments on the part of Conrector Paulmann and Registrator Heerbrand, profited nothing; and even the blue-eyed Veronica herself could not raise him from a certain moody humour, in which he had ever since been sunk. In fact, these friends regarded him as troubled in mind, and considered ways for diverting his thoughts; to which end, Registrator Heerbrand thought, there could nothing be so serviceable as copying Archivarius Lindhorst's manuscripts. The business, therefore, was to introduce the Student in some proper way to Archivarius Lindhorst; and so Registrator Heerbrand, knowing that the Archivarius used to visit a certain coffee house almost nightly, had invited the Student Anselmus to come every evening to that same coffee house, and drink a glass of beer and smoke a pipe, at his, the Registrator's charge, till such time as Archivarius Lindhorst should in one way or another see him, and the bargain for this copying work be settled; which offer the Student Anselmus had most gratefully accepted. "God will reward you, worthy Registrator, if you bring the young man to reason!" said Conrector Paulmann. "God will reward you!" repeated Veronica, piously raising her eyes to heaven, and vividly thinking that the Student Anselmus was already a most pretty young man, even without any reason.

Now accordingly, as Archivarius Lindhorst, with hat and staff, was making for the door, Registrator Heerbrand seized the Student Anselmus briskly by the hand, and stepping to meet the Herr Archivarius, he said: "Most esteemed Herr Archivarius, here is the Student Anselmus, who has an uncommon talent in calligraphy and drawing, and will undertake the copying of your rare manuscripts."

"I am most particularly glad to hear it," answered Archivarius Lindhorst sharply, then threw his three-cocked military hat on his head, and shoving Registrator Heerbrand and the Student Anselmus aside, rushed downstairs with great tumult, so that both of them were left standing in great confusion, gaping at the door, which he had slammed in their faces till the bolts and hinges of it rung again.

"He is a very strange old gentleman," said Registrator Heerbrand. "Strange old gentleman," stammered the Student Anselmus, with a feeling as if an ice-stream were creeping over all his veins, and he were stiffening into a statue. All the guests, however, laughed, and said: "Our Archivarius is on his high horse today: tomorrow, you shall see, he will be mild as a lamb again, and won't speak a word, but will look into the smoke-vortexes of his pipe, or read the newspapers; you must not mind these freaks."

"That is true too," thought the Student Anselmus: "who would mind such a thing, after all? Did not the Archivarius tell me he was most particularly glad to hear that I would undertake the copying of his manuscripts; and why did Registrator Heerbrand step directly in his way, when he was going home? No, no, he is a good man at bottom this Privy Archivarius Lindhorst, and surprisingly liberal. A little curious in his figures of speech; but what is that to me? Tomorrow at the stroke of twelve I will go to him, though fifty bronze Apple-wives should try to hinder me!"

FOURTH VIGIL

Gracious reader, may I venture to ask you a question? Have you ever had hours, perhaps even days or weeks, in which all your customary activities did nothing but cause you vexation and dissatisfaction; when everything that you usually consider worthy and important seemed trivial and worthless? At such a time you did not know what to do or where to turn. A dim feeling pervaded your breast that you had higher desires that must be fulfilled, desires that transcended the pleasures of this world, yet desires which your spirit, like a cowed child, did not even dare to utter. In this longing for an unknown Something, which longing hovered above you no matter where you were, like an airy dream with thin transparent forms that melted away each time you tried to examine them, you had no voice for the world about you. You passed to and fro with troubled look, like a hopeless lover, and no matter what you saw being attempted or attained in the bustle of varied existence, it awakened no sorrow or joy in you. It was as if you had no share in this sublunary world.

If, favourable reader, you have ever been in this mood, you know the state into which the Student Anselmus had fallen. I wish most heartily, courteous reader, that it were in my power to bring the Student Anselmus before your eyes with true vividness. For in these vigils in which I record his singular history, there is still so much more of the marvellous—which is likely to make the everyday life of ordinary mortals seem pallid—that I fear in the end you will believe in neither the Student Anselmus nor Archivarius Lindhorst; indeed, that you will even entertain doubts as to Registrator

Heerbrand and Conrector Paulmann, though these two estimable persons, at least, are still walking the pavements of Dresden. Favourable reader, while you are in the faery region of glorious wonders, where both rapture and horror may be evoked; where the goddess of earnestness herself will waft her veil aside and show her countenance (though a smile often glimmers in her glance, a sportive teasing before perplexing enchantments, comparable to mothers nursing and dandling their children)—while you are in this region which the spirit lays open to us in dreams, make an effort to recognize the well-known forms which hover around you in fitful brightness even in ordinary life. You will then find that this glorious kingdom lies much closer at hand than you ever supposed; it is this kingdom which I now very heartily desire, and am striving to show you in the singular story of the Student Anselmus.

So, as was hinted, the Student Anselmus, ever since that evening when he met with Archivarius Lindhorst, had been sunk in a dreamy musing, which rendered him insensible to every outward touch from common life. He felt that an unknown Something was awakening his inmost soul, and calling forth that rapturous pain, which is even the mood of longing that announces a loftier existence to man. He delighted most when he could rove alone through meads and woods; and as if released from all that fettered him to his necessary life, could, so to speak, again find himself in the manifold images which mounted from his soul.

It happened once that in returning from a long ramble, he passed by that notable elder-tree, under which, as if taken with faery, he had formerly beheld so many marvels. He felt himself strangely attracted by the green kindly sward; but no sooner had he seated himself on it than the whole vision which he had previously seen as in a heavenly trance, and which had since as if by foreign influence been driven from his mind, again came floating before him in the liveliest colours, as if he had been looking on it a second time. Nay, it was clearer to him now than ever, that the gentle blue eyes belonged to the gold-green snake, which had wound itself through the middle of the elder-tree; and that from the turnings of its tapering body all those glorious crystal tones, which had filled him with rapture, must have broken forth. As on Ascension Day, he again clasped the elder-tree to his bosom, and cried into the twigs and leaves: "Ah, once more shoot forth, and turn and wind yourself among the twigs, little fair green snake, that I may see you! Once more look at me with your gentle eyes! Ah, I love you, and must die in pain and grief, if you do not return!" All, however, remained quite dumb and still; and as before, the elder-tree rustled quite unintelligibly with its twigs and leaves. But the Student Anselmus now felt as if he knew what it was that so moved and worked within him, nay, that so tore his bosom in the pain of an infinite longing. "What else is it," said he, "but that I love you with my whole heart and soul, and even to the death, glorious little golden snake; nay, that without you I cannot live, and must perish in hopeless woe, unless I find you again, unless I have you as the beloved of my heart. But I know it, you shall be mine; and then all that glorious dreams have promised me of another higher world shall be fulfilled."

Henceforth the Student Anselmus, every evening, when the sun was scattering its bright gold over the peaks of the trees, was to be seen under the elder-bush, calling from the depths of his heart in most lamentable tones into the branches and leaves for a sight of his beloved, of his little gold-green snake. Once as he was going on with this, there suddenly stood before him a tall lean man, wrapped up in a wide light-gray surtout, who, looking at him with large fiery eyes, exclaimed: "Hey, hey, what whining and whimpering is this? Hey, hey, this is Herr Anselmus that was to copy my manuscripts." The Student Anselmus felt not a little terrified at hearing this voice, for it was the very same which on Ascension Day had called: "Hey, hey, what chattering and jingling is this," and so forth. For fright and astonishment, he could not utter a word. "What ails you, Herr Anselmus," continued Archivarius Lindhorst, for the stranger was no one else; "what do you want with the elder-tree, and why did you not come to me and set about your work?"

In fact, the Student Anselmus had never yet prevailed upon himself to visit Archivarius Lindhorst's house a second time, though, that evening, he had firmly resolved on doing it. But now at this moment, when he saw his fair dreams torn asunder, and that too by the same hostile voice which had once before snatched away his beloved, a sort of desperation came over him, and he broke out fiercely into these words: "You may think me mad or not, Herr Archivarius; it is all the same to me: but here in this bush, on Ascension Day, I saw the gold-green snake—ah! the beloved of my soul; and she spoke to me in glorious crystal tones; and you, you, Herr Archivarius, cried and shouted horribly over the water."

"How is this, my dear sir?" interrupted Archivarius Lindhorst, smiling quite inexpressibly, and taking snuff.

The Student Anselmus felt his breast becoming easy, now that he had succeeded in beginning this strange story; and it seemed to him as if he were quite right in laying the whole blame upon the Archivarius, and that it was he, and no one else, who had thundered so from the distance. He courageously proceeded: "Well, then, I will tell you the whole mystery that happened to me on Ascension evening; and then you may say and do, and think of me whatever you please." He accordingly disclosed the whole miraculous adventure, from his luckless upsetting of the apple basket, till the departure of the three gold-green snakes over the river; and how the people after that had thought him drunk or crazy. "All this," ended the Student Anselmus, "I actually saw with my eyes; and deep in my bosom those dear voices, which spoke to me, are still sounding in clear echo: it was in no way a dream; and if I am not to die of longing and desire, I must believe in these gold-green snakes, though I see by your smile, Herr Archivarius, that you hold these same snakes as nothing more than creatures of my heated and overstrained imagination."

"Not at all," replied the Archivarius, with the greatest calmness and composure; "the gold-green snakes, which you saw in the elder-bush, Herr Anselmus, were simply my three daughters; and that you have fallen over head and ears in love with the blue eyes of Serpentina the youngest, is now clear enough. Indeed, I knew it on Ascension Day myself: and as (on that occasion, sitting busied with my writing at home) I began to get annoyed with so much chattering and jingling, I called to the idle minxes that it was time to get home, for the sun was setting, and they had sung and basked enough."

The Student Anselmus felt as if he now merely heard in plain words something he had long dreamed of, and though he fancied he observed that elder-bush, wall and sward, and all objects about him were beginning slowly to whirl around, he took heart, and was ready to speak; but the Archivarius prevented him; for sharply pulling the glove from his left hand, and holding the stone of a ring, glittering in strange sparkles and flames before the Student's eyes, he said: "Look here, Herr Anselmus; what you see may do you good."

The Student Anselmus looked in, and O wonder! the stone emitted a cluster of rays; and the rays wove themselves together into a clear gleaming crystal mirror; in which, with many windings, now flying asunder, now twisted together, the three gold-green snakes were dancing and bounding. And when their tapering forms, glittering with a thousand sparkles, touched each other, there issued from them glorious tones, as of crystal bells; and the midmost of the three stretched forth her little head from the mirror, as if full of longing and desire, and her dark-blue eyes said: "Do you know me, then? Do you believe in me, Anselmus? In belief alone is love: can you love?"

"O Serpentina! Serpentina!" cried the Student Anselmus in mad rapture; but Archivarius Lindhorst suddenly breathed on the mirror, and with an electric sputter the rays sank back into their focus; and on his hand there was now nothing but a little emerald, over which the Archivarius drew his glove.

"Did you see the golden snakes, Herr Anselmus?" said the Archivarius.

"Ah, good heaven, yes!" replied the Student, "and the fair dear Serpentina."

"Hush!" continued Archivarius Lindhorst, "enough for now: for the rest, if you decide to work with me, you may see my daughter often enough; or rather I will grant you this real satisfaction: if you stick tightly and truly to your task, that is to say, copy every mark with the greatest clearness and correctness. But you have not come to me at all, Herr Anselmus, although Registrator Heerbrand promised I should see you immediately, and I have waited several days in vain."

Not until the mention of Registrator Heerbrand's name did the Student Anselmus again feel as if he was really standing with his two legs on the ground, and he was really the Student Anselmus, and the man talking to him really Archivarius Lindhorst. The tone of indifference, with which the latter spoke, in such rude contrast with the strange sights which like a genuine necromancer he had called forth, awakened a certain horror in the Student, which the piercing look of those fiery eyes, glowing from their bony sockets in the lean puckered visage, as from a leathern case, still farther aggravated: and the Student was again forcibly seized with the same unearthly feeling, which had before gained possession of him in the coffee house, when Archivarius Lindhorst had talked so wildly. With a great effort he retained his self-command, and as the Archivarius again asked, "Well, why did you not come?" the Student exerted his whole energies, and related to him what had happened at the street door.

"My dear Herr Anselmus," said the Archivarius, when the Student was finished; "dear Herr Anselmus, I know this Apple-wife of whom you speak; she is a vicious slut that plays all sorts of vile tricks on me; but that she has turned herself to bronze and taken the shape of a doorknocker, to deter pleasant visitors from calling, is indeed very bad, and truly not to be endured. Would you please, worthy Herr Anselmus, if you come tomorrow at noon and notice any more of this grinning and growling, just be so good as to let a drop or two of this liquor fall on her nose; it will put everything to rights immediately. And now, adieu, my dear Herr Anselmus! I must make haste, therefore I would not advise you to think of returning with me. Adieu, till we meet!—Tomorrow at noon!"

The Archivarius had given the Student Anselmus a little vial, with a gold-coloured fluid in it; and he walked rapidly off; so rapidly, that in the dusk, which had now come on, he seemed to be floating down to the valley rather than walking down to it. Already he was near the Kosel garden; the wind got within his wide greatcoat, and drove its breasts asunder; so that they fluttered in the air like a pair of large wings; and to the Student Anselmus, who was looking full of amazement at the course of the Archivarius, it seemed as if a large bird were spreading out its pinions for rapid flight. And now, while the Student kept gazing into the dusk, a white-gray kite with creaking cry soared up into the air; and he now saw clearly that the white flutter which he had thought to be the retiring Archivarius must have been this very kite, though he still could not understand where the Archivarius had vanished so abruptly.

"Perhaps he may have flown away in person, this Herr Archivarius Lindhorst," said the Student Anselmus to himself; "for I now see and feel clearly, that all these foreign shapes of a distant wondrous world, which I never saw before except in peculiarly remarkable dreams, have now come into my waking life, and are making their sport of me. But be this as it will! You live and glow in my breast, lovely, gentle Serpentina; you alone can still the infinite longing which rends my soul to pieces. Ah, when shall I see your kind eyes, dear, dear Serpentina!" cried the Student Anselmus aloud.

"That is a vile unchristian name!" murmured a bass voice beside him, which belonged to some promenader returning home. The Student Anselmus, reminded where he was, hastened off at a quick pace, thinking to himself: "Wouldn't it be a real misfortune now if Conrector Paulmann or Registrator Heerbrand were to meet me?"—But neither of these gentlemen met him.

FIFTH VIGIL

"There is nothing in the world that can be done with this Anselmus," said Conrector Paulmann; "all my good advice, all my admonitions, are fruitless; he will apply himself to nothing; though he is a fine classical scholar too, and that is the foundation of everything."

But Registrator Heerbrand, with a sly, mysterious smile, replied: "Let Anselmus take his time, my dear Conrector! he is a strange subject, this Anselmus, but there is much in him: and when I say much, I mean a Privy Secretary, or even a Court Councillor, a Hofrath."

"Hof——" began Conrector Paulmann, in the deepest amazement; the word stuck in his throat.

"Hush! hush!" continued Registrator Heerbrand, "I know what I know. These two days he has been with Archivarius Lindhorst, copying manuscripts; and last night the Archivarius meets me at the coffee house, and says: 'You have sent me a proper man, good neighbour! There is stuff in him!' And now think of Archivarius Lindhorst's influence—Hush! hush! we will talk of it this time a year from now." And with these words the Registrator, his face still wrinkled into the same sly smile, went out of the room, leaving the Conrector speechless with astonishment and curiosity, and fixed, as if by enchantment, in his chair.

But on Veronica this dialogue had made a still deeper impression. "Did I not know all along," she thought, "that Herr Anselmus was a most clever and pretty young man, to whom something great would come? Were I but certain that he really liked me! But that night when we crossed the Elbe, did he not press my hand twice? Did he not look at me, in our duet, with such glances that pierced into my very heart? Yes, yes! he really likes me; and I ——" Veronica gave herself up, as young maidens are wont, to sweet dreams of a gay future. She was Mrs. Hofrath, Frau Hofräthinn; she occupied a fine house in the Schlossgasse, or in the Neumarkt, or in the Moritzstrasse; her fashionable hat, her new Turkish shawl, became her admirably; she was breakfasting on the balcony in an elegant negligée, giving orders to her cook for the day: "And see, if you please, not to spoil that dish; it is the Hofrath's favourite." Then passing beaux glanced up, and she heard distinctly: "Well, she is a heavenly woman, that Hofräthinn; how prettily the lace cap suits her!" Mrs. Privy Councillor Ypsilon sends her servant to ask if it would please the Frau Hofräthinn to drive as far as the Linke Bath today? "Many compliments; extremely sorry, I am engaged to tea already with the Presidentinn Tz." Then comes the Hofrath Anselmus back from his office; he is dressed in the top of the mode: "Ten, I declare," cries he, making his gold watch repeat, and giving his young lady a kiss. "How are things, little wife? Guess what I have here for you?" he continues in a teasing manner, and draws from his waistcoat pocket a pair of beautiful earrings, fashioned in the newest style, and puts them on in place of the old ones. "Ah! What pretty, dainty earrings!" cried Veronica aloud; and started up from her chair, throwing aside her work, to see those fair earrings with her own eyes in the glass.

"What is this?" said Conrector Paulmann, roused by the noise from his deep study of *Cicero de Officiis*, and almost dropping the book from his hand; "are we taking fits, like Anselmus?" But at this moment, the Student Anselmus, who, contrary to his custom, had not been seen for several days, entered the room, to Veronica's astonishment and terror; for, in truth, he seemed altered in his whole bearing. With a certain precision, which was far from usual in him, he spoke of new tendencies of life which had become clear to his mind, of glorious prospects which were opening for him, but which many did not have the skill to discern. Conrector Paulmann, remembering Registrator Heerbrand's mysterious speech, was still more struck, and could scarcely utter a syllable, till the Student Anselmus, after letting fall some hints of urgent business at Archivarius Lindhorst's, and with elegant adroitness kissing Veronica's hand, was already down the stairs, off and away.

"This was the Hofrath," murmured Veronica to herself: "and he kissed my hand, without sliding on the floor, or treading on my foot, as he used to! He threw me the softest look too; yes, he really loves me!"

Veronica again gave way to her dreaming; yet now, it was as if a hostile shape were still coming forward among these lovely visions of her future household life as Frau Hofräthinn, and the shape were laughing in spiteful mockery, and saying: "This is all very stupid and trashy stuff, and lies to boot; for Anselmus will never, never, be Hofrath or your husband; he does not love you in the least, though you have blue eyes, and a fine figure, and a pretty hand." Then an ice-stream poured over Veronica's soul; and a deep sorrow swept away the delight with which, a little while ago, she had seen herself in the lace cap and fashionable earrings. Tears almost rushed into her eyes, and she said aloud: "Ah! it is too true; he does not love me in the least; and I shall never, never, be Frau Hofräthinn!"

"Romantic idiocy, romantic idiocy!" cried Conrector Paulmann; then snatched his hat and stick, and hastened indignantly from the house. "This was still wanting," sighed Veronica; and felt vexed at her little sister, a girl of twelve years, because she sat so unconcerned, and kept sewing at her frame, as if nothing had happened.

Meanwhile it was almost three o'clock; and now time to tidy up the apartment, and arrange the coffee table: for the Mademoiselles Oster had announced that they were coming. But from behind every workbox which Veronica lifted aside, behind the notebooks which she took away from the harpsichord, behind every cup, behind the coffeepot which she took from the cupboard, that shape peeped forth, like a little mandrake, and laughed in spiteful mockery, and snapped its little spider fingers, and cried: "He will not be your husband! he will not be your husband!" And then, when she threw everything away, and fled to the middle of the room, it peered out again, with long nose, in gigantic bulk, from behind the stove, and snarled and growled: "He will not be your husband!"

"Don't you hear anything, don't you see anything?" cried Veronica, shivering with fright, and not daring to touch anything in the room. Fränzchen rose, quite grave and quiet, from her embroidering frame, and said, "What ails you today, sister? You are just making a mess. I must help you, I see."

But at this time the visitors came tripping in in a lively manner, with brisk laughter; and the same moment, Veronica perceived that it was the stove handle which she had taken for a shape, and the creaking of the ill-shut stove door for those spiteful words. Yet, overcome with horror, she did not immediately recover her composure, and her excitement, which her paleness and agitated looks betrayed, was noticed by the Mademoiselles Oster. As they at once cut short their merry talk, and pressed her to tell them what, in Heaven's name, had happened, Veronica was obliged to admit that certain strange thoughts had come into her mind; and suddenly, in open day a dread of spectres, which she did not normally feel, had got the better of her. She described in such lively colours how a little gray mannikin, peeping out of all the corners of the room, had mocked and plagued her, that the Mademoiselles Oster began to look around with timid glances, and began to have all sorts of unearthly notions. But Fränzchen entered at this moment with the steaming coffeepot; and the three, taking thought again, laughed outright at their folly.

Angelica, the elder of the Osters, was engaged to an officer; the young man had joined the army; but his friends had been so long without news of him that there was too little doubt of his being dead, or at least grievously wounded. This had plunged Angelica into the deepest sorrow; but today she was merry, even to extravagance, a state of things which so much surprised Veronica that she could not but speak of it, and inquire the reason.

"Darling," said Angelica, "do you fancy that my Victor is out of heart and thoughts? It is because of him I am so happy. O Heaven! so happy, so blessed in my whole soul! For my Victor is well; in a little while he will be home, advanced to Rittmeister, and decorated with the honours which he has won. A deep but not dangerous wound, in his right arm, which he got from a sword cut by a French hussar, prevents him from writing; and rapid change of quarters, for he will not consent to leave his regiment, makes it impossible for him to send me tidings. But tonight he will be ordered home, until his wound is cured. Tomorrow he will set out for home; and just as he is stepping into the coach, he will learn of his promotion to Rittmeister."

"But, my dear Angelica," interrupted Veronica. "How do you know all this?"

"Do not laugh at me, my friend," continued Angelica; "and surely you will not laugh, for the little gray mannikin, to punish you, might peep out from behind the mirror there. I cannot lay aside my belief in certain mysterious things, since often enough in life they have come before my eyes, I might say, into my very hands. For example, I cannot consider it so strange and incredible as many others do, that there should be people gifted with a certain faculty of prophecy. In the city, here, is an old woman, who possesses this gift to a high degree. She does not use cards, nor molten lead, nor coffee grounds, like ordinary fortune tellers, but after certain preparations, in which you yourself take a part, she takes a polished metallic mirror, and the strangest mixture of figures and forms, all intermingled rise up in it. She interprets these and answers your question. I was with her last night, and got those tidings of my Victor, which I have not doubted for a moment."

Angelica's narrative threw a spark into Veronica's soul, which instantly kindled with the thought of consulting this same old prophetess about Anselmus and her hopes. She learned that the crone was called Frau Rauerin, and lived in a remote street near the Seethor; that she was not to be seen except on Tuesdays, Thursdays, and Fridays, from seven o'clock in the evening, but then, indeed, through the whole night till sunrise; and that she preferred her customers to come alone. It was now Thursday, and Veronica determined, under pretext of accompanying the Osters home, to visit this old woman, and lay the case before her.

Accordingly, no sooner had her friends, who lived in the Neustadt, parted from her at the Elbe Bridge, than she hastened towards the Seethor; and before long, she had reached the remote narrow street described to her, and at the end of it saw the little red house in which Frau Rauerin was said to live. She could not rid herself of a certain dread, nay, of a certain horror, as she approached the door. At last she summoned resolution, in spite of inward terror, and made bold to pull the bell: the door opened, and she groped through the dark passage for the stair which led to the upper story, as Angelica had directed. "Does Frau Rauerin live here?" cried she into the empty lobby as no one appeared; but instead of an answer, there rose a long clear "Mew!" and a large black cat, with its back curved up, and whisking its tail to and fro in wavy coils, stepped on before her, with much gravity, to the door of the apartment, which, on a second mew, was opened.

"Ah, see! Are you here already, daughter? Come in, love; come in!" exclaimed an advancing figure, whose appearance rooted Veronica to the floor. A long lean woman, wrapped in black rags!—while she spoke, her peaked projecting chin wagged this way and that; her toothless mouth, overshadowed by a bony hawk-nose, twisted itself into a ghastly smile, and gleaming cat's-eyes flickered in sparkles through the large spectacles. From a party-coloured clout wrapped round her head, black wiry hair was sticking out; but what deformed her haggard visage to absolute horror, were two large burn marks which ran from the left cheek, over the nose. Veronica's breathing stopped; and the scream, which was about to lighten her choked breast, became a deep sigh, as the witch's skeleton hand took hold of her, and led her into the chamber. Here everything was awake and astir; nothing but din and tumult, and squeaking, and mewing, and croaking, and piping all at once, on every hand. The crone struck the table with her fist, and screamed: "Peace, ye vermin!" And the meer-cats, whimpering, clambered to the top of the high bed; and the little meer-swine all ran beneath the stove, and the raven fluttered up to the round mirror; and the black cat, as if the rebuke did not apply to him, kept sitting at his ease on the cushioned chair, to which he had leapt directly after entering.

So soon as the room became quiet, Veronica took heart; she felt less frightened than she had outside in the hall; nay, the crone herself did not seem so hideous. For the first time, she now looked round the room. All sorts of odious stuffed beasts hung down from the ceiling: strange unknown household implements were lying in confusion on the floor; and in the grate was a scanty blue fire, which only now and then sputtered up in yellow sparkles; and at every sputter, there came a rustling from above and monstrous bats, as if with human countenances in distorted laughter, went flitting to and fro; at times, too, the flame shot up, licking the sooty wall, and then there sounded cutting howling tones of woe, which shook Veronica with fear and horror. "With your leave, Mamsell!" said the crone, knitting her brows, and seizing a brush; with which, having dipped it in a copper skillet, she then besprinkled the grate. The fire went out; and as if filled with thick smoke, the room grew pitch-dark: but the crone, who had gone aside into a closet, soon returned with a lighted lamp; and now Veronica could see no beasts or implements in the apartment; it was a common meanly furnished room. The crone came up to her, and said with a creaking voice: "I know what you wish, little daughter: tush, you would have me tell you whether you shall wed Anselmus, when he is Hofrath."

Veronica stiffened with amazement and terror, but the crone continued: "You told me the whole of it at home, at your father's, when the coffeepot was standing before you: I was the coffeepot; didn't you know me? Daughterkin, hear me! Give up, give up this Anselmus; he is a nasty creature; he trod my little sons to pieces, my dear little sons, the Apples with the red cheeks, that glide away, when people have bought them, whisk! out of their pockets, and roll back into my basket. He trades with the Old One: it was but the day before yesterday, he poured that cursed Auripigment on my face, and I nearly went blind with it. You can see the burn marks yet. Daughterkin, give him up, give him up! He does not love you, for he loves the gold-green snake; he will never be Hofrath, for he has joined the salamanders, and he means to wed the green snake: give him up, give him up!"

Veronica, who had a firm, steadfast spirit of her own, and could conquer girlish terror, now drew back a step, and said, with a serious resolute tone: "Old woman! I heard of your gift of looking into the future; and wished, perhaps too curiously and thoughtlessly, to learn from you whether Anselmus, whom I love and value, could ever be mine. But if, instead of fulfilling my desire, you keep vexing me with your foolish unreasonable babble, you are doing wrong; for I have asked of you nothing but what you grant to others, as I well know. Since you are acquainted with my inmost thoughts apparently, it might perhaps have been an easy matter for you to unfold to me much that now pains and grieves my mind;

but after your silly slander of the good Anselmus, I do not care to talk further with you. Goodnight!"

Veronica started to leave hastily, but the crone, with tears and lamentation, fell upon her knees; and, holding the young lady by the gown, exclaimed: "Veronica! Veronica! have you forgotten old Liese? Your nurse who has so often carried you in her arms, and dandled you?"

Veronica could scarcely believe her eyes; for here, in truth, was her old nurse, defaced only by great age and by the two burns; old Liese, who had vanished from Conrector Paulmann's house some years ago, no one knew where. The crone, too, had quite another look now: instead of the ugly many-pieced clout, she had on a decent cap; instead of the black rags, a gay printed bedgown; she was neatly dressed, as of old. She rose from the floor, and taking Veronica in her arms, proceeded: "What I have just told you may seem very mad; but, unluckily, it is too true. Anselmus has done me much mischief, though it is not his own fault: he has fallen into Archivarius Lindhorst's hands, and the Old One means to marry him to his daughter. Archivarius Lindhorst is my deadliest enemy: I could tell you thousands of things about him, which, however, you would not understand, or at best be too much frightened at. He is the Wise Man, it seems; but I am the Wise Woman: let this stand for that! I see now that you love this Anselmus; and I will help you with all my strength, that so you may be happy, and wed him like a pretty bride, as you wish."

"But tell me, for Heaven's sake, Liese——" interrupted Veronica.

"Hush! child, hush!" cried the old woman, interrupting in her turn: "I know what you would say; I have become what I am, because it was to be so: I could do no other. Well, then! I know the means which will cure Anselmus of his frantic love for the green snake, and lead him, the prettiest Hofrath, into your arms; but you yourself must help."

"Tell me, Liese; I will do anything and everything, for I love Anselmus very much!" whispered Veronica, scarcely audibly.

"I know you," continued the crone, "for a courageous child: I could never frighten you to sleep with the *Wauwau*; for that instant, your eyes were open to what the *Wauwau* was like. You would go without a light into the darkest room; and many a time, with papa's powder-mantle, you terrified the neighbours' children. Well, then, if you are in earnest about conquering Archivarius Lindhorst and the green snake by my art; if you are in earnest about calling Anselmus Hofrath and husband; then, at the next Equinox, about eleven at night, glide from your father's house, and come here: I will go with you to the crossroads, which cut the fields hard by here: we shall take what is needed, and whatever wonders you may see shall do you no whit of harm. And now, love, goodnight: Papa is waiting for you at supper."

Veronica hastened away: she had the firmest purpose not to neglect the night of the Equinox; "for," thought she, "old Liese is right; Anselmus has become entangled in strange fetters; but I will free him from them, and call him mine forever; mine he is, and shall be, the Hofrath Anselmus."

SIXTH VIGIL

"It may be, after all," said the Student Anselmus to himself, "that the superfine strong stomachic liqueur, which I took somewhat freely in Monsieur Conradi's, might really be the cause of all these shocking phantasms, which tortured me so at Archivarius Lindhorst's door. Therefore, I will go quite sober today, and so bid defiance to whatever farther mischief may assail me." On this occasion, as before when equipping himself for his first call on Archivarius Lindhorst, the Student Anselmus put his pen-drawings, and calligraphic masterpieces, his bars of Indian ink, and his well-pointed crow-pens, into his pockets; and was just turning to go out, when his eye lighted on the vial with the yellow liquor, which he had received from Archivarius Lindhorst. All the strange adventures he had met again rose on his mind in glowing colours; and a nameless emotion of rapture and pain thrilled through his breast. Involuntarily he exclaimed, with a most piteous voice: "Ah, am not I going to the Archivarius solely for a sight of you, gentle lovely Serpentina!" At that moment, he felt as if Serpentina's love might be the prize of some laborious perilous task which he had to undertake; and as if this task were nothing else but the copying of the Lindhorst manuscripts. That at his very entrance into the house, or more properly, before his entrance, all sorts of mysterious things might happen, as before, was no more than he anticipated. He thought no more of Conradi's strong drink, but hastily put the vial of liquor in his waistcoat pocket, that he might act strictly by the Archivarius' directions, should the bronze Apple-woman again take it upon her to make faces at him.

And the hawk-nose actually did peak itself, the cat-eyes actually did glare from the knocker, as he raised his hand to it, at the stroke of twelve. But now, without farther ceremony, he dribbled his liquor into the pestilent visage; and it folded and moulded itself, that instant, down to a glittering bowl-round knocker. The door opened, the bells sounded beautifully over all the house: "Klingling, youngling, in, in, spring, spring, klingling." In good heart he mounted the fine broad stair; and feasted on the odours of some strange perfume that was floating through the house. In doubt, he paused in the hall; for he did not know at which of these many fine doors he was to knock. But Archivarius Lindhorst, in a white damask nightgown, emerged and said: "Well, it is a real pleasure to me, Herr Anselmus, that you have kept your word at last. Come this way, if you please; I must take you straight into the laboratory." And with this he stepped rapidly through the hall, and opened a little side door, which led into a long passage. Anselmus walked on in high spirits, behind the Archivarius; they passed from this corridor into a hall, or rather into a lordly greenhouse: for on both sides, up to the ceiling, grew all sorts of rare wondrous flowers, indeed, great trees with strangely formed leaves and blossoms. A magic dazzling light shone over the whole, though you could not discover where it came from, for no window whatever was to be seen. As the Student Anselmus looked in through the bushes and trees, long avenues appeared to open into remote distance. In the deep shade of thick cypress groves lay glittering marble fountains, out of which rose wondrous figures, spouting crystal jets that fell with pattering spray into the gleaming lily-cups. Strange voices cooed and rustled through the wood of curious trees; and sweetest perfumes streamed up and down.

The Archivarius had vanished: and Anselmus saw nothing but a huge bush of glowing fire-lilies before him. Intoxicated with the sight and the fine odours of this fairy-garden, Anselmus stood fixed to the spot. Then began on all sides of him a giggling and laughing; and light little voices railed at him and mocked him: "Herr Studiosus! Herr Studiosus! how did you get in here? Why have you dressed so bravely, Herr Anselmus? Will you chat with us for a minute and tell us how grandmamma sat down upon the egg, and young master got a stain on his Sunday waistcoat?—Can you play the new tune, now, which you learned from Daddy Cockadoodle, Herr Anselmus?—You look very fine in your glass periwig, and brown-paper boots." So cried and chattered and sniggered the little voices, out of every corner, indeed, close by the Student himself, who now observed that all sorts of multicoloured birds were fluttering above him, and jeering at him. At that moment, the bush of fire-lilies advanced towards him; and he perceived that it was Archivarius Lindhorst, whose flowered nightgown, glittering in red and yellow, had deceived his eyes.

"I beg your pardon, worthy Herr Anselmus," said the Archivarius, "for leaving you alone: I wished, in passing, to take a peep at my fine cactus, which is to blossom tonight. But how do you like my little house-garden?"

"Ah, Heaven! It is inconceivably beautiful, Herr Archivarius," replied the Student; "but these multicoloured birds have been bantering me a little."

"What chattering is this?" cried the Archivarius angrily into the bushes. Then a huge gray Parrot came fluttering out, and perched itself beside the Archivarius on a myrtle bough, and looking at him with an uncommon earnestness and gravity through a pair of spectacles that stuck on its hooked bill, it creaked out: "Don't take it amiss, Herr Archivarius; my wild boys have been a little free or so; but the Herr Studiosus has himself to blame in the matter, for——"

"Hush! hush!" interrupted Archivarius Lindhorst; "I know the varlets; but you must keep them in better discipline, my friend!— Now, come along, Herr Anselmus."

And the Archivarius again stepped forth through many a strangely decorated chamber, so that the Student Anselmus, in following him, could scarcely give a glance at all the glittering wondrous furniture and other unknown things with which all the rooms were filled. At last they entered a large apartment, where the Archivarius, casting his eyes aloft, stood still; and Anselmus got time to feast himself on the glorious sight, which the simple decoration of this hall afforded. Jutting from the azure-coloured walls rose gold-bronze trunks of high palm-trees, which wove their colossal leaves, glittering like bright emeralds, into a ceiling far up: in the middle of the chamber, and resting on three Egyptian lions, cast out of dark bronze, lay a porphyry plate; and on this stood a simple flower pot made of gold, from which, as soon as he beheld it, Anselmus could not turn away his eyes. It was as if, in a thousand gleaming reflections, all sorts of shapes were sporting on the bright polished gold: often he perceived his own form, with arms stretched out in longing—ah! beneath the elder-bush—and Serpentina was winding and shooting up and down, and again looking at him with her kind eyes. Anselmus was beside himself with frantic rapture.

"Serpentina! Serpentina!" he cried aloud; and Archivarius Lindhorst whirled round abruptly, and said: "What, Herr Anselmus? If I am not wrong, you were pleased to call for my daughter; she is in the other side of the house at present, and indeed taking her lesson on the harpsichord. Let us go along."

Anselmus, scarcely knowing what he did, followed his conductor; he saw or heard nothing more till Archivarius Lindhorst suddenly grasped his hand and said: "Here is the place!" Anselmus awoke as from a dream and now perceived that he was in a high room lined on all sides with bookshelves, and nowise differing from a common library and study. In the middle stood a large writing table, with a stuffed armchair before it. "This," said Archivarius Lindhorst, "is your workroom for the present: whether you may work, some other time, in the blue library, where you so suddenly called out my daughter's name, I do not know yet. But now I would like to convince myself of your ability to execute this task appointed you, in the way I wish it and need it." The Student here gathered full courage; and not without internal self-complacence in the certainty of highly gratifying Archivarius Lindhorst, pulled out his drawings and specimens of penmanship from his pocket. But no sooner had the Archivarius cast his eye on the first leaf, a piece of writing in the finest English style, than he smiled very oddly and shook his head. These motions he repeated at every succeeding leaf, so that the Student Anselmus felt the blood mounting to his face, and at last, when the smile became quite sarcastic and contemptuous, he broke out in downright vexation: "The Herr Archivarius does not seem contented with my poor talents."

"My dear Herr Anselmus," said Archivarius Lindhorst, "you have indeed fine capacities for the art of calligraphy; but, in the meanwhile, it is clear enough, I must reckon more on your diligence and good-will, than on your attainments."

The Student Anselmus spoke at length of his often-acknowledged perfection in this art, of his fine Chinese ink, and most select crow-quills. But Archivarius Lindhorst handed him the English sheet, and said: "Be the judge yourself!" Anselmus felt as if struck by a thunderbolt, to see the way his handwriting looked: it was miserable, beyond measure. There was no rounding in the turns, no hair-stroke where it should be; no proportion between the capital and single letters; indeed, villainous schoolboy pot-hooks often spoiled the best lines. "And then," continued Archivarius Lindhorst, "your ink will not last." He dipped his finger in a glass of water, and as he just skimmed it over the lines, they vanished without a trace. The Student Anselmus felt as if some monster were throttling him: he could not utter a word. There stood he, with the unfortunate sheet in his hand; but Archivarius Lindhorst laughed aloud, and said: "Never mind, Herr Anselmus; what you could not do well before you will perhaps do better here. At any rate, you shall have better materials than you have been accustomed to. Begin, in Heaven's name!"

From a locked press, Archivarius Lindhorst now brought out a black fluid substance, which diffused a most peculiar odour; also pens, sharply pointed and of strange colour, together with a sheet of special whiteness and smoothness; then at last an Arabic manuscript: and as Anselmus sat down to work, the Archivarius left the room. The Student Anselmus had often copied Arabic manuscripts before; the first problem, therefore, seemed to him not so very difficult to solve. "How those pot-hooks came into my fine English script, heaven and Archivarius Lindhorst know best," said he; "but that they are not from *my* hand, I will testify to the death!" At every new word that stood fair and perfect on the parchment, his courage increased, and with it his adroitness. In truth, these pens wrote exquisitely well; and the mysterious ink flowed pliantly, and black as jet, on the bright white parchment. And as he worked along so diligently, and with such strained attention, he began to feel more and more at home in the solitary room; and already he had quite fitted himself into his task, which he now hoped to finish well, when at the stroke of three the Archivarius called him into the side room to a savoury dinner. At table, Archivarius Lindhorst was in an especially good humour. He inquired about the Student Anselmus' friends, Conrector Paulmann and Registrator Heerbrand, and of the latter he had a store of merry anecdotes to tell. The good old Rhenish was particularly pleasing to the Student Anselmus, and made him more talkative than he usually was. At the stroke of four, he rose to resume his labour; and this punctuality appeared to please the Archivarius.

If the copying of these Arabic manuscripts had prospered in his hands before dinner, the task now went forward much better; indeed, he could not himself comprehend the rapidity and ease with which he succeeded in transcribing the twisted strokes of this foreign character. But it was as if, in his inmost soul, a voice were whispering in audible words: "Ah! could you accomplish it, if you were not thinking of *her*, if you did not believe in *her* and in her love?" Then there floated whispers, as in low, low, waving crystal tones, through the room: "I am near, near, near! I help you: be bold, be steadfast, dear Anselmus! I toil with you so that you may be mine!" And as, in the fullness of secret rapture, he caught these sounds, the unknown characters grew clearer and clearer to him;

he scarcely needed to look at the original at all; nay, it was as if the letters were already standing in pale ink on the parchment, and he had nothing more to do but mark them black. So did he labour on, encompassed with dear inspiring tones as with soft sweet breath, till the clock struck six and Archivarius Lindhorst entered the apartment. He came forward to the table, with a singular smile; Anselmus rose in silence: the Archivarius still looked at him, with that mocking smile: but no sooner had he glanced over the copy, than the smile passed into deep solemn earnestness, which every feature of his face adapted itself to express. He seemed no longer the same. His eyes which usually gleamed with sparkling fire, now looked with unutterable mildness at Anselmus; a soft red tinted the pale cheeks; and instead of the irony which at other times compressed the mouth, the softly curved graceful lips now seemed to be opening for wise and soul-persuading speech. His whole form was higher, statelier; the wide nightgown spread itself like a royal mantle in broad folds over his breast and shoulders; and through the white locks, which lay on his high open brow, there wound a thin band of gold.

"Young man," began the Archivarius in solemn tone, "before you were aware of it, I knew you, and all the secret relations which bind you to the dearest and holiest of my interests! Serpentina loves you; a singular destiny, whose fateful threads were spun by enemies, is fulfilled, should she become yours and if you obtain, as an essential dowry, the Golden Flower Pot, which of right belongs to her. But only from effort and contest can your happiness in the higher life arise; hostile Principles assail you; and only the interior force with which you withstand these contradictions can save you from disgrace and ruin. While labouring here, you are undergoing a season of instruction: belief and full knowledge will lead you to the near goal, if you but hold fast, what you have begun well. Bear *her* always and truly in your thoughts, her who loves you; then you will see the marvels of the Golden Pot, and be happy forevermore. Farewell! Archivarius Lindhorst expects you tomorrow at noon in his cabinet. Farewell!" With these words Archivarius Lindhorst softly pushed the Student Anselmus out of the door, which he then locked; and Anselmus found himself in the chamber where he had dined, the single door of which led out to the hallway.

Completely stupefied by these strange phenomena, the Student Anselmus stood lingering at the street door; he heard a window open above him, and looked up: it was Archivarius Lindhorst, quite the old man again, in his light-gray gown, as he usually appeared.

The Archivarius called to him: "Hey, worthy Herr Anselmus, what are you studying over there? Tush, the Arabic is still in your head. My compliments to Herr Conrector Paulmann, if you see him; and come tomorrow precisely at noon. The fee for this day is lying in your right waistcoat pocket." The Student Anselmus actually found the speziesthaler in the pocket indicated; but he derived no pleasure from it. "What is to come of all this," said he to himself, "I do not know: but if it is some mad delusion and conjuring work that has laid hold of me, my dear Serpentina still lives and moves in my inward heart; and before I leave her, I will die; for I know that the thought in me is eternal, and no hostile Principle can take it from me: and what else is this thought but Serpentina's love?"

SEVENTH VIGIL

At last Conrector Paulmann knocked the ashes out of his pipe, and said: "Now, then, it is time to go to bed." "Yes, indeed," replied Veronica, frightened at her father's sitting so late: for ten had struck long ago. No sooner, accordingly, had the Conrector withdrawn to his study and bedroom, and Fränzchen's heavy breathing signified that she was asleep, than Veronica, who to save appearances had also gone to bed, rose softly, softly, out of it again, put on her clothes, threw her mantle round her, and glided out of doors.

Ever since the moment when Veronica had left old Liese, Anselmus had continually stood before her eyes; and it seemed as if a voice that was strange to her kept repeating in her soul that he was reluctant because he was held prisoner by an enemy and that Veronica, by secret means of the magic art, could break these bonds. Her confidence in old Liese grew stronger every day; and even the impression of unearthliness and horror by degrees became less, so that all the mystery and strangeness of her relation to the crone appeared before her only in the colour of something singular, romantic, and so not a little attractive. Accordingly, she had a firm purpose, even at the risk of being missed from home, and encountering a thousand inconveniences, to undertake the adventure of the Equinox. And now, at last, the fateful night, in which old Liese had promised to afford comfort and help, had come; and Veronica, long used to thoughts of nightly wandering, was full of heart and hope. She sped through the solitary streets; heedless of the storm which was howling in the air and dashing thick raindrops in her face.

With a stifled droning clang, the Kreuzthurm clock struck eleven, as Veronica, quite wet, reached old Liese's house. "Are you here, dear! wait, love; wait, love—" cried a voice from above; and in a moment the crone, laden with a basket, and attended by her cat, was also standing at the door. "We will go, then, and do what is proper, and can prosper in the night, which favours the work." So speaking, the crone with her cold hand seized the shivering Veronica, to whom she gave the heavy basket to carry, while she herself produced a little cauldron, a trivet, and a spade. By the time they reached the open fields, the rain had ceased, but the storm had become louder; howlings in a thousand tones were flitting through the air. A horrible heart-piercing lamentation sounded down from the black clouds, which rolled themselves together in rapid flight and veiled all things in thickest darkness. But the crone stepped briskly forward, crying in a shrill harsh voice: "Light, light, my lad!" Then blue forky gleams went quivering and sputtering before them; and Veronica perceived that it was the cat emitting sparks, and bounding forward to light the way; while his doleful ghastly screams were heard in the momentary pauses of the storm. Her heart almost failed; it was as if ice-cold talons were clutching into her soul; but, with a strong effort, she collected herself, pressed closer to the crone, and said: "It must all be accomplished now, come of it what may!"

"Right, right, little daughter!" replied the crone; "be steady, like a good girl; you shall have something pretty, and Anselmus to boot."

At last the crone paused, and said: "Here is the place!" She dug a hole in the ground, then shook coals into it, put the trivet over them, and placed the cauldron on top of it. All this she accompanied with strange gestures, while the cat kept circling round her. From his tail there sputtered sparkles, which united into a ring of fire. The coals began to burn; and at last blue flames rose up around the cauldron. Veronica was ordered to lay off her mantle and veil, and to cower down beside the crone, who seized her hands, and pressed them hard, glaring with her fiery eyes at the maiden. Before long the strange materials (whether flowers, metals, herbs, or beasts, you could not determine), which the crone had taken from her basket and thrown into the cauldron, began to seethe and foam. The crone let go Veronica, then clutched an iron ladle, and plunged it into the glowing mass, which she began to stir, while Veronica, as she directed, was told to look steadfastly into the cauldron and fix her thoughts on Anselmus. Now the crone threw fresh ingredients, glittering pieces of metal, a lock of hair which Veronica had cut from her head, and a little ring which she had long worn, into the pot, while the old woman howled in dread yelling tones through the gloom, and the cat, in quick, incessant motion, whimpered and whined—

I wish very much, favorable reader, that on this twenty-third of September, you had been on the road to Dresden. In vain, when night sank down upon you, the people at the last stage-post tried to keep you there; the friendly host represented to you that the storm and the rain were too bitter, and moreover, for unearthly reasons, it was not safe to rush out into the dark on the night of the Equinox; but you paid no heed to him, thinking to yourself, "I will give the postillion a whole thaler as a tip, and so, at latest, by one o'clock I shall reach Dresden. There in the Golden Angel or the Helmet or the City of Naumburg a good supper and a soft bed await me."

And now as you ride toward Dresden through the dark, you suddenly observe in the distance a very strange, flickering light. As you come nearer, you can distinguish a ring of fire, and in its center, beside a pot out of which a thick vapour is mounting with quivering red flashes and sparkles, there sit two very different forms. Right through the fire your road leads, but the horses snort, and stamp, and rear; the postillion curses and prays, and does not spare his whip; the horses will not stir from the spot. Without thinking, you leap out of the stagecoach and hasten forward toward the fire.

And now you clearly see a pretty girl, obviously of gentle birth, who is kneeling by the cauldron in a thin white nightdress. The storm has loosened her braids, and her long chestnut-brown hair is floating freely in the wind. Full in the dazzling light from the flame flickering from beneath the trivet hovers her sweet face; but in the horror which has poured over it like an icy stream, it is stiff and pale as death; and by her updrawn eyebrows, by her mouth, which is vainly opened for the shriek of anguish which cannot find its way from her bosom compressed with unnamable torment— you perceive her terror, her horror. She holds her small soft hands aloft, spasmodically pressed together, as if she were calling with prayers her guardian angel to deliver her from the monsters of the Pit, which, in obedience to this potent spell are to appear at any moment! There she kneels, motionless as a figure of marble. Opposite her a long, shrivelled, copper-yellow crone with a peaked hawk-nose and glistering cat-eyes sits cowering. From the black cloak which is huddled around her protrude her skinny naked arms; as she stirs the Hell-broth, she laughs and cries with creaking voice through the raging, bellowing storm.

I can well believe that unearthly feelings might have arisen in you, too—unacquainted though you are otherwise with fear and dread— at the aspect of this picture by Rembrandt or Hell-Breughel, taking place in actual life. Indeed, in horror, the hairs of your head might have stood on end. But your eye could not turn away from the gentle girl entangled in these infernal doings; and the electric stroke that quivered through all your nerves and fibres, kindled in you with the speed of lightning the courageous thought of defying the mysterious powers of the ring of fire; and at this thought your horror disappeared; nay, the thought itself came into being from your feelings of horror, as their product. Your heart felt as if you yourself were one of those guardian angels to whom the maiden, frightened almost to death, was praying; nay, as if you must instantly whip out your pocket pistol and without further ceremony blow the hag's brains out. But while you were thinking of all of this most vividly, you cried aloud, "Holla!" or "What the matter here?" or "What's going on there?" The postillion blew a clanging blast on his horn; the witch ladled about in her brewage, and in a trice everything vanished in thick smoke. Whether you would have found the girl, for whom you were groping in the darkness with the most heart-felt longing, I cannot say: but you surely would have destroyed the witch's spell and undone the magic circle into which Veronica had thoughtlessly entered.

Alas! Neither you, favourable reader, nor any other man either drove or walked this way, on the twenty-third of September, in the tempestuous witch-favouring night; and Veronica had to abide by the cauldron, in deadly terror, till the work was near its close. She heard, indeed, the howling and raging around her; all sorts of hateful voices bellowed and bleated, and yelled and hummed; but she did not open her eyes, for she felt that the sight of the abominations and the horrors with which she was encircled might drive her into incurable destroying madness. The hag had ceased to stir the pot: its smoke grew fainter and fainter; and at last, nothing but a light spirit-flame was burning in the bottom. Then she cried: "Veronica, my child! my darling! look into the grounds there! What do you see? What do you see?"

Veronica could not answer, yet it seemed as if all sorts of perplexing shapes were dancing and whirling in the cauldron; and suddenly, with friendly look, reaching her his hand, the Student

Anselmus rose from the cavity of the vessel. She cried aloud: "It is Anselmus! It is Anselmus!"

Instantly the crone turned the cock fixed at the bottom of the cauldron, and glowing metal rushed forth, hissing and bubbling, into a little mould which she had placed beside it. The hag now sprang aloft, and shrieked, capering about with wild horrific gestures: "It is done! It is done! Thanks, my pretty lad; did you watch?—Pooh, pooh, he is coming! Bite him to death! Bite him to death!" But then there sounded a strong rushing through the air: it was as if a huge eagle were pouncing down, striking round him with his pinions; and there shouted a tremendous voice: "Hey, hey, vermin!—It is over! It is over!—Home with you!" The crone sank down with bitter howling, and Veronica's sense and recollection forsook her.

On her returning to herself, it was broad daylight, she was lying in her bed, and Fränzchen was standing before her with a cup of steaming tea and saying to her: "Tell me, sister, what in all the world ails you? I have been standing here this hour, and you have been lying senseless, as if in a fever, and moaning and whimpering so that we were frightened to death. Father has not gone to his class this morning because of you; he will be here directly with the doctor."

Veronica took the tea in silence: and while she was drinking it, the horrid images of the night rose vividly before her eyes. "So it was all nothing but a wild dream that tortured me? Yet last night, I surely went to that old woman; it was the twenty-third of September too? Well, I must have been very sick last night, and so fancied all this; and nothing has sickened me but my perpetual thinking of Anselmus and the strange old woman who gave herself out for Liese, but was no such thing, and only made a fool of me with that story."

Fränzchen, who had left the room, again came in with Veronica's mantle, all wet, in her hand. "Look, sister," said she, "what a sight your mantle is! The storm last night blew open the shutters and upset the chair where your mantle was hanging; and the rain has come in, and wet it for you."

This speech sank heavy on Veronica's heart, for she now saw that it was no dream which had tormented her, but that she had really been with the witch. Anguish and horror took hold of her at the thought, and a fever-frost quivered through all her frame. In spasmodic shuddering, she drew the bedclothes close over her; but with this, she felt something hard pressing on her breast, and on grasping it with her hand, it seemed like a medallion: she drew it out, as soon as Fränzchen went away with the mantle; it was a little, round, bright-polished metallic mirror. "This is a present from the woman," cried she eagerly; and it was as if fiery beams were shooting from the mirror, and penetrating into her inmost soul with benignant warmth. The fever-frost was gone, and there streamed through her whole being an unutterable feeling of contentment and cheerful delight. She could not but remember Anselmus; and as she turned her thoughts more and more intensely on him, behold, he smiled on her in friendly fashion out of the mirror, like a living miniature portrait. But before long she felt as if it were no longer the image which she saw; no! but the Student Anselmus himself alive and in person. He was sitting in a stately chamber, with the strangest furniture, and diligently writing. Veronica was about to step forward, to pat his shoulder, and say to him: "Herr Anselmus, look round; it is I!" But she could not; for it was as if a fire-stream encircled him; and yet when she looked more narrowly, this fire-stream was nothing but large books with gilt leaves. At last Veronica so far succeeded that she caught Anselmus's eye: it seemed as if he needed, in gazing at her, to bethink himself who she was; but at last he smiled and said: "Ah! Is it you, dear Mademoiselle Paulmann! But why do you like now and then to take the form of a little snake?"

At these strange words, Veronica could not help laughing aloud; and with this she awoke as from a deep dream; and hastily concealed the little mirror, for the door opened, and Conrector Paulmann with Doctor Eckstein entered the room. Dr. Eckstein stepped forward to the bedside; felt Veronica's pulse with long profound study, and then said: "Ey! Ey!" Thereupon he wrote out a prescription; again felt the pulse; a second time said: "Ey! Ey!" and then left his patient. But from these disclosures of Dr. Eckstein's, Conrector Paulmann could not clearly make out what it was that ailed Veronica.

EIGHTH VIGIL

The Student Anselmus had now worked several days with Archivarius Lindhorst; these working hours were for him the happiest of his life; still encircled with lovely tones, with Serpentina's encouraging voice, he was filled and overflowed with a pure delight, which often rose to highest rapture. Every difficulty, every little care of his needy existence, had vanished from his thoughts; and in the new life, which had risen on him as in serene sunny splendour, he comprehended all the wonders of a higher world, which before had filled him with astonishment, nay, with dread. His copying proceeded rapidly and lightly; for he felt more and more as if he were writing characters long known to him; and he scarcely needed to cast his eye upon the manuscript, while copying it all with the greatest exactness.

Except at the hour of dinner, Archivarius Lindhorst seldom made his appearance; and this always precisely at the moment when Anselmus had finished the last letter of some manuscript: then the Archivarius would hand him another, and immediately leave him, without uttering a word; having first stirred the ink with a little black rod, and changed the old pens for new sharp-pointed ones. One day, when Anselmus, at the stroke of twelve, had as usual mounted the stair, he found the door through which he commonly entered, standing locked; and Archivarius Lindhorst came forward from the other side, dressed in his strange flower-figured dressing gown. He called aloud: "Today come this way, good Herr Anselmus; for we must go to the chamber where the masters of Bhagavadgita are waiting for us."

He stepped along the corridor, and led Anselmus through the same chambers and halls as at the first visit. The Student Anselmus again felt astonished at the marvellous beauty of the garden: but he now perceived that many of the strange flowers, hanging on the dark bushes, were in truth insects gleaming with lordly colours, hovering up and down with their little wings, as they danced and whirled in clusters, caressing one another with their antennae. On the other hand again, the rose and azure-coloured birds were odoriferous flowers; and the perfume which they scattered, mounted from their cups in low lovely tones, which, with the gurgling of distant fountains, and the sighing of the high groves and trees, mingled themselves into mysterious accords of a deep unutterable longing. The mock-birds, which had so jeered and flouted him before, were again fluttering to and fro over his head, and crying incessantly with their sharp small voices: "Herr Studiosus, Herr Studiosus, don't be in such a hurry! Don't peep into the clouds so! They may fall about your ears—He! He! Herr Studiosus, put your powdermantle on; cousin Screech-Owl will frizzle your toupee." And so it went along, in all manner of stupid chatter, till Anselmus left the garden.

Archivarius Lindhorst at last stepped into the azure chamber: the porphyry, with the Golden Flower Pot, was gone; instead of it, in the middle of the room, stood a table overhung with violet-coloured satin, upon which lay the writing gear already known to Anselmus; and a stuffed armchair, covered with the same sort of cloth, was placed beside it.

"Dear Herr Anselmus," said Archivarius Lindhorst, "you have now copied for me a number of manuscripts, rapidly and correctly, to my no small contentment: you have gained my confidence; but the hardest is still ahead; and that is the transcribing or rather painting of certain works, written in a peculiar character; I keep them in this room, and they can only be copied on the spot. You will, therefore, in future, work here; but I must recommend to you the greatest foresight and attention; a false stroke, or, which may Heaven forfend, a blot let fall on the original, will plunge you into misfortune."

Anselmus observed that from the golden trunks of the palm-tree, little emerald leaves projected: one of these leaves the Archivarius took hold of; and Anselmus saw that the leaf was in truth a roll of parchment, which the Archivarius unfolded, and spread out before the Student on the table. Anselmus wondered not a little at these strangely intertwisted characters; and as he looked over the many points, strokes, dashes, and twirls in the manuscript, he almost lost hope of ever copying it. He fell into deep thought on the subject.

"Be of courage, young man!" cried the Archivarius; "if you have continuing belief and true love, Serpentina will help you."

His voice sounded like ringing metal; and as Anselmus looked up in utter terror, Archivarius Lindhorst was standing before him in the kingly form, which, during the first visit, he had assumed in the library. Anselmus felt as if in his deep reverence he could not but sink on his knee; but the Archivarius stepped up the trunk of a palm-tree, and vanished aloft among the emerald leaves. The Student Anselmus perceived that the Prince of the Spirits had been speaking with him, and was now gone up to his study; perhaps intending, by the beams which some of the Planets had despatched to him as envoys, to send back word what was to become of Anselmus and Serpentina.

"It may be too," he further thought, "that he is expecting news from the springs of the Nile; or that some magician from Lapland is paying him a visit: it behooves me to set diligently about my task." And with this, he began studying the foreign characters on the roll of parchment.

The strange music of the garden sounded over him, and encircled him with sweet lovely odours; the mock-birds, too, he still heard giggling and twittering, but could not distinguish their words, a thing which greatly pleased him. At times also it was as if the leaves of the palm-trees were rustling, and as if the clear crystal tones, which Anselmus on that fateful Ascension Day had heard under the elder-bush, were beaming and flitting through the room. Wonderfully strengthened by this shining and tinkling, the Student Anselmus directed his eyes and thoughts more and more intensely on the superscription of the parchment roll; and before long he felt, as it were from his inmost soul, that the characters could denote nothing else than these words: *Of the marriage of the Salamander with the green snake.* Then resounded a louder triphony of clear crystal bells: "Anselmus! dear Anselmus!" floated to him from the leaves; and, O wonder! on the trunk of the palm-tree the green snake came winding down.

"Serpentina! Serpentina!" cried Anselmus, in the madness of highest rapture; for as he gazed more earnestly, it was in truth a lovely glorious maiden that, looking at him with those dark blue eyes, full of inexpressible longing, as they lived in his heart, was slowly gliding down to meet him. The leaves seemed to jut out and expand; on every hand were prickles sprouting from the trunk; but Serpentina twisted and wound herself deftly through them; and so drew her fluttering robe, glancing as if in changeful colours, along with her, that, plying round the dainty form, it nowhere caught on the projecting points and prickles of the palm-tree. She sat down by Anselmus on the same chair, clasping him with her arm, and pressing him towards her, so that he felt the breath which came from her lips, and the electric warmth of her frame.

"Dear Anselmus," began Serpentina, "you shall now be wholly mine; by your belief, by your love, you shall obtain me, and I will bring you the Golden Flower Pot, which shall make us both happy forevermore."

"O, kind, lovely Serpentina!" said Anselmus. "If I have you, what do I care for anything else! If you are but mine, I will joyfully give in to all the wonderful mysteries that have beset me since the moment when I first saw you."

"I know," continued Serpentina, "that the strange and mysterious things with which my father, often merely in the sport of his humour, has surrounded you have raised distrust and dread in your mind; but now, I hope, it shall be so no more; for I came at this moment to tell you, dear Anselmus, from the bottom of my heart and soul, everything, to the smallest detail, that you need to know for understanding my father, and so for seeing clearly what your relation to him and to me really is."

Anselmus felt as if he were so wholly clasped and encircled by the gentle lovely form, that only with her could he move and live, and as if it were but the beating of her pulse that throbbed through his nerves and fibres; he listened to each one of her words till it sounded in his inmost heart, and, like a burning ray, kindled in him the rapture of Heaven. He had put his arm round that daintier than dainty waist; but the changeful glistering cloth of her robe was so smooth and slippery, that it seemed to him as if she could at any moment wind herself from his arms, and glide away. He trembled at the thought.

"Ah, do not leave me, gentlest Serpentina!" cried he; "you are my life."

"Not now," said Serpentina, "till I have told you everything that in your love of me you can comprehend:

"Know then, dearest, that my father is sprung from the wondrous race of the Salamanders; and that I owe my existence to his love for the green snake. In primeval times, in the Fairyland Atlantis, the potent Spirit-prince Phosphorus bore rule; and to him the Salamanders, and other spirits of the elements, were pledged by oath. Once upon a time, a Salamander, whom he loved before all others (it was my father), chanced to be walking in the stately garden, which Phosphorus' mother had decked in the lordliest fashion with her best gifts; and the Salamander heard a tall lily singing in low tones: 'Press down thy little eyelids, till my lover, the Morning-wind, awake thee.' He walked towards it: touched by his glowing breath, the lily opened her leaves: and he saw the lily's daughter, the green snake, lying asleep in the hollow of the flower. Then was the Salamander inflamed with warm love for the fair snake; and he carried her away from the lily, whose perfumes in nameless lamentation vainly called for her beloved daughter throughout all the garden. For the Salamander had borne her into the palace of Phosphorus, and was there beseeching him: 'Wed me with my beloved, and she shall be mine forevermore.'—'Madman, what do you ask?' said the Prince of the Spirits. 'Know that once the Lily was my mistress, and bore rule with me; but the Spark, which I cast into her, threatened to annihilate the fair Lily; and only my victory over the black Dragon, whom now the Spirits of the Earth hold in fetters, maintains her, that her leaves continue strong enough to enclose this Spark, and preserve it within them. But when you clasp the green snake, your fire will consume her frame; and a new being rapidly arising from her dust, will soar away and leave you.'

"The Salamander heeded not the warning of the Spirit-prince: full of longing ardour he folded the green snake in his arms; she crumbled into ashes; a winged being, born from her dust, soared away through the sky.   Then the madness of desperation caught the Salamander; and he ran through the garden, dashing forth fire and flames; and wasted it in his wild fury, till its fairest flowers and blossoms hung down, blackened and scathed; and their lamentation filled the air.   The indignant Prince of the Spirits, in his wrath, laid hold of the Salamander, and said: 'Your fire has burnt out, your flames are extinguished, your rays darkened: sink down to the Spirits of the Earth; let them mock and jeer you, and keep you captive, till the Fire-elements shall again kindle, and beam up with you as with a new being from the Earth.'   The poor Salamander sank down extinguished: but now the testy old earth-spirit, who was Phosphorus' gardener, came forth and said: 'Master! who has greater cause to complain of the Salamander than I?   Had not all the fair flowers, which he has burnt, been decorated with my gayest metals; had I not stoutly nursed and tended them, and spent many a fair hue on their leaves?   And yet I must pity the poor Salamander; for it was but love, in which you, O Master, have full often been entangled, that drove him to despair, and made him desolate the garden.   Remit his too harsh punishment!'—'His fire is for the present extinguished,' said the Prince of the Spirits; 'but in the hapless time, when the speech of nature shall no longer be intelligible to degenerate man; when the spirits of the elements, banished into their own regions, shall speak to him only from afar, in faint, spent echoes; when, displaced from the harmonious circle, an infinite longing alone shall give him tidings of the land of marvels, which he once might inhabit while belief and love still dwelt in his soul: in this hapless time, the fire of the Salamander shall again kindle; but only to manhood shall he be permitted to rise, and entering wholly into man's necessitous existence, he shall learn to endure its wants and oppressions.   Yet not only shall the remembrance of his first state continue with him, but he shall again rise into the sacred harmony of all Nature; he shall understand its wonders, and the power of his fellow-spirits shall stand at his behest.   Then, too, in a lily-bush, shall he find the green snake again: and the fruit of his marriage with her shall be three daughters, which, to men, shall appear in the form of their mother.   In the spring season these shall disport themselves in the dark elder-bush, and sound with their lovely crystal

voices. And then if, in that needy and mean age of inward stunted-
ness, there shall be found a youth who understands their song; nay,
if one of the little snakes look at him with her kind eyes; if the look
awaken in him forecastings of the distant wondrous land, to which,
having cast away the burden of the Common, he can courageously
soar; if, with love to the snake, there rise in him belief in the wonders
of nature, nay, in his own existence amid these wonders, then the
snake shall be his. But not till three youths of this sort have been
found and wedded to the three daughters, may the Salamander cast
away his heavy burden, and return to his brothers.'—'Permit me,
Master,' said the earth-spirit, to make these three daughters a
present, which may glorify their life with the husbands they shall
find. Let each of them receive from me a flower pot, of the fairest
metal which I have; I will polish it with beams borrowed from the
diamond; in its glitter shall our kingdom of wonders, as it now exists
in the harmony of universal nature be imaged back in glorious
dazzling reflection; and from its interior, on the day of marriage,
shall spring forth a fire-lily, whose eternal blossoms shall encircle
the youth that is found worthy, with sweet wafting odours. Soon
too shall he learn its speech, and understand the wonders of our
kingdom, and dwell with his beloved in Atlantis itself.'

"Thou perceivest well, dear Anselmus, that the Salamander of
whom I speak is no other than my father. In spite of his higher
nature, he was forced to subject himself to the paltriest contradictions
of common life; and hence, indeed, often comes the wayward
humour with which he vexes many. He has told me now and then,
that, for the inward make of mind, which the Spirit-prince Phosphorus required as a condition of marriage with me and my sisters,
men have a name at present, which, in truth, they frequently enough
misapply: they call it a childlike poetic character. This character,
he says, is often found in youths, who, by reason of their high simplicity of manners, and their total want of what is called knowledge
of the world, are mocked by the common mob. Ah, dear Anselmus!
beneath the elder-bush, you understood my song, my look: you love
the green snake, you believe in me, and will be mine for evermore!
The fair lily will bloom forth from the Golden Flower Pot; and we
shall dwell, happy, and united, and blessed, in Atlantis together!

"Yet I must not hide from you that in its deadly battle with the
Salamanders and spirits of the earth, the black Dragon burst from
their grasp, and hurried off through the air. Phosphorus, indeed,
again holds him in fetters; but from the black quills, which, in the
struggle, rained down on the ground, there sprang up hostile spirits,

which on all hands set themselves against the Salamanders and spirits of the earth. That woman who hates you so, dear Anselmus, and who, as my father knows full well, is striving for possession of the Golden Flower Pot; that woman owes her existence to the love of such a quill (plucked in battle from the Dragon's wing) for a certain beet beside which it dropped. She knows her origin and her power; for, in the moans and convulsions of the captive Dragon, the secrets of many a mysterious constellation are revealed to her; and she uses every means and effort to work from the outward into the inward and unseen; while my father, with the beams which shoot forth from the spirit of the Salamander, withstands and subdues her. All the baneful principles which lurk in deadly herbs and poisonous beasts, she collects; and, mixing them under favourable constellations, raises therewith many a wicked spell, which overwhelms the soul of man with fear and trembling, and subjects him to the power of those demons, produced from the Dragon when it yielded in battle. Beware of that old woman, dear Anselmus! She hates you, because your childlike pious character has annihilated many of her wicked charms. Keep true, true to me; soon you will be at the goal!"

"O my Serpentina! my own Serpentina!" cried the Student Anselmus, "how could I leave you, how should I not love you forever!" A kiss was burning on his lips; he awoke as from a deep dream: Serpentina had vanished; six o'clock was striking, and it fell heavy on his heart that today he had not copied a single stroke. Full of anxiety, and dreading reproaches from the Archivarius, he looked into the sheet; and, O wonder! the copy of the mysterious manuscript was fairly concluded; and he thought, on viewing the characters more narrowly, that the writing was nothing else but Serpentina's story of her father, the favourite of the Spirit-prince Phosphorus, in Atlantis, the land of marvels. And now entered Archivarius Lindhorst, in his light-gray surtout, with hat and staff: he looked into the parchment on which Anselmus had been writing; took a large pinch of snuff, and said with a smile: "Just as I thought! —Well, Herr Anselmus, here is your speziesthaler; we will now go to the Linkische Bath: please follow me!" The Archivarius walked rapidly through the garden, in which there was such a din of singing, whistling, talking, that the Student Anselmus was quite deafened with it, and thanked Heaven when he found himself on the street.

Scarcely had they walked twenty paces, when they met Registrator Heerbrand, who companionably joined them. At the Gate, they filled their pipes, which they had upon them: Registrator Heerbrand complained that he had left his tinder-box behind, and could not strike fire. "Fire!" cried Archivarius Lindhorst, scornfully; "here is fire enough, and to spare!" And with this he snapped his fingers, out of which came streams of sparks, and directly kindled the pipes. —"Observe the chemical knack of some men!" said Registrator Heerbrand; but the Student Anselmus thought, not without internal awe, of the Salamander and his history.

In the Linkische Bath, Registrator Heerbrand drank so much strong double beer, that at last, though usually a good-natured quiet man, he began singing student songs in squeaking tenor; he asked every-one sharply, whether he was his friend or not? and at last had to be taken home by the Student Anselmus, long after the Archivarius Lindhorst had gone his ways.

NINTH VIGIL

The strange and mysterious things which day by day befell the Student Anselmus, had entirely withdrawn him from his customary life. He no longer visited any of his friends, and waited every morning with impatience for the hour of noon, which was to unlock his paradise. And yet while his whole soul was turned to the gentle Serpentina, and the wonders of Archivarius Lindhorst's fairy king-dom, he could not help now and then thinking of Veronica; nay, often it seemed as if she came before him and confessed with blushes how heartily she loved him; how much she longed to rescue him from the phantoms, which were mocking and befooling him. At times he felt as if a foreign power, suddenly breaking in on his mind, were drawing him with resistless force to the forgotten Veronica; as if he must needs follow her whither she pleased to lead him, nay, as if he were bound to her by ties that would not break. That very night after Serpentina had first appeared to him in the form of a lovely maiden; after the wondrous secret of the Salamander's nup-tials with the green snake had been disclosed, Veronica came before him more vividly than ever. Nay, not till he awoke, was he clearly aware that he had only been dreaming; for he had felt persuaded that Veronica was actually beside him, complaining with an expres-sion of keen sorrow, which pierced through his inmost soul, that he should sacrifice her deep true love to fantastic visions, which only the distemper of his mind called into being, and which, moreover, would at last prove his ruin. Veronica was lovelier than he had ever seen her; he could not drive her from his thoughts: and in this perplexed and contradictory mood he hastened out, hoping to get rid of it by a morning walk.

A secret magic influence led him on the Pirna gate: he was just turning into a cross street, when Conrector Paulmann, coming after him, cried out: "Ey! Ey!—Dear Herr Anselmus!—*Amice! Amice!* Where, in Heaven's name, have you been buried so long? We never see you at all. Do you know, Veronica is longing very much to have another song with you. So come along; you were just on the road to me, at any rate."

The Student Anselmus, constrained by this friendly violence, went along with the Conrector. On entering the house, they were met by Veronica, attired with such neatness and attention, that Conrector Paulmann, full of amazement, asked her: "Why so decked, Mamsell? Were you expecting visitors? Well, here I bring you Herr Anselmus."

The Student Anselmus, in daintily and elegantly kissing Veronica's hand, felt a small soft pressure from it, which shot like a stream of fire over all his frame. Veronica was cheerfulness, was grace itself; and when Paulmann left them for his study, she contrived, by all manner of rogueries and waggeries, to uplift the Student Anselmus so much that he at last quite forgot his bashfulness, and jigged round the room with the playful girl. But here again the demon of awkwardness got hold of him: he jolted on a table, and Veronica's pretty little workbox fell to the floor. Anselmus lifted it; the lid had flown up; and a little round metallic mirror was glittering on him, into which he looked with peculiar delight. Veronica glided softly up to him; laid her hand on his arm, and pressing close to him, looked over his shoulder into the mirror also. And now Anselmus felt as if a battle were beginning in his soul: thoughts, images flashed out—Archivarius Lindhorst—Serpentina—the green snake —at last the tumult abated, and all this chaos arranged and shaped itself into distinct consciousness. It was now clear to him that he had always thought of Veronica alone; nay, that the form which had yesterday appeared to him in the blue chamber, had been no other than Veronica; and that the wild legend of the Salamander's marriage with the green snake had merely been written down by him from the manuscript, but nowise related in his hearing. He wondered greatly at all these dreams; and ascribed them solely to the heated state of mind into which Veronica's love had brought him, as well as to his working with Archivarius Lindhorst, in whose rooms there were, besides, so many strangely intoxicating odours. He could not help laughing heartily at the mad whim of falling in love with a little green snake; and taking a well-fed Privy Archivarius for a Salamander: "Yes, yes! It is Veronica!" cried he aloud; but on turning round his head, he looked right into Veronica's blue eyes, from which warmest love was beaming. A faint soft Ah! escaped her lips, which at that moment were burning on his.

"O happy I!" sighed the enraptured Student: "What I yester-night but dreamed, is in very deed mine today."

"But will you really marry me, then, when you are a Hofrath?" said Veronica.

"That I will," replied the Student Anselmus; and just then the door creaked, and Conrector Paulmann entered with the words:

"Now, dear Herr Anselmus, I will not let you go today. You will put up with a bad dinner; then Veronica will make us delight-ful coffee, which we shall drink with Registrator Heerbrand, for he promised to come here."

"Ah, Herr Conrector!" answered the Student Anselmus, "are you not aware that I must go to Archivarius Lindhorst's and copy?"

"Look, *Amice!*" said Conrector Paulmann, holding up his watch, which pointed to half-past twelve.

The Student Anselmus saw clearly that he was much too late for Archivarius Lindhorst; and he complied with the Conrector's wishes the more readily, as he might now hope to look at Veronica the whole day long, to obtain many a stolen glance, and little squeeze of the hand, nay, even to succeed in conquering a kiss. So high had the Student Anselmus's desires now mounted; he felt more and more contented in soul, the more fully he convinced himself that he should soon be delivered from all these fantasies, which really might have made a sheer idiot of him.

Registrator Heerbrand came, as he had promised, after dinner; and coffee being over, and the dusk come on, the Registrator, puck-ering his face together, and gaily rubbing his hands, signified that he had something about him, which, if mingled and reduced to form, as it were, paged and titled, by Veronica's fair hands, might be pleasant to them all, on this October evening.

"Come out, then, with this mysterious substance which you carry with you, most valued Registrator," cried Conrector Paulmann. Then Registrator Heerbrand shoved his hand into his deep pocket, and at three journeys, brought out a bottle of arrack, two lemons, and a quantity of sugar. Before half an hour had passed, a savoury bowl of punch was smoking on Paulmann's table. Veronica drank their health in a sip of the liquor; and before long there was plenty of gay, good-natured chat among the friends. But the Student

Anselmus, as the spirit of the drink mounted into his head, felt all the images of those wondrous things, which for some time he had experienced, again coming through his mind. He saw the Archivarius in his damask dressing gown, which glittered like phosphorus; he saw the azure room, the golden palm-trees; nay, it now seemed to him as if he must still believe in Serpentina: there was a fermentation, a conflicting tumult in his soul. Veronica handed him a glass of punch; and in taking it, he gently touched her hand. "Serpentina! Veronica!" sighed he to himself. He sank into deep dreams; but Registrator Heerbrand cried quite aloud: "A strange old gentleman, whom nobody can fathom, he is and will be, this Archivarius Lindhorst. Well, long life to him! Your glass, Herr Anselmus!"

Then the Student Anselmus awoke from his dreams, and said, as he touched glasses with Registrator Heerbrand: "That proceeds, respected Herr Registrator, from the circumstance, that Archivarius Lindhorst is in reality a Salamander, who in his fury laid waste the Spirit-prince Phosphorus' garden, because the green snake had flown away from him."

"What?" inquired Conrector Paulmann.

"Yes," continued the Student Anselmus; "and for this reason he is now forced to be a Royal Archivarius; and to keep house here in Dresden with his three daughters, who, after all, are nothing more than little gold-green snakes, that bask in elder-bushes, and traitorously sing, and seduce away young people, like so many sirens."

"Herr Anselmus! Herr Anselmus!" cried Conrector Paulmann, "is there a crack in your brain? In Heaven's name, what monstrous stuff is this you are babbling?"

"He is right," interrupted Registrator Heerbrand: "that fellow, that Archivarius, is a cursed Salamander, and strikes you fiery snips from his fingers, which burn holes in your surtout like red-hot tinder. Ay, ay, you are in the right, brotherkin Anselmus; and whoever says No, is saying No to me!" And at these words Registrator Heerbrand struck the table with his fist, till the glasses rung again.

"Registrator! Are you raving mad?" cried the enraged Conrector. "Herr Studiosus, Herr Studiosus! what is this you are about again?"

"Ah!" said the Student, "you too are nothing but a bird, a screech-owl, that frizzles toupees, Herr Conrector!"

"What?—I a bird?—A screech-owl, a frizzler?" cried the Conrector, full of indignation: "Sir, you are mad, born mad!"

"But the crone will get a clutch of him," cried Registrator Heerbrand.

"Yes, the crone is potent," interrupted the Student Anselmus, "though she is but of mean descent; for her father was nothing but a ragged wing-feather, and her mother a dirty beet: but the most of her power she owes to all sorts of baneful creatures, poisonous vermin which she keeps about her."

"That is a horrid calumny," cried Veronica, with eyes all glowing in anger: "old Liese is a wise woman; and the black cat is no baneful creature, but a polished young gentleman of elegant manners, and her cousin-german."

"Can *he* eat Salamanders without singeing his whiskers, and dying like a snuffed candle?" cried Registrator Heerbrand.

"No! no!" shouted the Student Anselmus, "that he never can in this world; and the green snake loves me, and I have looked into Serpentina's eyes."

"The cat will scratch them out," cried Veronica.

"Salamander, Salamander beats them all, all," hallooed Conrector Paulmann, in the highest fury: "But am I in a madhouse? Am I mad myself? What foolish nonsense am I chattering? Yes, I am mad too! mad too!" And with this, Conrector Paulmann started up; tore the peruke from his head, and dashed it against the ceiling of the room; till the battered locks whizzed, and, tangled into utter disorder, it rained down powder far and wide. Then the Student Anselmus and Registrator Heerbrand seized the punch-bowl and the glasses; and, hallooing and huzzaing, pitched them against the ceiling also, and the sherds fell jingling and tingling about their ears.

. "*Vivat* the Salamander!—*Pereat, pereat* the crone!—Break the metal mirror!—Dig the cat's eyes out!—Bird, little bird, from the air—*Eheu—Eheu—Evoe—Evoe*, Salamander!" So shrieked, and shouted, and bellowed the three, like utter maniacs. With loud weeping, Fränzchen ran out; but Veronica lay whimpering for pain and sorrow on the sofa.

At this moment the door opened: all was instantly still; and a little man, in a small gray cloak, came stepping in. His countenance had a singular air of gravity; and especially the round hooked nose, on which was a huge pair of spectacles, distinguished itself from all noses ever seen. He wore a strange peruke too; more like a feather-cap than a wig.

"Ey, many good-evenings!" grated and cackled the little comical mannikin. "Is the Student Herr Anselmus among you, gentlemen?

—Best compliments from Archivarius Lindhorst; he has waited today in vain for Herr Anselmus; but tomorrow he begs most respectfully to request that Herr Anselmus does not miss the hour."

And with this, he went out again; and all of them now saw clearly that the grave little mannikin was in fact a gray parrot. Conrector Paulmann and Registrator Heerbrand raised a horselaugh, which reverberated through the room; and in the intervals, Veronica was moaning and whimpering, as if torn by nameless sorrow; but, as to the Student Anselmus, the madness of inward horror was darting through him; and unconsciously he ran through the door, along the streets. Instinctively he reached his house, his garret. Ere long Veronica came in to him, with a peaceful and friendly look, and asked him why, in the festivity, he had so vexed her; and desired him to be upon his guard against figments of the imagination while working at Archivarius Lindhorst's. "Goodnight, goodnight, my beloved friend!" whispered Veronica scarcely audibly, and breathed a kiss on his lips. He stretched out his arms to clasp her, but the dreamy shape had vanished, and he awoke cheerful and refreshed. He could not but laugh heartily at the effects of the punch; but in thinking of Veronica, he felt pervaded by a most delightful feeling. "To her alone," said he within himself, "do I owe this return from my insane whims. Indeed, I was little better than the man who believed himself to be of glass; or the one who did not dare leave his room for fear the hens should eat him, since he was a barleycorn. But so soon as I am Hofrath, I shall marry Mademoiselle Paulmann, and be happy, and there's an end to it."

At noon, as he walked through Archivarius Lindhorst's garden, he could not help wondering how all this had once appeared so strange and marvellous. He now saw nothing that was not common; earthen flowerpots, quantities of geraniums, myrtles, and the like. Instead of the glittering multi-coloured birds which used to flout him, there were nothing but a few sparrows, fluttering hither and thither, which raised an unpleasant unintelligible cry at sight of Anselmus. The azure room also had quite a different look; and he could not understand how that glaring blue, and those unnatural golden trunks of palm-trees, with their shapeless glistening leaves, should ever have pleased him for a moment. The Archivarius looked at him with a most peculiar ironic smile, and asked: "Well, how did you like the punch last night, good Anselmus?"

"Ah, doubtless you have heard from the gray parrot how——" answered the Student Anselmus, quite ashamed; but he stopped short, thinking that this appearance of the parrot was all a piece of jugglery.

"I was there myself," said Archivarius Lindhorst; "didn't you see me? But, among the mad pranks you were playing, I almost got lamed: for I was sitting in the punch bowl, at the very moment when Registrator Heerbrand laid hands on it, to dash it against the ceiling; and I had to make a quick retreat into the Conrector's pipe-head. Now, adieu, Herr Anselmus! Be diligent at your task; for the lost day you shall also have a speziesthaler, because you worked so well before."

"How can the Archivarius babble such mad stuff?" thought the Student Anselmus, sitting down at the table to begin the copying of the manuscript, which Archivarius Lindhorst had as usual spread out before him. But on the parchment roll, he perceived so many strange crabbed strokes and twirls all twisted together in inexplicable confusion, offering no resting point for the eye, that it seemed to him well nigh impossible to copy all this exactly. Nay, in glancing over the whole, you might have thought the parchment was nothing but a piece of thickly veined marble, or a stone sprinkled over with lichens. Nevertheless he determined to do his utmost; and boldly dipped in his pen: but the ink would not run, do what he liked; impatiently he flicked the point of his pen against his fingernail, and—Heaven and Earth!—a huge blot fell on the outspread original! Hissing and foaming, a blue flash rose from the blot; and crackling and wavering, shot through the room to the ceiling. Then a thick vapour rolled from the walls; the leaves began to rustle, as if shaken by a tempest; and down out of them darted glaring basilisks in sparkling fire; these kindled the vapour, and the bickering masses of flame rolled round Anselmus. The golden trunks of the palm-trees became gigantic snakes, which knocked their frightful heads together with piercing metallic clang; and wound their scaly bodies round Anselmus.

"Madman! suffer now the punishment of what, in capricious irreverence, thou hast done!" cried the frightful voice of the crowned Salamander, who appeared above the snakes like a glittering beam in the midst of the flame: and now the yawning jaws of the snakes poured forth cataracts of fire on Anselmus; and it was as if the fire-streams were congealing about his body, and changing into a firm ice-cold mass. But while Anselmus's limbs, more and more pressed together, and contracted, stiffened into powerlessness, his senses passed away. On returning to himself, he could not stir a joint: he was as if surrounded with a glistening brightness, on which he struck if he but tried to lift his hand.—Alas! He was sitting in a well-corked crystal bottle, on a shelf, in the library of Archivarius Lindhorst.

TENTH VIGIL

I am probably right in doubting, gracious reader, that you were ever sealed up in a glass bottle, or even that you have ever been oppressed with such sorcery in your most vivid dreams. If you have had such dreams, you will understand the Student Anselmus's woe and will feel it keenly enough; but if you have not, then your flying imagination, for the sake of Anselmus and me, will have to be obliging enough to enclose itself for a few moments in the crystal. You are drowned in dazzling splendour; everything around you appears illuminated and begirt with beaming rainbow hues: in the sheen everything seems to quiver and waver and clang and drone. You are swimming, but you are powerless and cannot move, as if you were imbedded in a firmly congealed ether which squeezes you so tightly that it is in vain that your spirit commands your dead and stiffened body. Heavier and heavier the mountainous burden lies on you; more and more every breath exhausts the tiny bit of air that still plays up and down in the tight space around you; your pulse throbs madly; and cut through with horrid anguish, every nerve is quivering and bleeding in your dead agony. Favourable reader, have pity on the Student Anselmus! This inexpressible torture seized him in his glass prison: but he felt too well that even death could not release him, for when he had fainted with pain, he awoke again to new wretchedness when the morning sun shone into the room. He could move no limb, and his thoughts struck against the glass, stunning him with discordant clang; and instead of the words which the spirit used to speak from within him he now heard only the stifled din of madness. Then he exclaimed in his despair: "O Serpentina! Serpentina! Save me from this agony of Hell!" And it was as if faint sighs breathed around him, which spread like transparent green elder-leaves over the glass; the clanging ceased; the dazzling, perplexing glitter was gone, and he breathed more freely.

"Haven't I myself solely to blame for my misery? Ah! Haven't I sinned against you, kind, beloved Serpentina? Haven't I raised vile doubts of you? Haven't I lost my belief, and with it, all, all that was to make me so blessed? Ah! You will now never, never be mine; for me the Golden Pot is lost, and I shall not behold its wonders any more. Ah, could I but see you but once more; but once more hear your kind, sweet voice, lovely Serpentina!"

So wailed the Student Anselmus, caught with deep piercing sorrow: then a voice spoke close by him: "What the devil ails you, Herr Studiosus? What makes you lament so, out of all compass and measure?"

The Student Anselmus now perceived that on the same shelf with him were five other bottles, in which he perceived three Kreuzkirche Scholars, and two Law Clerks.

"Ah, gentlemen, my fellows in misery," cried he, "how is it possible for you to be so calm, nay, so happy, as I read in your cheerful looks? You are sitting here corked up in glass bottles, as well as I, and cannot move a finger, nay, not think a reasonable thought, but there rises such a murder-tumult of clanging and droning, and in your head itself a tumbling and rumbling enough to drive one mad. But of course you do not believe in the Salamander, or the green snake."

"You are pleased to jest, Mein Herr Studiosus," replied a Kreuzkirche Scholar; "we have never been better off than at present: for the speziesthalers which the mad Archivarius gave us for all kinds of pot-hook copies, are chinking in our pockets; we have now no Italian choruses to learn by heart; we go every day to Joseph's or other beer gardens, where the double-beer is sufficient, and we can look a pretty girl in the face; so we sing like real Students, *Gaudeamus igitur*, and are contented!"

"They of the Cross are quite right," added a Law Clerk; "I too am well furnished with speziesthalers, like my dearest colleague beside me here; and we now diligently walk about on the Weinberg, instead of scurvy law-copying within four walls."

"But, my best, worthiest masters!" said the Student Anselmus, "do you not observe, then, that you are all and sundry corked up in glass bottles, and cannot for your hearts walk a hairsbreadth?"

Here the Kreuzkirche Scholars and the Law Clerks set up a loud laugh, and cried: "The Student is mad; he fancies himself to be sitting in a glass bottle, and is standing on the Elbe Bridge and looking right down into the water. Let us go on our way!"

"Ah!" sighed the Student, "they have never seen the kind Serpentina; they do not know what Freedom, and life in Love, and Belief, signify; and so by reason of their folly and low-mindedness, they do not feel the oppression of the imprisonment into which the Salamander has cast them. But I, unhappy I, must perish in want and woe, if she whom I so inexpressibly love does not rescue me!"

Then, waving in faint tinkles, Serpentina's voice flitted through the room: "Anselmus! Believe, love, hope!" And every tone beamed into Anselmus's prison; and the crystal yielded to his pressure and expanded, till the breast of the captive could move and heave.

The torment of his situation became less and less, and he saw clearly that Serpentina still loved him; and that it was she alone, who had rendered his confinement tolerable. He disturbed himself no more about his inane companions in misfortune; but directed all his thoughts and meditations on the gentle Serpentina. Suddenly, however, there arose on the other side a dull, croaking repulsive murmur. Before long he could observe that it came from an old coffeepot, with half-broken lid, standing opposite him on a little shelf. As he looked at it more narrowly, the ugly features of a wrinkled old woman unfolded themselves gradually; and in a few moments the Apple-wife of the Schwarzthor stood before him. She grinned and laughed at him, and cried with screeching voice: "Ey, ey, my pretty boy, must you lie in limbo now? In the crystal you ended! Didn't I tell you so long ago?"

"Mock and jeer me, you cursed witch!" said Anselmus, "you are to blame for it all; but the Salamander will catch you, you vile beet!"

"Ho, ho!" replied the crone, "not so proud, my fine copyist. You have squashed my little sons and you have scarred my nose; but I still love you, you knave, for once you were a pretty fellow, and my little daughter likes you, too. Out of the crystal you will never get unless I help you: I cannot climb up there, but my friend the rat, that lives close behind you, will eat the shelf in two; you will jingle down, and I shall catch you in my apron so that your nose doesn't get broken or your fine sleek face get injured at all. Then I will carry you to Mamsell Veronica, and you shall marry her when you become Hofrath."

"Get away, you devil's brood!" shouted the Student Anselmus in fury. "It was you alone and your hellish arts that made me commit the sin which I must now expiate. But I will bear it all patiently: for only here can I be encircled with Serpentina's love and consolation. Listen to me, you hag, and despair! I defy your power: I love Serpentina and none but her forever. I will not become Hofrath, I will not look at Veronica; by your means she is enticing me to evil. If the green snake cannot be mine, I will die in sorrow and longing. Away, filthy buzzard!"

The crone laughed, till the chamber rang: "Sit and die then," cried she: "but now it is time to set to work; for I have other trade to follow here." She threw off her black cloak, and so stood in hideous nakedness; then she ran round in circles, and large folios came tumbling down to her; out of these she tore parchment leaves, and rapidly patching them together in artful combination, and fixing them on her body, in a few instants she was dressed as if in strange multi-colored armor. Spitting fire, the black cat darted out of the ink-glass, which was standing on the table, and ran mewing towards the crone, who shrieked in loud triumph, and along with him vanished through the door.

Anselmus observed that she went towards the azure chamber; and directly he heard a hissing and storming in the distance; the birds in the garden were crying; the Parrot creaked out: "Help! help! Thieves! thieves!" That moment the crone returned with a bound into the room, carrying the Golden Flower Pot on her arm, and with hideous gestures, shrieking wildly through the air; "Joy! joy, little son!—Kill the green snake! To her, son! To her!"

Anselmus thought he heard a deep moaning, heard Serpentina's voice. Then horror and despair took hold of him: he gathered all his force, he dashed violently, as if every nerve and artery were bursting, against the crystal; a piercing clang went through the room, and the Archivarius in his bright damask dressing gown was standing in the door.

"Hey, hey! vermin!—Mad spell!—Witchwork!—Here, holla!" So shouted he: then the black hair of the crone started up in tufts; her red eyes glanced with infernal fire, and clenching together the peaked fangs of her abominable jaws, she hissed: "Hiss, at him! Hiss, at him! Hiss!" and laughed and neighed in scorn and mockery, and pressed the Golden Flower Pot firmly to her, and threw out of it handfuls of glittering earth on the Archivarius; but as it touched the dressing gown, the earth changed into flowers, which rained down on the ground. Then the lilies of the dressing gown flickered and flamed up; and the Archivarius caught these lilies blazing in sparky fire and dashed them on the witch; she howled with agony, but as she leaped aloft and shook her armor of parchment the lilies went out, and fell away into ashes.

"To her, my lad!" creaked the crone: then the black cat darted through the air, and bounded over the Archivarius's head towards the door; but the gray parrot fluttered out against him; caught him by the nape with his crooked bill, till red fiery blood burst down over his neck; and Serpentina's voice cried: "Saved! Saved!" Then the crone, foaming with rage and desperation, darted at the Archivarius: she threw the Golden Flower Pot behind her, and holding up the long talons of her skinny fists, tried to clutch the Archivarius by the throat: but he instantly doffed his dressing gown, and hurled it against her. Then, hissing, and sputtering, and bursting, blue flames shot from the parchment leaves, and the crone rolled around howling in agony, and strove to get fresh earth from the Flower Pot, fresh parchment leaves from the books, that she might stifle the blazing flames; and whenever any earth or leaves came down on her, the flames went out. But now, from the interior of the Archivarius issued fiery crackling beams, which darted on the crone.

"Hey, hey! To it again! Salamander! Victory!" clanged the Archivarius's voice through the chamber; and a hundred bolts whirled forth in fiery circles round the shrieking crone. Whizzing and buzzing flew cat and parrot in their furious battle; but at last the parrot, with his strong wing, dashed the cat to the ground; and with his talons transfixing and holding fast his adversary, which, in deadly agony, uttered horrid mews and howls, he, with his sharp bill, picked out his glowing eyes, and the burning froth spouted from them. Then thick vapour streamed up from the spot where the crone, hurled to the ground, was lying under the dressing gown: her howling, her terrific, piercing cry of lamentation, died away in the remote distance. The smoke, which had spread abroad with penetrating stench, cleared away; the Archivarius picked up his dressing gown; and under it lay an ugly beet.

"Honoured Herr Archivarius, here let me offer you the vanquished foe," said the parrot, holding out a black hair in his beak to Archivarius Lindhorst.

"Very right, my worthy friend," replied the Archivarius: "here lies my vanquished foe too: be so good now as manage what remains. This very day, as a small douceur, you shall have six coconuts, and a new pair of spectacles also, for I see the cat has villainously broken the glasses of these old ones."

"Yours forever, most honoured friend and patron!" answered the parrot, much delighted; then took the withered beet in his bill, and fluttered out with it by the window, which Archivarius Lindhorst had opened for him.

The Archivarius now lifted the Golden Flower Pot, and cried, with a strong voice, "Serpentina! Serpentina!" But as the Student Anselmus, rejoicing in the destruction of the vile witch who had hurried him into misfortune, cast his eyes on the Archivarius, behold, here stood once more the high majestic form of the Spirit-prince, looking up to him with indescribable dignity and grace. "Ansel-mus," said the Spirit-prince, "not you, but a hostile principle, which strove destructively to penetrate into your nature, and divide you against yourself, was to blame for your unbelief. You have kept your faithfulness: be free and happy." A bright flash quivered through the spirit of Anselmus: the royal triphony of the crystal bells sounded stronger and louder than he had ever heard it: his nerves and fibres thrilled; but, swelling higher and higher, the melodious tones rang through the room; the glass which enclosed Anselmus broke; and he rushed into the arms of his dear and gentle Serpentina.

ELEVENTH VIGIL

"But tell me, best Registrator! how could the cursed punch last night mount into our heads, and drive us to all kinds of *allotria*?" So said Conrector Paulmann, as he next morning entered his room, which still lay full of broken sherds; with his hapless peruke, dissolved into its original elements, soaked in punch among the ruin. For after the Student Anselmus ran out, Conrector Paulmann and Registrator Heerbrand had kept trotting and hobbling up and down the room, shouting like maniacs, and butting their heads together; till Fränzchen, with much labour, carried her dizzy papa to bed; and Registrator Heerbrand, in the deepest exhaustion, sank on the sofa, which Veronica had left, taking refuge in her bedroom. Registrator Heerbrand had his blue handkerchief tied about his head; he looked quite pale and melancholic, and moaned out: "Ah, worthy Conrector, it was not the punch which Mamsell Veronica most admirably brewed, no! but it was simply that cursed Student who was to blame for all the mischief. Do you not observe that he has long been *mente captus*? And are you not aware that madness is infectious? One fool makes twenty; pardon me, it is an old proverb: especially when you have drunk a glass or two, you fall into madness quite readily, and then involuntarily you manoeuvre, and go through your exercise, just as the crack-brained fugleman makes the motion. Would you believe it, Conrector? I am still giddy when I think of that gray parrot!"

"Gray fiddlestick!" interrupted the Conrector: "it was nothing but Archivarius Lindhorst's little old Famulus, who had thrown a gray cloak over himself, and was looking for the Student Anselmus."

"It may be," answered Registrator Heerbrand; "but, I must confess, I am quite downcast in spirit; the whole night through there was such a piping and organing."

"That was I," said the Conrector, "for I snore loud."

"Well, may be," answered the Registrator: "but, Conrector, Conrector! I had reason to raise some cheerfulness among us last night—And that Anselmus spoiled it all! You do not know—O Conrector, Conrector!" And with this, Registrator Heerbrand started up; plucked the cloth from his head, embraced the Conrector, warmly pressed his hand, and again cried, in quite heartbreaking tone: "O Conrector, Conrector!" and snatching his hat and staff, rushed out of doors.

"This Anselmus will not cross my threshold again," said Conrector Paulmann; "for I see very well, that, with this moping madness of his, he robs the best gentlemen of their senses. The Registrator has now gone overboard, too: I have hitherto kept safe; but the Devil, who knocked hard last night in our carousal, may get in at last, and play his tricks with me. So *Apage, Satanas!* Off with thee, Anselmus!" Veronica had grown quite pensive; she spoke no word; only smiled now and then very oddly, and seemed to wish to be left alone. "She, too, has Anselmus in her head," said the Conrector, full of spleen: "but it is well that he does not show himself here; I know he fears me, this Anselmus, and so he will never come."

These concluding words Conrector Paulmann spoke aloud; then the tears rushed into Veronica's eyes, and she said, sobbing: "Ah! how can Anselmus come? He has been corked up in the glass bottle for a long time."

"What? What?" cried Conrector Paulmann. "Ah Heaven! Ah Heaven! she is doting too, like the Registrator: the loud fit will soon come! Ah, you cursed, abominable, thrice-cursed Anselmus!" He ran forth directly to Dr. Eckstein; who smiled, and again said: "Ey! Ey!" This time, however, he prescribed nothing; but added, to the little he had uttered, the following words, as he walked away: "Nerves! Come round of itself. Take the air; walks; amusements; theatre; playing *Sonntagskind, Schwestern von Prag.* Come around of itself."

"I have seldom seen the Doctor so eloquent," thought Conrector Paulmann; "really talkative, I declare!"

Several days and weeks and months passed. Anselmus had vanished; but Registrator Heerbrand did not make his appearance either: not till the fourth of February, when, in a fashionable new coat of the finest cloth, in shoes and silk stockings, notwithstanding the keen frost, and with a large nosegay of fresh flowers in his hand, the Registrator entered precisely at noon the parlour of Conrector Paulmann, who wondered not a little to see his friend so well dressed. With a solemn air, Registrator Heerbrand came forward to Conrector Paulmann; embraced him with the finest elegance, and then said: "Now at last, on the Saint's-day of your beloved and most honoured Mamsell Veronica, I will tell you out, straightforward, what I have long had lying at my heart. That evening, that unfortunate evening, when I put the ingredients of our noxious punch in my pocket, I intended to tell to you a piece of good news, and to celebrate the happy day in convivial joys. I had learned that I was to be made Hofrath; for which promotion I have now the patent, *cum nomine et sigillo Principis*, in my pocket."

"Ah! Herr Registr—Herr Hofrath Heerbrand, I meant to say," stammered the Conrector.

"But it is you, most honoured Conrector," continued the new Hofrath; "it is you alone that can complete my happiness. For a long time, I have in secret loved your daughter, Mamsell Veronica; and I can boast of many a kind look which she has given me, evidently showing that she would not reject me. In one word, honoured Conrector! I, Hofrath Heerbrand, do now entreat of you the hand of your most amiable Mamsell Veronica, whom I, if you have nothing against it, purpose shortly to take home as my wife."

Conrector Paulmann, full of astonishment, clapped his hands repeatedly, and cried: "Ey, Ey, Ey! Herr Registr—Herr Hofrath, I meant to say—who would have thought it? Well, if Veronica does really love you, I for my share cannot object: nay, perhaps, her present melancholy is nothing but concealed love for you, most honoured Hofrath! You know what freaks women have!"

At this moment Veronica entered, pale and agitated, as she now commonly was. Then Hofrath Heerbrand approached her; mentioned in a neat speech her Saint's-day, and handed her the odorous nosegay, along with a little packet; out of which, when she opened it, a pair of glittering earrings gleamed up at her. A rapid flying blush tinted her cheeks; her eyes sparkled in joy, and she cried: "O Heaven! These are the very earrings which I wore some weeks ago, and thought so much of."

"How can this be, dearest Mamsell," interrupted Hofrath Heerbrand, somewhat alarmed and hurt, "when I bought them not an hour ago, in the Schlossgasse, for cash?"

But Veronica paid no attention to him; she was standing before the mirror to witness the effect of the trinkets, which she had already suspended in her pretty little ears. Conrector Paulmann disclosed to her, with grave countenance and solemn tone, his friend Heerbrand's preferment and present proposal. Veronica looked at the Hofrath with a searching look, and said: "I have long known that you wished to marry me. Well, be it so! I promise you my heart and hand; but I must now unfold to you, to both of you, I mean, my father and my bridegroom, much that is lying heavy on my heart; yes, even now, though the soup should get cold, which I see Fränzchen is just putting on the table."

Without waiting for the Conrector's or the Hofrath's reply, though the words were visibly hovering on the lips of both, Veronica continued: "You may believe me, father, I loved Anselmus from my heart, and when Registrator Heerbrand, who is now become Hofrath himself, assured us that Anselmus might possibly rise that high, I resolved that he and no other should be my husband. But then it seemed as if alien hostile beings tried snatching him away from me: I had recourse to old Liese, who was once my nurse, but is now a wise woman, and a great enchantress. She promised to help me, and give Anselmus wholly into my hands. We went at midnight on the Equinox to the crossing of the roads: she conjured certain hellish spirits, and by aid of the black cat, we manufactured a little metallic mirror, in which I, directing my thoughts on Anselmus, had but to look, in order to rule him wholly in heart and mind. But now I heartily repent having done all this; and here abjure all Satanic arts. The Salamander has conquered old Liese; I heard her shrieks; but there was no help to be given: so soon as the parrot had eaten the beet, my metallic mirror broke in two with a piercing clang." Veronica took out both the pieces of the mirror, and a lock of hair from her workbox, and handing them to Hofrath Heerbrand, she proceeded: "Here, take the fragments of the mirror, dear Hofrath; throw them down, tonight, at twelve o'clock, over the Elbe Bridge, from the place where the Cross stands; the stream is not frozen there: the lock, however, wear on your faithful breast. I here abjure all magic: and heartily wish Anselmus joy of his good fortune, seeing he is wedded with the green snake, who is much prettier and richer than I. You dear Hofrath, I will love and reverence as becomes a true honest wife."

"Alack! Alack!" cried Conrector Paulmann, full of sorrow; "she is cracked, she is cracked; she can never be Frau Hofräthinn; she is cracked!"

"Not in the smallest," interrupted Hofrath Heerbrand; "I know well that Mamsell Veronica has had some kindness for the loutish Anselmus; and it may be that in some fit of passion, she has had recourse to the wise woman, who, as I perceive, can be no other than the card-caster and coffee-pourer of the Seethor; in a word, old Rauerin. Nor can it be denied that there are secret arts, which exert their influence on men but too banefully; we read of such in the ancients, and doubtless there are still such; but as to what Mamsell Veronica is pleased to say about the victory of the Salamander, and the marriage of Anselmus with the green snake, this, in reality, I take for nothing but a poetic allegory; a sort of song, wherein she sings her entire farewell to the Student."

"Take it for what you will, my dear Hofrath!" cried Veronica; "perhaps for a very stupid dream."

"That I will not do," replied Hofrath Heerbrand; "for I know well that Anselmus himself is possessed by secret powers, which vex him and drive him on to all imaginable mad escapades."

Conrector Paulmann could stand it no longer; he burst out: "Hold! For the love of Heaven, hold! Are we overtaken with that cursed punch again, or has Anselmus's madness come over us too? Herr Hofrath, what stuff is this you are talking? I will suppose, however, that it is love which haunts your brain: this soon comes to rights in marriage; otherwise, I should be apprehensive that you too had fallen into some shade of madness, most honoured Herr Hofrath; then what would become of the future branches of the family, inheriting the *malum* of their parents? But now I give my paternal blessing to this happy union; and permit you as bride and bridegroom to take a kiss."

This immediately took place; and thus before the soup had grown cold, a formal betrothment was concluded. In a few weeks, Frau Hofräthinn Heerbrand was actually, as she had been in vision, sitting in the balcony of a fine house in the Neumarkt, and looking down with a smile at the beaux, who passing by turned their glasses up to her, and said: "She is a heavenly woman, the Hofräthinn Heerbrand."

TWELFTH VIGIL

How deeply did I feel, in the centre of my spirit, the blessedness of the Student Anselmus, who now, indissolubly united with his gentle Serpentina, has withdrawn to the mysterious land of wonders, recognized by him as the home towards which his bosom, filled with strange forecastings, had always longed.   But in vain was all my striving to set before you, favourable reader, those glories with which Anselmus is encompassed, or even in the faintest degree to shadow them to you in words.   Reluctantly I could not but acknowledge the feebleness of my every expression.   I felt myself enthralled amid the paltrinesses of everyday life; I sickened in tormenting dissatisfaction; I glided about like a dreamer; in brief, I fell into that condition of the Student Anselmus, which, in the Fourth Vigil, I endeavoured to set before you.   It grieved me to the heart, when I glanced over the Eleven Vigils, now happily accomplished, and thought that to insert the Twelfth, the keystone of the whole, would never be permitted me.   For whenever, in the night I set myself to complete the work, it was as if mischievous spirits (they might be relations, perhaps cousins-german, of the slain witch) held a polished glittering piece of metal before me, in which I beheld my own mean self, pale, drawn, and melancholic, like Registrator Heerbrand after his bout of punch.   Then I threw down my pen, and hastened to bed, that I might behold the happy Anselmus and the fair Serpentina at least in my dreams.   This had lasted for several days and nights, when at length quite unexpectedly I received a note from Archivarius Lindhorst, in which he wrote to me as follows:

> Respected Sir,—It is well known to me that you have written down, in Eleven Vigils, the singular fortunes of my good son-in-law Anselmus, whilom student, now poet; and are at present cudgelling your brains very sore, that in the Twelfth and Last Vigil you may tell somewhat of his happy life in Atlantis, where he now lives with my daughter, on the pleasant freehold, which I possess in that country. Now, notwithstanding I much regret that hereby my own peculiar nature is unfolded to the reading world; seeing it may, in my office as Privy Archivarius, expose me to a thousand inconveniences; nay, in the Collegium even give rise to the question: How far a Salamander can justly, and with binding consequences, plight himself by oath, as a Servant of the State? and how far, on the whole, important affairs may be intrusted to him, since, according to Gabalis and Swedenborg, the spirits of the elements are not to be trusted at all?—notwithstanding, my best friends must now avoid my embrace; fearing lest, in some sudden anger, I dart out a flash or two, and singe their hair-curls, and Sunday frocks; notwithstanding all this, I say, it is still my purpose to assist you in the completion of the work, since much good of me and of my dear married daughter (would the other two were off my hands also!) has therein been said.
>
> If you would write your Twelfth Vigil, descend your cursed five flights of stairs, leave your garret, and come over to me.   In the blue

palmtree-room, which you already know, you will find fit writing materials; and you can then, in few words, specify to your readers, what you have seen; a better plan for you than any long-winded description of a life which you know only by hearsay. With esteem,

Your obedient servant,

The Salamander Lindhorst,

P. T. Royal Archivarius.

This somewhat rough, yet on the whole friendly note from Archivarius Lindhorst, gave me high pleasure. It seemed clear enough, indeed, that the singular manner in which the fortunes of his son-in-law had been revealed to me, and which I, bound to silence, must conceal even from you, gracious reader, was well known to this peculiar old gentleman; yet he had not taken it so ill as I might have apprehended. Nay, here was he offering me a helping hand in the completion of my work; and from this I might justly conclude, that at bottom he was not averse to having his marvellous existence in the world of spirits thus divulged through the press.

"It may be," thought I, "that he himself expects from this measure, perhaps, to get his two other daughters married sooner: for who knows but a spark may fall in this or that young man's breast, and kindle a longing for the green snake; whom, on Ascension Day, under the elder-bush, he will forthwith seek and find? From the misery which befell Anselmus, when he was enclosed in the glass bottle, he will take warning to be doubly and trebly on his guard against all doubt and unbelief."

Precisely at eleven o'clock, I extinguished my study lamp; and glided forth to Archivarius Lindhorst, who was already waiting for me in the lobby.

"Are you there, my worthy friend? Well, this is what I like, that you have not mistaken my good intentions: follow me!"

And with this he led the way through the garden, now filled with dazzling brightness, into the azure chamber, where I observed the same violet table, at which Anselmus had been writing.

Archivarius Lindhorst disappeared: but soon came back, carrying in his hand a fair golden goblet, out of which a high blue flame was sparkling up. "Here," said he, "I bring you the favourite drink of your friend the Bandmaster, Johannes Kreisler. It is burning arrack, into which I have thrown a little sugar. Sip a little of it: I will doff my dressing gown, and to amuse myself and enjoy your worthy company while you sit looking and writing, I shall just bob up and down a little in the goblet."

"As you please, honoured Herr Archivarius," answered I: "but if I am to ply the liquor, you will get none."

"Don't fear that, my good fellow," cried the Archivarius; then hastily throwing off his dressing gown, he mounted, to my no small amazement, into the goblet, and vanished in the blaze. Without fear, softly blowing back the flame, I partook of the drink: it was truly precious!

Stir not the emerald leaves of the palm-trees in soft sighing and rustling, as if kissed by the breath of the morning wind? Awakened from their sleep, they move, and mysteriously whisper of the wonders, which from the far distance approach like tones of melodious harps! The azure rolls from the walls, and floats like airy vapour to and fro; but dazzling beams shoot through it; and whirling and dancing, as in jubilee of childlike sport, it mounts and mounts to immeasurable height, and vaults over the palm-trees. But brighter and brighter shoots beam upon beam, till in boundless expanse the grove opens where I behold Anselmus. Here glowing hyacinths, and tulips, and roses, lift their fair heads; and their perfumes, in loveliest sound, call to the happy youth: "Wander, wander among us, our beloved; for you understand us! Our perfume is the longing of love: we love you, and are yours for evermore!" The golden rays burn in glowing tones: "We are fire, kindled by love. Perfume is longing; but fire is desire: and do we not dwell in your bosom? We are yours!" The dark bushes, the high trees rustle and sound: "Come to us, beloved, happy one! Fire is desire; but hope is our cool shadow. Lovingly we rustle round your head: for you understand us, because love dwells in your breast!" The brooks and fountains murmur and patter: "Loved one, do not walk so quickly by: look into our crystal! Your image dwells in us, which we preserve with love, for you have understood us." In the triumphal choir, bright birds are singing: "Hear us! Hear us! We are joy, we are delight, the rapture of love!" But anxiously Anselmus turns his eyes to the glorious temple, which rises behind him in the distance. The fair pillars seem trees; and the capitals and friezes acanthus leaves, which in wondrous wreaths and figures form splendid decorations. Anselmus walks to the Temple: he views with inward delight the variegated marble, the steps with their strange veins of moss. "Ah, no!" cries he, as if in the excess of rapture, "she is not far from me now; she is near!" Then Serpentina advances, in the fullness of beauty and grace, from the Temple; she bears the Golden Flower Pot, from which a bright lily has sprung. The nameless rapture of infinite longing glows in her meek eyes; she looks at Anselmus, and says: "Ah! Dearest, the Lily has opened her blossom: what we longed for is fulfilled; is there a happiness to equal ours?" Anselmus clasps her with the tenderness of warmest ardour: the lily burns in flaming beams over his head. And louder move the trees and bushes; clearer and gladder play the brooks; the birds, the shining insects dance in the waves of perfume: a gay, bright rejoicing tumult, in the air, in the water, in the earth, is holding the festival of love! Now sparkling streaks rush, gleaming over all the bushes; diamonds look from the ground like shining eyes: strange vapours are wafted hither on sounding wings: they are the spirits of the elements, who do homage to the lily, and proclaim the happiness of Anselmus. Then Anselmus raises his head, as if encircled with a beamy glory. Is it looks? Is it words? Is it song? You hear the sound: "Serpentina! Belief in you, love of you has unfolded to my soul the inmost spirit of nature! You have brought me the lily, which sprang from gold, from the primeval force of the world, before Phosphorus had kindled the spark of thought; this lily is knowledge of the sacred harmony of all beings; and in this I live in highest blessedness for evermore. Yes, I, thrice happy, have perceived what was highest: I must indeed love thee forever, O Serpentina! Never shall the golden blossoms of the lily grow pale; for, like belief and love, this knowledge is eternal."

For the vision, in which I had now beheld Anselmus bodily, in his freehold of Atlantis, I stand indebted to the arts of the Salamander; and it was fortunate that when everything had melted into air, I found a paper lying on the violet-table, with the foregoing statement of the matter, written fairly and distinctly by my own hand. But now I felt myself as if transpierced and torn in pieces by sharp sorrow. "Ah, happy Anselmus, who has cast away the burden of everyday life, who in the love of kind Serpentina flies with bold pinion, and now lives in rapture and joy on your freehold in Atlantis! while I—poor I!—must soon, nay, in few moments, leave even this fair hall, which itself is far from a Freehold in Atlantis; and again be transplanted to my garret, where, enthralled among the pettinesses of existence, my heart and my sight are so bedimmed with thousand mischiefs, as with thick fog, that the fair lily will never, never be beheld by me."

Then Archivarius Lindhorst patted me gently on the shoulder, and said: "Softly, softly, my honoured friend! Do not lament so!

Were you not even now in Atlantis; and have you not at least a pretty little copyhold farm there, as the poetical possession of your inward sense? And is the blessedness of Anselmus anything else but a living in poesy? Can anything else but poesy reveal itself as the sacred harmony of all beings, as the deepest secret of nature?"

AUTOMATA

A considerable time ago I was invited to a little evening gathering, where our friend Vincent was, along with some other people. I was detained by business, and did not arrive till very late. I was all the more surprised not to hear the slightest sound as I came up to the door of the room. Could it be that nobody had been able to come? I gently opened the door. There sat Vincent, opposite me, with the others, around a little table; and they were all staring, stiff and motionless like so many statues, in the profoundest silence up at the ceiling. The lights were on a table at some distance, and nobody took any notice of me. I went nearer, full of amazement, and saw a glittering gold ring suspended from the ceiling, swinging back and forth in the air, and presently beginning to move in circles. One after another they said, "Wonderful!" "Most wonderful!" "Most inexplicable!" "Curious!" and so on. I could no longer contain myself, and cried out, "For Heaven's sake, tell me what you are doing."

At this they all jumped up. But Vincent cried, in that shrill voice of his: "Creeping Tom! You come slinking in like a sleep-walker, interrupting the most important and interesting experiments. Let me tell you that a phenomenon which the incredulous have classed without a moment's hesitation as fabulous, has just been verified by this company. We wished to see whether the pendulum swings of a suspended ring can be controlled by the concentrated human will. I undertook to fix my will upon it; and thought as hard as I could of circular oscillations. The ring, which is fixed to the ceiling by a silk thread, remained motionless for a very long time, but at last it began to swing, and it was just beginning to go in circles when you came in and interrupted us."

"But what if it were not your will," I said, "so much as the draught of air when I opened the door which set the ring in motion?"

"Materialist!" cried Vincent. Everybody laughed.

"The pendulum oscillations of rings nearly drove me crazy at one time," said Theodore. "This is absolutely certain, and anyone can convince himself of it: the oscillations of a plain gold ring, suspended by a fine thread over the palm of the hand, unquestionably take the direction which the unspoken will directs them to take. I cannot tell you how profoundly and how eerily this phenomenon affected me. I used to sit for hours at a time making the ring go swinging in the most varied directions, as I willed it; and at last I went to the length of making an oracle of it. I would say, mentally, 'If such and such a thing is going to happen, let the ring swing between my thumb and little finger; if it is not going to happen, let it swing at right angles to that direction,' and so on."

"Delightful," said Lothair. "You set up within yourself a higher spiritual principle to speak to you mystically when you conjure it up. Here we have the true 'spiritus familiaris,' the Socratic daemon. From here there is only a very short step to ghosts and supernatural stories, which might easily have their *raison d'être* in the influence of some exterior spiritual principle."

"And I mean to take just this step," said Cyprian, "by telling you, right here and now, the most terrible supernatural story I have ever heard. The peculiarity of this story is that it is vouched for by persons of credibility, and that the manner in which it has been brought to my knowledge, or recollection, has to do with the excited or (if you prefer) disorganized condition which Lothair observed me to be in a short time ago."

Cyprian stood up; and, as was his habit when his mind was occupied, and he needed a little time to arrange his words, he walked several times up and down the room. Presently he sat down, and began:—

"You may remember that some little time ago, just before the last campaign, I was paying a visit to Colonel von P—— at his country house. The colonel was a good-tempered, jovial man, and his wife quietness and simpleness personified. At the time I speak of, the son was away with the army, so that the family circle consisted, besides the colonel and his lady, of two daughters and an elderly French lady who was trying to persuade herself that she was fulfilling the duties of a governess—though the young ladies appeared to be beyond the period of being 'governed.' The elder of the two daughters was a most lively and cheerful girl, vivacious even to ungovernability; not without plenty of brains, but so constituted that she could not go five yards without cutting at least three entrechats. She sprang in the same fashion in her conversation and everything that she did, restlessly from one thing to another.

I myself have seen her within the space of five minutes work at needlework, read, draw, sing, dance, or cry about her poor cousin who was killed in battle and then while the tears were still in her eyes burst into a splendid infectious burst of laughter when the Frenchwoman spilled the contents of her snuffbox over the pug. The pug began to sneeze frightfully, and the old lady cried, 'Ah, che fatalità! Ah carino! Poverino!'" (She always spoke to the dog in Italian because he was born in Padua.) Moreover, this young lady was the loveliest blonde ever seen, and for all her odd caprices, full of the utmost charm, goodness, kindliness and attractiveness, so that whether she wanted to or not she exerted the most irresistible charm over everyone.

"Her younger sister was the greatest possible contrast to her (her name was Adelgunda). I try in vain to find words in which to express to you the extraordinary impression which this girl produced upon me when I first saw her. Picture to yourselves the most exquisite figure, and the most marvellously beautiful face; but her cheeks and lips wear a deathly pallor, and she moves gently, softly, slowly, with measured steps; and then, when you hear a low-toned word from her scarcely opened lips you feel a sort of shudder of spectral awe. Of course I soon got over this eerie feeling, and, when I managed to get her to emerge from her deep self-absorbed condition and converse, I was obliged to admit that the strangeness, the eeriness, was only external; and by no means came from within. In the little she said she displayed a delicate womanliness, a clear head, and a kindly disposition. She had not a trace of over-excitability, though her melancholy smile, and her glance, heavy as if with tears, seemed to speak of some morbid bodily condition producing a hostile influence on her mental state. It struck me as very strange that the whole family, not excepting the French lady, seemed to get into a state of anxiety as soon as anyone began to talk to this girl, and tried to interrupt the conversation, often breaking into it in a very forced manner. But the most extraordinary thing of all was that, as soon as it was eight o'clock in the evening, the young lady was reminded, first by the French lady and then by her mother, sister, and father, that it was time to go to her room, just as little children are sent to bed so that they will not overtire themselves. The French lady went with her, so that neither of them ever appeared at supper, which was at nine o'clock. The lady of the house, probably noticing my surprise at those proceedings, threw out (by way of preventing indiscreet inquiries) a sort of sketchy statement to the effect that Adelgunda was in very poor health, that, particularly about nine in the evening, she was liable to feverish attacks, and that the doctors had ordered her to have complete rest at that time. I saw there must be more in the affair than this, though I could not imagine what it might be; and it was only today that I ascertained the terrible truth, and discovered what the events were which have wrecked the peace of that happy circle in the most frightful manner.

"Adelgunda was at one time the most blooming, vigorous, cheerful creature to be seen. Her fourteenth birthday came, and a number of her friends and companions had been invited to spend it with her. They were all sitting in a circle in the shrubbery, laughing and amusing themselves, taking little heed that the evening was getting darker and darker, for the soft July breeze was blowing refreshingly, and they were just beginning thoroughly to enjoy themselves. In the magic twilight they set about all sorts of dances, pretending to be elves and woodland sprites. Adelgunda cried, 'Listen, children! I shall go and appear to you as the White Lady whom our gardener used to tell us about so often while he was alive. But you must come to the bottom of the garden, where the old ruins are.' She wrapped her white shawl round her, and went lightly dancing down the leafy path, the girls following her, in full tide of laughter and fun. But Adelgunda had scarcely reached the old crumbling arches, when she suddenly stopped, and stood as if paralyzed in every limb. The castle clock struck nine.

"'Look, look!' cried she, in a hollow voice of the deepest terror. 'Don't you see it? the figure—close before me—stretching her hand out at me. Don't you see her?'

"The children saw nothing whatever; but terror came upon them, and they all ran away, except one, more courageous than the rest, who hastened up to Adelgunda, and was going to take her in her arms. But Adelgunda, turning pale as death, fell to the ground. At the screams of the other girl everybody came hastening from the castle, and Adelgunda was carried in. At last she recovered from her faint, and, trembling all over, told them that as soon as she reached the ruins she saw an airy form, as if shrouded in mist, stretching its hand out towards her. Of course everyone ascribed this vision to some deceptiveness of the twilight; and Adelgunda recovered from her alarm so completely that night that no further evil consequences were anticipated, and the whole affair was supposed to be at an end. However, it turned out altogether otherwise. The next evening, when the clock struck nine, Adelgunda sprang up, in the midst of the people about her, and cried, 'There she is! there she is. Don't you see her—just before me?'

"Since that unlucky evening, Adelgunda declared that as soon as the clock struck nine, the figure stood before her, remaining visible for several seconds, although no one but herself could see anything of it, or trace by any psychic sensation the proximity of an unknown spiritual principle. So that poor Adelgunda was thought to be out of her mind; and, in a strange perversion of feeling, the family were ashamed of this condition of hers. I have told you already how she was dealt with in consequence. There was, of course, no lack of doctors, or of plans of treatment for ridding the poor soul of the *idée fixe*, as people were pleased to term the apparition which she said she saw. But nothing had any effect; and she implored, with tears, to be left in peace, inasmuch as the form which in its vague, uncertain traits had nothing terrible or alarming about it no longer caused her any fear; although for a time after seeing it she felt as if her inner being and all her thoughts and ideas were turned out from her, and were hovering, bodiless, outside of her. At last the colonel made the acquaintance of a celebrated doctor who had the reputation of being specially clever in the treatment of the mentally afflicted. When this doctor heard Adelgunda's story he laughed aloud, and said nothing could be easier than to cure a condition of the kind, which resulted solely from an overexcited imagination. The idea of the appearing of the spectre was so intimately associated with the striking of nine o'clock that the mind could not dissociate them. So that all that was necessary was to effect this separation by external means. About this there would be no difficulty, as it was only necessary to deceive the patient as to the time, and let nine o'clock pass without her being aware of it. If the apparition did not then appear, she would be convinced herself that it was an illusion; and measures to give tone to the general system would be all that would then be necessary to complete the cure.

"This unfortunate advice was taken. One night all the clocks at the castle were put back an hour—the hollow, booming tower clock included—so that, when Adelgunda awoke in the morning, although she did not know it, she was really an hour wrong in her time. When evening came, the family were assembled, as usual, in a cheerful corner room; no stranger was present, and the mother constrained herself to talk about all sorts of cheerful subjects. The colonel began (as was his habit, when in specially good humour) to carry on an encounter of wit with the old French lady, in which

Augusta, the older of the daughters, aided and abetted him. Everybody was laughing, and more full of enjoyment than ever. The clock on the wall struck eight (although it was really nine o'clock) and Adelgunda fell back in her chair, pale as death. Her work dropped from her hands; she rose, with a face of horror, stared before her into the empty part of the room, and murmured, in a hollow voice, 'What! an hour early! Don't you see it? Don't you see it? Right before me!'

"Everyone rose up in alarm. But as none of them saw the smallest vestige of anything, the colonel cried, 'Calm yourself, Adelgunda, there is nothing there! It is a vision of your brain, only your imagination. We see nothing, nothing whatever; and if there really were a figure close to you we should see it as well as you! Calm yourself.'

"'Oh God!' cried Adelgunda, 'they think I am out of my mind. See! it is stretching out its long arm, it is making signs to me!'

"And, as though she were acting under the influence of another, without exercise of her own will, with eyes fixed and staring, she put her hand back behind her, took up a plate which chanced to be on the table, held it out before her into vacancy, and let it go.

"The plate did not drop, but floated about among the persons present, and then settled gently on the table. Augusta and her mother fainted; and these fainting fits were succeeded by violent nervous fever. The colonel forced himself to retain his self-control, but the profound impression which this extraordinary occurrence made on him was evident in his agitated and disturbed condition.

"The French lady had fallen on her knees and prayed in silence with her face turned to the floor, and both she and Adelgunda remained free from evil consequences. The mother very soon died. Augusta survived the fever; but it would have been better had she died. She who, when I first saw her, was an embodiment of vigorous, magnificent youthful happiness, is now hopelessly insane, and that in a form which seems to me the most terrible and gruesome of all the forms of *idée fixe* ever heard of. For she thinks she is the invisible phantom which haunts Adelgunda; and therefore she avoids everyone, or, at all events, refrains from speaking, or moving if anybody is present. She scarce dares to breathe, because she firmly believes that if she betrays her presence in any way everyone will die. Doors are opened for her, and her food is set down, she slinks in and out, eats in secret, and so forth. Can a more painful condition be imagined?

"The colonel, in his pain and despair, followed the colours to the next campaign, and fell in the victorious engagement at W——. It is remarkable, most remarkable that since then Adelgunda has never seen the phantom. She nurses her sister with the utmost care, and the French lady helps her. Only this very day Sylvester told me that the uncle of these poor girls is here, taking the advice of our celebrated R——, as to the means of cure to be tried in Augusta's case. God grant that the cure may succeed, improbable as it seems."

When Cyprian finished, the friends all kept silence, looking meditatively before them. At last Lothair said, "It is certainly a very terrible ghost story. I must admit it makes me shudder, although the incident of the hovering plate is rather trifling and childish."

"Not so fast, my dear Lothair," Ottmar interrupted. "You know my views about ghost stories, and the manner in which I swagger towards visionaries; maintaining, as I do, that often as I have thrown down my glove to the spirit world challenging it to enter the lists with me, it has never taken the trouble to punish me for my presumption and irreverence. But Cyprian's story suggests another consideration. Ghost stories may often be mere chimeras; but, whatever may have been at the bottom of Adelgunda's phantom, and the hovering plate, this much is certain: that on that evening, in the family of Colonel Von P—— something happened which produced in three of the persons present such a shock to the system that the result was the death of one and the insanity of another; if we do not ascribe at least indirectly the colonel's death to it, too. For I happen to remember that I heard from officers who were on the spot, that he suddenly dashed into the thick of the enemy's fire as if impelled by the furies. Then the incident of the plate differs so completely from anything in the ordinary *mise en scène* of supernatural stories. The hour when it happened is so remote from ordinary supernatural use and wont, and the event so simple that its improbability acquires probability, and thereby becomes gruesome to me. But if one were to assume that Adelgunda's imagination carried along those of her father, mother and sister— that it was only within her brain that the plate moved about—would not this vision of the imagination striking three people dead in a moment, like a shock of electricity, be the most terrible supernatural event imaginable?"

"Certainly," said Theodore, "and I share with you, Ottmar, your opinion that the very horror of the incident lies in its utter simplicity. I can imagine myself enduring fairly well the sudden alarm produced by some fearful apparition; but the weird actions of some invisible thing would infallibly drive me mad. The sense of the most utter, most helpless powerlessness must grind the spirit to dust. I remember that I could hardly resist the profound terror which made me afraid to sleep in my room alone, like a silly child, when I once read of an old musician who was haunted in a terrible manner for a long time (almost driving him out of his mind) by an invisible being which used to play on his piano in the night, compositions of the most extraordinary kind, with the power and the technique of the most accomplished master. He heard every note, saw the keys going up and down, but never any form of a player."

"Really," Lothair said, "the way in which this class of subject is flourishing among us is becoming unendurable, I have admitted that the incident of that accursed plate produced the profoundest impression on me. Ottmar is right; if events are to be judged by their results, this is the most terrible supernatural story conceivable. Therefore I pardon the disturbed condition which Cyprian displayed earlier in the evening, and which has passed away considerably now. But not another word on the subject of supernatural horrors. I have seen a manuscript peeping out of Ottmar's breast-pocket for some time, as if craving for release; let him release it."

"No, no," said Theodore, "the flood which has been rolling along in such stormy billows must be gently led away. I have a manuscript well adapted for that end, which some peculiar circumstances led to my writing at one time. Although it deals pretty largely with the mystical, and contains plenty of psychic marvels and strange hypotheses, it is tied on pretty closely to affairs of everyday life." He read:

AUTOMATA

The Talking Turk was attracting universal attention, and setting the town in commotion. The hall where this automaton was exhibited was thronged by a continual stream of visitors, of all sorts and conditions, from morning till night, all eager to listen to the oracular utterances which were whispered to them by the motionless lips of this wonderful quasi-human figure. The manner of the construction and arrangement of this automaton distinguished it very much from ordinary mechanical figures. It was, in fact, a very remarkable automaton. In the center of a room of moderate size, containing only a few indispensable articles of furniture, sat this figure, about the size of a human being, handsomely formed, dressed in a rich and tasteful Turkish costume, on a low seat shaped like a tripod. The exhibitor would move this seat if desired, to show that there was no means of communication between it and the ground.

The Turk's left hand was placed in an easy position on its knee, and its right rested on a small movable table. Its appearance, as has been said, was that of a well-proportioned, handsome man, but the most remarkable part of it was its head. A face expressing a genuine Oriental astuteness gave it an appearance of life rarely seen in wax figures, even when they represent the characteristic countenances of talented men.

A light railing surrounded the figure, to prevent the spectators from crowding too closely about it; and only those who wished to inspect the construction of it (so far as the exhibitor could allow this to be seen without divulging his secret), and the person whose turn it was to put a question to it, were allowed to go inside this railing, and close up to the Turk. The usual procedure was to whisper the question you wished to ask into the Turk's right ear; on which he would turn, first his eyes, and then his whole head, towards you; and since you were aware of a gentle stream of air, like breath coming from his lips, you assumed that the low reply which was given to you really did proceed from the interior of the figure.

From time to time, after a few answers had been given, the exhibitor would apply a key to the Turk's left side, and wind up some clockwork with a good deal of noise. Here, also, he would, if desired, open a sort of lid, so that inside the figure you could see a complicated mechanism consisting of a number of wheels; and although you might not think it probable that this had anything to do with the automaton's speech, it was still evident that it occupied so much space that no human being could possibly be concealed inside, even if he were no bigger than Augustus's dwarf who was served up in a pasty. Besides the movement of the head, which always took place before an answer was given, the Turk would sometimes also raise his right hand, and either make a warning gesture with a finger, or, as it were, brush the question aside with his whole hand. Whenever this happened, nothing but repeated urging by the questioner could extract an answer, which was then generally ambiguous or angry. It might have been that the wheelwork was connected with, or answerable for, those motions of the head and hands, although even in this the agency of a sentient being seemed essential. People wearied themselves with conjectures concerning the source and agent of this marvellous intelligence.   The walls, the adjoining room, the furniture, everything connected with the exhibition, were carefully examined and scrutinized, all completely in vain. The figure and its exhibitor were watched and scanned most closely by the eyes of the most expert in mechanical science; but the more close and minute the scrutiny, the more easy and unconstrained were the actions and proceedings of both.   The exhibitor laughed and joked in the farthest corner of the room with the spectators, leaving the figure to make its gestures and give its replies as a wholly independent thing, having no need of any connection with him. Indeed he could not wholly restrain a slightly ironical smile when the table and the figure and tripod were being overhauled and peered at in every direction, taken as close to the light as possible, and inspected by powerful magnifying glasses.   The upshot of it all was, that the mechanical geniuses said the devil himself could make neither head nor tail of the confounded mechanism.   And a hypothesis that the exhibitor was a clever ventriloquist, and gave the answers himself (the breath being conveyed to the figure's mouth through hidden valves) fell to the ground, for the exhibitor was to be heard talking loudly and distinctly to people among the audience at the very time when the Turk was making his replies.

Despite the puzzling, mysterious nature of this exhibition, perhaps the interest of the public might soon have grown fainter, if it had not been kept alive by the nature of the answers which the Turk gave.   These were sometimes cold and severe, while occasionally they were sparkling and witty—even broadly so at times; at others they evinced strong sense and deep astuteness, and in some instances they were to a high degree painful and tragic.   But they were always strikingly apposite to the character and affairs of the questioner, who would frequently be startled by a mystical reference to the future, only possible, as it would seem, to one cognizant of the hidden thoughts and feelings which dictated the question.   And it often happened that the Turk, questioned in German, would reply in some other language known to the questioner, in which case it would be found that the answer could not have been expressed with equal point, force, and conciseness in any other language than that selected.   In short, no day passed without some fresh instance of a striking and ingenious answer of the wise Turk's becoming the subject of general remark.

It chanced, one evening, that Lewis and Ferdinand, two college friends, were in a company where the Talking Turk was the subject of conversation.   People were discussing whether the strangest feature of the matter was the mysterious and unexplained human influence which seemed to endow the figure with life, or the wonderful insight into the individuality of the questioner, or the remarkable talent of the answers. Lewis and Ferdinand were both rather ashamed to confess that they had not seen the Turk as yet, for it was *de rigueur* to see him, and everyone had some tale to tell of a wonderful answer to some skilfully devised question.

"All figures of this sort," said Lewis, "which can scarcely be said to counterfeit humanity so much as to travesty it—mere images of living death or inanimate life—are most distasteful to me. When I was a little boy, I ran away crying from a waxwork exhibition I was taken to, and even to this day I never can enter a place of the sort without a horrible, eerie, shuddery feeling. When I see the staring, lifeless, glassy eyes of all the potentates, celebrated heroes, thieves, murderers, and so on, fixed upon me, I feel disposed to cry with Macbeth

> Thou hast no speculation in those eyes
> Which thou dost glare with.

And I feel certain that most people experience the same feeling, though perhaps not to the same extent. For you may notice that scarcely anyone talks, except in a whisper, in waxwork museums. You hardly ever hear a loud word. But it is not reverence for the Crowned Heads and other great people that produces this universal pianissimo; it is the oppressive sense of being in the presence of something unnatural and gruesome; and what I detest most of all is the mechanical imitation of human motions. I feel sure this wonderful, ingenious Turk will haunt me with his rolling eyes, his turning head, and his waving arm, like some necromantic goblin, when I lie awake nights; so, the truth is I should very much prefer not going to see him. I should be quite satisfied with other people's accounts of his wit and wisdom."

"You know," said Ferdinand, "I fully agree with you about the disagreeable feeling produced by the sight of such imitations of human beings. But they are not all alike. Much depends on their workmanship, and on what they do. Now there was Ensler's rope dancer, one of the finest automata I have ever seen. There was a vigour about his movements which was most effective, and when he suddenly sat down on his rope, and bowed in an affable manner, he was utterly delightful. I do not suppose anyone ever experienced the gruesome feeling you speak of in looking at him. As for the Turk, I consider his case different altogether. The figure (which everyone says is a handsome-looking one, with nothing ludicrous or repulsive about it)—the figure really plays a very subordinate part in the business, and I think there can be little doubt that the turning of the head and eyes, and so forth, are intended to divert our attention for the very reason that it is elsewhere that the key to the mystery is to be found. That the breath comes out of the figure's mouth is very likely, perhaps certain; those who have been there say it does. It by no means follows that this breath is set in motion by the words which are spoken. There cannot be the smallest doubt that some human being is so placed as to be able, by means of acoustical and optical contrivances which we do not trace, to see and hear the persons who ask questions, and whisper answers back to them. Not a soul, even among our most ingenious mechanicians, has the slightest inkling of the process and this shows that it is a remarkably ingenious one; and that, of course, is one thing which renders the exhibition very interesting. But much the most wonderful part of it, in my opinion, is the spiritual power of this unknown human being, who seems to read the very depths of the questioner's soul. The answers often display an acuteness and sagacity, and, at the same time, a species of dread half-light, half-darkness, which really entitle them to be styled 'oracular' in the highest sense of the term. Several of my friends have told me instances of the sort which have fairly astounded me, and I can no longer refrain from putting the wonderful seer-gift of this unknown person to the test. I intend to go there tomorrow forenoon; and you must lay aside your repugnance to 'living puppets,' and come with me."

Although Lewis did his best to get off, he was obliged to yield, on pain of being considered eccentric, so many were the entreaties to him not to spoil a pleasant party by his absence, for a party had been made up to go the next forenoon, and, so to speak, take the miraculous Turk by the very beard. They went accordingly, and although there was no denying that the Turk had an unmistakable air of Oriental *grandezza*, and that his head was handsome and effective, as soon as Lewis entered the room, he was struck with a sense of the ludicrous about the whole affair. When the exhibitor put the key to the figure's side, and the wheels began their whirring, he made some rather silly joke to his friends about "the Turkish gentleman's having a roasting-jack inside him." Everyone laughed; and the exhibitor—who did not seem to appreciate the joke very much—stopped winding up the machinery. Whether it was that the hilarious mood of the company displeased the wise Turk, or that he chanced not to be "in the vein" on that particular day, his replies—though some were to very witty and ingenious questions—seemed empty and poor; and Lewis, in particular, had the misfortune to find that he was scarcely ever properly understood by the oracle, so that he received for the most part crooked answers. The exhibitor was clearly out of temper, and the audience were on the point of going away, ill-pleased and disappointed, when Ferdinand said, "Gentlemen, none of us seems to be much satisfied with the wise Turk, but perhaps we may be partly to blame ourselves; perhaps our questions may not have been altogether to his taste; the fact that he is turning his head at this moment, and raising his arm" (the figure was really doing so), "seems to indicate that I am not mistaken. A question has occurred to me to put to him; and if he gives one of his apposite answers to it, I think he will have quite redeemed his character."

Ferdinand went up to the Turk, and whispered a word or two in his ear. The Turk raised his arm as if unwilling to answer. Ferdinand persisted, and then the Turk turned his head towards him.

Lewis saw that Ferdinand instantly turned pale; but after a few seconds he asked another question, to which he got an answer at once. It was with a most constrained smile that Ferdinand, turning to the audience, said, "I can assure you, gentlemen, that as far as I am concerned the Turk has redeemed his character. I must beg you to pardon me if I conceal the question and the answer from you; of course the secrets of the Oracle may not be divulged."

Though Ferdinand strove hard to hide what he felt, it was evident from his efforts to be at ease that he was very deeply moved, and the cleverest answer could not have produced in the spectators the strange sensation, amounting to a sort of awe, which his unmistakable emotion gave rise to in them. The fun and the jests were at an end; hardly another word was spoken, and the audience dispersed in uneasy silence.

"My dear Lewis," said Ferdinand, as soon as they were alone together, "I must tell you all about this. The Turk has broken my heart; for I believe I shall never get over the blow he has given me until I die to fulfil his terrible prophecy."

Lewis gazed at him in amazement; and Ferdinand continued:

"I see, now, that the mysterious being who communicates with us by the medium of the Turk, has powers at his command which compel our most secret thoughts with magic might; it may be that this strange intelligence clearly and distinctly beholds that germ of the future which is being formed within us in mysterious connection with the outer world, and knows what will happen to us in the far future, like people with the second-sight who can predict the hour of death."

"You must have put an extraordinary question," Lewis answered; "but I should think you are tacking some unduly important meaning onto the oracle's ambiguous reply. Chance, I should imagine, has educed something which by accident is appropriate to your question; and you are attributing this to the mystic power of the person (most probably quite an everyday sort of creature) who speaks to us through the Turk."

"What you say," answered Ferdinand, "is quite at variance with all the conclusions you and I have come to on the subject of what is ordinarily termed 'chance.' However, you cannot be expected to comprehend my condition without my telling you all about an affair which happened to me some time ago. I have never breathed a syllable of it to anyone till now.

"Several years ago I was on my way back to B——, from a place a long way off in East Prussia, belonging to my father. In K——, I met with some young Courland fellows who were going back to B—— too. We travelled together in three post carriages; and, as we had plenty of money, and were all about the time of life when spirits are pretty high, you may imagine the manner of our journey. We were continually playing the maddest pranks of every kind. I remember that we got to M—— about noon, and set to work to plunder the landlady's wardrobe. A crowd collected in front of the inn, and we marched up and down, dressed in some of her clothes, smoking, till the postilion's horn sounded, and off we set again. We reached D—— in the highest possible spirits, and were so delighted with the place and scenery, that we determined to stay there several days. We made a number of excursions in the neighbourhood, and so once, when we had been out all day at the Karlsberg, finding a grand bowl of punch waiting for us on our return, we dipped into it pretty freely. Although I had not taken more of it than was good for me, still, I had been in the grand sea-breeze all day, and I felt all my pulses throbbing, and my blood seemed to rush through my veins in a stream of fire. When we went to our rooms at last, I threw myself down on my bed; but, tired as I was, my sleep was scarcely more than a kind of dreamy, half-conscious condition, in which I was cognizant of all that was going on about me. I fancied I could hear soft conversation in the next room, and at last I plainly made out a male voice saying, 'Well, good night, now; mind and be ready in good time.'

"A door opened and closed again, and then came a deep silence; but this was soon broken by one or two chords of a pianoforte.

"You know the magical effect of music sounding in that way in the stillness of night. I felt as though some beautiful spirit voice was speaking to me in these chords. I lay listening, expecting something in the shape of a fantasia—or some such piece of music—to follow; but imagine what it was like when a most gloriously, exquisitely beautiful lady's voice sang, to a melody that went to my heart, the words I am going to repeat to you:

Mio ben ricordati
S' avvien ch' io mora
Quanto quest' anima
    Fedel t' amò;
Io se pur amano
Le fredde ceneri,
Nel urna ancora
T' adorerò.*

"How can I ever hope to give you the faintest idea of the effect of those long-drawn swelling and dying notes upon me. I had never imagined anything approaching it. The melody was marvellous—quite unlike anything I had ever heard. It was itself the deep, tender sorrow of the most fervent love. As it rose in simple phrases, the clear upper notes like crystal bells, and sank till the rich low tones died away like the sighs of a despairing plaint, a rapture which words cannot describe took possession of me—the pain of a boundless longing seized my heart like a spasm. I could scarcely breathe, my whole being was merged in an inexpressible, superearthly delight. I did not dare to move; I could only listen; soul and body were merged in ear. It was not until the voice had been silent for some time that tears, coming to my eyes, broke the spell, and restored me to myself. I suppose that sleep then came upon me, for when I was roused by the shrill notes of a posthorn, the bright morning sun was shining into my room, and I found that it had been only in my dreams that I had been enjoying a bliss more deep, a happiness more ineffable, than the world could

*Darling! remember well,
    When I have passed away,
How this unchanging soul
    Loves Thee for aye!
Though my poor ashes rest
    Deep in my silent grave,
Ev'n in the urn of Death
    Thee I adore!

otherwise have afforded me. For a beautiful lady came to me—it was the lady who had sung the song—and said to me, very fondly and tenderly, 'Then you *did* recognize me, my own dear Ferdinand! I knew that I had only to sing, and I should live again in you wholly, for every note was sleeping in your heart.'

"Then I recognized, with unspeakable rapture, that she was the beloved of my soul, whose image had been enshrined in my heart since childhood. Though an adverse fate had torn her from me for a time, I had found her again now; but my deep and fervent love for her melted into that wonderful melody of sorrow, and our words and our looks grew into exquisite swelling tones of music, flowing together into a river of fire. Now, however, that I had awakened from this beautiful dream, I was obliged to confess to myself that I never had seen the beautiful lady before.

"I heard someone talking loudly and angrily in front of the house, and rising mechanically, I went to the window. An elderly gentleman, well dressed, was scolding the postilion, who had damaged something on an elegant travelling carriage. At last this was put to rights, and the gentleman called upstairs to someone, 'We're all ready now; come along, it's time to be off.' I found that there had been a young lady looking out of the window next to mine; but as she drew back quickly, and had on a broad travelling hat, I did not see her face. When she went out, however, she turned round and looked up at me, and heavens! I saw that she was the singer! she was the lady of my dream! For a moment her beautiful eyes rested upon me, and the beam of a crystal tone seemed to pierce my heart like the point of a burning dagger, so that I felt an actual physical smart: all my members trembled, and I was transfixed with an indescribable bliss. She quickly got into the carriage, the postilion blew a cheerful tune as if in jubilant defiance, and in a moment they had disappeared around the corner of the street. I remained at the window like a man in a dream.

"My Courland friends came in to fetch me for an excursion which had been arranged: I never spoke; they thought I was ill. How could I have uttered a single word connected with what had occurred? I abstained from making any inquiries in the hotel about the occupants of the room next to mine. I felt that every word relating to her uttered by any lips but mine would be a desecration of my secret. I resolved to keep it faithfully from thenceforth, to bear it about with me always, and to be forever true to her —my only love for evermore—although I might never see her again.

"You can quite understand my feelings. I know you will not blame me for having immediately given up everybody and everything but the most eager search for the very slightest trace of my unknown love. My jovial Courland friends were now perfectly unendurable to me; I slipped away from them quietly in the night, and was off as fast as I could travel to B——, to go on with my work there. You know I was always pretty good at drawing. Well, in B—— I took lessons in miniature painting from good masters, and got on so well that in a short time I was able to carry out the idea which had set me on this tack—to paint a portrait of her, as like as it could be made. I worked at it secretly, behind locked doors. No human eye has ever seen it; for I had a locket made for another picture of the same size, and I put her portrait into the frame instead of it, myself. Ever since, I have worn it next to my heart.

"I have never mentioned this affair—much the most important event in my life—until today; and you are the only creature in the world, Lewis, to whom I have breathed a word of my secret. Yet this very day a hostile influence—I know not whence or what— came piercing into my heart and life! When I went up to the Turk, I asked, thinking of my beloved: 'Will there ever again be a time for me like that which was the happiest in my life?'

"The Turk was most unwilling to answer me, as I daresay you observed; but at last, as I persisted, he said, 'I am looking into your breast; but the glitter of the gold, which is towards me, distracts me. Turn the picture around.'

"Have I words for the feeling which went shuddering through me? I am sure you must have seen how startled I was. The picture was really placed on my breast as the Turk had said; I turned it around, unobserved, and repeated my question. Then the figure said, in a sorrowful tone, 'Unhappy man! At the very moment when next you see her, you will be lost to her forever!'"

Lewis was about to try to cheer up his friend, who had fallen into a deep reverie, but some mutual acquaintances came in, and they were interrupted.

The story of this fresh instance of a mysterious answer by the Turk spread in the town, and people busied themselves in conjectures as to the unfavourable prophecy which had so upset the unprejudiced Ferdinand. His friends were besieged with questions, and Lewis had to invent a marvellous tale, which had all the more universal a success in that it was remote from the truth. The coterie with whom Ferdinand had been induced to go and see the Turk was in the habit of meeting once a week, and at their next meeting the Turk was necessarily the topic of conversation, as efforts were universally being made to obtain, from Ferdinand himself, full particulars of an adventure which had thrown him into such obvious despondency.   Lewis felt most deeply how bitter a blow it was to Ferdinand to find the secret of his romantic love, preserved so long and faithfully, penetrated by a fearful, unknown power; and he, like Ferdinand, was almost convinced that the mysterious link which attaches the present to the future must be clear to the vision of that power to which the most hidden secrets were thus manifest. Lewis could not help believing the oracle; but the malevolence, the relentlessness with which the misfortune impending over his friend had been announced, made him indignant with the undiscovered being who spoke by the mouth of the Turk.   He placed himself in persistent opposition to the automaton's many admirers; and while they considered that there was much impressiveness about its most natural movements, enhancing the effect of its oracular sayings, he maintained that it was those very turnings of the head and rollings of the eyes which he considered so absurd, and that this was the reason why he could not help making a joke on the subject; a joke which had put the exhibitor out of temper, and probably the invisible agent as well.   Indeed the latter had shown that this was so by giving a number of stupid and unmeaning answers.

"I must tell you," said Lewis, "that the moment I went into the room the figure reminded me of a most delightful nutcracker which a cousin of mine once gave me at Christmas when I was a little boy. The little fellow had the gravest and most comical face ever seen, and when he had a hard nut to crack there was some arrangement inside him which made him roll his great eyes, which projected far out of his head, and this gave him such an absurdly lifelike effect that I could play with him for hours.   In fact, in my secret soul, I almost thought he was real.   All the marionettes I have seen since then, however perfect, I have thought stiff and lifeless compared to my glorious nutcracker.   I had heard much of some wonderful automatons in the Arsenal at Dantzig, and I made it a point to go and see them when I was there some years ago.   Soon after I got there, an old-fashioned German soldier came marching up to me, and fired off his musket with such a bang that the great vaulted hall reverberated.   There were other similar tricks which I forget now; but at length I was taken into a room where I found the God of War—the terrible Mars himself—with all his suite.   He was seated, in a rather grotesque dress, on a throne ornamented with arms of all sorts; heralds and warriors were standing around him.   As soon as we came before the throne, a set of drummers began to roll their drums, and fifers blew on their fifes in the most horrible way—all out of tune—so that one had to put one's fingers in one's ears. My remark was that the God of War was very badly off for a band, and everyone agreed with me. The drums and fifes stopped; the heralds began to turn their heads about, and stamp with their halberds, and finally the God of War, after rolling his eyes for a time, started up from his seat, and seemed to be coming straight at us. However, he soon sank back on his throne again, and after a little more drumming and fifing, everything reverted to its state of wooden repose. As I came away from seeing these automatons, I said to myself, 'Nothing like my nutcracker!' And now that I have seen the sage Turk, I say again, 'Give me my Nutcracker.'"

People laughed at this, of course; though it was believed to be "more jest than earnest," for, to say nothing of the remarkable cleverness of many of the Turk's answers, the undiscoverable connection between him and the hidden being who, besides speaking through him, must produce the movements which accompanied his answers, was unquestionably very wonderful, at all events a masterpiece of mechanical and acoustical skill.

Lewis was himself obliged to admit this; and everyone was extolling the inventor of the automaton, when an elderly gentleman who, as a general rule, spoke very little, and had been taking no part in the conversation on the present occasion, rose from his chair (as he was in the habit of doing when he finally did say a few words, always greatly to the point) and began, in his usual polite manner, as follows:

"Will you be good enough to allow me, gentlemen,—I beg you to pardon me. You have reason to admire the curious work of art which has interested us all for so long; but you are wrong in supposing the commonplace person who exhibits it to be its inventor. The truth is that he really has no hand at all in what are the truly remarkable features of it. The originator of them is a gentleman highly skilled in matters of the kind—one who lives among us, and has done so for many years—whom we all know very well, and greatly respect and esteem."

Universal surprise was created by this, and the elderly gentleman was besieged with questions, on which he continued, "The gentleman to whom I allude is none other than Professor X———. The Turk had been here a couple of days, and nobody had taken any particular notice of him, though Professor X——— took care to go and see him at once, because everything in the shape of an automaton

interests him in the highest degree.   When he had heard one or two
of the Turk's answers, he took the exhibitor aside and whispered a
word or two in his ear.   The man turned pale, and shut up his
exhibition as soon as the two or three people who were in the room
had gone away.   The bills disappeared from the walls, and nothing
more was heard of the Talking Turk for a fortnight.   Then new
bills came out, and the Turk was found with the fine new head, and
all the other arrangements as they are at present—an unsolvable
riddle.   It is since that time that his answers have been so clever
and so interesting.   That all this is the work of Professor X——
admits of no question.   The exhibitor, in the interval when the
figure was not being exhibited, spent all his time with him.   Also it
is well known that the Professor passed several days in succession in
the room where the figure is.   Besides, gentlemen, you are no doubt
aware that the Professor himself possesses a number of most extraordinary automats, chiefly musical, which he has long vied with
Hofrath B—— in producing, keeping up with him a correspondence
concerning all sorts of mechanical, and, people say, even *magical*
acts and pursuits.   If he chose, he could astonish the world with
them.   But he works in complete privacy, although he is always
ready to show his extraordinary inventions to anyone who takes a
real interest in such matters."

It was, in fact, a matter of notoriety that this Professor X——,
whose principal pursuits were natural philosophy and chemistry,
delighted, next to them, in occupying himself with mechanical re-
search; but no one in the assemblage had had the slightest idea that
he had had any connection with the Talking Turk, and it was from
the merest hearsay that people knew anything concerning the
curiosities which the old gentleman had referred to.   Ferdinand
and Lewis felt strangely and vividly impressed by the old gentleman's account of Professor X——, and the influence which he had
brought to bear on that strange automaton.

"I cannot hide from you," said Ferdinand, "that hope is dawn-
ing upon me.   If I get nearer to this Professor X——, I may perhaps
come upon a clue to the mystery which is weighing so terribly upon
me at present.   And it is possible that the true significance and
import of the relations which exist between the Turk (or rather the
hidden entity which employs him as the organ of its oracular utterances) and myself, if I could comprehend it, might perhaps comfort
me, and weaken the impression of those words, for me so terrible.
I have made up my mind to make the acquaintance of this mysterious man on the pretext of seeing his automata; and as they are

musical ones, it will not be devoid of interest for you to come with me."

"As if it were not sufficient for me," said Lewis, "to be able to aid you, when you need it, with advice and help! But I cannot deny that even today, when the old gentleman was mentioning Professor X——'s connection with the Turk, strange ideas came into my mind; although perhaps I am going a long way about in search of what lies close at hand, could one but see it. For instance, to look as close at hand as possible for the solution of the mystery: is it not possible that the invisible being knew that you wore the picture next your heart, so that a mere lucky guess might account for the rest? Perhaps it was taking its revenge upon you for the rather discourteous style in which we were joking about the Turk's wisdom?"

"Not one soul," Ferdinand answered, "has ever set eyes on the picture; I told you this before. And I have never told anyone but yourself of the adventure which has had such an immensely important influence on my whole life. It is an utter impossibility that the Turk can have got to know of this in any ordinary manner. Much more probably, 'the long roundabout way' may be much nearer the truth."

"Well then," said Lewis, "what I mean is this: that this automaton, strongly as I appeared today to assert the contrary, is really one of the most extraordinary phenomena ever beheld, and that everything goes to prove that whoever controls and directs it has at his command higher powers than is supposed by those who go there simply to gape at things, and do no more than wonder at what is wonderful. The figure is nothing more than the outward form of the communication; but that form has been cleverly selected. Its shape, appearance, and movements are well adapted to occupy our attention in such a manner that its secrets are preserved and to give us a favourable opinion of the intelligence which gives the answers. There cannot be any human being concealed inside the figure; that is as good as proved, so it is clearly the result of some acoustic deception that we think the answers come from the Turk's mouth. But how this is accomplished—how the being who gives the answers is placed in a position to hear the questions and see the questioners, and at the same time to be audible to them—certainly remains a complete mystery to me. Of course all this merely implies great acoustic and mechanical skill on the part of the inventor, and remarkable acuteness—or, I might say, systematic craftiness—in overlooking nothing in the process of deceiving us.

"Still, this part of the riddle does not interest me too much, since it is completely overshadowed by the circumstance that the Turk often reads the very soul of the questioner. This is what I find remarkable. Does this being which answers our questions acquire, by some process unknown to us, a psychic influence over us, and does it place itself in spiritual rapport with us? How can it comprehend and read our minds and thoughts, and more than that, know our whole inner being? Even if it does not clearly speak out secrets dormant within us, it evokes, in a sort of ecstasy induced by its rapport with us, the suggestions, the outlines, the shadowings of everything in our minds, all of which are seen by the eye of our spirit, brightly illuminated. On this assumption the Turk strikes strings within us and makes them give forth a clear chord, audible and intelligible to us, instead of being a mere murmur as they usually are. As a result it is we who answer our own question; the voice which we hear is produced from within ourselves by the operation of this unknown spiritual power, and our vague presentiments and anticipations of the future are heightened into spoken prophecy. It is much the same thing in dreams when a strange voice tells us things we did not know, or about which we are in doubt; it is in really a voice proceeding from ourselves, although it seems to convey to us knowledge which we did not previously possess. No doubt the Turk (that is to say, the hidden power which is connected with him) seldom finds it necessary to place himself in rapport with people in this way. Hundreds of spectators can be dealt with in the cursory, superficial manner adapted to their questions and their characters, and it is seldom that a question is put which calls for the exercise of anything besides ready wit. But if the questioner is in a strained or exalted state the Turk would be affected in quite a different way, and he would then employ those means which render possible the production of a psychic rapport, giving him the power to answer from the inner depths of the questioner. His hesitation in replying to deep questions of this kind may be due to the delay which he grants himself to gain a few moments to bring into play the power in question. This is my true and genuine opinion; and you see that I have not that contemptuous notion of this work of art (or whatever may be the proper term to apply to it) that I would have had you believe I had. But I do not wish to conceal anything from you; though I see that if you adopt my idea, I shall not have given you any real comfort at all."

"You are wrong there, my dear friend," said Ferdinand. "The very fact that your opinion does agree with a vague notion which I felt dimly in my own mind comforts me very much. It is only myself that I have to take into account; my precious secret is not discovered, for I know that you will guard it as a sacred treasure. And, by-the-bye, I must tell you of a most extraordinary feature of the matter, which I had forgotten till now. Just as the Turk was speaking his last words, I fancied that I heard one or two broken phrases of the sorrowful melody, '*mio ben ricordati*,' and then it seemed to me that one single, long-drawn note of the glorious voice which I heard on that eventful night went floating by."

"Well," said Lewis, "and I remember, too, that, just as your answer was being given to you, I happened to place my hand on the railing which surrounds the figure. I felt it thrill and vibrate in my hand, and I fancied also that I could hear a kind of musical sound, for I cannot say it was a vocal note, passing across the room. I paid no attention to it, because, as you know, my head is always full of music, and I have several times been wonderfully deceived in a similar way; but I was very much astonished in my own mind when I traced the mysterious connection between that sound and your adventure in D———."

The fact that Lewis, too, had heard the sound was to Ferdinand a proof of the psychic rapport which existed between them; and as they further discussed the marvels of the affair, he began to feel the heavy burden lifted away which had weighed upon him since he heard the fatal answer, and was ready to go forward bravely to meet whatever the future might have in store.

"It is impossible that I can lose her," he said. "She is my heart's queen, and will always be there, as long as my own life endures."

They called on Professor X———, in high hope that he would be able to throw light on many questions relating to occult sympathies and the like, in which they were deeply interested. They found him to be an old man, dressed in an old-fashioned French style, exceedingly keen and lively, with small gray eyes which had an unpleasant way of fixing themselves on one, and a sarcastic smile, not very attractive, playing about his mouth.

When they had expressed their wish to see some of his automata, he said, "Ah! and you really take an interest in mechanical matters, do you? Perhaps you have done something in that direction yourselves? Well, I can show you in this house here what you will look for in vain in the rest of Europe: I may say, in the known world."

There was something most unpleasant about the Professor's voice; it was a high-pitched, screaming sort of discordant tenor, exactly suited to the mountebank manner in which he proclaimed his treasures. He fetched his keys with a great clatter, and opened the door of a tastefully and elegantly furnished hall, where the automata were. There was a piano in the middle of the room on a raised platform; beside it, on the right, a life-sized figure of a man, with a flute in his hand; on the left, a female figure, seated at an instrument somewhat resembling a piano; behind her were two boys with a drum and a triangle. In the background our two friends noticed an orchestrion (which was an instrument already known to them), and all around the walls were a number of musical clocks. The Professor passed in an offhand way close by the orchestrion and the clocks, and just touched the automata, almost imperceptibly; then he sat down at the piano, and began to play, pianissimo, an andante in the style of a march. He played it once through by himself; and as he commenced it for the second time the flute player put his instrument to his lips, and took up the melody; then one of the boys drummed softly on his drum in the most accurate time, and the other just touched his triangle, so that you could hear it and no more. Presently the lady came in with full chords sounding something like those of a harmonica, which she produced by pressing down the keys of her instrument; and then the whole room kept growing more and more alive; the musical clocks came in one by one, with the utmost rhythmical precision; the boy drummed louder; the triangle rang through the room, and lastly the orchestrion set to work, and drummed and trumpeted fortissimo, so that the whole place shook. This went on till the Professor wound up the whole business with one final chord, all the machines finishing also, with the utmost precision. Our friends bestowed the applause which the Professor's complacent smile (with its undercurrent of sarcasm) seemed to demand of them. He went up to the figures to set about exhibiting some further similar musical feats; but Lewis and Ferdinand, as if by a preconcerted arrangement, declared that they had pressing business which prevented their making a longer stay, and took their leave of the inventor and his machines.

"Most interesting and ingenious, wasn't it?" said Ferdinand; but Lewis's anger, long restrained, broke out.

"Oh! Damn that wretched Professor!" he cried. "What a terrible, terrible disappointment! Where are all the revelations we expected? What became of the learned, instructive discourse which we thought he would deliver to us, as to disciples at Sais?"

"At the same time," said Ferdinand, "we have seen some very ingenious mechanical inventions, curious and interesting from a

musical point of view. Clearly, the flute player is the same as
Vaucanson's well-known machine; and a similar mechanism applied
to the fingers of the female figure is, I suppose, what enables her to
bring out those beautiful tones from her instrument. The way in
which all the machines work together is really astonishing."

"It is exactly that which drives me so wild," said Lewis. "All
that machine music (in which I include the Professor's own playing)
makes every bone in my body ache. I am sure I do not know when
I shall get over it! The fact of any human being's doing anything
in association with those lifeless figures which counterfeit the appearance and movements of humanity has always, to me, something
fearful, unnatural, I may say terrible, about it. I suppose it would
be possible, by means of certain mechanical arrangements inside
them, to construct automata which would dance, and then to set
them to dance with human beings, and twist and turn about in all
sorts of figures; so that we should have a living man putting his
arms about a lifeless partner of wood, and whirling round and
round with her, or rather it. Could you look at such a sight, for
an instant, without horror? At all events, all mechanical music
seems monstrous and abominable to me; and a good stocking-loom
is, in my opinion, worth all the most perfect and ingenious musical
clocks in the universe put together. For is it the breath, merely,
of the performer on a wind-instrument, or the skillful, supple fingers
of the performer on a stringed instrument which evoke those tones
which lay upon us a spell of such power, and awaken that inexpressible feeling, akin to nothing else on earth—the sense of a
distant spirit world, and of our own higher life in it? Is it not,
rather, the mind, the soul, the heart, which merely employ those
bodily organs to give forth into our external life what we feel in our
inner depths? so that it can be communicated to others, and awaken
kindred chords in them, opening, in harmonious echoes, that marvellous kingdom, from which those tones come darting, like beams
of light? To set to work to make music by means of valves, springs,
levers, cylinders, or whatever other apparatus you choose to employ,
is a senseless attempt to make the means to an end accomplish what
can result only when those means are animated and, in their
minutest movements, controlled by the mind, the soul, and the
heart. The gravest reproach you can make to a musician is that he
plays without expression; because, by so doing, he is marring the
whole essence of the matter. Yet the coldest and most unfeeling
executant will always be far in advance of the most perfect machines. For it is impossible that any impulse whatever from the inner

man shall not, even for a moment, animate his rendering; whereas, in the case of a machine, no such impulse can ever do so. The attempts of mechanicians to imitate, with more or less approximation to accuracy, the human organs in the production of musical sounds, or to substitute mechanical appliances for those organs, I consider tantamount to a declaration of war against the spiritual element in music; but the greater the forces they array against it, the more victorious it is. For this very reason, the more perfect that this sort of machinery is, the more I disapprove of it; and I infinitely prefer the commonest barrel-organ, in which the mechanism attempts nothing but to be mechanical, to Vaucanson's flute player, or the harmonica girl."

"I entirely agree with you," said Ferdinand, "and indeed you have merely put into words what I have always thought; and I was much struck with it today at the Professor's. Although I do not live and move and have my being in music so wholly as you do, and consequently am not so sensitively alive to imperfections in it, I, too, have always felt a repugnance to the stiffness and lifelessness of machine music; and, I can remember, when I was a child at home, how I detested a large, ordinary musical clock, which played its little tune every hour. It is a pity that those skillful mechanicians do not try to apply their knowledge to the improvement of musical instruments, rather than to puerilities of this sort."

"Exactly," said Lewis. "Now, in the case of instruments of the keyboard class a great deal might be done. There is a wide field open in that direction to clever mechanical people, much as has been accomplished already; particularly in instruments of the pianoforte genus. But it would be the task of a really advanced system of the 'mechanics of music' to observe closely, study minutely, and discover carefully that class of sounds which belong, most purely and strictly, to Nature herself, to obtain a knowledge of the tones which dwell in substances of every description, and then to take this mysterious music and enclose it in some sort of instrument, where it should be subject to man's will, and give itself forth at his touch. All the attempts to evoke music from metal or glass cylinders, glass threads, slips of glass, or pieces of marble; or to cause strings to vibrate or sound in ways unlike the ordinary ways, are to me interesting in the highest degree. The obstacle in the way of real progress in the discovery of the marvellous acoustical secrets which lie hidden all around us in nature is that every imperfect attempt at an experiment is at once lauded as a new and perfect invention. This is why so many new instruments have started into existence—most of them with grand or ridiculous names—and have disappeared and been forgotten just as quickly."

"Your 'higher mechanics of music' seems to be a most interesting subject," said Ferdinand, "although, for my part, I do not as yet quite perceive the object at which it aims."

"The object at which it aims," said Lewis, "is the discovery of the most absolutely perfect kind of musical sound; and according to my theory, musical sound would be the nearer to perfection the more closely it approximated such of the mysterious tones of nature as are not wholly dissociated from this earth."

"I presume," said Ferdinand, "that it is because I have not penetrated so deeply into this subject as you have, but you must allow me to say that I do not quite understand you."

"Then," said Lewis, "let me give you some sort of an idea how this question looks to me.

"In the primeval condition of the human race (to make use of almost the very words of a talented writer—Schubert—in his *Glimpses of the Night Side of Natural Science*) mankind still lived in pristine holy harmony with nature, richly endowed with a heavenly instinct of prophecy and poetry. Mother Nature continued to nourish from the fount of her own life the wondrous being to whom she had given birth, and she encompassed him with a holy music, like the afflatus of a continual inspiration. Wondrous tones spoke of the mysteries of her unceasing activity. There has come down to us an echo from the mysterious depths of those primeval days— that beautiful notion of the music of the spheres, which filled me with the deepest and most devout reverence when I first read of it in *The Dream of Scipio*. I often used to listen, on quiet moonlight nights, to hear if those wondrous tones would come to me, borne on the wings of the whispering airs. However, as I said to you, those nature tones have not yet all departed from this world, for we have an instance of their survival, and occurrence in that 'music of the air' or 'voice of the demon,' mentioned by a writer on Ceylon—a sound which so powerfully affects the human system that even the least impressionable persons, when they hear those tones of nature imitating, in such a terrible manner, the expression of human sorrow and suffering, are struck with painful compassion and pro-found terror! Indeed, I once met with an instance of a pheno-menon of a similar kind myself at a place in East Prussia. I had been living there for some time; it was about the end of autumn, when, on quiet nights, with a moderate breeze blowing, I used dis-tinctly to hear tones, sometimes resembling the deep, stopped, pedal pipe of an organ, and sometimes like the vibrations from a deep, soft-toned bell. I often distinguished, quite clearly, the low F, and the fifth above it (the C), and often the minor third above, E flat, was perceptible as well; and then this tremendous chord of the seventh, so woeful and so solemn, produced on one the effect of the most intense sorrow, and even of terror!

"There is, about the imperceptible commencement, the swelling and the gradual dying of those nature tones—a something which has a most powerful and indescribable effect upon us; and any instrument which should be capable of producing this would, no doubt, affect us in a similar way. So that I think the glass harmonica comes the nearest, as regards its tone, to that perfection, which is to be measured by its influence on our minds. And it is fortunate that this instrument (which chances to be the very one which imitates those nature tones with such exactitude) happens to be just the very one which is incapable of lending itself to frivolity or ostentation, but exhibits its characteristic qualities in the purest of simplicity. The recently invented 'harmonichord' will doubtless accomplish much in this direction. This instrument, as you no doubt know, sets strings vibrating and sounding (not bells, as in the harmonica) by means of a mechanism, which is set in motion by the pressing down of keys, and the rotation of a cylinder. The performer has under his control the commencement, the swelling out and the diminishing of the tones much more than is the case with the harmonica, though as yet the harmonichord has not the tone of the harmonica, which sounds as if it came straight from another world."

"I have heard that instrument," said Ferdinand, "and certainly the tone of it went to the very depths of my being, although I thought the performer was doing it scant justice. As regards the rest, I think I quite understand you, although I do not, as yet, quite see into the closeness of the connection between those 'nature tones' and music."

Lewis answered, "Can the music which dwells within us be any other than that which lies buried in nature as a profound mystery, comprehensible only by the inner, higher sense, uttered by instruments, as the organs of it, merely in obedience to a mighty spell, of which we are the masters? But, in the purely psychical action and operation of the spirit—that is to say, in dreams—this spell is broken; and then, in the tones of familiar instruments, we are enabled to recognize those nature tones as wondrously engendered in the air, they come floating down to us, and swell and die away."

"I am thinking of the Æolian harp," said Ferdinand. "What is your opinion about that ingenious invention?"

"Every attempt," said Lewis, "to tempt Nature to give forth her tones is glorious, and highly worthy of attention. Only, it seems to me that as yet we have only offered her trifling toys, which she has often shattered to pieces in her indignation. A much grander idea than all those playthings (like Æolian harps) was the 'storm harp' which I have read of. It was made of thick cords of wire, which were stretched out at considerable distances apart, in the open country, and gave forth great, powerful chords when the wind smote them.

"Altogether, there is still a wide field open to thoughtful inventors in this direction, and I quite believe that the impulse recently given to natural science in general will be perceptible in this branch of it, and bring into practical existence much which is, as yet, nothing but speculation."

Just at this moment there suddenly came floating through the air an extraordinary sound, which, as it swelled and became more distinguishable, seemed to resemble the tone of a glass harmonica. Lewis and Ferdinand stood rooted to the spot in amazement, not unmixed with awe; the tones took the form of a profoundly sorrowful melody sung by a female voice. Ferdinand grasped Lewis by the hand, whilst the latter whispered the words,

Mio ben, ricordati, s' avvien ch' io mora.

At the time when this occurred they were outside the town, and before the entrance to a garden which was surrounded by lofty trees and tall hedges. There was a pretty little girl—whom they had not observed before—sitting playing in the grass near them, and she sprang up crying, "Oh, how beautifully my sister is singing again! I must take her some flowers, for she always sings sweeter and longer when she sees a beautiful carnation." And with that she gathered a bunch of flowers, and went skipping into the garden with it, leaving the gate ajar, so that our friends could see through it. What was their astonishment to see Professor X—— standing in the middle of the garden, beneath a lofty ash-tree! Instead of the repellent ironic grin with which he had received them at his house, his face wore an expression of deep melancholy earnestness, and his gaze was fixed upon the heavens, as if he were contemplating that world beyond the skies, of which those marvellous tones, floating in the air like the breath of a zephyr, were telling. He walked up and down the central path, with slow and measured steps; and, as he passed along, everything around him seemed to waken into life and movement. In every direction crystal tones came scintillating out of the dark bushes and trees, and, streaming through the air like flame, united in a wondrous concert, penetrating the inmost heart, and waking in the soul the most rapturous emotions of a higher world. Twilight was falling fast; the Professor disappeared among the hedges, and the tones died away in pianissimo. At length our friends went back to the town in profound silence; but, as Lewis was about to leave Ferdinand, the latter clasped him firmly, saying:

"Be true to me! Do not abandon me! I feel, too clearly, some hostile foreign influence at work upon my whole existence, smiting upon all its hidden strings, and making them resound at its pleasure. I am helpless to resist it, though it should drive me to my destruction! Can that diabolical, sneering irony, with which the Professor received us at his house, have been anything other than the expression of this hostile principle? Was it with any other intention than of getting his hands washed of me forever, that he fobbed us off with those automata of his?"

"You are very probably right," said Lewis, "for I have a strong suspicion myself that, in some manner which is as yet an utter riddle to me, the Professor does exercise some sort of power or influence over your fate, or, I should rather say, over that mysterious psychical relationship, or affinity, which exists between you and this lady. It may be that, being mixed up in some way with this affinity, in his character of an element hostile to it, he strengthens it by the very fact that he opposes it: and it may also be that the quality which renders you so extremely unacceptable to him is that your presence awakens and sets into lively movement all the strings and chords of this mutually sympathetic condition. This may be contrary to his desire, and, very probably, in opposition to some conventional family arrangement."

Our friends determined to leave no stone unturned in their efforts to make a closer approach to the Professor, with the hope that they might succeed, sooner or later, in clearing up this mystery which so affected Ferdinand's destiny and fate, and they were to have paid him a visit on the following morning as a preliminary step. However, a letter, which Ferdinand unexpectedly received from his father, summoned him to B——; it was impossible for him to permit himself the smallest delay, and in a few hours he was off, as fast as post-horses could convey him, assuring Lewis, as he started, that nothing should prevent his return in a fortnight, at the very latest.

It struck Lewis as a singular circumstance that soon after Ferdinand's departure, the same old gentleman who had at first spoken of the Professor's connection with the Talking Turk took an opportunity of enlarging to him on the fact that X——'s mechanical inventions were simply the result of an extreme enthusiasm for mechanical pursuits, and of deep and searching investigations in natural science. He also praised the Professor's wonderful discoveries in music, which, he said, he had not as yet communicated to anyone, adding that his mysterious laboratory was a pretty garden outside the town, and that passers-by had often heard wondrous tones and melodies there, just as if the whole place were peopled by fays and spirits.

The fortnight elapsed, but Ferdinand did not come back. At length, when two months had gone by, a letter came from him to the following effect:

Read and marvel; though you will learn only what, perhaps, you strongly suspected would be the case, when you got to know more of the Professor. As the horses were being changed in the village of P——, I was standing, gazing into the distance, not thinking specially of anything in particular. A carriage drove by, and stopped at the church, which was open. A young lady, simply dressed, stepped out of the carriage, followed by a young gentleman in a Russian Jaeger uniform, wearing several decorations. Two gentlemen got down from a second carriage. The innkeeper said, "Oh, this is the stranger couple our clergyman is marrying today." Mechanically I went into the church, just as the clergyman was concluding the service with the blessing. I looked at the couple—the bride was my sweet singer. She looked at me, turned pale, and fainted. The gentleman who was behind her caught her in his arms. It was Professor X——. What happened further I do not know, nor have I any recollection as to how I got here; probably Professor X—— can tell you all about it. But a peace and a happiness, such as I have never known before, have now taken possession of my soul. The mysterious prophecy of the Turk was a cursed falsehood, a mere result of blind groping with unskillful antennae. Have I lost her? Is she not mine forever in the glowing inner life?

It will be long before you hear from me, for I am going on to K——, and perhaps to the extreme north, as far as P——.

Lewis gathered the distracted condition of his friend's mind only too plainly from his language, and the whole affair became the greater a riddle to him when he ascertained that it was a matter of certainty that Professor X—— had not left town.

"Could all this," he thought, "be only a result of the conflict of mysterious psychical relations (existing, perhaps, between several people) making their way out into everyday life, and involving in their circle even outward events independent of them, so that the deluded inner sense looks upon them as phenomena proceeding unconditionally from itself, and believes in them accordingly? It may be that the hopeful anticipation which I feel within me will be realized—for my friend's consolation. For the Turk's mysterious prophecy is fulfilled, and perhaps, through that very fulfilment, the mortal blow which menaced my friend is averted.

"Well," said Ottmar, as Theodore came to a sudden stop, "is that all? Where is the explanation? What became of Ferdinand, the beautiful singer, Professor X——, and the Russian officer?"

"You know," said Theodore, "that I told you at the beginning that I was only going to read you a fragment, and I consider that the story of the Talking Turk *is* only a fragment. I mean that the imagination of the reader, or listener, should merely receive one or two more or less powerful impulses, and then go on swinging, pendulum-like, of its own accord. But if you, Ottmar, are really anxious to have your mind set at rest over Ferdinand's future, remember the dialogue on opera which I read to you some time since. This is the same Ferdinand who appears there, sound of mind and body; in the Talking Turk he is at an earlier stage of his career. So probably his somnambulistic love affair ended satisfactorily enough."

"To which," said Ottmar, "has to be added that Theodore used to take a delight in exciting people's imaginations by means of the most extraordinary—nay, wild and insane—stories, and then suddenly break them off. Not only this, but everything he did at that time was a fragment. He read second volumes only, not troubling himself about the firsts or thirds; saw only the second and third acts of plays; and so on."

"And," said Theodore, "I still have that inclination; to this hour nothing is so distasteful to me as when, in a story or a novel, the stage on which the imaginary world has been in action is swept so clean by the historic broom that not the smallest grain or particle of dust is left on it; when you go home so completely sated and satisfied that you have not the faintest desire left to have another peep behind the curtain. On the other hand, many a fragment of a clever story sinks deep into my soul, and the continuance of the play of my imagination, as it goes along on its own swing, gives me an enduring pleasure. Who has not felt this over Goethe's 'Nut-brown Maid'! And, above all, his fragment of that most delightful tale of the little lady whom the traveller always carried about with him in a little box always exercises an indescribable charm upon me."

"Enough," interrupted Lothair. "We are not to hear any more about the Talking Turk, and the story was really all told, after all."

A NEW YEAR'S EVE ADVENTURE

FOREWORD BY THE EDITOR

The Travelling Enthusiast, from whose journals we are presenting another "fancy-flight in the manner of Jacques Callot," has apparently not separated the events of his inner life from those of the outside world; in fact we cannot determine where one ends and the other begins. But even if you cannot see this boundary very clearly, dear reader, the Geisterseher may beckon you to his side, and before you are even aware of it, you will be in a strange magical realm where figures of fantasy step right into your own life, and are as cordial with you as your oldest friends. I beg of you—take them as such, go along with their remarkable doings, yield to the shudders and thrills that they produce, since the more you go along with them, the better they can operate. What more can I do for the Travelling Enthusiast who has encountered so much strangeness and madness, everywhere and at all times, but especially on New Year's Eve in Berlin?

MY BELOVED

I had a feeling of death in my heart—ice-cold death—and the sensation branched out like sharp, growing icicles into nerves that were already boiling with heat. I ran like a madman—no hat, no coat—out into the lightless stormy winter night. The weather vanes were grinding and creaking in the wind, as if Time's eternal gearwork were audibly rotating and the old year were being rolled away like a heavy weight, and ponderously pushed into a gloom-filled abyss.

You must surely know that on this season, Christmas and New Year's, even though it's so fine and pleasant for all of you, I am always driven out of my peaceful cell onto a raging, lashing sea. Christmas! Holidays that have a rosy glow for me. I can hardly wait for it, I look forward to it so much. I am a better, finer man than the rest of the year, and there isn't a single gloomy, misanthropic thought in my mind. Once again I am a boy, shouting with joy. The faces of the angels laugh to me from the gilded fretwork decorations in the shops decorated for Christmas, and the awesome tones of the church organ penetrate the noisy bustle of the streets, as if coming from afar, with "Unto us a child is born." But after the holidays everything becomes colorless again, and the glow dies away and disappears into drab darkness.

Every year more and more flowers drop away withered, their buds eternally sealed; there is no spring sun that can bring the warmth of new life into old dried-out branches. I know this well enough, but the Enemy never stops maliciously rubbing it in as the year draws to an end. I hear a mocking whisper: "Look what you have lost this year; so many worthwhile things that you'll never see again. But all this makes you wiser, less tied to trivial pleasures, more serious and solid—even though you don't enjoy yourself very much."

Every New Year's Eve the Devil keeps a special treat for me. He knows just the right moment to jam his claw into my heart, keeping up a fine mockery while he licks the blood that wells out. And there is always someone around to help him, just as yesterday the Justizrat came to his aid. He (the Justizrat) holds a big celebration every New Year's Eve, and likes to give everyone something special as a New Year's present. Only he is so clumsy and bumbling about it, for all his pains, that what was meant to give pleasure usually turns into a mess that is half slapstick and half torture.

I walked into his front hall, and the Justizrat came running to meet me, holding me back for a moment from the Holy of Holies out of which the odors of tea and expensive perfumes were pouring. He looked especially pleased with himself. He smirked at me in a very strange way and said, "My dear friend, there's something nice waiting for you in the next room. Nothing like it for a New Year's surprise. But don't be afraid!"

I felt that sinking feeling in my heart. Something was wrong, I knew, and I suddenly began to feel depressed and edgy. Then the doors were opened. I took up my courage and stepped forward, marched in, and among the women sitting on the sofa I saw *her*.

Yes, it was she. She herself. I hadn't seen her for years, and yet in one lightning flash the happiest moments of my life came back to me, and gone was the pain that had resulted from being separated from her.

What marvellous chance brought her here? What miracle introduced her into the Justizrat's circle—I didn't even know that he knew her. But I didn't think of any of these questions; all I knew was that she was mine again.

I must have stood there as if halted magically in midmotion. The Justizrat kept nudging me and muttering, "Mmmm? Mmmm? How about it?"

I started to walk again, mechanically, but I saw only her, and it was all that I could do to force out, "My God, my God, it's Julia!" I was practically at the tea table before she even noticed me, but then she stood up and said coldly, "I'm so delighted to see you here. You are looking well." And with that she sat down again and asked the woman sitting next to her on the sofa, "Is there going to be anything interesting at the theatre the next few weeks?"

You see a miraculously beautiful flower, glowing with beauty, filling the air with scent, hinting at even more hidden beauty. You hurry over to it, but the moment that you bend down to look into its chalice, the glistening petals are pushed aside and out pops a smooth, cold, slimy, little lizard that tries to cut you down with its glare.

That's just what happened to me. Like a perfect oaf I made a bow to the ladies, and since spite and idiocy often go together, as I stepped back I knocked a cup of hot tea out of the Justizrat's hand— he was standing right behind me—and all over his beautifully pleated jacket. The company roared at the Justizrat's mishap, and even more at me. In short, everything was going along smoothly enough for a madhouse, but I just gave up.

Julia, however, hadn't laughed, and as I looked at her again I thought for a moment that a gleam of our wonderful past came through to me, a fragment of our former life of love and poetry. At this point someone in the next room began to improvise on the piano, and the company began to show signs of life. I heard that this was someone I did not know, a great pianist named Berger, who played divinely, and that you had to listen to him.

"Will you stop making that noise with the teaspoons, Minchen," bawled the Justizrat, and with a coyly contorted hand and a languorous "Eh bien!" he beckoned the ladies to the door, to approach the virtuoso. Julia arose too and walked slowly into the next room.

There was something strange about her whole figure, I thought. Somehow she seemed larger, more developed, almost lush. Her blouse was cut low, only half covering her breasts, shoulders and

Doctor Dapertutto and Giuletta *(detail from illustration following page 230).*

neck; her sleeves were puffed, and reached only to her elbows; and her hair was parted at the forehead and pulled back into plaits—all of which gave her an antique look, much like one of the young women in Mieris's paintings. Somehow it seemed to me as if I had seen her like this before. She had taken off her gloves, and ornate bracelets on her wrist helped carry through the complete identity of her dress with the past and awaken more vividly dark memories.

She turned toward me before she went into the music room, and for an instant her angel-like, normally pleasant face seemed strained into a sneer. An uncomfortable, unpleasant feeling arose in me, like a cramp running through my nervous system.

"Oh, he plays divinely," lisped a girl, apparently inspired by the sweet tea, and I don't know how it happened, but Julia's arm was in mine, and I led her, or rather she led me, into the next room. Berger was raising the wildest hurricanes, and like a roaring surf his mighty chords rose and fell. It did me good.

Then Julia was standing beside me, and said more softly and more sweetly than before, "I wish you were sitting at the piano, singing softly about pleasures and hopes that have been lost." The Enemy had left me, and in just the name, "Julia!" I wanted to proclaim the bliss that filled me. But the crowd pushed between us and we were separated. Now she was obviously avoiding me, but I was lucky enough to touch her clothing and close enough to breathe in her perfume, and the springtime of the past arose in a hundred shining colors.

Berger let the hurricane blow itself out, the skies became clear, and pretty little melodies, like the golden clouds of dawn, hovered in pianissimo. Well-earned applause broke out when he finished, and the guests began to move around the room. It came about that I found myself facing Julia again. The spirit rose more mightily in me. I wanted to seize her and embrace her, but a bustling servant crowded between us with a platter of drinks, calling in a very offensive way, "Help yourself, please, help yourself."

The tray was filled with cups of steaming punch, but in the very middle was a huge cut-crystal goblet, also apparently filled with punch. How did that get there, among all the ordinary punch cups? He knows—the Enemy that I'm gradually coming to understand. Like Clemens in Tieck's "Oktavian" he walks about making a pleasant squiggle with one foot, and is very fond of red capes and feathers. Julia picked up this sparkling, beautifully cut goblet and offered it to me, saying, "Are you still willing to take a glass from my hand?" "Julia, Julia," I sighed.

As I took the glass, my fingers brushed against hers, and electric sensations ran through me. I drank and drank, and it seemed to me that little flickering blue flames licked around the goblet and my lip. Then the goblet was empty, and I really don't know myself how it happened, but I was now sitting on an ottoman in a small room lit only by an alabaster lamp, and Julia was sitting beside me, demure and innocent-looking as ever. Berger had started to play again, the andante from Mozart's sublime E-flat Symphony, and on the swan's wings of song my sunlike love soared high. Yes, it was Julia, Julia herself, as pretty as an angel and as demure; our talk a longing lament of love, more looks than words, her hand resting in mine.

"I will never let you go," I was saying. "Your love is the spark that glows in me, kindling a higher life in art and poetry. Without you, without your love, everything is dead and lifeless. Didn't you come here so that you could be mine forever?"

At this very moment there tottered into the room a spindle-shanked cretin, eyes a-pop like a frog's, who said, in a mixture of croak and cackle, "Where the Devil is my wife?"

Julia stood up and said to me in a distant, cold voice, "Shall we go back to the party? My husband is looking for me. You've been very amusing again, darling, as overemotional as ever; but you should watch how much you drink."

The spindle-legged monkey reached for her hand and she followed him into the living room with a laugh.

"Lost forever," I screamed aloud.

"Oh, yes; codille, darling," bleated an animal playing ombre.

I ran out into the stormy night.

IN THE BEER CELLAR

Promenading up and down under the linden trees can be a fine thing, but not on a New Year's Eve when it is bitter cold and snow is falling. Bareheaded and without a coat I finally felt the cold when icy shivers began to interrupt my feverishness. I trudged over the Opern Bridge, past the Castle, over the Schleusen Bridge, past the Mint. I was on Jaegerstrasse close to Thiermann's shop. Friendly lights were burning inside. I was about to go in, since I was freezing and I needed a good drink of something strong, when a merry group came bursting out, babbling loudly about fine oysters and good Eilfer wine. One of them—I could see by the lantern light that he was a very impressive-looking officer in the uhlans—was shouting, "You know, he was right, that fellow who cursed them out in Mainz last year for not bringing out the Eilfer, he was right!" They all laughed uproariously.

Without thinking, I continued a little farther, then stopped in front of a beer cellar out of which a single light was shining. Wasn't it Shakespeare's Henry V who once felt so tired and discouraged that he "remembered the poor creature, small beer?" Indeed, the same thing was happening to me. My tongue was practically cracking with thirst for a bottle of good English beer. I hastened down into the cellar.

"Yes, sir?" said the owner of the beer cellar, touching his cap amiably as he came toward me.

I asked for a bottle of good English beer and a pipe of good tobacco, and soon found myself sublimely immersed in fleshly comforts which even the Devil had to respect enough to leave me alone. Ah, Justizrat! If you had seen me descend from your bright living room to a gloomy beer cellar, you would have turned away from me in contempt and muttered, "It's not surprising that a fellow like that can ruin a first-class jacket."

I must have looked very odd to the others in the beer cellar, since I had no hat or coat. The waiter was just about to say something about it when there was a bang on the window, and a voice shouted down, "Open up! Open up! It's me!"

The tavern keeper went outside and came right back carrying two torches high; following him came a very tall, slender stranger who forgot to lower his head as he came through the low doorway and received a good knock. A black beretlike cap, though, kept him from serious injury. The stranger sidled along the wall in a very peculiar manner, and sat down opposite me, while lights were placed upon the table. You could characterize him briefly as pleasant but unhappy. He called for beer and a pipe somewhat grumpily, and then with a few puffs, created such a fog bank that we seemed to be swimming in a cloud. His face had something so individual and attractive about it that I liked him despite his dark moroseness. He had a full head of black hair, parted in the middle and hanging down in small locks on both sides of his head, so that he looked like someone out of a Rubens picture. When he threw off his heavy cloak, I could see that he was wearing a black tunic with lots of lacing, and it struck me as very odd that he had slippers pulled on over his boots. I became aware of this when he knocked out his pipe on his foot after about five minutes of smoking.

We didn't converse right away, for the stranger was preoccupied with some strange plants which he took out of a little botanical case and started to examine closely. I indicated my astonishment at the plants and asked him, since they seemed freshly gathered, whether he had been at the botanical garden or Boucher the florist's. He smiled in a strange way, and replied slowly, "Botany does not seem to be your speciality, or else you would not have asked such a . . ." he hesitated and I supplied in a low voice, "foolish . . ." ". . . question," he finished, waving aside my assertion. "If you were a botanist, you would have seen at a glance that these are alpine flora and that they are from Chimborazo." He said the last part very softly, and you can guess that I felt a little strange. This reply prevented further questions, but I kept having the feeling more and more strongly that I knew him—perhaps not "physically" but "mentally."

At this point there came another rapping at the window. The tavern keeper opened the door and a voice called in, "Be so good as to cover your mirrors."

"Aha!" said the host, "General Suvarov is late tonight," and he threw a cloth covering over the mirror. A short, dried-up-looking fellow came tumbling in with frantic, clumsy haste. He was engulfed in a cloak of peculiar brownish color, which bubbled and flapped around him as he bounced across the room toward us, so that in the dim light it looked as if a series of forms were dissolving and emerging from one another, as in Ensler's magic lantern show. He rubbed his hands together inside his overlong sleeves and cried, "Cold! Cold! It's so cold! Altogether different in Italy." Finally he took a seat between me and the tall man and said, "Horrible smoke . . . tobacco on tobacco . . . I wish I had a pipeful."

In my pocket I had a small steel tobacco box, polished like a mirror; I reached it out to the little man. He took one look at it, and thrust out both hands, shoving it away, crying, "Take that damned mirror away." His voice was filled with horror, and as I stared at him with amazement I saw that he had become a different person. He had burst into the beer cellar with a pleasant, youthful face, but now a deathly pale, shrivelled, terrified old man's face glared at me with hollow eyes. I turned in horror to the tall man. I was almost ready to shout, "For God's sake, look at him!" when I saw that the tall stranger was not paying any attention, but was completely engrossed in his plants from Chimborazo. At that moment the little man called, "Northern wine!" in a very affected manner.

After a time the conversation became more lively again. I wasn't quite at ease with the little man, but the tall man had the ability of offering deep and fascinating insights upon seemingly insignificant things, although at times he seemed to struggle to express himself and groped for words, and at times used words improperly, which often gave his statements an air of droll originality. In this way, by appealing to me more and more, he offset the bad impression created by the little man.

The little man seemed to be driven by springs, for he slid back and forth on his chair and waved his hands about in perpetual gesticulations, and a shudder, like icewater down my back, ran through me when I saw very clearly that he had two different faces, the pleasant young man's and the unlovely demonic old man's. For the most part he turned his old man's face upon the tall man, who sat impervious and quiet, in contrast to the perpetual motion of the small man in brown, although it was not as unpleasant as when it had looked at me for the first time.—In the masquerade of life our true inner essence often shines out beyond our mask when we meet a similar person, and it so happened that we three strange beings in a beer cellar looked at one another and knew what we were. Our conversation ran along morbid lines, in the sardonic humor that emerges only when you are wounded, almost to the point of death.

"There are hidden hooks and snares there, too," said the tall man.

"Oh, God," I joined in, "the Devil has set so many hooks for us everywhere, walls, arbors, hedge roses, and so on, and as we brush past them we leave something of our true self caught there. It seems to me, gentlemen, that all of us lose something this way, just as right now I have no hat or coat. They are both hanging on a hook at the Justizrat's, as you may know."

Both the tall and the short man visibly winced, as if they had been unexpectedly struck. The little man looked at me with hatred from his old man's face, leaped up on his chair and fussily adjusted the cloth that hung over the mirror, while the tall man made a point of pinching the candle wicks. The conversation limped along, and in its course a fine young artist named Philipp was mentioned, together with a portrait of a princess painted with intense love and longing, which she must have inspired in him. "More than just a likeness, a true image," said the tall man. "So completely true," I said, "that you could almost say it was stolen from a mirror."

The little man leaped up in a frenzy, and transfixing me with his flaming eyes, showing his old man's face, he screamed, "That's idiotic, crazy—who can steal your reflection? Who? Perhaps you think the Devil can? He would break the glass with his clumsy claws and the girl's fine white hands would be slashed and bloody. Erkhhhh. Show me a reflection, a stolen reflection, and I'll leap a thousand yards for you, you stupid fool!"

The tall man got up, strode over to the little man, and said in a contemptuous voice, "Don't make such a nuisance of yourself, my friend, or I'll throw you out and you'll be as miserable as your own reflection."

"Ha, ha, ha," laughed the little man with furious scorn. "You think so? Do you think so? You miserable dog, I at least still have my shadow, I still have my shadow!" And he leaped out of his chair and rushed out of the cellar. I could hear his nasty neighing laughter outside, and his shouts of "I still have my shadow!"

The tall man, as if completely crushed, sank back into his chair as pale as death. He took his head in both his hands and sighed deeply and groaned. "What's wrong?" I asked sympathetically. "Sir," he replied somewhat incoherently, "that nasty little fellow— followed me here, even in this tavern, where I used to be alone—nobody around, except once in a while an earth-elemental would dive under the table for bread crumbs—he's made me miserable—there's no getting it back—I've lost . . . I've lost . . . my . . . oh, I can't go on . . ." and he leaped up and dashed out into the street.

He happened to pass the lights, and I saw that—he cast no shadow! I was delighted, for I recognized him and knew all about him. I ran out after him. "Peter Schlemihl, Peter Schlemihl," I shouted. But he had kicked off his slippers, and I saw him striding away beyond the police tower, disappearing into the night.

I was about to return to the cellar, but the owner slammed the door in my face, proclaiming loudly, "From guests like these the Good Lord deliver me!"

MANIFESTATIONS

Herr Mathieu is a good friend of mine and his porter keeps his eyes open. He opened the door for me right away when I came to the Golden Eagle and pulled at the bell. I explained matters: that I had been to a party, had left my hat and coat behind, that my house key was in my coat pocket, and that I had no chance of waking my deaf landlady. He was a goodhearted fellow (the porter) and found a room for me, set lights about in it, and wished me a good night. A beautiful wide mirror, however, was covered, and though I don't know why I did it, I pulled off the cloth and set both my candles on the table in front of the mirror. When I looked in, I was so pale and tired-looking that I could hardly recognize myself. Then it seemed to me that from the remote background of the reflection there came floating a dark form, which as I focused my attention upon it, took on the features of a beautiful woman—Julia —shining with a magic radiance. I said very softly, "Julia, Julia!"

At this I heard a groaning and moaning which seemed to come from behind the drawn curtains of a canopy bed which stood in the farthest corner of the room. I listened closely. The groaning grew louder, seemingly more painful. The image of Julia had disappeared, and resolutely I seized a candle, ripped the curtains of the bed apart, and looked in. How can I describe my feelings to you when I saw before me the little man whom I had met at the beer cellar, asleep on the bed, youthful features dominant (though contorted with pain), muttering in his sleep, "Giuletta, Giuletta!" The name enraged me. I was no longer fearful, but seized the little man and gave him a good shake, shouting, "Heigh, my friend! What are you doing in my room? Wake up and get the Devil out of here!"

The little man blinked his eyes open and looked at me darkly. "That was really a bad dream," he said. "I must thank you for waking me." He spoke softly, almost murmured. I don't know why but he looked different to me; the pain which he obviously felt aroused my sympathy, and instead of being angry I felt very sorry for him. It didn't take much conversation to learn that the porter had inadvertently given me the room which had already been assigned to the little man, and that it was I who had intruded, disturbing his sleep.

"Sir," said the little man. "I must have seemed like an utter lunatic to you in the beer cellar. Blame my behavior on this: every now and then, I must confess, a mad spirit seizes control of me and makes me lose all concept of what is right and proper. Perhaps the same thing has happened to you at times?"

"Oh, God, yes," I replied dejectedly. "Just this evening, when I saw Julia again."

"Julia!" crackled the little man in an unpleasant tone. His face suddenly aged and his features twitched. "Let me alone.

And please be good enough to cover the mirror again," he said, looking sadly at his pillow.

"Sir," I said. "The name of my eternally lost love seems to awaken strange memories in you; so much so that your face has changed from its usual pleasant appearance. Still, I have hopes of spending the night here quietly with you, so I am going to cover the mirror and go to bed."

He raised himself to a sitting position, looked at me with his pleasant young face, and seized my hand, saying, while pressing it gently, "Sleep well, my friend. I see that we are companions in misery. Julia . . . Giuletta. . . . Well, if it must be, it must be. I cannot help it; I must tell you my deepest secret, and then you will hate and despise me."

He slowly climbed out of bed, wrapped himself in a generous white robe, and crept slowly, almost like a ghost, to the great mirror and stood in front of it. Ah—Brightly and clearly the mirror reflected the two lighted candles, the furniture, me—but the little man was not there! He stood, head bowed toward it, in front of the mirror, but he cast no reflection! Turning to me, deep despair on his face, he pressed my hands and said, "Now you know the depths of my misery. Schlemihl, a goodhearted fellow, is to be envied, compared to me. He was irresponsible for a moment and sold his shadow. But—I—I gave my reflection to her . . . to her!"

Sobbing deeply, hands pressed over his eyes, the little man turned to the bed and threw himself on it. I simply stood in astonishment, with suspicion, contempt, disgust, sympathy and pity all intermingled, for and against the little man. But while I was standing there, he began to snore so melodiously that it was contagious, and I couldn't resist the narcotic power of his tones. I quickly covered the mirror again, put out the candles, threw myself upon the bed like the little man, and immediately fell asleep.

It must have been early morning when a light awakened me, and I opened my eyes to see the little man, still in his white dressing gown, nightcap on his head, back turned to me, sitting at the table busily writing by the light of the two candles. There was a weird look about him, and I felt the chill of the supernatural. I fell into a waking-dream then, and was back at the Justizrat's again, sitting beside Julia on the ottoman. But the whole party seemed to be only a comic candy display in the window of Fuchs, Weide and Schoch (or somewhere similar) for Christmas, and the Justizrat was a splendid gumdrop with a coat made of pleated notepaper. Trees and rosebushes rose higher and higher about us, and Julia stood up, handing me the crystal goblet, out of which blue flames licked. Someone tugged at my arm and there was the little brown man, his old man's face on, whispering loudly to me, "Don't drink it, don't drink it. Look at her closely. Haven't you seen her and been warned against her in Brueghel and Callot and Rembrandt?"

I looked at Julia with horror, and indeed, with her pleated dress and ruffled sleeves and strange coiffure, she did look like one of the alluring young women, surrounded by demonic monsters, from the work of those masters.

"What are you afraid of?" said Julia. "I have you and your reflection, once and for all." I seized the goblet, but the little man leaped to my shoulder in the form of a squirrel, and waved his tail through the blue flames, chattering, "Don't drink it, don't drink it." At this point the sugar figures in the display came alive and moved their hands and feet ludicrously. The Justizrat ran up to me and called out in a thin little voice, "Why all the uproar, my friend? Why all the commotion? All you have to do is get to your feet; for quite a while I've been watching you stride away over tables and chairs."

The little man had completely disappeared. Julia no longer held the goblet in her hand. "Why wouldn't you drink?" she asked. "Wasn't the flame streaming out of the goblet simply the kisses you once got from me?"

I wanted to take her in my arms, but Schlemihl stepped between us and said, "This is Mina, who married my servant, Rascal." He stepped on a couple of the candy figures, who made groaning noises. They started to multiply enormously, hundreds and thousands of them, and they swarmed all over me, buzzing like a hive of bees. The gumdrop Justizrat, who had continued to climb, had swung up as far as my neckcloth, which he kept pulling tighter and tighter. "Justizrat, you confounded gumdrop," I screamed out loud, and startled myself out of sleep. It was bright day, already eleven o'clock.

I was just thinking to myself that the whole adventure with the little brown man had only been an exceptionally vivid dream, when the waiter who brought in my breakfast told me that the stranger who had shared his room with me had left early, and presented his compliments. Upon the table where I had seen the weird little man sitting and writing I found a fresh manuscript, whose content I am sharing with you, since it is unquestionably the remarkable story of the little man in brown. It is as follows.

THE STORY OF THE LOST REFLECTION

Things finally worked out so that Erasmus Spikher was able to fulfill the wish that he had cherished all his life. He climbed into the coach with high spirits and a well-filled knapsack. He was leaving his home in the North and journeying to the beautiful land of Italy. His devoted wife was weeping copiously, and she lifted little Rasmus (after carefully wiping his mouth and nose) into the coach to kiss his father goodbye.

"Farewell, Erasmus Spikher," said his wife, sobbing. "I will keep your house well for you. Think of me often, remain true to me, and do not lose your hat if you fall asleep near the window, as you always do." Spikher promised.

In the beautiful city of Florence Spikher found some fellow Germans, young men filled with high spirits and *joie de vivre*, who spent their time revelling in the sensual delights which Italy so well affords. He impressed them as a good fellow and he was often invited to social occasions since he had the talent of supplying soberness to the mad abandon about him, and gave the party a highly individual touch.

One evening in the grove of a splendid fragrant public garden, the young men (Erasmus could be included here, since he was only twenty-seven) gathered for an exceptionally merry feast. Each of the men, except Spikher, brought along a girl. The men were dressed in the picturesque old Germanic costume, and the women wore bright dresses, each styled differently, often fantastically, so that they seemed like wonderful mobile flowers. Every now and then one of the girls would sing an Italian love song, accompanied by the plaintive notes of mandolins, and the men would respond with a lusty German chorus or round, as glasses filled with fine Syracuse wine clinked. Yes, indeed, Italy is the land of love.

The evening breezes sighed with passion, oranges and jasmine breathed out perfume through the grove, and it all formed a part in the banter and play which the girls (delightfully merry as only Italian women can be) began. Wilder and noisier grew the fun. Friedrich, the most excited of all, leaped to his feet, one arm around his mistress, waving high a glass of sparkling Syracuse wine with the other, and shouted, "You wonderful women of Italy! Where can true, blissful love be found except with you? You are love incarnate! But you, Erasmus," he continued, turning to Spikher, "You don't seem to understand this. You've violated your promise, propriety and the custom. You didn't bring a girl with you, and

you have been sitting here moodily, so quiet and self-concerned that
if you hadn't been drinking and singing with us I'd believe you
were suffering an attack of melancholy."

"Friedrich," replied Erasmus, "I have to confess that I cannot
enjoy myself like that. You know that I have a wife at home,
and I love her. If I took up with a girl for even one night it would
be betraying my wife. For you young bachelors it's different, but
I have a family."

The young men laughed uproariously, for when Erasmus
announced his family obligations his pleasant young face became
very grave, and he really looked very strange. Friedrich's mistress,
when Spikher's words had been translated for her (for the two men
had spoken German), turned very seriously to Erasmus, and said,
half-threateningly, finger raised, "Cold-blooded, heartless German
—watch out, you haven't seen Giuletta yet."

At that very instant a rustling noise indicated that someone was
approaching, and out of the dark night into the area lighted by the
candles strode a remarkably beautiful girl. Her white dress, which
only half-hid her bosom, shoulders and neck, fell in rich broad folds;
her sleeves, puffed and full, came only to her elbows; her thick hair,
parted in the front, fell in braids at the back. Golden chains
around her throat, rich bracelets upon her wrists, completed her
antique costume. She looked exactly if she were a woman from
Mieris or Rembrandt walking about. "Giuletta," shrieked the
girls in astonishment and delight.

Giuletta, who was by far the most beautiful of all the women
present, asked in a sweet, pleasant voice, "Good Germans, may I
join you? I'll sit with that gentleman over there. He doesn't
have a girl, and he doesn't seem to be having a very good time,
either." She turned very graciously to Erasmus, and sat down
upon the empty seat beside him—empty because everyone thought
Erasmus would bring a girl along, too. The girls whispered to each
other, "Isn't Giuletta beautiful tonight," and the young men said,
"How about Erasmus? Was he joking with us? He's got the
best-looking girl of all!"

As for Erasmus, at the first glance he cast at Giuletta, he was so
aroused that he didn't even know what powerful passions were
working in him. As she came close to him, a strange force seized
him and crushed his breast so that he couldn't even breathe. Eyes
fixed in a rigid stare at her, mouth agape, he sat there not able to
utter a syllable, while all the others were commenting upon
Giuletta's charm and beauty.

Giuletta took a full goblet, and standing up, handed it with a friendly smile to Erasmus. He seized the goblet, touching her soft fingers, and as he drank, fire seemed to stream through his veins. Then Giuletta asked him in a bantering way, "Am I to be your girl friend?" Erasmus threw himself wildly upon the ground in front of her, pressed her hands to his breast, and cried in maudlin tones, "Yes, yes, yes! You goddess! I've always been in love with you. I've seen you in my dreams, you are my fortune, my happiness, my higher life!"

The others all thought the wine had gone to Erasmus's head, since they had never seen him like this before; he seemed to be a different man.

"You are my life! I don't care if I am destroyed, as long as it's with you," Erasmus shouted. "You set me on fire!" But Giuletta just took him gently in her arms. He became quieter again, and took his seat beside her. And once again the gaiety which had been interrupted by Erasmus and Giuletta began with songs and laughter. Giuletta sang, and it was as if the tones of her beautiful voice aroused in everyone sensations of pleasure never felt before but only suspected to exist. Her full but clear voice conveyed a secret ardor which inflamed them all. The young men clasped their mistresses more closely, and passion leaped from eye to eye.

Dawn was breaking with a rosy shimmer when Giuletta said that she had to leave. Erasmus got ready to accompany her home, but she refused but gave him the address at which he could find her in the future. During the chorus which the men sang to end the party, Giuletta disappeared from the grove and was seen walking through a distant *allée*, preceded by two linkmen. Erasmus did not dare follow her.

The young men left arm in arm with their mistresses, full of high spirits, and Erasmus, greatly disturbed and internally shattered by the torments of love, followed, preceded by his boy with a torch. After leaving his friends, he was passing down the distant street which led to his dwelling, and his servant had just knocked out the torch against the stucco of the house, when a strange figure mysteriously appeared in the spraying sparks in front of Erasmus. It was a tall, thin, dried-out-looking man with a Roman nose that came to a sharp point, glowing eyes, mouth contorted into a sneer, wrapped in a flame-red cloak with brightly polished steel buttons. He laughed and called out in an unpleasant yelping voice, "Ho, ho, you look as if you came out of a picture book with that cloak, slit doublet and plumed hat. You show a real sense of humor, Signor

Erasmus Spikher, but aren't you afraid of being laughed at on the streets? Signor, signor, crawl quietly back into your parchment binding."

"What the Devil is my clothing to you?" said Erasmus with anger, and shoving the red-clad stranger aside, he was about to pass by when the stranger called after him, "Don't be in such a hurry. You won't get to Giuletta that way."

"What are you saying about Giuletta?" cried Erasmus wildly. He tried to seize the red-clad man by the breast, but he turned and disappeared so rapidly that Erasmus couldn't even see where he went, and Erasmus was left standing in astonishment, in his hand a steel button that had been ripped from the stranger's cloak.

"That's the Miracle Doctor Dapertutto. What did he want?" asked Erasmus's servant. But Erasmus was seized with horror, and without replying, hastened home.

When, some time later, Erasmus called on Giuletta, she received him in a very gracious and friendly manner, yet to Erasmus's fiery passion she opposed a mild indifference. Only once in a while did her eyes flash, whereupon Erasmus would feel shudders pass through him, from his innermost being, when she regarded him with an enigmatic stare. She never told him that she loved him, but her whole attitude and behaviour led him to think so, and he found himself more and more deeply entangled with her. He seldom saw his old friends, however, for Giuletta took him into other circles.

Once Erasmus met Friedrich at a time when Erasmus was depressed, thinking about his native land and his home. Friedrich said, "Don't you know, Spikher, that you are moving in a very dangerous circle of acquaintances? You must realize by now that the beautiful Giuletta is one of the craftiest courtesans on earth. There are all sorts of strange stories going around about her, and they put her in a very peculiar light. I can see from you that she can exercise an irresistible power over men when she wants to. You have changed completely and are totally under her spell. You don't think of your wife and family any more."

Erasmus covered his face with his hands and sobbed, crying out his wife's name. Friedrich saw that a difficult internal battle had begun in Spikher. "Erasmus," he said, "let us get out of here immediately."

"Yes, Friedrich," said Erasmus heavily. "You are right. I don't know why I am suddenly overcome by such dark horrible foreboding—I must leave right away, today."

The two friends hastened along the street, but directly across from them came Signor Dapertutto, who laughed in Erasmus's face, and cried nasally, "Hurry, hurry; a little faster. Giuletta is waiting; her heart is full of longing, and her eyes are full of tears. Make haste. Make haste."

Erasmus stood as if struck by lightning.

"This scoundrel," said Friedrich, "this charlatan—I cannot stand him. He is always in and out of Giuletta's, and he sells her his magical potions."

"What!" cried Erasmus. "That disgusting creature visits Giuletta, Giuletta?"

"Where have you been so long? Everything is waiting for you. Didn't you think of me at all," breathed a soft voice from the balcony. It was Giuletta, in front of whose house the two friends, without noticing it, had stopped. With a leap Erasmus was in the house.

"He is gone, and cannot be saved," said Friedrich to himself, and walked slowly away.

Never before had Giuletta been more amiable. She wore the same clothing that she had worn when she first met Erasmus, and beauty, charm and youth shone from her. Erasmus completely forgot his conversation with Friedrich, and now more than ever his irresistible passion seized him. This was the first time that Giuletta showed without reservation her deepest love for him. She seemed to see only him, and to live for him only. At a villa which Giuletta had rented for the summer, a festival was being celebrated, and they went there. Among the company was a young Italian with a brutal ugly face and even worse manners, who kept paying court to Giuletta and arousing Erasmus's jealousy. Fuming with rage, Erasmus left the company and paced up and down in a side path of the garden. Giuletta came looking for him. "What is wrong with you? Aren't you mine alone?" she asked. She embraced him and planted a kiss upon his lips. Sparks of passion flew through Erasmus, and in a passion he crushed her to himself, crying, "No, I will not leave you, no matter how low I fall." Giuletta smiled strangely at these words, and cast at him that peculiar oblique glance which never failed to arouse a chilly feeling in him.

They returned to the company, and the unpleasant young Italian now took over Erasmus's role. Obviously enraged with jealousy, he made all sorts of pointed insults against Germans, particularly Spikher. Finally Spikher could bear it no longer, and he strode up to the Italian and said, "That's enough of your insults, unless you'd like to get thrown into the pond and try your hand at swimming." In an instant a dagger gleamed in the Italian's hand, but Erasmus dodged, seized him by the throat, threw him to the ground, and shattered his neck with a kick. The Italian gasped out his life on the spot.

Pandemonium broke loose around Erasmus. He lost consciousness, but felt himself being lifted and carried away. When he awoke later, as if from a deep enchantment, he lay at Giuletta's feet in a small room, while she, head bowed over him, held him in both her arms.

"You bad, bad German," she finally said, softly and mildly. "If you knew how frightened you've made me! You've come very close to disaster, but I've managed to save you. You are no longer safe in Florence, though, or even Italy. You must leave, and you must leave me, and I love you so much."

The thought of leaving Giuletta threw Erasmus into pain and sorrow. "Let me stay here," he cried. "I'm willing to die. Dying is better than living without you."

But suddenly it seemed to him as if a soft, distant voice was calling his name painfully. It was the voice of his wife at home. Erasmus was stricken dumb. Strangely enough, Giuletta asked him, "Are you thinking of your wife? Ah, Erasmus, you will forget me only too soon!"

"If I could only remain yours forever and ever," said Erasmus. They were standing directly in front of the beautiful wide mirror, which was set in the wall, and on the sides of it tapers were burning brightly. More firmly, more closely, Giuletta pressed Erasmus to her, while she murmured softly in his ear, "Leave me your reflection, my beloved; it will be mine and will remain with me forever."

"Giuletta," cried Erasmus in amazement. "What do you mean? My reflection?" He looked in the mirror, which showed him himself and Giuletta in sweet, close embrace. "How can you keep my reflection? It is part of me. It springs out to meet me from every clear body of water or polished surface."

"Aren't you willing to give me even this dream of your ego? Even though you say you want to be mine, body and soul? Won't you even give me this trivial thing, so that after you leave, it can accompany me in the loveless, pleasureless life that is left to me?"

Hot tears started from Giuletta's beautiful dark eyes.

At this point Erasmus, mad with pain and passion, cried, "Do I have to leave? If I have to, my reflection will be yours forever and a day. No power—not even the Devil—can take it away from you until you own me, body and soul."

Giuletta's kisses burned like fire on his mouth as he said this, and then she released him and stretched out her arms longingly to the mirror. Erasmus saw his image step forward independent of his movements, glide into Giuletta's arms, and disappear with her in a strange vapor. Then Erasmus heard all sorts of hideous voices bleating and laughing in demoniac scorn, and, seized with a spasm of terror, he sank to the floor. But his horror and fear aroused him, and in thick dense darkness he stumbled out the door and down the steps. In front of the house he was seized and lifted into a carriage, which rolled away with him rapidly.

"Things have changed somewhat, it seems," said a man in German, who had taken a seat beside him. "Nevertheless, everything will be all right if you give yourself over to me completely. Dear Giuletta has done her share, and has recommended you to me. You are a fine, pleasant young man and you have a strong inclination to pleasant pranks and jokes—which please Giuletta and me nicely. That was a real nice German kick in the neck. Did you see how Amoroso's tongue protruded—purple and swollen—it was a fine sight and the strangling noises and groans—ha, ha, ha." The man's voice was so repellent in its mockery, his chatter so gruesomely unpleasant, that his words felt like dagger blows in Erasmus's chest.

"Whoever you are," he said, "don't say any more about it. I regret it bitterly."

"Regret? Regret?" replied the unknown man. "I'll be bound that you probably regret knowing Giuletta and winning her love."

"Ah, Giuletta, Giuletta!" sighed Spikher.

"Now," said the man, "you are being childish. Everything will run smoothly. It is horrible that you have to leave her, I know, but if you were to remain here, I could keep your enemies' daggers away from you, and even the authorities."

The thought of being able to stay with Giuletta appealed strongly to Erasmus. "How, how can that be?"

"I know a magical way to strike your enemies with blindness, in short, that you will always appear to them with a different face, and they will never recognize you again. Since it is getting on toward daylight, perhaps you will be good enough to look long and attentively into any mirror. I shall then perform certain operations upon your reflection, without damaging it in the least, and you will be hidden and can live forever with Giuletta. As happy as can be; no danger at all."

"Oh, God," screamed Erasmus.

"Why call upon God, my most worthy friend," asked the stranger with a sneer.

"I—I have . . ." began Erasmus.

"Left your reflection behind—with Giuletta—" interrupted the other. "Fine. Bravissimo, my dear sir. And now you course through floods and forests, cities and towns, until you find your wife and little Rasmus, and become a paterfamilias again. No reflection, of course—though this really shouldn't bother your wife since she has you physically. Even though Giuletta will eternally own your dream-ego."

A torch procession of singers drew near at this moment, and the light the torches cast into the carriage revealed to Erasmus the sneering visage of Dr. Dapertutto. Erasmus leaped out of the carriage and ran toward the procession, for he had recognized Friedrich's resounding bass voice among the singers. It was his friends returning from a party in the countryside. Erasmus breathlessly told Friedrich everything that had happened, only withholding mention of the loss of his reflection. Friedrich hurried with him into the city, and arrangements were made so rapidly that when dawn broke, Erasmus, mounted on a fast horse, had already left Florence far behind.

Spikher set down in his manuscript the many adventures that befell him upon his journey. Among the most remarkable is the incident which first caused him to appreciate the loss of his reflection. He had stopped over in a large town, since his tired horse needed a rest, and he had sat down without thinking at a well-filled inn table, not noticing that a fine clear mirror hung before him. A devil of a waiter, who stood behind his chair, noticed that the chair seemed to be empty in the reflection and did not show the person who was sitting in it. He shared his observation with Erasmus's neighbor, who in turn called it to the attention of his. A murmuring and whispering thereupon ran all around the table, and the guests first stared at Erasmus, then at the mirror. Erasmus, however, was unaware that the disturbance concerned him, until a grave gentleman stood up, took Erasmus to the mirror, looked in, and then turning to the company, cried out loudly, "'Struth. He's not there. He doesn't reflect."

"What? No reflection? He's not in the mirror?" everyone cried in confusion. "He's a *mauvais sujet*, a *homo nefas*. Kick him out the door!"

Raging and filled with shame, Erasmus fled to his room, but he had hardly gotten there when he was informed by the police that he must either appear with full, complete, impeccably accurate reflection before the magistrate within one hour or leave the town. He rushed away, followed by the idle mob, tormented by street urchins, who called after him, "There he goes. He sold his reflection to the Devil. There he goes!" Finally he escaped. And from then on, under the pretext of having a phobia against mirrors, he insisted on having them covered. For this reason he was nicknamed General Suvarov, since Suvarov acted the same way.

When he finally reached his home city and his house, his wife and child received him with joy, and he began to think that calm, peaceful domesticity would heal the pain of his lost reflection. One day, however, it happened that Spikher, who had now put Giuletta completely out of his mind, was playing with little Rasmus. Rasmus's little hands were covered with soot from the stove, and he dragged his fingers across his father's face. "Daddy! I've turned you black. Look, look!" cried the child, and before Spikher could prevent it or avoid it, the little boy held a mirror in front of him, looking into it at the same time. The child dropped the mirror with a scream of terror and ran away to his room.

Spikher's wife soon came to him, astonishment and terror plainly on her face. "What has Rasmus told me—" she began. "Perhaps that I don't have a reflection, dear," interrupted Spikher with a forced smile, and he feverishly tried to prove that the story was too foolish to believe, that one could not lose a reflection, but if one did, since a mirror image was only an illusion, it didn't matter much, that staring into a mirror led to vanity, and pseudo-philosophical nonsense about the reflection dividing the ego into truth and dream. While he was declaiming, his wife removed the covering from a mirror that hung in the room and looked into it. She fell to the floor as if struck by lightning. Spikher lifted her up, but when she regained consciousness, she pushed him away with horror. "Leave me, get away from me, you demon! You are not my husband. No! You are a demon from Hell, who wants to destroy my chance of heaven, who wants to corrupt me. Away! Leave me alone! You have no power over me, damned spirit!"

Her voice screamed through the room, through the halls; the domestics fled the house in terror, and in rage and despair Erasmus rushed out of the house. Madly he ran through the empty walks of the town park. Giuletta's form seemed to arise in front of him, angelic in beauty, and he cried aloud, "Is this your revenge,

Giuletta, because I abandoned you and left you nothing but my reflection in a mirror? Giuletta, I will be yours, body and soul. I sacrificed you for her, Giuletta, and now she has rejected me. Giuletta, let me be yours—body, life, and soul!"

"That can be done quite easily, *caro signore*," said Dr. Dapertutto, who was suddenly standing beside him, clad in scarlet cloak with polished steel buttons. These were words of comfort to Erasmus, and he paid no heed to Dapertutto's sneering, unpleasant face. Erasmus stopped and asked in despair, "How can I find her again? She is eternally lost to me."

"On the contrary," answered Dapertutto, "she is not far from here, and she longs for your true self, honored sir; you yourself have had the insight to see that a reflection is nothing but a worthless illusion. And as soon as she has the real you—body, life, and soul—she will return your reflection, smooth and undamaged with the utmost gratitude."

"Take me to her, take me to her," cried Erasmus. "Where is she?"

"A certain trivial matter must come first," replied Dapertutto, "before you can see her and redeem your reflection. You are not entirely free to dispose of your worthy self, since you are tied by certain bonds which have to be dissolved first. Your worthy wife. Your promising little son."

"What do you mean?" cried Erasmus wildly.

"This bond," continued Dapertutto, "can be dissolved incontrovertibly, easily and humanely. You may remember from your Florentine days that I have the knack of preparing wonder-working medications. I have a splendid household aid here at hand. Those who stand in the way of you and your beloved Giuletta—let them have the benefit of a couple of drops, and they will sink down quietly, no pain, no embarrassment. It is what they call dying, and death is said to be bitter; but don't bitter almonds taste very nice? The death in this little bottle has only that kind of bitterness. Immediately after the happy collapse, your worthy family will exude a pleasant odor of almonds. Take it, honored sir."

He handed a small phial to Erasmus.*

"I should poison my wife and child?" shrieked Erasmus.

* Dr. Dapertutto's phial almost certainly contained prussic (hydrocyanic) acid, which is prepared from laurel leaves and bitter almonds. A very small quantity of this liquid, less than an ounce, produces the effects described. Cf. *Horns Archiv für mediz. Erfahrung*, 1813, May to December, page 510.

"Who spoke of poison?" continued the red-clad man, very calmly. "It's just a delicious household remedy. It's true that I have other ways of regaining your freedom for you, but for you I would like the process to be natural, humane, if you know what I mean. I really feel strongly about it. Take it and have courage, my friend."

Erasmus found the phial in his hand, he knew not how.

Without thinking, he ran home, to his room. His wife had spent the whole night amid a thousand fears and torments, asserting continually that the person who had returned was not her husband but a spirit from Hell who had assumed her husband's form. As a result, the moment Erasmus set foot in the house, everyone ran. Only little Rasmus had the courage to approach him and ask in childish fashion why he had not brought his reflection back with him, since Mother was dying of grief because of it. Erasmus stared wildly at the little boy, Dapertutto's phial in his hand. His son's pet dove was on his shoulder, and it so happened that the dove pecked at the stopper of the phial, dropped its head, and toppled over, dead. Erasmus was overcome with horror.

"Betrayer," he shouted. "You cannot make me do it!"

He threw the phial out through the open window, and it shattered upon the concrete pavement of the court. A luscious odor of almonds rose in the air and spread into the room, while little Rasmus ran away in terror.

Erasmus spent the whole day in torment until midnight. More and more vividly each moment the image of Giuletta rose in his mind. On one occasion, in the past, her necklace of red berries (which Italian women wear like pearls) had broken, and while Erasmus was picking up the berries he concealed one and kept it faithfully, because it had been on Giuletta's neck. At this point he took out the berry and fixed his gaze upon it, focusing his thought on his lost love. It seemed to him that a magical aroma emerged from the berry, the scent which used to surround Giuletta.

"Ah, Giuletta, if I could only see you one more time, and then go down in shame and disgrace . . ."

He had hardly spoken, when a soft rustling came along the walk outside. He heard footsteps—there was a knock on the door. Fear and hope stopped his breath. He opened the door, and in walked Giuletta, as remarkably beautiful and charming as ever. Mad with desire, Erasmus seized her in his arms.

"I am here, beloved," she whispered softly, gently. "See how well I have preserved your reflection?"

Peter Schlemihl and Erasmus Spikher *(detail from illustration following page 230).*

She took the cloth down from the mirror on the wall, and Erasmus saw his image nestled in embrace with Giuletta, independent of him, not following his movements. He shook with terror.

"Giuletta," he cried, "must you drive me mad? Give me my reflection and take me—body, life, soul!"

"There is still something between us, dear Erasmus," said Giuletta. "You know what it is. Hasn't Dapertutto told you?"

"For God's sake, Giuletta," cried Erasmus. "If that is the only way I can become yours, I would rather die."

"You don't have to do it the way Dapertutto suggested," said Giuletta. "It is really a shame that a vow and a priest's blessing can do so much, but you must loose the bond that ties you or else you can never be entirely mine. There is a better way than the one that Dapertutto proposed."

"What is it?" asked Spikher eagerly. Giuletta placed her arm around his neck, and leaning her head upon his breast whispered up softly, "You just write your name, Erasmus Spikher, upon a little slip of paper, under only a few words: 'I give to my good friend Dr. Dapertutto power over my wife and over my child, so that he can govern and dispose of them according to his will, and dissolve the bond which ties me, because I, from this day, with body and immortal soul, wish to belong to Giuletta, whom I have chosen as wife, and to whom I will bind myself eternally with a special vow.'"

Erasmus shivered and twitched with pain. Fiery kisses burned upon his lips, and he found the little piece of paper which Giuletta had given to him in his hand. Gigantic, Dapertutto suddenly stood behind Giuletta and handed Erasmus a steel pen. A vein on Erasmus's left hand burst open and blood spurted out.

"Dip it, dip it, write, write," said the red-clad figure harshly.

"Write, write, my eternal, my only lover," whispered Giuletta.

He had filled the pen with his blood and started to write when the door suddenly opened and a white figure entered. With staring eyes fixed on Erasmus, it called painfully and leadenly, "Erasmus, Erasmus! What are you doing? For the sake of our Saviour, don't do this horrible deed."

Erasmus recognized his wife in the warning figure, and threw the pen and paper far from him.

Sparks and flashes shot out of Giuletta's eyes; her face was horribly distorted; her body seemed to glow with rage.

"Away from me, demon; you can have no part of my soul. In the name of the Saviour, begone. Snake—Hell glows through you," cried Erasmus, and with a violent blow he knocked back

Giuletta, who was trying to embrace him again.   A screaming and
howling broke loose, and a rustling, as of raven feathers.   Giuletta
and Dapertutto disappeared in a thick stinking smoke, which as it
poured out of the walls put out the lights.

Dawn finally came, and Erasmus went to his wife.   He found her
calm and restrained.   Little Rasmus sat very cheerfully upon her
bed.   She held out her hand to her exhausted husband and said,
"I now know everything that happened to you in Italy, and I pity
you with all my heart.   The power of the Enemy is great.   He is
given to ill-doing and he could not resist the desire to make away
with your reflection and use it to his own purposes.   Look into the
mirror again, husband."

Erasmus, trembling, looked into the mirror, completely dejected.
It remained blank and clear; no other Erasmus Spikher looked back
at him.

"It is just as well that the mirror does not reflect you," said his
wife, "for you look very foolish, Erasmus.   But you must recognize
that if you do not have a reflection, you will be laughed at, and you
cannot be the proper father for a family; your wife and children
cannot respect you.   Rasmus is already laughing at you and next
will paint a mustache on you with soot, since you cannot see it.

"Go out into the world again, and see if you can track down your
reflection, away from the Devil.   When you have it back, you will
be very welcome here.   Kiss me" (Erasmus did) "and now—
goodbye.   Send little Rasmus new stockings every once in a while,
for he keeps sliding on his knees and needs quite a few pairs.   If you
get to Nuremberg, you can also send him a painted soldier and a
spice cake, like a devoted father.   Farewell, dear Erasmus."

His wife turned upon her other side and went back to sleep.
Spikher lifted up little Rasmus and hugged him to his breast.   But
since Rasmus cried quite a bit, Spikher set him down again, and
went into the wide world.   He struck upon a certain Peter Schlemihl,
who had sold his shadow; they planned to travel together, so that
Erasmus Spikher could provide the necessary shadow and Peter
Schlemihl could reflect properly in a mirror.   But nothing came
of it.

The end of the story of the lost reflection.

POSTSCRIPT BY THE TRAVELLING ENTHUSIAST

What is it that looks out of that mirror there?   Is it really I?
Julia, Giuletta—divine image, demon from Hell; delights and

torments; longing and despair. You can see, my dear Theodore Amadeus Hoffmann, that a strange dark power manifests itself in my life all too often, steals the best dreams away from sleep, pushing strange forms into my life. I am completely saturated with the manifestations of this New Year's Eve, and I more than half believe that the Justizrat is a gumdrop, that his tea was a candy display for Christmas or New Year's, that the good Julia was a picture of a siren by Rembrandt or Callot—who betrayed the unfortunate Spikher to get his alter ego, his reflection in the mirror. Forgive me. . . .

NUTCRACKER AND THE KING OF MICE

CHRISTMAS EVE

On the twenty-fourth of December, Dr. Stahlbaum's children were not allowed on any pretext whatever at any time that day to go into the small drawing-room, much less into the best drawing-room into which it opened. Fritz and Marie were sitting cowering together in a corner of the back parlour when the evening twilight fell, and they began to feel terribly eerie. Seeing that no candles were brought, as was generally the case on Christmas Eve, Fritz, whispering in a mysterious fashion, confided to his young sister (who was just seven) that he had heard rattlings and rustlings going on all day, since early morning, inside the forbidden rooms, as well as distant hammering. Further, that a short time ago a little dark-looking man had gone slipping and creeping across the floor with a big box under his arm, though he was well aware that this little man was no other than Godpapa Drosselmeier. At this news Marie clapped her little hands with joy, and cried:

"Oh! I do wonder what pretty things Godpapa Drosselmeier has been making for us *this* time!"

Godpapa Drosselmeier was anything but a nice-looking man. He was small and lean, with a great many wrinkles on his face, a big patch of black plaster where his right eye ought to have been, and not a hair on his head; which was why he wore a fine white wig, made of glass, and a very beautiful work of art. But he was a very, very clever man, who even knew and understood all about clocks and watches, and could make them himself. So that when one of the beautiful clocks that were in Dr. Stahlbaum's house was out of sorts and couldn't sing, Godpapa Drosselmeier would come, take off his glass periwig and his little yellow coat, gird himself with a blue apron, and proceed to stick sharp-pointed instruments into the inside of the clock in a way that made little Marie quite miserable to witness. However, this didn't really hurt the poor clock, which, on the contrary, would come to life again, and begin to whirr and sing and strike as merrily as ever; which caused everybody the greatest satisfaction. Of course, whenever he came he always brought something delightful in his pockets for the children—perhaps a little man, who would roll his eyes and make bows and scrapes, most comic to behold; or a box, out of which a little bird would jump; or something else of the kind. But for Christmas he always had some specially charming piece of ingenuity; something which had cost him infinite pains and labour—for which reason it was always taken away and put aside with the greatest care by the children's parents.

"Oh! what can Godpapa Drosselmeier have been making for us *this* time," Marie cried, as we have said.

Fritz was of the opinion that this time it could hardly be anything but a great castle, a fortress, where all sorts of pretty soldiers would be drilling and marching about; and then, that other soldiers would come and try to get into the fortress, upon which the soldiers inside would fire away at them, as pluckily as you please, with cannon, till everything banged and thundered like anything.

"No, no," Marie said. "Godpapa Drosselmeier once told me about a beautiful garden with a great lake in it, and beautiful swans swimming about with great gold collars, singing lovely music. And then a lovely little girl comes down through the garden to the lake, and calls the swans and feeds them with shortbread and cake."

"Swans don't eat cake and shortbread," Fritz cried, rather rudely (with masculine superiority), "and Godpapa Drosselmeier couldn't make a whole garden. After all, we have got very few of his playthings; whatever he brings is always taken away from us. So I like the things papa and mamma give us much better; we keep them, all right, ourselves, and can do what we like with them."

The children went on discussing what he might have in store for them this time. Marie called Fritz's attention to the fact that Miss Gertrude (her biggest doll) appeared to be failing a good deal as time went on, inasmuch as she was more clumsy and awkward than ever, tumbling on to the floor every two or three minutes. This did not occur without leaving very ugly marks on her face, and of course proper condition of her clothes became out of the question altogether. Scolding was of no use. Mamma too had laughed at her for being so delighted with Miss Gertrude's little new parasol. Fritz, again, remarked that a good fox was needed for his small zoological collection, and that his army was quite without cavalry, as his papa was well aware. But the children knew that their elders had got all sorts of charming things ready for them, and that the Christ Child, at Christmas time, took special care for their wants. Marie sat in thoughtful silence, but Fritz murmured quietly to himself:

"All the same, I should like a fox and some hussars!"

It was now quite dark. Fritz and Marie, sitting close together, did not dare to utter another syllable; they felt as if there were a fluttering of gentle, invisible wings around them, while a very distant, but unutterably beautiful strain of music could dimly be heard. Then a bright gleam of light passed quickly across the wall, and the children knew that the Christ Child had sped away on shining wings to other happy children. At this moment a silvery bell said, "Kling-ling! Kling-ling!" the doors flew open, and such a brilliance of light came streaming from the drawing-room that the children stood rooted where they were with cries of "Oh! Oh!"

Papa and mamma came and took their hands, saying, "Come now, darlings, and see what the blessed Christ Child has brought for you."

THE CHRISTMAS PRESENTS

I appeal to you, kind reader (or listener)—Fritz, Theodore, Ernest, or whatsoever your name may be—and I beg you to bring vividly before your mind's eye your last Christmas table, all glorious with its various delightful Christmas presents; and then perhaps you will be able to form some idea of the manner in which the two children stood speechless with their eyes fixed on all the beautiful things; how after a while, Marie, with a sigh, cried, "Oh, how lovely! how lovely!" and Fritz gave several jumps of delight.

The children had certainly been very, very good and well-behaved all the foregoing year to be thus rewarded; for never before had so many beautiful and delightful things been provided for them. The great Christmas tree on the table bore many apples of silver and gold, and all its branches were heavy with bud and blossom, consisting of sugar almonds, many-tinted bon-bons, and all sorts of things to eat. Perhaps the prettiest thing about this wonder-tree, however, was the fact that in all the recesses of its spreading branches hundreds of little tapers glittered like stars, inviting the children to pluck its flowers and fruit. Also, all around the tree on every side everything shone and glittered in the loveliest manner. Oh, how many beautiful things there were! Who, oh who, could describe them all? Marie gazed there at the most delicious dolls, and all kinds of toys, and (what was the prettiest thing of all) a little silk dress with many-tinted ribbons was hung upon a projecting branch so that she could admire it on all sides; which she accordingly did, crying out several times, "Oh! what a lovely, lovely, darling little dress! And I suppose, I do believe, I shall really be allowed to put it on!" Fritz, in the meantime, had had two or three trials of how his new fox (which he had found tied to the table) could gallop and now stated that he seemed a wildish sort of brute; but, no matter, he felt sure he would soon get him well in order; and he set to work to muster his new squadron of hussars, admirably equipped, in red and gold uniforms, with real silver swords, and mounted on such shining white horses that you would have thought they were of pure silver too.

When the children had sobered down a little, and were beginning upon the beautiful picture books (which were open, so that you could see all sorts of most beautiful flowers and people of every hue, to say nothing of lovely children playing, all as naturally represented as if they were really alive and could speak), there came another tinkling of a bell, to announce the display of Godpapa Drosselmeier's Christmas present, which was on another table, against the wall, concealed by a curtain. When this curtain was drawn, what did the children behold?

On a green lawn, bright with flowers, stood a lordly castle with a great many shining windows and golden towers. A chime of bells was going on inside it; doors and windows opened, and you saw very small but beautiful ladies and gentlemen with plumed hats, and long robes down to their heels walking up and down in the rooms of it. In the central hall, which seemed all in a blaze, there were quantities of little candles burning in silver chandeliers; children in little short doublets were dancing to the chimes of the bells. A gentleman in an emerald green mantle came to a window, made signs, and then disappeared inside again; also, even Godpapa Drosselmeier himself (but scarcely taller than papa's thumb) came now and then, and stood at the castle door, then went in again.

Fritz had been looking on with the rest at the beautiful castle and the people walking about and dancing in it, with his arms leant on the table; then he said:

"Godpapa Drosselmeier, let *me* go into your castle for a little while."

Drosselmeier answered that this could not possibly be done. In which he was right; for it was silly of Fritz to want to go into a castle which was not so tall as himself, golden towers and all. And Fritz saw that this was so.

After a short time, as the ladies and gentlemen kept on walking about just in the same fashion, the children dancing, and the emerald man looking out at the same window, and Godpapa Drosselmeier coming to the door, Fritz cried impatiently:

"Godpapa Drosselmeier, please come out at that other door!"

"That can't be done, dear Fritz," answered Drosselmeier.

"Well," resumed Fritz, "make that green man that looks out so often walk about with the others."

"And that can't be done, either," said his godpapa, once more.

"Make the children come down, then," said Fritz.   "I want to see them nearer."

"Nonsense, nothing of that sort can be done," cried Drosselmeier with impatience.   "The machinery must work as it's doing now; it can't be altered, you know."

"Oh," said Fritz, "it can't be done, eh?   Very well, then, Godpapa Drosselmeier, I'll tell you what it is.   If your little creatures in the castle there can only always do the same thing, they're not much worth, and I think precious little of them!   No, give me my hussars.   They've got to maneuver backwards and forwards just as I want them, and are not fastened up in a house."

With which he made off to the other table, and set his squadron of silver horse trotting here and there, wheeling and charging and slashing right and left to his heart's content.   Marie had slipped away softly, too, for she was tired of the promenading and dancing of the puppets in the castle, though, kind and gentle as she was, she did not like to show it as her brother did.   Drosselmeier, somewhat annoyed, said to the parents, "After all, an ingenious piece of mechanism like this is not a matter for children, who don't understand it; I shall put my castle back in its box again."   But mother came to the rescue, and made him show her the clever machinery which moved the figures, Drosselmeier taking it all to pieces, putting it together again, and quite recovering his temper in the process. So that he gave the children all sorts of delightful brown men and women with golden faces, hands and legs, which were made of ginger cake, and with which they were greatly content.

MARIE'S PET AND PROTÉGÉ

But there was a reason why Marie found it against the grain to come away from the table where the Christmas presents were laid out; and this was, that she had just noticed something there which she had not observed at first. Fritz's hussars having taken ground to the right at some distance from the tree, in front of which they had previously been paraded, there became visible a most delicious little man, who was standing there quiet and unobtrusive, as if waiting patiently till it should be his turn to be noticed.

Objection, considerable objection, might, perhaps, have been taken to him on the score of his figure, for his body was rather too tall and stout for his legs, which were short and slight; moreover, his head was a good deal too large. But much of this was atoned for by the elegance of his costume, which showed him to be a person of taste and cultivation. He had on a very pretty violet hussar's jacket, knobs and braid all over, pantaloons of the same, and the loveliest little boots ever seen even on a hussar officer—fitting his little legs just as if they had been painted on them. It was funny, certainly, that dressed in this style as he was he had a little, rather absurd, short cloak on his shoulders, which looked almost as if it were made of wood, and on his head a cap like a miner's. But Marie remembered that Godpapa Drosselmeier often appeared in a terribly ugly morning jacket, and with a frightful-looking cap on his head, and yet was a very very darling godpapa.

As Marie kept looking at this little man, whom she had quite fallen in love with at first sight, she saw more and more clearly what a sweet nature and disposition were legible in his countenance. Those green eyes of his (which stuck, perhaps, a little more prominently out of his head than was quite desirable) beamed with kindliness and benevolence. It was one of his beauties, too, that his chin was set off with a well-kept beard of white cotton, as this drew attention to the smile which his bright red lips always expressed.

"Oh, papa, dear!" cried Marie at last, "whose is that most darling little man beside the tree?"

"Well," was the answer, "that little fellow is going to do plenty of good service for all of you; he's going to crack nuts for you, and he is to belong to Louise just as much as to you and Fritz." With which papa took him up from the table, and on his lifting the end of the wooden cloak, the little man opened his mouth wider and wider, displaying two rows of very white, sharp teeth. Marie, directed by her father, put a nut into his mouth, and—knack—he had bitten it in two, so that the shells fell down, and Marie got the kernel. So then it was explained to all that this charming little man belonged to the Nutcracker family, and was practicing the profession of his ancestors. "And," said papa, "as friend Nutcracker seems to have made such an impression on you, Marie, he shall be given over to your special care and charge, though, as I said, Louise and Fritz are to have the same right to his services as you."

Marie took him into her arms at once, and made him crack some more nuts; but she picked out all the smallest, so that he might not have to open his mouth so terribly wide, because that was not nice for him. Then sister Louise came, and he had to crack some nuts for her too, which duty he seemed very glad to perform, as he kept on smiling most courteously.

Meanwhile, Fritz was a little tired, after so much drill and maneuvering, so he joined his sisters, and laughed beyond measure at the funny little fellow, who (as Fritz wanted his share of the nuts) was passed from hand to hand, and was continually snapping his mouth open and shut. Fritz gave him all the biggest and hardest nuts he could find, but all at once there was a "crack—crack," and three teeth fell out of Nutcracker's mouth, and his lower jaw became loose and wobbly.

"Ah! my poor darling Nutcracker," Marie cried, and took him away from Fritz.

"A nice sort of chap he is!" said Fritz. "Calls himself a nut-cracker, and can't give a decent bite—doesn't seem to know much about his business. Hand him over here, Marie! I'll keep him biting nuts if he drops all the rest of his teeth, and his jaw into the bargain. What's the good of a chap like him!"

"No, no," said Marie, in tears; "you shan't have him, my darling Nutcracker; see how he's looking at me so mournfully, and showing me his poor sore mouth. You're a hard-hearted creature! You beat your horses, and you've had one of your soldiers shot."

"Those things must be done," said Fritz, "and you don't understand anything about such matters. But Nutcracker's as much mine as yours, so hand him over!"

Marie began to cry bitterly, and quickly wrapped the wounded Nutcracker up in her little pocket handkerchief. Papa and mamma came with Drosselmeier, who took Fritz's part, to Marie's regret. But papa said, "I have put Nutcracker in Marie's special charge, and as he seems to have need just now of her care, she has full power over him, and nobody else has anything to say in the matter. And I'm surprised that Fritz should expect further service from a man wounded in the execution of his duty. As a good soldier, he ought to know better than that."

Fritz was much ashamed, and, troubling himself no further as to nuts or nutcrackers, crept off to the other side of the table, where his hussars (having established the necessary outposts and videttes) were bivouacking for the night. Marie got Nutcracker's lost teeth together, bound a pretty white ribbon, taken from her dress, about his poor chin, and then wrapped the poor little fellow, who was looking very pale and frightened, more tenderly and carefully than before in her handkerchief. Thus she held him, rocking him like a child in her arms, as she looked at the picture books. She grew quite angry (which was not usual with her) with Godpapa Drosselmeier because he laughed so, and kept asking how she could make such a fuss about an ugly little fellow like that. That odd and peculiar likeness to Drosselmeier, which had struck her when she saw Nutcracker at first, occurred to her mind again now, and she said, with much earnestness:

"Who knows, godpapa, if you were to be dressed the same as my darling Nutcracker, and had on the same shining boots—who knows whether you mightn't look almost as handsome as he does?"

Marie did not understand why papa and mamma laughed so heartily, nor why Godpapa Drosselmeier's nose got so red, nor why he did not join so much in the laughter as before. Probably there was some special reason for these things.

WONDERFUL EVENTS

We must now explain that in the sitting-room on the left hand as you go in there stands against the wall a high, glass-fronted cupboard, where all the children's Christmas presents are yearly put away to be kept. Louise, the elder sister, was still quite little when her father had this cupboard constructed by a very skillful workman, who had put in it such transparent panes of glass, and altogether made the whole affair so splendid, that the things, when inside it, looked almost more shining and lovely than when one had them actually in one's hands.

In the upper shelves, which were beyond the reach of Fritz and Marie, were stowed Godpapa Drosselmeier's works of art; immediately under them was the shelf for the picture books. Fritz and Marie were allowed to do what they liked with the two lower shelves, but it always came about that the lowest one of all was where Marie put her dolls, as their place of residence, while Fritz utilized the shelf above this as cantonments for his troops. So that on the evening about which we are speaking, Fritz had quartered his hussars in his—the upper—shelf of these two. Marie had put

Miss Gertrude rather in a corner, established her new doll in the well-appointed chamber there, with all its appropriate furniture, and invited herself to tea and cakes with her. This chamber was splendidly furnished, everything on a first-rate scale, and in good and admirable style, as I have already said. I don't know if you, my observant reader, have the satisfaction of possessing an equally well-appointed room for your dolls: a little beautifully-flowered sofa, a number of the most charming little chairs, a nice little tea-table, and, above all, a beautiful little white bed, where your pretty darlings of dolls go to sleep? All this was in a corner of the shelf, the walls of which, in this part, had beautiful little pictures hanging on them; and you may well imagine that, in such a delightful chamber as this, the new doll (whose name, as Marie had discovered, was Miss Clara) thought herself extremely comfortably settled, and remarkably well off.

It was getting very late, not so very far from midnight, indeed, before the children could tear themselves away from all these Yule-tide fascinations, and Godpapa Drosselmeier had been gone a considerable time. They remained riveted beside the glass cupboard, although their mother several times reminded them that it was long after bedtime. "Yes," said Fritz, "I know well enough that these poor fellows (meaning his hussars) are tired enough, and awfully anxious to turn in for the night, though as long as I'm here, not a man-jack of them dares to nod his head." With which he went off. But Marie earnestly begged for just a little while longer, saying she had such a number of things to see to, and promising that as soon as she had them all settled she would go to bed at once. Marie was a very good and reasonable child, and therefore her mother allowed her to remain a little longer with her toys; but lest she should be too much occupied with her new doll and the other playthings and would forget to put out the candles which were lighted all around on the wall sconces, she herself put all of them out, leaving merely the lamp which hung from the ceiling to give a soft and pleasant light. "Come to bed soon, Marie, or you'll never be up in time in the morning," cried her mother as she went away into the bedroom.

As soon as Marie was alone, she set rapidly to work to do what she wanted most to do, which, though she scarcely knew why, she somehow did not like to set about in her mother's presence. She had been holding Nutcracker, wrapped in the handkerchief, carefully in her arms all this time, and she now laid him softly down on the table, gently unrolled the handkerchief, and examined his wounds.

Nutcracker was very pale, but at the same time he was smiling with a melancholy and pathetic kindliness which went straight to Marie's heart.

"Oh, my darling little Nutcracker!" said she, very softly, "don't you be vexed because brother Fritz has hurt you so: he didn't mean it, you know; he's only a little bit hardened with his soldiering and that, but he's a good, nice boy, I assure you. I'll take the greatest care of you, and nurse you, till you're quite, quite better and happy again. And your teeth shall be put in again for you, and your shoulder set right. Godpapa Drosselmeier will see to that; he knows how to do things of that kind —"

Marie could not finish what she was going to say, because at the mention of Godpapa Drosselmeier, friend Nutcracker made a most horrible, ugly face. A sort of sharp green sparkle seemed to dart out of his eyes. This was only for an instant, however; and just as Marie was going to be terribly frightened, she found that she was looking at the very same nice, kindly face, with the pathetic smile which she had seen before, and she saw plainly that it was nothing but some draught of air making the lamp flicker that had seemed to produce the change.

"Well!" she said, "I certainly am a silly girl to be so easily frightened, and think that a wooden doll could make faces at me! But I'm too fond, really, of Nutcracker, because he's so funny, and so kind and nice; and so he must be taken the greatest care of, and properly nursed till he's well."

With which she took him in her arms again, approached the cupboard, and kneeling down beside it, said to her new doll:

"I'm going to ask a favour of you, Miss Clara—that you will give up your bed to this poor sick, wounded Nutcracker, and make yourself as comfortable as you can on the sofa here. Remember that you're well and strong yourself, or you wouldn't have such fat, red cheeks, and that there are very few dolls who have as comfortable a sofa as this to lie upon."

Miss Clara, in her Christmas full-dress, looked very grand and disdainful, and said not so much as "Boo!"

"Very well," said Marie, "why should I make such a fuss, and stand on any ceremony?"—took the bed and moved it forward; laid Nutcracker carefully and tenderly down on it; wrapped another pretty ribbon taken from her own dress about his hurt shoulder, and drew the bedclothes up to his nose.

"But he shan't stay with that nasty Clara," she said, and moved the bed, with Nutcracker in it, to the upper shelf, so that it was

placed near the village in which Fritz's hussars had their cantonments.   She closed the cupboard, and was moving away to go to
bed, when—listen, children!—there began a low soft rustling and
rattling, and a sort of whispering noise, all round, in all directions,
from all quarters of the room—behind the stove, under the chairs,
behind the cupboards.

The clock on the wall "warned" louder and louder, but could
not strike.   Marie looked at it, and saw that the big gilt owl which
was on the top of it had drooped its wings so that they covered the
whole of the clock, and had stretched its catlike head, with the
crooked beak, a long way forward.   And the "warning" kept
growing louder and louder, with distinct words: "Clocks, clocks,
stop ticking.   No sound, but cautious 'warning.'   Mouse-King's
ears are fine.   Prr-prr.   Only sing poom, poom; sing the olden
song of doom! prr-prr; poom, poom.   Bells go chime!   Soon rings
out the fated time!"   And then came "Poom! poom!" quite
hoarsely and smothered, twelve times.

Marie grew terribly frightened, and was going to rush away as
best she could, when she noticed that Godpapa Drosselmeier was
up on the top of the clock instead of the owl, with his yellow coattails
hanging down on both sides like wings.   But she manned herself,
and called out in a loud voice of anguish:

"Godpapa! godpapa! what are you up there for?   Come down
to me, and don't frighten me so terribly, you naughty, naughty
Godpapa Drosselmeier!"

But then there began a sort of wild kickering and squeaking,
everywhere, all about, and presently there was a sound as of running
and trotting, as of thousands of little feet behind the walls, and
thousands of little lights began to glitter out between the chinks of
the woodwork.   But they were not lights; no, no! little glittering
eyes; and Marie became aware that, everywhere, mice were peeping
and squeezing themselves out through every chink.   Presently they
were trotting and galloping in all directions over the room; orderly
bodies, continually increasing, of mice, forming themselves into
regular troops and squadrons, in good order, just as Fritz's soldiers
did when maneuvers were going on.

As Marie was not afraid of mice (as many children are), she
could not help being amused by this, and her first alarm had nearly
left her, when suddenly there came such a sharp and terrible piping
noise that the blood ran cold in her veins.   Ah! what did she see
then?   Well, truly, kind reader, I know that your heart is in the
right place, just as much as my friend Field Marshal Fritz's is, but

if you had seen what now came before Marie's eyes, you would have made a clean pair of heels of it; nay, I consider that you would have plumped into your bed, and drawn the blankets further over your head than necessity demanded.

But poor Marie hadn't it in her power to do any such thing, because right at her feet, as if impelled by some subterranean power, sand, and lime, and broken stone came bursting up, and then seven mouse-heads with seven shining crowns upon them rose through the floor, hissing and piping in a most horrible way. Quickly the body of the mouse which had these seven crowned heads forced its way up through the floor. This enormous creature shouted, with its seven heads, aloud to the assembled multitude, squeaking to them with all the seven mouths in full chorus. Then the entire army set itself in motion, and went trot, trot, right up to the cupboard—and, in fact, to Marie, who was standing beside it.

Marie's heart had been beating so with terror that she had thought it must jump out of her breast, and she must die. But now it seemed to her as if the blood in her veins stood still. Half-fainting, she leant backwards, and then there was a "klirr, klirr, prr," and a pane of the cupboard, broken by her elbow, fell in shivers to the floor. She felt for a moment a sharp, stinging pain in her arm, but this seemed to make her heart lighter; she heard no more of the queaking and piping. Everything was quiet; and though she didn't dare to look, she thought the noise of the breaking glass had frightened the mice back to their holes.

But what came to pass then? Right behind Marie a movement seemed to commence in the cupboard, and small, faint voices began to be heard, saying:

> Come, awake, measures take;
> Out to the fight, out to the fight;
> Shield the right, shield the right;
> Arm and away, this is the night.

And harmonica bells began ringing as prettily as you please.

"Oh! that's my little peal of bells!" cried Marie, and went nearer and looked in. Then she saw that there was bright light in the cupboard, and everything was busily in motion there; dolls and little figures of various kinds all running about together, and struggling with their little arms. At this point, Nutcracker rose from his bed, cast off the bedclothes, and sprang with both feet onto the floor (of the shelf), crying out at the top of his voice:

> Knack, knack, knack,
> Stupid mousey pack,

All their skulls we'll crack.
Mousey pack, knack, knack,
Mousey pack, crick and crack,
Cowardly lot of schnack!

And with this he drew his little sword, waved it in the air, and cried:

"Ye, my trusty vassals, brethren and friends, are ye ready to stand by me in this great battle?"

Immediately three scaramouches, one pantaloon, four chimney-sweeps, two zither-players, and a drummer cried, in eager accents:

"Yes, your highness; we will stand by you in loyal duty; we will follow you to death, victory, and the fray!" And they precipitated themselves after Nutcracker (who, in the excitement of the moment, had dared that perilous leap) to the bottom shelf. Now *they* might well dare this perilous leap, for not only had they got plenty of clothes on, of cloth and silk, but besides, there was not much in their insides except cotton and sawdust, so that they plumped down like little wool-sacks. But as for poor Nutcracker, he would certainly have broken his arms and legs; for, bethink you, it was nearly two feet from where he had stood to the shelf below, and his body was as fragile as if he had been made of elm-wood. Yes, Nutcracker would have broken his arms and legs, had not Miss Clara started up at the moment of his spring, and received the hero, drawn sword and all, in her tender arms.

"Oh! you dear, good Clara!" cried Marie, "how I did misunderstand you. I believe you were quite willing to let dear Nutcracker have your bed."

But Miss Clara now cried, as she pressed the young hero gently to her silken breast:

"Oh, my lord! go not into this battle and danger, sick and wounded as you are. See how your trusty vassals, clowns and pantaloon, chimney-sweeps, zithermen and drummer, are already arrayed below; and the puzzle-figures in my shelf here are in motion and preparing for the fray! Deign, oh my lord, to rest in these arms of mine, and contemplate your victory from a safe coign of vantage."

Thus spoke Clara. But Nutcracker behaved so impatiently, and kicked so with his legs, that Clara was obliged to put him down on the shelf in a hurry. However, he at once sank gracefully on one knee, and expressed himself as follows:

"Oh, lady! the kind protection and aid which you have afforded me will ever be present to my heart, in battle and in victory!"

On this, Clara bowed herself so as to be able to take hold of him by his arms, raised him gently up, quickly loosed her girdle, which was ornamented with many spangles, and would have placed it about his shoulders. But the little man swiftly drew himself two steps back, laid his hand upon his heart, and said, with much solemnity:

"Oh, lady! do not bestow this mark of your favour upon me; for—" He hesitated, gave a deep sigh, took the ribbon with which Marie had bound him from his shoulders, pressed it to his lips, put it on as a token, and, waving his glittering sword, sprang like a bird over the ledge of the cupboard down to the floor.

You will observe, kind reader, that Nutcracker, even before he really came to life, had felt and understood all Marie's goodness and regard, and that it was because of his gratitude and devotion to her that he would not take or even wear Miss Clara's ribbon, although it was exceedingly pretty and charming. This good, true-hearted Nutcracker preferred Marie's much commoner and less pretentious token.

But what is going to happen now? At the moment when Nutcracker sprang down, the squeaking and piping began again worse than ever. Alas! under the big table, the hordes of the mouse army had taken up a position, densely massed, under the command of the terrible mouse with the seven heads. So what is to be the result?

THE BATTLE

"Beat the *Generale*, trusty vassal-drummer!" cried Nutcracker, very loudly, and immediately the drummer began to roll his drum in the most splendid style, so that the windows of the glass cupboard rattled and resounded. Then there began a cracking and a clattering inside, and Marie saw all the lids of the boxes in which Fritz's army was quartered bursting open. The soldiers all came out and jumped down to the bottom shelf, where they formed up in good order. Nutcracker hurried up and down the ranks, speaking words of encouragement.

"There's not a dog of a trumpeter taking the trouble to sound a call!" he cried in a fury. Then he turned to the pantaloon (who was looking decidedly pale), and wobbling his long chin a good deal, said in a solemn tone:

"I know how brave and experienced you are, General! What is essential here is a rapid comprehension of the situation, and immediate utilization of the passing moment. I entrust you with the

command of the cavalry and artillery.   You can do without a horse;
your own legs are long, and you can gallop on them as fast as is
necessary.   Do your duty!"

Immediately Pantaloon put his long, lean fingers to his mouth,
and gave such a piercing crow that it rang as if a hundred little
trumpets had been sounding lustily.   Then there began a tramping
and a neighing in the cupboard; and Fritz's dragoons and cuirassiers
—but above all, the new glittering hussars—marched out, and then
came to a halt, drawn up on the floor.   They then marched past
Nutcracker by regiments, with *guidons* flying and bands playing.
After this they wheeled into line, and formed up at right angles to
the line of march.   Upon this, Fritz's artillery came rattling up,
and formed action front in advance of the halted cavalry.   Then it
went "boom-boom!" and Marie saw the sugar-plums doing terrible
execution amongst the thickly-massed mouse-battalions, which
were powdered quite white by them, and greatly put to shame.
But a battery of heavy guns, which had taken up a strong position
on mamma's footstool, was what did the greatest execution; and
"poom-poom-poom!" kept up a murderous fire of gingerbread
nuts into the enemy's ranks with most destructive effect, mowing
the mice down in great numbers.

The enemy, however, was not materially checked in his advance,
and had even possessed himself of one or two of the heavy guns,
when there came "prr-prr-prr!" and Marie could scarcely see what
was happening for smoke and dust; but this much is certain, that
every corps engaged fought with the utmost bravery and determination, and it was for a long time doubtful which side would gain
the day.   The mice kept on developing fresh bodies of their forces,
as they were advanced to the scene of action; their little silver balls
—like pills in size—which they delivered with great precision (their
musketry practice being especially fine) took effect even inside the
glass cupboard.   Clara and Gertrude ran up and down in utter
despair, wringing their hands, and loudly lamenting.

"Must I—the very loveliest doll in all the world—perish miser-
ably in the very flower of my youth?" cried Miss Clara.

"Oh! was it for this," wept Gertrude, "that I have taken such
pains to *conserver* myself all these years?   Must I be shot here in my
own drawing-room after all?"

On this, they fell into each other's arms, and howled so terribly
that you could hear them above all the din of the battle.   For you
have no idea of the hurly-burly that went on now, dear auditor!
It went prr-prr-poof, piff-schnetterdeng—schnetterdeng—boom-

booroom—boom-booroom—boom—all confusedly and higgledy-piggledy; and the mouse-king and the mice squeaked and screamed; and then again Nutcracker's powerful voice was heard shouting words of command, and issuing important orders, and he was seen striding along amongst his battalions in the thick of the fire.

Pantaloon had made several most brilliant cavalry charges, and covered himself with glory. But Fritz's hussars were subjected—by the mice—to a heavy fire of very evil-smelling shot, which made horrid spots on their red tunics; this caused them to hesitate, and hang rather back for a time. Pantaloon made them take ground to the left, in échelon, and in the excitement of the moment he, with his dragoons and cuirassiers, executed a somewhat analogous movement. That is to say, they brought up the right shoulder, wheeled to the left, and marched home to their quarters. This had the effect of bringing the battery of artillery on the footstool into imminent danger, and it was not long before a large body of exceedingly ugly mice delivered such a vigorous assault on this position that the whole of the footstool, with the guns and gunners, fell into the enemy's hands.

Nutcracker seemed much disconcerted, and ordered his right wing to commence a retrograde movement. A soldier of your experience, my dear Fritz, knows well that such a movement is almost tantamount to a regular retreat, and you grieve with me in anticipation, for the disaster which threatens the army of Marie's beloved little Nutcracker. But turn your glance in the other direction, and look at this left wing of Nutcracker's, where all is still going well, and you will see that there is still much hope for the commander-in-chief and his cause.

During the hottest part of the engagement, masses of mouse cavalry had been quietly debouching from under the chest of drawers, and had subsequently made a most determined advance upon the left wing of Nutcracker's force, uttering loud and horrible squeakings. But what a reception they met with! Very slowly, as the nature of the terrain necessitated (for the ledge at the bottom of the cupboard had to be passed), the regiment of motto figures, commanded by two Chinese Emperors, advanced, and formed a square. These fine, brilliantly uniformed troops, consisting of gardeners, Tyrolese, Tungooses, hairdressers, harlequins, Cupids, lions, tigers, unicorns, and monkeys, fought with the utmost courage, coolness, and steady endurance.

This *bataillon d'élite* would have wrested the victory from the enemy had not one of the mouse cavalry captains, pushing forward in a rash and foolhardy manner, made a charge upon one of the Chinese Emperors and bitten off his head. This Chinese Emperor, in his fall, knocked over and smothered a couple of Tungooses and a unicorn, and this created a gap through which the enemy effected a rush, which resulted in the whole battalion being bitten to death. But the enemy gained little advantage by this; for as soon as one of the mouse-cavalry soldiers bit one of these brave adversaries to death, he found that there was a small piece of printed paper sticking in his throat, of which he died in a moment. Still, this was of small advantage to Nutcracker's army, which, having once commenced a retrograde movement, went on retreating farther and farther, suffering greater and greater loss. The unfortunate Nutcracker soon found himself driven back close to the front of the cupboard, with a very small remnant of his army.

"Bring up the reserves! Pantaloon! Scaramouch! Drummer! where the devil have you got to?" shouted Nutcracker, who was still reckoning on reinforcements from the cupboard. And there did, in fact, advance a small contingent of brown gingerbread men and women, with gilt faces, hats, and helmets; but they laid about them so clumsily that they never hit any of the enemy, and soon knocked off the cap of their commander-in-chief, Nutcracker himself. And the enemy's chasseurs soon bit their legs off, so that they tumbled topsy-turvy, and killed several of Nutcracker's companions-in-arms into the bargain.

Nutcracker was now hard pressed, and closely hemmed in by the enemy, and in a position of extreme peril. He tried to jump the bottom ledge of the cupboard, but his legs were not long enough. Clara and Gertrude had fainted; so they could give him no assistance. Hussars and heavy dragoons came charging up at him, and he shouted in wild despair:

"A horse! a horse! My kingdom for a horse!"

At this moment two of the enemy's riflemen seized him by his wooden cloak, and the king of the mice went rushing up to him, squeaking in triumph out of all his seven throats.

Marie could contain herself no longer. "Oh! my poor Nutcracker!" she sobbed, took her left shoe off, without very distinctly knowing what she was about, and threw it as hard as she could into the thick of the enemy, straight at their king.

Instantly everything vanished and disappeared. All was silence. Nothing was to be seen. But Marie felt a more stinging pain than before in her left arm, and fell on the floor insensible.

THE INVALID

When Marie awoke from a deathlike sleep she was lying in her little bed; and the sun was shining brightly in at the window, which was all covered with frost-flowers. There was a strange gentleman sitting beside her, whom she recognized as Dr. Wendelstern. "She's awake," he said softly, and her mother came and looked at her very scrutinizingly and anxiously.

"Oh, mother!" whispered Marie, "are all those horrid mice gone away, and is Nutcracker quite safe?"

"Don't talk such nonsense, Marie," answered her mother. "What have the mice to do with Nutcracker? You're a very naughty girl, and have caused us all a great deal of anxiety. See what comes of children not doing as they're told! You were playing with your toys so late last night that you fell asleep. I don't know whether or not some mouse jumped out and frightened you, though there are no mice here, generally. But you broke a pane of the glass cupboard with your elbow, and cut your arm so badly that Dr. Wendelstern (who has just taken a number of pieces of the glass out of your arm) thinks that if it had been a little higher up you might have had a stiff arm for life, or even have bled to death. Thank Heaven, I awoke about twelve o'clock and missed you; and I found you lying insensible in front of the glass cupboard, bleeding frightfully, with a number of Fritz's lead soldiers scattered round you, and other toys, broken motto figures, and gingerbread men; and Nutcracker was lying on your bleeding arm, with your left shoe not far off."

"Oh, mother, mother," said Marie, "these were the remains of the tremendous battle between the toys and the mice; and what frightened me so terribly was that the mice were going to take Nutcracker (who was the commander-in-chief of the toy army) prisoner. Then I threw my shoe in among the mice, and after that I know nothing more that happened."

Dr. Wendelstern gave a significant look at the mother, who said very gently to Marie:

"Never mind, dear, keep yourself quiet. The mice are all gone away, and Nutcracker's in the cupboard, quite safe and sound."

Here Marie's father came in, and had a long consultation with Dr. Wendelstern. Then he felt Marie's pulse, and she heard them talking about "wound-fever." She had to stay in bed and take medicine for some days, although she didn't feel at all ill, except that her arm was rather stiff and painful. She knew Nutcracker had got safe out of the battle, and she seemed to remember, as if in a dream, that he had said, quite distinctly, in a very melancholy tone:

"Marie! dearest lady! I am most deeply indebted to you. But it is in your power to do even more for me."

She thought and thought what this could possibly be, but in vain; she couldn't make it out. She wasn't able to play on account of her arm; and when she tried to read, or look through the picture books, everything wavered before her eyes so strangely that she was obliged to stop. The days seemed very long to her, and she could scarcely pass the time till evening, when her mother came and sat at her bed-side, telling and reading her all sorts of nice stories. She had just finished telling her the story of Prince Fakardin, when the door opened and in came Godpapa Drosselmeier, saying:

"I've come to see with my own eyes how Marie's getting on."

When Marie saw Godpapa Drosselmeier in his little yellow coat, the scene of the night when Nutcracker lost the battle with the mice came so vividly back to her that she couldn't help crying out:

"Oh! Godpapa Drosselmeier, how nasty you were! I saw you quite well when you were sitting on the clock, covering it all over with your wings to prevent it from striking and frightening the mice. I heard you quite well when you called the Mouse-King. Why didn't you help Nutcracker? Why didn't you help *me*, you nasty god-papa? It's nobody's fault but yours that I'm lying here with a bad arm."

Her mother, in much alarm, asked what she meant. But Drosselmeier began making extraordinary faces, and said, in a snarling voice, like a sort of chant in monotone:

"Pendulums could only rattle—couldn't tick, ne'er a click; all the clocks stopped their ticking: no more clicking; then they all struck loud, cling-clang. Dolls! Don't your heads hang down! Hink and hank, and honk and hank. Doll-girls! don't hang your heads! Cling and ring! The battle's over—Nutcracker all safe in clover. Comes the owl, on downy wing—Scares away the mouses' king. Pak and pik and pik and pook—clocks, bim-boom— grr-grr. Pendulums must click again. Tick and tack, grr and brr, prr and purr."

Marie fixed wide eyes of terror upon Godpapa Drosselmeier, because he was looking quite different and far more horrid than usual, and was jerking his right arm backwards and forwards as if he were some puppet moved by a handle. She was beginning to grow terribly frightened at him when her mother came in, and Fritz (who had arrived in the meantime) laughed heartily, crying, "Why, godpapa, you *are* going on funnily! You're just like my old Jumping Jack that I threw away last month."

But the mother looked very grave, and said, "This is a most extraordinary way of going on, Mr. Drosselmeier. What can you mean by it?"

"My goodness!" said Drosselmeier, laughing, "did you never hear my nice Watchmaker's Song? I always sing it to little invalids like Marie." Then he hastened to sit down beside Marie's bed, and said to her, "Don't be vexed with me because I didn't gouge out all the Mouse-King's fourteen eyes. That couldn't be managed exactly; but to make up for it, here's something which I know will please you greatly."

He dived into one of his pockets, and what he slowly, slowly brought out of it was—Nutcracker! whose teeth he had put in again quite firmly, and set his broken jaw completely to rights. Marie shouted for joy, and her mother laughed and said, "Now you see for yourself how nice Godpapa Drosselmeier is to Nutcracker."

"But you must admit, Marie," said her godpapa, "that Nutcracker is far from being what you might call a handsome fellow, and you can't say he has a pretty face. If you like, I'll tell you how it was that the ugliness came into his family, and has been handed down in it from one generation to another. Did ever you hear about the Princess Pirlipat, the witch Mouserink, and the clever Clockmaker?"

"I say, Godpapa Drosselmeier," interrupted Fritz at this juncture, "you've put Nutcracker's teeth in again all right, and his jaw isn't wobbly as it was; but what's become of his sword? Why haven't you given him a sword?"

"Oh," cried Drosselmeier, annoyed, "you must always be bothering and finding fault with something or other, boy. What have I to do with Nutcracker's sword? I've put his mouth to rights for him; he must look out for a sword for himself."

"Yes, yes," said Fritz, "so he must, of course, if he's a right sort of fellow."

"So tell me, Marie," continued Drosselmeier, "if you know the story of Princess Pirlipat?"

"Oh no," said Marie. "Tell it me, please—do tell it me!"

"I hope it won't be as strange and terrible as your stories generally are," said her mother.

"Oh no, nothing of the kind," said Drosselmeier. "On the contrary, it's quite a funny story which I'm going to have the honour of telling this time."

"Go on then—do tell it to us," cried the children; and Drosselmeier commenced as follows:—

THE STORY OF THE HARD NUT

Pirlipat's mother was a king's wife, so that, of course, she was a queen; and Pirlipat herself was a princess by birth as soon as ever she was born. The king was quite beside himself with joy over his beautiful little daughter as she lay in her cradle, and he danced round and round upon one leg, crying again and again.

"Hurrah! hurrah! hip, hip, hurrah! Did anybody ever see anything so lovely as my little Pirlipat?"

And all the ministers of state, and the generals, the presidents, and the officers of the staff, danced about on one leg, as the king did, and cried as loud as they could, "No, no—never!"

Indeed, there was no denying that a lovelier baby than Princess Pirlipat was never born since the world began. Her little face looked as if it were woven of the most delicate white and rose-coloured silk; her eyes were of sparkling azure, and her hair all in little curls like threads of gold. Moreover, she had come into the world with two rows of little pearly teeth, with which, two hours after her birth, she bit the Lord High Chancellor in the fingers when he was making a careful examination of her features, so that he cried, "Oh! Gemini!" quite loudly.

There are persons who assert that "Oh Lord" was the expression he employed, and opinions are still considerably divided on this point. At all events, she bit him in the fingers; and the realm learned, with much gratification, that both intelligence and discrimination dwelt within her angelical little frame.

All was joy and gladness, as I have said, save that the queen was very anxious and uneasy, nobody could tell why. One remarkable circumstance was that she had Pirlipat's cradle most scrupulously guarded. Not only were there always guards at the doors of the nursery, but—over and above the two head nurses close to the cradle —there always had to be six other nurses all around the room at night. And what seemed rather a funny thing, which nobody could understand, was that each of these six nurses always had to have a cat in her lap, and to keep on stroking it all night long, so that it would never stop purring.

It is impossible that you, my reader, should know the reason of all these precautions; but I do, and shall proceed to tell you at once.

Once upon a time, many great kings and very grand princes were assembled at Pirlipat's father's court, and very great doings were afoot. Tournaments, theatricals, and state balls were going on on the grandest scale, and the king, to show that he had no lack of gold and silver, made up his mind to make a good hole in the crown revenues for once, and launch out regardless of expense. Wherefore (having previously ascertained privately from the state head master cook that the court astronomer had indicated a propitious hour for pork-butchering), he resolved to give a grand pudding-and-sausage banquet. He jumped into a state carriage, and personally invited all the kings and the princes—to a basin of soup, merely—that he might enjoy their astonishment at the magnificence of the entertainment. Then he said to the queen, very graciously, "My darling, *you* know exactly how I like my puddings and sausages!"

The queen quite understood what this meant. It meant that she should undertake the important duty of making the puddings and the sausages herself, which was a thing she had done on one or two previous occasions. So the chancellor of the exchequer was ordered to issue out of store the great golden sausage kettle, and the silver casseroles. A great fire of sandalwood was kindled, the queen put on her damask kitchen apron, and soon the most delicious aroma of pudding broth rose steaming out of the kettle. This sweet smell penetrated into the very council chamber. The king could not control himself.

"Excuse me for a few minutes, my lords and gentlemen," he cried, rushed to the kitchen, embraced the queen, stirred in the kettle a little with his golden sceptre, and then went back easier in his mind to the council chamber.

The important moment had now arrived when the fat had to be cut up into little square pieces, and browned on silver spits. The ladies-in-waiting retired, because the queen, from motives of love and duty to her royal consort, thought it proper to perform this important task in solitude. But when the fat began to brown, a delicate little whispering voice made itself audible, saying, "Give me some of that, sister! I want some of it, too; I am a queen as well as yourself; give me some."

The queen knew well who was speaking. It was Dame Mouserink, who had been established in the palace for many years. She claimed relationship to the royal family, and she was queen of the realm of Mousolia herself, and lived with a considerable retinue of her own under the kitchen hearth. The queen was a kind-hearted, benevolent woman; and, although she didn't exactly care to recognize Dame Mouserink as a sister and a queen, she was willing, at this festive season, to spare her the tidbits she had a mind to. So she said, "Come out, then, Dame Mouserink; of course you shall taste my browned fat."

So Dame Mouserink came running out as fast as she could, held up her pretty little paws, and took morsel after morsel of the browned fat as the queen held them out to her. But then all Dame Mouserink's uncles, and her cousins, and her aunts, came jumping out too; and her seven sons (who were terrible ne'er-do-wells) into the bargain; and they all set to at the browned fat, and the queen was too frightened to keep them at bay. Most fortunately the mistress of the robes came in, and drove these importunate visitors away, so that a little of the browned fat was left; and then, when the court mathematician (an ex-senior wrangler of his university) was called in (which he had to be, on purpose), it was found possible, by means of skillfully devised apparatus provided with special micrometer screws, and so forth, to apportion and distribute the fat among the whole of the sausages, etc., under construction.

The kettledrums and the trumpets summoned all the great princes and potentates to the feast. They assembled in their robes of state; some of them on white palfreys, some in crystal coaches. The king received them with much gracious ceremony, and took his seat at the head of the table, with his crown on, and his sceptre in his hand. Even during the serving of the white pudding course, it was observed that he turned pale, and raised his eyes to heaven; sighs heaved his bosom; some terrible inward pain was clearly raging within him. But when the black puddings were handed round, he fell back in his seat, loudly sobbing and groaning.

Everyone rose from the table, and the court physician tried in vain to feel his pulse. Ultimately, after the administration of most powerful remedies—burnt feathers, and the like—His Majesty seemed to recover his senses to some extent, and stammered, scarce audibly, the words: "Too little fat!"

The queen cast herself down at his feet in despair, and cried, in a voice broken by sobs, "Oh, my poor unfortunate royal consort! Ah, what tortures you are doomed to endure! But see the culprit here at your feet. Punish her severely! Alas! Dame Mouserink, her uncles, her seven sons, her cousins and her aunts, came and ate up nearly all the fat—and—"

Here the queen fell back insensible.

But the king jumped up, all anger, and cried in a terrible voice, "Mistress of the robes, what is the meaning of this?"

The mistress of the robes told all she knew, and the king resolved to take revenge on Dame Mouserink and her family for eating up the fat which ought to have been in the sausages. The privy council was summoned, and it was resolved that Dame Mouserink should be tried for her life, and all her property confiscated. But as His Majesty was of opinion that she might go on consuming the fat, which was his appanage, the whole matter was referred to the court Clockmaker and Arcanist—whose name was the same as mine—Christian Elias Drosselmeier, and he undertook to expel Dame Mouserink and all her relations from the palace precincts forever, by means of a certain politico-diplomatic procedure. He invented certain ingenious little machines, into which pieces of browned fat were inserted; and he placed these machines down all about the dwelling of Dame Mouserink. Now she herself was much too knowing not to see through Drosselmeier's artifice; but all her remonstrances and warnings to her relations were unavailing. Enticed by the fragrant odour of the browned fat, all her seven sons, and a great many of her uncles, cousins and aunts, walked into Drosselmeier's little machines and were immediately taken prisoners by the fall of a small grating, after which they met with a shameful death in the kitchen.

Dame Mouserink left this scene of horror with her small following. Rage and despair filled her breast. The court rejoiced greatly; the queen was very anxious, because she knew Dame Mouserink's character, and knew well that she would never allow the death of her sons and other relatives to go unavenged. And, in fact, one day when the queen was cooking a fricassée of sheep's lights for the king (a dish to which he was exceedingly partial), Dame Mouserink suddenly made her appearance, and said: "My sons and my uncles, my cousins and my aunts, are now no more. Have a care, lady, lest the queen of the mice bites your little princess in two! Have a care!"

With which she vanished, and was no more seen. But the queen was so frightened that she dropped the fricassée into the fire; so this was the second time Dame Mouserink spoiled one of the king's favorite dishes, at which he was very irate.

But this is enough for tonight; we'll go on with the rest of it another time—said Drosselmeier.

Sorely as Marie—who had ideas of her own about this story— begged Godpapa Drosselmeier to go on with it, he would not be persuaded, but jumped up, saying, "Too much at a time wouldn't be good for you; the rest tomorrow."

Just as Drosselmeier was going out of the door, Fritz said: "I say, Godpapa Drosselmeier, was it really you who invented mousetraps?"

"How can you ask such silly questions?" cried his mother. But Drosselmeier laughed oddly, and said, "Well, you know I'm a clever clockmaker. Mousetraps had to be invented some time or other."

And now you know, children, said Godpapa Drosselmeier the next evening, why it was the queen took such precautions about her little Pirlipat. Had she not always the fear before her eyes of Dame Mouserink coming back and carrying out her threat of biting the princess to death? Drosselmeier's ingenious machines were of no avail against the clever, crafty Dame Mouserink, and nobody save the court astronomer, who was also state astrologer and reader of the stars, knew that the family of the Cat Purr had the power to keep her at bay. This was the reason why each of the lady nurses was obliged to keep one of the sons of that family (each of whom was given the honorary rank and title of "privy councillor of legation") in her lap, and render his onerous duty less irksome by gently scratching his back.

One night, just after midnight, one of the chief nurses stationed close to the cradle, woke suddenly from a profound sleep. Everything lay buried in slumber. Not a purr to be heard—deep, death-like silence, so that the death-watch ticking in the wainscot sounded quite loud. What were the feelings of this principal nurse when she saw, close beside her, a great, hideous mouse, standing on its hind legs, with its horrid head laid on the princess's face! She sprang up with a scream of terror. Everybody awoke; but then Dame Mouserink (for she was the great big mouse in Pirlipat's cradle) ran quickly away into the corner of the room. The privy councillors of legation dashed after her, but too late! She was off and away through a chink in the floor. The noise awoke Pirlipat, who cried terribly. "Heaven be thanked, she is still alive!" cried all the nurses; but what was their horror when they looked at Pirlipat, and saw what the beautiful, delicate little thing had turned into. An enormous bloated head (instead of the pretty little golden-haired one) at the top of a diminutive, crumpled-up body, and green, wooden-looking eyes staring where the lovely azure-blue pair had been, whilst her mouth had stretched across from the one ear to the other.

Of course the queen nearly died of weeping and loud lamentation, and the walls of the king's study had all to be hung with padded arras, because he kept on banging his head against them, crying:

"Oh! wretched king that I am! Oh, wretched king that I am!"

Of course he might have seen then, that it would have been much better to eat his puddings with no fat in them at all, and let Dame Mouserink and her folk stay on under the hearthstone. But Pirlipat's royal father did not think of that. What he did was to lay all the blame on the court Clockmaker and Arcanist, Christian Elias Drosselmeier, of Nuremberg. Wherefore he promulgated a sapient edict to the effect that said Drosselmeier should within the space of four weeks restore Princess Pirlipat to her pristine condition—or, at least, indicate an unmistakable and reliable process whereby that might be accomplished—or else suffer a shameful death by the axe of the common headsman.

Drosselmeier was not a little alarmed; but he soon began to place confidence in his art, and in his luck; so he proceeded to execute the first operation which seemed to him to be expedient. He took Princess Pirlipat very carefully to pieces, screwed off her hands and feet, and examined her interior structure. Unfortunately, he found that the bigger she got the more deformed she would be, so that he didn't see what was to be done at all. He put her carefully together again, and sank down beside her cradle—which he wasn't allowed to go away from—in the deepest dejection.

The fourth week had come, and Wednesday of the fourth week, when the king came in with eyes gleaming with anger, made threatening gestures with his sceptre, and cried:

"Christian Elias Drosselmeier, restore the princess, or prepare for death!"

Drosselmeier began to weep bitterly. The little princess kept on cracking nuts, an occupation which seemed to afford her much quiet satisfaction. For the first time the Arcanist was struck by Pirlipat's remarkable appetite for nuts, and the circumstance that she had been born with teeth. And the fact had been that immediately after her transformation she had begun to cry, and she had gone on crying till by chance she got hold of a nut. She at once cracked it, and ate the kernel, after which she was quite quiet. From that time her nurses found that nothing would do but to go on giving her nuts.

"Oh, holy instinct of nature—eternal, mysterious, inscrutable Interdependence of Things!" cried Drosselmeier, "thou pointest out to me the door of the secret.   I will knock, and it shall be opened unto me."

He at once begged for an interview with the Court Astronomer, and was conducted to him closely guarded.   They embraced with many tears for they were great friends, and then retired into a private closet, where they referred to many books treating of sympathies, antipathies, and other mysterious subjects.   Night came on.   The Court Astronomer consulted the stars, and with the assistance of Drosselmeier (himself an adept in astrology) drew the princess's horoscope.   This was an exceedingly difficult operation, for the lines kept getting more and more entangled and confused for ever so long.   But at last—oh what joy!—it lay plain before them that all the princess had to do to be delivered from the enchantment which made her so hideous and get back her former beauty was to eat the sweet kernel of the nut Crackatook.

Now this nut Crackatook had a shell so hard that you might have fired a forty-eight pounder at it without producing the slightest effect on it.   Moreover, it was essential that this nut should be cracked, in the princess's presence, by the teeth of a man whose beard had never known a razor, and who had never had on boots. This man had to hand the kernel to her with his eyes closed, and he might not open them till he had made seven steps backwards without a stumble.

Drosselmeier and the astronomer had been at work on this problem uninterruptedly for three days and three nights; and on the Saturday the king was sitting at dinner when Drosselmeier—who was to have been beheaded on the Sunday morning—burst in joyfully to announce that he had found out what had to be done to restore Princess Pirlipat to her pristine beauty.   The king embraced him in a burst of rapture, and promised him a diamond sword, four decorations, and two Sunday suits.

"Set to work immediately after dinner," the monarch cried, adding kindly, "Take care, dear Arcanist, that the young unshaven gentleman in shoes, with the nut Crackatook all ready in his hand, is on the spot; and be sure that he touches no liquor beforehand, so that he mayn't trip up when he makes his seven backward steps like a crab.   He can get as drunk as a lord afterwards, if he likes."

Drosselmeier was dismayed at this utterance of the king's, and stammered out, not without trembling and hesitation, that, though the remedy was discovered, both the nut Crackatook and the young gentleman who was to crack it had still to be searched for, and that it was matter of doubt whether they ever would be found at all.

The king, greatly incensed, whirled his sceptre round his crowned head, and shouted in the voice of a lion:

"Very well, then you must be beheaded!"

It was exceedingly fortunate for the wretched Drosselmeier that the king had thoroughly enjoyed his dinner that day, and was consequently in an admirable temper, and disposed to listen to the sensible advice which the queen, who was very sorry for Drosselmeier, did not hesitate to give him. Drosselmeier took heart and represented that he really had fulfilled the conditions, discovered the necessary measures, and gained his life, consequently. The king said this was all bosh and nonsense; but at length, after two or three glasses of liqueurs decreed that Drosselmeier and the astronomer should start off immediately, and not come back without the nut Crackatook in their pockets. The man who was to crack it (by the queen's suggestion) might be heard of by means of advertisements in the local and foreign newspapers and gazettes.

Godpapa Drosselmeier interrupted his story at this point, and promised to finish it on the following evening.

Next evening, as soon as the lights were brought, Godpapa Drosselmeier duly arrived, and went on with his story as follows:—

Drosselmeier and the court astronomer had been journeying for fifteen long years without finding the slightest trace of the nut Crackatook. I might go on for more than four weeks telling you where all they had been and what extraordinary things they had seen. I shall not do so, however, but merely mention that Drosselmeier in his profound discouragement at last began to feel a most powerful longing to see his dear native town of Nuremberg once again. And he was more powerfully moved by this longing than usual one day, when he happened to be smoking a pipe of kanaster with his friend in the middle of a great forest in Asia, and he cried:

"Oh, Nuremberg, Nuremberg, dear native town—he who still knows thee not, place of renown—though far he has travelled, and great cities seen—as London, and Paris, and Peterwardein— knoweth not what it is happy to be—still must his longing heart languish for thee—for thee, O Nuremberg, exquisite town—where the houses have windows both upstairs and down!"

As Drosselmeier lamented dolefully, the astronomer, seized with compassionate sympathy, began to weep and howl so terribly that he was heard throughout the length and breadth of Asia. But he collected himself again, wiped the tears from his eyes, and said:

"After all, dearest colleague, why should we sit and weep and howl here? Why not go to Nuremberg? Does it matter a brass farthing, after all, where and how we search for this horrible nut Crackatook?"

"That's true, too," answered Drosselmeier, consoled. They both got up immediately, knocked the ashes out of their pipes, started off, and travelled straight on without stopping from that forest right in the centre of Asia till they came to Nuremberg. As soon as they got there, Drosselmeier went straight to his cousin the toymaker and doll-carver, and gilder and varnisher, whom he had not seen for a great many long years. To him he told all the tale of Princess Pirlipat, Dame Mouserink, and the nut Crackatook, so that he clapped his hands repeatedly and cried in amazement:

"Dear me, cousin, these things are really wonderful—very wonderful, indeed!"

Drosselmeier told him, further, some of the adventures he had met with on his long journey—how he had spent two years at the court of the King of Dates; how the Prince of Almonds had expelled him with ignominy from his territory; how he had applied in vain to the Natural History Society at Squirreltown—in short, how he had been everywhere utterly unsuccessful in discovering the faintest trace of the nut Crackatook. During this narrative, Christoph Zacharias had kept frequently snapping his fingers, twisting himself round on one foot, smacking with his tongue, etc.; then he cried:

"Ey—aye—oh!—that really would be the very deuce and all."

At last he threw his hat and wig in the air, warmly embraced his cousin, and cried:

"Cousin, cousin, you're a made man—a made man you are—for either I am much deceived, or I have the nut Crackatook myself!"

He immediately produced a little cardboard box, out of which he took a gilded nut of medium size.

"Look there!" he said, showing this nut to his cousin; "the state of matters as regards this nut is this. Several years ago at Christmas time a stranger came here with a sack of nuts, which he offered for sale. Just in front of my shop he got into a quarrel, and put the sack down the better to defend himself from the nutsellers of the place, who attacked him. Just then a heavily loaded wagon drove over the sack, and all the nuts were smashed but one. The stranger, with an odd smile, offered to sell me this nut for a twenty-kreuzer piece of the year 1796. This struck me as strange. I found just such a coin in my pocket, so I bought the nut, and I gilt it, though I didn't know why I took the trouble, or should have given so much for it."

All question as to its being really the long-sought nut Crackatook was dispelled when the Court Astronomer carefully scraped away the gilding, and found the word "Crackatook" graven on the shell in Chinese characters.

The joy of the exiles was great, as you may imagine; and the cousin was even happier, for Drosselmeier assured him that *he* was a made man too, as he was sure of a good pension, and all the gold leaf he would want for the rest of his life for his gilding, free, gratis, for nothing.

The Arcanist and the Astronomer both had on their nightcaps, and were going to turn into bed, when the astronomer said:

"I tell you what it is, my dear colleague, one piece of good fortune never comes alone. I feel convinced that we've not only found the nut, but the young gentleman who is to crack it, and hand the beauty-restoring kernel to the princess, into the bargain. I mean none other than your cousin's son here, and I don't intend to close an eye this night till I've drawn that youngster's horoscope."

With which he threw away his nightcap, and at once set to work to consult the stars. The cousin's son was a nice-looking, well-grown young fellow, had never been shaved, and had never worn boots. True, he had been a Jumping Jack for a Christmas or two in his earlier days, but there was scarcely any trace of this discoverable about him, his appearance had been so altered by his father's care. He had appeared last Christmas in a beautiful red coat with gold trimmings, a sword by his side, his hat under his arm, and a fine wig with a pigtail. Thus apparelled, he stood in his father's shop exceedingly lovely to behold, and from his native *galanterie* he occupied himself in cracking nuts for the young ladies, who called him "the handsome nutcracker."

Next morning the Astronomer fell, with much emotion, into the Arcanist's arms, crying:

"This is the very man!—we have him!—he is found! Only, dearest colleague, two things we must keep carefully in view. In the first place, we must construct a most substantial pigtail for this precious nephew of yours, which shall be connected with his lower jaw in such sort that it shall be capable of communicating a very powerful pull to it. And next, when we get back to the Residenz, we must carefully conceal the fact that we have brought the young gentleman who is to shiver the nut back with us. He must not make his appearance for a considerable time after us.   I read in the horoscope that if two or three others bite at the nut unsuccessfully to begin with, the king will promise the man who breaks it—and as a consequence, restores her good looks to the princess—the princess's hand and the succession to the crown."

The doll-maker cousin was immensely delighted with the idea of his son's marrying Princess Pirlipat and being a prince and king, so he gave him wholly over to the envoys to do what they liked with him.   The pigtail which Drosselmeier attached to him proved to be a very powerful and efficient instrument, as he exemplified by cracking the hardest of peach-stones with the utmost ease.

Drosselmeier and the Astronomer, having at once sent news to the Residenz of the discovery of the nut Crackatook, the necessary advertisements were at once put in the newspapers, and by the time that our travellers got there, several nice young gentlemen had arrived, among whom there were even princes, who had sufficient confidence in their teeth to try to disenchant the princess.   The ambassadors were horrified when they saw poor Pirlipat again. The diminutive body with tiny hands and feet was not big enough to support the great shapeless head.   The hideousness of the face was enhanced by a beard like white cotton, which had grown about the mouth and chin.   Everything had turned out as the court astronomer had read it in the horoscope.   One milksop in shoes after another bit his teeth and his jaws into agonies over the nut without doing the princess the slightest good in the world.   And then, when he was carried out on the verge of insensibility by the dentists who were in attendance on purpose, he would sigh:

"Ah dear, that *was* a hard nut."

Now when the king, in the anguish of his soul, had promised to him who should disenchant the princess his daughter and the kingdom, the charming, gentle young Drosselmeier made his appearance, and begged to be allowed to make an attempt.   None of the previous ones had pleased the princess so much.   She pressed her little hands to her heart and sighed:

"Ah, I hope it will be he who will crack the nut and be my husband."

When he had politely saluted the king, the queen, and the Princess Pirlipat, he received the nut Crackatook from the hands of the Clerk of the Closet, put it between his teeth, made a strong effort with his head, and—crack—crack—the shell was shattered into a number of pieces.   He neatly cleared the kernel from the pieces of husk which were sticking to it, and making a leg presented it courteously to the princess, after which he closed his eyes and began his backward steps. The princess swallowed the kernel, and—oh marvel!—the monstrosity vanished, and in its place there stood a wonderfully beautiful lady with a face which seemed woven of delicate lily-white and rose-red silk, eyes of sparkling azure, and hair all in little curls like threads of gold.

Trumpets and kettledrums mingled in the loud rejoicings of the populace. The king and all his court danced about on one leg, as they had done at Pirlipat's birth, and the queen had to be treated with Eau de Cologne, having fallen into a fainting fit from joy and delight. All this tremendous tumult interfered not a little with young Drosselmeier's self-possession, for he still had to make his seven backward steps. But he collected himself as best he could, and was just stretching out his right foot to make his seventh step, when up came Dame Mouserink through the floor, making a horrible weaking and squeaking, so that Drosselmeier, as he was putting his foot down, trod upon her and stumbled so that he almost fell. Oh misery!—all in an instant he was transmogrified, just as the princess had been before: his body all shrivelled up, and could scarcely support the great shapeless head with enormous projecting eyes and the wide gaping mouth. In the place where his pigtail used to be a scanty wooden cloak hung down, controlling the movements of his nether jaw.

The clockmaker and the astronomer were wild with terror and consternation, but they saw that Dame Mouserink was wallowing in her gore on the floor. Her wickedness had not escaped punishment, for young Drosselmeier had squashed her so in the throat with the sharp point of his shoe that she was mortally hurt.

But as Dame Mouserink lay in her death agony she squeaked and cheeped lamentably and cried:

"Oh, Crackatook, thou nut so hard!—Oh, fate, which none may disregard!—Hee hee, pee pee, woe's me, I cry!—since I through that hard nut must die.—But, brave young Nutcracker, I see—you soon must follow after me.—My sweet young son, with sevenfold crown—will soon bring Master Cracker down.—His mother's death he will repay—so, Nutcracker, beware that day!—Oh, life most sweet, I feebly cry—I leave you now, for I must die. Queak!"

With this cry died Dame Mouserink, and her body was carried out by the Court Stovelighter. Meantime nobody had been troubling himself about young Drosselmeier. But the princess reminded the king of his promise, and he at once directed that the young hero should be conducted to his presence. But when the poor wretch came forward in his transmogrified condition the princess put both her hands to her face, and cried:

"Oh please take away that horrid Nutcracker!"

The Lord Chamberlain seized him immediately by his little shoulders, and shied him out at the door. The king, furious at the idea of a nutcracker being brought before him as a son-in-law, laid all the blame upon the clockmaker and the astronomer, and ordered them both to be banished for ever.

The horoscope which the astronomer had drawn in Nuremberg had said nothing about this; but that didn't hinder him from taking some fresh observations. And the stars told him that young Drosselmeier would conduct himself so admirably in his new condition that he would still be a prince and a king, in spite of his transmogrification; but also that his deformity would only disappear after the son of Dame Mouserink, the seven-headed king of the mice (whom she had borne after the death of her original seven sons) should perish by his hand, and a lady should fall in love with him notwithstanding his deformity.

That is the story of the hard nut, children, and now you know why people so often use the expression "that was a hard nut to crack," and why Nutcrackers are so ugly.

Thus did Godpapa Drosselmeier finish his tale. Marie thought the Princess Pirlipat was a nasty ungrateful thing. Fritz, on the other hand, was of the opinion that if Nutcracker had been a proper sort of fellow he would soon have settled the Mouse-King's hash, and got his good looks back again.

UNCLE AND NEPHEW

Should any of my respected readers or listeners ever have happened to be cut by glass they will know what an exceedingly nasty thing it is, and how long it takes to heal. Marie was obliged to stay in bed a whole week because she felt so terribly giddy whenever she tried to stand up; but at last she was quite well again, and able to jump about as of old. Things in the glass cupboard looked very fine indeed —everything new and shiny, trees and flowers and houses—toys of every kind. Above all, Marie found her dear Nutcracker again, smiling at her in the second shelf, with his teeth all sound and right.

As she looked at this pet of hers with much fondness, it suddenly struck her that all Godpapa Drosselmeier's story had been about

Nutcracker, and his family feud with Dame Mouserink and her people. And now she knew that her Nutcracker was none other than young Mr. Drosselmeier, of Nuremberg, Godpapa Drosselmeier's delightful nephew, unfortunately under the spells of Dame Mouserink. For while the story was being told, Marie couldn't doubt for a moment that the clever clockmaker at Pirlipat's father's court was Godpapa Drosselmeier himself.

"But why didn't your uncle help you? Why didn't he help you?" Marie cried, sorrowfully, as she felt more and more clearly every moment that in the battle which she had witnessed the question in dispute had been no less a matter than Nutcracker's crown and kingdom. Weren't all the other toys his subjects? And wasn't it clear that the astronomer's prophecy that he was to be rightful King of Toyland had come true?

While the clever Marie was weighing all these things in her mind, she kept expecting that Nutcracker and his vassals would give some indications of being alive, and make some movements as she looked at them. This, however, was by no means the case. Everything in the cupboard kept quite motionless and still. Marie thought this was the effect of Dame Mouserink's enchantments, and those of her seven-headed son, which still were keeping up their power.

"But," she said, "though you're not able to move, or to say the least little word to me, dear Mr. Drosselmeier, I know you understand me and see how very well I wish you. Always reckon on my assistance when you require it. At all events, I will ask your uncle to aid you with all his great skill and talents, whenever there may be an opportunity."

Nutcracker still kept quiet and motionless. But Marie fancied that a gentle sigh came breathing through the glass cupboard, which made its panes ring in a wonderful, though all but imperceptible, manner—while something like a little bell-toned voice seemed to sing:

"Marie fine, angel mine! I will be thine, if thou wilt be mine!"

Although a sort of cold shiver ran through her at this, still it caused her the keenest pleasure.

Twilight came on. Marie's father came in with Godpapa Drosselmeier, and presently Louise set out the tea-table, and the family took their places round it, talking in the pleasantest and merriest manner about all sorts of things. Marie had taken her little stool, and sat down at her godpapa's feet in silence. When everybody happened to cease talking at the same time, Marie looked her godpapa full in the face with her great blue eyes, and said:

"I know now, godpapa, that my Nutcracker is your nephew, young Mr. Drosselmeier from Nuremberg. The prophecy has come true: he is a king and a prince just as your friend the astronomer said he would be. But you know as well as I do that he is at war with Dame Mouserink's son—that horrid king of the mice. Why don't you help him?"

Marie told the whole story of the battle, as she had witnessed it, and was frequently interrupted by the loud laughter of her mother and sister; but Fritz and Drosselmeier listened quite gravely.

"Where in the name of goodness has the child got her head filled with all that nonsense?" cried her father.

"She has such a lively imagination, you see," said her mother; "she dreamt it all when she was feverish with her arm."

"It is all nonsense," cried Fritz, "and it isn't true! My red hussars are not such cowards as all that. If they were, do you suppose I should command them?"

But godpapa smiled strangely, and took little Marie on his knee, speaking more gently to her than ever he had been known to do before.

"More is given to you, Marie dear," he said, "than to me, or the others. You are a born princess, like Pirlipat, and reign in a bright beautiful country. But you still have much to suffer, if you mean to befriend poor transformed Nutcracker; for the king of the mice lies in wait for him at every turn. But I cannot help him; you, and you alone, can do that. So be faithful and true."

Neither Marie nor any of the others knew what Godpapa Drosselmeier meant by these words. But they struck Dr. Stahlbaum—Marie's father—as being so strange that he felt Drosselmeier's pulse, and said:

"There seems a good deal of congestion about the head, my dear sir. I'll write you a little prescription."

But Marie's mother shook her head meditatively, and said:

"I have a strong idea what Mr. Drosselmeier means, though I can't exactly put it in words."

VICTORY

It was not very long before Marie was awakened one bright moonlight night by a curious noise which came from one of the corners of her room. There was a sound as of small stones being thrown, and rolled here and there; and intermittently there came a horrid cheeping and squeaking.

"Oh, dear me! here come these abominable mice again!" cried Marie in terror, and she wanted to awaken her mother. But the noise suddenly ceased; and she could not move a muscle—for she saw the king of the mice working himself out through a hole in the wall. At last he came into the room, ran about in it, and got onto the little table at the head of her bed with a great jump.

"Hee-hehee!" he cried; "give me your candy! out with your cakes, marzipan and sugar-stick, gingerbread cakes! Don't pause to argue! If yield them you won't, I'll chew up Nutcracker! See if I don't!"

As he cried out these terrible words, he gnashed and chattered his teeth most frightfully, and then made off again through the hole in the wall. This frightened Marie so that she was quite pale in the morning, and so upset that she scarcely could utter a word. A hundred times she felt impelled to tell her mother or her sister, or at all events her brother, what had happened. But she thought, "Of course none of them would believe me. They would only laugh at me."

But she saw well enough that to succour Nutcracker she would have to sacrifice all her sweet things; so she laid out all she had of them at the bottom of the cupboard next evening.

"I can't make out how the mice have got into the sitting-room," said her mother. "This is something quite new. There never were any there before. See, Marie, they've eaten up all your candy."

And so it was: the epicure Mouse-King hadn't found the marzipan altogether to his taste, but had gnawed all round the edges of it, so that what he had left of it had to be thrown into the ash-pit. Marie did not mind about her candy, being delighted to think that she had saved Nutcracker by means of it. But what were her feelings when next night there again came a squeaking close by her ear. Alas! The king of the mice was there again, with his eyes glaring worse than the night before.

"Give me your sugar toys," he cried; "give them you must, or else I'll chew Nutcracker up into dust!"

Then he was gone again.

Marie was very sorry. She had as beautiful a collection of sugar-toys as ever a little girl could boast of. Not only had she a charming little shepherd, with his shepherdess, looking after a flock of milk-white sheep, with a nice dog jumping about them, but two postmen with letters in their hands, and four couples of prettily dressed young gentlemen and most beautifully dressed young ladies, swinging in a Russian swing. Then there were two or three dancers, and behind them Farmer Feldkuemmel and the Maid of Orleans. Marie didn't much care about *them*; but back in the corner there was a little baby with red cheeks, and this was Marie's darling. The tears came to her eyes.

"Ah!" she cried, turning to Nutcracker, "I really will do all I can to help you. But it's very hard."

Nutcracker looked at her so piteously that she determined to sacrifice everything—for she remembered the Mouse-King with all his seven mouths wide open to swallow the poor young fellow; so that night she set down all her sugar figures in front of the cupboard, as she had the candy the night before. She kissed the shepherd, the shepherdess, and the lambs; and at last she brought her best beloved of all, the little red-cheeked baby from its corner, but did put it a little further back than the rest. Farmer Feldkuemmel and the Maid of Orleans had to stand in the front rank.

"This is really getting too bad," said Marie's mother the next morning; "some nasty mouse or other must have made a hole in the glass cupboard, for poor Marie's sugar figures are all eaten and gnawed." Marie really could not restrain her tears. But she was soon able to smile again; for she thought, "What does it matter? Nutcracker is safe."

In the evening Marie's mother was telling her father and Godpapa Drosselmeier about the mischief which some mouse was doing in the children's cupboard, and her father said:

"It's a regular nuisance! What a pity that we can't get rid of it. It's destroying all the poor child's things."

Fritz intervened, and remarked, "The baker downstairs has a fine grey Councillor-of-Legation; I'll go and get hold of him, and he'll soon put a stop to it, and bite the mouse's head off, even if it's Dame Mouserink herself, or her son, the king of the mice."

"Oh, yes!" said his mother, laughing, "and jump up on to the chairs and tables, knock down the cups and glasses, and do ever so much mischief besides."

"No, no!" answered Fritz; "the baker's Councillor-of-Legation's a very clever fellow. I wish I could walk about on the edge of the roof, as he does."

"Don't let us have a nasty cat in the house in the night-time," said Louise, who hated cats.

"Fritz is quite right though," said their mother; "unless we set a trap. Haven't we got such a thing in the house?"

"Godpapa Drosselmeier's the man to get us one," said Fritz; "it was he who invented them, you know." Everybody laughed. And when their mother said they did not possess such a thing, Drosselmeier said he had plenty; and he actually sent a very fine one round that day. When the cook was browning the fat, Marie—with her head full of the marvels of her godpapa's tale—called out to her:

"Ah, take care, Queen! Remember Dame Mouserink and her people." But Fritz drew his sword, and cried, "Let them come if they dare! I'll give an account of them." But everything about the hearth remained quiet and undisturbed. As Drosselmeier was fixing the browned fat on a fine thread, and setting the trap gently down in the glass cupboard, Fritz cried:

"Now, Godpapa Clockmaker, mind that the Mouse-King doesn't play you some trick!"

Ah, how did it fare with Marie that night? Something as cold as ice went tripping about on her arm, and something rough and nasty laid itself on her cheek, and cheeped and squeaked in her ear. The horrible Mouse-King came and sat on her shoulder, foamed a blood-red foam out of all his seven mouths, and chattering and grinding his teeth, he hissed into Marie's ear:

"Hiss, hiss!—keep away—don't go in there—beware of that house—don't you be caught—death to the mouse—hand out your picture books—none of your scornful looks!—Give me your dresses—also your laces—or, if you don't, leave you I won't—Nutcracker I'll bite—drag him out of your sight—his last hour is near—so tremble for fear!—Fee, fa, fo, fum—his last hour is come!—Hee hee, pee pee—squeak—squeak!"

Marie was overwhelmed with anguish and sorrow, and was looking quite pale and upset when her mother said to her next morning:

"This horrid mouse hasn't been caught. But never mind, dear, we'll catch the nasty thing yet, never fear. If the traps won't work, Fritz shall fetch the grey Councillor-of-Legation."

As soon as Marie was alone, she went up to the glass cupboard, and said to Nutcracker, in a voice broken by sobs:

"Ah, my dear, good Mr. Drosselmeier, what can I do for you, poor unfortunate girl that I am! Even if I give that horrid king of the mice all my picture books, and my new dress which the Christ Child gave me at Christmas as well, he's sure to go on asking for more."

Soon I shan't have anything more left, and he'll want to eat *me*! Oh, poor thing that I am! What shall I do? What shall I do?"

As she was thus crying and lamenting, she noticed that a great spot of blood had been left, since the eventful night of the battle, upon Nutcracker's neck. Since she had known that he was really young Mr. Drosselmeier, her godpapa's nephew, she had given up carrying him in her arms, and petting and kissing him; indeed, she felt a delicacy about touching him at all. But now she took him carefully out of his shelf, and began to wipe off this blood spot with her handkerchief. What were her feelings when she found that Nutcracker was growing warmer and warmer in her hand, and beginning to move! She put him back into the cupboard as fast as she could. His mouth began to wobble backwards and forwards, and he began to whisper, with much difficulty:

"Ah, dearest Miss Stahlbaum—most precious of friends! How deeply I am indebted to you for everything—for *everything*! But don't, don't sacrifice any of your picture books or pretty dresses for me. Get me a sword—a sword is what I want. If you get me that, I'll manage the rest—though—he may—"

There Nutcracker's speech died away, and his eyes, which had been expressing the most sympathetic grief, grew staring and lifeless again.

Marie felt no fear; she jumped for joy, rather, now that she knew how to help Nutcracker without further painful sacrifices. But where on earth was she to get hold of a sword for him? She re-solved to take counsel with Fritz; and that evening when their father and mother had gone out, and they two were sitting beside the glass cupboard, she told him what had passed between her and Nutcracker with the king of the mice, and what it was that was required to rescue Nutcracker.

The thing which chiefly exercised Fritz's mind was Marie's statement as to the unexemplary conduct of his red hussars in the great battle. He asked her once more, most seriously, to assure him that it really was the truth; and when she had repeated her state-ment on her word of honour, he advanced to the cupboard and made his hussars a most affecting address. As a punishment for their behaviour, he solemnly took their plumes one by one out of their busbies, and prohibited them from sounding the march of the hussars of the guard for the space of a twelvemonth. When he had performed this duty, he turned to Marie and said:

"As far as the sword is concerned, I have it in my power to assist Nutcracker. I placed an old Colonel of Cuirassiers on retirement on a pension yesterday, so that he has no further occasion for his sabre, which is sharp."

This Colonel was settled, on his pension, in the back corner of the third shelf. He was fetched out and his sabre—still a bright and handsome silver weapon—taken off, and girt about Nutcracker.

Next night Marie could not close an eye for anxiety. About midnight she fancied she heard a strange stirring and noise in the sitting-room—a rustling and a clanging—and suddenly there came a shrill "Queak!"

"The king of the mice! The king of the mice!" she cried, and jumped out of bed, all terror. Everything was silent; but soon there came a gentle tapping at the door of her room, and a soft voice made itself heard, saying:

"Please open your door, dearest Miss Stahlbaum! Don't be in the least degree alarmed; good, happy news!"

It was Drosselmeier's voice—young Drosselmeier's, I mean. She threw on her dressing-gown and opened the door as quickly as possible. There stood Nutcracker, with his sword all covered with blood in his right hand, and a little wax taper in his left. When he saw Marie, he knelt down on one knee, and said:

"It was you, and you only, dearest lady, who inspired me with knightly valour, and steeled me with strength to do battle with the insolent caitiff who dared to insult you. The treacherous king of the mice lies vanquished and writhing in his gore! Deign, lady, to accept these tokens of victory from the hand of him who is, till death, your true and faithful knight."

With this Nutcracker took from his left arm the seven crowns of the Mouse-King, which he had ranged upon it, and handed them to Marie, who received them with the keenest pleasure. Nutcracker rose and continued as follows:

"Oh! my best beloved Miss Stahlbaum, if you would only take the trouble to follow me for a few steps, what glorious and beautiful things I could show you, at this supreme moment when I have overcome my hereditary foe! Do—do come with me, dearest lady!"

TOYLAND

I feel quite convinced, children, that none of you would have hesitated for a moment to go with good, kind Nutcracker, who had always shown himself to be such a charming person, and Marie was all the more disposed to do as he asked her, because she knew what her just claims on his gratitude were, and was sure that he would keep his word, and show her all sorts of beautiful things. So she said:

"I will go with you, dear Mr. Drosselmeier; but it mustn't be very far, and it won't do to be very long, because, you know, I haven't had any sleep yet."

"Then we will go by the shortest route," said Nutcracker, "although it is, perhaps, rather the most difficult."

He went on in front, followed by Marie, till he stopped before the big old wardrobe. Marie was surprised to see that though it was generally shut, the doors of it were now wide open, so that she could see her father's travelling cloak of fox-fur hanging in the front. Nutcracker clambered deftly up this cloak, by the edgings and trimmings of it, so as to get hold of the big tassel which was fastened at the back of it by a thick cord. He gave this tassel a tug, and a pretty little ladder of cedarwood let itself quickly down through one of the arm-holes of the cloak.

"Now, Miss Stahlbaum, step up that ladder, if you will be so kind," said Nutcracker. Marie did so. But as soon as she had got up through the armhole, and began to look out at the neck, a dazzling light came streaming on her, and she found herself standing on a lovely, sweet-scented meadow, from which millions of sparks were streaming upward, like the glitter of beautiful gems.

"This is Candy Mead, where we are now," said Nutcracker. "But we'll go in at that gate there."

Marie looked up and saw a beautiful gateway on the meadow, only a few steps off. It seemed to be made of white, brown, and raisin-coloured marble; but when she came close to it she saw it was all of baked sugar-almonds and raisins, which—as Nutcracker said when they were going through it—was the reason it was called "Almond and Raisin Gate." There was a gallery running round the upper part of it, apparently made of barley sugar, and in this gallery six monkeys, dressed in red doublets, were playing on brass instruments in the most delightful manner ever heard. It was all that Marie could do to notice that she was walking along upon a beautiful variegated marble pavement, which, however, was really a mosaic of lozenges of all colours. Presently the sweetest of odours came breathing round her, streaming from a beautiful little wood on both sides of the way. There was such a glittering and sparkling among the dark foliage that one could see all the gold and silver fruits hanging on the many-tinted stems, and these stems and branches were all ornamented and dressed up in ribbons and bunches of flowers like brides and bridegrooms and festive wedding guests. And as the orange perfume came wafted, as if on the wings of gentle zephyrs, there was a soughing among the leaves and branches, and all the gold-leaf and tinsel rustled and tinkled like beautiful music, to which the sparkling lights could not help dancing.

"Oh, how charming this is!" cried Marie, enraptured.

"This is Christmas Wood, dearest Miss Stahlbaum," said Nutcracker.

"Ah!" said Marie, "if I could only stay here for a little! Oh, it is so lovely!"

Nutcracker clapped his little hands, and immediately there appeared a number of little shepherds and shepherdesses, and hunters and huntresses, so white and delicate that you would have thought they were made of pure sugar, whom Marie had not noticed before, although they had been walking about in the wood. They brought a beautiful gold reclining chair, laid a white satin cushion in it, and politely invited Marie to take a seat. As soon as she did so, the shepherds and shepherdesses danced a pretty ballet, to which the hunters and huntresses played music on their horns, and then they all disappeared among the thickets.

"I must really apologize for the poor style in which this dance was executed, dearest Miss Stahlbaum," said Nutcracker. "These people all belong to our Wire Ballet Troupe, and can only do the same thing over and over again. Had we not better go on a little farther?"

"Oh, I'm sure it was all most delightful, and I enjoyed it immensely!" said Marie, as she stood up and followed Nutcracker, who was leading the way. They went by the side of a gently rippling brook, which seemed to be what was giving out all the perfume which filled the wood.

"This is Orange Brook," said Nutcracker; "but, except for its sweet scent, it is nowhere nearly as fine a water as the River Lemonade, a beautiful broad stream, which falls—as this one does also—into the Almond-milk Sea."

And, indeed, Marie soon heard a louder plashing and rushing, and came in sight of the River Lemonade, which went rolling along in swelling waves of a yellowish colour, between banks covered with a herbage and underbrush which shone like green carbuncles. A remarkable freshness and coolness, strengthening heart and breast, exhaled from this fine river. Not far from it a dark yellow stream crept sluggishly along, giving out a most delicious odour; and on its banks sat numbers of pretty children, angling for little fat fishes, which they ate as soon as they caught them. These fish were very much like filberts, Marie saw when she came closer. A short distance farther, on the banks of this stream, stood a nice little village. The houses of this village, and the church, the parsonage, the barns, and so forth, were all dark brown with gilt roofs, and many of the walls looked as if they were plastered over with lemon peel and shelled almonds.

"That is Gingerthorpe on the Honey River," said Nutcracker. "It is famed for the good looks of its inhabitants; but they are very short-tempered people, because they suffer so much from toothache. So we won't go there at present."

At this moment Marie caught sight of a little town where the houses were all sorts of colours and quite transparent, exceedingly pretty to look at. Nutcracker went on towards this town, and Marie heard a noise of bustle and merriment, and saw some thousands of nice little folks unloading a number of wagons which were drawn up in the market place. What they were unloading from the wagons looked like packages of coloured paper and tablets of chocolate.

"This is Bonbonville," Nutcracker said. "An embassy has just arrived from Paperland and the King of Chocolate. These poor Bonbonville people have been vexatiously threatened lately by the Fly-Admiral's forces, so they are covering their houses over with their presents from Paperland, and constructing fortifications with the fine pieces of workmanship which the Chocolate-King has sent them. But oh! dearest Miss Stahlbaum, we are not going to restrict ourselves to seeing the small towns and villages of this country. Let us be off to the metropolis."

He stepped quickly onwards, and Marie followed him, all expectation. Soon a beautiful rosy vapour began to rise, suffusing everything with a soft splendour. She saw that this was reflected from rose-red, shining water, which went plashing and rushing away in front of them in wavelets of roseate silver. And on this delightful water, which kept broadening and broadening out wider and wider, like a great lake, the loveliest swans were floating, white as silver, with collars of gold. And, as if vying with each other, they were singing the most beautiful songs, at which little fish, glittering like diamonds, danced up and down in the rosy ripples.

"Oh!" cried Marie, in the greatest delight, "this must be the lake which Godpapa Drosselmeier was once going to make for me, and I am the girl who is to play with the swans."

Nutcracker gave a sneering sort of laugh, such as she had never seen in him before, and said:

"My uncle could never make a thing of this kind. You would be much more likely to do it yourself. But don't let us bother about that. Rather let us go sailing over the water, Lake Rosa here, to the metropolis."

THE METROPOLIS

Nutcracker clapped his little hands again, and the waves of Lake Rosa began to sound louder and to splash higher, and Marie became aware of a sort of car approaching from the distance, made wholly of glittering precious stones of every colour, and drawn by two dolphins with scales of gold. Twelve of the dearest little Negro boys, with headdresses and doublets made of hummingbirds' feathers woven together, jumped to land, and carried first Marie and then Nutcracker, gently gliding above the water, into the car, which immediately began to move along over the lake of its own accord. Ah! how beautiful it was when Marie went over the waters in the shell-shaped car, with the rose-perfume breathing around her, and the rosy waves splashing. The two golden-scaled dolphins lifted their nostrils, and sent streams of crystal high in the air; and as these fell down in glittering, sparkling rainbows, there was a sound as of two delicate, silvery voices, singing, "Who comes over the rosy sea?—Fairy is she. Bim-bim—fishes; sim-sim—swans; sfa-sfa—golden birds; tratrah, rosy waves, wake you, and sing, sparkle and ring, sprinkle and kling—this is the fairy we languish to see—coming at last to us over the sea. Rosy waves dash—bright dolphins play—merrily, merrily on!"

But the twelve little boys at the back of the car seemed to take some umbrage at this song of the water jets; for they shook the sun shades they were holding so that the palm leaves they were made of clattered and rattled together; and as they shook them they stamped an odd sort of rhythm with their feet, and sang:

"Klapp and klipp, and klipp and klapp, and up and down."

"These are merry, amusing fellows," said Nutcracker, a little put out, "but they'll set the whole lake into a state of regular mutiny on my hands!" And in fact there did begin a confused and confusing noise of strange voices which seemed to be floating both in the water and in the air. However, Marie paid no attention to it, but went on looking into the perfumed rosy waves, from each of which a pretty girl's face smiled back to her.

"Oh! look at Princess Pirlipat," she cried, clapping her hands with gladness, "smiling at me so charmingly down there! Do look at her, Mr. Drosselmeier."

But Nutcracker sighed, almost sorrowfully, and said:

"That is not Princess Pirlipat, dearest Miss Stahlbaum, it is only yourself; always your own lovely face smiling up from the rosy waves." At this Marie drew her head quickly back, closed her eyes as tightly as she could, and was terribly ashamed. But just then the twelve Negroes lifted her out of the car and set her on shore. She found herself in a small thicket or grove, almost more beautiful even than Christmas Wood, everything glittered and sparkled so in it. And the fruit on the trees was extraordinarily wonderful and beautiful, and not only of very curious colours, but with the most delicious perfume.

"Ah!" said Nutcracker, "here we are in Comfit Grove, and yonder lies the metropolis."

How shall I set about describing all the wonderful and beautiful sights which Marie now saw, or give any idea of the splendour and magnificence of the city which lay stretched out before her on a flowery plain? Not only did the walls and towers of it shine in the brightest and most gorgeous colours, but the shapes and appearance of the buildings were like nothing to be seen on earth. Instead of roofs the houses had on beautiful twining crowns, and the towers were garlanded with beautiful leaf-work, sculptured and carved into exquisite, intricate designs. As they passed in at the gateway, which looked as if it was made entirely of macaroons and sugared fruits, silver soldiers presented arms, and a little man in a brocade dressing gown threw himself upon Nutcracker's neck, crying:

"Welcome, dearest prince! welcome to Sweetmeatburgh!"

Marie wondered not a little to see such a very grand personage recognize young Mr. Drosselmeier as a prince. But she heard such a number of small delicate voices making such a loud clamouring and talking, and such a laughing and chattering going on, and such a singing and playing, that she couldn't give her attention to anything else, but asked Drosselmeier what was the meaning of it all.

"Oh, it is nothing out of the common, dearest Miss Stahlbaum," he answered. "Sweetmeatburgh is a large, populous city, full of mirth and entertainment. This is only the usual thing that is always going on here every day. Please come on a little farther."

After a few paces more they were in the great market place, which presented the most magnificent appearance. All the houses which were round it were of filagreed sugarwork, with galleries towering above galleries; and in the centre stood a lofty cake covered with sugar, by way of obelisk, with fountains round it spouting orgeat, lemonade, and other delicious beverages into the air. The runnels at the sides of the footways were full of creams, which you might have ladled up with a spoon if you had chosen. But prettier than all this were the delightful little people who were crowding about everywhere by the thousand, shouting, laughing, playing, and singing, in short, producing all that jubilant uproar which Marie had heard from the distance. There were beautifully dressed ladies and gentlemen, Greeks and Armenians, Tyrolese and Jews, officers and soldiers, clergymen, shepherds, jack-puddings, in short, people of every conceivable kind to be found in the world.

The tumult grew greater towards one of the corners; the people streamed asunder. For the Great Mogul happened to be passing along there in his palanquin, attended by three-and-ninety grandees of the realm, and seven hundred slaves. But it chanced that the Fishermen's Guild, about five hundred strong, were keeping a festival at the opposite corner of the place; and it was rather an unfortunate coincidence that the Grand Turk took it in his head just at this particular moment to go out for a ride, and crossed the square with three thousand Janissaries. And, as if this were not enough, the grand procession of the Interrupted Sacrifice came along at the same time, marching up towards the obelisk with a full orchestra playing, and the chorus singing: "Hail! all hail to the glorious sun!"

So there was a thronging and a shoving, a driving and a squeaking; and soon lamentations arose, and cries of pain, for one of the fishermen had knocked a Brahmin's head off in the throng, and the Great Mogul had been very nearly run down by a jack-pudding. The din grew wilder and wilder. People were beginning to shove one another, and even to come to fisticuffs; when the man in the brocade dressing gown who had welcomed Nutcracker as prince at the gate, clambered up to the top of the obelisk, and, after a very clear-tinkling bell had rung thrice, shouted very loudly three times: "Pastrycook! pastrycook! pastrycook!"

Instantly the tumult subsided. Everybody tried to save himself as quickly as he could; and after the entangled processions had been disentangled, the dirt properly brushed off the Great Mogul, and the Brahmin's head stuck on again all right, the merry noise went on just the same as before.

"Tell me why that gentleman called out 'Pastrycook,' Mr. Drosselmeier, please," said Marie.

"Ah! dearest Miss Stahlbaum," said Nutcracker, "in this place 'Pastrycook' means a certain unknown and very terrible Power, which it is believed can do with people just what it chooses. It represents the Fate or Destiny which rules these happy little people, and they stand in such awe and terror of it that the mere mention of its name quells the wildest tumult in a moment, as the burgomaster has just shown. Nobody thinks further of earthly matters, cuffs in the ribs, broken heads, or the like. Every one retires within himself, and says: 'What is man? and what his ultimate destiny?'"

Marie could not forbear a cry of admiration and utmost astonishment as she now found herself suddenly before a castle shining in roseate radiance, with a hundred beautiful towers. Here and there at intervals upon its walls were rich bouquets of violets, narcissuses, tulips, carnations, whose dark, glowing colours heightened the dazzling whiteness, inclining to rose-colour, of the walls. The great dome of the central building, as well as the pyramidal roofs of the towers, were set all over with thousands of sparkling gold and silver stars.

"Aha!" said Nutcracker, "here we are at Marzipan Castle at last!"

Marie was sunk and absorbed in contemplation of this magic palace. But the fact did not escape her that the roof was wanting to one of the principal towers, and that little men up upon a scaffold made of sticks of cinnamon were busy putting it on again. But before she had had time to ask Nutcracker about this, he said:

"This beautiful castle a short time ago was threatened with tremendous havoc, if not with total destruction. Sweet-tooth the giant happened to be passing by, and he bit off the top of that tower there, and was beginning to gnaw at the great dome. But the Sweetmeatburgh people brought him a whole quarter of the town by way of tribute, and a considerable slice of Comfit Grove into the bargain. This stopped his mouth, and he went on his way."

At this moment, soft, beautiful music was heard, and out came twelve little pages with lighted clove-sticks, which they held in their little hands by way of torches. Each of their heads was a pearl, their bodies were emeralds and rubies, and their feet were beautifully worked pure gold. After them came four ladies about the size of Marie's Miss Clara, but so gloriously and brilliantly attired that Marie saw in a moment that they could be nothing but princesses of the blood royal. They embraced Nutcracker most tenderly, and shed tears of gladness, saying, "Oh, dearest prince! beloved brother!"

Nutcracker seemed deeply affected. He wiped away his tears, which flowed thick and fast, and then he took Marie by the hand and said with much pathos and solemnity:

"This is Miss Marie Stahlbaum, the daughter of a most worthy medical man and the preserver of my life. Had she not thrown her slipper just in the nick of time—had she not procured me the pensioned Colonel's sword—I should have been lying in my cold grave at this moment, bitten to death by the accursed king of the mice. I ask you to tell me candidly, can Princess Pirlipat, princess though she is, compare for a moment with Miss Stahlbaum here in beauty, in goodness, in virtues of every kind? My answer is, emphatically 'No.'"

All the ladies cried "No;" and they fell upon Marie's neck with sobs and tears, and cried: "Ah! noble preserver of our beloved royal brother! Excellent Miss Stahlbaum!"

They now conducted Marie and Nutcracker into the castle, to a hall whose walls were composed of sparkling crystal. But what delighted Marie most of all was the furniture. There were the most darling little chairs, bureaus, writing-tables, and so forth, standing about everywhere, all made of cedar or Brazil-wood, covered with golden flowers. The princesses made Marie and Nutcracker sit down, and said that they would themselves prepare a banquet. So they went and brought quantities of little cups and dishes of the finest Japanese porcelain, and spoons, knives and forks, graters and stew pans, and other kitchen utensils of gold and silver. Then they fetched the most delightful fruits and sugar things—such as Marie had never seen the like of—and began to squeeze the fruit in the daintiest way with their little hands, and to grate the spices and rub down the sugar-almonds; in short, they set to work so skillfully that Marie could see very well how accomplished they were in kitchen matters, and what a magnificent banquet there was going to be. Knowing her own skill in this line, she wished in her secret heart, that she might be allowed to go and help the princesses and have a finger in all these pies herself. And the prettiest of Nutcracker's sisters, just as if she had read the wishes of Marie's heart, handed her a little gold mortar, saying:

"Sweet friend, dear preserver of my brother, would you mind pounding a little of this sugar-candy?"

Now as Marie went on pounding in the mortar with good will and the utmost enjoyment—and the sound of it was like a lovely song—Nutcracker began to relate with much minuteness all that had happened on the occasion of the terrible engagement between his forces and the army of the king of the mice; how he had had the worst of it on account of the bad behaviour of his troops; how the horrible mouse king had all but bitten him to death, so that Marie had had to sacrifice a number of his subjects who were in her service, etc., etc.

During all this it seemed to Marie as if what Nutcracker was saying—and even the sound of her own mortar—kept growing more and more indistinct, and going farther and farther away.   Presently she saw a silver mistiness rising up all about, like clouds, in which the princesses, the pages, Nutcracker, and she herself were floating. And a curious singing and a buzzing and humming began, which seemed to die away in the distance; and then she seemed to be going up—up—up, as if on waves constantly rising and swelling higher and higher, higher and higher, higher and higher.

CONCLUSION

And then came a "prr-poof," and Marie fell down from some inconceivable height.

That was a crash and a tumble!

However, she opened her eyes, and, lo and behold, there she was in her own bed! It was broad daylight, and her mother was standing at her bedside, saying:

"Well, what a sleep you have had! Breakfast has been ready for ever so long."

Of course, dear audience, you see how it was. Marie, confounded and amazed by all the wonderful things she had seen, had at last fallen asleep in Marzipan Castle, and the Negroes or the pages, or perhaps the princesses themselves, had carried her home and put her to bed.

"Oh, mother darling," said Marie, "what a number of places young Mr. Drosselmeier has taken me to in the night, and what beautiful things I have seen!"   And she gave very much the same faithful account of it all as I have given to you.

Her mother listened, looking at her with astonishment, and when she had finished, said:

"You have had a long, beautiful dream, Marie; but now you must put it all out of your head."

Marie firmly maintained that she had not been dreaming at all; so her mother took her to the glass cupboard, lifted out Nutcracker from his usual position on the third shelf, and said:

"You silly girl, how can you believe that this wooden figure can have life and motion?"

"Ah, mother," answered Marie, "I know perfectly well that Nutcracker is young Mr. Drosselmeier from Nuremberg, Godpapa Drosselmeier's nephew."

Her father and mother both burst out into laughter.

"It's all very well your laughing at poor Nutcracker, father," cried Marie, almost weeping, "but he spoke very highly of *you*; for when we arrived at Marzipan Castle, and he was introducing me to his sisters, the princesses, he said you were a most worthy medical man."

The laughter grew louder, and Louise and even Fritz joined in it. Marie ran into the next room, took the Mouse-King's seven crowns from her little box, and handed them to her mother, saying, "Look there, then, dear mother; those are the Mouse-King's seven crowns which young Mr. Drosselmeier gave me last night as a proof that he had got the victory."

Her mother gazed in amazement at the little crowns, which were made of some very brilliant, wholly unknown metal, and worked more beautifully than any human hands could have worked them. Dr. Stahlbaum could not cease looking at them with admiration and astonishment either, and both the father and the mother enjoined Marie most earnestly to tell them where she really had got them from. But she could only repeat what she had said before; and when her father scolded her and accused her of untruthfulness, she began to cry bitterly, and said, "Oh, dear me; what can I tell you except the truth!"

At this moment the door opened, and Godpapa Drosselmeier came in, crying, "Hullo! hullo! what's all this? My little Marie crying? What's all this? what's all this?"

Dr. Stahlbaum told him all about it, and showed him the crowns. As soon as he had looked at them, however, he cried out:

"Stuff and nonsense! stuff and nonsense! These are the crowns I used to wear on my watch-chain. I gave them as a present to Marie on her second birthday. Do you mean to tell me you don't remember?"

None of them *did* remember anything of the kind. But Marie, seeing that her father and mother's faces were clear of clouds again, ran up to her godpapa, crying:

"You know all about the affair, Godpapa Drosselmeier; tell it to them. Let them know from your own lips that my Nutcracker is your nephew, young Mr. Drosselmeier from Nuremberg, and that it was he who gave me the crowns." But Drosselmeier made a very angry face, and muttered, "Stupid stuff and nonsense!" upon which Marie's father took her in front of him, and said with much earnestness:

"Now look here, Marie; let there be an end of all this foolish trash and absurd nonsense for once and for all; I'm not going to allow any more of it; and if ever I hear you say again that that idiotic, misshapen Nutcracker is your godpapa's nephew, I shall throw, not only Nutcracker, but all your other playthings—Miss Clara not excepted—out of the window."

Of course poor Marie dared not utter another word concerning that which her whole mind was full of, for you may well suppose that it was impossible for anyone who had seen all that she had seen to forget it. And I regret to say that even Fritz himself at once turned his back on his sister whenever she wanted to talk to him about the wondrous realm in which she had been so happy. Indeed, he is said to have frequently murmured, "Stupid goose!" between his teeth, though I can scarcely think this compatible with his proved kindness of heart. This much, however, is matter of certainty, that as he no longer believed what his sister said, he now at a public parade formally recanted what he had said to his red hussars, and in the place of the plumes he had deprived them of, gave them much taller and finer ones of goose quills and allowed them to sound the march of the hussars of the guard as before.

Marie did not dare to say anything more of her adventures. But the memories of that fairy realm haunted her with a sweet intoxication, and the music of that delightful, happy country still rang sweetly in her ears. Whenever she allowed her thoughts to dwell on all those glories, she saw them again, and so it came about that, instead of playing as she used to, she sat quiet and meditative, absorbed within herself. Everybody found fault with her for being such a little dreamer.

It chanced one day that Godpapa Drosselmeier was repairing one of the clocks in the house, and Marie was sitting beside the glass cupboard, sunk in her dreams and gazing at Nutcracker. All at once she said, as if involuntarily:

"Ah, dear Mr. Drosselmeier, if you really were alive, *I* shouldn't be like Princess Pirlipat and despise you because you had had to give up being a nice handsome gentleman for my sake!"

"Stupid stuff and nonsense!" cried Godpapa Drosselmeier.

But, as he spoke, there came such a tremendous bang and shock that Marie fell from her chair insensible.

When she came back to her senses her mother was busied about her and said, "How could you go and tumble off your chair in that way, a big girl like you? Here is Godpapa Drosselmeier's nephew come from Nuremberg. See how good you can be."

Marie looked up. Her godpapa had on his yellow coat and his glass wig, and was smiling in the highest good humour. By the hand he was holding a very small but very handsome young gentleman. His little face was red and white; he had on a beautiful red coat trimmed with gold lace, white silk stockings and shoes, with a lovely bouquet of flowers in his shirt frill. He was beautifully frizzed and powdered, and had a magnificent queue hanging down his back. The little sword at his side seemed to be made entirely of jewels, it sparkled and shone so, and the little hat under his arm was woven of flocks of silk. He gave proof of the fineness of his manners in that he had brought for Marie a quantity of the most delightful toys—above all, the very same figures as those which the Mouse-King had eaten up—as well as a beautiful sabre for Fritz. He cracked nuts at table for the whole party; the very hardest did not withstand him. He placed them in his mouth with his left hand, tugged at his pigtail with his right, and crack! they fell in pieces.

Marie grew red as a rose at the sight of this charming young gentleman; and she grew redder still when after dinner young Drosselmeier asked her to go with him to the glass cupboard in the sitting-room.

"Play nicely together, children," said Godpapa Drosselmeier; "now that my clocks are all nicely in order, I can have no possible objection."

But as soon as young Drosselmeier was alone with Marie, he went down on one knee, and spoke as follows:

"Ah! my most dearly beloved Miss Stahlbaum! see here at your feet the fortunate Drosselmeier, whose life you saved here on this very spot. You were kind enough to say, plainly and unmistakably, in so many words, that *you* would not have despised me, as Princess Pirlipat did, if I had been turned ugly for your sake. Immediately I ceased to be a contemptible Nutcracker, and resumed my former not altogether ill-looking person and form. Ah! most exquisite lady! bless me with your precious hand; share with me my crown and kingdom, and reign with me in Marzipan Castle, for there I am now king."

Marie raised him, and said gently, "Dear Mr. Drosselmeier, you are a kind, nice gentleman; and as you reign over a delightful country of charming, funny, pretty people, I accept your hand."

So then they were formally betrothed; and when a year and a day had come and gone, they say he came and fetched her away in a golden coach, drawn by silver horses. At the marriage there danced two-and-twenty thousand of the most beautiful dolls and other figures, all glittering in pearls and diamonds; and Marie is to this day the queen of a realm where all kinds of sparkling Christmas Woods, and transparent Marzipan Castles—in short, the most wonderful and beautiful things of every kind—are to be seen—by those who have the eyes to see them.

So this is the end of the tale of Nutcracker and the King of the Mice.

THE SAND-MAN

NATHANAEL TO LOTHAIR

I know you are all very uneasy because I have not written for such a long, long time. Mother, to be sure, is angry, and Clara, I dare say, believes I am living here in riot and revelry, and quite forgetting my sweet angel, whose image is so deeply engraved upon my heart and mind. But that is not so; daily and hourly I think of you all, and my lovely Clara's form comes to gladden me in my dreams, and smiles upon me with her bright eyes, as graciously as she used to do in the days when I used to associate daily with you.

Oh! how could I write to you in the distracted state of mind in which I have been, and which, until now, has quite bewildered me! A terrible thing has happened to me. Dark forebodings of some awful fate threatening me are spreading themselves out over my head like black clouds, impenetrable to every friendly ray of sunlight. I must now tell you what has taken place; I must, that I see well enough, but only to think of it makes the wild laughter burst from my lips. Oh! my dear, dear Lothair, what shall I say to make you feel, if only in an inadequate way, that what happened to me a few days ago could thus really exercise such a hostile and disturbing influence upon my life? I wish you were here to see for yourself! But now you will, I suppose, take me for a superstitious ghost-seer. In a word, the terrible thing which I have experienced, the fatal effect of which I in vain exert every effort to shake off, is simply that some days ago, namely, on the thirtieth of October, at twelve o'clock at noon, a peddler of weather glasses and thermometers came into my room and wanted to sell me one of his wares. I bought nothing, and threatened to kick him downstairs, whereupon he went away of his own accord.

You will conclude that it can only be very peculiar relations— relations intimately intertwined with my life—that can give significance to this event, and that it must be the peddler himself who had such a very unpleasant effect upon me. And so it really is. I will summon up all my faculties in order to narrate to you calmly and patiently enough about the early days of my youth to put matters before you in such a way that your keen sharp intellect can grasp everything clearly and distinctly, in bright and living pictures.

Just as I am beginning, I hear you laugh and Clara say, "What's all this childish nonsense about!" Well, laugh at me, laugh heartily at me, pray do. But, good God! my hair is standing on end, and I seem to be entreating you to laugh at me in the same sort of frantic despair in which Franz Moor [in Schiller's *Die Räuber*] entreated Daniel to laugh him to scorn. But to my story.

Except at dinner we, i.e., I and my brothers and sisters, saw little of our father all day long. His business no doubt took up most of his time. After our evening meal, which usually was served at seven o'clock, we all went, mother with us, into father's room, and took our places around a round table. My father smoked his pipe, drinking a large glass of beer at the same time. Often he told us many wonderful stories, and got so excited over them that his pipe would go out; I used then to light it for him with a spill, and this formed my chief amusement. Often, again, he would give us picture books to look at, while he sat silent and motionless in his easy chair, puffing out such dense clouds of smoke that we were all as it were enveloped in mist.

On such evenings mother was very sad; and as soon as it struck nine she said, "Come, children! off to bed! Come! The Sand-man is come, I see." And I always did seem to hear something trampling upstairs with slow heavy steps; that must be the Sand-man. Once in particular I was very much frightened at this dull trampling and knocking; as mother was leading us out of the room I asked her, "O mamma! who is this nasty Sand-man who always sends us away from papa? What does he look like?"

"There is no Sand-man, my dear," mother answered; "when I say the Sand-man is come, I only mean that you are sleepy and can't keep your eyes open, as if somebody had put sand in them." This answer of mother's did not satisfy me; nay, in my childish mind the thought clearly unfolded itself that mother denied there was a Sand-man only to prevent us from being afraid,—why, I always heard him come upstairs.

Full of curiosity to learn something more about this Sand-man and what he had to do with us children, I finally asked the old woman who acted as my youngest sister's nurse, what sort of man he was—the Sand-man?

"Why, 'thanael, darling, don't you know?" she replied. "Oh! he's a wicked man, who comes to little children when they won't go to bed and throws handfuls of sand in their eyes, so that they jump out of their heads all bloody; and he puts them into a bag and takes them to the half-moon as food for his little ones; and they sit there in the nest and have hooked beaks like owls, and they pick naughty little boys' and girls' eyes out with them."

After this I formed in my own mind a horrible picture of the cruel Sand-man. When anything came blundering upstairs at night I trembled with fear and dismay; and all that my mother could get out of me were the stammered words "The Sand-man! the Sand-man!" whilst the tears coursed down my cheeks. Then I ran into my bedroom, and the whole night through tormented myself with the terrible apparition of the Sand-man. I was quite old enough to perceive that the old woman's tale about the Sand-man and his little ones' nest in the half-moon couldn't be altogether true; nevertheless the Sand-man continued to be for me a fearful incubus, and I was always seized with terror—my blood always ran cold, not only when I heard anybody come up the stairs, but when I heard anybody noisily open the door to my father's room and go in. Often the Sand-man stayed away for a long time altogether; then he would come several times in close succession.

This went on for years, without my being able to accustom myself to this fearful apparition, without the image of the horrible Sand-man growing any fainter in my imagination. His intercourse with my father began to occupy my fancy ever more and more; I was restrained from asking my father about him by an unconquerable shyness; but as the years went on the desire waxed stronger and stronger within me to fathom the mystery myself and to see the fabulous Sand-man. He had been the means of disclosing to me the path of the wonderful and the adventurous, which so easily find lodgment in the mind of the child. I liked nothing better than to hear or read horrible stories of goblins, witches, dwarfs, and so on; but always at the head of them all stood the Sand-man, whose picture I scribbled in the most extraordinary and repulsive forms with both chalk and coal everywhere, on the tables, and cupboard doors, and walls.

When I was ten years old my mother removed me from the nursery into a little chamber off the corridor not far from my father's room. We still had to withdraw hastily whenever, on the stroke of nine, the mysterious unknown was heard in the house. As I lay in my little chamber I could hear him go into father's room, and soon afterwards I fancied there was a fine and peculiar smelling steam spreading itself through the house.

As my curiosity waxed stronger, my resolve to make the Sand-man's acquaintance somehow or other took deeper root. Often when my mother had gone past, I slipped quickly out of my room into the corridor, but I could never see anything, for always before I could reach the place where I could get sight of him, the Sand-man was well inside the door. At last, unable to resist the impulse any longer, I determined to conceal myself in father's room and wait there for the Sand-man.

One evening I perceived from my father's silence and mother's sadness that the Sand-man would come; accordingly, pleading that I was excessively tired, I left the room before nine o'clock and concealed myself in a hiding place close beside the door. The street door creaked, and slow, heavy, echoing steps crossed the passage towards the stairs. Mother hurried past me with my brothers and sisters. Softly—softly—I opened the door to father's room. He sat as usual, silent and motionless, with his back towards the door; he did not hear me; and in a moment I was in and behind a curtain drawn before my father's open wardrobe, which stood just inside the room. Nearer and nearer and nearer came the echoing footsteps. There was a strange coughing and shuffling and mumbling outside. My heart beat with expectation and fear. A quick step now close, close beside the door, a noisy rattle of the handle, and the door flies open with a bang. Recovering my courage with an effort, I take a cautious peep out. In the middle of the room in front of my father stands the Sand-man, the bright light of the lamp falling full upon his face. The Sand-man, the terrible Sand-man, is the old lawyer Coppelius who often comes to dine with us.

But the most hideous figure could not have awakened greater trepidation in my heart than this Coppelius did. Picture to yourself a large broad-shouldered man, with an immensely big head, a face the colour of yellow ochre, gray bushy eyebrows, from beneath which two piercing, greenish, cat-like eyes glittered, and a prominent Roman nose hanging over his upper lip. His distorted mouth was often screwed up into a malicious sneer; then two dark-red spots appeared on his cheeks, and a strange hissing noise proceeded from between his tightly clenched teeth. He always wore an ash-gray coat of an old-fashioned cut, a waistcoat of the same, and nether extremities to match, but black stockings and buckles set with stones on his shoes. His little wig scarcely extended beyond the

Nathanael eavesdrops on Coppelius

crown of his head, his hair was curled round high up above his big red ears, and plastered to his temples with cosmetic, and a broad closed hair-bag stood out prominently from his neck, so that you could see the silver buckle that fastened his folded neck-cloth. Altogether he was a most disagreeable and horribly ugly figure; but what we children detested most of all was his big coarse hairy hands; we could never fancy anything that he had once touched. This he had noticed; and so, whenever our good mother quietly placed a piece of cake or sweet fruit on our plates, he delighted to touch it under some pretext or other, until the tears stood in our eyes, and from disgust and loathing we lost the enjoyment of the tit-bit that was intended to please us. And he did just the same thing when father gave us a glass of sweet wine on holidays. Then he would quickly pass his hand over it, or even sometimes raise the glass to his blue lips, and he laughed quite sardonically when all we dared do was to express our vexation in stifled sobs. He habitually called us the "little brutes"; and when he was present we might not utter a sound; and we cursed the ugly spiteful man who deliberately and intentionally spoilt all our little pleasures.

Mother seemed to dislike this hateful Coppelius as much as we did; for as soon as he appeared, her cheerfulness and bright and natural manner were transformed into sad, gloomy seriousness. Father treated him as if he were a being of some higher race, whose ill manners were to be tolerated, while no efforts ought to be spared to keep him in good humour. Coppelius had only to give a slight hint, and his favourite dishes were cooked for him and rare wine uncorked.

As soon as I saw this Coppelius, therefore, the fearful and hideous thought arose in my mind that he, and he alone, must be the Sand-man; but I no longer conceived of the Sand-man as the bugbear in the old nurse's fable, who fetched children's eyes and took them to the half-moon as food for his little ones—no! but as an ugly spectre-like fiend bringing trouble and misery and ruin, both temporal and everlasting, everywhere he appeared.

I was spellbound on the spot. At the risk of being discovered, and as I well enough knew, of being severely punished, I remained as I was, with my head thrust through the curtains listening. My father received Coppelius in a ceremonious manner.

"Come, to work!" cried the latter, in a hoarse snarling voice, throwing off his coat. Gloomily and silently my father took off his dressing gown, and both put on long black smock-frocks. Where they took them from I forgot to notice.' Father opened the folding doors of a cupboard in the wall; but I saw that what I had so long taken to be a cupboard was really a dark recess, in which was a little hearth. Coppelius approached it, and a blue flame crackled upwards from it. Round about were all kinds of strange utensils.

Good God! as my father bent down over the fire how different he looked! His gentle features seemed to be drawn up by some dreadful convulsive pain into an ugly, repulsive Satanic mask. He looked like Coppelius. Coppelius plied the red-hot tongs and drew bright glowing masses out of the thick smoke and began assiduously to hammer them. I fancied that there were men's faces visible round about, but without eyes, having ghastly deep black holes where the eyes should have been.

"Eyes here! Eyes here!" cried Coppelius, in a hollow sepulchral voice. My blood ran cold with horror; I screamed and tumbled out of my hiding place onto the floor. Coppelius immediately seized me. "You little brute! You little brute!" he bleated, grinding his teeth. Then, snatching me up, he threw me on the hearth, so that the flames began to singe my hair. "Now we've got eyes—eyes—a beautiful pair of children's eyes," he whispered and, thrusting his hands into the flames he took out some red-hot grains and was about to throw them into my eyes.

Then my father clasped his hands and entreated him, saying, "Master, master, let my Nathanael keep his eyes—oh! let him keep them." Coppelius laughed shrilly and replied, "Well then, the boy may keep his eyes and whine and pule his way through the world; but we will at any rate examine the mechanism of the hand and the foot." And thereupon he roughly laid hold of me, so that my joints cracked, and twisted my hands and my feet, pulling them now this way, and now that, "That's not quite right altogether! It's better as it was!—the old fellow knew what he was about." Thus lisped and hissed Coppelius; but all around me grew black and dark; a sudden convulsive pain shot through all my nerves and bones; I knew nothing more.

I felt a soft warm breath fanning my cheek; I awakened as if out of the sleep of death; my mother was bending over me. "Is the Sand-man still here?" I stammered. "No, my dear child; he's been gone a long, long time; he'll not hurt you." Thus spoke my mother, as she kissed her recovered darling and pressed him to her heart. But why should I tire you, my dear Lothair? why do I dwell at such length on these details, when there's so much remains to be said? Enough—I was detected in my eavesdropping, and roughly handled by Coppelius. Fear and terror brought on a violent fever, of which I lay ill several weeks. "Is the Sand-man still there?" these were the first words I uttered on coming to myself again, the first sign of my recovery, of my safety. Thus, you see, I have only to relate to you the most terrible moment of my youth for you to thoroughly understand that it must not be ascribed to the weakness of my eyesight if all that I see is colourless, but to the fact that a mysterious destiny has hung a dark veil of clouds about my life, which I shall perhaps only break through when I die.

Coppelius did not show himself again; it was reported he had left the town.

It was about a year later when, in our old manner, we sat around the round table in the evening. Father was in very good spirits, and was telling us amusing tales about his youthful travels. As it was striking nine we all at once heard the street door creak on its hinges, and slow ponderous steps echoed across the passage and up the stairs. "That is Coppelius," said my mother, turning pale. "Yes, it is Coppelius," replied my father in a faint broken voice. The tears started from my mother's eyes. "But, father, father," she cried, "must it be so?" "This is the last time," he replied; "this is the last time he will come to me, I promise you. Go now, go and take the children. Go, go to bed—good-night."

As for me, I felt as if I were converted into cold, heavy stone; I could not get my breath. As I stood there immovable, my mother seized me by the arm. "Come, Nathanael! come along!" I suffered myself to be led away; I went into my room. "Be a good boy and keep quiet," mother called after me; "get into bed and go to sleep." But, tortured by indescribable fear and uneasiness, I could not close my eyes. It seemed that hateful, hideous Coppelius stood before me with his glittering eyes, smiling maliciously down upon me; in vain did I strive to banish the image. Somewhere about midnight there was a terrific explosion, as if a cannon were being fired off. The whole house shook; something went rustling and clattering past my door; the house door was pulled to with a bang.

"That is Coppelius," I cried, terror-stricken, and leaped out of bed. Then I heard a wild heart-rending scream; I rushed into my father's room; the door stood open, and clouds of suffocating smoke came rolling towards me. The servant maid shouted, "Oh! my master! my master!" On the floor in front of the smoking hearth lay my father, dead, his face burned black and fearfully distorted, my sisters weeping and moaning around him, and my mother lying near them in a swoon.

"Coppelius, you atrocious fiend, you've killed my father," I shouted. My senses left me. Two days later, when my father was placed in his coffin, his features were mild and gentle again as they had been when he was alive. I found great consolation in the thought that his association with the diabolical Coppelius could not have ended in his everlasting ruin.

Our neighbours had been awakened by the explosion; the affair got talked about, and came before the magisterial authorities, who wished to cite Coppelius to clear himself. But he had disappeared from the place, leaving no traces behind him.

Now when I tell you, my dear friend, that the peddler I spoke of was the villain Coppelius, you will not blame me for seeing impending mischief in his inauspicious reappearance. He was differently dressed; but Coppelius's figure and features are too deeply impressed upon my mind for me to be capable of making a mistake in the matter. Moreover, he has not even changed his name. He proclaims himself here, I learn, to be a Piedmontese mechanician, and styles himself Giuseppe Coppola.

I am resolved to enter the lists against him and avenge my father's death, let the consequences be what they may.

Don't say a word to mother about the reappearance of this odious monster. Give my love to my darling Clara; I will write to her when I am in a somewhat calmer frame of mind. Adieu, &c.

CLARA TO NATHANAEL

You are right, you have not written to me for a very long time, but nevertheless I believe that I still retain a place in your mind and thoughts. It is a proof that you were thinking a good deal about me when you were sending off your last letter to brother Lothair, for instead of directing it to him you directed it to me. With joy I tore open the envelope, and did not perceive the mistake until I read the words, "Oh! my dear, dear Lothair."

Now I know I ought not to have read any more of the letter, but ought to have given it to my brother. But as you have so often in innocent raillery made it a sort of reproach against me that I possessed such a calm and, for a woman, cool-headed temperament that I should be like the woman we read of—if the house was threatening to tumble down, I should stop before hastily fleeing, to smooth down a crumple in the window curtains—I need hardly tell you that the beginning of your letter quite upset me. I could scarcely breathe; there was a bright mist before my eyes.

Oh! my darling Nathanael! what could this terrible thing be that had happened? Separation from you—never to see you again, the thought was like a sharp knife in my heart. I read on and on. Your description of that horrid Coppelius made my flesh creep. I now learned for the first time what a terrible and violent death your good old father died. Brother Lothair, to whom I handed over his property, sought to comfort me, but with little success. *such an impact* That horrid peddler Giuseppe Coppola followed me everywhere; and I am almost ashamed to confess it, but he was able to disturb my sleep, which is usually sound and calm, with all sorts of wonderful dream shapes. But soon—the next day—I saw everything in a different light. Oh! do not be angry with me, my best beloved, if, despite your strange presentiment that Coppelius will do you some mischief, Lothair tells you I am in quite as good spirits, and just the same as ever.

I will frankly confess, it seems to me that all the horrors of which you speak, existed only in your own self, and that the real true outer world had but little to do with it. I can quite admit that old Coppelius may have been highly obnoxious to you children, but your real detestation of him arose from the fact that he hated children.

Naturally enough, the gruesome Sand-man of the old nurse's story was associated in your childish mind with old Coppelius, who even though you had not believed in the Sand-man, would have been to you a ghostly bugbear, especially dangerous to children. His mysterious labours along with your father at nighttime were, I daresay, nothing more than secret experiments in alchemy, with which your mother could not be over-well pleased, owing to the large sums of money that most likely were thrown away upon them; and besides, your father, his mind full of the deceptive striving after higher knowledge, may probably have become rather indifferent to his family, as so often happens in the case of such experimentalists.

So also it is equally probable that your father brought about his death by his own imprudence, and that Coppelius is not to blame for it. I must tell you that yesterday I asked our experienced neighbour, the chemist, whether in experiments of this kind an explosion could take place which would have a momentarily fatal effect. He said, "Oh, certainly!" and described to me in his prolix and circumstantial way how it could be occasioned, mentioning at the same time so many strange and funny words that I could not remember them at all. Now I know you will be angry at your Clara, and will say, "Of the Mysterious which often clasps man in its invisible arms there's not a ray can find its way into her cold heart. She sees only the varied surface of the things of the world and, like the little child, is pleased with the golden glittering fruit, at the kernel of which lies the fatal poison."

Oh! my beloved Nathanael, do you believe then that the intuitive prescience of a dark power working within us to our own ruin cannot exist also in minds which are cheerful, natural, free from care? But please forgive me that I, a simple girl, presume in any way to indicate to you what I really think of such an inward strife. After all, I should not find the proper words, and you would only laugh at me, not because my thoughts were stupid, but because I was so foolish as to attempt to tell them to you.

If there is a dark and hostile power which traitorously fixes a thread in our hearts in order that, laying hold of it and drawing us by means of it along a dangerous road to ruin, which otherwise we should not have trod—if, I say, there is such a power, it must assume within us a form like ourselves, nay, it must be ourselves; for only in that way can we believe in it, and only so understood do we yield to it so far that it is able to accomplish its secret purpose. So long as we have sufficient firmness, fortified by cheerfulness, always to acknowledge foreign hostile influences for what they really are, while we quietly pursue the path pointed out to us by both inclination and calling, then this mysterious power perishes in its futile struggles to attain the form which is to be the reflected image of ourselves.

It is also certain, Lothair adds, that if we have once voluntarily given ourselves up to this dark physical power, it often reproduces within us the strange forms which the outer world throws in our way, so that thus it is we ourselves who engender within ourselves the spirit which by some remarkable delusion we imagine to speak in that outer form. It is the phantom of our own self whose intimate relationship with, and whose powerful influence upon our soul either plunges us into hell or elevates us to heaven.

Thus you will see, my beloved Nathanael, that I and brother Lothair have talked over the subject of dark powers and forces well; and now, after I have written down the principal results of our discussion with some difficulty, they seem to me to contain many really profound thoughts. Lothair's last words, however, I don't quite understand; I only dimly guess what he means; and yet I cannot help thinking it is all very true.

I beg you, dear, strive to forget the ugly lawyer Coppelius as well as the peddler Giuseppe Coppola. Try and convince yourself that these foreign influences can have no power over you, that it is only belief in their hostile power which can in reality make them dangerous to you.

If every line of your letter did not betray the violent excitement of your mind, and if I did not sympathize with your condition from the bottom of my heart, I could in truth jest about the lawyer Sand-man and peddler Coppelius. Pluck up your spirits! Be cheerful! I have resolved to appear to you as your guardian angel if that ugly man Coppola should dare take it into his head to bother you in your dreams, and drive him away with a good hearty laugh. I'm not afraid of him and his nasty hands, not the least little bit; I won't let him either as lawyer spoil any dainty tit-bit I've taken, or as Sand-man rob me of my eyes.

My darling, darling Nathanael,
Eternally your, &c. &c.

NATHANAEL TO LOTHAIR

I am very sorry that Clara opened and read my last letter to you; of course the mistake is to be attributed to my own absence of mind. She has written me a very deep philosophical letter, proving conclusively that Coppelius and Coppola only exist in my own mind and are phantoms of my own self, which will at once be dissipated, as soon as I look upon them in that light. In very truth one can hardly believe that the mind which so often sparkles in those bright, beautifully smiling, childlike eyes of hers like a sweet lovely dream could draw such subtle and scholastic distinctions. She also mentions your name. You have been talking about me. I suppose you have been giving her lectures, since she sifts and refines everything so acutely. But enough of this! I must now tell you it is most certain that Giuseppe Coppola is not Coppelius. I am attending the lectures of our recently appointed Professor of Physics, who, like the distinguished naturalist, is called Spalanzani, and is of Italian origin. He has known Coppola for many years; and it is also easy to tell from Coppola's accent that he really is a Pied-montese. Coppelius was a German, though no honest German, I fancy.

Nevertheless I am not quite satisfied. You and Clara will perhaps take me for a gloomy dreamer, but in no way can I get rid of the impression which Coppelius's cursed face made upon me. I am glad to learn from Spalanzani that he has left town.

This Professor Spalanzani is a very queer fish. He is a little fat man, with prominent cheekbones, thin nose, projecting lips, and small piercing eyes. You cannot get a better picture of him than by turning over one of the Berlin pocket almanacs and looking at Cagliostro's portrait engraved by Chodowiecki; Spalanzani looks just like him.

Once lately, as I went up the steps to his house, I perceived that beside the curtain which generally covered a glass door there was a small chink. What it was that excited my curiosity I cannot explain; but I looked through. In the room I saw a female, tall, very slender, but of perfect proportions, and splendidly dressed, sitting at a little table, on which she had placed both her arms, her hands being folded together. She sat opposite the door, so that I could easily see her angelically beautiful face. She did not appear to notice me, and there was moreover a strangely fixed look about her eyes. I might almost say they appeared as if they had no power of vision; I thought she was sleeping with her eyes open. I felt quite uncomfortable, and so I slipped away quietly into the Professor's lecture-room, which was close at hand.

Afterwards I learned that the figure which I had seen was Spalanzani's daughter, Olimpia, whom he keeps locked up in a most wicked and unaccountable way. No man is ever allowed to come near her. Perhaps, however, there is something peculiar about her after all; perhaps she's an idiot or something of that sort.

But why am I telling you all this? I could tell you it all better and in more detail when I see you. For in a fortnight I shall be among you. I must see my dear sweet angel, my Clara, again. Then the little bit of ill-temper which, I must confess, took possession of me after her fearfully sensible letter, will be blown away. And that is the reason why I am not writing to her as well today.

With all best wishes, &c.

Nothing more strange and extraordinary can be imagined, gracious reader, than what happened to my poor friend, the young student Nathanael, and which I have undertaken to relate to you. Have you ever experienced anything that completely took possession of your heart and mind and thoughts to the utter exclusion of everything else? All was seething and boiling within you; your blood, heated to fever pitch, leaped through your veins and inflamed your cheeks. Your gaze was so peculiar, as if seeking to

grasp in empty space forms not seen by any other eye, and all your
words ended in sighs betokening some mystery.

Then your friends asked you, "What is the matter with you, my
dear friend? What do you see?" And, wishing to describe the inner
pictures in all their vivid colours, with their lights and their shades,
you struggled in vain to find words with which to express yourself.
But you felt as if you must gather up all the events that had happened,
wonderful, splendid, terrible, jocose, and awful, in the very first
word, so that the whole might be revealed by a single electric
discharge, so to speak.

Yet every word and everything that partook of the nature of
communication by intelligible sounds seemed to be colourless, cold,
and dead. Then you try and try again, and stutter and stammer,
while your friends' prosy questions strike like icy winds upon your
heart's hot fire until they extinguish it. But if, like a bold painter,
you had first sketched in a few audacious strokes the outline of the
picture you had in your soul, you would then easily have been able
to deepen and intensify the colours one after the other, until the
varied throng of living figures carried your friends away and they,
like you, saw themselves in the midst of the scene that had proceeded
out of your own soul.

Strictly speaking, indulgent reader, I must indeed confess to you,
nobody has asked me for the history of young Nathanael; but you
are very well aware that I belong to that remarkable class of authors
who, when they bear anything about in their minds in the manner I
have just described, feel as if everybody who comes near them, and
also the whole world to boot, were asking, "Oh! what is it? Oh!
do tell us, my good sir?"

Hence I was most powerfully impelled to narrate to you
Nathanael's ominous life. I was completely captivated by the
elements of marvel and alienness in his life; but, for this very reason,
and because it was necessary in the very beginning to dispose you,
indulgent reader, to bear with what is fantastic—and that is not a
small matter—I racked my brain to find a way of commencing the
story in a significant and original manner, calculated to arrest your
attention. To begin with "Once upon a time," the best beginning
for a story, seemed to me too tame; with "In the small country
town S—— lived," rather better, at any rate allowing plenty of
room to work up to the climax; or to plunge at once *in medias res*,
"'Go to the devil!' cried the student Nathanael, his eyes blazing
wildly with rage and fear, when the weather-glass peddler Giuseppe
Coppola"—well, that is what I really had written, when I thought

I detected something of the ridiculous in Nathanael's wild glance; and the history is anything but laughable. I could not find any words which seemed fitted to reflect in even the feeblest degree the brightness of the colours of my mental vision.

I determined not to begin at all. So I pray you, gracious reader, accept the three letters which my friend Lothair has been so kind as to communicate to me as the outline of the picture, into which I will endeavour to introduce more and more colour as I proceed with my narrative. Perhaps, like a good portrait painter, I may succeed in depicting Nathanael in such a way that you will recognize it as a good likeness without being acquainted with the original, and will feel as if you had very often seen him with your own bodily eyes. Perhaps, too, you will then believe that nothing is more wonderful, nothing more fantastic than real life, and that all that a writer can do is to present it as "in a glass, darkly."

In order to make the beginning more intelligible, it is necessary to add to the letters that, soon after the death of Nathanael's father, Clara and Lothair, the children of a distant relative, who had likewise died, leaving them orphans, were taken by Nathanael's mother into her own house. Clara and Nathanael conceived a warm affection for each other, to which there could be no objection. When therefore Nathanael left home to prosecute his studies in G——, they were engaged. It is from G—— that his last letter is written, where he is attending the lectures of Spalanzani, the distinguished Professor of Physics.

I might now proceed comfortably with my narration, if at this moment Clara's image did not rise up so vividly before my eyes that I cannot turn them away from it, just as I never could when she looked upon me and smiled so sweetly. Nowhere would she have passed for beautiful; that was the unanimous opinion of everyone who professed to have any technical knowledge of beauty. But while architects praised the pure proportions of her figure and form, painters averred that her neck, shoulders, and bosom were almost too chastely modelled, and yet, on the other hand, one and all were in love with her glorious Magdalene hair, and talked a good deal of nonsense about Battoni-like colouring. One of them, a veritable romanticist, strangely enough likened her eyes to a lake by Ruisdael, in which is reflected the pure azure of the cloudless sky, the beauty of woods and flowers, and all the bright and varied life of a living landscape. Poets and musicians went still further and said, "What's all this talk about seas and reflections? How can we look upon the girl without feeling that wonderful heavenly songs and melodies beam upon us from her eyes, penetrating deep down into our hearts, till everything becomes awake and throbbing with emotion? And if we cannot sing anything at all passable then, why, we are not worth much; and this we can also plainly read in the rare smile which flits around her lips when we have the hardihood to squeak out something in her presence which we pretend to call singing, in spite of the fact that it is nothing more than a few single notes confusedly linked together."

And it really was so. Clara had the powerful fancy of a bright, innocent, unaffected child, a woman's deep and sympathetic heart, and an understanding clear, sharp, and discriminating. Dreamers and visionaries had a bad time of it with her; for without saying very much—she was not by nature of a talkative disposition—she plainly asked, by her calm steady look and rare ironical smile, "How can you imagine, my dear friends, that I can take these fleeting shadowy images for true living and breathing forms?" For this reason many found fault with her as being cold, unimaginative, and devoid of feeling; others, however, who had reached a clearer and deeper conception of life, were extremely fond of the intelligent, childlike, large-hearted girl.

No one else had such an affection for her as Nathanael, who was a zealous and cheerful cultivator of the fields of science and art. Clara clung to her lover with all her heart; the first clouds she encountered in life were when he had to separate from her. With what delight did she fly into his arms when, as he had promised in his last letter to Lothair, he really came back to his native town and entered his mother's room! And as Nathanael had foreseen, the moment he saw Clara again he no longer thought about either the lawyer Coppelius or her sensible letter; his ill-humour had quite disappeared.

Nevertheless Nathanael was right when he told his friend Lothair that the repulsive vendor of weather glasses, Coppola, had exercised a fatal and disturbing influence upon his life. It was quite patent to all; for even during the first few days he showed that he was completely and entirely changed. He gave himself up to gloomy reveries, and moreover acted so strangely; they had never observed anything at all like it in him before. Everything, even his own life, was to him but dreams and presentiments. His constant theme was that every man who delusively imagined himself to be free was merely the plaything of the cruel sport of mysterious powers, and it was vain for man to resist them; he must humbly submit to whatever destiny had decreed for him. He went so far as to maintain that it was foolish to believe that a man could do anything in art or science of his own accord; for the inspiration in which alone any true artistic work could be done did not proceed from the spirit within outwards, but was the result of the operation directed inwards of some Higher Principle existing without and beyond ourselves.

This mystic extravagance was in the highest degree repugnant to Clara's clear intelligent mind, but it seemed vain to enter upon any attempt at refutation.   Yet when Nathanael went on to prove that Coppelius was the Evil Principle which had entered into him and taken possession of him at the time he was listening behind the curtain, and that this hateful demon would in some terrible way ruin their happiness, then Clara grew grave and said, "Yes, Nathanael.   You are right; Coppelius is an Evil Principle; he can do dreadful things, as bad as could a Satanic power which should assume a living physical form, but only—only if you do not banish him from your mind and thoughts.   As long as you believe in him he exists and is at work; your belief in him is his only power."

Whereupon Nathanael, quite angry because Clara would only grant the existence of the demon in his own mind, began to dilate at large upon the whole mystic doctrine of devils and awful powers, but Clara abruptly broke off the theme by making, to Nathanael's very great disgust, some quite commonplace remark.

Such deep mysteries are sealed books to cold, unsusceptible characters, he thought, without its being clearly conscious to himself that he counted Clara among these inferior natures, and accordingly he did not remit his efforts to initiate her into these mysteries.   In the morning, when she was helping to prepare breakfast, he would take his stand beside her, and read all sorts of mystic books to her, until she begged him—"But, my dear Nathanael, I shall have to scold you as the Evil Principle which exercises a fatal influence upon my coffee.   For if I do as you wish, and let things go their own way, and look into your eyes while you read, the coffee will all boil over into the fire, and you will none of you get any breakfast."   Then Nathanael hastily banged the book shut and ran away in great displeasure to his own room.

Formerly he had possessed a peculiar talent for writing pleasing, sparkling tales, which Clara took the greatest delight in hearing; but now his productions were gloomy, unintelligible, and wanting in form, so that, although Clara out of forbearance towards him did not say so, he nevertheless felt how very little interest she took in them.   There was nothing that Clara disliked so much as what was tedious; at such times her intellectual sleepiness was not to be overcome; it was betrayed both in her glances and in her words. Nathanael's effusions were, in truth, exceedingly tedious.

His ill-humour at Clara's cold prosaic temperament continued to increase; Clara could not conceal her distaste for his dark, gloomy, wearying mysticism; and thus both began to be more and more estranged from each other without exactly being aware of it themselves. The image of the ugly Coppelius had, as Nathanael was obliged to confess to himself, faded considerably in his fancy, and it often cost him great pains to present him in vivid colours in his literary efforts, in which Coppelius played the part of the ghoul of Destiny.

At length it entered into his head to make his dismal presentiment that Coppelius would ruin his happiness the subject of a poem. He made himself and Clara, united by true love, the central figures, but represented a black hand as being from time to time thrust into their life, plucking out a joy that had blossomed for them. At length, as they were standing at the altar, the terrible Coppelius appeared and touched Clara's lovely eyes, which leaped into Nathanael's own bosom, burning and hissing like bloody sparks. Then Coppelius laid hold of him, and hurled him into a blazing circle of fire, which spun round with the speed of a whirlwind, and storming and blustering, dashed away with him. The fearful noise it made was like a furious hurricane lashing the foaming sea waves until they rise up like black, white-headed giants in the midst of the raging struggle. But through the midst of the savage fury of the tempest he heard Clara's voice calling, "Can you not see me, dear? Coppelius has deceived you; they were not my eyes which burned so in your bosom; they were fiery drops of your own heart's blood. Look at me, I have got my own eyes still." Nathanael thought, "Yes, that is Clara, and I am hers forever." Then this thought laid a powerful grasp upon the fiery circle so that it stood still, and the riotous turmoil died away, rumbling down into a dark abyss. Nathanael looked into Clara's eyes; but it was death whose gaze rested so kindly upon him.

While Nathanael was writing this work he was very quiet and sober-minded; he filed and polished every line, and as he had chosen to submit himself to the limitations of meter, he did not rest until all was pure and musical. When, however, he had at length finished it and read it aloud to himself he was seized with horror and awful dread, and he screamed, "Whose hideous voice is this?" But he soon came to see in it again nothing beyond a very successful poem, and he confidently believed it would enkindle Clara's cold temperament, though to what end she should be thus aroused was not quite clear to his own mind, nor yet what would be the real purpose served by tormenting her with these dreadful pictures, which prophesied a terrible and ruinous end to her affection.

Nathanael and Clara sat in his mother's little garden. Clara was bright and cheerful, since for three entire days her lover, who had been busy writing his poem, had not teased her with his dreams or forebodings. Nathanael, too, spoke in a gay and vivacious way of things of merry import, as he formerly used to do, so that Clara said, "Ah! now I have you again. We have driven away that ugly Coppelius, you see." Then it suddenly occurred to him that he had got the poem in his pocket which he wished to read to her. He at once took out the manuscript and began to read.

Clara, anticipating something tedious as usual, prepared to submit to the infliction, and calmly resumed her knitting. But as the sombre clouds rose up darker and darker she let her knitting fall on her lap and sat with her eyes fixed in a set stare upon Nathanael's face. He was quite carried away by his own work, the fire of enthusiasm coloured his cheeks a deep red, and tears started from his eyes. At length he concluded, groaning and showing great lassitude; grasping Clara's hand, he sighed as if he were being utterly melted in inconsolable grief, "Oh! Clara! Clara!" She drew him softly to her heart and said in a low but very grave and impressive tone, "Nathanael, my darling Nathanael, throw that foolish, senseless, stupid thing into the fire."

Then Nathanael leaped indignantly to his feet, crying, as he pushed Clara from him, "You damned lifeless automaton!" and rushed away. Clara was cut to the heart, and wept bitterly. "Oh! he has never loved me, for he does not understand me," she sobbed.

Lothair entered the arbour. Clara was obliged to tell him all that had taken place. He was passionately fond of his sister; and every word of her complaint fell like a spark upon his heart, so that the displeasure which he had long entertained against his dreamy friend Nathanael was kindled into furious anger. He hastened to find Nathanael, and upbraided him in harsh words for his irrational behaviour towards his beloved sister.

The fiery Nathanael answered him in the same style. "A fantastic, crack-brained fool," was retaliated with, "A miserable, common, everyday sort of fellow." A meeting was the inevitable consequence. They agreed to meet on the following morning behind the garden wall, and fight, according to the custom of the students of the place, with sharp rapiers. They went about silent and gloomy; Clara had both heard and seen the violent quarrel, and also observed the fencing master bring the rapiers in the dusk of the evening. She had a presentiment of what was to happen. They both appeared at the appointed place wrapped up in the same gloomy silence, and threw off their coats. Their eyes flaming with the bloodthirsty light of pugnacity, they were about to begin their contest when Clara burst through the garden door. Sobbing, she screamed, "You savage, terrible men! Cut me down before you attack each other; for how can I live when my lover has slain my brother, or my brother slain my lover?"

Lothair let his weapon fall and gazed silently at the ground, while Nathanael's heart was rent with sorrow, and all the affection which he had felt for his lovely Clara in the happiest days of her golden youth was reawakened within him. His murderous weapon, too, fell from his hand; he threw himself at Clara's feet. "Oh! can you ever forgive me, my only, my dearly loved Clara? Can you, my dear brother Lothair, also forgive me?" Lothair was touched by his friend's great distress; the three young people embraced each other amid endless tears, and swore never again to break their bond of love and fidelity.

Nathanael felt as if a heavy burden that had been weighing him down to the earth was now rolled from off him, nay, as if by offering resistance to the dark power which had possessed him, he had rescued his own self from the ruin which had threatened him. Three happy days he now spent amidst the loved ones, and then returned to G——, where he had still a year to stay before settling down in his native town for life.

Everything having reference to Coppelius had been concealed from Nathanael's mother, for they knew she could not think of Coppelius without horror, since she as well as Nathanael believed him to be guilty of causing her husband's death.

. . . . . .

When Nathanael came to the house where he lived in G——, he was greatly astonished to find it burned down to the ground, so that nothing but the bare outer walls were left standing amid a heap of ruins. Although the fire had broken out in the laboratory of the chemist who lived on the ground floor, and had therefore spread upwards, some of Nathanael's bold, active friends had succeeded in time in forcing a way into his room in the upper story and saving his books and manuscripts and instruments. They had carried them all uninjured into another house, where they engaged a room for him; this he now at once took possession of.

That he lived opposite Professor Spalanzani did not strike him particularly, nor did it occur to him as anything more singular that he could, as he observed, by looking out of his window, see straight into the room where Olimpia often sat alone. Her figure he could plainly distinguish, although her features were uncertain and confused. It did at length occur to him, however, that she remained for hours together in the same position in which he had first discovered her through the glass door, sitting at a little table without any occupation whatever, and it was evident that she was constantly gazing across in his direction. He could not but confess to himself that he had never seen a finer figure. However, with Clara mistress of his heart, he remained perfectly unaffected by Olimpia's stiffness and apathy; and it was only occasionally that he sent a fugitive glance over his compendium across to her—that was all.

He was writing to Clara; a light tap came at the door. At his summons to "Come in," Coppola's repulsive face appeared peeping in. Nathanael felt his heart beat with trepidation; but, recollecting what Spalanzani had told him about his fellow countryman Coppola, and what he himself had so faithfully promised his beloved in respect to the Sand-man Coppelius, he was ashamed at himself for this childish fear of specters. Accordingly, he controlled himself with an effort, and said, as quietly and as calmly as he possibly could, "I don't want to buy any weather glasses, my good friend; you had better go elsewhere."

Then Coppola came right into the room, and said in a hoarse voice, screwing up his wide mouth into a hideous smile, while his little eyes flashed keenly from beneath his long gray eyelashes, "Eh! No want weather glass? No weather glass? I got eyes-a too. Fine eyes-a." In some fright, Nathanael cried, "You idiot, how can you have eyes?—eyes—eyes?" But Coppola, laying aside his barometers, thrust his hands into his big coat pockets and brought out several spy-glasses and spectacles, and put them on the table. "Looka! Looka! Spettacles for nose. Spettacles. Those my eyes-a." And he continued to produce more and more spectacles from his pockets until the table began to gleam and flash all over. Thousands of eyes were looking and blinking convulsively and staring up at Nathanael; he could not avert his gaze from the table. Coppola went on heaping up his spectacles, while wilder and ever wilder burning flashes crossed through and through each other and darted their blood-red rays into Nathanael's breast.

Quite overcome and frantic with terror, he shouted, "Stop! stop! you fiend!" and he seized Coppola by the arm, which Coppola had again thrust into his pocket in order to bring out still more spectacles, although the whole table was covered all over with them. With a harsh disagreeable laugh Coppola gently freed himself; and with the words "So! want none! Well, here fine glass!" he swept all his spectacles together, and put them back into his coat pockets, while from a breast pocket he produced a great number of larger and smaller perspectives. As soon as the spectacles were gone Nathanael recovered his equanimity again; and, bending his thoughts upon Clara, he clearly discerned that the gruesome incubus had proceeded only from himself, and that Coppola was an honest mechanician and optician, and far from being Coppelius's dreaded double and ghost. And then, besides, none of the glasses which Coppola now placed on the table had anything at all singular about them, at least nothing so weird as the spectacles; so, in order to square accounts with himself Nathanael now really determined to buy something of the man. He took up a small, very beautifully cut pocket perspective, and by way of proving it looked through the window.

Never before in his life had he had a glass in his hands that brought out things so clearly and sharply and distinctly. Involuntarily he directed the glass upon Spalanzani's room; Olimpia sat at the little table as usual, her arms laid upon it and her hands folded. Now he saw for the first time the regular and exquisite beauty of her features. The eyes, however, seemed to him to have a singular look of fixity and lifelessness. But as he continued to look closer and more carefully through the glass he fancied a light like humid moonbeams came into them. It seemed as if their power of vision was now being enkindled; their glances shone with ever-increasing vivacity.

Nathanael remained standing at the window as if glued to the spot by a wizard's spell, his gaze riveted unchangeably upon the divinely beautiful Olimpia. A coughing and shuffling of the feet awakened him out of his enchaining dream, as it were. Coppola stood behind him, "Tre zechini" (three ducats). Nathanael had completely forgotten the optician; he hastily paid the sum demanded. "Ain't 't? Fine-a glass? Fine-a glass?" asked Coppola in his harsh unpleasant voice, smiling sardonically. "Yes, yes, yes," rejoined Nathanael impatiently; "adieu, my good friend." But Coppola did not leave the room without casting many peculiar side glances upon Nathanael; and the young student heard him laughing loudly on the stairs. "Ah well!" thought he, "he's laughing at me because I've paid him too much for this little perspective —because I've given him too much money—that's it."

As he softly murmured these words he fancied he detected a gasping sigh as of a dying man stealing awfully through the room; his heart stopped beating with fear. But to be sure he had heaved a deep sigh himself; it was quite plain. "Clara is quite right," said he to himself, "in holding me to be an incurable ghost-seer; and yet it's very ridiculous—more ridiculous, that the stupid thought of having paid Coppola too much for his glass should cause me this strange anxiety; I can't see any reason for it."

Now he sat down to finish his letter to Clara; but a glance through the window showed him Olimpia still in her former posture. Urged by an irresistible impulse he jumped up and seized Coppola's perspective; nor could he tear himself away from the fascinating Olimpia until his friend Siegmund called for him to go to Professor Spalanzani's lecture. The curtains before the door of the all-important room were closely drawn, so that he could not see Olimpia. Nor could he even see her from his own room during the two following days, notwithstanding that he scarcely ever left his window, and maintained a scarce interrupted watch through Coppola's perspective upon her room.

On the third day curtains were drawn across the window. Plunged into the depths of despair,—goaded by longing and ardent desire, he hurried outside the walls of the town. Olimpia's image hovered about his path in the air and stepped forth out of the bushes, and peeped up at him with large and lustrous eyes from the bright surface of the brook. Clara's image was completely faded from his mind; he had no thoughts except for Olimpia. He uttered his love plaints aloud and in a lachrymose tone, "Oh! my glorious, noble star of love, have you only risen to vanish again, and leave me in the darkness and hopelessness of night?"

Returning home, he became aware that there was a good deal of noisy bustle going on in Spalanzani's house. All the doors stood wide open; men were taking in all kinds of gear and furniture; the windows of the first floor were all lifted off their hinges; busy maid-servants with immense hair-brooms were driving backwards and forwards dusting and sweeping, while from inside could be heard the knocking and hammering of carpenters and upholsterers. Utterly astonished, Nathanael stood still in the street; then Siegmund joined him, laughing, and said, "Well, what do you say to our old Spalanzani?" Nathanael assured him that he could not say anything, since he did not know what it all meant. To his great astonishment, he could hear, however, that they were turning the quiet gloomy house almost inside out with their dusting and cleaning and alterations. Then he learned from Siegmund that Spalanzani intended giving a great concert and ball on the following day, and that half the university was invited. It was generally reported that Spalanzani was going to let his daughter Olimpia, whom he had so long so jealously guarded from every eye, make her first appearance.

Nathanael received an invitation. At the appointed hour, when the carriages were rolling up and the lights were gleaming brightly in the decorated halls, he went across to the Professor's, his heart beating high with expectation. The company was both numerous and brilliant.

Olimpia was richly and tastefully dressed. One could not but admire her figure and the regular beauty of her features. Yet the striking inward curve of her back, as well as the wasplike smallness of her waist, appeared to be the result of too-tight lacing, and there was something stiff and measured in her gait and bearing that made an unfavourable impression upon many. It was ascribed to the constraint imposed upon her by the company.

The concert began. Olimpia played on the piano with great skill; and sang as skillfully an *aria di bravura*, in a voice which was, if anything, almost too brilliant, but clear as glass bells. Nathanael was transported with delight; he stood in the background farthest from her, and owing to the blinding lights could not quite distinguish her features. So, without being observed, he took Coppola's glass out of his pocket, and directed it upon the beautiful Olimpia. Oh! then he perceived how her yearning eyes sought him, how every note only reached its full purity in the loving glance which penetrated to and inflamed his heart. Her roulades seemed to him to be the exultant cry towards heaven of the soul refined by love; and when at last, after the cadenza, the long trill rang loudly through the hall, he felt as if he were suddenly grasped by burning arms and could no longer control himself—he could not help shouting aloud in his mingled pain and delight, "Olimpia!" All eyes were turned upon him; many people laughed.

The concert came to an end, and the ball began. Oh! to dance with her—with her—that was now the aim of all Nathanael's wishes, of all his desires. But how should he have courage to request her, the queen of the ball, to grant him the honour of a dance? And yet he couldn't tell how it came about, just as the dance began, he found himself standing close beside her, nobody having as yet asked her to be his partner. So, with some difficulty stammering out a few words, he grasped her hand. It was cold as ice; he shook with an awful, frosty shiver. But, fixing his eyes upon her face, he saw that her glance was beaming upon him with love and longing, and at the same moment he thought that the pulse began to beat in her cold hand, and the warm life-blood to course through her veins. And passion burned more intensely in his own heart also; he threw his arm round her beautiful waist and whirled her round the hall. He had always thought that he kept good and accurate time in dancing, but from the perfectly rhythmical evenness with which Olimpia danced, and which frequently put him quite out, he perceived how very faulty his own time really was. Notwithstanding, he would not dance with any other lady; and everybody else who approached Olimpia to call upon her for a dance, he would have liked to kill on the spot. This, however, only happened twice; to his astonishment Olimpia remained after this without a partner, and he did not fail on each occasion to take her out again.

If Nathanael had been able to see anything else except the beautiful Olimpia, there would inevitably have been a good deal of unpleasant quarrelling and strife; for it was evident that Olimpia was the object of the smothered laughter suppressed only with difficulty, which was heard in various corners amongst the young people; and they followed her with very curious looks.

Nathanael, excited by dancing and the plentiful supply of wine he had consumed, had laid aside the shyness which at other times characterized him. He sat beside Olimpia, her hand in his own, and declared his love enthusiastically and passionately in words which neither of them understood, neither he nor Olimpia. And yet perhaps she did, for she sat with her eyes fixed unchangeably upon his, sighing repeatedly, "Ah! Ah! Ah!" Upon this Nathanael would answer, "Oh, you glorious heavenly lady! You ray from the promised paradise of love! Oh! what a profound soul you have! my whole being is mirrored in it!" and a good deal more in the same strain. But Olimpia only continued to sigh "Ah! Ah!" again and again.

Professor Spalanzani passed by the two happy lovers once or twice, and smiled with a look of peculiar satisfaction. All at once it seemed to Nathanael, albeit he was far away in a different world, as if it were growing perceptibly darker down below at Professor Spalanzani's. He looked about him, and to his very great alarm became aware that there were only two lights left burning in the

hall, and they were on the point of going out. The music and dancing had long ago ceased. "We must part—part!" he cried, wildly
and despairingly; he kissed Olimpia's hand; he bent down to her
mouth, but ice-cold lips met his burning ones. As he touched her
cold hand, he felt his heart thrill with awe; the legend of "The
Dead Bride" shot suddenly through his mind. But Olimpia had
drawn him closer to her, and the kiss appeared to warm her lips
into vitality.

Professor Spalanzani strode slowly through the empty apartment,
his footsteps giving a hollow echo; and his figure had, as the flickering shadows played about him, a ghostly, awful appearance. "Do
you love me? Do you love me, Olimpia? Only one little word—
do you love me?" whispered Nathanael, but she only sighed, "Ah!
Ah!" as she rose to her feet.

"Yes, you are my lovely, glorious star of love," said Nathanael,
"and will shine for ever, purifying and ennobling my heart."
"Ah! Ah!" replied Olimpia, as she moved along. Nathanael
followed her; they stood before the Professor. "You have had an
extraordinarily animated conversation with my daughter," said he,
smiling. "Well, well, my dear Mr. Nathanael, if you find pleasure
in talking to the stupid girl, I am sure I shall be glad for you to come
and do so." Nathanael took his leave, his heart singing and leaping
in a perfect delirium of happiness.

During the next few days Spalanzani's ball was the general topic
of conversation. Although the Professor had done everything to
make the thing a splendid success, yet certain gay spirits related
more than one thing that had occurred which was quite irregular
and out of order. They were especially keen in pulling Olimpia
to pieces for her taciturnity and rigid stiffness; in spite of her beautiful form they alleged that she was hopelessly stupid, and in this fact
they discerned the reason why Spalanzani had so long kept her concealed from publicity. Nathanael heard all this with inward wrath,
but nevertheless he held his tongue; for, thought he, would it indeed
be worth while to prove to these fellows that it is their own stupidity
which prevents them from appreciating Olimpia's profound and
brilliant parts?

One day Siegmund said to him, "Pray, brother, have the kindness to tell me how you, a clever fellow, came to lose your head over
that Miss Wax-face—that wooden doll across there?" Nathanael
was about to fly into a rage, but he recollected himself and replied,
"Tell me, Siegmund, how came it that Olimpia's divine charms
could escape your eye, so keenly alive as it always is to beauty, and

your acute perception as well? But Heaven be thanked for it, otherwise I should have had you for a rival, and then the blood of one of us would have had to be spilled."

Siegmund, perceiving how matters stood with his friend, skillfully changed his tactics and said, after remarking that all argument with one in love about the object of his affections was out of place, "Yet it's very strange that several of us have formed pretty much the same opinion about Olimpia. We think she is—you won't take it ill, brother?—that she is singularly statuesque and soulless. Her figure is regular, and so are her features, that can't be gainsaid; and if her eyes were not so utterly devoid of life, I may say, of the power of vision, she might pass for a beauty. She is strangely measured in her movements, they all seem as if they were dependent upon some wound-up clockwork. Her playing and singing have the disagreeably perfect, but insensitive timing of a singing machine, and her dancing is the same. We felt quite afraid of this Olimpia, and did not like to have anything to do with her; she seemed to us to be only acting *like* a living creature, and as if there was some secret at the bottom of it all."

Nathanael did not give way to the bitter feelings which threatened to master him at these words of Siegmund's; he fought down and got the better of his displeasure, and merely said, very earnestly, "You cold prosaic fellows may very well be afraid of her. It is only to its like that the poetically organized spirit unfolds itself. Upon me alone did her loving glances fall, and through my mind and thoughts alone did they radiate; and only in her love can I find my own self again. Perhaps, however, she doesn't do quite right not to jabber a lot of nonsense and stupid talk like other shallow people. It is true, she speaks but few words; but the few words she does speak are genuine hieroglyphs of the inner world of Love and of the higher cognition of the intellectual life revealed in the intuition of the Eternal beyond the grave. But you have no understanding for all these things, and I am only wasting words."

"God be with you, brother," said Siegmund very gently, almost sadly, "but it seems to me that you are in a very bad way. You may rely upon me, if all—No, I can't say any more." It all at once dawned upon Nathanael that his cold prosaic friend Siegmund really and sincerely wished him well, and so he warmly shook his proffered hand.

Nathanael had completely forgotten that there was a Clara in the world, whom he had once loved—and his mother and Lothair. They had all vanished from his mind; he lived for Olimpia alone.

He sat beside her every day for hours together, rhapsodizing about his love and sympathy enkindled into life, and about psychic elective affinity—all of which Olimpia listened to with great reverence.

He fished up from the very bottom of his desk all the things that he had ever written—poems, fancy sketches, visions, romances, tales, and the heap was increased daily with all kinds of aimless sonnets, stanzas, canzonets. All these he read to Olimpia hour after hour without growing tired; but then he had never had such an exemplary listener. She neither embroidered, nor knitted; she did not look out of the window, or feed a bird, or play with a little pet dog or a favourite cat, neither did she twist a piece of paper or anything of that kind round her finger; she did not forcibly convert a yawn into a low affected cough—in short, she sat hour after hour with her eyes bent unchangeably upon her lover's face, without moving or altering her position, and her gaze grew more ardent and more ardent still. And it was only when at last Nathanael rose and kissed her lips or her hand that she said, "Ah! Ah!" and then "Goodnight, dear."

Back in his own room, Nathanael would break out with, "Oh! what a brilliant—what a profound mind! Only you—you alone understand me." And his heart trembled with rapture when he reflected upon the wondrous harmony which daily revealed itself between his own and his Olimpia's character; for he fancied that she had expressed in respect to his works and his poetic genius the identical sentiments which he himself cherished deep down in his own heart, and even as if it was his own heart's voice speaking to him. And it must indeed have been so; for Olimpia never uttered any other words than those already mentioned. And when Nathanael himself in his clear and sober moments, as, for instance, directly after waking in a morning, thought about her utter passivity and taciturnity, he only said, "What are words—but words? The glance of her heavenly eyes says more than any tongue. And anyway, how can a child of heaven accustom herself to the narrow circle which the exigencies of a wretched mundane life demand?"

Professor Spalanzani appeared to be greatly pleased at the intimacy that had sprung up between his daughter Olimpia and Nathanael, and showed the young man many unmistakable proofs of his good feeling towards him. When Nathanael ventured at length to hint very delicately at an alliance with Olimpia, the Professor smiled all over his face at once, and said he should allow his daughter to make a perfectly free choice.

Encouraged by these words, and with the fire of desire burning in his heart, Nathanael resolved the very next day to implore Olimpia to tell him frankly, in plain words, what he had long read in her sweet loving glances—that she would be his for ever. He looked for the ring which his mother had given him at parting; he would present it to Olimpia as a symbol of his devotion, and of the happy life he was to lead with her from that time onwards.

While looking for it he came across his letters from Clara and Lothair; he threw them carelessly aside, found the ring, put it in his pocket, and ran across to Olimpia. While still on the stairs, in the entrance passage, he heard an extraordinary hubbub; the noise seemed to proceed from Spalanzani's study. There was a stamping —a rattling—pushing—knocking against the door, with curses and oaths intermingled. "Leave hold—leave hold—you monster—you rascal—put your life's work into it?—Ha! ha! ha! ha!—That was not our wager—I, I made the eyes—I the clockwork.—Go to the devil with your clockwork—you damned dog of a watchmaker—be off—Satan—stop—you paltry turner—you infernal beast—stop— begone—let me go." The voices which were thus making all this racket and rumpus were those of Spalanzani and the fearsome Coppelius.

Nathanael rushed in, impelled by some nameless dread. The Professor was grasping a female figure by the shoulders, the Italian Coppola held her by the feet; and they were pulling and dragging each other backwards and forwards, fighting furiously to get possession of her.

Nathanael recoiled with horror on recognizing that the figure was Olimpia. Boiling with rage, he was about to tear his beloved from the grasp of the madmen, when Coppola by an extraordinary exertion of strength twisted the figure out of the Professor's hands and gave him such a terrible blow with her, that Spalanzani reeled backwards and fell over the table among the phials and retorts, the bottles and glass cylinders, which covered it: all these things were smashed into a thousand pieces. But Coppola threw the figure across his shoulder, and, laughing shrilly and horribly, ran hastily down the stairs, the figure's ugly feet hanging down and banging and rattling like wood against the steps.

Nathanael was stupefied—he had seen only too distinctly that in Olimpia's pallid waxed face there were no eyes, merely black holes in their stead; she was an inanimate puppet. Spalanzani was rolling on the floor; the pieces of glass had cut his head and breast and arm; the blood was escaping from him in streams. But he gathered his strength together by an effort.

"After him—after him! What do you stand staring there for? Coppelius—Coppelius—he's stolen my best automaton—at which I've worked for twenty years—my life work—the clockwork—speech—movement—mine—your eyes—stolen your eyes—damn him—curse him—after him—fetch me back Olimpia—there are the eyes." And now Nathanael saw a pair of bloody eyes lying on the floor staring at him; Spalanzani seized them with his uninjured hand and threw them at him, so that they hit his breast.

Then madness dug her burning talons into Nathanael and swept down into his heart, rending his mind and thoughts to shreds. "Aha! aha! aha! Fire-wheel—fire-wheel! Spin round, fire-wheel! merrily, merrily! Aha! wooden doll! spin round, pretty wooden doll!" and he threw himself upon the Professor, clutching him fast by the throat.

He would certainly have strangled him had not several people, attracted by the noise, rushed in and torn away the madman; and so they saved the Professor, whose wounds were immediately dressed. Siegmund, with all his strength, was not able to subdue the frantic lunatic, who continued to scream in a dreadful way, "Spin round, wooden doll!" and to strike out right and left with his doubled fists. At length the united strength of several succeeded in overpowering him by throwing him on the floor and binding him. His cries passed into a brutish bellow that was awful to hear; and thus raging with the harrowing violence of madness, he was taken away to the madhouse.

Before continuing my narration of what happened further to the unfortunate Nathanael, I will tell you, indulgent reader, in case you take any interest in that skillful mechanician and fabricator of automata, Spalanzani, that he recovered completely from his wounds. He had, however, to leave the university, for Nathanael's fate had created a great sensation; and the opinion was pretty generally expressed that it was an imposture altogether unpardonable to have smuggled a wooden puppet instead of a living person into intelligent tea-circles—for Olimpia had been present at several with success. Lawyers called it a cunning piece of knavery, and all the harder to punish since it was directed against the public; and it had been so craftily contrived that it had escaped unobserved by all except a few preternaturally acute students, although everybody was very wise now and remembered to have thought of several facts which occurred to them as suspicious. But these latter could not succeed in making out any sort of a consistent tale. For was it, for instance, a thing likely to occur to anyone as suspicious that, according to the declaration of an elegant beau of these tea-parties, Olimpia had, contrary to all good manners, sneezed oftener than she had yawned? The former must have been, in the opinion of this elegant gentleman, the winding up of the concealed clockwork; it had always been accompanied by an observable creaking, and so on.

The Professor of Poetry and Eloquence took a pinch of snuff, and, slapping the lid to and clearing his throat, said solemnly, "My most honourable ladies and gentlemen, don't you see then where the rub is? The whole thing is an allegory, a continuous metaphor. You understand me? *Sapienti sat.*"

But several most honourable gentlemen did not rest satisfied with this explanation; the history of this automaton had sunk deeply into their souls, and an absurd mistrust of human figures began to prevail. Several lovers, in order to be fully convinced that they were not paying court to a wooden puppet, required that their mistress should sing and dance a little out of time, should embroider or knit or play with her little pug, &c., when being read to, but above all things else that she should do something more than merely listen—that she should frequently speak in such a way as to really show that her words presupposed as a condition some thinking and feeling. The bonds of love were in many cases drawn closer in consequence, and so of course became more engaging; in other instances they gradually relaxed and fell away. "I cannot really be made responsible for it," was the remark of more than one young gallant.

At the tea-gatherings everybody, in order to ward off suspicion, yawned to an incredible extent and never sneezed. Spalanzani was obliged, as has been said, to leave the place in order to escape a criminal charge of having fraudulently imposed an automaton upon human society. Coppola, too, had also disappeared.

When Nathanael awoke he felt as if he had been oppressed by a terrible nightmare; he opened his eyes and experienced an indescribable sensation of mental comfort, while a soft and most beautiful sensation of warmth pervaded his body. He lay on his own bed in his own room at home; Clara was bending over him, and at a little distance stood his mother and Lothair. "At last, at last, O my darling Nathanael; now we have you again; now you are cured of your grievous illness, now you are mine again." And Clara's words came from the depths of her heart; and she clasped him in her arms. The bright scalding tears streamed from his eyes, he was so overcome with mingled feelings of sorrow and delight; and he gasped forth, "My Clara, my Clara!"

Siegmund, who had staunchly stood by his friend in his hour of need, now came into the room. Nathanael gave him his hand—"My faithful brother, you have not deserted me." Every trace of insanity had left him, and in the tender hands of his mother and his beloved, and his friends, he quickly recovered his strength again. Good fortune had in the meantime visited the house; a niggardly old uncle, from whom they had never expected to get anything, had died, and left Nathanael's mother not only a considerable fortune, but also a small estate, pleasantly situated not far from the town. There they resolved to go and live, Nathanael and his mother, and Clara, to whom he was now to be married, and Lothair. Nathanael had become gentler and more childlike than he had ever been before, and now began really to understand Clara's supremely pure and noble character. None of them ever reminded him, even in the remotest degree, of the past. But when Siegmund took leave of him, Nathanael said, "By heaven, brother! I was in a bad way, but an angel came just at the right moment and led me back upon the path of light. Yes, it was Clara." Siegmund would not let him speak further, fearing lest the painful recollections of the past might arise too vividly and too intensely in his mind.

The time came for the four happy people to move to their little property. At noon they were going through the streets. After making several purchases they found that the lofty tower of the town hall was throwing its giant shadows across the market place. "Come," said Clara, "let us go up to the top once more and have a look at the distant hills." No sooner said than done. Both of them, Nathanael and Clara, went up the tower; their mother, however, went on with the servant-girl to her new home, and Lothair, not feeling inclined to climb up all the many steps, waited below. There the two lovers stood arm in arm on the topmost gallery of the tower, and gazed out into the sweet-scented wooded landscape, beyond which the blue hills rose up like a giant's city.

"Oh! do look at that strange little gray bush, it looks as if it were actually walking towards us," said Clara. Mechanically he put his hand into his side pocket; he found Coppola's perspective and looked for the bush; Clara stood in front of the glass.

Then a convulsive thrill shot through his pulse and veins; pale as a corpse, he fixed his staring eyes upon her; but soon they began to roll, and a fiery current flashed and sparkled in them, and he yelled fearfully, like a hunted animal. Leaping up high in the air and laughing horribly at the same time, he began to shout in a piercing voice, "Spin round, wooden doll! Spin round, wooden doll!" With the strength of a giant he laid hold upon Clara and tried to hurl her over, but in an agony of despair she clutched fast hold of the railing that went round the gallery.

Lothair heard the madman raging and Clara's scream of terror: a fearful presentiment flashed across his mind. He ran up the steps; the door of the second flight was locked. Clara's scream for help rang out more loudly. Mad with rage and fear, he threw himself against the door, which at length gave way. Clara's cries were growing fainter and fainter—"Help! save me! save me!" and her voice died away in the air. "She is killed—murdered by that madman," shouted Lothair. The door to the gallery was also locked.

Despair gave him the strength of a giant; he burst the door off its hinges. Good God! there was Clara in the grasp of the madman Nathanael, hanging over the gallery in the air, holding on to the iron bar with only one hand. Quick as lightning, Lothair seized his sister and pulled her back, at the same time dealing the madman a blow in the face with his doubled fist, which sent him reeling backwards, forcing him to let go his victim.

Lothair ran down with his insensible sister in his arms. She was saved. But Nathanael ran round and round the gallery, leaping up in the air and shouting, "Spin round, fire-wheel! Spin round, fire-wheel!" The people heard the wild shouting, and a crowd began to gather. In the midst of them towered the lawyer Coppelius, like a giant; he had only just arrived in the town, and had gone straight to the market place.

Some were for going up to overpower and take the madman, but Coppelius laughed and said, "Ha! ha! wait a bit; he'll come down of his own accord;" and he stood gazing up along with the rest.

All at once Nathanael stopped as if spellbound; he bent down over the railing and perceived Coppelius. With a piercing scream, "Eh! Fine eyes-a, fine eyes-a!" he leaped over the railing.

When Nathanael lay on the stone pavement with a shattered head, Coppelius had disappeared in the crush and confusion.

Several years afterwards it was reported that, outside the door of a pretty country house in a remote district, Clara had been seen sitting hand in hand with a pleasant gentleman, while two bright boys were playing at her feet. From this it may be concluded that she eventually found that quiet domestic happiness which her cheerful, blithesome character required, and which Nathanael, with his tempest-tossed soul, could never have been able to give her.

RATH KRESPEL

Councillor Krespel was one of the strangest, oddest men I ever met with in my life. When I went to live in H—— for a time the whole town was full of talk about him, as he happened just then to be in the midst of one of the very craziest of his schemes. Krespel was renowned as both a clever, learned lawyer and a skillful diplomat. One of the reigning princes of Germany—not, however, one of the most powerful—had turned to him for assistance in drawing up a memorial, which he was desirous of presenting at the Imperial Court with the view of furthering his legitimate claims upon a certain strip of territory. The project was crowned with the happiest success; and as Krespel had once complained that he could never find a dwelling sufficiently comfortable to suit him, the prince, to reward him for the memorial, undertook to defray the cost of building a house which Krespel might erect just as he pleased. Moreover, the prince was willing to purchase any site that Krespel should fancy. This offer, however, the Councillor would not accept; he insisted that the house should be built in his garden, which was situated in a very beautiful neighbourhood outside the town walls. So he bought all kinds of materials and had them carted out. Then he might have been seen day after day, attired in his curious garments (which he had made himself according to certain fixed rules of his own), slaking the lime, sifting the sand, piling up the bricks and stones in regular heaps, and so on. All this he did without once consulting an architect or thinking about a plan. One fine day, however, he went to an experienced builder of the town and requested him to be in his garden at daybreak the next morning, with all his journeymen and apprentices, and a large body of labourers, and so on, to build him his house. Naturally the builder asked for the architect's plan, and was not a little astonished when Krespel replied that none was needed, and that things would turn out all right in the end, just as he wanted them.

Next morning, when the builder and his men came to the place, they found a trench drawn out in the shape of an exact square; and Krespel said, "Here's where you must lay the foundations; then carry up the walls until I say they are high enough." "Without windows and doors, and without partition walls?" broke in the builder, as if alarmed at Krespel's mad folly. "Do what I tell you, my dear sir," replied the Councillor quite calmly; "leave the rest to me; it will be all right."

It was only the promise of high pay that could induce the builder to proceed with the ridiculous building; but none has ever been erected under merrier circumstances. As there was an abundant supply of food and drink, the workmen never left their work; and amidst their continuous laughter the four walls were run up with incredible quickness, until one day Krespel cried, "Stop!" Then the workmen, laying down trowel and hammer, came down from the scaffoldings and gathered round Krespel in a circle, while every face was asking, "Well, and what now?"

"Make way!" cried Krespel; and then running to one end of the garden, he strode slowly towards the square of brickwork. When he came close to the wall he shook his head in a dissatisfied manner, ran to the other end of the garden, again strode slowly towards the brickwork square, and proceeded to act as before. These tactics he pursued several times, until at length, running his sharp nose hard against the wall, he cried, "Come here, come here, men! break me a door in here! Here's where I want a door made!" He gave the exact dimensions in feet and inches, and they did as he bid them. Then he stepped inside the structure, and smiled with satisfaction as the builder remarked that the walls were just the height of a good two-story house. Krespel walked thoughtfully backwards and forwards across the space within, the bricklayers behind him with hammers and picks, and wherever he cried, "Make a window here, six feet high by four feet broad!" "There a little window, three feet by two!" a hole was made in a trice.

It was at this stage of the proceedings that I came to H——; and it was highly amusing to see how hundreds of people stood round about the garden and raised a loud shout whenever the stones flew out and a new window appeared where nobody had for a moment expected it. And in the same manner Krespel proceeded with the rest of the house, and with all the work necessary to that end; every-thing had to be done on the spot in accordance with the instructions which the Councillor gave from time to time. However, the ab-surdity of the whole business, the growing conviction that things would in the end turn out better than might have been expected, but above all, Krespel's generosity—which indeed cost him nothing —kept them all in good-humour. Thus were the difficulties overcome which necessarily arose out of this eccentric way of building, and in a short time there was a completely finished house, its outside, indeed, presenting a most extraordinary appearance, no two windows, etc., being alike; but on the other hand the interior arrangements suggested a peculiar feeling of comfort. All who entered the house bore witness to the truth of this; and I too experienced it myself when I was taken in by Krespel after I had become more intimate with him. For hitherto I had not exchanged a word with this eccentric man; his building had occupied him so much that he had not even once been to Professor M——'s to dinner, as he was in the habit of doing on Tuesdays. Indeed, in reply to a special invitation, he sent word that he should not set foot over the threshold before the housewarming of his new building took place.

All his friends and acquaintances, therefore, confidently looked forward to a great banquet; but Krespel invited nobody except the masters, journeymen, apprentices, and labourers who had built the house. He entertained them with the choicest viands: bricklayer's apprentices devoured partridge pies regardless of consequences; young joiners polished off roast pheasants with the greatest success; while hungry labourers helped themselves for once to the choicest morsels of *truffes fricassées.* In the evening their wives and daughters came, and there was a great ball. After waltzing a short while with the wives of the masters, Krespel sat down among the town musicians, took a violin in his hand, and directed the orchestra until daylight.

On the Tuesday after this festival, which exhibited Councillor Krespel in the character of a friend of the people, I at length saw him appear, to my no little joy, at Professor M——'s. Anything more strange and fantastic than Krespel's behaviour it would be impossible to find. He was so stiff and awkward in his movements that he looked every moment as if he would run up against something or do some damage. But he did not; and the lady of the house seemed to be well aware that he would not, for she did not grow a shade paler when he rushed with heavy steps round a table crowded with beautiful cups, or when he maneuvered near a large mirror that reached down to the floor, or even when he seized a flower pot of beautifully painted porcelain and swung it round in the air as if desirous of making its colours play. Moreover, before dinner he subjected everything in the Professor's room to a most minute examination; he also took down a picture from the wall and hung it up again, standing on one of the cushioned chairs to do so. At the same time he talked a good deal and vehemently; at one time his thoughts kept leaping, as it were, from one subject to another (this was most conspicuous during dinner); at another, he was unable to have done with an idea; seizing upon it again and again, he gave it all sorts of wonderful twists and turns, and couldn't get back into the ordinary track until something else took hold of his fancy. Sometimes his voice was rough and harsh and screeching, and sometimes it was low and drawling and singing; but at no time did it harmonize with what he was talking about.

Music was the subject of conversation; the praises of a new composer were being sung, when Krespel, smiling, said in his low singing tones, "I wish the devil with his pitchfork would hurl that atrocious garbler of music millions of fathoms down to the bottomless pit of hell!" Then he burst out passionately and wildly, "She is an angel of heaven, nothing but pure god-given music!—the paragon and queen of song!"—and tears stood in his eyes. To understand this, we had to go back to a celebrated artiste, who had been the subject of conversation an hour before.

Just at this time a roast hare was on the table; I noticed that Krespel carefully removed every particle of meat from the bones on his plate, and was most particular in his inquiries after the hare's feet; these the Professor's little five-year-old daughter now brought to him with a very pretty smile. Besides, the children had cast many friendly glances towards Krespel during dinner; now they rose and drew nearer to him, but not without signs of timorous awe. What's the meaning of that? thought I to myself. Dessert was brought in; then the Councillor took a little box from his pocket, in which he had a miniature steel lathe. This he immediately screwed fast to the table, and turning the bones with incredible skill and rapidity, he made all sorts of little fancy boxes and balls, which the children received with cries of delight.

Just as we were rising from table, the Professor's niece asked, "And what is our Antonia doing?"

Krespel's face was like that of one who has bitten of a sour orange and wants to look as if it were a sweet one; but his expression soon changed into the likeness of a hideous mask, whilst he laughed behind it with downright bitter, fierce, and as it seemed to me, satanic scorn. "Our Antonia? our dear Antonia?" he asked in his drawling, disagreeable singing way.

The Professor hastened to intervene; in the reproving glance which he gave his niece I read that she had touched a point likely to stir up unpleasant memories in Krespel's heart.

"How are you getting on with your violins?" interposed the Professor in a jovial manner, taking the Councillor by both hands. Then Krespel's countenance cleared up, and with a firm voice he replied, "Capitally, Professor; you recollect my telling you of the lucky chance which threw that splendid Amati into my hands. Well, I've only cut it open today—not before today. I hope Antonia has carefully taken the rest of it to pieces."

"Antonia is a good child," remarked the Professor.

"Yes, indeed, that she is," cried the Councillor, whisking himself round; then, seizing his hat and stick, he hastily rushed out of the room. I saw in the mirror that tears were in his eyes.

As soon as the Councillor was gone, I at once urged the Professor to explain to me what Krespel had to do with violins, and particularly with Antonia. "Well," replied the Professor, "not only is the Councillor a remarkably eccentric fellow altogether, but he practices violin making in his own crack-brained way." "Violin making!" I exclaimed, perfectly astonished. "Yes," continued the Professor, "according to the judgment of men who understand the thing, Krespel makes the very best violins that can be found nowadays; formerly he would frequently let other people play on those in which he had been especially successful, but that's been all over and done with now for a long time. As soon as he has finished a violin he plays on it himself for one or two hours, with very remarkable power and with the most exquisite expression; then he hangs it up beside the rest, and never touches it again or suffers anybody else to touch it. If a violin by any of the eminent old masters is hunted up anywhere, the Councillor buys it immediately, no matter what the price put upon it. But he plays it as he does his own violins, only once; then he takes it to pieces in order to examine closely its inner structure, and should he fancy he hasn't found exactly what he was looking for, in a pet he throws the pieces into a big chest, which is already full of the remains of broken violins."

"But who and what is Antonia?" I inquired, hastily and impetuously.

"Well, now, that," continued the Professor, "that is a thing which might very well make me conceive an unconquerable aversion to the Councillor, were I not convinced that there is some peculiar secret behind it, for he is such a good-natured fellow at bottom as to be sometimes guilty of weakness. When he came to H——, several

years ago, he led the life of an anchorite, along with an old housekeeper, in —— Street. Soon, by his oddities, he excited the curiosity of his neighbours; as soon as he became aware of this, he
sought and made acquaintances. Not only in my house but everywhere we became so accustomed to him that he grew to be indispensable. In spite of his rude exterior, even the children liked him,
without ever proving a nuisance to him; for notwithstanding all their
friendly passages together, they always retained a certain timorous
awe of him, which secured him against all overfamiliarity. You
have had today an example of the way in which he wins their hearts
by his ready skill in various things. We all took him at first for a
crusty old bachelor, and he never contradicted us.

"After he had been living here some time, he went away, nobody
knew where, and returned at the end of some months. The evening
following his return his windows were lit up to an unusual extent!
This alone was sufficient to arouse his neighbours' attention, and
they soon heard a surpassingly beautiful female voice singing to the
accompaniment of a piano. Then the music of a violin was heard
chiming in and entering upon a keen ardent contest with the voice.
They knew at once that the player was the Councillor. I myself
mixed in the large crowd which had gathered in front of his house
to listen to this extraordinary concert; and I must confess that,
beside this voice and the peculiar, deep, soul-stirring impression
which the execution made upon me, the singing of the most celebrated artistes whom I had ever heard seemed to me feeble and
void of expression. Until then I had had no conception of such
long-sustained notes, of such nightingale trills, of such undulations
of musical sound, of such swelling up to the strength of organ notes,
of such dying away to the faintest whisper. There was not one
whom the sweet witchery did not enthrall; and when the singer
ceased, nothing but soft sighs broke the impressive silence.

"About midnight the Councillor was heard talking violently, and
another male voice seemed, to judge from the tones, to be reproach-
ing him, while at intervals the broken words of a sobbing girl could
be detected. The Councillor continued to shout with increasing
violence, until he fell into that drawling, singing way that you
know. He was interrupted by a loud scream from the girl, and
then all was as still as death. Suddenly a loud racket was heard on
the stairs; a young man rushed out sobbing, threw himself into a
post-chaise which stood below, and drove rapidly away.

"The next day the Councillor was very cheerful, and nobody
had the courage to question him about the events of the previous

night. But on inquiring of the housekeeper, we gathered that the
Councillor had brought home with him an extraordinarily pretty
young lady whom he called Antonia, and she it was who had sung
so beautifully. A young man also had come along with them; he
had treated Antonia very tenderly, and must evidently have been
her fiancé. But he, since the Councillor peremptorily insisted on
it, had had to go away again in a hurry. What the relations
between Antonia and the Councillor are has remained a secret, but
this much is certain, that he tyrannizes over the poor girl in the
most hateful fashion. He watches her as Doctor Bartolo watches
his ward in the *Barber of Seville*; she hardly dares show herself at the
window; and if, yielding now and again to her earnest entreaties,
he takes her into society, he follows her with Argus' eyes, and will
on no account suffer a musical note to be sounded, far less let
Antonia sing—indeed, she is not permitted to sing in his own house.
Antonia's singing on that memorable night, has, therefore, come to
be regarded by the townspeople in the light of a tradition of some
marvellous wonder that suffices to stir the heart and the fancy; and
even those who did not hear it often exclaim, whenever any other
singer attempts to display her powers in the place, 'What sort of a
wretched squeaking do you call that? Nobody but Antonia knows
how to sing.'"

Having a singular weakness for such fantastic histories, I found it
necessary, as may easily be imagined, to make Antonia's acquaintance. I had myself often enough heard the popular saying about
her singing, but had never imagined that that exquisite artiste was
living in the place, held a captive in the bonds of this eccentric
Krespel like the victim of a tyrannous sorcerer. Naturally enough
I heard Antonia's marvellous voice in my dreams on the following
night, and as she besought me in the most touching manner in a
glorious adagio movement (very ridiculously it seemed to me, as if
I had composed it myself) to save her, I soon resolved, like a second
Astolpho, to penetrate into Krespel's house, as if into another
Alcina's magic castle, and deliver the queen of song from her
ignominious fetters.

It all came about in a different way from what I had expected; I
had seen the Councillor scarcely more than two or three times, and
eagerly discussed with him the best method of constructing violins,
when he invited me to call and see him. I did so; and he showed
me his treasures of violins. There were fully thirty of them hanging
up in a closet; one among them bore conspicuously all the marks of
great antiquity (a carved lion's head, and so on), and, hung up

higher than the rest and surmounted by a crown of flowers, it seemed to exercise a queenly supremacy over them.

"This violin," said Krespel, on my making some inquiry relative to it, "this violin is a very remarkable and curious specimen of the work of some unknown master, probably of Tartini's time. I am perfectly convinced that there is something especially exceptional in its inner construction, and that, if I took it to pieces, a secret would be revealed to me which I have long been seeking to discover, but—laugh at me if you like—this senseless thing which only gives signs of life and sound as I make it, often speaks to me in a strange way of itself. The first time I played upon it I somehow fancied that I was only the magnetizer who has the power of moving his subject to reveal of his own accord in words the visions of his inner nature. Don't go away with the belief that I am such a fool as to attach even the slightest importance to such fantastic notions, and yet it's certainly strange that I could never prevail upon myself to cut open that dumb lifeless thing there. I am very pleased now that I have not cut it open, for since Antonia has been with me I sometimes play to her upon this violin. For Antonia is fond of it—very fond of it."

As the Councillor uttered these words with visible signs of emotion, I felt encouraged to hazard the question, "Will you not play it to me, Councillor?" Krespel made a wry face, and falling into his drawling, singing way, said, "No, my good sir!" and that was an end of the matter. Then I had to look at all sorts of rare curiosities, the greater part of them childish trifles; at last thrusting his arm into a chest, he brought out a folded piece of paper, which he pressed into my hand, adding solemnly, "You are a lover of art; take this present as a priceless memento, which you must value at all times above everything else."

Therewith he took me by the shoulders and gently pushed me towards the door, embracing me on the threshold. That is to say, I was in a symbolical manner virtually kicked out of doors. Unfolding the paper, I found a piece of a first string of a violin about an eighth of an inch in length, with the words, "A piece of the treble string with which the deceased Stamitz strung his violin for the last concert at which he ever played."

This summary dismissal at mention of Antonia's name led me to infer that I should never see her; but I was mistaken, for on my second visit to the Councillor's I found her in his room, assisting him to put a violin together. At first sight Antonia did not make a strong impression; but soon I found it impossible to tear myself away from her blue eyes, her sweet rosy lips, her uncommonly graceful, lovely form.   She was very pale; but a shrewd remark or a merry sally would call up a winning smile on her face and suffuse her cheeks with a deep burning flush, which, however, soon faded away to a faint rosy glow.

My conversation with her was quite unconstrained, and yet I saw nothing whatever of the Argus-like watchings on Krespel's part which the Professor had imputed to him; on the contrary, his behaviour moved along conventional lines, nay, he even seemed to approve of my conversation with Antonia.   So often I stepped in to see the Councillor; and as we became accustomed to each other's society, a singular feeling of homeliness, taking possession of our little circle of three, filled our hearts with inward happiness.   I still continued to derive exquisite enjoyment from the Councillor's strange crotchets and oddities; but it was of course Antonia's irresistible charms alone which attracted me, and led me to put up with a good deal which I should otherwise, in the frame of mind in which I then was, have impatiently shunned.   For it happened only too often that in the Councillor's characteristic extravagance there was mingled much that was dull and tiresome; and it was particularly irritating to me that, as soon as I turned the conversation to music, particularly upon singing, he was sure to interrupt me, with that sardonic smile upon his face and those repulsive singing tones of his, by some remark of a quite opposite tendency, very often of a commonplace character.   From the great distress which at such times Antonia's glances betrayed, I perceived that he only did it to deprive me of a pretext for calling upon her for a song.   But I didn't relinquish my design.   The hindrances which the Councillor threw in my way only strengthened my resolution to overcome them; I *must* hear Antonia sing if I was not to pine away in reveries and dim aspirations for want of hearing her.

One evening Krespel was in an uncommonly good humour; he had been taking an old Cremona violin to pieces, and had discovered that the soundpost was fixed half a line more obliquely than usual—an important discovery! one of incalculable advantage in the practical work of making violins!   I succeeded in setting him off at full speed on his hobby of the true art of violin playing.   Mention of the way in which the old masters picked up their dexterity in execution from really great singers (which was what Krespel happened just then to be expatiating upon), naturally paved the way for the remark that now the practice was the exact opposite of this, the vocal score erroneously following the affected and abrupt transitions and rapid scaling of the instrumentalists.

"What is more nonsensical," I cried, leaping from my chair, running to the piano, and opening it quickly, "what is more nonsensical than such an execrable style as this, which, far from being music, is much more like the noise of peas rolling across the floor?"

At the same time I sang several of the modern *fermatas*, which rush up and down and hum like a well-spun peg-top, striking a few villainous chords by way of accompaniment.

Krespel laughed outrageously and screamed, "Ha! ha! I hear our German-Italians or our Italian-Germans struggling with an aria from Pucitta, or Portogallo, or some other *Maestro di capella*, or rather *schiavo d'un primo uomo.*"*

Now, thought I, now's the time; so turning to Antonia, I remarked, "Antonia knows nothing of such singing as that, I believe?" At the same time I struck up one of old Leonardo Leo's beautiful soul-stirring songs. Then Antonia's cheeks glowed; heavenly radiance sparkled in her eyes, which grew full of reawakened inspiration; she hastened to the piano; she opened her lips; but at that very moment Krespel pushed her away, grasped me by the shoulders, and with a shriek that rose up to a tenor pitch, cried, "My son—my son—my son!" And then he immediately went on, singing very softly, and grasping my hand with a bow that was the pink of politeness, "In very truth, my esteemed and honourable student friend, in very truth it would be a violation of the codes of social intercourse, as well as of all good manners, were I to express aloud and in a stirring way my wish that here, on this very spot, the devil from hell would softly break your neck with his burning claws, and so in a sense make short work of you; but, setting that aside, you must acknowledge, my dearest friend, that it is rapidly growing dark, and there are no lamps burning tonight so that, even though I did not kick you downstairs at once, your darling limbs might still run a risk of suffering damage. Go home by all means; and cherish a kind remembrance of your faithful friend, if it should happen that you never—pray, understand me—if you should never see him in his own house again."

Therewith he embraced me, and still keeping fast hold of me, turned with me slowly towards the door, so that I could not get another look at Antonia. Of course it is plain enough that in my position I couldn't thrash the Councillor, though that is what he really deserved. The Professor enjoyed a good laugh at my expense,

---

* "Slave of a primo uomo"—The male equivalent of a prima donna.

and assured me that I had ruined for ever all hopes of retaining the Councillor's friendship. Antonia was too dear to me, I might say too holy, for me to go and play the part of the languishing lover and stand gazing up at her window, or to fill the role of the lovesick adventurer. Completely upset, I went away from H——; but, as is usual in such cases, the brilliant colours of the picture of my fancy faded, and the recollection of Antonia, as well as of Antonia's singing (which I had never heard), often fell upon my heart like a soft faint trembling light, comforting me.

Two years afterwards I received an appointment in B——, and set out on a journey to the south of Germany. The towers of H—— rose before me in the red vaporous glow of the evening; the nearer I came the more was I oppressed by an indescribable feeling of the most agonizing distress; it lay upon me like a heavy burden; I could not breathe; I was obliged to get out of my carriage into the open air. But my anguish continued to increase until it became actual physical pain.

Soon I seemed to hear the strains of a solemn chorale floating in the air; the sounds continued to grow more distinct. I realized that they were men's voices chanting a church chorale. "What's that? what's that?" I cried, a burning stab darting as it were through my breast. "Don't you see?" replied the coachman, who was driving along beside me, "why, don't you see? they're burying somebody up yonder in yon churchyard." And indeed we were near the churchyard; I saw a circle of men clothed in black standing round a grave, which was on the point of being closed. Tears started to my eyes; I somehow fancied they were burying there all the joy and all the happiness of life.

Moving on rapidly down the hill, I was no longer able to see into the churchyard; the chorale came to an end, and I perceived not far distant from the gate some of the mourners returning from the funeral. The Professor, with his niece on his arm, both in deep mourning, went close past me without noticing me. The young lady had her handkerchief pressed close to her eyes, and was weeping bitterly.

In the frame of mind in which I then was I could not possibly go into the town, so I sent my servant on with the carriage to the hotel where I usually put up, while I took a turn in the familiar neighbourhood, to get rid of a mood that was possibly only due to physical causes, such as heating on the journey, and so forth.

On arriving at a very familiar avenue, which leads to a pleasure resort, I came upon a most extraordinary spectacle. Councillor

Krespel was being conducted by two mourners, from whom he appeared to be endeavouring to make his escape by all sorts of strange twists and turns. As usual, he was dressed in his own curious homemade gray coat; but from his little cocked hat, which he wore perched over one ear in military fashion, a long narrow ribbon of black crepe fluttered backwards and forwards in the wind. Around his waist he had buckled a black sword belt; but instead of a sword he had stuck a long fiddle bow into it.

A creepy shudder ran through my limbs: "He's insane," thought I, as I slowly followed them. The Councillor's companions led him as far as his house, where he embraced them, laughing loudly. They left him; and then his glance fell upon me, for I now stood near him. He stared at me fixedly for some time; then he cried in a hollow voice, "Welcome, my student friend! you also understand it!" Thereupon he took me by the arm and pulled me into the house, up the steps, into the room where the violins hung. They were all draped in black crepe; the violin of the old master was missing; in its place was a cypress wreath.

I knew what had happened. "Antonia! Antonia!" I cried in inconsolable grief. The Councillor, with his arms crossed on his breast, stood beside me as if turned into stone. I pointed to the cypress wreath. "When she died," he said in a very hoarse solemn voice, "the soundpost of that violin broke into pieces with a ringing crack, and the soundboard was split from end to end. The faithful instrument could only live with her and in her; it lies beside her in the coffin, it has been buried with her."

Deeply agitated, I sank down upon a chair, while the Councillor began to sing a gay song in a husky voice; it was truly horrible to see him hopping about on one foot, and the crepe strings (he still had his hat on) flying about the room and up to the violins hanging on the walls. Indeed, I could not repress a loud cry that rose to my lips when, on the Councillor making an abrupt turn, the crepe came all over me; I fancied he wanted to envelop me in it and drag me down into the horrible dark depths of insanity.

Suddenly he stood still and addressed me in his singing way, "My son! my son! why do you call out? Have you espied the angel of death? That always precedes the ceremony." Stepping into the middle of the room, he took the violin bow out of his sword belt and, holding it over his head with both hands, broke it into a thousand pieces. Then, with a loud laugh, he cried, "Now you imagine my sentence is pronounced, don't you, my son? but it's nothing of the kind—not at all! not at all! Now I'm free—free—

free—hurrah! I'm free! Now I shall make no more violins—no more violins—Hurrah! no more violins!" This he sang to a horrible mirthful tune, again spinning round on one foot.

Perfectly aghast, I was making the best of my way to the door, when he held me fast, saying quite calmly, "Stay, my student friend, pray don't think from this outbreak of grief, which is torturing me as if with the agonies of death, that I am insane; I only do it because a short time ago I made myself a dressing-gown in which I wanted to look like Fate or like God!" The Councillor then went on with a medley of silly and awful rubbish, until he fell down utterly exhausted. I called the old housekeeper, and was very pleased to find myself in the open air again.

I never doubted for a moment that Krespel had become insane. The Professor, however, asserted the contrary. "There are men," he remarked, "from whom nature or a special destiny has taken away the cover behind which the mad folly of the rest of us runs its course unobserved. They are like thin-skinned insects, which, as we watch the restless play of their muscles, seem to be misshapen; nevertheless everything soon comes back into its proper form again. Everything that stays on the level of mental process in us, becomes action in Krespel. That bitter scorn which the spirit that is wrapped up in the doings and dealings of the earth often has, Krespel gives vent to in outrageous gestures and agile caprioles. But these are his lightning conductor. What comes up out of the earth he gives again to the earth, but what is divine, that he keeps; and so I believe that his inner consciousness, in spite of the apparent madness which springs from it to the surface, is as right as a trivet. To be sure, Antonia's sudden death grieves him sorely, but I warrant that tomorrow will see him going along in his old jogtrot way as usual." And the Professor's prediction was almost literally filled. Next day the Councillor appeared to be just as he formerly was, only he averred that he would never make another violin, nor ever play on another. And, as I learned later, he kept his word.

Hints which the Professor let fall confirmed my own private conviction that the carefully guarded secret of the Councillor's relations with Antonia, nay, even her death, was a crime which must weigh heavily upon him, a crime that could not be atoned for. I determined that I would not leave H—— without taxing him with the offence which I conceived him to be guilty of. I determined to shake his heart down to its very roots, and compel him to make open confession of the terrible deed. The more I reflected upon the matter the clearer it grew in my own mind that Krespel must be a villain, and in the same proportion my intended reproach, which assumed of itself the form of a real rhetorical masterpiece, grew more fiery and more impressive. Thus equipped and mightily incensed, I hurried to his house.

I found him making toys, smiling calmly. "How can peace," I burst out, "find lodgment even for a single moment in your breast, as long as the memory of your horrible deed preys like a serpent upon you?"

He gazed at me in amazement, and laid his chisel aside. "What do you mean, my dear sir?" he asked; "pray take a seat." But my indignation chafing me more and more, I went on to accuse him directly of having murdered Antonia, and to threaten him with the vengeance of the Eternal.

Further, as a newly full-fledged lawyer, full of my profession, I went so far as to give him to understand that I would leave no stone unturned to get a clue to the business, and so deliver him here in this world into the hands of an earthly judge.

I must confess that I was considerably disconcerted when, at the conclusion of my violent and pompous harangue, the Councillor, without answering so much as a single word, calmly fixed his eyes upon me as though expecting me to go on again. And this I did indeed attempt to do, but it sounded so ill-founded and so stupid as well that I soon grew silent again.

Krespel gloated over my embarrassment, while a malicious ironic smile flitted across his face. Then he grew very grave, and addressed me in solemn tones. "Young man, no doubt you think I am foolish, insane; that I can pardon you, since we are both confined in the same madhouse; and you only blame me for deluding myself with the idea that I am God the Father because you imagine yourself to be God the Son. But how do you dare desire to insinuate yourself into the secrets and lay bare the hidden motives of a life that is strange to you and that must continue so? She has gone and there is no mystery."

He ceased speaking, rose, and crossed the room backwards and forwards several times. I ventured to ask for an explanation; he fixed his eyes upon me, grasped me by the hand, and led me to the window, which he threw wide open. Propping himself upon his arms, he leaned out, and, looking down into the garden, told me the history of his life. When he finished I left him, touched and ashamed.

In a few words, his relations with Antonia rose in the following way. Twenty years ago the Councillor had been led into Italy by his engrossing passion for hunting up and buying the best violins of the old masters. At that time he had not yet begun to make them himself, and so of course he had not begun to take to pieces those which he bought. In Venice he heard the celebrated singer Angela ——i, who at that time was playing with splendid success as prima donna at St. Benedict's Theatre.

His enthusiasm was awakened, not only in her art—which Signora Angela had indeed brought to a high pitch of perfection—but in her angelic beauty as well. He sought her acquaintance; and in spite of all his rugged manners he succeeded in winning her heart, principally through his bold and yet at the same time masterly violin playing.

Close intimacy led in a few weeks to marriage, which, however, was kept a secret, because Angela was unwilling to sever her connection with the theatre; neither did she wish to part with her professional name, by which she was celebrated, nor to add to it the cacophonous "Krespel." With the most extravagant irony he described to me what a strange life of worry and torture Angela led him as soon as she became his wife. Krespel was of the opinion that more capriciousness and waywardness were concentrated in Angela's little person than in all the rest of the prima donnas in the world put together. If now and then he presumed to stand up in his own defense, she let loose a whole army of abbots, music composers, and students upon him, who, ignorant of his true connection with Angela, soundly rated him as a most intolerable, ungallant lover for not submitting to all the Signora's caprices.

It was just after one of these stormy scenes that Krespel fled to Angela's country seat to try and forget in playing fantasias on his Cremona violin the annoyances of the day. But he had not been there long before the Signora, who had followed hard after him, stepped into the room. She was in an affectionate humour; she embraced her husband, overwhelmed him with sweet and languishing glances, and rested her pretty head on his shoulder. But Krespel, carried away into the world of music, continued to play on until the walls echoed again; thus he chanced to touch the Signora somewhat ungently with his arm and the fiddle bow.

She leaped back full of fury, shrieking, "*Bestia tedesca!*",* snatched the violin from his hands, and dashed it on the marble table into a thousand pieces. Krespel stood like a statue before her; but then, as if awakening out of a dream, he seized her with the strength of

* "You German beast!"

a giant and threw her out of the window of her own house and, without troubling himself about anything more, fled back to Venice —to Germany.

It was not, however, until some time had elapsed that he had a clear recollection of what he had done; although he knew that the window was scarcely five feet from the ground, and although he was fully cognizant of the necessity, under the above-mentioned circumstances, of throwing the Signora out of the window, he still felt troubled by a sense of painful uneasiness, the more so since she had imparted to him in no ambiguous terms an interesting secret as to her condition.

He did not dare to make inquiries; and he was surprised about eight months afterwards at receiving a tender letter from his beloved wife, in which she made not the slightest allusion to what had taken place in her country house, only adding to the intelligence that she had been safely delivered of a sweet little daughter the heartfelt prayer that her dear husband and now a happy father would come at once to Venice.

That, however, Krespel did not do; instead he appealed to a close friend for a more circumstantial account of the details, and learned that the Signora had alighted upon the soft grass as lightly as a bird, and that the sole consequences of the fall or shock had been mental. That is to say, after Krespel's heroic deed she had become completely altered; she never showed a trace of caprice, of her former freaks, or of her teasing habits; and the composer who wrote for the next carnival was the happiest fellow under the sun, since the Signora was willing to sing his music without the scores and hundreds of changes which she at other times had insisted upon. "To be sure," added his friend, "there was every reason for preserving the secret of Angela's cure, else every day would see lady singers flying through windows."

The Councillor was excited at this news; he engaged horses; he took his seat in the carriage. "Stop!" he cried suddenly. "Why, there's not a shadow of doubt," he murmured to himself, "that as soon as Angela sets eyes upon me again, the evil spirit will recover his power and once more take possession of her. And since I have already thrown her out of the window, what could I do if a similar case were to occur again? What would there be left for me to do?" He got out of the carriage, and wrote an affectionate letter to his wife, making graceful allusion to her tenderness in especially dwelling upon the fact that his tiny daughter had like him a little mole behind the ear, and—remained in Germany.

Fanciful map prepared by Hoffmann to indicate the location of his Berlin residence. It illustrates landmarks, Hoffmann's friends, and characters from his stories.

Restauration u. große Weinstube
bey Thiemer
Bernhardi
Ludwig Tieck
Brentano
ein Affe
Directions Zimmer
Graf Brühl
Kreisler
Damen
Restauration im Theater
Regierungs Rath Hoffmann
Fenster
Schlafkabinet
Arbeits Stube
Zimmer der Frau
Cabinet
Prunkzimmer
Küche
Vorzimmer
Flur
Treppe
Taubenstraße
eine Mausefalle
Glöckner
Kammergericht
Anonymus
ein Vogel im Fluge
eine Rose
Gensdarmes Markt

Now an active correspondence began between them. Assurances of unchanged affection—invitations—laments over the absence of the beloved one—thwarted wishes—hopes, etc.—flew backwards and forwards from Venice to H——, from H—— to Venice. At length Angela came to Germany, and, as is well known, sang with brilliant success as prima donna at the great theatre in F——. Despite the fact that she was no longer young, she won all hearts by the irresistible charm of her wonderfully splendid singing. At that time she had not lost her voice in the least degree.

Meanwhile, Antonia had been growing up; and her mother never tired of writing to tell her father that a singer of the first rank was developing in her. Krespel's friends in F—— also confirmed this intelligence, and urged him to come to F—— to see and admire this uncommon sight of two such glorious singers. They had not the slightest suspicion of the close relations in which Krespel stood to the pair. He would willingly have seen with his own eyes the daughter who occupied so large a place in his heart, and who moreover often appeared to him in his dreams; but as soon as he thought about his wife he felt very uncomfortable, and so he remained at home among his broken violins.

There was a certain promising young composer, B—— of F——, who was found to have suddenly disappeared, nobody knew where. This young man fell so deeply in love with Antonia that, as she returned his love, he earnestly besought her mother to consent to an immediate union, sanctified as it would further be by art. Angela had nothing to urge against his suit; and the Councillor the more readily gave his consent since the young composer's productions had found favour before his rigorous critical judgment.

Krespel was expecting to hear of the consummation of the marriage, when he received instead a black-sealed envelope addressed in a strange hand. Doctor R—— conveyed to the Councillor the sad intelligence that Angela had fallen seriously ill in consequence of a cold caught at the theatre, and that during the night immediately preceding what was to have been Antonia's wedding day, she had died. To him, the Doctor, Angela had disclosed the fact that she was Krespel's wife, and that Antonia was his daughter; he, Krespel, had better hasten therefore to take charge of the orphan. Notwithstanding that the Councillor was a good deal upset by this news of Angela's death, he soon began to feel that an antipathetic, disturbing influence had departed from his life, and that now for the first time he could begin to breathe freely.

The very same day he set out for F——. You could not credit
how heart-rending was the Councillor's description of the moment
when he first saw Antonia. Even in the fantastic oddities of his
expression there was such a marvellous power of description that I
am unable to give even so much as a faint indication of it. Antonia
inherited all her mother's amiability and all her mother's charms,
but not the repellent reverse of the medal. There was no chronic
moral ulcer, which might break out from time to time. Antonia's
betrothed put in an appearance, while Antonia herself, fathoming
with happy instinct the deeper-lying character of her wonderful
father, sang one of old Padre Martini's motets, which, she knew,
Krespel in the heyday of his courtship had never grown tired of
hearing her mother sing.

The tears ran in streams down Krespel's cheeks; even Angela he
had never heard sing like that. Antonia's voice was of a very
remarkable and altogether peculiar timbre; at one time it was like
the sighing of an æolian harp, at another like the warbled gush of
the nightingale. It seemed as if there was not room for such notes
in the human breast. Antonia, blushing with joy and happiness,
sang on and on—all her most beautiful songs, B—— playing the
piano as only enthusiasm that is intoxicated with delight can play.
Krespel was at first transported with rapture, then he grew thoughtful—still—absorbed in reflection. At length he leaped to his feet,
pressed Antonia to his heart, and begged her in a low husky voice,
"Sing no more if you love me—my heart is bursting—I fear—I fear
—don't sing again."

"No!" remarked the Councillor next day to Doctor R——,
"when, as she sang, her blushes gathered into two dark red spots on
her pale cheeks, I knew it had nothing to do with your nonsensical
family likenesses, I knew it was what I dreaded."

The Doctor, whose countenance had shown signs of deep distress
from the very beginning of the conversation, replied, "Whether it
arises from a too early taxing of her powers of song, or whether the
fault is Nature's—enough, Antonia labours under an organic
failure in the chest, while it is from it too that her voice derives its
wonderful power and its singular timbre, which I might almost say
transcend the limits of human capabilities of song. But it bears the
announcement of her early death; for, if she continues to sing, I
wouldn't give her at the most more than six months longer to live."

Krespel's heart was lacerated as if by the stabs of hundreds of
stinging knives. It was as though his life had been for the first time
overshadowed by a beautiful tree full of the most magnificent

blossoms, and now it was to be sawed to pieces at the roots, so that it could not grow green and blossom any more. His resolution was taken. He told Antonia everything; he put the alternatives before her—whether she would follow her fiancé and yield to his and the world's seductions, but with the certainty of dying early, or whether she would spread round her father in his old days that joy and peace which had hitherto been unknown to him, and so secure a long life.

She threw herself into his arms sobbing, and he, knowing the heart-rending trial that was before her, did not press for a more explicit declaration. He talked the matter over with her fiancé; but, although the latter swore that no note should ever cross Antonia's lips, the Councillor was only too well aware that even B—— could not resist the temptation of hearing her sing, at any rate, arias of his own composition. And the world, the musical public, even though acquainted with the nature of the singer's affliction, would certainly not relinquish its claims to hear her, for in cases where pleasure is concerned people of this class are very selfish and cruel.

The Councillor disappeared from F—— along with Antonia, and came to H——. B—— was in despair when he learned that they had gone. He set out on their track, overtook them, and arrived at H—— at the same time that they did. "Let me see him only once, and then die!" entreated Antonia. "Die! die!" cried Krespel, wild with anger, an icy shudder running through him. His daughter, the only creature in the wide world who had awakened in him the springs of unknown joy, who alone had reconciled him to life, tore herself away from his heart, and he—he suffered the terrible trial to take place.

B—— sat down at the piano; Antonia sang; Krespel fiddled away merrily, until the two red spots showed themselves on Antonia's cheeks. Then he bade her stop; and as B—— was taking leave of his betrothed, she suddenly fell to the floor with a loud scream.

"I thought," continued Krespel in his narration, "I thought that she was, as I had anticipated, really dead; but as I had prepared myself for the worst, my calmness did not leave me, nor my self-command desert me. I grasped B——, who stood like a silly sheep in his dismay, by the shoulders, and said (here the Councillor fell into his singing tone), 'Now that you, my estimable pianoforte player, have, as you wished and desired, really murdered your fiancée, you may quietly take your departure; at least have the goodness to make yourself scarce before I run my bright hanger through your heart.

My daughter, who, as you see, is rather pale, could very well do with some colour from your precious blood. Make haste and run, for I might also hurl a nimble knife or two after you.' I must, I suppose, have looked rather formidable as I uttered these words, for, with a cry of the greatest terror, B—— tore himself loose from my grasp, rushed out of the room, and down the steps." Directly after B—— was gone, when the Councillor tried to lift up his daughter, who lay unconscious on the floor, she opened her eyes with a deep sigh, but soon closed them again as if about to die.

Then Krespel's grief found vent aloud, and would not be comforted. The Doctor, whom the old housekeeper had called in, pronounced Antonia's case a somewhat serious but by no means dangerous attack; and she did indeed recover more quickly than her father had dared to hope. She now clung to him with the most confiding childlike affection; she entered into his favourite hobbies— into his mad schemes and whims. She helped him take old violins to pieces and glue new ones together. "I won't sing again any more, but will live for you," she often said, sweetly smiling upon him, after she had been asked to sing and had refused. Such appeals, however, the Councillor was anxious to spare her as much as possible; for this reason it was that he was unwilling to take her into society, and solicitously shunned all music. He well understood how painful it must be for her to forgo altogether the exercise of that art which she had brought to such a pitch of perfection.

When the Councillor bought the wonderful violin that he had buried with Antonia, and was about to take it to pieces, she met him with great sadness in her face and softly breathed the petition, "What! this as well?" By some power, which he could not explain, he felt impelled to leave this particular instrument unbroken, and to play upon it.

Scarcely had he drawn the first few notes from it than Antonia cried aloud with joy, "Why, that's me!—now I shall sing again." And, in truth, there was something remarkably striking about the clear, silvery, bell-like tones of the violin; they seemed to have been engendered in the human soul. Krespel's heart was deeply moved; he played, too, better than ever. As he ran up and down the scale, playing bold passages with consummate power and expression, she clapped her hands together and cried with delight, "I did that well! I did that well!"

From this time onwards her life was filled with peace and cheerfulness. She often said to the Councillor, "I should like to sing something, father." Then Krespel would take his violin down from the wall and play her most beautiful songs, and her heart was right glad and happy.

Shortly before my arrival in H——, the Councillor fancied one night that he heard somebody playing the piano in the adjoining room, and he soon made out distinctly that B—— was flourishing on the instrument in his usual style. He wished to get up, but felt himself held down as if by a dead weight, and lying as if fettered in iron bonds; he was utterly unable to move an inch. Then Antonia's voice was heard singing low and soft; soon, however, it began to rise and rise in volume until it became an ear-splitting fortissimo; and at length she passed over into a powerfully impressive song which B—— had once composed for her in the devotional style of the old masters.

Krespel described his condition as being incomprehensible, for terrible anguish was mingled with a delight he had never experienced before. All at once he was surrounded by a dazzling brightness, in which he beheld B—— and Antonia locked in a close embrace, and gazing at each other in a rapture of ecstasy. The music of the song and of the pianoforte accompanying it went on without any visible signs that Antonia was singing or that B—— touched the instrument.

Then the Councillor fell into a sort of dead faint, while the images vanished. On awakening he still felt the terrible anguish of his dream. He rushed into Antonia's room. She lay on the sofa, her hands devoutly folded, and looking as if asleep and dreaming of the joys and raptures of heaven. But she was—dead.

TOBIAS MARTIN, MASTER COOPER, AND HIS MEN

I

On the first of May of the year one thousand five hundred and eighty, the Honourable Guild of Coopers in the free imperial town of Nuremberg held its solemn annual meeting, according to use and wont. A short time previously one of its "Vorsteher," or "Candlemasters" as they were called, had been carried to his grave; so that it was necessary to appoint his successor. The choice fell upon Master Martin and in truth no one could equal him in strong and elegant building of vats; nor did anyone understand as he did the keeping of wine in cellar; for which reason he had the grandest lords and gentry for his customers, and lived in the utmost comfort; nay, in absolute wealth, so that the worthy town councillor, Jacobus Paumgartner (who was presiding at the meeting), said at the Guild meeting, "You have done right well, my worthy friends, to choose Master Martin for your presidency, which could not be in better hands. Master Martin is highly esteemed by all who have the pleasure of his acquaintance for his great ability, and his profound experience in the art of storing and caring for the noble wine. His ceaseless, honest industry, his life of piety, in spite of the wealth which he has amassed, are an example to you all.

"And, a thousand times welcome as our president, Master Martin."

Thus saying, Paumgartner rose from his chair, and stepped forward a pace or two with extended arms, expecting that Master Martin would advance towards him in reciprocation. Upon which Master Martin pressed his arms on the elbows of his chair, and raised himself slowly and heavily, as his well-nourished "corporation" caused him to do; after which, with equal deliberateness he walked into Paumgartner's hearty embrace, which he scarcely returned.

"Well, Master Martin," said Paumgartner, a little annoyed, "is there anything not quite to your liking in having been elected Candlemaster?"

Master Martin, as was his habit, threw his head well back, fingered his paunch with both hands, and looked around the assemblage with his eyes opened very wide, and his nether lip protruded; then, turning to Paumgartner, he said: "My dear and worthy sir! Why should it not be to my liking that I receive what is my just due? Who despises the reward of his hard work? Who sends from his door a bad debtor who comes at last to pay the money he has owed so long? My good sirs,"—here he turned to the masters—"it has struck you at last, has it, that *I—I have* to be president of our Honourable Guild? What are the qualifications you expect in your president? Ought he to be the best hand at his work?—Go and look at my two-fudder vat, hooped without firing, my fine masterpiece there, and then come and tell me if one of you can boast of a piece of work its equal in strength and beauty. Should your president be a man of money and property?—Call at my house, and I will open my chests and my coffers, and you shall gladden your eyes with the sight of the glittering gold and silver. Should he be honoured and esteemed by high and low, great and small?—Ask our honourable gentlemen of the Council; ask princes and lords all round our good town of Nuremberg; ask the Right Rev. Bishop of Bamberg; ask them all what they think of Master Martin—and I don't think you will hear much to his disadvantage."

With which Master Martin patted his fat corporation with much complacent contentment, twinkled his half-closed eyes, and as all were silent and only a half-suppressed throat-clearing, of a somewhat dubious character, audible here and there, he continued as follows:

"However, I perceive—in fact I am well aware—that I ought now to return thanks, to the best of my ability, that it has pleased the Lord at last to enlighten your minds to make this election. Well! When I am paid for my work, or when my debtor returns me the sum he borrowed, I always write at the bottom of the receipt, 'With thanks. Tobias Martin, master cooper in this town'; so I return you all my hearty thanks that you have paid off an old debt by electing me your Candlemaster. For the rest, I promise that I will perform the duties of my office with all truth and faithfulness; that I shall ever be ready to stand by the Guild, or any of its members, in word and deed in time of need, to the utmost of my power. It will be my heart's earnest desire to maintain our Honourable Company in all the honour and dignity which it possesses at present.

"My worthy fellow craftsmen, dear friends and masters, I invite you, one and all, to dinner on Sunday next, when, over a good glass of Hochheimer, Johannisberger, or whatever other good wine out of my cellar you may prefer, we may consider and discuss what further may be best for our common advantage.   Once more, consider yourselves all cordially invited."

The faces of the Honourable Society, which had darkened considerably at Martin's first arrogant words, now brightened again, and the gloomy silence was succeeded by lively conversation, in which much was said concerning the eminent merits of Master Martin, and of his celebrated cellar.   Everyone promised to appear on Sunday, and gave his hand to the newly elected president, who shook them all cordially—and he even pressed one or two of the masters just the least little bit against his waistcoat, as if he half thought of embracing them.

The meeting dispersed in the best of humour and the highest spirits.

II

It so chanced that Master Jacobus Paumgartner, on his way to his own dwelling, had to pass the door of Master Martin's house; and when together they had reached the said door and Paumgartner was about to proceed on his way, Master Martin, taking off his little cap and bowing as low as he could, said to the Councillor: "Ah! if you would not think it beneath you, my dear and honoured sir, to step into this poor house of mine for a brief hour; if you would but be so kind as to grant me the opportunity of profiting by and delighting in your wise conversation."

"I am sure, Master Martin," said the Councillor with a smile, "I shall only be too happy to accept your invitation to come in; though how you can call your house a poor one I cannot imagine.   I know well that the wealthiest of our citizens do not surpass you in the costliness of your furniture and appointments.   It is only the other day that you finished those additions to your house which have made it the ornament of our famous Imperial town; of the interior arrangements I say nothing, for I am aware that of them no patrician need be ashamed."

Old Paumgartner was right; for when the brightly waxed and polished door studded with rich brasswork was opened, the spacious entrance hall with its beautifully laid floor, fine pictures on the walls, rich carpets, and elegant cabinets and chairs, was seen to be like a fine drawing-room; so that everyone willingly obeyed the instruc-

tions which, according to an old custom, were inscribed on a tablet
hung up close to the door:

> If you would climb this stair,
> Take heed to wear clean shoon;
> Or better, leave them there,
> Then reproach there can be none.
> A proper man would know
> How his duty he should show.

It was warm weather, and the air in the rooms, now that the
evening twilight was falling, was heavy and steamy; for which reason
Master Martin took his guest into the cool, spacious "best kitchen";
such at that time was named the apartment which, in the houses of
wealthy merchants, was furnished like a kitchen and adorned—not
for use, but solely for display—with all manner of costly household
implements. As soon as they came in, Master Martin cried loudly,
"Rosa! Rosa!" The door presently opened, and Rosa, Master
Martin's only daughter, entered.

Gracious reader! I must here ask you to call to mind as vividly as
you can the masterpieces of our grand Albrecht Dürer. Let those
beautiful maidens whom he has portrayed, instinct with grace and
charm, sweetness, gentleness, pious meekness, rise before you. Think
of their noble, tender figures; the pure, rounded foreheads white as
snow; the rose-tint suffusing the cheeks; the delicate lips, red as
cherries; the eyes, looking far away, in dreamy longing, half shad-
owed by the dark lashes, as moonlight is by thick leafage. Think of
the silky hair, carefully gathered and knotted. Think of all the
heavenly beauty of those forms, and you will see the lovely
Rosa. He who relates this tale cannot hope otherwise to portray
her.

Let me, however, remind you of another great young painter into
whose soul a quickening ray from those ancient days has penetrated:
I mean our German Master Cornelius, in Rome. Just as he has made
Margaret (in his illustrations to Goethe's mighty *Faust*) appear, when
she says—

> I'm not a lady of rank; nor am I fair,

such was Rosa, when she felt constrained, bashfully and modestly,
to evade the ardent advances of some admirer.

She now bent low before Paumgartner, in childlike deference, took
his hand and pressed it to her lips. The old gentleman's pale cheeks
glowed. As the radiance of the evening sky, fading away into

darkness, brightens up suddenly for a last moment, gilding the dark foliage before it sinks into night, so did the fire of youth long-passed flash up in his eyes. "Ah, Master Martin!" he cried, "you are a wealthy, prosperous man, but by far the most precious gift that Heaven has bestowed on you is your charming Rosa. The sight of her makes the hearts of us old fellows beat, as we sit at the Council Board; and if *we* can't turn our eyes away from her, who can blame the young men if they stand staring like stone images when they meet her in the street; or see only *her* in church, and not the parson? What marvel that, when there is a festival in the common, they drive the other girls to despair by all running after *your* daughter, following exclusively *her* with their sighs, love-looks, and honeyed speeches? Well, Master Martin, you are aware you may pick and choose among the best patrician blood in the countryside for your son-in-law, or wherever else you have a mind."

Master Martin's face crumpled up into sombre folds. He told his daughter to go and bring some fine old wine; and when she, blushing over and over, with eyes fixed on the ground, had hurried away for it, he said to old Paumgartner:

"Ay, honourable sir! it is no doubt the truth that my daughter is gifted with exceptional beauty, and that Heaven has made me rich in that respect as well as in others; but how could you speak of it in the girl's presence?—and as to a patrician son-in-law, that cannot be."

"Nay, nay, Master Martin," answered Paumgartner; "'out of the abundance of the heart, the tongue speaketh,' you know. *My* old sluggish blood begins to dance in my veins when I look at Rosa; and there can't be much harm in my saying what she must know well enough to be true."

Rosa brought the wine and two magnificent goblets. Martin drew the richly carved great table to the center of the room; but just as the old fellows had taken their places, and Martin was filling the goblets, a tramping of horses was heard in front of the house. A horseman seemed to be drawing bridle; a voice was heard ringing loudly in the hall. Rosa hastened to the door, and came back to say that the old Junker Heinrich von Spangenberg was there and wished to speak with Master Martin.

"Well!" said Martin, "this is really a wondrous lucky evening, since my good friend—my oldest patron and customer—has come to pay me a call. New orders, no doubt; something fresh to lay down in the cellar." With which he made off as fast as he could, to greet his welcome guest.

III

The Hochheimer sparkled in the beautiful, cut goblets, and opened the hearts and loosened the tongues of the three old fellows. Spangenberg, advanced in years but still glowing with life and vigour, served up many a quaint tale and adventure of his younger days, so that Master Martin's paunch waggled heartily, and he had times without end to wipe tears of irrepressible laughter from his eyes. Paumgartner, too, forgot his senatorial gravity more than usual, and gave himself up thoroughly to the enjoyment of the noble liquor and the entertaining talk. Then Rosa came in with a pretty basket, whence she brought out table-linen dazzling as snow. She tripped here and there with housewifely eagerness, laid the table, and covered it with all sorts of appetizing dishes and begged the gentlemen, with sweetest smiles, not to disdain what had been made ready in haste. The laughter and the flow of conversation ceased. Paumgartner and Spangenberg could neither of them move his eyes away from the beautiful girl, and even Master Martin watched her housewifely activities with a smile of satisfaction as he leaned back in his chair with folded hands. When Rosa would have left them, old Spangenberg jumped up as briskly as a youth, took her by both shoulders and cried over and over again, with tears in his eyes, "Oh you good, precious angel!—you sweet, kind, charming girl!" Then he kissed her three times on the forehead and went back to his chair in deep reflection. Paumgartner drank a toast to her health.

"Yes!" began Spangenberg when she had left the room; "Yes, Master Martin! Heaven has, in that daughter of yours, bestowed on you a jewel which you cannot prize too highly. She will bring you to great honour one day. Who—of any rank whatever— wouldn't be delighted to be your son-in-law?"

"You see," said Paumgartner, "you see, Master Martin, the noble Herr von Spangenberg thinks exactly as I do. Already I see my darling Rosa a patrician's bride, with the rich pearls in her lovely fair hair!"

"My dear gentlemen!" cried Master Martin, looking quite out of temper, "why should you persist in talking about a matter which has not even begun to enter my thoughts? My daughter Rosa is just eighteen; she is too young to be thinking of a husband; and how matters may come to pass hereafter, I leave wholly in God's hands. But this much is certain—that neither a patrician nor any other man shall have my daughter's hand, except that cooper who proves himself, to my satisfaction, to be the most utterly perfect master of his craft—always supposing that my daughter loves him; for I am not going to constrain my darling daughter to anything whatever in the world, least of all to a marriage that does not please her."

Spangenberg and Paumgartner looked each other in the face, much astonished at this remarkable statement of the Master's. Presently, after clearing his throat a good deal, Spangenberg began:

"Then your daughter is not to rise out of her own class, is she?"

"God forbid that she should," answered Martin.

"But," continued Spangenberg, "suppose some doughty young master belonging to some other noble craft—say, a goldsmith, or perhaps a talented young painter—were to come wooing your daughter and pleased her very specially, much more than any of her other wooers, how would it be then?"

Master Martin answered, drawing himself up, and throwing back his head:

"'Show me,' I should say, 'show me, my good young sir, the two-fudder cask that you have built as your masterpiece.' And if he couldn't do that, I would open the door politely, and beg him, as civilly as I could, to try his luck elsewhere."

Spangenberg resumed:

"Suppose the young fellow said, 'I cannot show you a small-scale piece of work such as you speak of; but come with me to the market place, and look at that stately building, reaching its slender peaks proudly up to the skies. That is *my* masterpiece.'"

"Ah, my good sir!" Martin interrupted impatiently; "what is the good of your taking all this trouble to alter my determination? My son-in-law shall belong to my own craft and to no other; for I look upon my craft as being the most glorious that exists on earth. Do you suppose that all that is necessary to make a cask hold together is to fit the hoops onto the staves? Ah! ha! The glory and the beauty of our craft is that it presupposes a knowledge of the preservation and the nursing of that most precious of heaven's gifts—noble wine, that so it may ripen and penetrate us with its strength and sweetness, a glowing spirit of life. Then there is the construction of the cask itself. If the build is to be successful, we have to measure and calculate all the curves, and the other dimensions, with rule and compass with the utmost accuracy. Geometers and arithmeticians we must be, that we may compute the proportions and the capacities of our casks. Ah, good sir, I can tell you my very heart laughs within my body when I see a fair, well-proportioned cask laid on the end-stool, the staves all beautifully finished off with the riving knife and the broad axe, and the men set to with the mallets, and 'clipp, clapp' ring the strokes of the driver. Ha! ha! that is merry music. There stands the work, perfect; and I may well look round me with a dash of pride when I take my marking-iron and brand it with my own trademark on the head of the cask—my own mark, known and respected by all genuine wine masters in the land. You spoke of master builders, dear sir. Very good; a grand, stately house is a fine work beyond doubt. But if I were a master builder and passed by one of my works, and saw some dirty-minded creature, some good-for-nothing, despicable wretch who had happened to become the owner of that house, looking down at me from one of the balconies, I should feel shame at the bottom of my heart; I would long to tear down that work of mine from sheer annoyance and disgust. Nothing of that sort can ever happen to me, for in my works dwells ever the very purest thing on earth—good wine. God's blessing on my craft!"

"Your encomium," said Spangenberg, "was admirable and heartily felt on your part. It is to your honour that you hold your craft in high esteem. But please be patient with me if I do not leave you in peace even now. Suppose a patrician did actually come and ask you for your daughter. Sometimes, when a matter really comes very close to one, much in it begins to assume a different appearance from what one thought."

"Ah," cried Martin a little warmly, "what could I say, except with a polite bow, 'Honoured sir, if you were but a clever cooper; but as you are—'"

"Listen further," interrupted Spangenberg. "If some fine morning a handsome noble were to come on a splendid charger, with a brilliant following all in grand clothes, and rein up at your door and ask for Rosa for his wife?"

"Hey! hey!" cried Master Martin more impetuously than before; "I would run as fast as I could and bolt and bar the door. Then I would cry and shout, 'Ride on your road, your lordship. Roses such as mine do not bloom for you. I dare say my cellar and my cash-box please you well, and you'll take the girl into the bargain. On your way!'"

Old Spangenberg rose up, his face red as fire. He leaned both hands on the table and looked down before him. "Well," he began, after a short silence, "this is my last question, Master Martin. If the young noble at your door were my own son, if I myself were at your door with him, would you bar the door? Would you think we had come only for the sake of your cellar and your cash-box?"

"Most certainly not," answered Master Martin. "My honoured and dear sir, I should open the door politely to you; everything in my house should be at your and your son's command. But as regards Rosa, I should say, 'Had it pleased Heaven that your noble son had been a clever cooper, no one on earth would have been more welcome to me as a son-in-law. As it is, however—' But why should you plague me with all those extraordinary questions, honoured sir? Our delightful conversation has come to an end, and our glasses are standing full. Let us leave questions of the son-in-law and Rosa's marriage aside. I drink your son's good health. People say he is a fine, handsome gentleman."

Master Martin took up his goblet, and Paumgartner followed his example, saying, "A truce to captious conversation; here's to your noble son's health."

Spangenberg touched glasses with them, and then said with a forced smile, "You saw, of course, that I was only speaking in jest. My son, who has only to ask and have amongst the best and noblest in the land, would be a raving lunatic to come here begging for your daughter and so far to disregard his rank and birth as to sue for her. But you could have answered me in a more friendly way."

"Ah, my dear sir," answered Martin, "even if it were a joke I could answer it in no other manner, without loss of my proper self-respect. For you must confess, yourselves, that you are aware that I am justified in holding myself to be the best cooper in all the countryside; that all that can be known as to wine, I know; that I hold faithfully by the wine laws framed in the days of our departed Emperor Maximilian; that, as a pious man, I hate and despise all godlessness; that I never burn beyond an ounce of sulphur in a two-fudder cask, which is needful for the preservation thereof. All this, dear and honoured sirs, you can sufficiently trace the savour of, in my wine here."

Spangenberg, resuming his seat, strove to assume a happier expression of countenance again, and Paumgartner led the conversation to other topics. But as the strings of an instrument, when once they have gone out of tune, stretch and warp more and more, and the master cannot evoke from it the well-sounding chords which he could produce before, nothing that the three men tried to say would harmonize any longer. Spangenberg called his servants and went away depressed and out of temper from Martin's house, which he had come to in such a jovial mood.

IV

Master Martin was somewhat concerned at his old friend and patron's having gone away annoyed. He said to Paumgartner, who had finished his last goblet and was leaving too:

"I really cannot make out what the old gentleman was driving at with all those odd questions; and why should he be so vexed when he went away?"

"Dear Master Martin," answered Paumgartner, "you are a fine, grand, noble, upright fellow, and you are right to set a value on what, by the help of God, you have brought to such a prosperous issue and carried on so well, and what has been a source of wealth and fortune to you at the same time. Still, this should not lead you to ostentation and pride, which are contrary to all Christian feeling. It was hardly right in you to set yourself above all the other masters at the meeting today as you did. Very likely you do know more of your craft than all the rest of them put together; but to go and cast this straight in their teeth could only give rise to anger and annoyance. And then your conduct this evening; you surely could not have been so blind as not to see that what Spangenberg was driving at was to find out how far your headstrong pride would really carry you. It could not help hurting the worthy gentleman sorely to hear you attribute any young noble's wooing of your daughter to mere greed for your money. It would have all been well enough if you had got back into the right road when he began to talk about his own son. If you had said,'Ah, my good and honoured sir, if you were to come with your son to ask for my daughter (an honour on which, certainly, I never could have reckoned), I should waver in the firmness of my determination.' If you had said that, what would have been the consequence but that old Spangenberg, forgetting his previous wrongs, would have smiled and got back into the fine temper he was in before."

"Scold me well," said Master Martin, "I deserve it, I know. But when the old gentleman spoke such nonsense, I really could not bring myself to give him any other answer."

"Then," Paumgartner continued, "this silly notion of yours that you won't give your daughter to anybody but a cooper. Was ever such nonsense heard of? You say your daughter's destiny shall be left in God's hands, and yet you go and wrest it out of God's hands yourself, by deciding that you will choose your son-in-law out of one limited circle. This may be the very destruction of both her and you. Leave off such unchristian, childish folly, Master Martin.

Commit the matter to the Almighty. He will place the right decision in your daughter's heart."

"Ah, my dear sir," said Master Martin quite dejectedly, "I see now, for the first time, how wrong I was not to make a clean breast of the whole business at once. You, of course, suppose that it is merely an overhigh opinion of the cooper's craft which makes me resolve never to give Rosa to anybody but a master cooper. But that is by no means the case; there is another reason. I can't let you go away until I have told you all this. You shall not pass a single night, even, with a bad opinion of me in your mind. Sit down again; I beg it as a favour. See, here is still another bottle of my oldest wine; Spangenberg was too much offended to taste it. Sit, and stay but a few minutes longer."

Paumgartner was surprised at Master Martin's confidential insistence, which was not in his usual nature. It seemed as if something lay heavy on his mind which he felt eager to be clear of. When Paumgartner had resumed his seat, and taken some of the wine, Master Martin commenced as follows:

"You are aware, dear sir, that my beloved wife died soon after Rosa's birth from the effects of a difficult confinement. My own grandmother was still alive and very old (if one can call it being alive, to be stone deaf, blind, scarcely able to speak, paralyzed in every limb, and completely bedridden). My Rosa had been baptized, and the nurse was sitting with her in the room where my old grandmother lay. I was so sorrowful and (when I looked at the child) so wonderfully happy, and yet so sad—I was so deeply touched that I found it impossible to do any work, and I was standing sunk in my thoughts beside my grandmother's bed, envying her, and thinking how well for her it was that she had done with earthly pain. And as I was so looking into her pale face, all at once she began to smile in the strangest way; her wrinkled features seemed to smooth out, her pale cheeks took on a colour; she sat up in her bed and stretched her powerless arms, as she had not been able to do for a long time, and as if suddenly inspired by some miraculous power, she called out distinctly in a soft, sweet voice, 'Rosa! darling Rosa!' The nurse gave her the child. She took it and dandled it in her arms. But now, my dear sir, picture my amazement, nay, my terror, when the old lady began, in a strong, clear voice, a song, in the *hohe fröhliche Lobweis* of Herr Hans Bechler, of the Holy Ghost in Strasbourg:

> Little maiden, with cheeks of roses,
> Rosa, hear the decree.
> Never yield thee to dread or doubting,

Set God fast in thy heart.
Let not vain longings deride thee.
He prepares thee a brightsome dwelling,
Streams, of sweet savour, flowing therein,
Beauteous angels, singing full sweetly.
Pious of soul,
List to the truest of wooing,
Loveliest promise of love.
A House, resplendent and gleaming,
He whom thy heart goeth forth to
Shall to thy dwelling bring.
Needless to ask of thy father.
This is thy destined lord.
For this House, into thy dwelling
Bringeth good fortune and bliss.
Keep thine eyes open, then, maiden;
Watchful thine ears for the true word to come.
God's truest blessing be on thee,
Walking thy flowery way.

"And when my old grandmother had sung this song, she put the child gently and carefully down on the bedcover, and laying her withered, trembling hands upon its forehead, whispered words which were wholly unintelligible, though the expression of her face showed that she was praying. Then she sank back with her head on the pillow, and as the nurse lifted the child my old grandmother gave a deep sigh—she was gone."

"A wonderful story," said Paumgartner. "Still I don't see how this prophetic song of your old grandmother has any connection with your obstinate determination to give Rosa to nobody but a master cooper."

"What can be clearer," said Master Martin, "than that the old lady, specially enlightened by the Lord during the last moments of her life, declared in prophecy how matters are to go with Rosa, if she is to be happy and fortunate? The wooer who is to bring wealth, luck and happiness into her dwelling with a beautiful house; who can that be but a clever cooper, who shall finish his masterpiece, the beautiful house of his building, in my workshop? In what other house do streams of sweet savour flow up and down but in a wine-cask? And when the wine is working it rustles, and hums, and splashes; and that is the singing of the angels as they float on the tiny ripples. Ay, ay! no other bridegroom did the old grandmother mean but the master cooper. And that it shall be!"

"Good Master Martin," said Paumgartner, "you interpret the old lady's words after your own manner; I cannot agree with your interpretation, and I still maintain that you ought to leave the whole matter in the hands of God, and in your daughter's heart; for the true meaning and the proper deciding of it most certainly lie hidden there."

"And I, as far as I am concerned," said Master Martin impatiently, "stick to my own opinion, that my son-in-law *shall* be none but a clever cooper. This I hold to, for once and for all."

Paumgartner was almost beginning to lose his temper over Martin's obstinacy. But he controlled himself, and rose from his chair, saying, "It is getting late, Master Martin; I think we have had as much wine and as much conversation as are good for us."

As they stepped into the hall, there appeared a young woman with five boys, of whom the eldest might have been scarcely eight, and the youngest scarcely half a year old. The woman was weeping and sobbing. Rosa hastened to meet Martin and Paumgartner, crying, "Ah! Heavens! Valentine has just died. Here are his wife and children." "What? Valentine dead?" cried Master Martin, much shocked. "Oh, because of that accident, that accident! My dear sir, Valentine was the best of all my workmen; a hard-working, good, honest fellow. A short time ago he hurt himself dangerously with an adze, during the building of a big cask. His wound got worse and worse; he fell into a violent fever, and now he has had to die in the prime of his years." Master Martin went up to the disconsolate woman, who was bathed in tears, lamenting that she must perish in misery and distress.

"What do you think of *me*?" asked Master Martin. "Your husband came by his death at my service, and do you suppose I am going to abandon you in your need? God forbid! You all belong to my house henceforth. Tomorrow, or when you choose, we will bury your husband, poor fellow, and then you and your boys go to my farm before the Gate of Our Lady, where my great workshop is, and be there with my men. You can look after the housekeeping; I will bring up those fine young boys of yours as though they were my own. More than that, your old father shall come and live here too. He was a grand journeyman cooper while he had strength in his arms for the work. If he can't wield the mallet nowadays, or the notching-tool, or the hooping-iron, or take his stroke at the grooving-bench, why he can manage to turn out hoops with the rounding-knife. Whether or not, into my house he comes with the rest of you."

Had not Master Martin held the woman up, she would have fallen at his feet overwhelmed with emotion. The older boys hung upon his doublet, and the two youngest, whom Rosa had taken in her arms, held out their little hands to him as if they understood what he said.

Said old Paumgartner, smiling, with tears in his eyes, "One can't be vexed with you, Master Martin," and he betook himself to his dwelling.

V

The evening was falling as a young journeyman, very handsome and distinguished-looking, Friedrich by name, was lying on a little grassy hillock, shaded by leafy trees.   The sun had set, and a rosy glow flooded the horizon.   The famous imperial town of Nuremberg could be distinctly seen in the distance, broadening out in the valley, its proud towers stretching up into the evening red which shone brightly on their pinnacles.   The young artisan had his arm propped upon his bundle, or travelling knapsack, and was gazing down into the valley with longing eyes.   He plucked a flower or two from the grass, and cast them into the air towards the sunset sky; then once more he gazed mournfully before him, and the hot tears came to his eyes.   At length he lifted his head, stretched out his arms, as if he were embracing some beloved form, and sang the following song, in a clear, very pleasant voice:

> Again, again I see thee, my own beloved home,
> My faithful heart has never lost
> The faintest trace of thee.
> Rise on my sight, oh roseate sheen;
> Fain would I see nought else but roses.
> Love's own blossoms, glow on my heart,
> Gladden my bosom, cheer my soul.
> Ah, swelling heart, and must thou break?
> Beat firm through pain and sweetest joy.
> And thou, thou golden evening sky,
> Be thou to me a faithful herald;
> Bear down to her my sighs and tears
> And tell her, should I die, my heart
> Dissolved in love unchanging.

When Friedrich had finished this song, he took some wax from his bundle, warmed it in his breast, and began to model a beautiful rose, with its hundreds of delicate petals, in the most skillful and artistic manner.   As he worked at it, he kept singing detached phrases of his song; and, thus absorbed, he did not notice a handsome young man who had been standing behind him for a considerable time, eagerly watching as he worked.

"My friend," said this young fellow, "that is an exquisite piece of work you are doing."

Friedrich looked round, startled. But when he saw the stranger's kindly dark eyes, he felt as if he had known him long. So he answered, with a smile, "Ah, my dear sir, how can you care to look at this trifle, which is only to pass a little time on my journey?"

The stranger answered, "If you call that flower, so accurately studied and copied from nature, and so tenderly executed, a 'trifle,' a plaything, you must be a remarkably finished and accomplished artist in that line. You delight me in a double sense. First, your song, which you sang so charmingly (in the *Zarte Buchstabenweis* of Martin Haescher), went to my heart; and now I have to admire your masterly skill in modelling. Where are you bound today?"

"The goal of my journey," answered Friedrich, "lies there before our eyes. I am bound for my home there, the renowned imperial town of Nuremberg. Since the sun is far beneath the horizon, I shall pass the night down in the village there; but I shall push on as early as I can in the morning, and be in Nuremberg by noon."

"Ah, how well that falls in," cried the other; "I am bound for Nuremberg, too. I shall pass the night along with you in the village, and we can go on together in the morning. So let us talk together a little while."

The young man, whose name was Reinhold, threw himself down on the grass beside Friedrich, and went on as follows:

"If I am not mistaken, you are a splendid foundryman. I see that by your style of moulding. Or do you work in gold and silver?"

Friedrich looked sadly down, and began, quite dejectedly:

"Ah, my dear sir, you take me for something much higher and better than I really am. I must tell you candidly that I learned the craft of a cooper, and I wish to go and work with a well-known master of that craft in Nuremberg. You will despise me because I do not model and cast glorious images, figures, and groups, but just make casks and barrels."

"This is delightful," cried Reinhold, laughing aloud. "The idea of *my* despising you for being a cooper, when I am nothing else myself!"

Friedrich looked at him fixedly; he did not know what to think. Reinhold's dress was like anything rather than that of a journeyman cooper on his travels. The doublet of fine black cloth trimmed with

velvet, the delicate lace cravat, short sword, beret, with long drooping feather, seemed more appropriate to a well-to-do merchant; and
yet there was a certain strange something in his face and whole
bearing which excluded the idea of a merchant. Reinhold saw
Friedrich's doubts; he opened his knapsack, and brought out his
cooper's leather apron and case of tools, crying, "Look *there*, friend;
have you any doubt now as to my being your comrade? I daresay
my clothes may strike you a little; but I come from Strassburg, where
the coopers dress like gentry. Certainly, like yourself, I once had
ideas of something different; but now I think the cooper's craft the
finest in the world, and I have based many of my fairest life hopes on
it. Is not this *your* case, too, comrade? But it almost seems to me
as if some dark cloud-shadow had come over the happiness of your
life, preventing you from looking around you with any gladness.
Your song was all love-longing and sorrow; but there were tones in it
which seemed to come out of my own breast, and I feel as though I
knew everything which is imprisoned within you. That is all the
more reason why you should tell me all about it. As we are going to
be intimate friends and companions in Nuremberg, confide in me."
Reinhold put an arm about Friedrich, and looked him kindly in the
eyes.

"The more I look at you," Friedrich said, "the more I am drawn
to you. I distinctly hear a voice within me which tells me you are
my true friend. So I *must* tell you everything. Not that a poor
fellow such as I has anything really important to confide to you, but
merely because the breast of a true friend has room for a man's sorrows; and, from the first moment of our acquaintance, I felt that you
are the truest friend I possess. I am a cooper now, and I may say
I know my craft well. But all my devotion was given to another—
perhaps a better—art. From my childhood my desire was to be a
silversmith, a great master in the art of casting and working in silver,
like Peter Fischer, or the Italian Benvenuto Cellini. I worked at
this with fervent zeal under Master Johannes Holzschuer, the famous
silversmith in my native town, who, although he did not himself cast
images of the kind I refer to, was able to give me instruction. To
Herr Holzschuer's house Herr Tobias Martin, the master cooper,
occasionally came with his daughter, the beautiful charming Rosa.
I fell in love with her, without quite being aware of it myself. I left
home and went to Augsburg to learn image casting properly, and
it was not till then that the love flames blazed up in my heart. I
saw and heard only Rosa. I loathed every effort, every endeavour
that did not lead to *her*; so I started off on the only path which *did*

lead to her. Master Martin will give his daughter to no man except
the cooper who, in his house, shall make the most perfect masterpiece which a cooper can produce, and whom at the same time his
daughter shall look upon favourably into the bargain. I cast my
own art to one side, I learned the cooper's craft, and I am going to
Nuremberg to work in Master Martin's workshop. That is my
object and intention. But now that my home lies before me and
Rosa's image glows vividly before my eyes, I could faint for hesitation, anxiety, dread. I see *now* how foolishly I have acted. Can
I tell whether Rosa loves me, or ever will love me?"

Reinhold had listened with even closer attention. He now rested
his head on his arm, and, placing his hand over his eyes, asked, in a
hollow, gloomy voice:

"Has Rosa ever given you any sign that she cares for you?"

"Ah," said Friedrich, "when I left Nuremberg, Rosa was more a
child than a woman. She certainly did not dislike me. She used
to smile at me when I never wearied of gathering flowers and
making wreaths in Herr Holzschuer's garden. But—"

"Well, there is some hope in that case," Reinhold cried out suddenly, so violently, and in such an unpleasant, yelling tone, that
Friedrich felt almost frightened. Reinhold started to his feet, the
sword at his side rattled, and as he stood drawn up to his full height,
the evening shadows fell on his pale face, and distorted his gentle
features in such an unpleasant way that Friedrich cried, in real
anxiety:

"What has come over you so suddenly?"

As he spoke he stepped backward, knocking against Reinhold's
bundle with his foot. A sound of strings rang forth, and Reinhold
cried angrily:

"Don't smash my lute, you villain!"

He took the instrument from his bundle and struck its strings
stormily, as if he would tear them in pieces. But soon his touch
upon them grew soft and tuneful.

"Let us go on down to the village, brother!" he said in the same
gentle tone as before. "I have here a fine remedy against the evil
spirits which stand in our way, and may oppose me particularly."

"Why should evil spirits stand in our way, brother?" asked
Friedrich. "Your playing is beautiful. Please go on with it."

The golden stars had come forth in the dark azure of the heavens;
the night wind was breathing in soft whispers over the perfumed
meadows; the streams were murmuring more loudly; the dark trees
of the forest were rustling all around in the distance. Reinhold and

Friedrich went down into the valley, playing and singing; and clear and bright as on shining pinions, their songs of love and longing floated on the breeze.

When they reached their night quarters, Reinhold threw his lute and his knapsack down, and pressed Friedrich stormily to his heart. Friedrich felt tears upon his cheek; they came from Reinhold's eyes.

VI

When Friedrich awoke the next morning, he missed his new friend, who had thrown himself down by his side on the straw bed; and as he saw neither the lute nor the bundle, he thought Reinhold, for reasons unknown to him, had left him and taken another road. When he went out, however, he saw Reinhold with his lute under his arm, and his knapsack, but dressed quite differently from what he had been the day before. He had taken the feather from his cap, was not wearing his sword, and had on a homely citizen's doublet of sober hue instead of the velvet slashed one he had previously worn.

"*Now*, brother," he cried, with a merry laugh, "I am sure you see that I really am your comrade and fellow journeyman. However, I must say you slept wonderfully well for a man in love. Look how high the sun is. Let's be off at once."

Friedrich was silent and thoughtful; he scarcely answered Reinhold, or paid any attention to his jests, for he darted about hither and thither in the highest spirits, shouting aloud and throwing his cap into the air; but even he became quieter as they approached the town, quieter and quieter.

"I cannot go any further, I am so anxious, so uncertain, so filled with delicious unrest," said Friedrich, throwing himself down exhausted, when they had all but arrived at the gates of Nuremberg. Reinhold sat down beside him, and after a time said:—

"Last night I must have seemed to you to be a very strange creature, good brother, but when you told me of your love, and were so disconsolate, all manner of absurd nonsense came into my head, making me feel confused. I think I should have gone crazy at last, had not your singing and my lute driven the evil spirits away. This morning, when the first rays of the sun awoke me, all my sense of enjoyment in life had come back to me. I went out, and as I strolled up and down among the trees, all sorts of glorious thoughts came into my mind; the way in which I had met you—how my whole heart had so turned to you.

"I remembered a pretty tale of a matter which happened some time ago in Italy when I chanced to be there. I should like to tell it to you, as it shows very vividly what true friendship can accomplish.

"It so happened that a certain noble prince, a zealous friend and protector of the arts, offered a valuable prize for a picture, the subject of which, very interesting, and not overdifficult to treat, was duly announced. Two young painters, who were close friends, determined to compete for this prize. They were in the habit of working together; they told each other their respective ideas on the subject, showed each other their sketches for it, and talked much together as to the difficulties to be overcome. The older of the two, who had more experience than the other in drawing and composition, had soon grasped the idea of his picture, had sketched it, and was helping the younger with all his power; for the latter was so discouraged at the very threshold of his sketch for the picture, that he would have given up all idea of going on had not the elder unceasingly encouraged him, and given him advice and suggestions.

"Now when they began to paint their pictures, the younger, who was a master of colour, was able to give the elder many suggestions, which he skillfully used; thus, the elder had never coloured a picture so well, and the younger had never drawn one so well. When the pictures were finished, the masters embraced each other, each of them inwardly delighted with the work of the other, and each convinced that the well-earned prize belonged of right to the other.

"The younger, however, was the winner of the prize; upon which he cried out, thoroughly ashamed: 'Why should I have it? What is my merit compared to my friend's? I could not have accomplished anything worthy of praise but for his help.' But the elder said: 'And did you not help me with valuable counsel and advice? No doubt my picture is by no means bad; but you have got the prize, as was proper. To strive towards the same goal, bravely and openly, that is real friendship. Then the laurel which the victor gains honours the vanquished too. I like you all the more for your having laboured so doughtily, and brought me, too, honour and renown by your victory.' Now, Friedrich, that painter was right, was he not? Would it not rather truly and intimately unite than separate true friends to strive for the same prize, honestly, openly, genuinely, to the utmost of their power? Can petty envy or hatred find place in noble minds?"

"Never!" answered Friedrich; "assuredly never! We are now loving brethren; very likely we shall both ere long set to work to turn out the great Nuremberg 'masterpiece'—the two-fudder cask, without firing—each on his own account. But heaven forbid that I should be able to trace in myself the faintest tinge of envy, if yours, dear brother Reinhold, should be a better one than mine."

"Ha, ha, ha!" laughed Reinhold. "What does your 'masterpiece' signify? You will soon make *that*, I have no doubt, to the admiration of all competent coopers; and let me tell you that, as far as concerns the measurements, the proportions, curves, etc., you have found in me your man; moreover, you can trust me as to the choice of the timber, staves, of red oak, felled in the winter, free from wormholes, red or white stripes, or blemishes—that is what we will seek out. You can trust my eye; I will give you the best possible advice about everything, and my own 'masterpiece' will be none the worse for that."

"But" cried Friedrich, "why should we talk about 'masterpieces,' and which of us is going to succeed there? Is that what we are going to contend for? The real 'masterpiece' is winning Rosa; how are we to set about that? My head reels at it."

"Well, brother," cried Reinhold, still laughing; "really we were not saying anything about Rosa; you are a dreamer. Come along, let us get to the town."

Friedrich rose, and walked along, perplexed. As they were washing and brushing themselves in the inn, Reinhold said:

"For my part, I don't know in the least what master I am going to work with. I don't know a creature in the place, so I was thinking that perhaps you would take me with you to Master Martin's, brother; perhaps he would give me work."

"You take a weight from my heart," answered Friedrich; "for if you are with me I shall find it easier to overcome my anxiety and my uneasiness."

So they set out together stoutly for the house of the renowned cooper, Master Martin.

It happened to be the very Sunday on which Master Martin was giving his great official dinner in honour of his appointment, and it was exactly dinner time. Thus, when Reinhold and Friedrich crossed Master Martin's threshold, they became aware of a ringing of wine glasses, and the confused buzz of a merry dinner company.

"Ah!" said Friedrich sadly; "I fear we have come at an unfortunate time."

"I think just the contrary," said Reinhold; "for Master Martin will be in a fine temper, after all that good cheer, and disposed to grant our requests."

And presently Master Martin—to whom they had caused their coming to be announced—came out to them, in festal attire, and with no small amount of rubicundity of nose and cheeks. As soon as he saw Friedrich, he cried out, "Aha, Friedrich, good lad, you have come home again! That is well; and you have taken up the noblest of trades, cooper craft, too! Herr Holzschuer makes terrible faces when your name is mentioned, and says a really great artist is spoilt in you, and that you could very likely have cast all sorts of little niminy-piminy figures, like those in St. Sebald's—that, and trellis-work, such as there is in Fugger's house in Augsburg. Stupid stuff and nonsense; you have done the proper thing in turning to what is right; many thousand welcomes." With which Master Martin took him by the shoulders and embraced him, according to his wont when highly pleased. Friedrich completely revived at Master Martin's kind reception of him. All his bashfulness abandoned him; he not only boldly asked Master Martin to take him on, but begged him to take Reinhold into his service too.

"Well," said Master Martin, "you could not possibly have come at a better time; there is plenty of work, and I'm greatly in need of men. You are both heartily welcome. Put down your bundles and come in; dinner is nearly over, but there is room at the table, and Rosa will take every care of you." And Master Martin went in with the two journeymen.

The worthy and honourable masters were all seated there, Herr Paumgartner in the place of honour. Their faces were all aglow; dessert was just served, and a nobler wine was sparkling in the great drinking glasses. Matters had arrived at a point when each of the masters was talking, very loud, about something different from all the others, yet they all thought they quite followed and understood; and now one, and now another, laughed loud, without quite knowing why. But when Master Martin, with Friedrich and Reinhold in either hand, announced that two fine young journeymen, with good certificates, the sort of fellows after his own heart, had come offering to work for him, all grew silent, and everybody looked at the handsome lads with pleasant satisfaction. Reinhold glanced around him with his clear eyes, almost proudly; but Friedrich cast his down, and toyed with his beret. Master Martin gave the two men places at the bottom of the table. But they were the most glorious places of all, for presently Rosa came and sat down beside them, carefully helping and serving them with exquisite dishes and delicious wines. All this made a delightful picture to behold. The beautiful Rosa, the handsome lads, the bearded masters, one could not but think of some shining morning cloud rising up alone on a dark background of sky; or, perhaps, of pretty spring flowers, raising their heads from melancholy, colourless grass.

Friedrich could hardly breathe for rapture and delight; only by stealth did he now and then glance at her who was filling all his soul. He stared down at his plate; how was it possible for him to swallow a morsel? Reinhold, on the other hand, never moved his eyes (from which sparkling lightnings flashed) from the girl. He began to talk of his far travels in such a marvellous manner, that she had never heard anything like it before. All that he spoke of seemed to rise before her eyes in thousands of ever-changing images; she was all eye, all ear. She did not know where she was, or what was happening to her when Reinhold, in the fire of his discourse, grasped her hand and pressed it to his heart.

"Friedrich," he cried, "why are you sitting mum and sad? Have you lost your tongue? Come, let's clink our glasses to the health of this young lady, who is taking such care of us here." Friedrich took with trembling hand the tall goblet which Reinhold had filled to the brim, and which, as Reinhold did not draw breath, he had to empty to the last drop. "Here's to our brave master!" Reinhold cried again, filling the glasses; and once more Friedrich had to empty his bumper. Then the fire-spirit of the wine permeated him, and set his halting blood a-moving, till it coursed, seething and dancing, through all his veins. "What a blissful feeling," he muttered, as the glowing scarlet mantled in his cheeks; "I cannot express it; never have I felt so happy before."

Rosa—to whom those words might, perhaps, convey another sense —smiled on him with marvellous sweetness, and he, freed from all his bashfulness, said: "Dear Rosa, I suppose you don't remember me at all, do you?"

"Now, Friedrich," answered Rosa, with downcast eyes; "how could I forget you so soon? At old Herr Holzschuer's I was only a child, certainly, but you did not think it beneath you to play with me; and you always talked of such nice things. And that beautiful little basket of silver wire which you gave me one Christmas, I still have, and shall always prize it as a precious keepsake."

Tears stood in the lad's eyes, in the intoxication of his happiness. He tried to speak; but only the words, "Ah, Rosa! Dear Rosa!" came out of his heart like a deep sigh. Rosa went on to say: "I have always wished most heartily that I might see you again, but that you should take to the cooper's craft, I never could have imagined. Ah! when I think of the beautiful things you used to make at Herr

Holzschuer's, it is really a shame that you do not keep to you own art."

"Ah, Rosa," said Friedrich, "it was all for your sake that I was faithless to my own beloved art." Scarcely were the words spoken than he wanted to sink into the ground with shame and alarm. The most unintentional of avowals had come from his lips. Rosa, as if she saw it all, turned her face away from him. He strove in vain for words.

Just then, Herr Paumgartner rapped on the table loudly with a knife, and announced to the company that Herr Vollrad, a worthy master-singer, would favour them with a song. So Herr Vollrad stood up, cleared his throat, and sang such a beautiful song in Hans Vogelsang's *Güldne Tonweis* that all hearts throbbed for joy, and even Friedrich recovered from his serious embarrassment. After Herr Vollrad had sung other beautiful songs, in various other "tones" or "manners"—such as the *Süsser Ton*, the *Krummzinkenweis*, the *Geblümte Paradiesweis*, the *Frischepomeranzenweis*, etc.—he said that, should there be any at the table who knew anything of the gracious craft of the master-singers, he should now be so good as to sing a song.

At this Reinhold rose, and said that, if he might be permitted to accompany himself on the lute after the Italian manner he too would be happy to sing a song, keeping, however, wholly to the German "modes." No one saying anything to the contrary, he got out his lute, and after preluding a little in the loveliest way, went on with the following song:—

> Where is the little fount,
>   Where springs the flavourous wine?
> Deep in the ground.
> There found,
>   All men may see with joy its golden glory shine.
> Who found it, thought it out,
> With doughty might and thews,
> With craft and careful skill?
> Who but the cooper!
> None but he can build
> The precious fount and source.

This song pleased everyone beyond measure, but none so much as Master Martin, whose eyes beamed with pleasure and delight. Without attending to Herr Vollrad—who spoke more than was necessary concerning Herr Müller's *Stumpfe Schossweis*, which the journeyman had "hit off by no means badly"—Master Martin rose and, lifting his challenge glass on high, cried: "Come here—

proper cooper and fine master-singer—come here and drain this glass with me."

Reinhold had to do as he was told. As he came back to his seat he whispered to the thoughtful Friedrich, " *You* must sing now, what you sang last night."

"You are mad," Friedrich cried, in anger. But Reinhold spoke out to the company in a loud voice, saying:

"Honourable gentlemen and masters, my dear brother Friedrich here knows much more beautiful songs and has a far finer voice than I. But the dust of the journey has got into his throat, so that he will sing to you in all 'manners' on another occasion."

Then they all began praising and applauding Friedrich as if he had actually sung, and some of the masters even thought his voice was finer than Reinhold's. Herr Vollrad (after another glass) thought and said that Friedrich caught the beautiful German "modes" even better than Reinhold, who had just a little too much of the Italian school about him. But Master Martin threw his head back, smote his breast with his fist till it resounded again, and cried:

"Those are *my* men—mine, I say! Master Tobias Martin, the Cooper of Nuremberg's men."

And all the masters nodded their heads, and said, as they savoured the last drops out of their tall drinking glasses:

"Aye, aye, it is so! All right! Master Martin's, the Cooper of Nuremberg's fine, clever men."

At last they all went home to bed; and Master Martin gave each of his new journeymen a nice bright chamber in his house.

VII

After Friedrich and Reinhold had worked with Master Martin for a week or two, he observed that in measurements, rule and compass work, calculations, and correctness of eye, Reinhold was probably without a rival. But it was different with work at the bench with the adze or the mallet. At this Reinhold soon wearied, and the work would not progress, let him exert himself as he would. Friedrich, on the other hand, hammered and planed away sturdily, and did not get very tired of it. What they both had in common, however, was a refinement of manner, to which there joined themselves, chiefly at Reinhold's instigation, much innocent merriment and witty fun. Moreover (especially when Rosa was by) they did not spare their throats, but sang many a beautiful song, often together, when their voices went delightfully. And when Friedrich, turning his eyes to Rosa, would tend to fall into a melancholy and sentimental strain, Reinhold would immediately strike in with a comic ditty of his own devising, which began:

The vat is not the zither—the zither not the vat,

so that old Martin had often to drop the tool which he had in his hand, and hold his sides for inward laughter. On the whole both the journeymen, but especially Reinhold, stood high in Master Martin's favour; and one might almost fancy that Rosa too sometimes found a pretext for lingering oftener and longer in the workshop than perhaps she otherwise would have done.

One day Master Martin went thoughtfully to his open workshop outside the town gate, where work was carried on in the summertime. Friedrich and Reinhold were just setting up a small cask. Master Martin placed himself before them with folded arms, and said:

"I really cannot tell you how thoroughly I am satisfied with you. But I find myself in a considerable predicament. People write to me from the Rhine country that as regards crop this present year is going to be more blessed than any that has gone before it. A certain wise man has said that this comet which has appeared in the sky so fertilizes the earth with its wonderful rays, that the earth will give forth all the heat which breeds the noble metals in its deepest depths, which heat will so stream and exhale up into the thirsting vines, that they will yield crop upon crop brimful of the liquid fire which has heated them. It seems there has not been such a lucky constellation for well on to three hundred years. Very good; there will be a great deal of work. And, moreover, the Bishop of Bamberg has written to order a large vat. We shall not be able to finish it, so that I shall have to look out for another journeyman hand—a good one. All the same, I don't want to bring the first comer out of the street among us. And yet what's to be done? I see no choice. If you happen to know of a good hand anywhere whom you would have no objection to work with, say the word, and I'll send and get him though it should cost me no small sum."

Scarce had Master Martin said this, when a young man of tall, powerful figure cried in at the door, in a loud voice, "Hi, there! Is this Master Martin's?"

"Yes," said Master Martin, stepping up to the young man, "it is; but there's no occasion to shout so damnably loud. That is not the way to come at people."

"Ha, ha, ha!" laughed the young man. "I see you are Master Martin yourself. You answer exactly to the description of him given to me—fat belly, imposing double chin, flashing eyes, and red nose. My best respects to you, Master Martin."

"Well, sir," said Master Martin, greatly irritated, "and what may your business with Master Martin be?"

"I am a journeyman cooper," the young man answered, "and all I want is to know if you can give me a job of work here."

Master Martin took a step or two backward in sheer amazement at the notion that, just when he had made up his mind to look out for another hand, one should appear and offer himself; and he scanned the young man closely from head to foot. The latter met his gaze with eyes which flashed. Now, as Master Martin observed the broad chest, athletic build, and powerful hands of the young man, he thought to himself, "This is just the sort of fellow that I want." And he asked him for his certificates.

"I don't have them with me," the young man said, "but I will soon get them. In the meantime, I give you my word that I will do your work faithfully and honourably. That must suffice for the time." And thereupon, without waiting for Master Martin's leave, he strode into the workshop, threw down his beret and his bundle, tied on his apron, and said, "Now then, Master Martin, tell me what to do."

Master Martin, puzzled by this cool manner of setting about matters, had to take thought with himself for a moment. "Well," he said, "my lad, to show us that you are a trained cooper, set to with the notcher upon that cask there at the end stool."

The stranger journeyman accomplished the task told him with remarkable force, skill, and rapidity. And then, loudly laughing, he cried, "Now, master, have you any doubt that I am a trained cooper? But," he continued, as he strolled up and down the shop examining the tools, timber, and so on, "you seem to have a good deal of queer stuff about here. Now here's a funny little bit of a mallet. I suppose your children amuse themselves with that. And the broad-axe yonder, that's for your apprentice boys, I presume; isn't it?" With that he whirled the great heavy mallet—which Reinhold could not wield and which Friedrich could use only with difficulty—up to the rooftree, did the like with the ponderous broad-axe which Master Martin worked with, and then rolled great casks about as if they had been bowls; and, seizing a thick unshaped stave, he cried, "Master, this seems good sort of oak-heart. I reckon it will fly like glass!" and banged it against the grindstone, so that it broke right across into two pieces with a loud report.

"My good sir," Master Martin cried, "wouldn't you like to kick around that two-fudder cask, or knock the workshop apart? You might make a mallet of one of the rafters; and, by way of a broad-axe to your liking, I'll send to the Town Hall for Roland's sword, three ells long."

"That would do for me nicely," said the young man, with sparkling eyes. But presently he cast them down, and spoke in a gentler tone:

"All I was thinking, dear Master Martin, was that your work needed strong men. But perhaps I was a little hasty in showing off my strength. Take me into your employ all the same. I will do what work you give me in first-rate style, you will see."

Master Martin looked him in the face, and had to own to himself that he had probably never seen nobler or more thoroughly honest features. Indeed the young man's face stirred up a dim remembrance of someone whom he had known and esteemed for a very long time. But this memory would not become clear, although, for this cause, he at once agreed to employ the young man, merely stipulating that he should produce proper certificates to prove that he belonged to the craft.

Reinhold and Friedrich meanwhile had finished setting up the cask at which they were working, and were putting on the first hoops. At such times they were in the habit of singing, and they now began a pretty song, in the *Stieglitzweis* of Adam Puschmann. At this Conrad (such was the newcomer's name) shouted out from the planing bench where Master Martin had set him to work, "Ugh! what a cheeping and chirping. Sounds as though the mice were squeaking about the shop. If you're going to sing, sing something that will cheer a fellow up and put some heart into him to go on with his work. I sometimes sing a thing of that sort myself." With which he commenced a rough, wild hunting song, full of "Hulloh!" and "Hussah!" And he imitated the cry of the hounds and the shouts of the people in such a thundering, all-penetrating voice, that the workshop shook and resounded. Master Martin stopped both his ears with his hands, and the boys of Frau Martha (Valentine's widow), who were playing in the workshop, hid themselves in terror among the timber.

Just then Rosa came in astonished, nay terrified, at the prodigious shouting, for "singing" it could not be called. Conrad was silent the moment he saw Rosa. He rose and went up to her in the most courteous manner, saying, in a soft voice, and with gleaming fire in his bright brown eyes: "Beautiful lady, how this old workshop beamed with roseate splendour as soon as you entered it. Ah! had

I but seen you a little sooner I should not have offended your ears with my rough hunting song."

He turned to Master Martin and the other workmen, and cried, "Stop that abominable noise, every one of you! Whenever this beautiful lady deigns to show herself here, hammers and mallets must stop. We will hear only her sweet voice, and listen with bowed heads to such commands as she may deign to issue to us—her humblest servants."

Reinhold and Friedrich gazed at each other in amazement; but Master Martin shouted with laughter, and said, "Well, Conrad, I must say you are the very drollest rascal that ever put on an apron. You come here, and seem to be going to set to work to smash the whole place to atoms, like some great lumbering giant. Next you bellow till we're all obliged to hold our ears; and, by way of a worthy finale, you treat my little daughter here as if she were a noblewoman and you a love-stricken Junker."

"I know your lovely daughter quite well, Master Martin," answered Conrad unconcernedly; "and I tell you she is the most glorious lady that walks the earth, and she would honor the most noble Junker by letting him be her champion!"

Master Martin held his sides. He nearly suffocated himself before he made way for his laughter by dint of wheezing and coughing. He then managed to get out "Good! very good! my dear young sir. Take my little girl Rosa for a noblewoman if you will, but get back to your work at the bench there."

Conrad stood rooted to the spot with eyes fixed on the ground; rubbed his forehead, and said softly, "So I must." He did as he was ordered. Rosa sat down on a small barrel, as she usually did when she came to the workshop. Reinhold and Friedrich brought this barrel forward for her as they were wont to do; and then they sang together (as Master Martin bade them) the pretty song in which Conrad had interrupted them. The latter went on with his task, silent and thoughtful. When the song was ended Master Martin said, "Heaven has endowed you two dear lads with a precious gift. You have no idea how much I honour the glorious art of song. In fact I once wanted to be a Meistersinger myself. But it wouldn't do. I could make nothing of it, try as hard as I might. With all my endeavours I earned nothing but derision and jesting, when I tried my hand at the master-singing. In free-singing, I either added notes, or dropped notes, or lost track of the form, or made incorrect ornaments, or even sang false melodies. Well, well! you will make a better job of it. What the master couldn't manage, his men will.

Next Sunday there will be a master-singing at the usual time, after noonday service, at Saint Catherine's Church; and there you two, Reinhold and Friedrich, may gain praise and honour by means of your beautiful art. For before the principal singing a free-singing will be held, open to strangers, at which you may try your skill. Now, Conrad" (Master Martin called over to the planing bench), "mightn't *you* mount the singing stool too, and treat them to that beautiful hunting song of yours?"

"Don't jest, good master," answered Conrad, without looking up; "there's a place and time for everything: while you are edifying yourself at the master-singing, I shall go in search of my own pleasure, to the common."

Things turned out as Master Martin had expected. Reinhold mounted the singing stool and sang songs in various "manners," which delighted all the Meistersinger, but they were of opinion that, though the singer committed no actual errors, a certain "outlandish" or foreign style, which they could not quite define themselves, somewhat detracted from their merit. Soon after this, Friedrich seated himself on the singing stool, took off his beret, and after looking before him for a second or two, cast a glance at the assembly (which darted through Rosa's heart like a glowing arrow, so that she could not help sighing deeply), then began a glorious song, in the *Zarter Ton* of Heinrich Frauenlob. All the masters declared unanimously that none of them could surpass this young journeyman.

When evening came and the singing was over, Master Martin, by way of thoroughly completing the enjoyment of the day, betook himself with Rosa to the common. Reinhold and Friedrich were allowed to go with them. Rosa walked between the two. Friedrich, in a state of great glorification by reason of the praise of the Meistersinger, ventured, in the intoxication of his blissfulness, on many a daring word, which Rosa, drooping her eyes modestly, did not seem to wish to hear. She turned instead to Reinhold, who, in his usual way, chattered and made many a lively jest and sally, not hesitating to sling his arm round one of hers.

When they came where the young men were engaged in divers athletic sports (some of them of knightly sort), they heard the people crying, over and over again, "He has won again!—nobody can stand before him! There! he wins again!—the strong man!" When Master Martin had pressed his way through the crowd, he found that all this shouting and acclamation were for none other than his own journeyman, Conrad, who had excelled everybody at running, boxing, and throwing the javelin. Just as Master Martin came on the scene, Conrad was challenging all comers to a bout of fencing with blunted rapiers, and several young patrician bloods, skilled at this exercise, accepted; but he very soon conquered them all with little difficulty, so that there was no end to the applause for his strength and skill.

The sun had set; the evening sky was glowing red, and the twilight rapidly falling. Master Martin, Rosa, and the two journeymen had seated themselves beside a plashing fountain. Reinhold told many delightful things concerning faraway Italy; but Friedrich gazed, silent and happy, into Rosa's beautiful eyes. Then Conrad approached, with slow and hesitating steps, as if he had not quite made up his mind whether to join the others or not. So Master Martin called out, "Come along, come along, Conrad! You have held your own bravely; just as I like my journeymen to do. Don't be bashful, my lad; you have my full permission."

Conrad flashed a penetrating glance at the master, who was nodding to him condescendingly, and said, in a hollow tone: "So far, I have not asked your permission whether I might join you or not. It was not to *you* that I was thinking whether I should come or otherwise. I have laid all my opponents prostrate in the dust in knightly play, and what I wanted to do was to ask this beautiful lady if she would not mind giving me, as my guerdon, those flowers which she wears in her breast." With which Conrad knelt on one knee before Rosa, looked her honestly in the face with his clear brown eyes, and petitioned, "Give me the flowers, if you will be so kind, fair Rosa; you can hardly refuse me." Rosa at once took the flowers from her breast, and gave them to him, saying with a smile, "I am sure such a doughty knight deserves a prize of honour from a lady; so take my flowers, although they are beginning to wither a little." Conrad kissed them, and placed them in his beret; but Master Martin rose up crying, "Stupid nonsense! Let's go home; it'll soon be dark." Martin walked first; Conrad, in a courtier-like fashion, gave Rosa his arm, and Reinhold and Friedrich brought up the rear, not in the best of temper. The people who met them stopped and looked after them, saying:

"Ey! look there!—that is Master Martin, the rich cooper, with his pretty daughter and his fine journeymen; fine folks, these, I call them!"

VIII

Young girls usually live over again all the enjoyments of a festal day, in detail on the subsequent morning, and this secondary feast then seems almost more delicious to them than the original itself. Thus the fair Rosa on the subsequent morning sat pondering alone in her chamber, with her hands folded in her lap, and her head hung down in reverie, letting spindle and needlework rest. Probably she was mentally listening again to Reinhold and Friedrich's singing, and again watching the athletic Conrad vanquishing his adversaries, and receiving from her the victor's prize. Now and then she would hum a line or two of some song; then she would say, "You want my flowers?" and then a deeper crimson mantled in her cheeks; flashes darted through her half-closed eyelids, faint sighs stole forth from her innermost breast.

Frau Martha came in, and Rosa was delighted to have the opportunity of giving her a circumstantial account of all that had happened in Saint Catherine's Church and afterwards in the common. When she had finished, Martha said, smiling, "Well, Rosa dear, you will soon have to make up your mind which of those three brave wooers you are going to choose."

"What are you talking about, Frau Martha?" Rosa cried; "I haven't any wooers."

"Come, come," answered Martha, "don't pretend that you don't know what's going on. Anybody who has eyes, and is not as blind as a mole, sees well enough that all the three, Reinhold, Friedrich, and Conrad, are head over heels in love with you."

"What an idea!" cried Rosa, hiding her eyes with her hand.

"Come, come," said Martha, sitting down beside her and putting an arm about her; "take your hand away; look me straight in the face, and then deny, if you can, that you have known for many a day that all the three of them are devoted to you, heart and soul! You see that you *can't* deny it. It would be a miracle if a woman's eye should not see a thing of that sort in an instant. When you come into the workshop, all their eyes turn away from their work, to you, and everything goes on in a different way, three times as swimmingly. Reinhold and Friedrich begin singing their prettiest songs; even that wild fellow Conrad turns quiet and kindly. They all try to get beside you; and fire flashes out of the face of whichever of them has a kind glance or a friendly word from you. Aha! little daughter! you are a very fortunate girl to have three such men paying attention to you. Whether you will ever choose one of them— and if so, which—of course I cannot tell, for you are good and nice to them all; though I—but silence as to that! If you were to come to me, and say, 'Frau Martha, give me your advice,' I should freely answer, 'Doesn't your own heart speak out quite clearly and distinctly? Then *he* is the one.' Of course, they're all pretty much alike to *me*. I like Reinhold, and I like Friedrich too; and Conrad as well, for the matter of that; and still I have some objections to every one of them. Aye! the fact is, dear Rosa, when I look at those three young fellows at their work, I always think of my dear husband. And I must say, as far as the work which he did went, everything which he did was done in a different style from theirs. There was a swing and a *go* about it: you saw that his heart was in it; that he wasn't thinking of anything else. But *they* always seem to me to be doing it for the doing's sake, as if they all had something else at the bottom of their minds all the time; as if the work was a sort of task which they had taken up of their own accords, and were sticking to as well as they could, against the grain. I get on best with Friedrich. He is a nice, straightforward fellow. He seems more like *us*, somehow. One understands whatever he says. And what I like about him is that he loves you in such a silent sort of way, with all the bashfulness of a good child; that he hardly dares to look at you, and blushes whenever you say a word to him."

A tear came to Rosa's eye. She rose, turned to the window, and said: "Yes, I am very fond of Friedrich too; but you mustn't think too little of Reinhold, either."

"How should I?" said Martha; "he's the nicest-looking of them all, far and away. When he looks one through and through, with his eyes like lightning, one can hardly bear it. Still, there is a something about him so strange and wonderful, that I feel a little inclined to draw back from him in a sort of awe. I think the master must feel, when he is at work in the workshop, as I should if somebody brought a lot of pots and pans all sparkling with gold and jewels into my kitchen, and I had to set to work with them as if they were so many ordinary pots and pans. I wouldn't dare to touch them. He talks, and tells tales, and it all sounds like beautiful music, and carries you away. But when I think seriously about what he has been saying after he has done, I haven't understood a word of it, really. And then, when he will sometimes joke and jest just like one of ourselves, and I think he *is* only one of us after all, all of a sudden he will look up at you so proudly, and seem such a gentleman, that you feel frightened. It is not that he ever swaggers, as plenty of the young gentlefolk do; it's something quite different. In one word, it strikes me—God forgive me for saying it!—that he must have dealing with higher powers; as if he really belonged to another world altogether. Conrad is a rough, overbearing sort of fellow, but he has something aristocratic about him, too, which doesn't go a bit well with the cooper's apron; and he goes on as if it were his place to give orders, which everybody else had to obey. In the little time that he has been here, you see he has got so far that even Master Martin himself has to obey him, when he roars at him with that thundering voice of his. But then, at the same time, Conrad is so good-humoured, and so thoroughly straightforward and honourable, that one can't be vexed with him. In fact I must say that, in spite of his wildness, *I* like him better than Reinhold, almost; for though he *does* often speak roughly, yet you always understand what he is saying. I would wager he has once been a soldier, however he may pretend to disguise himself now. That's why he knows so well about weapons, and the knightly exercises, which become him so well. Now tell me, truly and sincerely, Rosa dear, which of them do *you* like the best?"

"Don't be so crafty with me, Frau Martha," Rosa replied. "One thing is certain—that I don't feel at all as you do about Reinhold. It is quite true that he is of quite a different sort from the others. When he talks, it seems as if some beautiful garden opened upon you, full of lovely flowers, blossoms, and fruit, the like of which are not to be found on earth; but it delights me to look into this garden. And many things strike me quite differently since Reinhold has been here. Many things which were dim and formless in my mind have grown so distinct and clear, that I can see them and understand them perfectly."

Frau Martha got up, and as she departed, she threatened Rosa with uplifted finger, saying, "Well, Rosa! I suppose Reinhold is to be the one: I never should have dreamed he would have been."

"I beg and pray you, Martha dear, neither dream, nor anticipate anything. Leave it all to the future. What the future brings will be the will of Heaven, and to that we must all submit with resignation."

Meanwhile things were very lively in Master Martin's workshop. To execute all his commissions he had taken on fresh hands and a few apprentices, and there was such a banging and hammering going on that it was audible far and wide. Reinhold had made out all the measurements for the Bishop of Bamberg's great vat, and set it up so cleverly that Master Martin's heart laughed in his body, and he cried out, over and over again, "*that* I *do* call a piece of work! that's going to be a cask such as I never turned out before—always excepting my *own* masterpiece." The three journeymen hooping the cask were hammering till the whole place rang. Old Valentine was shaving away busily with the hollowing-cramp. Frau Martha, with her two youngest children in her lap, was sitting just behind Conrad, while the others were playing and chasing each other about with the hoops. It was such a merry, boisterous affair altogether, that nobody noticed the entrance of old Master Johannes Holzschuer. However, Master Martin went up to him, and asked him courteously what might be his will.

"Well," said Master Holzschuer, "I wanted to see my dear Friedrich, who is working away so hard there. But, besides that, Master Martin, I want a fine cask for my cellar, and I was going to ask you to turn me one out. See! *there* is just the sort of cask I want —that one your men have in hand there, let me have that one. You have but to tell me the price."

Reinhold, who, being a little tired, was resting, said on his way on to the scaffold again, "Ah, Herr Holzschuer, you will have to do without this cask; we are making it for the Bishop of Bamberg."

Master Martin, folding his arms behind his back, advancing his left foot, and lifting his head proudly, blinked at the cask with his eyes, and said somewhat boastfully, "My dear master, you might know by the choiceness of the timber and the superiority of the workmanship that a masterpiece such as this is a thing for a Prince-Bishop's cellar alone. My journeyman Reinhold has said well. But when we have got the crop off our hands, I will turn you out a tidy simple little cask, such as will be suitable for your cellar."

Old Holzschuer, annoyed with Master Martin's haughtiness, thought, for his part, that *his* money was just as good as the Bishop of Bamberg's, and that he would probably get as good value for it elsewhere; and he said so. Master Martin, overwhelmed with anger, contained himself with difficulty. He scarcely dared to offend old Holzschuer, friend of the Council as he was, highly esteemed by all the town. But just at that moment, Conrad was making such a tremendous hammering with his mallet on the cask that the whole place was ringing and resounding; and Master Martin's boiling wrath ran over, so that he spluttered out, with a shout, "Conrad— dunderhead that you are—stop banging that cask like a madman! Do you want to break it?"

"Ho! ho, you funny little master," Conrad cried, looking round with an angry face, "why shouldn't I?" and set to work again, hammering at the cask with such violence that the largest of the hoops burst with a "clirr," knocking Reinhold off the narrow board of the scaffold, and from the hollow sound which followed, it was evident that one of the staves must have sprung as well. Overcome with rage and fury, Master Martin seized the stave which Valentine was shaving, and with a loud roar of "Damned dog!" dealt Conrad a heavy blow with it across the back.

When Conrad felt the blow, he turned quickly round, and stood for a moment as if unconscious, and then his eyes flamed with wild anger; he gnashed his teeth, howled out, "You hit me!" got down, with one spring, from the scaffold, seized the broad-axe which was on the ground, and aimed with it a tremendous stroke at the master, which would have split his skull, had not Friedrich pulled him aside, so that it missed his head; but it fell on his arm, whence the blood at once streamed out. Martin, stout and unwieldy, lost his balance and stumbled over the bench, at which an apprentice was working, and onto the ground. All the rest now threw themselves around Conrad, who was raging, and brandishing the bloody broad-axe in the air, yelling, in a terrible voice.

"To Hell with him!—to Hell with him!"

Exerting all his gigantic strength, he sent them flying from him in all directions, and was raising his weapon for a second stroke, which would certainly have given Master Martin his quietus as he lay coughing and groaning on the ground, but Rosa, pale as death, appeared at the door. The moment Conrad saw her, he paused like a stone image, with the uplifted weapon in his hand. Then he threw it away far from him, struck his hands together in front of his breast, cried—in a voice which went to every one's heart—"God in Heaven! what have I done?" and darted out of the building. Nobody thought of following him.

Master Martin was now set on his legs again, by dint of some effort, and it was found that the blade of the broad-axe had struck the fleshy part of his arm without doing very much mischief. Old Master Holzschuer, whom Martin had also dragged over in his fall, was pulled out from amid the timber; and Frau Martha's children, who were frightened and crying, were pacified. Master Martin was much confounded; but on the whole thought that if that devil of a wicked fellow had only not damaged the beautiful *cask*, he himself was not much the worse. Carrying chairs were brought for the old gentlemen, for Herr Holzschuer was more or less the worse for his tumble, too, and expressed a very mean opinion of a calling which was carried on where there were so many lethal weapons at hand, advising Friedrich to return to the beautiful metals, and casting, and that the sooner the better.

When the world was wrapped in twilight, Friedrich, and with him Reinhold, who had been hard hit by the hoop and felt sore in every bone of his body, crept, very unhappy, back to town. At the back of a hedge, they heard a low sobbing and sighing. They stopped; and presently a tall figure rose from the earth, which they at once recognized to be Conrad; and they started back, alarmed. "Ah! don't be afraid of me, my friends!" Conrad cried. "You think I am a diabolical, murdering dog; but I really am nothing of the kind. Only I couldn't help myself. I *had to* kill him. I really should go along with you and do it now, if possible—but no!—no, no! The whole thing is over! you won't see me any more. Give my deepest homage to beautiful Rosa, whom I love so dearly, so dearly. Tell her I will wear her flowers on my heart as long as I live, and that they shall be on me when I—but perhaps she may hear of me again. Goodbye! goodbye! dear old friends and comrades!" With which he ran off across the fields without a stop.

"There's something very strange about him." Reinhold said. "We can't judge what he does by everyday standards. Perhaps the future may unravel this mystery."

IX

Master Martin's workshop was now as melancholy a place as it had once been merry. Reinhold, unable to work, remained in his room. Master Martin, with his arm in a sling, railed and rated unceasingly on the subject of his late evil, incomprehensible journeyman. Rosa and Frau Martha with her children avoided the scene of the mad attempt, so that Friedrich's hammer on the wood sounded mournful and hollow as he went on, finishing the job by himself.

Soon his heart was filled with the deepest sorrow. For he fancied he now saw very clearly that what he had long dreaded was the truth. He was *sure* that Rosa loved Reinhold. It was not only that all her real friendliness, besides many a sweet word, had all along been given to him; but it was sufficient proof, now that Reinhold was unable to come to the workshop, that she never thought of leaving the house either—doubtless to nurse and take care of her lover. On Sunday, when everybody went out to make holiday and Master Martin—now nearly well—asked him to go with Rosa and him to the meadow, he declined, and went off alone to the village on the height, overpowered with grief and love anxiety. There, where he had first met Reinhold, he laid himself down on the flowery turf, and, as he thought how the beautiful Star of Hope, which had shone before him on all his journey home, had now—at the goal—vanished suddenly into the deepest night—how all his undertaking was now like the vain effort of a dreamer who stretches his longing arms to embrace empty images of air—the tears came to his eyes and rolled down his cheeks onto the grass, and the flowers, which hung their little heads as if in sorrow for his bitter fortune.   He scarce knew how it came that the sighs which heaved his distracted breast took the form of words and music.   But he sang the following song:—

> My star of hope! ah! whither has thou fled?
> Alas! for me, slid down beneath the marge,
> To rise, in splendour, upon happier hearts.
> Thou trembling night wind! smite upon this breast,
> And waken there the bliss which bringeth death,
> That so my heart, surcharged with tears of blood,
> May break, in longing ne'er to be assuaged.
> Dark trees! oh, tell me what mysterious words
> Ye whisper thus, in loving confidence.
> And ye, gold hems of heaven's wide-spread robe,
> Why shine ye down on me benignantly?
> Show me my grave! there is my hope's fair haven!
> There, and there only shall I rest in peace.

It sometimes happens that the deepest sorrow, if it can find tears and words, dissolves into a mild melancholy, so that perhaps even a gentle shimmer of hope begins to beam faintly through the heart. And so it was that Friedrich felt wondrously consoled and strengthened after he had sung this song.   The evening wind, and the dark trees which he had invoked, rustled and whispered as if with voices of comfort.   Golden streaks appeared in the dark sky like sweet dreams of coming glory and happiness still afar off.   He rose, and walked down to the village.   There he felt as if Reinhold was walking by his side as he had been when he first met him.   All that Reinhold had said came back upon his mind.   When he remembered Reinhold's story of the two painters who had tried for the prize, scales seemed to fall from his eyes.   It was quite clear that Reinhold must, before then, have seen and loved the fair Rosa. Nothing but this love had taken him to Master Martin's house in Nuremberg, and by the painter's contest he had meant nothing but his own and Friedrich's rivalry as regarded Rosa.   Friedrich listened once more to what Reinhold had then said, that "to strive towards the same goal, bravely and openly, was true friendship, and must truly in the depths of their hearts rather unite than separate real friends; for nobleness or littleness never can find place in hearts which are true."

"Yes, friend of my heart!" Friedrich cried aloud, "to you I will turn without reserve. You yourself shall tell me if all hope is over for me."

It was broad day when Friedrich knocked at Reinhold's door. As all was silent within, he opened it—it was not fastened, as it generally was—and entered. When he did so, he stood transfixed like a statue; for there, on an easel before him, stood a full-length portrait of Rosa, in all the pride of her beauty, lighted up by the rays of the rising sun. The maulstick on the table, where it had been thrown down—the colours still wet—showed that the portrait had just been worked upon.

"Rosa! Rosa! oh, Father of Heaven!" Friedrich cried. Reinhold tapped him on the shoulder, and asked him, with a smile, what he thought of the picture. Friedrich pressed him to his heart saying:

"Ah, glorious fellow! mighty artist!—it is all clear to me now. You have gained the prize for which I—wretch that I am!—was bold enough to try. What am I, compared to you; what is *my* art, to *yours?* Alas! I had great ideas in my mind, too! Don't laugh me altogether to scorn, dear Reinhold. I thought what a glorious thing it would be to make a mould model of Rosa's beautiful form in the finest silver. But that, of course, would be mere child's play. But as for *you!*—how she smiles in all the pride of her loveliness!— Ah! Reinhold! happiest of men! what you said long ago has now come true. We have striven for the prize. You have won it. You could not *but* win. But I am still yours, with all my soul! I must get away; I could not bear to stay here. I should die if I saw Rosa again. Forgive me this, my dear, dear, glorious friend! This very day—this very moment—I must go into the wide world, wherever my sorrow—my inconsolable misery—may drive me." With which he would have left the room; but Reinhold held him fast, saying gently:

"You shall not go, because things may possibly turn out far otherwise than you suppose. It is time now that I should tell you what I have kept silence about hitherto. That I am not a cooper at all, but a painter, you probably now have gathered; and I hope the portrait has proved to you that I am not one of the worst. When I was very young, I went to Italy, the land of art; and there it chanced that some great masters took an interest in me, and fanned the sparks which smouldered within me into living fire. Thus I soon rose to some eminence, and my pictures became celebrated all over Italy. The Grand Duke of Florence took me to his court. At that time I did not care to know anything of the German school of art, and, without having seen any German pictures, I talked largely of the woodenness, the bad drawing, and the hardness of your Dürer and your Cranach. However, one day, a dealer brought a small Madonna of old Albrecht's into the Duke's gallery, which went to my heart in a wonderful manner; so that I completely turned away from the luxury of the Italian school, and at that hour determined to see for myself, in my native Germany, those masterpieces on which my thoughts were now bent. I came to Nuremberg here; and when I saw Rosa, it seemed to me as though that Madonna which beamed so brightly in my heart were walking the earth. In my case, just as in yours, dear Friedrich, all my being flamed up in a blaze of affection. I saw and thought of nothing but Rosa. Even art was only precious in my sight because I could go on drawing and painting Rosa hundreds of times, over and over again. In the unceremonious Italian fashion, I thought I should have no difficulty in approaching her, but all my efforts in this direction were vain. There was no way of getting introduced, in honour, to Master Martin's house. At last I thought of going and straightforwardly announcing myself as one of her wooers, but then I heard of Master Martin's determination to give her to nobody but a real master cooper. On this, I came to the rather quixotic resolve that I would go and learn coopering at Strassburg, and then betake myself to Master Martin's workshop. The rest I left to Heaven's will. How I carried out my resolution, you know; but you have still to learn that a few days ago Master Martin told me I should make a first-rate cooper, and should be very acceptable to him as a son-in-law; for he saw well enough that I was trying to gain Rosa's favour, and that she liked me."

"How could it be otherwise?" Friedrich cried. "Yes, yes; she will be yours. How could I, most wretched of creatures, ever hope for such bliss!"

"My brother!" said Reinhold, "you forget that Rosa has by no means yet confirmed what wily Master Martin fancies he sees. It is true she has always been very charming and kindly with me; but that is not exactly how a loving heart displays itself. Promise me, my brother, to keep quiet for three days more, and work in the shop as usual. I might go back again there now, too; but since I have been busy at this picture, that miserable handicraft sickens me inexpressibly. I *cannot* take a hammer in my hand again, come what will! On the third day I will tell you distinctly how matters stand between me and Rosa. If I should really be the fortunate man to whom she has given her heart, you may depart; and you will learn that time heals the very deepest wounds."

Friedrich promised to abide his destiny.

On the third day (Friedrich had carefully shunned the sight of Rosa) his heart trembled with fear and anxious expectation. He crept about the workshop like one in a dream, and his awkwardness was such as to give Master Martin occasion to scold angrily, in a way unusual with him. Taking things all round, something seemed to have come to the master which had taken away all satisfaction from him. He talked much of wicked artfulness and ingratitude, without further explaining what he was driving at. When evening at length came and Friedrich was going back to town, near the city gate he saw a man on horseback, whom he at once knew to be Reinhold. As soon as this latter caught sight of him he cried out: "Ha, ha! here you are!—just as I wished!" He got off his horse, threw the reins on his arm, and took his friend by the hand: "Let us stroll along together for a while," he said; "I can tell you now how my love affair has turned out."

Friedrich noticed that Reinhold was dressed as he had been when they first met, and that the horse had a valise on him. Reinhold was looking rather pale and troubled. "Good luck to you, brother!" he cried, somewhat wildly. "You can go on hammering lustily away at your casks, for I am clearing out of your way. I have just said goodbye to lovely Rosa, and worthy old Martin."

"What!" cried Friedrich, who felt a kind of electric shock go through him. "You are going away—when Master Martin wants you for a son-in-law, and when Rosa loves you?"

"Dear brother," answered Reinhold, "that is what your jealousy has led you to imagine. It has turned out that Rosa would have married me from mere filial obedience, but that there is not a single spark of love for me in that ice-cold heart of hers. Ha, ha! I should have been a celebrated cooper! Shaving hoops on weekdays with my apprentices, and taking my worthy housekeeper wife on Sundays to St. Catherine's or St. Sebald's to service, and then to the meadow in the evening, one year after another, all my life long."

"Well, you needn't ridicule the simple, innocent life of the good townspeople," cried Friedrich, interrupting Reinhold in his laughter. "It's not Rosa's fault if she does not really love you. You are so angry—so wild!"

"You are right," said Reinhold; "it is only my stupid way of behaving like a spoiled child when I feel annoyed. You will understand that I told Rosa of my love for her, and of her father's goodwill. The tears streamed from her eyes; her hand trembled in mine; she turned away her face, and said, 'Of course I must do as my father wishes.' That was enough. This strange vexation of mine must have enabled you to read my inmost heart. You see that my efforts to gain Rosa were the result of a deception, which my mistaken feeling had prepared for itself. As soon as I had finished her portrait, my heart was at rest; and I often felt, in an inexplicable manner, as though Rosa had really been the picture, and the picture the real Rosa. The mean, wretched, mechanical handicraft grew detestable to me: the common style of life, and the whole business of having to get myself made a master cooper and marry, depressed me so that I felt as if I were going to be immured in a prison and chained to a block. How could that heavenly child whom I have worn in my heart—*as* I have worn her in my heart—ever become my wife? Ah, no! she must forever be resplendent in the master-works which my soul shall engender; in eternal youth, delightsome-ness, and beauty. Oh, how I long to be working at them! How could I ever sever myself from my heavenly calling! Soon shall I bathe once more in your fervid vapours, glorious land! home of all the arts!"

The friends had reached the point where the road which Reinhold meant to follow turned sharp off to the left. "Here we part!" he cried. He pressed Friedrich warmly to his heart, sprang into the saddle, and galloped away.

Friedrich gazed after him in silence, and then crept home, filled with the strangest thoughts.

X

The next day Master Martin was labouring away at the Bishop of Bamberg's cask, in moody silence; and Friedrich too, who was only now feeling fully what he had lost in Reinhold, was not capable of a word, far less of a song. At last Martin threw down his hammer, folded his arms, and said in a low voice:

"So Reinhold has gone too! He was a great, celebrated painter, and merely making a fool of me with his coopering. If I had but the slightest inkling of that when he came to my house with you, and seemed so handy and clever, shouldn't I just have shown him the door! Such an open, honest-looking face! and yet all deceit and falsehood! Well! he is gone; but *you* are going to stick to me and the craft with truth and honour.

"When you get to be a good master cooper—and if Rosa takes a fancy to you—well! you know what I mean, and can try if you can gain her liking." With which he took up his hammer, and went busily on with his work. Friedrich could not quite explain to himself why it was that Master Martin's words pained his heart—why some strange, anxious dread arose in him, darkening every shimmer of hope. Rosa came to the workshop, for the first time in a long while, but she was deeply thoughtful and (as Friedrich remarked to his sorrow) her eyes were red from weeping. "She has been crying about *him*; she loves him," a voice in his heart said; and he did not dare to raise his glance to her whom he loved so unutterably.

The cask was finished; and then, and only then, Master Martin, as he contemplated that highly successful piece of work, grew cheerful and light-hearted once more. "Ay, my lad," he said, slapping Friedrich on the shoulder, "it is a settled matter that, if you can turn out a right good masterpiece and win Rosa's good-will, my son-in-law you shall be. After that you can join the noble guild of the Meistersinger, and gain much renown."

At this time Master Martin's commissions so accumulated that he had to hire two new journeymen, capital workmen, but rough fellows who had picked up many evil habits during their long years of travel as journeymen away from home. In place of the old merry talk, the jokes, and the pretty singing which used to go on in the workshop, nothing was to be heard there now but obscene ditties. Rosa avoided the place, so that Friedrich only saw her at long intervals, and when he then looked at her with melancholy longing, and sighed out, "Ah! dearest Rosa! if I could but talk with you again! if you would only be kindly with me as you used to be when Reinhold was here!" she would cast her eyes bashfully down, and murmur, "Have you anything to say to me, dear Friedrich?" But he would stand transfixed and speechless. The lucky moment would pass, as quick as lightning which flashes in the evening sky, and has vanished ere one has noticed it almost.

Master Martin was now all insistence that Friedrich should set to work on his "Masterpiece." He had himself chosen, in his workshop, the finest, cleanest, most flawless timber, which had been stored there for over five years, and had not a vein or a streak in it; and nobody was to give Friedrich the slightest hand in the job except old Valentine.

More and more intensely disgusted with the whole thing as Friedrich now was, on account of those brutes of journeymen, the thought that all his future life hung upon this piece of work almost stifled him. The strange sense of dread and anxiety which had developed in him when Master Martin had lauded his faithful devotion to the craft, took shape now, more and more clearly. He felt convinced that he would come to the most utter and shameful failure in an occupation completely repugnant to his whole nature, filled as it was with the love of his own art. Reinhold, and Rosa's portrait he could not drive out of his mind; at the same time, his own branch of art shone upon him in the brightest splendour. Often, when the terrible sense of the full wretchedness of the trade he was engaged in seemed likely to overpower him as he was working at it, he would pretend to be unwell, and hurry off to the church of St. Sebald, where he would gaze for hours at Peter Fischer's marvellous monument, and then cry out, like one enchanted, "Oh, Father of Heaven! —to conceive, to execute such a work as that—could there be anything on earth more glorious!" and then when he had to go back to his staves and hoops, and remember that by means of *them* only, Rosa was to be won, the very devil's glowing talons seemed to touch his heart, and he felt as if he must perish in the terrible misery of it all. Reinhold often appeared to him in dreams, bringing to him lovely designs, in which Rosa was worked in, and displayed now as a flower, now as a beautifully winged angel. But there was always a something wanting. Reinhold had forgotten to put a *heart* in Rosa's image; and that he added himself. *Then* all the flowers and leaves of the design seemed to begin moving and singing, and breathing out the most delicious odours; and the noble metals reflected Rosa's form as in a gleaming mirror, seeming to stretch her longing arms to her lover—but the image would vanish in dim vapour, and the beautiful Rosa herself seemed to be clasping him to her loving heart, all blissful desire. His feelings towards the miserable coopering work grew more and more terribly unendurable, and he went for aid and consolation (as well as for advice) to his old master, Johannes Holzschuer. This master allowed Friedrich to set about a little piece of work, for which an idea had occurred to him and for the carrying out of which, with the necessary gold and silver, he had saved up the wages which Master Martin gave him for many a day.

Thus it came about that Friedrich, who was so very pale that there was but too much reason to believe (as he gave out) that he was suffering from strongly marked consumptive symptoms, scarcely ever went to Master Martin's workshop, and that months elapsed without his having made the very slightest progress with his masterpiece, the great two-fudder cask. Master Martin pressed him to work at least as much as his strength would permit him, and Friedrich was at length compelled to go once more to the hateful cutting-block, and take the broad-axe in hand again. As he was working, Master Martin came up and looked at the staves he had been finishing. He grew red in the face and cried out:

"Why, Friedrich! what do you call this? A nice job and a half! Are those staves turned out by a journeyman trying to pass as master, or by an apprentice boy who has been only a day or two in the shop! Bethink yourself, man; what demon has entered itself into you? My beautiful oak timber! The great masterpiece indeed! Clumsy, careless goose!"

Overcome by all the hellish torments which were burning in his heart, Friedrich could contain himself no longer. He sent the broad-axe flying with all his force, and cried, "Master, it's all over! If it costs me my life—if I perish in misery unnamed, I cannot go on labouring at this wretched handicraft another minute. I am drawn to my own glorious art with a power which I cannot withstand. Alas! I love your Rosa unutterably—as no other on earth can love her. It is for her sake alone that I have gone through with this abominable work in this place. I know I have lost her now. I shall soon die of grief for her. But I cannot help it. I must go back to my own glorious art, to my own dear master, Johannes Holzschuer, whom I deserted so shamefully."

Master Martin's eyes shone like flaming tapers. Scarce able to articulate for anger, he stammered out:

"What! you too! lies and cheatery! impose on *me*—talk of a 'miserable handicraft!' Out of my sight, you shameless scoundrel —get out from here!" with which he took Friedrich by the shoulders and chucked him out of the workshop.

The derisive laughter of the other journeymen and the apprentices followed him. But old Valentine folded his hands, looked thoughtfully at the ground, and said, "I always saw that good fellow had something very different in his head from casks."

Frau Martha cried a great deal, and her children lamented over Friedrich, who used to play with them, and bring them many a nice piece of sweet stuff.

XI

Notwithstanding Master Martin's anger with Reinhold and Friedrich, he could not but admit that with them all happiness and joy had fled from the workshop. His new journeymen caused him nothing but vexation and annoyance every day. He had to give himself trouble over every trifling detail of the work, and had difficulty in getting the very smallest matter done as he wished it. Wholly worn out with the worries of the day, he would often sigh, "Ah, Reinhold! ah, Friedrich! how I wish you had not deceived me so shamefully! Oh that you had only gone on being coopers, and not turned out to be something else!" This went so far, that he often thought of giving up business altogether.

He was sitting one evening in a gloomy frame of mind of this description, when Herr Jacobus Paumgartner, and with him Master Johannes Holzschuer, came in unexpectedly. He felt sure their visit related to Friedrich, and in fact Paumgartner soon led the conversation to him, and Master Holzschuer began to extol him in every possible way, stating his opinion that with Friedrich's talents and diligence he would not only become a first-class goldsmith, but actually tread in Peter Fischer's footsteps as an eminent sculptor. Then Herr Paumgartner set to work to inveigh vehemently against the undeserved treatment that the poor fellow had received from Master Martin, and they both of them urged the latter that, if Friedrich should turn out a fine goldsmith and modeller, he should give him Rosa to wife, provided she was really fond of him.

Master Martin allowed them both to finish what they had to say; then he took off his cap and answered with a smile, "Worthy sirs, you speak strongly in favour of the lad, who has—all the same— deceived me in a shameful manner. I forgive him that, however, but you must not expect me to alter my firm decision on his account. It is not the slightest use asking me to give him my Rosa—completely out of the question."

Just then, Rosa came in, pale as death, with eyes red from crying, and in silence placed glasses and wine on the table.

"Very well!" said Holzschuer; "then I suppose I shall be obliged to let Friedrich have his way, and leave this place altogether. He has just finished a beautiful piece of workmanship at my atelier, which—if you will allow him, Master Martin—he wishes to offer to Rosa as a keepsake. I have it with me; look at it."

He produced a small silver goblet, beautifully and artistically ornamented all over, and handed it to Master Martin who was a great admirer and "amateur" of such things. He took it and looked at it on all sides with great admiration; in fact it would have been difficult to meet a more beautiful piece of silverwork than this little vessel where lovely vine branches, with tendrils interwoven with roses were twining in all directions, while from among the grapes and the roses beautiful angels were peeping, and others, embracing, were graven inside it, on its gilt sides and bottom; so that when wine was poured into it, those angels seemed to hover up and down, in charming play.

"A very pretty thing indeed!" Master Martin said. "Beautiful work about it! I shall be glad to take it, if Friedrich will allow me to give him twice its worth in good gold pieces."

So saying, Master Martin filled the cup with wine, and set it to his lips.

Here the door opened gently, and Friedrich, with the deadly pain of parting forever from her he loved best on earth in his white face, came in. As soon as Rosa saw him, she gave a bitter cry of "Oh, my own dearest Friedrich!" and threw herself half-fainting on his breast.

Master Martin set the cup down, and when he saw Rosa in Friedrich's arms, he opened wide eyes, as if he were seeing ghosts. Then he took up the cup again without a word, and looked down into it. "Rosa," he cried in a loud voice, rising from his chair, "do you really love Friedrich?"

"Ah!" said Rosa in a whisper, "I·cannot hide it any longer—I love him as my life! My heart was broken when you sent him away."

"Take your wife to your heart then, Friedrich. Yes, yes, I say it —*your wife*," Master Martin cried out.

Paumgartner and Holzschuer looked at each other, lost in amazement; but Master Martin, holding the cup in his hands, went on, and said, "Oh Father of Heaven! has not everything turned out exactly as the old lady prophesied it should? 'A House resplendent and gleaming he shall to thy dwelling bring; streams of sweet savour flowing therein; beauteous angels sing full sweetly; he whom thy heart goeth forth to—needless to ask of thy father, this is thy Bridegroom beloved!' Oh fool that I have been! this is the bright little house! here are the angels, the bridegroom! Aha! gentlemen, my friends and patrons—my son-in-law is found!"

Anyone who has at any time been under the spell of an evil dream, and thought he was lying in the deep, black darkness of the grave, and then has suddenly awakened in the bright springtime, all perfume, sunshine and song, and she who is dearest to him on earth has come and put her arms about him, while he looked into the heaven of her beautiful face—that person will understand how Friedrich felt—will comprehend the exuberance of his happiness. Unable to utter a word, he held Rosa fast in his arms as if he would never let her go, till she gently extricated herself from his embrace and led him to her father. He then found words, and cried:

"Oh, dear master, is this really true, then? Do you give me Rosa for my wife, and may I go back to my own art?"

"Yes, yes, believe it!" answered Master Martin. "What else is there that I can do? You have fulfilled my grandmother's prophecy, and your masterpiece need not be finished."

Friedrich smiled, transfigured with happiness, and said: "No, dear master, you will allow me to finish my masterpiece, and then I will go back to my smelting furnace. For I should enjoy finishing my cask, as my last piece of coopering work."

"So let it be then, my dear, good son," cried Master Martin, with eyes sparkling with joy. "Finish your masterpiece, and then for the wedding!"

Friedrich kept his word. He duly finished his two-fudder cask, and all the masters averred that it would be hard to meet with a prettier piece of work; at which Master Martin was highly delighted, and thought that, all things considered, heaven could scarcely have awarded him a better son-in-law.

The wedding day had come at last. Friedrich's cask masterpiece, full of noble wine and garlanded with flowers, stood on the house floor. The masters of the craft, headed by Herr Paumgartner, duly arrived, with their wives, followed by the master goldsmiths. The procession was just setting out for St. Sebald's church, where the wedding was to be, when a blast of trumpets sounded in the streets, and horses were neighing and stamping in front of Master Martin's house. He hastened to the balcony window, and there he saw Herr von Spangenberg drawing up, in front of the house in festal array. A few yards behind him rode a young cavalier, a grand-looking young gentleman on a spirited charger, with a sword at his side and tall plumes waving in his beret which sparkled with jewels. At the cavalier's side Master Martin saw a most beautiful lady, also splendidly attired, and riding a palfrey as white as new-fallen snow. Pages and servants in fine liveries formed a circle about them. The trumpets ceased to sound, and old Baron von Spangenberg cried out, "Ha, ha! Master Martin. I am not come here on account of your cellar or your gold-ingots, but because it is Rosa's wedding day. Will you let me come in, dear Master Martin?"

Master Martin, remembering what he had said that night so long ago, was somewhat embarrassed, but hastened down to welcome the party. The old Baron dismounted, and came in, with courteous greetings. Pages hurried up, offering their arms to help the young lady to dismount; her cavalier gave her his hand, and followed the old Baron. But as soon as Master Martin looked upon the young cavalier, he started back three paces, clapped his hands and cried, "Good heavens! 'tis Conrad!"

The cavalier smiled, and said, "Yes, yes, Master Martin, I am your journeyman Conrad. You must pardon me for having given you that nasty wound. By rights, dear master, I ought to have sent you to kingdom come; you must see that yourself—however, things have all turned out differently."

Master Martin, in some confusion, answered that he "thought it was just as well that he had *not* been sent to 'kingdom come,'" and that he hadn't much minded the little bit of a cut with the broad-axe.

As Master Martin and his new guests now entered the chamber where the bridal pair were, with the others, everybody acclaimed the beauty of the lady, for she was so exactly like the bride that she might have been her twin sister. The cavalier went up to the bride courteously, saying, "Beautiful Rosa, I hope you will permit Conrad to be present at your wedding. You are no longer vexed with the wild thoughtless fellow who so nearly cost you a great sorrow?"

As the bride, the bridegroom, and Master Martin looked from one to another in utter perplexity, the old Baron cried out, "Well, well! suppose I must help you out of your dream. This is my son, Conrad, and there is his beautiful wife, whose name is Rosa, the same as the bride's. Remember, Master Martin, our conversation, when I asked you if you would refuse to give me your Rosa even to *my* son. It had a special purpose. The boy was head over heels in love with your Rosa. He persuaded me to throw all consideration to the winds, and agree to act as his mediator—his go-between. But when I told him how you had shown me the door, he went and sneaked into your service in the most foolish way, as a cooper, to gain Rosa's heart, with the view, I suppose, of carrying her off from you. Well! you cured him with that swinging blow you gave him on the back, and thanks to you for that, inasmuch as he has found a noble lady, who may perhaps be really the Rosa he had in his heart from the beginning."

Meanwhile the lady had saluted the bride with the gentlest courtesy, and placed round her neck a rich pearl necklace, as a wedding gift.

"Look, dear Rosa," she said, taking some withered flowers from among the fresh ones she wore on her breast, "these are the flowers which you gave to my Conrad as a prize of victory. He kept them faithfully till he saw me. But then he was false to you, and let me have them. Don't be angry."

Rosa, blushing deeply, and casting her eyes modestly down, answered, "Ah! my lady, how can you speak so? He never could have cared for *me*, certainly. *You* were his love alone; and because I happen to be called Rosa, too, and am—as these gentlemen say—a little like you, he made love to me, thinking all the time of you."

The procession was about to start for the second time, when a young gentleman came in, dressed in the Italian fashion, all in slashed black velvet, with a fine gold chain and a collar of rich lace.

"Oh, my Reinhold," cried Friedrich, and fell upon his neck; and the bride and Master Martin, too, rejoiced, and cried out, "Here is our beloved Reinhold!"

"Did I not say, my dearest friend," said Reinhold, cordially returning the embraces, "that everything would turn out gloriously for you after all? Let me celebrate your wedding day with you. I have come a long distance to do so. And as an everlasting memorial, hang up in your house the picture which I painted for you, and which I have brought with me." He called outside, and two servants came in carrying a large painting in a magnificent gold frame, representing Master Martin in his workshop with his journeymen Reinhold, Friedrich, and Conrad at work on the great cask, with Rosa just come in at the door. Everybody was amazed at the truthfulness and splendid colouring of this work of art.

"Ah," said Friedrich, "*that* is *your* cooper's masterpiece. Mine is downstairs. But I shall turn out another."

"I know," said Reinhold, "and you are a fortunate man; stick to your own art; very probably it is better suited to domesticity and the like than mine."

At the wedding dinner Friedrich sat between the two Rosas, with Master Martin opposite to him, between Reinhold and Conrad. Paumgartner filled Friedrich's goblet to the brim with noble wine, and drank to the health of Master Martin and his grand journeymen. The goblet went round, and first Baron von Spangenberg, and after him all the worthy masters, drained it to the same toast.

THE MINES OF FALUN

One bright, sunny day in July the whole population of Goethaborg was assembled at the harbour. A fine East Indiaman, happily returned from her long voyage, was lying at anchor, with her long, homeward-bound pennant and the Swedish flag fluttering gaily in the azure sky. Hundreds of boats, skiffs and other small craft, thronged with rejoicing seafolk, were going to and fro on the mirroring waters of the Goethaelf, and the cannon of Masthuggetorg thundered their far-echoing greeting out to sea. The gentlemen of the East India Company were walking up and down on the quay, reckoning up, with smiling faces, the plentiful profits they had netted, and rejoicing at the yearly increasing success of their hazardous enterprise and at the growing commercial importance of their good town of Goethaborg. For the same reasons everybody looked at these brave adventurers with pleasure and pride, and shared their rejoicing; for their success brought sap and vigour into the whole life of the place.

The crew of the East Indiaman, about a hundred strong, landed in a number of boats (gaily dressed with flags for the occasion) and prepared to hold their Hoensning. That is the name of the feast which the sailors hold on such occasions; it often goes on for several days. Musicians went before them in strange, gay dresses; some played lustily on violins, oboes, fifes and drums, while others sang merry songs. After them came the crew, walking two and two; some, with gay ribbons on their hats and jackets, waved fluttering streamers; others danced and skipped; and all of them shouted and cheered at the tops of their voices, till the sounds of merriment rang far and wide.

Thus the gay procession passed through the streets, and on to the suburb of Haga, where a feast was ready for them in a tavern.

Here the best of "Oel" flowed in rivers and bumper after bumper was quaffed. Women joined them, as is always the case when sailors come home from a long voyage; dancing began, and wilder and wilder grew the revel, and louder and louder the din.

One sailor only—a slender, handsome lad of about twenty or a little less—had slipped away and was sitting alone outside, on the bench at the door of the tavern.

Two or three of his shipmates came out to him, and one of them cried, laughing loudly:

"Now then, Elis Froebom! are you going to be a donkey, as usual, and sit out here sulking instead of joining the sport like a man? Why, you might as well part company from the old ship altogether, and set sail on your own hook as fight shy of the Hoensning. One would think you were a regular long-shore landlubber, and had never been afloat on blue water. All the same, you've got as good pluck as any sailor that walks a deck—ay, and as cool and steady a head in a gale of wind as ever I came athwart; but you see, you can't take your liquor! You'd sooner keep the ducats in your pocket than serve them out to the land-sharks ashore here. Here, lad! take a drink of that; or Naecken, the sea-devil, and all the Troll will be foul of your hawse before you know where you are!"

Elis Froebom jumped up quickly from the bench, glared angrily at his shipmates, took the tumbler—which was filled to the brim with brandy—and emptied it at a draught; then he said:

"You see I can take my glass with any man of you, Ivens; and you can ask the captain if I'm a good sailor or not; so stow away that long tongue of yours and sheer off! I don't care about all this drink and row here; and what I'm doing out here by myself's no business of yours; you have nothing to do with it."

"All right, my hearty!" answered Ivens. "I know all about it. You're one of these Nerica men—and a moony lot the whole cargo of them are too. They're the sort that would rather sit and pipe their eye about nothing particular than take a good glass and see what the women at home are made of, after a twelve-month's cruise! But just you belay there a bit. Steer full and bye, and stand off and on, and I'll send somebody out to you that'll cut you adrift in a pig's whisper from that old bench where you've cast your anchor."

They went, and presently a very pretty girl came out of the tavern and sat down beside the melancholy Elis, who was still sitting, silent and thoughtful, on the bench. From her dress and general appearance there could be no doubt as to her calling. But the life she was leading had not yet quite marred the delicacy of the wonderfully tender features of her beautiful face; there was no trace of repulsive boldness about the expression of her dark eyes—rather a quiet, melancholy longing.

"Aren't you coming to join your shipmates, Elis?" she said. "Now that you're back safe and sound, after all you've gone through on your long voyage, aren't you glad to be home in the old country again?"

The girl spoke in a soft, gentle voice, putting her arms about him. Elis Froebom looked into her eyes as if roused from a dream. He took her hand; he pressed her to his breast. It was evident that what she had said had made its way to his heart.

"Ah!" he said, as if collecting his thoughts, "it's no use talking about enjoying myself. I can't join in all that riot and uproar; there's no pleasure in it, for me. You go back. Sing and shout like the rest of them, if you can, and let gloomy, melancholy Elis stay out here by himself; he would only spoil your pleasure. Wait a minute, though! I like you, and I want you to think of me sometimes, when I'm away on the sea again."

With that he took two shining ducats out of his pocket and a beautiful Indian handkerchief from his breast, and gave them to the girl. Her eyes streamed with tears; she rose, laid the money on the bench, and said:

"Oh, keep your ducats; they only make me miserable; but I'll wear the handkerchief in remembrance of you. You're not likely to find me next year when you hold your Hoensning in the Haga."

And she crept slowly away down the street, with her hands pressed to her face.

Elis fell back into his gloomy reveries. At length, as the uproar in the tavern grew loud and wild, he cried:

"Oh, I wish I were deep, deep beneath the sea! for there's nobody left in the wide, wide world that I can be happy with now!"

A deep, harsh voice spoke, close behind him: "You must have been most unfortunate, youngster, to wish to die, just when life should be opening before you."

Elis looked round, and saw an old miner leaning with folded arms against the boarded wall of the tavern, looking down at him with a grave, penetrating stare.

As Elis looked at him, a feeling came to him as if some familiar figure had suddenly come into the deep, wild solitude in which he had thought himself lost. He pulled himself together, and told the old miner that his father had been a stout sailor, but had perished in the storm from which he himself had been saved as if by a miracle; that his two soldier brothers had died in battle, and he had supported his mother with the liberal pay he drew for sailing to the East Indies. He said he had been obliged to follow the life of a sailor, having been brought up to it from childhood, and it had been a great piece of good fortune that he got into the service of the East India Company. This voyage, the profits had been greater than usual, and each of the crew had been given a sum of money over and above his pay; so that he had hastened, in the highest spirits, with his pockets full of ducats, to the little cottage where his mother lived. But strange faces looked at him from the windows, and a young woman who opened the door to him at last told him in a cold, harsh tone that his mother had died three months earlier, and that he would find the few bits of things that were left, after paying the funeral expenses, waiting for him at the Town Hall.

The death of his mother broke his heart. He felt alone in the world—as much so as if he had been wrecked on some lonely reef, helpless and miserable. All his life at sea seemed to him to have been a mistaken, purposeless driving. And when he thought of his mother, perhaps badly looked after by strangers, he thought it a wrong and horrible thing that he should have gone to sea at all, instead of staying at home and taking proper care of her. His comrades had dragged him to the Hoensning in spite of himself, and he had thought too that the uproar and even the drink might deaden his pain; but instead of that, all the veins in his breast seemed to be bursting, and he felt as if he would bleed to death.

"Well," said the old miner, "you'll soon be off to sea again, Elis, and then your sorrow will soon be over. Old folks must die; there's no help for that. She has only gone from this miserable world to a better."

"Ah!" said Elis, "it is just because nobody believes in my sorrow, and that they all think me a fool to feel it—I say it's that which is driving me out of the world! I won't go to sea any more; I'm sick of living altogether. When the ship used to go flying along through the water, with all sails set, spreading like wings, the waves playing and dashing in exquisite music, and the wind singing in the rigging, my heart used to bound. Then I could hurrah and shout on deck like the best of them. And when I was on lookout duty of dark, quiet nights, I used to think about getting home, and how glad my dear old mother would be to have me back. I could enjoy a Hoensning like the rest of them then. And when I had shaken the ducats into mother's lap and given her the handkerchiefs and all the other pretty things I had brought home, her eyes would sparkle with pleasure, and she would clap her hands for joy, and run out and in, and fetch me ale which she had kept for my homecoming. And when I sat with her evenings, I would tell her of all the strange folks I had seen, and their ways and customs, and about the wonderful things I had come across in my long voyages. This delighted her; and she would tell me of my father's wonderful cruises in the far North, and lots of strange sailor's yarns which I had heard a hundred times but never could hear too often. Ah! who will give me that happiness back again? What should I do among my shipmates? They would only laugh at me. Where should I find any heart for my work? There would be no purpose to it."

"It gives me real satisfaction to listen to you, youngster," said the old miner. "I have been observing you, without your knowledge, for the last hour or two, and have had my own enjoyment in doing so. All that you have said and done has shown me that you have a very thoughtful mind, and a character and nature pious, simple, and sincere. Heaven could have given you no more precious gifts; but you were never in all your born days in the least cut out for a sailor. How could the wild, unsettled sailor's life suit a meditative, melancholy Neriker like you?—for I can see that you come from Nerica by your features and whole appearance. You are right to say goodbye to that life forever. But you're not going to walk about idle, with your hands in your pockets? Take my advice, Elis Froebom. Go to Falun, and be a miner. You are young and strong. You'll soon be a first-class pick-hand; then a hewer; presently a surveyor, and so get higher and higher. You have a lot of ducats in your pocket. Take care of them; invest them; add more to them. Very likely you'll soon get a 'Hemmans' of your own, and then a share in the works. Take my advice, Elis Froebom; be a miner."

The old man's words caused him a sort of fear.

"What?" he cried. "Would you have me leave the bright, sunny sky that revives and refreshes me, and go down into that hell-like abyss, and dig and tunnel like a mole for metals and ores, merely to gain a few wretched ducats? Oh, never!"

"The usual thing," said the old man. "People despise what they have had no chance of knowing anything about! As if all the constant wearing, petty anxieties inseparable from business up here on the surface, were nobler than the miner's work. To his skill, knowledge, and untiring industry Nature lays bare her most secret treasures. You speak of gain with contempt, Elis Froebom. Well, there's something infinitely higher in question here, perhaps: the mole tunnels the ground from blind instinct; but it may be, in the deepest depths, by the pale glimmer of the mine candle, men's eyes get to see clearer, and at length, growing stronger and stronger, acquire the power of reading in the stones, the gems, and the minerals, the mirroring of secrets which are hidden above the clouds. You know nothing about mining, Elis.   Let me tell you a little."

He sat down on the bench beside Elis, and began to describe the various processes minutely, placing all the details before him in the clearest and brightest colours.   He talked of the mines of Falun, in which he said he had worked since he was a boy; he described the great main-shaft, with its dark brown sides; he told how incalculably rich the mine was in gems of the finest water.   More and more vivid grew his words, more and more glowing his face.   He went, in his description, through the different shafts as if they had been the alleys of some enchanted garden.   The jewels came to life, the fossils began to move; the wondrous pyrosmalite and the almandine flashed in the light of the miner's candles; the rock crystals glittered, and darted their rays.

Elis listened intently.   The old man's strange way of speaking of all these subterranean marvels as if he were standing in the midst of them impressed him deeply.   His breast felt stifled; it seemed to him as if he were already down in these depths with the old man, and would never look upon the friendly light of day again. And yet it seemed as though the old man were opening to him a new and unknown world, to which he really properly belonged, and that he had somehow felt all the magic of that world in mystic forebodings since his boyhood.

"Elis Froebom," said the old man at last, "I have laid before you all the glories of a calling for which Nature really destined you. Think the subject over well, and then act as your better judgment counsels you."

He rose quickly from the bench and strode away without any goodbye to Elis, without looking at him even.   Soon he disappeared from his sight.

Meanwhile quietness had set in in the tavern.   The strong ale and brandy had got the upper hand.   Many of the sailors had gone away with the girls; others were lying snoring in corners. Elis—who could go no more to his old home—asked for, and was given, a little room to sleep in.

Scarcely had he thrown himself, worn and weary as he was, upon his bed, when dreams began to wave their pinions over him. He thought he was sailing in a beautiful vessel on a sea calm and clear as a mirror, with a dark, cloudy sky vaulted overhead.   But when he looked down into the sea he presently saw that what he had thought was water was a firm, transparent, sparkling substance, in the shimmer of which the ship, in a wonderful manner, melted away, so that he found himself standing upon this floor of crystal, with a vault of black rock above him, for that was rock which he had taken at first for clouds. Impelled by some power unknown to him he stepped onward, but at that moment everything around him began to move, and wonderful plants and flowers, of glittering metal, came shooting up out of the crystal mass he was standing on, and entwined their leaves and blossoms in the loveliest manner. The crystal floor was so transparent that Elis could distinctly see the roots of these plants. But soon, as his glance penetrated deeper and deeper, he saw, far, far down in the depths, innumerable beautiful maidens, embracing each other with white, gleaming arms; and it was from their hearts that the roots, plants, and flowers were growing. And when these maidens smiled, a sweet sound rang all through the vault above, and the wonderful metal-flowers shot up higher and waved their leaves and branches in joy. An indescribable sense of rapture came upon the lad; a world of love and passionate longing awoke in his heart.

"Down, down to you!" he cried, and threw himself with out-stretched arms down upon the crystal ground. But it gave way under him, and he seemed to be floating in shimmering ether.

"Ha! Elis Froebom; what do you think of this world of glory?" a strong voice cried. It was the old miner. But as Elis looked at him, he seemed to expand into gigantic size, and to be made of glowing metal. Elis was beginning to be terrified; but a brilliant light came darting like a sudden lightning flash out of the depths of the abyss, and the earnest face of a grand, majestic woman appeared. Elis felt the rapture of his heart swelling and swelling into destroying pain. The old man had hold of him, and cried:

"Take care, Elis Froebom! That is the queen. You may look up now."

He turned his head involuntarily, and saw the stars of the night sky shining through a cleft in the vault overhead. A gentle voice called his name as if in inconsolable sorrow. It was his mother's. He thought he saw her form up at the cleft. But it was a young and beautiful woman who was calling him, and stretching her hands down into the vault.

"Take me up!" he cried to the old man. "I tell you I belong to the upper world, and its familiar, friendly sky."

"Take care, Froebom," said the old man solemnly; "be faithful to the queen, whom you have devoted yourself to."

But now, when he looked down again into the immobile face of the majestic woman, he felt that his personality dissolved away into glowing molten stone. He screamed aloud in nameless fear and awoke from this dream of wonder, whose rapture and terror echoed deep within his being.

"I suppose I could scarcely help dreaming all this extraordinary stuff," he said to himself, as he collected his senses with difficulty; "the old miner told me so much about the glories of the subterranean world that of course my head's quite full of it. But I never in my life felt as I do now. Perhaps I'm still dreaming. No, no; I suppose I must be a little out of sorts. Let's get into the open air. The fresh sea breeze'll soon set me all right."

He pulled himself together, and ran to the Klippa Haven, where the uproar of the Hoensning was breaking out again. But he soon found that all enjoyment passed him by, that he couldn't hold any thought fast in his mind, that presages and wishes to which he could give no name went crossing each other in his mind. He thought of his dead mother with the bitterest sorrow; but then, again, it seemed to him that what he most longed for was to see that girl again— the one whom he gave the handkerchief to—who had spoken so nicely to him the evening before. And yet he was afraid that if she were to come to meet him out of some street, she would turn out in the end to be the old miner. And he was afraid of *him*; though, at the same time, he would have liked to hear more from him of the wonders of the mine.

Driven hither and thither by all these fancies, he looked down into the water, and then he thought he saw the silver ripples hardening into the sparkling glimmer in which the grand ships melted away, while the dark clouds, which were beginning to gather and obscure the blue sky, seemed to sink down and thicken into a vault of rock. He was in his dream again, gazing into the immobile face of the majestic woman, and the devouring pain of passionate longing took possession of him as before.

His shipmates roused him from his reverie to go and join one of their processions, but an unknown voice seemed to whisper in his ear:

"What are you doing here? Away, away! Your home is in the mines of Falun. There all the glories which you saw in your dream are waiting for you. Away, away to Falun!"

For three days Elis hung and loitered about the streets of Goethaborg, constantly haunted by the wonderful images of his dream, continually urged by the unknown voice. On the fourth day he was standing at the gate through which the road to Gefle goes, when a tall man walked through it, passing him. Elis fancied he recognized in this man the old miner, and he hastened on after him, but could not overtake him.

He followed him on and on, without stopping.

He knew he was on the road to Falun, and this circumstance quieted him in a curious way; for he felt certain that the voice of destiny had spoken to him through the old miner, and that it was he who was now leading him on to his appointed place and fate.

And in fact, many times—particularly if there was any uncertainty about the road—he saw the old man suddenly appear out of some ravine, or from thick bushes, or gloomy rocks, stalk away before him, without looking round, and then disappear again.

At last, after journeying for many weary days, Elis saw in the distance two great lakes with a thick vapour rising between them. As he mounted the hill to westward, he saw some towers and black roofs rising through the smoke. The old man appeared before him, grown to gigantic size, pointed with outstretched hand towards the vapour, and disappeared again among the rocks.

"There lies Falun," said Elis, "the end of my journey."

He was right; for people, coming up from behind him, said the town of Falun lay between the lakes Runn and Warpann, and that the hill he was ascending was the Guffrisberg, where the main shaft of the mine was.

He went bravely on. But when he came to the enormous gulf, like the jaws of hell itself, the blood curdled in his veins, and he stood as if turned to stone at the sight of this colossal work of destruction.

The main shaft of the Falun mines is some twelve hundred feet long, six hundred feet broad, and a hundred and eighty feet deep. Its dark brown sides go, at first for the most part, perpendicularly down, till about halfway they are sloped inwards towards the center by enormous accumulations of stones and refuse. In these, and on the sides, there peeped out here and there timberings of old shafts, formed of strong shores set close together and strongly rabbeted at the ends, in the way that log houses are built. Not a tree, not a blade of grass to be seen in all the bare, blank, crumbling congeries of stony chasms; the pointed, jagged, indented masses of rock tower aloft all round in wonderful forms, often like monstrous animals turned to stone, often like colossal human beings. In the abyss itself lie in wild confusion—pell-mell—stones, slag, and scoria, and an eternal, stupefying sulphurous vapour rises from the depths, as if the hell-broth, whose reek poisons and kills all the green gladsomeness of nature, were being brewed down below. One would think this was where Dante went down and saw the Inferno, with all its horror and immitigable pain.

As Elis looked down into this monstrous abyss, he remembered what an old sailor, one of his shipmates, had told him once. This shipmate of his, at a time when he was down with fever, thought the sea had suddenly all gone dry, and the boundless depths of the abyss had opened under him, so that he saw all the horrible creatures of the deep twining and writhing about in dreadful contortions among thousands of extraordinary shells and groves of coral, till they died, and lay dead, with their mouths all gaping. The old sailor said that to see such a vision meant death, ere long, in the waves; and in fact very soon he did fall overboard, no one knew exactly how, and was drowned without possibility of rescue. Elis thought of that: for indeed the abyss seemed to him to be a good deal like the bottom of the sea run dry; and the black rocks, and the blue and red slag and scoria, were like horrible monsters shooting out polyp-arms at him. Two or three miners happened just then to be coming up from work in the mine, and in their dark mining clothes, with their black, grimy faces, they were much like ugly, diabolical creatures of some sort, slowly and painfully crawling and forcing their way up to the surface.

Elis felt a shudder of dread go through him, and—what he had never experienced in all his career as a sailor—he became giddy. Unseen hands seemed to be dragging him down into the abyss.

He closed his eyes and ran a few steps away from it, and it was not till he began climbing up the Guffrisberg again, far from the shaft, and could look up at the bright, sunny sky, that he quite lost the feeling of terror which had taken possession of him. He breathed freely once more, and cried, from the depths of his heart:

"Lord of my Life! what are the dangers of the sea compared with the horror which dwells in that awful abyss of rock? The storm may rage, the black clouds may come whirling down upon the breaking billows, but the beautiful, glorious sun soon gets the mastery again and the storm is past. But never does the sun penetrate into these black, gloomy caverns; never a freshening breeze of spring can revive the heart down there. No! I shall not join you, black earthworms! Never could I bring myself to lead that terrible life."

He resolved to spend that night in Falun, and set off back to Goethaborg the first thing in the morning.

When he got to the market place, he found a crowd of people there. A train of miners with their mine candles in their hands, and musicians before them, was halted before a handsome house. A tall, slightly built middle-aged man came out, looking around him with kindly smiles. It was easy to see by his frank manner, his open brow, and his bright, dark-blue eyes that he was a genuine Dalkarl. The miners formed a circle around him, and he shook them each cordially by the hand, saying kindly words to them all.

Elis learned that this was Pehrson Dahlsjoe, Alderman, and owner of a fine "Fraelse" at Stora-Kopparberg. "Fraelse" is the name given in Sweden to landed property leased out for the working of the lodes of copper and silver contained in it. The owners of these lands have shares in the mines and are responsible for their management.

Elis was told, further, that the Assizes were just over that day, and that then the miners went round in procession to the houses of the aldermen, the chief engineers and the minemasters, and were hospitably entertained.

When he looked at these fine, handsome fellows, with their kindly, frank faces, he forgot all about the earthworms he had seen coming up the shaft. The healthy gladsomeness which broke out afresh in the whole circle, as if new-fanned by a spring breeze, when Pehrson Dahlsjoe came out, was of a different sort from the senseless noise and uproar of the sailors' Hoensning. The manner in which these miners enjoyed themselves went straight to the serious Elis's heart. He felt indescribably happy; but he could scarce restrain his tears when some of the young pickmen sang an ancient ditty in praise of the miner's calling, and of the happiness of his lot, to a simple melody which touched his heart and soul.

When this song was ended, Pehrson Dahlsjoe opened his door, and the miners all went into his house one after another. Elis followed involuntarily and stood at the threshold, so that he could see the whole spacious room where the miners took their places on benches. Then the doors at the side opposite to him opened, and a beautiful young lady in evening dress came in. She was in the full glory of the freshest bloom of youth, tall and slender with dark hair in many curls, and a bodice fastened with rich clasps. The miners all stood up, and a low murmur of pleasure ran through their ranks. "Ulla Dahlsjoe!" they said. "What a blessing Heaven has bestowed on our hearty alderman in her!" Even the oldest miners' eyes sparkled when she gave them her hand in kindly greeting, as she did to them all. Then she brought beautiful silver tankards, filled them with splendid ale (such as Falun is famous for), and handed them to the guests with a face beaming with kindness and hospitality.

When Elis saw her a lightning flash seemed to go through his heart, kindling all the heavenly bliss, the love-longings, the passionate ardour lying hidden and imprisoned there. For it was Ulla Dahlsjoe who had held out the hand of rescue to him in his mysterious dream. He thought he understood now the deep significance of that dream, and, forgetting the old miner, praised the stroke of fortune which had brought him to Falun.

Alas! he felt he was but an unknown, unnoticed stranger, standing there on the doorstep miserable, comfortless, alone—and he wished he had died before he saw Ulla, as he now must perish for love and longing. He could not move his eyes from the beautiful creature, and as she passed close to him, he pronounced her name in a low, trembling voice. She turned and saw him standing there with a face as red as fire, unable to utter a syllable. So she went up to him and said, with a sweet smile:

"I suppose you are a stranger, friend, since you are dressed as a sailor. Well! why are you standing at the door? Come in and join us."

Elis felt as if in the blissful paradise of some happy dream, from which he would presently waken to inexpressible wretchedness. He emptied the tankard which she had given him; and Pehrson Dahlsjoe came up, and after kindly shaking hands with him, asked him where he came from and what had brought him to Falun.

Elis felt the warming power of the noble liquor in his veins, and looking Dahlsjoe in the eye, he felt happy and courageous. He told him he was a sailor's son and had been at sea since his childhood, had just come home from the East Indies and found his mother dead; that he was now alone in the world; that the wild sea life had become altogether distasteful to him; that his keenest inclination led him to a miner's calling, and that he wished to get employment as a miner here in Falun. The latter statement, quite the reverse of his recent determination, escaped him involuntarily; it was as if he could not have said anything else to the alderman, as if it were the most ardent desire of his soul, although he had not known it himself till now.

Pehrson Dahlsjoe looked at him long and carefully, as if he would read his heart; then he said:

"I cannot suppose, Elis Froebom, that it is mere thoughtless fickleness and the love of change that lead you to give up the calling you have followed hitherto, nor that you have omitted to weigh maturely and consider all the difficulties and hardships of the miner's life before making up your mind to take to it.   It is an old belief with us that the mighty elements with which the miner has to deal, and which he controls so bravely, destroy him unless he strains all his being to keep command of them—if he gives place to other thoughts which weaken that vigour which he has to reserve wholly for his constant conflict with Earth and Fire.   But if you have properly tested the sincerity of your inward call and it has withstood the trial, you are come in a good hour.   Workmen are wanted in my part of the mine.   If you like, you can stay here with me, and tomorrow the Captain will take you down with him, and show you what to do."

Elis's heart swelled with gladness at this.   He thought no more of the terror of the awful, hell-like abyss into which he had looked. The thought that he was going to see Ulla every day and live under the same roof with her filled him with rapture and delight.   He gave way to the sweetest hopes.

Pehrson Dahlsjoe told the miners that a young hand had applied for employment, and presented him to them then and there.   They all looked approvingly at the well-knit lad, and thought he was quite cut out for a miner, what with his light, powerful figure, his industry and straightforwardness.

One of the men, well advanced in years, came and shook hands with him cordially, saying he was Head Captain in Pehrson Dahlsjoe's part of the mine, and would be very glad to give him any help and instruction in his power.   Elis had to sit down beside this man, who at once began, over his tankard of ale, to describe with much minuteness the sort of work which Elis would have to commence with.

Elis remembered the old miner whom he had seen at Goethaborg, and strangely enough found he was able to repeat nearly all that he had told him.

"Ay," cried the Head Captain.   "Where can you have learned all that?   It's most surprising!   There can't be a doubt that you will be the finest pickman in the mine in a very short time."

Ulla—going back and forth among the guests and attending to them—often nodded kindly to Elis, and told him to be sure and enjoy himself.   "You're not a stranger now, you know," she said, "but one of the household.   You have nothing more to do with the treacherous sea—the rich mines of Falun are your home."

A heaven of bliss and rapture dawned upon Elis at these words of Ulla's.   It was evident that she liked to be near him; and Pehrson Dahlsjoe watched his quiet earnestness of character with manifest approval.

But Elis's heart beat violently when he stood again by the reeking hell-mouth, and went down the mine with the Captain, in his miner's clothes, with the heavy, iron-shod Dalkarl shoes on his feet. Hot vapours soon threatened to suffocate him, and then presently the candles flickered in the cutting draughts of cold air that blew in the lower levels.   They went down deeper and deeper, on iron ladders at last scarcely a foot wide; and Elis found that his sailor's adroitness at climbing was not of the slightest service to him there.

They got to the lowest depths of the mine at last, and the Captain showed him what work he was to do.

Elis thought of Ulla.   Like some bright angel he saw her hovering over him, and he forgot all the terror of the abyss, and the hardness of the labour.

It was clear in all his thoughts that it was only if he devoted himself with all the power of his mind, and with all the exertion which his body would endure, to mining work here with Pehrson Dahlsjoe, that there was any possibility of his fondest hopes being some day realized.   Wherefore it came about that he was as good at his work as the most practiced hand in an incredibly short space of time.

Staunch Pehrson Dahlsjoe got to like this good, industrious lad better and better every day, and often told him plainly that he had found in him one whom he regarded as a dear son as well as a first-class mine-hand.   Also Ulla's regard for him became more and more unmistakable.   Often, when he was going to his work and there was any prospect of danger, she would enjoin him with tears in her eyes to be sure to take care of himself.   And she would come running to meet him when he came back, and always had the finest of ale or some other refreshment ready for him.   His heart danced for joy one day when Pehrson said to him that as he had brought a good sum of money with him, there could be no doubt that—with his habits of economy and industry—he would soon have a Hemmans, or perhaps even a Fraelse; and then not a mineowner in all Falun would refuse if he asked for his daughter.   Elis would have liked to tell him at once how unspeakably he loved Ulla, and how all his hopes of happiness were based upon her.   But unconquerable shyness and the doubt whether Ulla really liked him—though he often thought she did—sealed his lips.

One day it chanced that Elis was at work in the lowest depths of the mine, shrouded in thick, sulphurous vapour, so that his candle only shed a feeble glimmer and he could scarcely distinguish the run of the lode. Suddenly he heard—as if coming from some still deeper cutting—a knocking as if somebody was at work with a pick-hammer. As that sort of work was scarcely possible at such a depth, and as he knew nobody was down there that day but himself—because the Captain had all the men employed in another part of the mine—this knocking and hammering struck him as strange and uncanny. He stopped working and listened to the hollow sounds, which seemed to come nearer and nearer. All at once he saw, close by him, a black shadow and—as a keen draught of air blew away the sulphur vapour—the old miner whom he had seen in Goethaborg.

"Good luck," he cried, "good luck to Elis Froebom, down here among the stones! What do you think of the life, comrade?"

Elis would have liked to ask in what wonderful way the old man had got into the mine; but he kept striking his hammer on the rocks with such force that the sparks went whirling all round, and the mine rang as if with distant thunder. Then he cried, in a terrible voice:

"There's a grand run of trap just here; but a scurvy, ignorant scoundrel like you sees nothing in it but a narrow streak of 'trumm' not worth a beanstalk. Down here you're a sightless mole, and you'll always be a mere abomination to the Metal Prince. You're of no use up above either—trying to get hold of the pure Regulus; which you never will—hey! You want to marry Pehrson Dahlsjoe's daughter; that's what you've taken to mine work for, not from any love of it. Mind what you're after, doubleface; take care that the Metal Prince, whom you are trying to deceive, doesn't take you and dash you down so that the sharp rocks tear you limb from limb. And Ulla will never be your wife; that much I tell you."

Elis's anger was kindled at the old man's insulting words.

"What are you doing," he cried, "here in my master, Herr Pehrson Dahlsjoe's shaft, where I am doing my duty and working as hard at it as I can? Be off out of this the way you came, or we'll see which of us two will dash the other's brains out down here."

With which he placed himself in a threatening attitude and swung his hammer about the old man's ears; he only gave a sneering laugh, and Elis saw with terror how he swarmed up the narrow ladder rungs like a squirrel, and disappeared amongst the black labyrinths of the chasms.

The young man felt paralyzed in all his limbs; he could not go on with his work, but went up. When the old Head Captain—who had been busy in another part of the mine—saw him, he cried:

"For God's sake, Elis, what has happened to you? You're as pale as death. I suppose it's the sulphur gas; you're not accustomed to it yet. Here, take a drink, my lad; that'll do you good."

Elis took a good mouthful of brandy out of the flask which the Head Captain handed to him; and then, feeling better, told him what had happened down in the mine, as also how he had made the uncanny old miner's acquaintance in Goethaborg.

The Head Captain listened silently; then dubiously shook his head and said:

"That must have been old Torbern that you met, Elis; and I see now that there really is something in the tales that people tell about him. More than one hundred years ago, there was a miner here of the name of Torbern. He seems to have been one of the first to bring mining into a flourishing condition at Falun here, and in his time profits far exceeded anything that we know of now. Nobody at that time knew so much about mining as Torbern, who had great scientific skill and thoroughly understood all the ins and outs of the business. The richest lodes seemed to disclose themselves to him, as if he was endowed with higher powers peculiar to himself; and as he was a gloomy, meditative man, without wife or child—with no regular home, indeed—and very seldom came up to the surface, it couldn't fail that a story soon went about that he was in compact with the mysterious power which dwells in the bowels of the earth and creates metals. Disregarding Torbern's solemn warnings—for he always prophesied that some calamity would happen as soon as the miners' impulse to work ceased to be sincere love for the marvellous metals and ores—people went on enlarging the excavations more and more for the sake of mere profit, till on St. John's Day of the year 1678, came the terrible landslip and subsidence which formed our present enormous main shaft, laying waste the whole of the works, as they were then, in the process. It was only after many months' labour that several of the shafts were with much difficulty put into workable order again. Nothing was seen or heard of Torbern. There seemed to be no doubt that he had been at work down below at the time of the catastrophe, so that there could be no question what his fate had been. But not long after, particularly when the work was beginning to go better again, the miners said they had seen old Torbern in the mine, and that he had given them valuable advice and pointed out rich lodes to them. Others had come across him at the top of the main shaft, walking round it, sometimes lamenting, sometimes shouting in wild anger. Other young fellows have come here in the way you yourself did, saying that an old miner had advised them to take to mining and shown them the way to Falun. This always happened when there was a scarcity of hands; very likely it was Torbern's way of helping on the cause. But if it really was he whom you had those words with in the mine, and if he spoke of a fine run of trap there isn't a doubt that there must be a grand vein of ore thereabouts, and we must see tomorrow if we can come across it. Of course you remember that we call rich veins of the kind 'trap-runs,' and that a 'trumm' is a vein which goes subdividing into several smaller ones, and probably gets lost altogether."

When Elis, tossed hither and thither by various thoughts went into Pehrson Dahlsjoe's, Ulla did not come to meet him as usual. She was sitting with downcast looks and—as he thought—eyes which had been weeping; and beside her was a handsome young fellow, holding her hand and trying to say all sorts of kind and amusing things to which she seemed to pay little attention. Pehrson Dahlsjoe took Elis—who, seized by gloomy presentiments, was keeping a dark glance riveted on the pair—into another room, and said:

"Well, Elis, you will soon have it in your power to give me a proof of your regard and sincerity. I have always looked upon you as a son, but you will soon take the place of one altogether. The man whom you see in there is a well-to-do merchant, Eric Olavsen by name, from Goethaborg. I am giving him my daughter for his wife, at his desire. He will take her to Goethaborg, and then you will be left alone with me, my only support in my declining years. Well, you say nothing? You turn pale? I trust this step doesn't displease you, and that now that I'm going to lose my daughter you are not going to leave me too? But I hear Olavsen mentioning my name; I must go in."

With which he went back to the room.

Elis felt a thousand red-hot irons tearing at his heart. He could find no words, no tears. In wild despair he ran out, out of the house, away to the great mine shaft.

That monstrous chasm had a terrible appearance by day; but now, when night had fallen and the moon was just peeping down into it, the desolate crags looked like a numberless horde of horrible monsters, the dire brood of hell, rolling and writhing in wildest confusion all about its reeking sides and clefts, and flashing up fiery eyes and shooting forth glowing claws to clutch the race of mortals.

"Torbern, Torbern," Elis cried in a terrible voice which made the rocks re-echo. "Torbern, I am here; you were not wrong— I was a wretched fool to fix my hopes on any earthly love, up on the surface here. My treasure, my life, everything for me, is down below. Torbern! take me down with you! Show me the richest veins, the lodes of ore, the glowing metal! I will dig and bore, and toil and labour. Never, never more will I come back to see the light of day. Torbern! Torbern! take me down to you!"

He took his flint and steel from his pocket, lighted his candle, and went quickly down the shaft, into the deep cutting where he had been on the previous day, but he saw nothing of the old man. But what was his amazement when, at the deepest point, he saw the vein of metal with the utmost clearness and distinctness, so that he could trace every one of its ramifications and its risings and fallings. But as he kept his gaze fixed more and more firmly on this wonderful vein, a dazzling light seemed to come shining through the shaft, and the walls of rock grew transparent as crystal. That mysterious dream which he had had in Goethaborg came back upon him. He was looking upon those Elysian Fields of glorious metallic trees and plants on which, by way of fruits, buds, and blossoms, hung jewels streaming with fire. He saw the maidens and he looked on the face of the mighty queen. She put out her arms, drew him to her, and pressed him to her breast. Then a burning ray darted through his heart, and all his consciousness was merged in a feeling of floating in waves of some blue, transparent, glittering mist.

"Elis Froebom! Elis Froebom!" a powerful voice from above cried out, and the reflection of torches began shining in the shaft. It was Pehrson Dahlsjoe who had come down with the Captain to search for the lad, who had been seen running in the direction of the main shaft like a mad creature.

They found him standing as if turned to stone, with his face pressed against the cold, hard rock.

"What are you doing down here in the nighttime, you foolish fellow?" cried Pehrson. "Pull yourself together, and come up with us. Who knows what good news you may hear."

Elis went up in profound silence after Dahlsjoe, who did not cease to rate him soundly for exposing himself to such danger. It was broad daylight when they got to the house.

Ulla threw herself into Elis's arms with a great cry and called him the fondest names, and Pehrson said to him:

"You foolish fellow! How could I help seeing, long ago, that you were in love with Ulla, and that it was on her account, in all probability, that you were working so hard in the mine? Neither could I help seeing that she was just as fond of you. Could I wish for a better son-in-law than a fine, hearty, hard-working, honest miner—than just yourself, Elis? What vexed me was that you never would speak."

"We scarcely knew ourselves," said Ulla, "how fond we were of each other."

"However that may be," said Pehrson, "I was annoyed that Elis didn't tell me openly and candidly of his love for you, and that was why I made up the story about Eric Olavsen, which was so nearly being the death of you, you silly fellow. Not but what I wished to try you, Ulla, into the bargain. Eric Olavsen has been married for many a day, and I give my daughter to you, Elis Froebom, for, I say again, I couldn't wish for a better son-in-law."

Tears of joy and happiness ran down Elis's cheeks. The highest bliss which his imagination had pictured had come to pass so suddenly and unexpectedly that he could scarcely believe it was anything but another blissful dream. The work people came to dinner, at Dahlsjoe's invitation, in honour of the event. Ulla had dressed in her prettiest attire, and looked more charming than ever, so that they all cried, over and over again, "Eh! what a sweet and charming creature Elis has for his wife! May God bless them and make them happy!"

Yet the terror of the previous night still lay upon Elis's pale face, and he often stared about him as if he were far away from all that was going on round him. "Elis, darling, what is the matter?" Ulla asked anxiously. He pressed her to his heart and said, "Yes, yes, you are my own, and all is well." But in the midst of all his happiness he often felt as though an icy hand clutched at his heart, and a dismal voice asked him:

"Is it your highest aim to be engaged to Ulla? Wretched fool! Have you not looked upon the face of the queen?"

He felt himself overpowered by an indescribable feeling of anxiety. He was haunted and tortured by the thought that one of the workmen would suddenly assume gigantic proportions, and to his horror he would recognize in him Torbern, come to remind him, in a terrible manner, of the subterranean realm of gems and metals to which he had devoted himself.

And yet he could see no reason why the spectral old man should be hostile to him, or what connection there was between his mining work and his love.

Pehrson, seeing Elis's disordered condition, attributed it to the trouble he had gone through and his nocturnal visit to the mine. Not so Ulla, who, seized by a secret presentiment, implored her lover to tell her what terrible thing had happened to him to tear him away from her so entirely. This almost broke his heart. It was in vain that he tried to tell her of the wonderful face which had revealed itself to him in the depths of the mine. Some unknown power seemed to seal his lips forcibly; he felt as though the terrible face of the queen were looking out from his heart, so that if he mentioned her, everything about him would turn to stone, to dark, black rock, as at the sight of the Medusa's frightful head. All the glory and magnificence which had filled him with rapture in the abyss appeared to him now as a pandemonium of immitigable torture, deceptively decked out to allure him to his ruin.

Dahlsjoe told him he must stay at home for a few days to shake off the sickness which he seemed to have fallen into. And during this time Ulla's affection, which now streamed bright and clear from her candid, childlike heart, drove away the memory of his fateful adventure in the mine depths. Joy and happiness brought him back to life and to belief in his good fortune, and in the impossibility of its being ever interfered with by any evil power.

When he went down the pit again, everything appeared quite different to what it used to be. The most glorious veins lay clear and distinct before his eyes. He worked twice as zealously as before; he forgot everything else. When he got to the surface again, it cost him an effort to remember Pehrson Dahlsjoe, even his Ulla. He felt as if divided into two halves, as if his better self, his real personality, went down to the central point of the earth, and there rested in bliss in the queen's arms, whilst *he* went to his dark dwelling in Falun. When Ulla spoke of their love, and the happiness of their future life together, he would begin to talk of the splendours of the depths, and the inestimably precious treasures that lay hidden there, and in so doing would get entangled in such wonderful, incomprehensible sayings that alarm and terrible anxiety took possession of the poor child, who could not divine why Elis should be so completely altered from his former self. He kept telling the Captain and Dahlsjoe himself with the greatest delight, that he had discovered the richest veins and the most magnificent trap-runs, and when these turned out to be nothing but unproductive rock, he would laugh contemptuously and say that none but he understood the secret signs, the significant writing, fraught with hidden meaning, which the queen's own hand had inscribed on the rocks, and that it was sufficient to understand those signs without bringing to light what they indicated.

The old Captain looked sorrowfully at Elis, who spoke, with wild gleaming eyes of the glorious paradise which glowed down in the depths of the earth. "That terrible old Torbern has been at him," he whispered in Dahlsjoe's ear.

"Pshaw! don't believe these miners' yarns," cried Dahlsjoe. "He's a deep-thinking serious fellow, and love has turned his head, that's all. Wait till the marriage is over, then we'll hear no more of the trap-runs, the treasures, and the subterranean paradise."

The wedding day fixed by Dahlsjoe came at last. For a few days previously Elis had been more tranquil, more serious, more sunk in deep reflection than ever. But, on the other hand, never had he shown such affection for Ulla as at this time. He could not leave her for a moment, and never went down the mine at all. He seemed to have forgotten his restless excitement about mining work, and never a word of the subterranean kingdom crossed his lips. Ulla was all rapture. Her fear lest the dangerous powers of the subterranean world, of which she had heard old miners speak, had been luring him to his destruction, had left her; and Dahlsjoe too said, laughing to the Captain, "You see, Elis was only a little light-headed for love of my Ulla."

Early on the morning of the wedding day, which was St. John's Day as it chanced, Elis knocked at the door of Ulla's room. She opened it, and started back terrified at the sight of Elis, dressed in his wedding clothes, deadly pale, with dark gloomy fire sparkling in his eyes.

"I only want to tell you, my beloved Ulla," he said, in a faint, trembling voice, "that we are just arrived at the summit of the highest good fortune which it is possible for mortals to attain. Everything has been revealed to me in the night which is just over. Down in the depths below, hidden in chlorite and mica, lies the cherry-coloured sparkling almandine, on which the tablet of our lives is graven. I have to give it to you as a wedding present. It is more splendid than the most glorious blood-red carbuncle, and when, united in truest affection, we look into its streaming splendour together, we shall see and understand the peculiar manner in which our hearts and souls have grown together into the wonderful branch which shoots from the queen's heart, at the central point of the globe.

All that is necessary is that I go and bring this stone to the surface, and that I will do now, as fast as I can. Take care of yourself meanwhile, darling. I will be back in a little while."

Ulla implored him with bitter tears to give up all idea of such a dreamlike undertaking, for she felt a strong presentiment of disaster; but Ellis declared that without this stone he should never know a moment's peace or happiness, and that there was not the slightest danger of any kind. He pressed her fondly to his heart, and was gone.

The guests were all assembled to accompany the bridal pair to the church of Copparberg, where they were to be married, and a crowd of girls, who were to be the bridesmaids and walk in procession before the bride (as is the custom of the place), were laughing and playing round Ulla. The musicians were tuning their instruments to begin a wedding march. It was almost noon, but Elis had not made his appearance. Suddenly some miners came running up, horror in their pale faces, with the news that there had been a terrible catastrophe, a subsidence of the earth, which had destroyed the whole of Pehrson Dahlsjoe's part of the mine.

"Elis! oh, Elis! you are gone!" screamed Ulla, wildly, and fell as if dead. Then for the first time Dahlsjoe learned from the Captain that Elis had gone down the main shaft in the morning. Nobody else had been in the mine, the rest of the men having been invited to the wedding. Dahlsjoe and all the others hurried off to search, at the imminent danger of their own lives. In vain! Elis Froebom was not to be found. There could be no question but that the earth-fall had buried him in the rock. And thus came desolation and mourning upon the house of brave Pehrson Dahlsjoe, at the moment when he thought he was assured of peace and happiness for the remainder of his days.

Long had stout Pehrson Dahlsjoe been dead, his daughter Ulla long lost sight of and forgotten. Nobody in Falun remembered them. More than fifty years had gone by since Froebom's luckless wedding day, when it chanced that some miners who were making a connection passage between two shafts found, at a depth of three hundred yards, buried in vitriolated water, the body of a young miner, which seemed when they brought it to the daylight to be turned to stone.

The young man looked as if he were lying in a deep sleep, so perfectly preserved were the features of his face, so wholly without trace of decay his new suit of miner's clothes, and even the flowers in his breast.   The people of the neighbourhood all collected round the young man, but no one recognized him or could say who he had been, and none of the workmen missed any comrade.

The body was going to be taken to Falun, when out of the distance an old, old woman came creeping slowly and painfully up on crutches.

"Here's the old St. John's Day grandmother!" the miners said. They had given her this name because they had noticed that every year she came up to the main shaft on Saint John's Day, and looked down into its depths, weeping, lamenting, and wringing her hands as she crept round it, then went away again.

The moment she saw the body she threw away her crutches, lifted her arms to Heaven, and cried, in the most heart-rending way.

"Oh! Elis Froebom! Oh, my sweet, sweet bridegroom!"

And she huddled down beside the body, took the stone hands and pressed them to her heart, chilled with age, but throbbing still with the fondest love, like some naphtha flame under the surface ice.

"Ah!" she said, looking round at the spectators, "nobody, nobody among you remembers poor Ulla Dahlsjoe, this poor boy's happy bride fifty long years ago.   When I went away, in my terrible sorrow and despair, to Ornaes, old Torbern comforted me, and told me I should see my poor Elis, who was buried in the rock upon our wedding day, once more here upon earth.   And I have come every year and looked for him.   And now this blessed meeting has been granted me this day.   Oh, Elis! Elis! my beloved husband!"

She wound her arms about him as if she would never part from him more, and the people all stood around in the deepest emotion.

Fainter and fainter grew her sobs and sighs, till they ceased to be audible.

The miners closed around.   They would have raised poor Ulla, but she had breathed out her life upon her bridegroom's body. The spectators noticed now that it was beginning to crumble into dust.   The appearance of petrifaction had been deceptive.

In the church of Copparberg, where they were to have been married fifty years earlier, the miners laid in the earth the ashes of Elis Froebom, and with them the body of her who had been thus "Faithful unto death."

SIGNOR FORMICA

I

Celebrated people often have many ill things said of them, whether well-founded or not. And no exception was made in the case of that admirable painter Salvator Rosa, whose vivid, living pictures cannot fail to impart a keen and characteristic delight to those who look upon them.

At the time that Salvator's fame was ringing through Naples, Rome, and Tuscany—indeed, through all Italy—and painters who were desirous of gaining applause were trying to imitate his highly individual style, his malicious and envious rivals were spreading all sorts of evil reports intended to cast ugly black stains upon the glorious splendour of his artistic fame. They claimed that he had at a former period of his life belonged to a gang of banditti, and that it was to his experiences during this lawless time that he owed all the wild, fierce, fantastically attired figures which he introduced into his pictures, just as the gloomy fearful wildernesses of his landscapes (the *selve selvagge*, savage woods, to use Dante's expression) were faithful representations of the haunts where the banditti lay hidden. What was worse still, they openly charged him with having been concerned in the atrocious and bloody revolt which had been set on foot by the notorious Masaniello in Naples. They even described the share he had taken in it, down to the minutest details.

The rumour ran that Aniello Falcone, the painter of battle pieces, one of the best of Salvator's masters, had been stung into fury and filled with bloodthirsty vengeance because the Spanish soldiers had slain one of his relatives in a street brawl. Without delay he gathered a band of wild and desperate young men, mostly painters, put arms into their hands, and gave them the name of the "Company of Death." And in truth this band inspired all the fear and consternation suggested by its terrible name. At all hours of the day they wandered the streets of Naples in gangs, and cut down without mercy every Spaniard whom they met. They did more—they forced their way into the holy sanctuaries, and relentlessly murdered their unfortunate enemies who had taken refuge there. At night they gathered around their chief, the bloody-minded madman Masaniello, and painted him by torchlight, so that in a short time there were hundreds of these little pictures circulating in Naples and the surrounding area.

This is the ferocious band of which Salvator Rosa was alleged to have been a member, working hard at butchering his fellow men by day, and by night working just as hard at painting. The truth about him has however been stated, by a celebrated art critic, Taillasson, I believe. "Salvator Rosa's works are characterized by arrogant and defiant originality, and by fantastic energy both of conception and of execution. Nature revealed herself to him not in the lovely peacefulness of green meadows, flourishing fields, sweet-smelling groves, murmuring springs, but in the awful and the sublime as seen in towering masses of rock, in the wild seashore, in savage inhospitable forests; and the voices that he loved to hear were not the whisperings of the evening breeze or the musical rustle of leaves, but the roaring of the hurricane and the thunder of the cataract. To one viewing his desolate landscapes, with the strange savage figures stealthily moving about in them, here singly, there in troops, the uncomfortable thoughts arise unbidden, 'Here's where a fearful murder took place, there's where the bloody corpse was hurled into the ravine.' "

Admitting all this, and even that Taillasson is also right when he maintains that Salvator's "Plato," indeed, that even his "Holy St. John Proclaiming the Advent of the Saviour in the Wilderness," look just a little like highway robbers—admitting this, I say, it is nevertheless unjust to argue from the character of the works to the character of the artist himself, and to assume that an artist who represents savage and terrible subjects with lifelike fidelity must himself have been a savage, terrible man. He who prates most about the sword is often he who wields it the worst; he who feels in the depths of his soul all the horrors of a bloody deed, so that, taking the palette or the pencil or the pen in his hand, he is able to give living form to his feelings, is often the one least capable of practicing similar deeds.

Enough! I don't believe a single word of all those evil reports, by which men sought to brand the excellent Salvator an abandoned murderer and robber, and I hope that you, kindly reader, will share my opinion. Otherwise, I see grounds for fearing that you might perhaps entertain some doubts respecting what I am about to tell you of this artist. The Salvator I wish to put before you in this tale—that is, according to my conception of him—is a man bubbling over with the exuberance of life and fiery energy, but at the same time a man endowed with the noblest and most loyal character—a character which, like that of all men who think and feel deeply, is able even to control the bitter irony which arises from a clear view of the significance of life. I need scarcely add that Salvator was no less renowned as a poet and musician than as a painter. His genius was revealed in rays thrown in many directions.

I repeat again, I do not believe that Salvator had any share in Masaniello's bloody deeds; on the contrary, I think it was the horrors of that fearful time which drove him from Naples to Rome, where he arrived a poverty-stricken fugitive, just at the time that Masaniello fell.

Not over well dressed, and with a scanty purse containing not more than a few bright sequins in his pocket, he crept through the gate just after nightfall. Somehow or other, he didn't exactly know how, he wandered as far as the Piazza Navona. In better times he had once lived there in a large house near the Pamfili Palace. With an ill-tempered growl, he gazed up at the large plate-glass windows glistening and glimmering in the moonlight. "Hm!" he exclaimed ironically. "It'll cost me dozens of yards of coloured canvas before I can open my studio up there again." But suddenly he felt paralyzed in every limb, and at the same moment more weak and feeble than he had ever felt in his life before. "But shall I," he murmured between his teeth as he sank down upon the stone steps leading up to the house door, "really be able to finish canvas enough in the way the fools want it done? I have a notion that that will be the end of it!"

A cold cutting night wind was blowing down the street. Salvator realized that he must find shelter. Rising with difficulty, he staggered on into the Corso, and then turned into the Via Bergognona. At last he stopped before a little house with only a couple of windows, inhabited by a poor widow and her two daughters. This woman had housed him for little money the first time he came to Rome, an unknown stranger ignored by everyone; and so he hoped to find a lodging with her again, such as would be best suited to his reduced circumstances.

He knocked at the door, and several times shouted out his name. At last he heard the old woman slowly and reluctantly waking out of her sleep. She shuffled to the window in her slippers, and began to rain down a shower of abuse upon the scoundrel who was disturbing her in this way in the middle of the night; her house was not an inn, and so on. Then there ensued a good deal of talk back and forth before she recognized her former lodger's voice. But when Salvator complained that he had fled from Naples and was unable to find a shelter in Rome, the old woman cried, "By all the blessed saints of Heaven! Is that you, Signor Salvator? Your little room above, that looks onto the court, is still empty, and the old fig-tree has pushed its branches right through the window and into the room, so that you can sit and work like you was in a beautiful cool arbour. Yes, and how pleased my girls will be that you have come back, Signor Salvator. But, d'ye know, my Margarita's grown a big girl and fine-looking? You won't give her any more rides on your knee now. And—and your cat, you know, three months ago she choked on a fishbone. But you know, my fat neighbour that you used to laugh at and draw cartoons of—she *did* marry that young fellow, Signor Luigi, after all. Ah well! *nozze e magistrati sono da dio destinati* [marriages and magistrates are made in heaven], they say."

"Signora Caterina," cried Salvator, interrupting the old woman, "I beg you by the blessed saints, let me in, and then tell me all about your fig-tree and your daughters, the cat and your fat neighbour— I am dying of weariness and cold."

"Bless me, how impatient we are," rejoined the old woman. "*Chi va piano va sano, chi va presto more lesto* [walk slowly and have a long life; make haste and a widow's your wife], I tell you. But you are tired, you are cold; where are the keys? Quick with the keys!"

But the old woman still had to wake her daughters and kindle a fire—and she was a long time about it, such a long, long time. At last she opened the door and let poor Salvator in. Scarcely had he crossed the threshold than, overcome by fatigue and illness, he dropped on the floor as if dead. Happily the widow's son, who lived at Tivoli, chanced to be at his mother's that night. He at once gave up his bed to make room for the sick man.

The old woman was very fond of Salvator, and she rated him above all other painters in the world. In everything that he did she took the greatest pleasure. She was therefore quite beside herself to see him in this sad condition, and wanted to run off to the neighbouring monastery to have her father confessor come and fight against the adverse power of the disease with consecrated candles or some powerful amulet or other. On the other hand, her son thought it would be almost better to see about getting an experienced physician at once, and off he ran there and then to the Piazza di Spagna, where he knew the distinguished Dr. Splendiano Accoramboni dwelt. No sooner did the doctor learn that the painter

Salvator Rosa lay ill in the Via Bergognona than he declared himself ready to call and see the patient.

Salvator lay unconscious, struck down by a most severe attack of fever. The old woman had hung up two or three pictures of saints above his bed, and was praying fervently. The girls, though bathed in tears, tried from time to time to get the sick man to swallow a few drops of the cooling lemonade which they had made, while their brother, who had taken his place at the head of the bed, wiped the cold sweat from Salvator's brow. And so morning found them, when with a loud creak the door opened, and the celebrated Dr. Splendiano Accoramboni entered the room.

If Salvator had not been so seriously ill that the two girl's hearts were melted in grief, they would, I think (for they were in general frolicsome and saucy), have enjoyed a hearty laugh at the doctor's extraordinary appearance, instead of retiring shyly, as they did, into the corner. It will indeed be worth while to describe the outward appearance of this little man who presented himself at Dame Caterina's in the Via Bergognona in the gray of the morning. In spite of being rather tall as a boy, Dr. Splendiano Accoramboni had not been able to advance beyond the altitude of four feet. Moreover, in the days of his youth, he had been distinguished for his elegant figure. Before his head, always indeed somewhat ill-shaped, and his big cheeks, and his stately double chin had put on too much fat; before his nose had grown bulky and spread owing to overmuch indulgence in Spanish snuff; and before his little belly had assumed the shape of a wine-tub from too much fattening on macaroni—the garments of an Abbate, which he at that time affected, suited him down to the ground. He was then in truth a pretty little man, and accordingly the Roman ladies had styled him their *caro puppazetto* [sweet little doll].

But these days were gone. A German painter, seeing Dr. Splendiano walking across the Piazza di Spagna, said—and he was perhaps not far wrong—that it looked as if some strapping fellow of six feet or so had walked away from his own head, which had fallen on the shoulders of a little marionette clown, who now had to carry it about as his own.

This curious little figure walked about in patchwork—an immense quantity of pieces of Venetian damask of a large flower pattern that had been cut up in making a dressing-gown; high up around his waist he had buckled a broad leather belt, from which an excessively long rapier hung; while his snow-white wig was surmounted by a high conical cap, not unlike the obelisk in the Piazza

San Pietro. Since the said wig, all tumbled and tangled, spread out thick and wide all over his back, it might very well have been taken for the cocoon out of which a fine silkworm had crept.

The worthy Splendiano Accoramboni stared through his big, bright spectacles, with his eyes wide open, first at his patient, then at Dame Caterina. Calling her aside, he croaked with bated breath, "There lies the great painter Salvator Rosa, and he's lost if my skill doesn't save him, Signora Caterina. Tell me when he came to lodge with you? Did he bring many beautiful large pictures with him?"

"Ah! my dear doctor," replied Signora Caterina, "the poor fellow only came last night. And as for pictures—why, I don't know nothing about them; but there's a big box below, and Salvator begged me to take very good care of it, before he became senseless like he now is. I suppose there's a fine picture packed in it, as he painted in Naples."

What Signora Caterina said, however, was a falsehood; but we shall soon see that she had good reasons for imposing upon the doctor in this way.

"Good! Very good!" said the doctor, simpering and stroking his beard; then, with as much solemnity as his long rapier, which kept catching in all the chairs and tables, would allow, he approached the sick man and felt his pulse, snorting and wheezing, so that it had a most curious effect in the midst of the reverential silence which had fallen upon all the rest. Then he ran over in Greek and Latin the names of a hundred and twenty diseases that Salvator had not, then almost as many which he might have had, and concluded by saying that on the spur of the moment he didn't recollect the name of his disease, but that he would within a short time find a suitable one for it, and the proper remedies as well. Then he took his departure with the same solemnity with which he had entered, leaving them all full of trouble and anxiety.

At the bottom of the steps the doctor requested to see Salvator's box; Signora Caterina showed him one—in which were two or three of her deceased husband's cloaks now laid aside, and some old worn-out shoes. The doctor smilingly tapped the box, on this side and on that, and remarked in a tone of satisfaction "We shall see! we shall see!" Some hours later he returned with a very beautiful name for his patient's disease, and brought with him some big bottles of an evil-smelling potion, which he directed to be given to the patient constantly. This was a work of no little trouble, for Salvator resisted as well as he could, and obviously showed the greatest aversion for the stuff, which looked, and smelt, and tasted, as if it had been concocted from Acheron itself.

Whether the disease, since it had now received a name, and in consequence really signified something, had only just begun to put forth its virulence, or whether Splendiano's potion made too much of a disturbance inside the patient—it is at any rate certain that the poor painter grew weaker and weaker from day to day, from hour to hour. And notwithstanding Dr. Splendiano Accoramboni's assurance that after the vital process had reached a state of perfect equilibrium, he would give it a new start like the pendulum of a clock, they were all very doubtful as to Salvator's recovery, and thought that the doctor had perhaps already given the pendulum such a rough jolt that the mechanism was damaged.

Now it happened one day that when Salvator seemed scarcely able to move a finger he was suddenly seized with the paroxysm of fever; in a momentary accession of strength he leapt out of bed, seized the full medicine bottles, and hurled them fiercely out of the window. Just at this moment Dr. Splendiano Accoramboni was entering the house, when two or three bottles came bang upon his head, smashing all to pieces, while the brown liquid ran in streams all down his face and wig and ruff. Hastily rushing into the house, he screamed like a madman, "Signor Salvator has gone out of his mind, he's delirious; no skill can save him now, he'll be dead in ten minutes. Give me the picture, Signora Caterina, give me the picture —it's mine, the scanty reward of all my trouble. Give me the picture, I say."

But when Signora Caterina opened the box, and Dr. Splendiano saw nothing but the old cloaks and torn shoes, his eyes spun round in his head like a pair of fire-wheels; he gnashed his teeth; he stamped; he consigned poor Salvator, the widow, and all the family to the devil; then he rushed out of the house like an arrow from a bow, or as if he had been shot from a cannon.

After the violence of the paroxysm had spent itself, Salvator again relapsed into a deathlike condition. Signora Caterina was fully persuaded that his end was really come, and away she sped as fast as she could to the monastery, to fetch Father Boniface to administer the sacrament to the dying man. Father Boniface came and looked at the sick man; he said he was well acquainted with the peculiar signs which approaching death stamps on the human face, but that for the present there were no indications of them on the face of the insensible Salvator. Something might still be done, and he would procure help at once, only Dr. Splendiano Accoramboni with his

Greek names and infernal medicines was not to be allowed to cross the threshold again. The good Father set out at once, and we shall see later that he kept his word about sending the promised help.

Salvator recovered consciousness again; he fancied he was lying in a beautiful flower-scented arbour, for green boughs and leaves were interlacing above his head. He felt a salutary warmth glowing in his veins, but it seemed to him as if somehow his left arm was bound fast.

"Where am I?" he asked in a faint voice. Then a handsome young man, who had stood at his bedside, but whom he had not noticed until just now, threw himself upon his knees, and grasping Salvator's right hand, kissed it and bathed it with tears, as he cried again and again, "Oh! Signor! my noble master! now it's all right; you are saved, you'll get better."

"Tell me—" began Salvator, when the young man begged him not to exert himself, for he was too weak to talk; he would tell him all that had happened. "You see, my esteemed and excellent sir," began the young man, "you were very ill when you came from Naples, but your condition was not really dangerous; a few simple remedies would soon have set you, with your strong constitution, on your legs again, if you hadn't, through Carlos's well-intentioned blunder in running off for the nearest physician, fallen into the hands of the Pyramid Doctor, who did his best to put you in your grave."

"What do you say?" exclaimed Salvator, laughing heartily, notwithstanding the feeble state he was in. "What do you say?—the Pyramid Doctor? Yes, although I was very ill, I saw that the little fellow in damask patchwork, who condemned me to drink his vile devil's brew, wore on his head the obelisk from the Piazza San Pietro—and so that's why you call him the Pyramid Doctor?"

"Why," said the young man, likewise laughing, "Dr. Splendiano Accoramboni must have come to see you in his mysterious conical nightcap; and, do you know, you can see it flashing every morning from his window like some bad omen in the sky. But it's not for this cap that he's called the Pyramid Doctor; for that there's a very different reason. Dr. Splendiano is a great lover of pictures and has quite a choice collection, which he has gained in a peculiar way. He keeps a close eye on painters and their illnesses. He's particularly eager to get at artists who are strangers in Rome. If they eat an ounce or two too much macaroni, or drink a glass more Syracuse than is altogether good for them, he will afflict them with first one and then the other disease, designating it by a formidable name, and proceeding at once to cure them of it. He generally bargains for a picture as the price of his attendance; and as only specially obstinate constitutions can withstand his remedies, it generally happens that he gets his picture out of the chattels left by the poor foreigner, who meanwhile has been carried to the Pyramid of Cestius, and buried there. It hardly need be said that Signor Splendiano always picks out the best of the pictures the painter has finished, and also does not forget to bid the men take several others along with it. The cemetery near the Pyramid of Cestius is Dr. Splendiano Accoramboni's cornfield, which he diligently cultivates, and for that reason he is called the Pyramid Doctor. Dame Caterina took great pains, of course with the best intentions, to make the doctor believe that you had brought a fine picture with you; you may imagine with what eagerness he concocted his medicines for you. It was fortunate that you threw the doctor's bottles at his head, it was also fortunate that he left you in anger, and no less fortunate that Signora Caterina, who believed you were in the agonies of death, fetched Father Boniface to administer to you the sacrament. Father Boniface understands something of the art of healing; he formed a correct diagnosis of your condition and sent for me."

"Then you also are a doctor?" asked Salvator in a faint voice.

"No," replied the young man, a deep blush mantling his cheeks, "no, my estimable and worthy sir, I am not in the least a doctor like Signor Splendiano Accoramboni; I am a barber-surgeon. I felt that I would sink into the earth with fear—with joy—when Father Boniface came and told me that Salvator Rosa was almost at the point of death in the Via Bergognona, and required my help. I came as fast as I could, opened a vein in your left arm, and you were saved. Then we brought you up into this cool airy room that you once occupied. Look, there's the easel which you left behind you; there are a few sketches which Signora Caterina has treasured as if they were relics. You've passed the crisis of your illness; simple remedies such as Father Boniface can prepare are all that you want, except good nursing, to bring back your strength again. And now permit me once more to kiss this hand—this creative hand that charms her deepest secrets from Nature and clothes them in living form. Permit poor Antonio Scacciati to pour out all the gratitude and immeasurable joy of his heart that Heaven has granted him to save the life of our great and noble painter, Salvator Rosa." Thereupon the young barber-surgeon threw himself on his knees again, and, seizing Salvator's hand, kissed it and bathed it in tears as before.

"I don't understand," said the artist, raising himself up a little, though with considerable difficulty, "I don't understand, my dear Antonio, what makes you show me all this respect. You are, you say, a barber-surgeon, and we don't in a general way find this trade going hand in hand with art—"

"As soon," replied the young man, casting down his eyes, "as you have picked up your strength again, my dear sir, I have a good deal to tell you that now lies heavy on my heart."

"Do so," said Salvator; "you may have every confidence in me—that you may, for I don't know that any man's face has made a more direct appeal to my heart than yours. The more I look at you the more plainly I seem to trace in your features a resemblance to that incomparable young painter—I mean Sanzio Raphael."

Antonio's eyes were lit up with a proud, radiant light—he vainly struggled for words with which to express his feelings.

At this moment Signora Caterina appeared, followed by Father Boniface, who brought Salvator a medicine which he had mixed and which the patient swallowed with more relish and felt to have a more beneficial effect upon him than the Acheronian waters of the Pyramid Doctor Splendiano Accoramboni.

II

And Antonio's words proved true. The simple remedies of Father Boniface, the careful nursing of good Signora Caterina and her daughters, the warmer weather which now came—all co-operated so well together with Salvator's naturally robust constitution that he soon felt sufficiently well to think about work again; first of all he made a few sketches which he thought of working out afterwards.

Antonio scarcely ever left Salvator's room; he was all eyes when the painter drew out his sketches; while his judgment on many points showed that he must have been initiated into the secrets of art.

"See here Antonio," said Salvator to him one day, "you understand art matters so well that I believe you have not merely cultivated your critical judgment, but must have wielded the brush as well."

"You may remember," rejoined Antonio, "when you were just about coming to yourself again after your long unconsciousness, that I had several things to tell you which lay heavy on my mind. Now is the time for me to unfold all my heart to you. You must know then, that though I am called Antonio Scacciati the barber-surgeon, who opened the vein in your arm for you, I really belong to art—to the art to which, after bidding farewell to my hateful trade, I intend to devote myself for once and for all."

"Ho! ho!" exclaimed Salvator, "Ho! ho! Antonio, weigh well what you are about to do. You *are* a clever surgeon, and perhaps will never be anything more than a bungling painter all your life long; for, with your permission, as young as you are, you are decidedly too old to begin to use the charcoal now. Believe me, a man's whole lifetime is scarce long enough to acquire a knowledge of the True—still less the practical ability to represent it."

"Ah! but, my dear sir," replied Antonio, smiling blandly, "don't imagine that I should now have come to entertain the foolish idea of taking up the difficult art of painting if I hadn't practiced it on every possible occasion from my childhood. In spite of the fact that my father obstinately kept me away from everything connected with art, Heaven was graciously pleased to throw me in the way of some celebrated artists. I must tell you that the great Annibal Caracci interested himself in the orphan boy, and also that I may with justice call myself Guido Reni's pupil."

"Well then," said Salvator somewhat sharply, a way of speaking he sometimes had, "my good Antonio, you have indeed had great masters, and so without detriment to your surgical practice, you must have been a great pupil. Only I don't understand how you, a faithful disciple of the gentle, elegant Guido, whom you perhaps outdo in elegance in your own pictures—for pupils do this in their enthusiasm—can find any pleasure in my productions, and can really regard me as a master in the Art."

At these words, which indeed sounded a good deal like derisive mockery, the hot blood rushed into the young man's face.

"Let me be frank and lay bare the thoughts I have in my mind. I tell you, Salvator, I have never honoured any master from the depths of my soul as I do you. What I am amazed at in your works is the sublime grandeur of conception which is often revealed. You grasp the deepest secrets of Nature: you understand the mysterious hieroglyphics of her rocks, trees, and waterfalls; you hear her sacred voice, you understand her language, and possess the power to write down what she has said to you. Yes, I can call your bold free style of painting nothing else than *writing down*. Man and his doings do not satisfy you; you see him only as a part of Nature, and as his essential character is conditioned by natural phenomena; and in these facts I see why you are truly great only in your landscapes with their wonderful figures. Historical painting confines you to limits which clog your genius for reproducing your higher intuitions of Nature."

"That's talk you've picked up from envious historical painters," said Salvator, interrupting his young companion; "like them, Antonio, you throw me the bone of landscape painting that I may gnaw away at it, and so spare their own good flesh. Don't I understand the human figure and all that is dependent upon it? But this silly criticism, repeated from others—"

"Don't be angry," interrupted Antonio, "don't be angry, my good sir; I am not blindly repeating anybody's words, and I should not for a moment think of trusting to the judgment of our painters here in Rome. Who can help admiring the bold draughtmanship, the powerful expression, but above all the living movement of your figures? It's plain to see that you don't work from a stiff, inflexible model, or even from a lifeless manikin; it is evident that you yourself are your own breathing, living model, and that when you sketch or paint, you have the figure you want to put on your canvas reflected in a great mirror opposite to you."

"The devil! Antonio," exclaimed Salvator, laughing, "I believe you must have been peeping into my studio when I was not aware of it, since you have such an accurate knowledge of what goes on in it."

"Perhaps I may," replied Antonio; "but let me go on. I am not so anxious to classify the pictures which your powerful mind suggests to you as are your pedantic critics. In fact, I think that the word 'landscape,' as generally employed, has an indifferent application to your productions; I should prefer to call them historical representations in the highest sense of the word. If we fancy that this or that rock or this or that tree is gazing at us like a gigantic being with thoughtful earnest eyes, so again, on the other hand, this or that group of fantastically attired men resembles some remarkable stone which has been endowed with life; all Nature, breathing and moving in harmonious unity, lends accents to the sublime thought which leapt into existence in your mind. This is the spirit in which I have studied your pictures, and so in this way it is, my grand and noble master, that I owe to you my truer perceptions in matters of art. But don't imagine that I have fallen into childish imitation. However much I would like to have your free bold pencil, I do not attempt to conceal the fact that Nature's colours appear to me different from what I see in your pictures. It is useful, I think, for the sake of acquiring technique, for the pupil to imitate the style of this or that master, but as soon as he comes to stand in any sense on his own feet, he ought to aim at representing Nature as he himself sees her. Nothing but this true method of perception, this unity with oneself, can give rise to character and truth. Guido shared these sentiments; and that fiery man Preti, who, as you are aware, is called *Il Calabrese*—a painter who certainly, more than any other man, has reflected upon his art—also warned me against all imitation. Now you know, Salvator, why I admire you beyond all other painters, but do not imitate you."

While the young man had been speaking, Salvator had kept his eyes fixed unchangeably upon him; he now clasped him tumultuously to his heart.

"Antonio," he then said, "what you have just now said are wise and thoughtful words. Young as you are, you are nevertheless, as far as the true perception of art is concerned, a long way ahead of many of our old and much vaunted masters, who have a good deal of stupid foolish twaddle about their painting, but never get at the true root of the matter. Body alive, man! When you were talking about my pictures, I began to understand myself for the first time, I believe; and because you do not imitate my style—do not, like a good many others, take a tube of black paint in your hand, or dab on a few glaring colours, or even make two or three crippled figures with repulsive faces look up from the midst of filth and dirt, and then say, 'There's a Salvator for you!'—just for these very reasons I think a good deal of you. I tell you, my lad, you'll not find a more faithful friend than I am—that I can promise you with all my heart and soul."

Antonio was beside himself with joy at the kind way in which the great painter thus testified to his interest in him. Salvator expressed an earnest desire to see his pictures. Antonio took him immediately to his studio.

Salvator had really expected to find something fairly good from the young man who spoke so intelligently about art, and who, it appeared, had a good deal in him; but nevertheless he was greatly surprised at the sight of Antonio's fine pictures. Everywhere he found boldness in conception, and correctness in drawing; and the freshness of the colouring, the good taste in the arrangement of the drapery, the uncommon delicacy of the extremities, the exquisite grace of the heads, were all so many evidences that Antonio was no unworthy pupil of the great Reni. But Antonio had avoided this master's besetting sin of trying, all too obviously, to sacrifice expression to beauty. It was plain that Antonio was aiming to reach Annibal's strength, without having as yet succeeded.

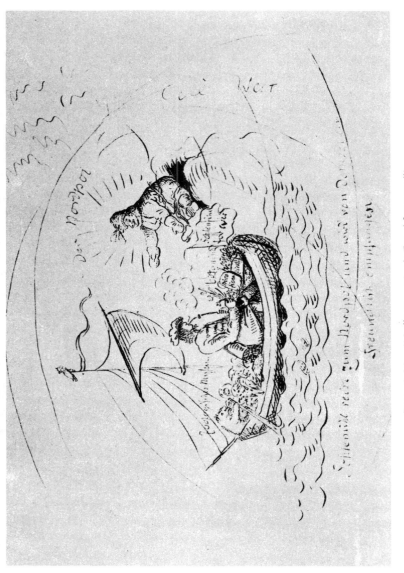

Peter Schlemihl (*"A New Year's Eve Adventure"*)

Salvator spent some considerable time of thoughtful silence in the examination of each of the pictures. Then he said, "Listen, Antonio: it is indeed undeniable that you were born to follow the noble art of painting. For not only has Nature endowed you with the creative spirit from which the finest thoughts pour forth in an inexhaustible stream, but she has also granted you the rare ability to surmount in a short space of time the difficulties of technique. It would only be false flattery if I were to tell you that you had yet advanced to the level of your masters, that you are equal to Guido's exquisite grace or Annibal's strength; but I am certain that you far excel all the painters who hold up their heads so proudly in the Academy of San Luca here—Tiarini, Gessi, Sementa, and all the rest of them, even Lanfranco himself, for he only understands fresco painting. And yet, Antonio, if I were in your place, I should deliberate a while before throwing away the lancet altogether, and confining myself entirely to the pencil. That sounds rather strange, but listen to me. Art seems to be having a bad time of it just now, or rather the devil seems to be very busy amongst our painters nowadays, setting them against one another. If you cannot make up your mind to put up with all sorts of annoyances, to endure more and more scorn and abuse in proportion as you advance in art, and as your fame spreads to meet with malicious scoundrels everywhere, who with a friendly face will force themselves upon you in order to ruin you the most surely afterwards—if you cannot, I say, make up your mind to endure all this—let painting alone. Think of the fate of your teacher, the great Annibal, whom a rascally band of rivals persecuted in Naples, so that he did not receive one single commission for a great work, and was everywhere rejected with contempt. This is said to have been instrumental in his early death. Think of what happened to Domenichino when he was painting the dome of the chapel of St. Januarius. Didn't the villains of painters—I won't mention a single name, not even the rascals Belisario and Ribera—didn't they bribe Domenichino's servant to strew ashes in the lime, so the plaster wouldn't stick fast on the walls, and the painting have no permanence? Think of all that, and examine yourself well whether your spirit is strong enough to endure things like that; if not, your artistic power will be broken, and along with the resolute courage for work you will also lose your ability."

"But, Salvator," replied Antonio, "it would hardly be possible for me to have more scorn and abuse to endure, supposing I took up painting entirely and exclusively, than I have already endured while merely a barber-surgeon. You have been pleased with my pictures, you have indeed! and at the same time declared from inner conviction that I am capable of doing better things than several of our painters of the Academy. But these are just the men who turn up their noses at all that I have produced, and say contemptuously, 'Look, here's our barber-surgeon who wants to be a painter!' And for this very reason my resolve is only more unshaken; I will sever myself from a trade that grows more hateful every day. Upon you, my honoured master, I now stake all my hopes. Your word is powerful; if you would speak a good word for me, you might overthrow my envious persecutors at a single blow, and put me in the place where I ought to be."

"You repose great confidence in me," rejoined Salvator. "And now that we thoroughly understand each other's views on painting, and I have seen your works, I don't really know that there is anybody for whom I would rather take up the cudgels than for you."

Salvator once more inspected Antonio's pictures, and stopped before one representing a "Magdalene at the Saviour's feet," which he especially praised.

"In this Magdalene," he said, "you have deviated from the usual mode of representation. Your Magdalene is not a thoughtful virgin, but a lovely artless child rather, and yet she is such a marvellous child that hardly anybody else but Guido could have painted her. There is a unique charm in her dainty figure; you must have painted with enthusiasm; and if I am not mistaken, the original of this Magdalene is alive and to be found in Rome. Come, confess, Antonio, you are in love!"

Antonio looked down, while he said in a low shy voice, "Nothing escapes your penetration, my dear sir; perhaps it is as you say, but do not blame me for it. That picture I set the highest store by, and hitherto I have guarded it as a holy secret from all men's eyes."

"What do you say?" interrupted Salvator. "None of the painters here has seen your picture?"

"No, not one," was Antonio's reply.

"All right then, Antonio," continued Salvator, his eyes sparkling with delight. "Very well then, you may rely upon it, I will overwhelm your enemies, and get you the honour you deserve. Entrust your picture to me; bring it to my studio secretly by night, and then leave all the rest to me. Will you do so?"

"Gladly, with all my heart," replied Antonio. "And now I should very much like to talk to you about my love-troubles as well; but I feel as if I ought not to do so today, after we have opened our minds to each other on the subject of art. I also entreat you to grant me your assistance both in word and deed later on in this matter of my love."

"I am at your service," said Salvator, "for both, both when and where you require me." Then as he was going away, he once more turned round and said, smiling, "See here, Antonio, when you disclosed to me the fact that you were a painter, I was very sorry that I had spoken about your resemblance to Sanzio. I took it for granted that you were as silly as most of our young folk, who, if they bear but the slightest resemblance in the face to any great master, at once trim their beard or hair as he does, and from this fancy it their business to imitate the style of the master in their art achievements, even though it is a manifest violation of their natural talents to do so. Neither of us has mentioned Raphael's name, but I assure you that I have seen in your pictures clear indications that you have grasped the full significance of the inimitable thoughts which are reflected in the works of the greatest painter of this age. You understand Raphael, and would give me a different answer than Velásquez did when I asked him not long ago what he thought of Sanzio. 'Titian,' he replied, 'is the greatest painter; Raphael knows nothing about carnation.' This Spaniard, I think, understands flesh but not criticism; and yet these men in San Luca elevate him to the clouds because he once painted cherries which the sparrows picked at."

It happened not many days afterwards that the Academicians of San Luca met together in their church to judge the works of painters who had applied for admission to the Academy. There Salvator had sent Scacciati's fine picture. In spite of themselves the painters were greatly struck with its grace and power; and from all lips there was heard nothing but the most extravagant praise when Salvator informed them that he had brought the picture with him from Naples, as the legacy of a young painter who had died prematurely.

It was not long before all Rome was crowding to see and admire the picture by the young unknown master who had died so young; it was unanimously agreed that no such work had been done since Guido Reni's time; some even went so far in their enthusiasm as to place this exquisitely lovely Magdalene above Guido's creations of a similar kind.

Among the crowd of people who were gathered round Scacciati's picture, Salvator one day observed a man who, besides presenting a most extraordinary appearance, behaved as if he were crazy. Well advanced in years, he was tall, thin as a spindle, with a pale face, a long sharp nose, a chin equally long, a little, pointed beard, and gray, gleaming eyes. On the top of his light sand-coloured wig he had set a high hat with a magnificent feather; he wore a short dark red mantle or cape with many bright buttons, a sky-blue doublet slashed in the Spanish style, immense leather gauntlets with silver fringes, a long rapier at his side, light gray stockings drawn up above his bony knees and gartered with yellow ribbons, and bows of the same sort of yellow ribbon on his shoes.

This remarkable figure was standing before the picture as if enraptured: he raised himself on tiptoe; he stooped down till he became quite small; then he jumped up with both feet at once, heaved deep sighs, groaned, nipped his eyes so close together that the tears began to trickle down his cheeks, opened them wide again, fixed his gaze immovably upon the charming Magdalene, sighed again, lisped in a thin, querulous castrato-like voice, "*Ah! carissima—bebedettissima! Ah! Marianna—Mariannina—bellissima.*" ["Oh! dearest—most adored! Ah! Marianna—sweet Marianna! my most beautiful!"]

Salvator, who delighted in such eccentricities, drew near the old fellow, intending to engage him in conversation about Scacciati's work, which seemed to afford him so much exquisite delight. Without paying any particular heed to Salvator, the old gentleman stood cursing his poverty, because he could not give a million sequins for the picture, and place it under lock and key where nobody else could set his cursed eyes upon it. Then, hopping up and down again, he blessed the Virgin and all the holy saints that the scoundrel of an artist who had painted the heavenly picture which was driving him to despair and madness was dead.

Salvator concluded that the man either was out of his mind, or was an Academician of San Luca with whom he was unacquainted.

All Rome was full of Scacciati's wonderful picture; people could scarcely talk about anything else, and this of course was convincing proof of the excellence of the work. And when the painters were again assembled in the church of San Luca, to decide about the admission of certain other pictures which had been announced for exhibition, Salvator Rosa suddenly asked, whether the painter of the "Magdalene at the Saviour's Feet" was not worthy of being admitted a member of the Academy. They all with one accord, including even that hairsplitter in criticism, Cavalierè Josepin, declared that such a great artist would have been an ornament to the Academy, and expressed their sorrow at his death in the choicest phrases, although, like the old madman, they were praising Heaven in their hearts that he was dead. Still more, they were so far carried away by their enthusiasm that they passed a resolution that the admirable young painter whom death had snatched away from art so early should be nominated a member of the Academy in his grave, and that masses should be read for the benefit of his soul in the church of San Luca. They therefore begged Salvator to inform them what was the full name of the deceased, the date of his birth, the place where he was born, and so forth.

Then Salvator rose and said in a loud voice, "Signors, the honour you are anxious to render to a dead man you can more easily bestow upon a living man who walks in your midst. The 'Magdalene at the Saviour's Feet'—the picture which you so justly exalt above all other artistic productions that the last few years have given us, is not the work of a dead Neapolitan painter as I pretended (this I did simply to get an unbiased judgment from you); that painting, that masterpiece, which all Rome is admiring, is from the hand of Signor Antonio Scacciati, the barber-surgeon."

The painters sat staring at Salvator as if suddenly thunderstruck, incapable of either moving or uttering a single sound. After quietly exulting over their embarrassment for some minutes, Salvator continued, "Well now, signors, you would not tolerate the worthy Antonio among you because he is a surgeon; but I think that the illustrious Academy of San Luca has great need of a surgeon to set the limbs of the many crippled figures which emerge from the studios of a good many among your number. But of course you will no longer scruple to do what you ought to have done long ago, namely, elect that excellent painter Antonio Scacciati a member of the Academy."

The Academicians, swallowing Salvator's bitter pill, feigned to be highly delighted that Antonio had in this way given such incontestable proofs of his talent, and with all due ceremony nominated him a member of the Academy.

As soon as it became known in Rome that Antonio was the author of the wonderful picture, he was overwhelmed with congratulations, and even with commissions for great works, which poured in upon him from all sides. Thus by Salvator's shrewd and cunning stratagem the young man emerged all at once out of obscurity, and with the first real step he took in his artistic career rose to great honour.

Antonio revelled in ecstasies of delight. So much the more therefore did Salvator wonder, some days later, to see him appear with his face pale and distorted, utterly miserable and woebegone. "Ah!

Salvator!" said Antonio, "what advantage has it been to me that you have helped me to rise to a level far beyond my expectations, that I am now overwhelmed with praise and honour, that the prospect of a most successful artistic career is opening out before me? I am utterly miserable, for the picture to which, next to you, my dear sir, I owe my great triumph, has proved the cause of lasting misfortune to me."

"Stop!" replied Salvator, "don't sin against your art or your picture. I don't believe a word about the terrible misfortune which you say has befallen you. You are in love, and I presume you can't get all your wishes gratified at once, on the spur of the moment; that's all it is. Lovers are like children; they scream and cry if anyone touches their doll. Stop your moaning and groaning; that's something I cannot stand. Come, sit down there and tell all about your fair Magdalene, quietly, and give me the history of your love affair, and let me know what the stumbling blocks are that we have to remove. I promise you my help beforehand. The more adventurous, the more I shall like them. In fact, my blood is coursing hot in my veins again, and I must work off some energy in a few wild pranks. But go on with your story, Antonio, and as I said, let's have it quietly without any sighs and lamentations, without any Ohs! and Ahs!"

Antonio took his seat on the stool which Salvator had pushed up to the easel at which he was working, and began as follows:—

"There is a high house in the Via Ripetta, with a balcony which projects far over the street so that it immediately strikes the eye of anyone entering through the Porta del Popolo. In it lives the biggest fool in all Rome—an old bachelor with every fault that a bachelor could have—he is avaricious, vain, anxious to appear young, amorous, foppish. He is tall, as thin as a switch, wears a gay Spanish costume, a sandy wig, a conical hat, leather gauntlets, a rapier at his side—"

"Stop, stop!" cried Salvator, interrupting him, "excuse me a minute or two, Antonio." Then, turning over the picture which he was painting, he seized his charcoal and in a few free, bold strokes sketched on the back of the canvas the old man whom he had seen behaving so strangely in front of Antonio's picture at San Luca.

"By all the saints!" cried Antonio, as he leaped to his feet, and forgetful of his unhappiness, he burst out into a loud laugh. "That's the man! That's Signor Pasquale Capuzzi, whom I was just describing, that's Capuzzi to the very T."

"So you see," said Salvator calmly, "that I am already acquainted with the worthy gentleman who most probably is your bitter enemy. But go on."

"Signor Pasquale Capuzzi," continued Antonio, "is as rich as Croesus, but at the same time, as I have just told you, a miser and an impossible ass. The best thing about him is that he loves art, particularly music and painting; but he mixes up so much folly with it all, that even here there's no standing him. He considers himself the greatest composer in the world, and thinks that there's not a singer in the Papal Choir who can approach him. Accordingly he looks down on our Frescobaldi with contempt; and when the Romans talk about the wonderful charm of Ceccarelli's voice, he informs them that Ceccarelli knows as much about singing as a pair of top-boots, and that he, Capuzzi, knows which is the right way to delight the world. And since the first singer of the Pope bears the proud name of Signor Odoardo Ceccarelli di Merania, our Capuzzi is delighted when anybody calls him Signor Pasquale Capuzzi di Senigaglia; for it was in Senigaglia that he was born. Rumour goes that his mother, being startled at the sight of a seal suddenly rising to the surface, gave birth to him in a fisherman's boat, and this accounts, it is said, for a good deal of the currishness in his nature.

"Several years ago he produced one of his operas on the stage. He was hissed off, but that hasn't cured him of his mania for writing execrable music. Indeed, when he heard Francesco Cavalli's opera *Le Nozze di Teti e Peleo*, he swore that Cavalli had stolen the most sublime parts from *his* immortal works, for which he barely escaped being thrashed or even stabbed. He still has a craze for singing arias, and accompanies his hideous squalling on a jarring, jangling guitar, all out of tune. His faithful Pylades is an ill-bred eunuch dwarf, whom the Romans call Pitichinaccio. There is a third member of the company—guess who it is? None other than the Pyramid Doctor, who makes a noise like a melancholy ass and yet fancies he's singing an excellent bass, as good as Martinelli of the Papal Choir. These three fine people are in the habit of meeting in the evening on the balcony of Capuzzi's house, where they sing Carissimi's motets until all the dogs and cats in the neighbourhood break out miaowing and howling, and all the neighbors heartily wish the devil would run away with all blessed three.

"With this old idiot, my father was very intimate, since he trimmed Capuzzi's wig and beard. When my father died, I undertook this business, and Capuzzi was most satisfied with me, because, as he once stated, I knew better than anybody else how to give his mustaches a bold upward twirl. But the real reason was that I was satisfied with the few pence which he gave me for my trouble. He firmly believed that he overpaid me, since, while I was trimming his beard, he would always close his eyes and croak through an aria from his own compositions. My ears used to split, and yet the old fellow's crazy antics afforded me a good deal of amusement, so that I continued to attend him.

"One day, I quietly ascended the stairs, knocked at the door, and opened it, when lo, a girl—an angel of light—came to meet me. You know my Magdalene; it was she. I stood stock still, rooted to the spot. No, Salvator, you shall have no Ohs! and Ahs! Well, the first sight of this, the most lovely girl I had ever seen, enkindled in me the most passionate love. The old man informed me with a smirk that the young lady was the daughter of his brother Pietro, who had died at Senigaglia, that her name was Marianna, and that she was an orphan. Since he was her uncle and guardian, he had taken her into his house. You can easily imagine that after this Capuzzi's house was Paradise to me. But no matter what plans I made, I could never succeed in getting a téte-à-téte with Marianna, even for a single moment. Her glances, however, and many a stolen sigh, and many a soft pressure of the hand, let me know my good fortune.

The old man divined what I was after—which was not a very difficult thing for him to do. He informed me that my behaviour towards his niece was not such as to please him altogether, and he asked me what was the real purport of my attentions. Then I frankly confessed that I loved Marianna with all my heart, and that the greatest earthly happiness I could conceive was a union with her. At this Capuzzi, after measuring me from top to toe, burst out in a guffaw of contempt, and declared that he never had any idea that such lofty thoughts could haunt the brain of a paltry barber. I was almost boiling with rage; I said he knew very well that I was no paltry barber but rather a good surgeon, and, moreover, in painting, a faithful pupil of the great Annibal Caracci and of the unrivalled Guido Reni. But Capuzzi only replied by a still louder guffaw of laughter, and in his horrible falsetto squeaked, 'See here, my sweet Signor barber, my excellent Signor surgeon, my honoured Annibal Caracci, my beloved Guido Reni, be off to the devil, and don't ever show yourself here again, if you don't want your legs broken.' And then the knock-kneed old fool laid hold of me with no less an intention than to kick me out of the room, and hurl me down the stairs. But that, you know, was the limit. My anger got the better of me, I seized the old lunatic and threw him so that his legs stuck up in the air; and there I left him screaming, while I ran down the stairs and out of the house door which, I need hardly say, has been closed to me ever since.

"And that's how matters stood when you came to Rome and when Heaven inspired Father Boniface with the happy idea of bringing me to you. Then as soon as your clever trick had brought me the success for which I had been vainly striving so long, that is, when I was accepted by the Academy of San Luca, and all Rome was heaping up praise and honour on me lavishly, I went straight to the old man and suddenly presented myself before him in his own room, like a threatening apparition. Such at least he must have thought me, for he grew as pale as a corpse, and retreated behind a great table, trembling in every limb. And in a firm and earnest way I represented to him that it was not now a paltry barber or a surgeon, but a celebrated painter and Academician of San Luca, Antonio Scacciati, to whom he would not, I hoped, refuse the hand of his niece Marianna.

You should have seen into what a passion the old fool flew. He screamed; he flourished his arms about like one possessed of devils; he yelled that I, a ruffianly murderer, was seeking his life, that I had stolen his Marianna from him since I had portrayed her in my picture, and it was driving him mad, driving him to despair, for all the world, all the world, were fixing their covetous, lustful eyes upon his Marianna, his life, his hope, his all; but I had better take care, he would burn my house over my head, and me and my picture in it. And therewith he kicked up such a din, shouting, 'Fire! Murder! Thieves! Help!' that I was completely confused, and thought only of making my way out of the house.

"The crackbrained old fool is head over ears in love with his niece; he keeps her under lock and key; and as soon as he succeeds in getting a dispensation from the Pope, he will force her to a shameful marriage with himself. All hope for me is lost!"

"No, no, not quite," said Salvator, laughing, "I am of the opinion that things could not be better for you. Marianna loves you, of that you are convinced; and all we have to do is to get her out of the power of that old lunatic, Signor Pasquale Capuzzi. I should like to know what there is to hinder a couple of enterprising fellows like you and me from accomplishing this. Pluck up your courage, Antonio. Instead of wailing, and sighing, and fainting like a lovesick swain, it would be better to set to work to think out some plan for rescuing your Marianna. You wait and see, Antonio, how finely we'll circumvent the old dotard; the wildest extravagance hardly seems wild enough to me. I'll set about it at once, and learn what I can about the old man, and about his habits of life. But you must not be seen in this affair, Antonio. Go home quietly, and come back to me early tomorrow morning, then we'll consider our first plan of attack."

Herewith Salvator shook the paint out of his brush, threw on his mantle, and hurried to the Corso, while Antonio betook himself home as Salvator had bidden him—his heart comforted and full of hope again.

III

Next morning Salvator, having in the meantime inquired into Capuzzi's habits of life, very greatly surprised Antonio by a description of them, even down to the minutest details.

"Poor Marianna," said Salvator, "leads a sad life of it with the crazy old fellow. There he sits sighing and ogling the whole day long, and what is worse still, in order to soften her heart towards him, he sings her all sorts of love ditties that he has composed or intends to compose. At the same time he is so damnably jealous that he will not even permit the poor young girl to have the usual female attendance, for fear of intrigues and amours, which a maid might be induced to engage in. Instead, a hideous little monster with hollow eyes and pale flabby cheeks appears every morning and evening to perform for sweet Marianna the services of a tiring-maid. And this little apparition is nobody else but that dwarf Pitichinaccio, who has to wear women's clothing. Capuzzi, whenever he leaves, carefully locks and bolts every door; besides which there is always a confounded fellow keeping watch below, who was formerly a bravo, and then a gendarme, and now lives under Capuzzi's rooms. It seems, therefore, almost impossible to enter his house; nevertheless I promise you, Antonio, that this very night you shall be in Capuzzi's own room and shall see your Marianna, though this time it will only be in Capuzzi's presence."

"What do you say?" cried Antonio, quite excited; "what do you say? We shall manage it tonight? I thought it was impossible."

"There, there," continued Salvator, "keep still, Antonio, and let us quietly consider how we may safely carry out the plan I have conceived. But in the first place I must tell you that I have already scraped an acquaintance with Signor Pasquale Capuzzi without knowing it. That wretched spinet, which stands in the corner there, belongs to him, and he wants me to pay him the preposterous sum of ten ducats for it. When I was convalescent I longed for some music, which always comforts me and does me a deal of good, so I begged my landlady to get me some such instrument as that. Signora Caterina learned that there was an old man living in the Via Ripetta who had a fine spinet to sell. I got the instrument brought here. I did not trouble myself either about the price or about the owner. It was only yesterday evening that I learned quite by chance that the gentleman who intended to cheat me with this rickety old thing was Signor Pasquale Capuzzi. Signora Caterina had enlisted the services of an acquaintance living in the same house, and indeed on the same floor as Capuzzi—and now you can easily guess whence I have got all my news."

"Yes," replied Antonio, "then the way to get in is found; your landlady—"

"I know very well, Antonio," said Salvator, cutting him short, "I know what you're going to say. You think you can find a way to your Marianna through Signora Caterina. But you'll find that we can't do anything of that sort; she is far too talkative; she can't keep the least secret, and so we can't for a single moment think of employing her in this business. Now listen to me quietly. Every evening when it's dark, Signor Pasquale, although it's very hard work for him owing to his knock-knees, carries his little friend the eunuch home in his arms, as soon as he has finished his duties as maid. Nothing in the world could induce the timid Pitichinaccio to set foot on the pavement at that time of night. So that when—"

At this moment somebody knocked at Salvator's door, and to the consternation of both, Signor Pasquale stepped in in all the splendour of his gala attire. On catching sight of Scacciati he stood stock still as if paralyzed, and then, opening his eyes wide, he gasped for air as though he had some difficulty in breathing. But Salvator hastily ran to meet him, and took him by both hands, saying, "My dear Signor Pasquale, your presence in my humble dwelling is, I feel, a very great honour. May I presume that it is your love for art which brings you to me? You wish to see the newest things I have done, perhaps to give me a commission for some work. In what, my dear Signor Pasquale, can I serve you?"

"I have a word or two to say to you, my dear Signor Salvator," stammered Capuzzi painfully, "but—alone—when you are alone.

With your leave I will withdraw and come again at a more season-able time."

"By no means," said Salvator, holding the old gentleman fast, "by no means, my dear sir. You need not stir a step; you could not have come at a more seasonable time, for, since you are a great admirer of the noble art of painting, and the patron of all good painters, I am sure you will be greatly pleased for me to introduce to you Antonio Scacciati here, the first painter of our time, whose glorious work—the wonderful 'Magdalene at the Saviour's Feet'—has excited the most enthusiastic admiration throughout all Rome. *You* too, I need hardly say, have also formed a high opinion of the work, and must be very anxious to know the great artist himself."

The old man was seized with a violent trembling; he shook as if he had a shivering fit of the ague, and shot fiery wrathful looks at poor Antonio. He however approached the old gentleman, and, bowing with polished courtesy, assured him that he esteemed him-self happy at meeting in such an unexpected way with Signor Pasquale Capuzzi, whose great learning in music as well as in paint-ing was a theme for wonder not only in Rome but throughout all Italy, and he concluded by requesting the honour of his patronage.

This behaviour of Antonio, in pretending to meet the old gentle-man for the first time in his life, and in addressing him in such flattering phrases, soon brought him around again. He forced his features into a simpering smile, and, as Salvator now let his hands loose, gave his mustache an elegant upward curl, at the same time stammering out a few unintelligible words. Then, turning to Salvator, he requested payment of the ten ducats for the spinet he had sold him.

"Oh! that trifling little matter we can settle afterwards, my good sir," was Salvator's answer. "First have the goodness to look at this sketch of a picture which I have drawn, and drink a glass of Syracuse while you do so." Salvator meanwhile placed his sketch on the easel and moved up a chair for the old gentleman, and then, when he had taken his seat, he presented him with a large and handsome wine-cup full of good Syracuse—the little pearl-like bubbles rising gaily to the top.

Signor Pasquale was very fond of a glass of good wine—when he did not have to pay for it; and now he ought to have been in an especially happy frame of mind, for, besides nourishing his heart with the hope of getting ten ducats for a rotten, worn-out spinet, he was sitting before a splendid, boldly designed picture, the rare beauty of which he was quite capable of estimating at its full worth. And that he was in this happy frame of mind he evidenced in divers ways; he simpered ingratiatingly; he half closed his little eyes; he assiduously stroked his chin and mustache; and lisped time after time, "Splendid! delicious!" but they did not know to which he was referring, the picture or the wine.

When he had thus worked himself into a quiet cheerful humour, Salvator suddenly began—"They tell me, my dear sir, that you have a most beautiful and amiable niece, named Marianna—is it so? All the young men of the city are so smitten with love that they do nothing but run up and down the Via Ripetta stupidly, almost dislocating their necks in their efforts to look up at your balcony for a sight of your sweet Marianna, to snatch a single glance from her heavenly eyes."

Suddenly all the charming simpers, all the good humour which had been called up into the old gentleman's face by the good wine, were gone. Looking gloomily before him, he said sharply, "Ah! that's an instance of the corruption of our abandoned young men. They fix their infernal eyes, the shameful seducers, upon mere children. For I tell you, my good sir, that my niece Marianna is a child, still a child, only just outgrown her nurse's care."

Salvator turned the conversation upon something else; the old gentleman recovered himself. But just as he, his face again radiant with sunshine, was on the point of putting the full wine-cup to his lips, Salvator began anew. "But tell me, my dear sir, if it is indeed true that your niece, with her sixteen summers, really has beautiful auburn hair, and eyes full of heaven's own loveliness and joy, like Antonio's 'Magdalene?' It is generally maintained that she has."

"I don't know," replied the old gentleman, still more sharply than before, "I don't know. But let us leave my niece in peace; rather let us exchange a few instructive words on the noble subject of art, as your fine picture here invites me to do."

Every time that Capuzzi raised the wine-cup to his lips to take a good draught, Salvator began to talk again about the beautiful Marianna, so that at last the old gentleman leaped from his chair in a perfect passion, banged the cup down upon the table and almost broke it, screaming in a high shrill voice, "By the infernal pit of Pluto! by all the furies! you will turn my wine into poison—into poison I tell you. But I see through you, you and your fine friend Signor Antonio, you think to make sport of me. But you'll find yourselves deceived. Pay me the ten ducats you owe me immediately, and then I will leave you and your associate, that barber-fellow Antonio, to make your way to the devil."

Salvator shouted, as if mastered by the most violent rage, "What! you have the audacity to treat me in this way in my own house! Do you think I'm going to pay you ten ducats for that rotten box? The worms have long ago eaten all the goodness and all the music out of it. Not ten—not five—not three—not one ducat shall you have for it, it's not worth a farthing. Away with the tumble-down thing!" and he kicked over the little instrument again and again, till the strings were all jarring and jangling together.

"Ha!" screeched Capuzzi, "justice is still to be had in Rome; I will have you arrested, sir—arrested and cast into the deepest dungeon," and he was about to rush out of the room, blustering like a hailstorm. But Salvator took fast hold of him with both hands, and drew him down into the chair again, softly murmuring in his ear, "My dear Signor Pasquale, don't you perceive that I was only jesting with you? You shall have for your spinet, not ten, but *thirty* ducats cash down." And he went on repeating, "thirty bright ducats in ready money," until Capuzzi said in a faint and feeble voice, "What do you say, my dear sir? Thirty ducats for the spinet without its being repaired?" Then Salvator released his hold of the old gentleman, and asserted on his honour that within an hour the instrument should be worth thirty—nay, forty ducats, and that Signor Pasquale should receive as much for it.

Taking in a fresh supply of breath, and sighing deeply, the old gentleman murmured, "Thirty—forty ducats!" Then he began, "But you have greatly offended me, Signor Salvator—" "Thirty ducats," repeated Salvator. Capuzzi simpered, but then began again, "But you have grossly wounded my feelings, Signor Salvator—" "Thirty ducats," exclaimed Salvator, cutting him short; and he continued to repeat, "Thirty ducats! thirty ducats!" as long as the old gentleman continued to sulk—till at length Capuzzi said, radiant with delight, "If you will give me thirty—I mean forty ducats for the spinet, all shall be forgiven and forgotten, my dear sir."

"But," began Salvator, "before I can fulfill my promise, I still have one little condition to make, which you, my honoured Signor Pasquale Capuzzi di Senigaglia, can easily grant. You are the first composer in all Italy, besides being the foremost singer of the day. When I heard in the opera *Le Nozze di Teti e Peleo* the great scene which that shameless Francesco Cavalli has stolen from your works, I was enraptured. If you would only sing me that aria while I put the spinet to rights you would confer upon me the greatest pleasure I can conceive."

Puckering up his mouth into the most winning of smiles, and blinking his little gray eyes, the old gentleman replied, "I perceive, my good sir, that you are yourself a clever musician, for you possess taste and know how to value the deserving better than these ungrateful Romans. Listen—listen—to the aria of all arias."

Thereupon he rose to his feet, and stretching himself up to his full height, spread out his arms and closed both eyes, so that he looked like a cock preparing to crow; and he at once began to screech in such a way that the walls rang again, and Signora Caterina and her two daughters soon came running in, fully under the impression that such screaming must betoken some accident or other. At the sight of the crowing old gentleman they stopped on the threshold utterly astonished; and thus they formed the audience of the incomparable musician Capuzzi.

Meanwhile Salvator, having picked up the spinet and thrown back the lid, took his palette in hand, and in bold firm strokes began on the lid of the instrument the most remarkable piece of painting that ever was seen. The central idea was a scene from Cavalli's opera *Le Nozze di Teti*, but there was a multitude of other personages mixed up with it in the most fantastic way. Among them were the recognizable features of Capuzzi, Antonio, Marianna (faithfully reproduced from Antonio's picture), Salvator himself, Signora Caterina and her two daughters—and even the Pyramid Doctor was not wanting—and all grouped so intelligently, judiciously, and ingeniously, that Antonio could not conceal his astonishment, both at the artist's intellectual power as well as at his technique.

Meanwhile old Capuzzi had not been content with the aria which Salvator had requested him to give, but carried away by his musical madness, he went on singing or rather screeching without cease, working his way through the most awful recitatives from one execrable scene to another. He must have been going on for nearly two hours when he sank back in his chair, breathless, and with his face as red as a cherry. And just at this same time also Salvator had so far worked out his sketch that the figures began to wear a look of vitality, and the whole, viewed at a little distance, had the appearance of a finished work.

"I have kept my word with respect to the spinet, my dear Signor Pasquale," breathed Salvator in the old man's ear. Pasquale started up as if awakening out of a deep sleep. Immediately his glance fell upon the painted instrument, which stood directly opposite him. Then, opening his eyes wide as if he saw a miracle, and throwing his conical hat on the top of his wig, he took his crutch-stick under his arm, made one bound to the spinet, tore the lid off the hinges, and holding it above his head, ran like a madman out of the house altogether, followed by the hearty laughter of Signora Caterina and both her daughters.

"The old miser," said Salvator, "knows very well that he has only to take that painted lid to Count Colonna or to my friend Rossi and he will at once get forty ducats for it, or even more."

Salvator and Antonio then both deliberated how they should carry out the plan of attack which was to be made when night came. We shall soon see what the two adventurers resolved upon, and what success they had in their adventure.

As soon as it was dark, Signor Pasquale, after locking and bolting the door of his house, carried the little monster of an eunuch home as usual. The whole way the little wretch was whining and growling, complaining that not only did he sing Capuzzi's arias till he got hoarse and burnt his fingers cooking the macaroni, but he had now to lend himself to duties which brought him nothing but sharp boxes of the ear and rough kicks, which Marianna lavishly distributed to him whenever he came near her. Old Capuzzi consoled him as well as he could, promising to provide him an ampler supply of sweets than he had hitherto done; indeed, as the little man would not cease his growling and querulous complaining, Pasquale even laid himself under the obligation to get a natty abbot's coat made for the little torment out of an old black plush wasitcoat which he (the dwarf) had often set covetous eyes upon. He demanded a wig and a sword as well. Parleying upon these points, they arrived at the Via Bergognona, for that was where Pitichinaccio dwelt, only four doors from Salvator.

The old man set the dwarf down cautiously and opened the street door; and then, the dwarf in front, they both began to climb up the narrow stairs, which were more like a rickety ladder for hens and chickens than steps for respectable people. But they had hardly mounted half way up when a terrible racket began up above, and the coarse voice of some wild drunken fellow was heard cursing and swearing, and demanding to be shown the way out of the damned house. Pitichinaccio squeezed himself close to the wall, and entreated Capuzzi, in the name of all the saints, to go on first. But before Capuzzi had ascended two steps, the fellow who was up above came tumbling headlong downstairs, caught hold of the old man, and whisked him away like a whirlwind out through the open

door below into the middle of the street. There they both lay—
Capuzzi at bottom and the drunken brute like a heavy sack on top
of him. The old gentleman screamed piteously for help; two men
came up at once and with considerable difficulty freed him from
the heavy weight lying upon him; the other fellow, as soon as he
was lifted up, reeled away cursing.

"Good God! what's happened to you, Signor Pasquale? What
are you doing here at this time of night? What quarrel have you
been getting mixed up in in that house there?" asked Salvator
and Antonio, for these were the two men.

"Oh, I shall die!" groaned Capuzzi; "that son of the devil has
crushed all my limbs; I can't move."

"Let me look," said Antonio, feeling all over the old gentleman's
body, and suddenly he pinched Capuzzi's right leg so sharply that
the old man screamed loudly.

"By all the saints!" cried Antonio in consternation, "My dear
Signor Pasquale, you've broken your right leg in the most dangerous
place. If you don't get speedy help you will be a dead man within
a short time, or at any rate be lame all your life long."

A terrible scream escaped the old man's breast. "Calm yourself, my dear sir," continued Antonio, "although I'm now a painter,
I haven't altogether forgotten my surgical practice. We will carry
you to Salvator's house and I will at once bind up—"

"My dear Signor Antonio," whined Capuzzi, "you nourish
hostile feelings towards me, I know." "But," broke in Salvator,
"this is now no longer the time to talk about enmity; you are in
danger, and that is enough for honest Antonio to exert all his skill
on your behalf. Lay hold, friend Antonio."

Gently and cautiously they lifted up the old man between them,
and carried him to Salvator's dwelling. All the way Capuzzi
screamed with the unspeakable pain caused by his broken leg.

Signora Caterina said that she had had a foreboding that something was going to happen, and so she had not gone to bed. As
soon as she caught sight of old Pasquale and heard what had befallen him, she began to heap reproaches upon him for his bad
conduct. "I know," she said, "I know very well, Signor Pasquale,
whom you've been taking home again. Now that you've got your
beautiful niece Marianna in the house with you, you think you've
no further call to have womenfolk about you, and you treat that
poor Pitichinaccio most shameful and infamous, putting him in
petticoats. But look to it. *Ogni carne ha il suo osso* [Every house
has its skeleton]. Why if you have a girl about you, don't you need

womenfolk? *Fate il passo secondo la gamba* [Cut your clothes according to your cloth], and don't you require anything either more or less from your Marianna than what is right. Don't lock her up as if she were a prisoner, nor make your house a dungeon. *Asino punto convien che trotti* [If you are in the stream, you had better swim with it]; you have a beautiful niece and you must alter your ways to suit her, that is, you must only do what she wants you to do. But you are an ungallant and hard-hearted man, yes, and even in love, and jealous as well, they say, which I hope at your years is not true. Your pardon for telling you it all straight, but *chi ha nel petto fiele non puo sputar miele* [when there's bile in the heart there can't be honey in the mouth]. So now, if you don't die of your broken leg, which at your age is not at all unlikely, let this be a warning to you; and leave your niece free to do what she likes, and let her marry the fine young gentleman as I know very well."

And so the stream went on uninterruptedly, while Salvator and Antonio cautiously undressed the old gentleman and put him to bed. Signora Caterina's words were like knives cutting deeply into his breast; but whenever he attempted to interrupt, Antonio warned him that all speaking was dangerous, and so he had to swallow his bitter gall. At length Salvator sent Signora Caterina away, to fetch some ice-cold water that Antonio wanted.

Salvator and Antonio satisfied themselves that the fellow who had been sent to Pitichinaccio's house had done his duty well. Notwithstanding the apparently terrible fall, Capuzzi had not received the slightest damage beyond a slight bruise or two. Antonio put the old gentleman's right foot in splints and bandaged it up so tight that he could not move. Then they wrapped him up in cloths that had been soaked in ice-cold water, as a precaution, they alleged, against inflammation, so that Capuzzi shook as if with the ague.

"My good Signor Antonio," he groaned feebly, "tell me if it is all over with me. Must I die?"

"Compose yourself," replied Antonio. "If you will only compose yourself, Signor Pasquale! As you have come through the first dressing with so much nerve and without fainting, I think we may say that the danger is past; but you will require the most attentive nursing. At present we mustn't let you out of the doctor's sight."

"Oh! Antonio," whined the old gentleman, "you know how I like you, how highly I esteem your talents. Don't leave me. Give me your dear hand—so! You won't leave me, will you, my dear good Antonio?"

"Although I am now no longer a surgeon," said Antonio, "although I've given up that trade which I hated, in your case, Signor Pasquale, I will make an exception, and will undertake to attend you, for which I shall ask nothing except that you give me your friendship, your confidence again. You were a little hard upon me—"

"Say no more," lisped the old gentleman, "not another word, my dear Antonio—"

"Your niece will be half dead with anxiety," said Antonio again, "at your not returning home. You are, considering your condition, brisk and strong enough, and so as soon as day dawns we'll carry you home to your own house. There I will again look at your bandage, and arrange your bed as it ought to be, and give your niece her instructions, so that you may soon get well again."

The old gentleman heaved a deep sigh and closed his eyes, remaining some minutes without speaking. Then, stretching out his hand towards Antonio, he drew him down close beside him, and whispered, "It was only a joke that you had with Marianna, was it not, my dear sir?"

"Think no more about that, Signor Pasquale," replied Antonio. "Your niece did, it is true, strike my fancy; but I have now quite different things in my head, and—to confess it honestly—I am very pleased that you did return a sharp answer to my foolish suit. I thought I was in love with your Marianna, but what I really saw in her was only a fine model for my 'Magdalene.' And this probably explains how it is that, now that my picture is finished, I feel quite indifferent toward her."

"Antonio," cried the old man, in a strong voice, "Antonio, you glorious fellow! What comfort you give me—what help—what consolation! Now that you don't love Marianna I feel as if all my pain had gone."

"Why, I declare, Signor Pasquale," said Salvator, "if we didn't know you to be a grave and sensible man, with a true perception of what is becoming to your years, we might easily believe that you were yourself by some infatuation in love with your sixteen-year-old niece."

Again the old gentleman closed his eyes, and groaned and moaned at the horrible pain, which now returned with redoubled violence.

The first red streaks of morning came shining in through the window. Antonio announced to the old man that it was now time to take him to his own house in the Via Ripetta. Signor Pasquale's reply was a deep and pitiful sigh. Salvator and Antonio lifted him out of bed and wrapped him in a wide mantle which had belonged to Signora Caterina's husband, and which she lent them for this purpose. The old man implored them by all the saints to take off the villainous cold bandages in which his bald head was swathed, and to give him his wig and plumed hat. And also, if it were possible, Antonio was to put his mustache a little in order, that Marianna might not be too much frightened at sight of him.

Two porters with a litter were standing ready before the door. Signora Caterina, still storming at the old man, and mixing a great many proverbs in her abuse, carried down the bed, in which they then carefully packed him; and so, accompanied by Salvator and Antonio, he was taken home to his own house.

No sooner did Marianna see her uncle in this wretched plight than she began to scream, while a torrent of tears gushed from her eyes; without noticing her lover, who had come along with him, she grasped the old man's hands and pressed them to her lips, bewailing the terrible accident that had befallen him—so much pity had the good child for the old man who plagued and tormented her with his amorous folly. Yet at this same moment the inherent nature of woman asserted itself in her; for it only required a few significant glances from Salvator to put her in full possession of all the facts of the case. Now, for the first time, she stole a glance at the happy Antonio, blushing hotly as she did so; and a pretty sight it was to see how a roguish smile gradually routed and broke through her tears. Salvator, despite the "Magdalene," had not expected to find the little maiden half so charming, or so sweetly pretty as he now really discovered her to be; and while, almost feeling inclined to envy Antonio his good fortune, he felt that it was all the more necessary to get poor Marianna away from her hateful uncle, let the cost be what it might.

Signor Pasquale forgot his trouble in being received so affectionately by his lovely niece, which was indeed more than he deserved. He simpered and pursed up his lips so that his mustache was all of a totter, and groaned and whined, not with pain, but simply and solely with amorous longing.

Antonio arranged his bed professionally, and, after Capuzzi had been laid on it, tightened the bandage still more, at the same time so muffling up his left leg as well that he had to lay there motionless like a log of wood. Salvator withdrew and left the lovers alone with their happiness.

The old gentleman lay buried in cushions; moreover, as an extra precaution, Antonio had bound a thick piece of cloth well steeped in water round his head, so that he might not hear the lovers whispering together. This was the first time they unburdened all their hearts to each other, swearing eternal fidelity in the midst of tears and rapturous kisses. The old gentleman could have no idea of what was going on, for Marianna from time to time asked him how he felt, and even permitted him to press her little white hand to his lips.

When the morning began to be well advanced, Antonio hastened away to procure, as he said, all the things that the old gentleman required, but in reality to invent some means for putting him, for some hours at least, in a still more helpless condition, as well as to consult with Salvator what further steps were then to be taken.

IV

Next morning Antonio came to Salvator, melancholy and dejected.

"Well, what's the matter?" cried Salvator when he saw him coming, "What are you hanging your head about? What's happened to you now, you happy dog? Can you not see your mistress every day, and kiss her and press her to your heart?"

"Oh! Salvator, it's all over with my happiness, it's gone for ever," cried Antonio. "The devil is making sport of me. Our stratagem has failed, and we now are open enemies with that cursed Capuzzi."

"So much the better," said Salvator; "so much the better. But come, Antonio, tell me what's happened."

"Just imagine, Salvator," began Antonio, "yesterday when I went back to the Via Ripetta after an absence of at the most two hours, with all sorts of medicines, whom should I see but old Pasquale standing in his own doorway, fully dressed. The Pyramid Doctor and that damned bravo were standing behind him, while a confused something was bobbing around their legs. I believe it was that little monster Pitichinaccio. As soon as the old man saw me, he shook his fist at me, and began to heap curses on me, swearing that if I approached his door, he would have all my bones broken. 'Be off to the devil, you dirty barber-fellow,' he shrieked; 'you think you can outwit me with your lying and tricks! Like the devil himself you lie in wait for my poor innocent Marianna, and think you are going to get her into your toils—but stop a moment! I will spend my last ducat to have the life stamped out of you, before you know it. And your fine patron, Signor Salvator, the murderer—bandit—who's escaped the halter—he shall be sent to join his captain Masaniello in hell—I'll have him run out of Rome; that won't cost me much trouble.'

"The old fellow raged on, and since that damned bravo, set on by the Pyramid Doctor, looked as if he was getting ready to attack me, and a crowd of curious onlookers began to assemble, what could I do but leave as fast as I could? I didn't like to come to you in my trouble, for I know you would only laugh at me and my complaints. Why, you can hardly keep back your laughter now."

As Antonio ceased speaking, Salvator did indeed burst out laughing heartily.

"Now," he cried, "now the situation is beginning to be interesting. And now, my worthy Antonio, I will tell you in detail what took place at Capuzzi's after you left. You hardly left the house when Signor Splendiano Accoramboni, who learned—God knows in what way—that his bosom friend Capuzzi had broken his right leg during the night, drew near in all solemnity with a surgeon. Your bandages and the whole way of treatment you adopted with Signor Pasquale was bound to excite suspicion. The surgeon removed the splints and bandages, and they discovered, what we both knew very well, that there was nothing wrong, not even an ossicle dislocated, let alone broken. It didn't require any uncommon intelligence to figure out the rest."

"But," said Antonio, utterly astonished, "my dear, good sir, tell me how you learned all that? Tell me how you get into Capuzzi's house and know everything that takes place there?"

"I have already told you," replied Salvator, "that an acquaintance of Signora Caterina lives in the same house, and on the same floor as Capuzzi. This acquaintance, the widow of a wine-dealer, has a daughter whom my little Margaret often goes to see. Girls have a special instinct for finding other girls of the same sort and so it came about that Rose—that's the name of the wine-dealer's daughter—and Margaret soon discovered a small vent in the living room, leading into a dark closet that adjoins Marianna's apartment. Marianna had heard the whispering and murmuring of the two girls, and she noticed the vent-hole, and so the way to a mutual exchange of communications was soon open and used. Whenever old Capuzzi takes his afternoon nap, the girls gossip away to their heart's content. You may have noticed that little Margaret, Signora Caterina's and my favourite, is not so serious and reserved as her elder sister, Anna, but is pert and mischievous. Without expressly mentioning your love affair I have told her to get

Marianna to tell her everything that takes place in Capuzzi's house. She is a very apt pupil in the matter; and if I laughed at your pain and despondency just now it was because I knew what would comfort you, knew I could prove to you that the affair has now taken a most favourable turn. I have plenty of excellent news for you."

"Salvator!" cried Antonio, his eyes sparkling with joy, "how you cause my hopes to rise! Thank God for the vent-hole! I will write to Marianna; Margaret can take the letter with her—"

"No, no, we can have none of that, Antonio," replied Salvator. "Margaret can be useful to us without being your love messenger exactly. Besides, accident, which often plays fine tricks, might carry your love notes into old Capuzzi's hands, and bring an endless amount of fresh trouble upon Marianna, just when she is on the point of getting the lovesick old fool under her thumb. Listen to what happened. The way in which Marianna received the old fellow when we took him home has reformed him. He is fully convinced that she no longer loves you, but that she has given him at least one half of her heart, and that all he has to do is to win the other half. And Marianna, since she imbibed the poison of your kisses, has advanced three years in shrewdness, artfulness, and experience. She has convinced the old man, not only that she had no share in our trick, but that she hates our goings-on, and will meet with scorn every device on your part to approach her. In his excessive delight the old man was too hasty, and swore that if he could do anything to please his adored Marianna he would do it immediately, she only has to mention it. At this Marianna modestly asked for nothing except that her *zio carissimo* [dearest uncle] would take her to see Signor Formica in the theatre outside the Porta del Popolo. This rather stumped Capuzzi; he consulted with the Pyramid Doctor and with Pitichinaccio; at last Signor Pasquale and Signor Splendiano came to the resolution that they really would take Marianna to this theatre tomorrow. Pitichinaccio will accompany them in the disguise of a handmaid. He gave his consent only on condition that Signor Pasquale would make him a present, not only of the plush wasitcoat, but also of a wig, and at night would, alternately with the Pyramid Doctor, carry him home. That bargain they finally made; and so this remarkable trinity will certainly go along with pretty Marianna to see Signor Formica tomorrow, in the theatre outside the Porta del Popolo."

It is now necessary to say who Signor Formica was, and what he had to do with the theatre outside the Porta del Popolo.

At the time of the Carnival in Rome, nothing is more sad than when the theatre managers have been unlucky in their choice of a musical composer, or when the primo tenore at the Argentina theatre has lost his voice on the way, or when the male prima donna of the Valle theatre is laid up with a cold—in brief, when the chief source of recreation which the Romans were hoping to find does not work out. Then comes Holy Thursday and cuts off all the hopes that otherwise might have been realized. It was just after one of these unlucky carnivals—almost before the strict fastdays were past, when a certain Nicolo Musso opened a theatre outside the Porta del Popolo, where he stated his intention of putting nothing but light impromptu comic sketches in the manner of the Commedia dell' arte on the boards. His advertisement was ingenious and witty, and consequently the Romans formed a favourable preconception of Musso's enterprise. But even without this they were so desperate for entertainment that they would have snatched eagerly at the poorest show.

The interior arrangements of the theatre, or rather of the small shed, did not say much for the financial resources of the enterprising manager. There was no orchestra, nor were there boxes. Instead, a gallery was put up at the back, where the arms of the house of Colonna were conspicuous—a sign that Count Colonna had taken Musso and his theatre under his special protection. A low platform covered with carpets and hung around with painted sheets of paper (which, according to the requirements of the piece, had to represent a wood or a room or a street)—this was the stage. Add to this that the spectators had to content themselves with hard uncomfortable wooden benches, and it was no wonder that Signor Musso's patrons on first entering were pretty loud in their grumblings against him for calling a miserable shed a theatre. But no sooner had the first two actors who appeared exchanged a few words than the attention of the audience was arrested; as the piece proceeded their interest took the form of applause, their applause grew to admiration, their admiration to the wildest pitch of enthusiastic excitement, which found vent in loud and continuous laughter, clapping of hands, and screams of "Bravo! Bravo!"

And indeed it would not have been very easy to find anything finer than these extemporized representations of Nicolo Musso; they overflowed with wit, humour, and imagination, and they lashed the follies of the day with an unsparing scourge. The audience was carried away by the incomparable powers of characterization that all the actors showed, but particularly by the inimitable mimicry of

Pasquarello, by his marvellously natural imitations of the voice, gait and postures of well-known personages. By his inexhaustible humour, and the point and appositeness of his impromptu sallies, he quite carried his audience away. The man who played the role of Pasquarello and who called himself Signor Formica was animated by a spirit of great originality; often there was something so strange in his tone and gestures that the audience, even in the midst of the most unrestrained burst of laughter, felt a cold shiver run through them. He was excellently supported by Dr. Gratiano, who in pantomime, in voice, and in his talent for saying the most delightful things mixed up with apparently the most extravagant nonsense, seemed to have no equal in the world. This role was played by an old Bolognese named Maria Agli.

Thus in a short time all cultured Rome was seen hastening in a continuous stream to Nicolo Musso's little theatre outside the Porta del Popolo, while Formica's name was on everybody's lips, and people shouted with wild enthusiasm, "*Oh! Formica! Formica benedetto! Oh! Formicissimo!*"—not only in the theatre but also in the streets. They regarded him as a supernatural visitant, and many an old lady who had split her sides with laughing in the theatre, would suddenly look grave and say solemnly, "*Scherza coi fanti e lascia star santi*" [Jest with children but let the saints alone], if anybody ventured to say the least thing in disparagement of Formica's acting. This arose from the fact that outside the theatre Signor Formica was an inscrutable mystery. Never was he seen anywhere and all efforts to discover traces of him were vain, while Nicolo Musso on his part refused to say a word about Formica's life off the stage.

And this was the theatre that Marianna was anxious to go to.

"Let us make a decisive onslaught on our foes," said Salvator; "we couldn't have a finer chance than when they're returning home from the theatre." Then he imparted to Antonio the details of a plan, which, though it appeared venturesome and dangerous, Antonio embraced with joy, since it held out to him a prospect of carrying off his Marianna from the hated old Capuzzi. He was also delighted to hear that Salvator was especially concerned to chastise the Pyramid Doctor.

When night came, Salvator and Antonio each took a guitar and went to the Via Ripetta, where, with the express view of causing old Capuzzi annoyance, they complimented lovely Marianna with the finest serenade that ever was heard. For Salvator played and sang in masterly style, while Antonio, as far as the capabilities of his fine tenor would allow him, almost rivalled Odoardo Ceccarelli. Although Signor Pasquale appeared on the balcony and tried to silence the singers with abuse, his neighbours, attracted to their windows by the good singing, shouted to him that he and his companions howled and screamed like so many cats and dogs, and yet he wouldn't listen to good music when it did come into the street; let him go in and stop up his ears if he didn't want to listen to good singing. And so Signor Pasquale had to bear the torture nearly all night long of hearing Salvator and Antonio sing songs which either were the sweetest of love songs or else mocked at the folly of amorous old fools. They plainly saw Marianna standing at the window, even though Signor Pasquale begged her in the sweetest of phrases and protestations not to expose herself to the noxious night air.

Next evening the most remarkable company that ever was seen proceeded down the Via Ripetta towards the Porta del Popolo. All eyes were turned upon them, and people asked each other if these were maskers left from the Carnival. Signor Pasquale Capuzzi, spruce and smug, all elegance and politeness, wearing his gay Spanish suit well brushed, parading a new yellow feather in his conical hat, and stepping along in shoes too small for him, as if he were walking among eggs, was leading pretty Marianna on his arm; her slender figure could not be seen, still less her face, since she was smothered up in her veil and wraps. On the other side marched Dr. Splendiano Accoramboni in his great wig, which covered the whole of his back, so that from behind he appeared to be a huge head walking along on two little legs. Close behind Marianna, and almost clinging to her, waddled the eunuch dwarf Pitichinaccio, dressed in fiery red petticoats, his head hideously covered with bright-coloured flowers.

This evening Signor Formica outdid even himself. As a new number, which he had not done before, he introduced short songs into his performance, burlesquing the style of certain well-known singers. Old Capuzzi's passion for the operatic stage, which in his youth had almost amounted to a mania, was now stirred up in him anew. In a rapture of delight he kissed Marianna's hand time after time, and protested that he would not miss an evening at Nicolo Musso's theatre with her. Signor Formica he extolled to the very skies, and joined hand and foot in the boisterous applause of the rest of the spectators. Signor Splendiano was less satisfied, and kept continually admonishing Signor Capuzzi and lovely Marianna not to laugh so immoderately. In a single breath he ran over the names of twenty or more diseases which might arise from splitting the sides with laughing. But neither Marianna nor Capuzzi heeded him in the least. As for Pitichinaccio, he felt very uncomfortable. He had been obliged to sit behind the Pyramid Doctor, whose great wig completely overshadowed him. He could not see a single thing on the stage, nor any of the actors, and he was also repeatedly bothered and annoyed by two forward women who had placed themselves near him. They called him a dear, comely little lady, and asked him if he was married, though to be sure, he was very young, and whether he had any children, who they swore must be sweet little creatures, and so forth. The cold sweat stood in beads on poor Pitichinaccio's brow; he whined and whimpered, and cursed the day he was born.

After the conclusion of the performance, Signor Pasquale waited until the spectators had left the theatre. The last light was extinguished just as Signor Splendiano lit a small piece of wax torch at it; and then Capuzzi, with his worthy friends and Marianna, slowly and circumspectly set out on their return journey.

Pitichinaccio wept and screamed; Capuzzi, greatly to his vexation, had to take him on his left arm, while with the right he led Marianna. Dr. Splendiano showed the way with his miserable little bit of torch, which only burned with difficulty, and even then in a feeble sort of a way, so that the wretched light it cast merely served to reveal to them the thick darkness of the night.

While they were still a good distance from the Porta del Popolo they suddenly found themselves surrounded by several tall figures closely enveloped in mantles. The torch was knocked out of the doctor's hand, and went out on the ground. Capuzzi, as well as the doctor, stood still without uttering a sound. Then, from some invisible source, a pale reddish light fell upon the muffled figures, and four grisly skulls fixed their hollow ghastly eyes upon the Pyramid Doctor. "Woe—woe—woe betide thee, Splendiano Accoramboni!" the terrible spectres shrieked in deep, sepulchral tones. Then one of them wailed, "Do you know me? do you know me, Splendiano? I am Cordier, the French painter, who was buried last week; your medicines brought me to my grave." Then the second, "Do you know me, Splendiano? I am Küfner, the German painter, whom you poisoned with your infernal electuary." Then the third, "Do you know me, Splendiano? I am Liers, the Fleming, whom you killed with your pills, and whose brother you defrauded of a picture." Then the fourth, "Do you know me, Splendiano? I am Ghigi, the Neapolitan painter, whom you despatched with your powders." And lastly all four together,

"Woe—woe—woe upon thee, Splendiano Accoramboni, cursed Pyramid Doctor! We bid you come—come down with us beneath the earth. Away—away—away with you!" and so saying they threw themselves upon the unfortunate doctor, and raising him in their arms, whisked him away like a whirlwind.

Now, although Signor Pasquale was a good deal overcome by terror, yet it is surprising how promptly he recovered courage as soon as he saw that it was only his friend Accoramboni with whom the spectres were concerned. Pitichinaccio had stuck his head, with the flower-bed that was on it, under Capuzzi's mantle, and clung so fast around his neck that all efforts to shake him off proved futile.

"Pluck up your spirits," Capuzzi exhorted Marianna, when nothing more was to be seen of the spectres or of the Pyramid Doctor; "pluck up your spirits, and come to me, my sweet little dove! As for my worthy friend Splendiano, it's all over with him. May St. Bernard, who also was an able physician and gave many a man a lift on the road to happiness, may he help him, if the revengeful painters whom he hastened to get to his Pyramid break his neck! But who'll sing the bass of my canzonas now? And this booby, Pitichinaccio, is squeezing my throat so, that, besides the fright caused by Splendiano's abduction, I fear I shall not be able to produce a pure note for six weeks to come. Don't be alarmed, my Marianna, my darling! It's all over now."

She assured him that she had quite recovered from her alarm, and begged him to let her walk alone without support, so that he could free himself from his troublesome pet Pitichinaccio. But Signor Pasquale only took faster hold of her, saying that he wouldn't let her leave his side a yard in that pitch darkness for anything in the world.

Just as Signor Pasquale, now at his ease again, was about to proceed on his road, four frightful fiend-like figures rose up in front of him, as if out of the earth; they wore short flaring red mantles and fixed their keen glittering eyes upon him, at the same time making horrible noises—yelling and whistling. "Ugh! ugh! Pasquale Capuzzi! You cursed fool! You amorous old devil! We belong to your fraternity; we are the evil spirits of love, and have come to carry you off to hell—to hell-fire—you and your crony Pitichinaccio." Thus screaming, the Satanic figures fell upon the old man. Capuzzi fell heavily to the ground and Pitichinaccio along with him, both raising a shrill piercing cry of distress and fear, like that of a whole troop of cudgelled asses.

Marianna had meanwhile torn herself away from the old man and leaped aside. Then one of the devils clasped her softly in his arms, whispering the sweet glad words, "O Marianna! my Marianna! At last we've managed it! My friends will carry the old man a long, long way from here, while we get to safety."

"O my Antonio!" whispered Marianna softly.

But suddenly the scene was illuminated by the light of several torches, and Antonio felt a stab in his shoulder. Quick as lightning he turned around, drew his sword, and attacked a bravo, who with his stiletto upraised was just preparing to deliver a second blow. He saw that his three companions were defending themselves against a superior number of gendarmes. He managed to beat off the fellow who had attacked him, and joined his friends. Although they were maintaining their ground bravely, the contest was too unequal; the gendarmes would certainly have proved victorious if two newcomers had not suddenly ranged themselves with a shout on the side of the young men, one of them immediately cutting down the fellow who was pressing Antonio the hardest.

In a few minutes the contest was decided against the police. Several lay stretched on the ground seriously wounded; the rest fled with loud yells towards the Porta del Popolo.

Salvator Rosa (for he it was who had hastened to Antonio's assistance and cut down his opponent) wanted to take Antonio and the young painters who were disguised in the devil's masks and then and there chase the police into the city.

Maria Agli, however, who had come along with him, and, notwithstanding his advanced age, had tackled the police as stoutly as any of the rest, urged that this would be imprudent, for the guard at the Porta del Popolo would be certain to know of the affair and would arrest them. So they all betook themselves to Nicolo Musso, who gladly received them into his narrow little house not far from the theatre. The artists took off their devils' masks and laid aside their mantles, which had been rubbed over with phosphorus, while Antonio, who, beyond an insignificant scratch on his shoulder, was not wounded, exercised his surgical skill in binding up the wounds of the rest—Salvator, Agli, and his young comrades—for all the others had been wounded, though none of them at all dangerously.

The adventure, despite its foolhardiness, would undoubtedly have been successful, if Salvator and Antonio had not to a certain extent overlooked one person, who upset everything. The *ci-devant* bravo and gendarme Michele, who lived below in Capuzzi's house, and was his general servant, had, in accordance with Capuzzi's directions, followed Capuzzi's party to the theatre, but at some distance off, for the old gentleman was ashamed of the tattered reprobate. In the same way Michele was following them homewards. And when the spectres appeared, Michele who, be it remarked, feared neither death nor devil, suspecting that something was wrong, hurried back as fast as he could run in the darkness to the Porta del Popolo, raised an alarm, and returned with all the gendarmes he could find, just at the moment when, as we know, the devils fell upon Signor Pasquale, and were about to carry him off as the dead men had the Pyramid Doctor.

In the very hottest moment of the fight, one of the young painters observed that one of the gendarmes, taking Marianna in his arms (for she had fainted), made off for the gate, while Signor Pasquale ran after him with incredible swiftness, as if he had quicksilver in his legs. At the same time, by the light of the torches, the artist caught a glimpse of something gleaming, clinging to Capuzzi's mantle and whimpering; no doubt it was Pitichinaccio.

Next morning Dr. Splendiano was found near the Pyramid of Cestius, fast asleep, doubled up like a ball and squeezed into his wig, as if into a warm soft nest. When he awakened, he rambled in his talk, and there was some difficulty in convincing him that he was still on the surface of the earth, and in Rome to boot. And when at length he reached his own house, he returned thanks to the Virgin and all the saints for his rescue, threw all his tinctures, essences, electuaries, and powders out of the window, burned his prescriptions, and vowed to heal his patients in the future by no other means than by anointing and laying on of hands, as some celebrated physician of former ages, who was at the same time a saint (his name I cannot recall just at this moment), had done with great success before him.

"I can't tell you," said Antonio next day to Salvator, "how my heart boils with rage since my blood has been spilled. Death and destruction overtake that villain Capuzzi! I tell you, Salvator, that I am determined to *force* my way into his house. I will cut him down if he opposes me, and carry off Marianna."

"An excellent plan!" replied Salvator, laughing. "An excellent plan! Splendidly contrived! Of course I am sure you have also found the same means for transporting Marianna through the air to the Piazza di Spagna, so that they don't seize you and hang you before you can reach sanctuary. No, my dear Antonio, violence can do nothing for you this time. You may lay your life on it too that Signor Pasquale will now take steps to guard against any open attack. Moreover, our adventure has made a good deal of noise, and the public laughter at the absurd way in which we have read a lesson to Splendiano and Capuzzi has roused the police out of their light slumber, and they, you may be sure, will now exert all their feeble efforts to trap us. No, Antonio, let us have recourse to craft. *Con arte e con inganno si vive mezzo l'anno, con inganno e con arte si vive l'altra parte* [If cunning and scheming will help us six months through, scheming and cunning will help us the other six too], says Signora Caterina, and she isn't far wrong. Besides, I can't help laughing to see how we've behaved and acted for all the world like brainless boys, and I shall have to bear most of the blame, for I am a good bit older than you. Tell me, Antonio, supposing our scheme had been successful, and you had actually carried off Marianna from the old man, where would you have fled to, where would you have hidden her, and how would you have managed to get united to her by the priest before the old man could interfere to prevent it? You shall, however, in a few days, really and truly run away with your Marianna. I have let Nicolo Musso as well as Signor Formica into all the secret, and in common with them devised a plan which can scarcely fail. So cheer up, Antonio; Signor Formica will help you."

"Signor Formica?" replied Antonio in a tone of indifference which almost amounted to contempt. "Signor Formica! In what way can a buffoon help me?"

"Ho! ho!" laughed Salvator. "Please bear in mind, that Signor Formica is worthy of your respect. Don't you know he is a sort of magician who in secret is master of the most mysterious arts? I tell you, Signor Formica will help you. Old Maria Agli, the clever Bolognese Dr. Gratiano, is also a sharer in the plot, and will have an important part to play in it. You shall abduct your Marianna from Musso's theatre."

"You are deluding me with false hopes, Salvator," said Antonio. "You have just said that Signor Pasquale will take care to avoid all open attacks. How can you suppose after his recent unpleasant experience that he can possibly be willing to visit Musso's theatre again?"

"It will not be as difficult as you imagine to entice him there," replied Salvator. "What will be more difficult will be to get him to the theatre without his followers. But, be that as it may, what you have now got to do, Antonio, is to have everything prepared and arranged with Marianna, to flee from Rome the moment a favourable opportunity comes. You must go to Florence; your skill as a painter will recommend you there; and you shall have no lack of acquaintances, nor of honourable patronage and assistance—that you may leave to me to provide for. After we have had a few days' rest, we will then see what is to be done further. Once more, Antonio—live in hope; Formica will help you."

V

Signor Pasquale was only too well aware who had been at the bottom of the mischief that had happened to him and the poor Pyramid Doctor near the Porta del Popolo, and so it may be imagined how enraged he was against Antonio, and against Salvator Rosa, whom he rightly judged to be the ringleader. He was untiring in his efforts to comfort poor Marianna, who was quite ill from fear—so she said; but in reality she was furious that the scoundrel Michele with his gendarmes had come up, and torn her from her Antonio's arms. Meanwhile Margaret was very active in bringing her tidings of her lover; and Marianna based all her hopes upon the enterprising mind of Salvator. With impatience she waited from day to day for something fresh to happen, and by a thousand petty tormenting ways let the old gentleman feel the effects of this impatience; but though she thus tamed his amorous folly and made him humble enough, she failed to reach the evil spirit of love that haunted his heart. After she made him experience to the full all the tricksy humours of the most wayward girl, she then suffered him to press his withered lips upon her tiny hand just once. He then swore in his excessive delight that he would never cease kissing the Pope's toe until he had obtained dispensation to wed his niece, the paragon of beauty and amiability. Marianna was particularly careful not to interrupt him in these outbreaks of passion, for by encouraging these gleams of hope in the old man's breast she fanned the flame of hope in her own, for the more he could be lulled into the belief that he held her fast in the indissoluble chains of love, the more easy it would be for her to escape him.

Some time passed, when one day at noon Michele came stamping upstairs. After he had knocked a good many times to induce Signor Pasquale to open the door, he announced with considerable prolixity that there was a gentleman below who urgently requested to see Signor Pasquale Capuzzi, who he knew lived there.

"By all the blessed saints of Heaven!" cried the old gentleman, exasperated; "doesn't the rascal know that on no account do I receive strangers in my own house?"

But the gentleman was of very respectable appearance, reported Michele, rather oldish, talked well, and called himself Nicolo Musso.

"Nicolo Musso," murmured Capuzzi reflectively; "Nicolo Musso, who owns the theatre beyond the Porta del Popolo; what can he want with me?" Whereupon, carefully locking and bolting the door, he went downstairs with Michele, in order to converse with Nicolo in the street before the house.

"My dear Signor Pasquale," began Nicolo, approaching to meet him, and bowing with polished ease, "that you deign to honour me with your acquaintance affords me great pleasure. You lay me under a very great obligation. Since the Romans saw you in my theatre—you, a man of the most approved taste, of the soundest knowledge, and a master in art—not only has my fame increased, but my receipts have doubled. I am therefore all the more deeply pained to learn that certain young criminals made a murderous attack on you and your friends as you were returning from my theatre at night. But I pray you, Signor Pasquale, by all the saints, don't cherish any grudge against me or my theatre on account of this outrage, which shall be severely punished. Don't deprive me of the honour of your presence at my performances!"

"My dear Signor Nicolo," replied the old man, simpering, "be assured that I never enjoyed myself more than I did when I visited your theatre. Your Formica and your Algi—why, they are actors who cannot be matched anywhere. But the fright almost killed my friend Dr. Splendiano Accoramboni, indeed it almost proved the death of me—no, it was too great; and though it has not turned me against your theatre, it certainly has from the road there. If you will put up your theatre in the Piazza del Popolo, or in the Via Babuina, or in the Via Ripetta, I certainly will not fail to visit you every evening; but there's no power on earth shall ever get me outside the Porta del Popolo at nighttime again."

Nicolo sighed deeply, as if greatly troubled. "That is very hard upon me," said he then, "harder perhaps than you will believe, Signor Pasquale. For unfortunately—I had based all my hopes upon you. I came to solicit your assistance."

"My assistance?" asked the old gentleman in astonishment. "My assistance, Signor Nicolo? In what way could it profit you?"

"My dear Signor Pasquale," replied Nicolo, drawing his handkerchief across his eyes, as if brushing away the trickling tears, "my most excellent Signor Pasquale, you will remember that my actors are in the habit of including songs in their performances. This practice I was thinking of extending imperceptibly more and more, then to get together an orchestra, and, frankly, get around the prohibitions against it, and establish what would amount to an opera house. You, Signor Capuzzi, are the first composer in all Italy; and we can attribute it to nothing but the inconceivable frivolity of the Romans and the malicious envy of your rivals that we hear anything else but your pieces exclusively at all the theatres. Signor Pasquale, I came to request you on my bended knees to allow me to put your immortal works, as far as circumstances will admit, on my humble stage."

"My dear Signor Nicolo," said the old gentleman, his face all sunshine, "why are we talking here in the public street? Pray have the goodness to climb up one or two rather steep flights of stairs. Come along with me up to my poor dwelling."

Almost before Nicolo got into the room, the old gentleman brought forward a great pile of dusty music manuscript, opened it, and, taking his guitar in his hands, began to deliver himself of a series of the frightful high-pitched screams which he considered singing.

Nicolo behaved like one in raptures. He sighed; he uttered extravagant expressions of approval; he exclaimed at intervals, *"Bravo! Bravissimo! Benedettissimo Capuzzi!"* until at last he threw himself at the old man's feet as if utterly beside himself with ecstatic delight, and grasped his knees. But he nipped them so hard that the old gentleman jumped off his seat, calling out with pain, and saying to Nicolo, "By the saints! Let me go, Signor Nicolo; you'll kill me."

"No," replied Nicolo, "no, Signor Pasquale, I will not rise until you have promised that Formica may sing in my theatre the day after tomorrow the divine arias which you have just executed."

"You are a man of taste," groaned Pasquale—"a man of deep insight. To whom could I better entrust my compositions than to you? You shall take all my arias with you. Only let go of me. But, good God! I shall not hear them—my divine masterpieces! Oh! let go of me, Signor Nicolo."

"No," replied Nicolo, still on his knees, and tightly pressing the old gentleman's thin spindle-shanks together, "no, Signor Pasquale, I will not let go until you give me your word that you will be present in my theatre the night after tomorrow. You need not fear any new attack! Why, don't you see that the Romans, once they have heard your work, will bring you home in triumph by the light of hundreds of torches? But in case that does not happen, I myself and my faithful comrades will take our arms and accompany you home ourselves."

"You yourself will accompany me home, with your comrades?" asked Pasquale. "And how many may that be?"

"Eight or ten persons will be at your command, Signor Pasquale. Yield to my intercession and resolve to come, I beg of you."

"Formica has a fine voice," lisped Pasquale. "How finely he will execute my arias."

"Come, oh! come!" exhorted Nicolo again, giving the old gentleman's knees an extra squeeze.

"You will pledge yourself that I shall reach my own house without being molested?" asked the old gentleman.

"I pledge my honour and my life," was Nicolo's reply, as he gave the knees a still sharper squeeze.

"Agreed!" cried the old gentleman; "I will be in your theatre the day after tomorrow."

Then Nicolo leapt to his feet and pressed Pasquale in so close an embrace that he gasped and panted for lack of breath.

At this moment Marianna entered the room. Signor Pasquale tried to frighten her away again by the look of resentment which he hurled at her; she took not the slightest notice of it, but going straight up to Musso, addressed him as if in anger—"It is in vain for you, Signor Nicolo, to attempt to entice my dear uncle to go to your theatre. You are forgetting that the infamous trick lately played by some dissolute seducers, who were lying in wait for me, almost cost the life of my dearly beloved uncle, and of his worthy friend Splendiano; yes, that it almost cost my life too. I will never give my consent to my uncle's again exposing himself to such danger. Desist from your entreaties, Nicolo. And you, my dearest uncle, you will stay quietly at home, will you not, and not venture out beyond the Porta del Popolo again at nighttime, which is a friend to nobody?"

Signor Pasquale was thunderstruck. He opened his eyes wide and stared at his niece. Then he rewarded her with the sweetest endearments, and set forth at considerable length how Signor Nicolo had pledged himself to arrange matters so that there would be no danger on the return home.

"Nonetheless," said Marianna, "I stick to my word, and beg you most earnestly, my dearest uncle, not to go to the theatre outside the Porta del Popolo. I ask your pardon, Signor Nicolo, for speaking my suspicions frankly in your presence. You are, I know, acquainted with Salvator Rosa and also with Antonio Scacciati. What if you are acting with our enemies? What if you are only trying to entice my dear uncle into your theatre so that they can carry out some fresh villainous scheme, for I know that my uncle will not go without me?"

"What a suspicion!" cried Nicolo, quite alarmed. "What a terrible suspicion, Signora! Have you such a bad opinion of me? Have I such a bad reputation that you think I could be guilty of treachery like that? But if you think so unfavourably of me, if you mistrust the assistance I have promised you, let Michele, who I know rescued you out of the hands of the robbers, accompany you, and let him take a large body of gendarmes with him, who can wait for you outside the theatre, for you cannot of course expect me to fill my auditorium with police."

Marianna fixed her eyes steadily upon Nicolo's, and then said, earnestly and gravely, "What do you say? Michele and gendarmes should accompany us? Now I see plainly, Signor Nicolo, that you mean honestly by us, and that my suspicions were unfounded. Pray forgive me my thoughtless words. And yet I cannot banish my nervousness and anxiety about my dear uncle; I must still beg him not to take this dangerous step."

Signor Pasquale had listened to all this conversation with expressions on his face that clearly showed the nature of the struggle that was going on within him. But now he could no longer contain himself; he threw himself on his knees before his beautiful niece, seized her hands, kissed them, bathed them with the tears which ran down his cheeks, exclaiming as if beside himself, "My adored, my angelic Marianna! Fierce and devouring are the flames of the passion which burns at my heart. Oh! this nervousness, this anxiety—it is indeed the sweetest confession that you love me." And he besought her not to give way to fear, but to go and listen in the theatre to the finest arias which the most divine of composers had ever written.

Nicolo too did not stop his entreaties, plainly showing his disappointment, until Marianna permitted her scruples to be overcome; and she promised to lay all fear aside and accompany the best and dearest of uncles to the theatre outside the Porta del Popolo. Signor Pasquale was in ecstasies, was in the seventh heaven of delight. He was convinced that Marianna loved him; and he now might hope to hear his music on the stage, and win the laurel wreath which had so long been the object of his desires; he was on the point of seeing his dearest dreams fulfilled. Now he would let his light shine in perfect glory before his true and faithful friends, for he fully expected that Signor Splendiano and little Pitichinaccio would go with him as on the first occasion.

The night that Signor Splendiano had slept in his wig near the Pyramid of Cestius he had had, besides the spectres who ran away with him, all sorts of sinister apparitions visit him. The whole cemetery seemed alive, and hundreds of corpses had stretched out their skeleton arms towards him, moaning and wailing that even in their graves they could not get over the torture caused by his essence and electuaries. Accordingly the Pyramid Doctor, although he could not contradict Signor Pasquale's opinion that it was only a wild trick played on him by a gang of dissolute young men, grew melancholy; and, although not ordinarily inclined to superstition, he now saw spectres everywhere, and was tormented by forebodings and bad dreams.

As for Pitichinaccio, he could not be convinced that it was not real devils come straight from the flames of hell that had fallen on Signor Pasquale and himself, and the bare mention of that dreadful night was enough to make him scream. All the claims of Signor Pasquale that there had been nobody behind the masks but Antonio Scacciati and Salvator Rosa were of no effect, for Pitichinaccio wept and swore that in spite of his terror and apprehension he had clearly recognized both the voice and the behaviour of the devil Fanfarelli in the one who had pinched his belly black and blue.

It may therefore be imagined what an almost endless amount of trouble it cost Signor Pasquale to persuade the two to go with him once more to Nicolo Musso's theatre. Splendiano was the first to decide to go—after he had procured from a monk of St. Bernard's order a small consecrated bag of musk, the perfume of which neither dead man nor devil could endure; with this he intended to arm himself against all assaults. Pitichinaccio could not resist the temptation of a promised box of candied grapes, but Signor Pasquale had to consent that the dwarf might wear his new abbot's coat, instead of petticoats, which he affirmed had proved an immediate source of attraction to the devil.

What Salvator feared seemed therefore as if it would really take place; and yet his plan depended entirely, he continued to repeat, upon Signor Pasquale's being in Nicolo's theatre alone with Marianna, without his companions. Both Antonio and Salvator racked their brains to prevent Splendiano and Pitichinaccio from going along with Signor Pasquale. Every scheme that occurred to them had to be given up for lack of time, for the principal plan in

Nicolo's theatre had to be carried out on the evening of the following day. But Providence, which often employs the most unlikely instruments for the chastisement of fools, interposed on behalf of the distressed lovers, and put it into Michele's head to practice some of his blundering, thus accomplishing what Salvator and Antonio's craft was unable to accomplish.

That same night there was heard in the Via Ripetta before Signor Pasquale's house such a chorus of fearful screams and of cursing and raving and abuse that all the neighbours were startled up out of their sleep, and a body of gendarmes, who had been pursuing a murderer as far as the Piazza di Spagna, hastened up with torches, supposing that some fresh deed of violence was being committed. But when they, and a crowd of other people whom the noise had attracted, came upon the anticipated scene of murder, they found poor little Pitichinaccio lying as if dead on the ground, whilst Michele was thrashing the Pyramid Doctor with a formidable bludgeon. And they saw the doctor reel to the ground just at the moment when Signor Pasquale painfully scrambled to his feet, drew his rapier, and furiously attacked Michele. Round about were pieces of broken guitars. If several people had not grasped the old man's arm he would assuredly have run Michele right through the heart. The ex-bravo, now becoming aware by the light of the torches whom he had attacked, stood as if petrified, his eyes almost starting out of his head, "a painted desperado, on the balance between will and power," as it is said somewhere. Then, uttering a fearful scream, he tore his hair and begged for pardon and mercy. Neither the Pyramid Doctor nor Pitichinaccio was seriously injured, but they had been so soundly cudgelled that they could neither move nor stir, and had to be carried home.

Signor Pasquale had himself brought this mishap upon his own shoulders. We know that Salvator and Antonio had complimented Marianna with the finest serenade that could be heard; but I have forgotten to say that to the old gentleman's great indignation they repeated it for several successive nights. At length Signor Pasquale, whose rage was kept in check by his neighbours, was foolish enough to have recourse to the authorities of the city, urging them to forbid the two painters to sing in the Via Ripetta. The authorities, however, replied that it would be a thing unheard of in Rome to prevent anybody from singing and playing the guitar where he pleased, and it was irrational to ask such a thing. So Signor Pasquale, determined to put an end to the nuisance himself, had promised Michele a large reward if he seized the first opportunity to fall upon the singers and give them a good sound drubbing. Michele at once procured a stout bludgeon, and lay in wait every night behind the door. But it happened that Salvator and Antonio judged it prudent to omit their serenading in the Via Ripetta for some nights before they carried out their plan, so as not to remind the old gentleman of his adversaries. Marianna remarked quite innocently that though she hated Antonio and Salvator, yet she liked their singing, for nothing was so nice as to hear music floating upwards in the night air.

This Signor Pasquale made a mental note of, and as the essence of gallantry intended to surprise his love with a serenade on his part, which he had himself composed and carefully practiced with his faithful friends. On the very night before the one in which he was hoping to celebrate his greatest triumph in Nicolo Musso's theatre, he stealthily slipped out of the house and went and fetched his associates, with whom he had previously arranged matters. But no sooner had they sounded the first few notes on their guitars than Michele, whom Signor Pasquale had thoughtlessly forgotten to inform of his design, burst forth from behind the door, highly delighted that the opportunity which was to bring him the promised reward had at last come, and began to cudgel the musicians most unmercifully. We are already acquainted with the result. Of course there was no further possibility of either Splendiano or Pitichinaccio's accompanying Signor Pasquale to Nicolo's theatre, for they were both confined to their beds beplastered all over. Signor Pasquale, however, was unable to stay away, although his back and shoulders smarted considerably from the drubbing he had himself received; every note in his arias was a cord which drew him there with irresistible power.

"Well," said Salvator to Antonio, "since the obstacle which we took to be insurmountable has been removed from our way of itself, it all depends now upon you not to let the favourable moment slip for carrying off your Marianna from Nicolo's theatre. But I needn't talk, you won't fail; I will greet you now as the fiancé of Capuzzi's lovely niece, who in a few days will be your wife. I wish you happiness, Antonio, and yet I feel a shiver run through me when I think about your marriage."

"What do you mean, Salvator?" asked Antonio, utterly astounded.

"Call it a crotchet, call it a foolish fancy, or what you will, Antonio," rejoined Salvator—"I love the fair sex, but there is not a woman (not even one that I was madly in love with, and would die for) who doesn't make me tremble with fear when I think of marriage to her. Their inscrutability perplexes all men. A woman that we believe has surrendered herself to us entirely, heart and soul, and that we think has unfolded all her character to us, is the first to deceive us, and along with the sweetest of her kisses we drink the most pernicious of poisons."

"And my Marianna?" asked Antonio, amazed.

"Pardon me, Antonio," continued Salvator, "even your Marianna, who is loveliness and grace personified, has given me a fresh proof of how dangerous the mysterious nature of woman is to us. Just call to mind what the behaviour of that innocent, inexperienced child was when we carried her uncle home, how at a single glance from me she understood everything—everything, I tell you, and as you yourself admitted, proceeded to play her part with the greatest cleverness. But that is not to be compared at all with what took place when Musso visited the old man. The most practiced address, the most impenetrable cunning—in short, all the arts of the most experienced woman of the world could not have done more than little Marianna did to deceive old Capuzzi with perfect success. She could not have acted in any better way to prepare the road for us for any kind of enterprise. Our feud with the cranky old fool—any sort of cunning scheme seems justified—

"But—come, my dear Antonio, never mind my fanciful crotchets, be happy with your Marianna; as happy as you can."

If a monk had taken his place beside Signor Pasquale when he set out along with his niece to go to Nicolo Musso's theatre, everybody would have thought that the strange pair were being led to execution. First went valiant Michele, repulsive in appearance, and armed to the teeth; then came Signor Pasquale and Marianna, followed by fully twenty gendarmes.

Nicolo received the old gentleman and his lady with every mark of respect at the entrance to the theatre, and conducted them to the seats which had been reserved for them, immediately in front of the stage. Signor Pasquale felt highly flattered by this mark of honour, and gazed about him with proud and sparkling eyes, whilst his pleasure, his joy, was greatly enhanced to find that all the seats near and behind Marianna were occupied by women alone. A couple of violins and a bass-fiddle were being tuned behind the curtains of the stage; the old gentleman's heart beat with expectation; and when all at once the orchestra struck up the *ritornello* of his work, he felt an electric thrill tingling in every nerve.

Formica came forward in the character of Pasquarello, and sang —sang in Capuzzi's own voice, and with all his characteristic gestures, the most hopeless aria that ever was heard. The theatre shook with the loud and boisterous laughter of the audience. They shouted, they screamed wildly, "O Pasquale Capuzzi! Our most illustrious composer and artist! Bravo! Bravissimo!" The old gentleman, not perceiving the ridicule and irony of the laughter, was in raptures of delight. The aria came to an end, and the people cried "Sh! sh!" for Dr. Gratiano, played on this occasion by Nicolo Musso himself, appeared on the stage, holding his hands over his ears and shouting to Pasquarello for God's sake to stop this ridiculous screeching.

Then the doctor asked Pasquarello how long he had taken to the confounded habit of singing, and where he had got that execrable piece of music.

Whereupon Pasquarello replied that he didn't know what the doctor wanted; the doctor was like the Romans, and had no taste for real music, since he failed to recognize the most talented of musicians. The aria had been written by the greatest of living composers, in whose service he had the good fortune to be, receiving instruction in both music and singing from the master himself.

Gratiano then began guessing, and mentioned the names of a great number of well-known composers and musicians, but at every distinguished name Pasquarello only shook his head contemptuously.

At length Pasquarello said that the doctor was only exposing gross ignorance, since he did not know the name of the greatest composer of the time. It was no other than Signor Pasquale Capuzzi, who had done him the honour of taking him into his service. Could he not see that he was the friend and servant of Signor Pasquale?

Then the doctor broke out into a loud long roar of laughter, and cried, What! Had he (Pasquarello) after leaving him (the doctor), in whose service he had gotten plenty of tips besides wages and food —had he gone and taken service with the worst old idiot who ever stuffed himself with macaroni, to a patched carnival fool who strutted about like a satisfied old hen after a shower of rain, to the snarling skinflint, the lovesick old poltroon, who infected the air of the Via Ripetta with the disgusting bleating which he called singing? and so forth.

To which Pasquarello, quite incensed, replied that it was nothing but envy which showed in the doctor's words; he (Pasquarello) was of course speaking with his heart in his mouth [*parla col cuore in mano*]; the doctor was not at all the man to pass an opinion upon Signor Pasquale Capuzzi di Senigaglia; he was speaking with his heart in his mouth. The doctor himself had a strong tang of all that he blamed in the excellent Signor Pasquale; but he was speaking with his heart in his mouth; he (Pasquarello) had himself often heard fully six hundred people at once laugh most heartily at Dr. Gratiano. and so forth. Then Pasquarello spoke a long panegyric upon his new master, Signor Pasquale, attributing to him all the virtues under the sun; and he concluded with a description of his character, which he portrayed as being the very essence of amiability and grace.

"Heaven bless you, Formica!" lisped Signor Capuzzi to himself. "Heaven bless you, Formica! I see you have arranged this to make my triumph perfect, since you are upbraiding the Romans for all their envious and ungrateful persecution of me, and are letting them know *who* I really am."

"Ha! here comes my master himself," cried Pasquarello at this moment, and there entered on the stage—Signor Pasquale Capuzzi himself, just as he breathed and walked, his very clothes, face, gestures, gait, postures; in fact so perfectly like Signor Capuzzi in the auditorium, that the latter, quite aghast, let go Marianna's hand, which hitherto he had held fast in his own, and tapped himself, his nose, his wig, in order to discover whether he was not dreaming, or seeing double, whether he was really sitting in Nicolo Musso's theatre and dare credit the miracle.

Capuzzi on the stage embraced Dr. Gratiano with great kindness, and asked how he was. The doctor replied that he had a good appetite, and slept soundly, at his service [*per servirlo*]; and as for his purse—well, it was suffering from a galloping consumption. Only yesterday he had spent his last ducat for a pair of rosemary-coloured stockings for his sweetheart, and was just going to walk around to one or two moneylenders to see if he could borrow thirty ducats—

"How can you pass over your best friends?" said Capuzzi. "Here, my dear sir, here are fifty ducats, come take them."

"Pasquale, what are you about?" said the real Capuzzi under his breath.

Dr. Gratiano began to talk about a bond and about interest; but Signor Capuzzi declared that he could not think of asking for either from such a friend as the doctor.

"Pasquale, have you gone out of your senses?" exclaimed the real Capuzzi a little louder.

After many grateful embraces Dr. Gratiano took his leave. Now Pasquarello drew near with a good many bows, and extolled Signor Capuzzi to the skies, adding, however, that his purse was suffering from the same complaint as Gratiano's, and he begged for some of the same excellent medicine that had cured his. Capuzzi on the stage laughed, and said he was pleased to find that Pasquarello knew how to turn his good humour to advantage, and threw him several glittering ducats.

"Pasquale, you must be mad, possessed of the devil," cried the real Capuzzi aloud. The listeners told him to be quiet.

Pasquarello went still further in his eulogy of Capuzzi, and came at last to speak of the aria which he (Capuzzi) had composed, and with which he (Pasquarello) hoped to enchant everybody. The fictitious Capuzzi clapped Pasquarello heartily on the back, and went on to say that he might venture to tell him (Pasquarello), his faithful servant, in confidence, that in reality he knew nothing whatever of the science of music, and in respect to the aria of which he (Pasquarello) had just spoken, as well as all pieces that he (Capuzzi) had ever composed, why, he had stolen them out of Frescobaldi's canzonas and Carissimi's motets.

"I tell you you're lying in your throat, you dog," shouted the Capuzzi off the stage, rising from his seat. Again he was told to keep still, and the woman who sat next to him drew him down on the bench.

"It's now time to think about other and more important matters," continued Capuzzi on the stage. He was going to give a grand banquet the next day, and Pasquarello must look alive and have everything ready that was necessary. Then he produced and read over a list of all the rarest and most expensive dishes, making Pasquarello tell him how much each would cost, at the same time giving him the money for them.

"Pasquale! You're insane! You've gone mad! You good-for-nothing scamp! You spendthrift!" shouted the real Capuzzi at intervals, growing more and more enraged the higher the cost of this the most nonsensical of dinners arose.

At length, when the list was finished, Pasquarello asked what had induced him to give such a splendid banquet.

"Tomorrow will be the happiest and most joyous day of my life," replied the fictitious Capuzzi. "For let me tell you, my good Pasquarello, that I am going to celebrate the auspicious marriage of my dear niece Marianna tomorrow. I am going to give her hand to that fine young man, the best of all artists, Scacciati."

Hardly had the words fallen from his lips when the real Capuzzi leapt to his feet, utterly beside himself, quite out of his mind, his face aflame with the most fiendish rage, and doubling his fists and shaking them at his counterpart on the stage, he yelled at the top of his voice, "No, you won't, no, you won't, you rascal! You scoundrel, you—Pasquale! Do you mean to cheat yourself out of your Marianna, you hound? Are you going to throw her into the arms of that scoundrel—sweet Marianna, your life, your hope, your all? Ah! watch out! watch out! you infatuated fool. Remember what sort of a reception you will meet with from yourself. You shall beat yourself black and blue with your own hands, so that you have no relish for banquets and weddings!"

But the Capuzzi on the stage doubled his fists like the Capuzzi below, and shouted in exactly the same furious way, and in the same high-pitched voice, "May all the spirits of hell sit at your heart, you abominable simpleton of a Pasquale, you atrocious skinflint—you lovesick old fool—you gaudy-tricked-out ass with the cap and bells dangling about your ears. Take care lest I snuff out the candle of your life, and put an end to the dirty tricks which you try to work upon the good, honest, modest Pasquale Capuzzi."

Amid the most fearful cursing and swearing of the real Capuzzi, the one on the stage dished up one fine anecdote after the other about him.

"Don't you dare," shouted the fictitious Capuzzi at last, "you amorous old ape, interfere with the happiness of these two young people, whom Heaven has destined for each other."

At this moment there appeared at the back of the stage Antonio Scacciati and Marianna locked in each other's arms. Although the old man was at other times somewhat feeble on his legs, now fury gave him strength and agility. With a single bound he was on the stage, had drawn his sword, and was about to charge upon the pretended Antonio. He found, however, that he was held fast from behind. An officer of the Papal guard had stopped him, and said in a serious voice, "Recollect where you are, Signor Pasquale; you are in Nicolo Musso's theatre. Without intending it, you have played a most ridiculous role today. You will not find either Antonio or Marianna here."

The two persons whom Capuzzi had taken for his niece and her lover now drew near, along with the rest of the actors. The faces were all completely strange to him. His rapier fell from his trembling hand; he took a deep breath as if awakening out of a bad dream; he grasped his brow with both hands; he opened his eyes wide. The presentiment of what had happened suddenly struck him, and he shouted, "Marianna!" in such a stentorian voice that the walls rang.

But she was beyond reach of his shouts. Antonio had taken advantage of the opportunity while Pasquale, oblivious of everything around him and even of himself, was quarrelling with his double, to make his way to Marianna, and escape with her through the audience, and out a side door, where a carriage stood ready waiting; and away they went as fast as their horses could gallop towards Florence.

"Marianna!" screamed the old man again, "Marianna! she is gone. She has fled. That knave Antonio has stolen her from me. Away! after them! Have pity on me, good people, and take torches and help me look for my little darling. Oh! you serpent!"

He tried to make for the door. But the officer held him fast, saying, "Do you mean that pretty young lady who sat beside you? I believe I saw her slip out with a young man—I think Antonio Scacciati—a long time ago, when you began your silly quarrel with one of the actors who wore a mask like your face. You needn't make trouble about it; every inquiry shall at once be set on foot, and Marianna shall be brought back to you as soon as she is found. But as for yourself, Signor Pasquale, your behaviour here and your murderous attempt on the life of that actor compel me to arrest you."

Signor Pasquale, his face as pale as death, incapable of uttering a single word or even a sound, was led away by the very same gendarmes who were to have protected him against masked devils and spectres. Thus it came to pass that on the selfsame night on which he had hoped to celebrate his triumph, he was plunged into the midst of trouble and all the frantic despondency which amorous old fools feel when they are deceived.

VI

Everything here below beneath the sun is subject to continual change; and perhaps there is nothing which can be called more inconstant than opinion, which turns round in an everlasting circle like the wheel of fortune. He who reaps great praise today is overwhelmed with biting censure tomorrow; today we trample under foot the man who tomorrow will be raised far above us.

Of all those who in Rome had ridiculed and mocked at old Pasquale Capuzzi, with his sordid avarice, his foolish amorousness, his insane jealousy, was there one who did not wish poor tormented Marianna her liberty? But now that Antonio had successfully carried off his mistress, all their ridicule and mockery was suddenly changed into pity for the old fool, whom they saw wandering about the streets of Rome with his head hanging on his breast, utterly disconsolate. Misfortunes seldom come singly; and so it happened that Signor Pasquale, soon after Marianna had been taken from him, lost his best bosom friends also. Little Pitichinaccio choked himself in foolishly trying to swallow an almond in the middle of a cadenza; and a sudden stop was put to the life of the illustrious Pyramid Doctor Signor Splendiano Accoramboni by a slip of the pen, for which he had only himself to blame. Michele's drubbing made such work with him that he fell into a fever. He determined to make use of a remedy which he claimed to have discovered, so, calling for pen and ink, he wrote down a prescription in which, by employing a wrong sign, he increased the quantity of a powerful substance to a dangerous extent. Scarcely had he swallowed the medicine than he sank back on the pillows and died, establishing, however, by his own death in the most splendid and satisfactory manner the efficacy of the last tincture which he ever prescribed.

As already remarked, those who had laughed loudest and who had repeatedly wished Antonio success in his schemes, had now nothing but pity for the old gentleman; and the bitterest blame was heaped, not so much upon Antonio, as upon Salvator Rosa, whom, to be sure, they regarded as the instigator of the whole plan.

Salvator's enemies, who were many, exerted all their efforts to fan the flame. "You see," they said, "he was one of Masaniello's cutthroats, and he is ready to turn his hand to any deed of mischief, to any disreputable enterprise; we shall be the next to suffer from his presence in the city; he is a dangerous man."

And the jealous faction who had leagued together against Salvator actually did succeed in stemming the tide of his prosperous career. He produced one remarkable picture after another, all bold in conception, and splendidly executed; but the so-called critics shrugged their shoulders, now pointing out that the hills were too blue, the trees too green, the figures now too long, now too broad, finding fault everywhere where there was no fault to be found, and seeking to detract from his hard-earned reputation in all the ways they could think of. Especially bitter in their persecution of him were the Academicians of San Luca, who could not forget how he had taken them in with the surgeon; they even went beyond the limits of their own profession, and decried the clever stanzas which Salvator at that time wrote, hinting very plainly that he did not cultivate his own fruit but plundered that of his neighbours. For these reasons, therefore, Salvator could not regain the splendor, which he had formerly enjoyed in Rome. Instead of being visited by the most eminent Romans in a large studio, he had to remain with Signora Caterina and his green fig-tree; but amid these poor surroundings he sometimes found both consolation and tranquility of mind.

Salvator took the malicious machinations of his enemies to heart more than he should have; he even began to feel that an insidious disease, resulting from chagrin and dejection, was gnawing at his vitals. In this unhappy frame of mind he designed and executed two large pictures which caused quite an uproar in Rome. Of these one represented the transitoriness of all earthly things, and in the principal figure, that of a wanton female bearing all the indications of her degrading calling, was recognizable the mistress of one of the cardinals; the other portrayed the Goddess of Fortune dispensing her rich gifts. But cardinals' hats, bishops' mitres, gold medals, decorations of orders, were falling upon bleating sheep, braying asses, and other such contemptible animals, while well-made men in ragged clothes were vainly straining their eyes upwards to get even the smallest gift. Salvator had given free rein to his embittered mood, and the animals' heads bore the closest resemblance to the features of various eminent persons. It is easy to imagine, therefore, that the tide of hatred against him rose; and he was more bitterly persecuted than ever.

Signora Caterina warned him, with tears in her eyes, that as soon as it began to be dark suspicious characters were beginning to lurk about the house, apparently dogging his every footstep. Salvator saw that it was time to leave Rome; and Signora Caterina and her beloved daughters were the only people whom it caused him pain to part from.

In response to the repeated invitations of the Duke of Tuscany, he went to Florence; and here at length he was richly paid for all the mortification and worry which he had had to struggle against in Rome, and here all the honour and all the fame which he so truly deserved were freely conferred upon him. The Duke's presents and the high prices which he received for his pictures soon enabled him to remove into a large house and to furnish it in the most magnificent style. There he gathered around him the most illustrious authors and scholars of the day, among whom it will be sufficient to mention Evangelista Toricelli, Valerio Chimentelli, Battista Ricciardi, Andrea Cavalcanti, Pietro Salvati, Filippo Apolloni, Volumnio Bandelli, Francesco Rovai. They formed an association for the prosecution of artistic and scientific pursuits, while Salvator was able to contribute an element of whimsicality to the meetings, which had a singular effect in animating and enlivening the mind. The banqueting hall was like a beautiful grove with fragrant bushes and flowers and splashing fountains; and the dishes even, which were served up by pages in eccentric costumes, were very wonderful to look at, as if they came from some distant land of magic. These meetings of writers and savants in Salvator Rosa's house were called at that time the Accademia de' Percossi.

Though Salvator's mind was in this way devoted to science and art, yet his real true nature came to life again when he met with his friend Antonio Scacciati, who, along with his lovely Marianna, led the pleasant carefree life of an artist. They often recalled poor old Signor Pasquale whom they had deceived, and all that had taken place in Nicolo Musso's theatre.

Antonio once asked Salvator how he had contrived to enlist in his cause the active interest not only of Musso but of the excellent Formica, and of Agli too. Salvator replied that it had been very easy, for Formica was his most intimate friend in Rome, so that it had been a work of both pleasure and love to arrange everything on the stage in accordance with the instructions Salvator gave him. Antonio protested that, though still he could not help laughing over the scene which had paved the way to his happiness, he yet wished with all his heart to be reconciled to the old man, even if he never touched a penny of Marianna's fortune, which the old gentleman had confiscated; the practice of his art brought him in a sufficient income. Marianna too was often unable to restrain her tears when she thought that her father's brother might go to his grave without having forgiven her the trick which she had played upon him; and so Pasquale's hatred overshadowed like a dark cloud the brightness of their happiness. Salvator comforted them both—Antonio and Marianna—by saying that time had adjusted still worse difficulties, and that chance would perhaps bring the old gentleman near them in some less dangerous way than if they had remained in Rome, or were to return there now.

We shall see that a prophetic spirit spoke in Salvator.

A considerable time had elapsed, when one day Antonio burst into Salvator's studio breathless and pale as death. "Salvator!" he cried, "Salvator, my friend, my protector! I am lost if you do not help me. Pasquale Capuzzi is here; he has procured a warrant for my arrest for seducing his niece."

"What can Signor Pasquale do against you now?" asked Salvator. "Haven't you been married to Marianna by the Church?"

"Oh!" replied Antonio, giving way completely to despair, "the blessing of the Church herself cannot save me from ruin. Heaven knows by what means the old man has been able to approach the Pope's nephew. At any rate the Pope's nephew has taken the old man under his protection, and has given him hope that the Holy Father will declare my marriage with Marianna to be null and void; and more, that he will grant him (the old man) dispensation to marry his niece."

"Stop!" cried Salvator, "now I see it all; now I see it all. What threatens to be your ruin, Antonio, is this man's hatred against me. For I must tell you that this nephew of the Pope's, a proud, coarse, boorish clown, was among the animals in my picture to whom the Goddess of Fortune is dispensing her gifts. That it was I who helped you to win Marianna, though indirectly, is well known, not only to this man, but to all Rome—which is quite reason enough to persecute you since they cannot do anything to me. And so, Antonio, having brought this misfortune on you, I must make every effort to assist you, all the more since you are my dearest and most intimate friend. But, by the saints! I don't see in what way I can frustrate your enemies' little game—"

Therewith Salvator, who had continued to paint at a picture all the time, laid aside brush, palette, and maul-stick, and, rising from his easel, began to pace the room backwards and forwards, his arms crossed over his breast, Antonio meanwhile being quite wrapt up in his own thoughts, with his eyes fixed upon the floor.

At length Salvator paused before him and said with a smile, "See here, Antonio, I cannot do anything myself against your powerful enemies, but I know a man who can help you, and who will help you, and that is—Signor Formica."

"Oh!" said Antonio, "don't joke with an unhappy man, whom nothing can save."

"What! you are despairing again?" exclaimed Salvator, who was now suddenly in the merriest humour, and he laughed aloud. "I tell you, Antonio, my friend Formica shall help you in Florence just as he helped you in Rome. Go quietly home and comfort your Marianna, and calmly wait and see how things turn out. I trust you will be ready at the shortest notice to do what Signor Formica, who is really here in Florence at the present time, shall require of you." This Antonio promised most faithfully, and hope revived in him again, and confidence.

Signor Pasquale Capuzzi was not a little astonished at receiving a formal invitation from the Accademia de' Percossi. "Ah!" he exclaimed, "Florence is the place then where a man's merits are recognized, where Pasquale Capuzzi di Senigaglia, a man gifted with the most excellent talents, is known and valued." Thus the thought of his knowledge and his art, and the honour that was shown him on their account, overcame the hatred which he would otherwise have felt against a society at the head of which stood Salvator Rosa. His Spanish gala-dress was more carefully brushed than ever; his conical hat was equipped with a new feather; his shoes were provided with new ribbons; and so Signor Pasquale appeared at Salvator's as brilliant as an iridescent beetle, his face all sunshine. The magnificence which he saw on all sides of him, even Salvator himself, who had received him dressed in the richest apparel, inspired him with deep respect, and, after the manner of little souls, who, though at first proud and puffed up, immediately grovel in the dust whenever they come into contact with what they feel to be superior to themselves, Pasquale's behaviour towards Salvator, whom he would gladly have done a mischief to in Rome, was nothing but humility and submissive deference.

So much attention was paid to Signor Pasquale from all sides, his judgment was appealed to so unconditionally, and so much was said about his services to art, that he felt new life infused into his veins; and an unusual spirit was awakened within him, so that his utterances on many points were more sensible than might have been expected. If it be added that never in his life before had he been so splendidly entertained, and never had he drunk such inspiriting wine, it will readily be conceived that his pleasure was intensified from moment to moment, and that he forgot all the wrong which had been done him at Rome as well as the unpleasant business which had brought him to Florence. Often after their banquets the Academicians used to amuse themselves with short impromptu dramatic representations, and this evening the distinguished playwright and poet Filippo Apolloni called upon those who generally took part in them to bring the festivities to a fitting conclusion with one of their usual performances. Salvator at once withdrew to make all the necessary preparations.

Not long afterwards the bushes at the farther end of the banquet hall began to move, the branches with their foliage were parted, and a little theatre provided with seats for the spectators became visible.

"By the saints!" exclaimed Pasquale Capuzzi, terrified, "where am I? Surely that's Nicolo Musso's theatre."

Without heeding his exclamation, Evangelista Toricelli and Andrea Cavalcanti—both of them grave, respectable, venerable men—took him by the arm and led him to a seat immediately in front of the stage, taking their places on each side of him.

This was no sooner done that there appeared on the boards— Formica in the character of Pasquarello.

"You dirty scoundrel, Formica!" shouted Pasquale, leaping to his feet and shaking his doubled fist at the stage. Toricelli and Cavalcanti's stern, reproving glances bade him sit still and keep quiet.

Pasquarello wept and sobbed, and cursed his destiny, which brought him nothing but grief and heartbreak, declaring he didn't know how he should ever set about it if he wanted to laugh again. He concluded by saying that if he could look upon blood without fainting, he should certainly cut his throat, or should throw himself in the Tiber if he could only stop that cursed swimming when he got into the water.

Doctor Gratiano now joined him and inquired what was the cause of his trouble.

Whereupon Pasquarello asked him whether he did not know anything about what had taken place in the house of his master, Signor Pasquale Capuzzi di Senigaglia, whether he did not know that an infamous scoundrel had carried off pretty Marianna, his master's niece?

"Ah!" murmured Capuzzi, "I see you want to make your excuses to me, Formica; you wish for my pardon—well, we shall see."

Dr. Gratiano expressed his sympathy, and observed that the scoundrel must have gone to work very cunningly to have eluded all the inquiries which had been instituted by Capuzzi.

"Ho! ho!" rejoined Pasquarello. "The doctor need not imagine that the scoundrel, Antonio Scacciati, had succeeded in escaping the sharpness of Signor Pasquale Capuzzi who was supported by powerful friends. Antonio had been arrested, his marriage with Marianna annulled, and Marianna herself had again come into Capuzzi's power."

"Has he got her again?" shouted Capuzzi, beside himself; "has he got her again, good Pasquale? Has he got his little darling, his Marianna? Is the scoundrel Antonio arrested? Heaven bless you, Formica!"

"You take a too keen interest in the play, Signor Pasquale," said Cavalcanti gravely. "Pray permit the actors to proceed with their parts without interrupting them in this disturbing fashion."

Ashamed of himself, Signor Pasquale resumed his seat, for he had again risen to his feet.

Dr. Gratiano asked what had taken place then.

A wedding, continued Pasquarello, a wedding had taken place. Marianna had repented of what she had done; Signor Pasquale had obtained the desired dispensation from the Holy Father, and had married his niece.

"Yes, yes," murmured Pasquale Capuzzi to himself, whilst his eyes sparkled with delight, "yes, yes, my dear, good Formica; he will marry his sweet Marianna, the happy Pasquale. He knew that the dear little darling had always loved him, and that it was only Satan who had led her astray."

"Why then, everything is all right," said Dr. Gratiano, "and there's no cause for lamentation."

Pasquarello began, however, to weep and sob more violently than before, till at length, as if overcome by the terrible nature of his pain, he fainted away. Dr. Gratiano ran backwards and forwards in great distress, was so sorry he had no smelling salts with him, felt in all his pockets, and at last produced a roasted chestnut, and put it under the insensible Pasquarello's nose. Pasquarello immediately recovered, sneezing violently, and attributing his faintness to his weak nerves, he related that immediately after the marriage Marianna had been afflicted with the saddest melancholy, continually calling upon Antonio, and treating the old gentleman with contempt and aversion. But the old fellow, quite infatuated by his passion and jealousy, had not ceased to torment the poor girl with his folly in the most abominable way. And here Pasquarello mentioned a host of mad tricks which Pasquale had done, and which were really widely known in Rome. Signor Capuzzi sat on thorns; he murmured at intervals, "Curse you, Formica! You are lying! What evil spirit is in you?" He was only prevented from bursting out into a violent passion by Toricelli and Cavalcanti, who sat watching him with earnest gaze.

Pasquarello concluded his narration by saying that Marianna had at last succumbed to her unsatisfied longing for her lover, her great distress of mind, and the innumerable tortures which were inflicted upon her by the execrable old fellow, and had died in the flower of her youth.

At this moment was heard a mournful *De profundis* sung by hollow, husky voices, and men clad in long black robes appeared on the stage, bearing an open coffin, within which was seen the corpse of lovely Marianna wrapped in white shrouds. Behind it came Signor Pasquale Capuzzi in the deepest mourning, feebly staggering along and wailing aloud, beating his breast, and crying in a voice of despair, "O Marianna! Marianna!"

So soon as the real Capuzzi caught sight of his niece's corpse he broke out into loud lamentations, and both Capuzzis, the one of the stage and the one off, gave vent to their grief in the most heart-rending wails and groans, "O Marianna! O Marianna! O unhappy me! Alas! Alas for me!"

Let the reader picture to himself the open coffin with the corpse of the lovely girl, surrounded by the hired mourners singing their dismal *De profundis* in hoarse voices, and then the comical masks of Pasquarello and Dr. Gratiano, who were expressing their grief in the most ridiculous gestures, and lastly the two Capuzzis, wailing and screeching in despair. Indeed, everyone who witnessed the extra-ordinary spectacle could not help feeling, even in the midst of the unrestrained laughter they had burst out into at sight of the mar-vellous actor who portrayed Capuzzi, that their hearts were chilled by a most uncomfortable feeling of awe.

Now the stage grew dark, and there was thunder and lightning. A pale ghostly figure, which bore most unmistakably the features of Capuzzi's dead brother, Pietro of Senigaglia, Marianna's father, rose seemingly from the ground.

"O you infamous brother, Pasquale! what have you done with my daughter? what have you done with my daughter?" wailed the figure, in a dreadful and hollow voice. "Despair, you atrocious murderer of my child. You shall find your reward in hell."

Capuzzi on the stage dropped on the floor as if struck by lightning, and at the same moment the real Capuzzi reeled from his seat un-conscious. The bushes rustled together again, and the stage was gone, and also Marianna and Capuzzi and the ghastly spectre Pietro. Signor Pasquale Capuzzi lay in such a dead faint that it cost a good deal of trouble to revive him.

At length he came to himself with a deep sigh, and stretching out both hands before him as if to ward off the horror that had seized him, he cried in a husky voice, "Leave me alone, Pietro." Then a torrent of tears ran down his cheeks, and he sobbed and cried, "Oh! Marianna, my darling child—my—my Marianna." "But recollect yourself," said Cavalcanti, "recollect yourself, Signor Pasquale, it was only on the stage that you saw your niece dead. She is alive; she is here to crave pardon for the thoughtless step which love and also your own inconsiderate conduct drove her to take."

And Marianna, and behind her Antonio Scacciati, now ran for-ward from the back part of the hall and threw themselves at the old gentleman's feet—for he had meanwhile been placed in an easy chair. Marianna, looking most charming and beautiful, kissed his hands and bathed them with tears, beseeching him to pardon both her and Antonio, to whom she had been united by the blessing of the Church.

Suddenly the hot blood surged into the old man's pallid face, fury flashed from his eyes, and he cried in half-choked voice, "Oh! you abominable scoundrel! You poisonous serpent whom I nourished in my bosom!" Then old Toricelli, with grave and thoughtful dignity, put himself in front of Capuzzi, and told him that he (Capuzzi) had seen a representation of the fate that would inevitably and irremediably overtake him if he had the hardihood to carry out his wicked purpose against Antonio and Marianna's peace and happiness. He depicted in startling colours the folly and madness of amorous old men, who call down upon their own heads the most ruinous mischief which Heaven can inflict upon a man, since all the love which might have fallen to their share is lost, and instead hatred and contempt shoot their fatal darts at them from every side.

At intervals lovely Marianna cried in a tone that went to everybody's heart, "O my uncle, I will love and honour you as my own father; you will kill me by a cruel death if you rob me of my Antonio." And all the eminent men by whom the old gentleman was surrounded cried with one accord that it would not be possible for a man like Signor Pasquale Capuzzi di Senigaglia, a patron of art and himself an artist, not to forgive the young people, and assume the part of father to the most lovely of ladies, not possible that he could refuse to accept with joy as his son-in-law such an artist as Antonio Scacciati, who was highly esteemed throughout all Italy and richly crowned with fame and honour.

Then it was patent to see that a violent struggle went on within the old gentleman. He sighed, moaned, clasped his hands before his face, and, while Toricelli was continuing to speak in a most impressive manner, and Marianna was appealing to him in the most touching accents, and the rest were extolling Antonio all they knew how, he kept looking down—now upon his niece, now upon Antonio, whose splendid clothes and rich chains of honour bore testimony to the truth of what was said about the artistic fame he had earned.

All rage left Capuzzi's countenance; he sprang up with radiant eyes, and pressed Marianna to his heart, saying, "Yes, I forgive you, my dear child; I forgive you, Antonio. Far be it from me to disturb your happiness. You are right, my worthy Signor Toricelli;

Formica has shown me in the tableau on the stage all the mischief and ruin that would have befallen me had I carried out my insane design. I am cured, quite cured of my folly. But where is Signor Formica, where is my good physician? let me thank him a thousand times for my cure; it is he alone who has accomplished it. The terror that he has caused me to feel has brought about a complete revolution within me."

Pasquarello stepped forward. Antonio threw himself upon his neck, crying, "O Signor Formica, you to whom I owe my life, my all—oh! take off your mask, so that I may see your face, so that Formica will not be any longer a mystery to me."

Pasquarello took off his cap and his mask, which looked like a natural face, since it offered not the slightest hindrance to the play of countenance, and Formica, Pasquarello, was transformed into— Salvator Rosa.

"Salvator!" exclaimed Marianna, Antonio, and Capuzzi, utterly astounded.

"Yes," said that wonderful man, "it is Salvator Rosa, whom the Romans would not recognize as painter and poet, but who in the character of Formica drew from them almost every evening for more than a year, in Nicolo Musso's wretched little theatre, the most noisy and most demonstrative storms of applause, from whose mouth they willingly took all the scorn, and all the satiric mockery of what is bad, which they would on no account listen to and see in Salvator's poems and pictures. It is Salvator Formica who has helped you, Antonio."

"Salvator," began old Capuzzi, "Salvator Rosa, I have always regarded you as my worst enemy; yet I have always prized your artistic skill very highly; and now I love you as the worthiest friend I have, and beg you to accept my friendship in return."

"Tell me," replied Salvator, "tell me, my worthy Signor Pasquale, what service I can render you, and accept my assurances beforehand, that I will leave no stone unturned to accomplish whatever you may ask of me."

And now the genial smile which had not been seen upon Capuzzi's face since Marianna had been carried off, began to steal back again. Taking Salvator's hand he lisped in a low voice, "My dear Signor Salvator, you possess an unlimited influence over good Antonio; beseech him in my name to permit me to spend my few remaining days with him, and my dear daughter Marianna, and to accept at my hands the inheritance left her by her mother, as well as the good dowry which I was thinking of adding to it. And he must not look jealous if I occasionally kiss her white hand; and ask him—every Sunday at least when I go to Mass, to trim my rough mustache, for there's nobody in all the world understands it as well as he does."

It cost Salvator an effort to repress his laughter at the strange old man; but before he could make any reply, Antonio and Marianna, embracing the old gentleman, assured him that they should not believe he was fully reconciled to them, and should not be really happy, until he came to live with them as their dear father, never to leave them again. Antonio added that not only on Sunday, but every other day, he would trim Capuzzi's mustache as elegantly as he knew how, and accordingly the old gentleman was perfectly radiant with delight. Meanwhile a splendid supper had been prepared, to which the entire company now turned in the best of spirits.

In taking my leave of you, beloved reader, I wish with all my heart that, while you have been reading the story of the wonderful Signor Formica, you have derived as much pure pleasure from it as Salvator and all his friends felt on sitting down to their supper.

THE KING'S BETROTHED

It was a blessed year. In the fields the corn, the wheat and the barley were growing most gloriously. The boys waded in the grass, and the cattle in the clover. The trees hung so full of cherries that a whole army of sparrows, though determined to peck everything bare, were forced to leave half the fruit for a future feast. Every creature filled itself full every day at the great guest table of nature. Above all, however, the vegetables in Herr Dapsul von Zabelthau's kitchen garden had turned out to be such a splendid and beautiful crop that it was no wonder Fräulein Aennchen was unable to contain herself with joy on the subject.

This would be a good place to explain who Herr Dapsul von Zabelthau and Aennchen were.

Perhaps, dear reader, at some time or other you have found yourself in that beautiful country which is watered by the pleasant, kindly river Main. Soft morning breezes breathe their perfumed breath over the plain as it shimmers in the golden splendour of the newly risen sun. It is so beautiful that you cannot stand being cooped up in your stuffy carriage, and you alight and wander into the little grove, through the trees of which, as you descend towards the valley, you come in sight of a little village. And as you stand gazing, there suddenly comes toward you, through the trees, a tall, lanky man, whose strange dress and appearance rivet your attention. He wears a small gray felt hat on top of a black periwig; all his clothes are gray—coat, vest, breeches, stockings—even his walking stick. He comes towards you with long swinging strides, seemingly unaware of your existence, and almost runs you down. "Good morning, sir!" you cry, whereupon like a man startled out of a dream, he replies "Good morning." In a moment he adds, "Oh, sir, how thankful we ought to be that we have a good, fine morning. The poor people at Santa Cruz have just had two earthquakes, and now—at this moment—rain is falling in torrents." While you have been thinking what to reply to this strange creature, he, with an "Allow me, sir," gently passes his hand across your brow, and inspects the palm of your hand.   And saying, in the same melancholy accents as before, "God bless you, sir!   You have a favorable constellation," he goes striding on his way.

This odd personage was none other than Herr Dapsul von Zabelthau, whose sole—rather miserable—possession is the village, or hamlet, of Dapsulheim, which lies before you in this most pleasant and smiling country which you are now entering.   You are looking forward to something in the shape of breakfast, but in the little inn things have a rather gloomy aspect.   Its small store of provisions was cleaned out at the fair, and as you can't be expected to be content with nothing but milk, they tell you to go to the Manor House, where the gracious Fräulein Anna will entertain you hospitably with whatever is available there.   Accordingly, you betake yourself there without further ceremony.

Concerning this Manor House, there is nothing further to be said than that it has doors and windows, like that of Baron Tonderton-tonk in Westphalia.   But above the hall door the family coat-of-arms, carved in wood with a skill that would do credit to a native New Zealander, makes a fine show.   And this Manor House derives a peculiar character of its own from the circumstances that its north side looks upon the enceinte, or outer line of a defense belonging to an old ruined castle, so that the back entrance is what was formerly the castle gate, and through it one passes at once into the courtyard of that castle, in the middle of which the tall watchtower still stands undamaged.

From the hall door, above which is the coat-of-arms, a red-cheeked young lady comes to meet you; with her clear blue eyes and fair hair she might be called very pretty indeed, although her figure may be considered just the least bit too roundly substantial.   A personification of friendly kindliness, she begs you to go in, and as soon as she ascertains your wants, serves you up the most delicious milk, a liberal allowance of first-rate bread and butter, uncooked ham—as good as you would find in Bayonne—and a small glass of beet brandy.   Meanwhile, this young lady, who is none other than Fräulein Anna von Zabelthau, talks to you gaily and pleasantly of rural matters, displaying anything but a limited knowledge of such subjects.   Suddenly, however, there resounds a loud and terrible voice, as if from the skies, crying "Anna, Anna, Anna!"   This rather startles you, but Fräulein Anna says pleasantly, "There's papa back from his walk, calling from his study for his breakfast." "Calling from his study," you repeat, or enquire, astonished.

"Yes," says Fräulein Anna, or Fräulein Aennchen, as the people call her. "Yes; papa's study is up in the tower there, and he calls down through the speaking trumpet." And you see Aennchen open the narrow door of the old tower, with a *dejeuner à la fourchette* similar to that which you have had yourself—namely, a liberal helping of bread and ham, not forgetting the brandy—and go briskly in. But she is back directly, and taking you around the charming kitchen garden, has so much to say about feather leaf, rampion, English turnips, Little Green Heading, Montrue, Great Mogul, Yellow Prince's Head, and so forth, that you would have no idea that all these fine names merely mean various cabbages and salad greens.

I think, dear reader, that this little glimpse which you have had of Dapsulheim is sufficient to enable you to understand all the outs and ins of the establishment, concerning which I have to narrate to you all sorts of extraordinary, barely comprehensible matters and occurrences. Herr Dapsul von Zabelthau had during his youth very rarely left his parents' castle. They had been people of considerable means. His tutor, a strange, elderly man, after teaching him foreign languages, particularly those of the East, fostered his natural inclination to mysticism, or more exactly, occultism. This tutor died, leaving to young Dapsul as a legacy a whole library of the hidden sciences, into the very depths of which he proceeded to plunge. His parents dying, he betook himself to long journeyings, and (as his tutor had impressed him with the necessity of doing) to Egypt and India. When he got home again after many years, a cousin had looked after his affairs with such zeal that there was nothing left but the little hamlet of Dapsulheim. Herr Dapsul was too eagerly occupied in the pursuit of sun-born gold of a higher sphere to trouble himself about earthly things. He rather felt obliged to his cousin for preserving for him pleasant, friendly Dapsulheim, with its fine, tall tower, which had been built for astrological operations. In the upper story he at once established his study.

This careful cousin now pointed out that Herr Dapsul von Zabelthau was bound to marry. Dapsul immediately admitted the necessity, and without more ado at once married the lady whom his cousin had selected for him. This lady disappeared almost as quickly as she had appeared on the scene. She died, after bearing him a daughter. The cousin attended to the marriage, the baptism, and the funeral; so that Dapsul, up in his tower, paid very little attention to any of it. For there was a very remarkable comet visible most of this time, and Dapsul, ever melancholy and anticipative of evil, considered that he was involved in its influence.

His little daughter, under the careful upbringing of an old grandaunt, developed a remarkable aptitude for rural affairs. She had to begin at the very beginning, and, so to speak, rise from the ranks, serving successively as goose-girl, maid-of-all-work, upper farm-maid, housekeeper, and finally, as mistress, so that Theory was all along illustrated and impressed upon her mind by a salutary share of Practice. She was exceedingly fond of ducks and geese, hens and pigeons, and even the tender broods of well-shaped piglings she was by no means indifferent to, though she did not put a ribbon and a bell round a little white sucking pig's neck and make it into a sort of lapdog, as a certain young lady, in another place, was once known to do.

But more than anything—more than even to the fruit-trees— she was devoted to the kitchen garden. From her grandaunt's attainments in this line she had derived very remarkable theoretical knowledge of vegetable culture (which the reader has seen for himself), as regarded digging of the ground, sowing the seed, and setting the plants. Fräulein Aennchen not only superintended all these operations, but lent most valuable manual aid. She wielded a most vigorous spade—her bitterest enemy would have admitted this. So that while Herr Dapsul von Zabelthau was immersed in astrological observations and other important matters, Fräulein Aennchen carried on the management of the place in the ablest possible manner, Dapsul looking after the celestial part of the business, and Aennchen managing the terrestrial side of things with unceasing vigilance and care.

As above said, it was small wonder that Aennchen was almost beside herself with delight at the magnificence of the yield which this season had produced in the kitchen garden. But the carrot bed was what surpassed everything else in the garden in its promise.

"Oh, my dear, beautiful carrots!" cried Anna over and over again, and she clapped her hands, danced, and jumped about, and conducted herself like a child who has been given a grand Christmas present.

And indeed it seemed as though the carrot-children underground were taking part in Aennchen's gladness, for some extremely delicate laughter, which just made itself heard, was undoubtedly proceeding from the carrot bed. Aennchen, however, didn't pay much heed to it, but ran to meet one of the farm men who was coming, holding up a letter, and calling out to her, "For you, Fräulein Aennchen. Gottlieb brought it from the town."

Aennchen saw immediately from the handwriting that it was from none other than young Herr Amandus von Nebelstern, the son of a neighbouring proprietor, now at the university. During the time when he was living at home, and in the habit of running over to Dapsulheim every day, Amandus had arrived at the conviction that all his life he never could love anybody except Aennchen. Similarly, Aennchen was perfectly certain that she could never really care the least bit about anybody else but this brown-locked Amandus. Thus both Aennchen and Amandus had come to the conclusion and arrangement that they were to be married as soon as they could— the sooner the better—and be the very happiest married couple in the wide world.

Amandus had at one time been a bright enough natural sort of lad, but at the university he had got into the hands of god knows whom, and had been induced to fancy himself a marvellous poetical genius, and to indulge himself to an extreme amount of absurd extravagance in expression of ideas. He carried this so far that he soon soared far away beyond everything which prosaic idiots term Sense and Reason (maintaining at the same time, as they do, that both are perfectly coexistent with the utmost liveliness of imagination).

It was from this young Amandus that the letter came which Aennchen opened and read, as follows:—

Heavenly Maiden—
Dost thou see, dost thou feel, dost thou not image and figure to thyself, thy Amandus, how, circumambiated by the orange-flower-laden breath of the dewy evening, he is lying on his back in the grass, gazing heavenward with eyes filled with the holiest love and the most longing adoration? The thyme and the lavender, the rose and the gilliflower, as also the yellow-eyed narcissus and the shame-faced violet—he weaveth into garlands. And the flowers are love-thoughts—thoughts of thee, oh Anna! But doth feeble prose beseem inspired lips? Listen! oh, listen how I can only love, and speak of my love, sonnetically!

Love flames aloft in thousand eager sunspheres,
   Joy wooeth joy within the heart so warmly:
   Down from the darkling sky soft stars are shining,
Back-mirrored from the deep, still wells of love-tears.

Delight, alas! doth die of joy too burning—
   The sweetest fruit hath aye the bitt'rest kernel—
   While longing beckons from the violet distance,
In pain of love my heart to dust is turning.

In fiery billows' rage the ocean surges,
  Yet the bold swimmer dares the plunge full arduous,
  And soon amid the waves his strong course urges.

And on the shore, now near, the jacinth shoots:
  The faithful heart holds firm: 'twill bleed to death;
  But heart's blood is the sweetest of all roots.

Oh, Anna! when thou readest this sonnet of all sonnets, may all the heavenly rapture permeate thee in which all my being was dissolved when I wrote it down, and then read it out, to kindred minds, conscious, like myself, of life's highest. Think, oh, think! sweet maiden of

Thy faithful, enraptured,
  Amandus von Nebelstern.

P.S.—Don't forget, oh, sublime maiden! when answering this, to send a pound or two of that Virginia tobacco which you grow yourself. It burns splendidly, and has a far better flavour than the Porto Rico which the Bürschen smoke when they go to the Kneipe.

Fräulein Aennchen pressed the letter to her lips, and said, "Oh, how dear, how beautiful! And the darling verses, rhyming so beautifully. Oh, if I were only clever enough to understand it all; but I suppose nobody can do that but a student. I wonder what that about the 'roots' means? I suppose it must be the long red English carrots, or, who knows, it may be the rampion."

That very day Fräulein Aennchen made it her business to pack up the tobacco, and she took a dozen of her finest goose quills to the schoolmaster, to get him to make them into pens. Her intention was to sit down at once and begin her answer to the precious letter. As she was going out of the kitchen garden, she was again followed by a very faint almost imperceptible sound of delicate laughter; and if she had paid a little attention to what was going on, she would have been sure to hear a little delicate voice saying, "Pull me, pull me! I am ripe—ripe—ripe!" However, as we have said, she paid no attention, and did not hear this.

II

Herr Dapsul von Zabelthau generally came down from his astronomical tower about noon, to partake of a frugal repast with his daughter, which usually lasted a very short time, and during which there was generally a great predominance of silence, for Dapsul did not like to talk. And Aennchen did not trouble him by speaking much, and this all the more for the reason that if her papa did actually begin to talk, he would come out with all sorts of curious unintelligible nonsense, which made a body's head giddy. This day, however, her head was so full, and her mind so excited and taken up with the flourishing state of the kitchen garden, and the letter from her beloved Amandus, that she talked of both subjects incessantly, mixed up, without leaving off. At last Herr Dapsul von Zabelthau laid down his knife and fork, stopped his ears with his hands, and cried out, "Oh, damn this empty gabbling!"

Aennchen stopped, alarmed, and he went on to say, in the melancholy sustained tones which were characteristic of him, "With regard to the vegetables, my dear daughter, I have long been cognizant that the manner in which the stars have worked together this season has been eminently favourable to those growths, and the earthly man will be amply supplied with cabbage, radishes, and lettuce, so that the earthly matter may duly increase and withstand the fire of the world-spirit, like a properly kneaded pot. The gnomic principle will resist the attacks of the salamander, and I shall have the enjoyment of eating the parsnips which you cook so well. With regard to young Amandus von Nebelstern, I have not the slightest objection to your marrying him as soon as he comes back from the university. Simply send Gottlieb up to tell me when your marriage is going to take place, so that I may go with you to the church."

Herr Dapsul kept silence for a few seconds, and then, without looking at Aennchen, whose face was glowing with delight, he went on, smiling and striking his glass with his fork (two things which he seldom did at all, though he always did them together) to say, "Your Amandus is a man who has to, must do something— that is to say, a gerund. I shall merely tell you, my dear Aennchen, that I drew up his horoscope a long while ago. His constellation is favourable enough on the whole. He has Jupiter in the ascending node, Venus regarding in the sextile. The trouble is, that the path of Sirius cuts across, and just at the point of intersection, there is a great danger from which Amandus delivers his betrothed. The danger—what it is—is undiscoverable, because some strange being, which appears to set at defiance all astrological science, seems to be concerned in it. At the same time, it is evident and certain that it is only the strange physical condition which mankind terms craziness, or mental derangement, which will enable Amandus to accomplish this deliverance. Oh, my daughter!" (here Herr Dapsul fell again into his usual pathetic tones), "may no mysterious power, which keeps itself hidden from my seer-eyes, come suddenly across your path, so that young Amandus von Nebelstern may not have to rescue you from any other danger but that of being an old maid." He sighed several times consecutively, and then continued, "But the path of Sirius breaks off abruptly after this danger, and Venus and Jupiter, divided before, come together again, reconciled."

Herr Dapsul von Zabelthau had not spoken so much for years as on this occasion. He arose exhausted, and went back up into his tower.

Aennchen had her answer to Herr von Nebelstern ready in good time next morning. It was as follows:—

My Own Dearest Amandus—

You cannot believe what joy your letter has given me. I have told papa about it, and he has promised to go to church with us when we're married. Be sure to come back from the university as soon as ever you can. Oh! if I only could *quite* understand your darling verses, which rhyme so beautifully. When I read them to myself aloud they sound wonderful, and *then* I think I *do* understand them quite well. But soon everything grows confused, and seems to get away from me, and I feel as if I had been reading a lot of mere words that somehow don't belong to each other at all. The schoolmaster says this must be so, and that it's the new fashionable way of speaking. But, you see, I'm—oh, well!—I'm only a stupid, foolish creature. Please to write and tell me if I couldn't be a student for a little time, without neglecting my housework. I suppose that couldn't be, though, could it? Well, well: when once we're husband and wife, perhaps I may pick up a little of your learning, and learn a little of this new, fashionable way of speaking.

I send you the Virginian tobacco, my dearest Amandus. I've packed my bonnet box full of it, as much as ever I could get into it; and, in the meantime, I've put my new straw hat on Charlemagne's head—you know he stands in the spare bedroom, although he has no feet, being only a bust, as you remember.

Please don't laugh, Amandus dear; but I have made some poetry myself, and it rhymes quite nicely, some of it. Write and tell me how a person, without learning, can know so well what rhymes to what? Just listen, now—

> I love you, dearest, as my life.
> And long at once to be your wife.
> The bright blue sky is full of light,
> When evening comes the stars shine bright.
> So you must love me always truly,
> And never cause me pain unduly,
> I pack up the 'baccy you asked me to send,
> And I hope it will yield you enjoyment no end.

There! you must take the will for the deed, and when I learn the fashionable way of speaking, I'll do some better poetry. The yellow lettuces are promising splendidly this year—never was such a crop; so are the French beans; but my little dachshund, Feldmann, gave the big gander a terrible bite in the leg yesterday. However, we can't have everything perfect in this world. A hundred kisses in imagination, my dearest Amandus, from

Your most faithful fiancée,
Anna von Zabelthau.

P.S.—I've been writing in an awful hurry, and that's the reason the letters are rather crooked here and there.

P.S.—But you mustn't mind about that. Though I may write a little crookedly, my heart is all straight, and I am

Always your faithful
Anna.

P.S.—Oh, good gracious! I had almost forgot—thoughtless thing that I am. Papa sends you his kind regards, and says you are to rescue me from a terrible danger some day. Now, I'm very glad of this, and remain, once more,

Your most true and loving
Anna von Zabelthau.

It was a good weight off Fräulein Aennchen's mind when she had written this letter; it had cost her a considerable effort. So she felt lighthearted and happy when she had put it in its envelope, sealed it up without burning the paper or her own fingers, and given it, together with the bonnet-boxful of tobacco, to Gottlieb to take to the post office in the town. When she had seen properly to the poultry in the yard, she ran as fast as she could to the place she loved best—the kitchen garden. When she got to the carrot bed she thought it was about time to be thinking of the gourmets in the town, and be pulling the earliest of the carrots. The servant-girl was called in to help in this process. Fräulein Aennchen walked, gravely and seriously, into the middle of the bed, and grasped a stately carrot plant. But when she pulled at it a strange sound was heard. Do not, reader, think of the witches' mandrake root, and the horrible whining and howling which pierces the heart of man when it is drawn from the earth. No; the tone which was heard on this occasion was like very delicate, joyous laughter. But Fräulein Aennchen let the carrot plant go, and cried out, rather frightened, "Eh! Who's that laughing at me?" But there being nothing more to be heard she took hold of the carrot plant again—which seemed to be finer and better grown than any of the rest—and notwithstanding the laughing, which began again, pulled up the very finest and most splendid carrot ever beheld by mortal eye. When

she looked at it more closely she gave a cry of joyful surprise, so
that the maidservant came running up; and she also exclaimed
aloud at the beautiful miracle which disclosed itself to her eyes.
For there was a beautiful ring firmly attached to the carrot, with a
shining topaz mounted in it.

"Oh," cried the maid, "that's for you!   It's your wedding ring.
Put it on right away!"

"Stupid nonsense!" said Fräulein Aennchen.   "I must get my
wedding ring from Herr Amandus von Nebelstern, not from a
carrot."

However, the longer she looked at the ring, the better she was
pleased with it; and, indeed, it was of such wonderfully fine workmanship that it seemed to surpass anything ever produced by
human skill.   On the ring part of it there were hundreds and
hundreds of tiny little figures twined together in the most manifold
groupings, hardly to be made out with the naked eye at first, so
microscopically minute were they.   But when one looked at them
closely for a little while they appeared to grow bigger and more
distinct, and to come to life, and dance in pretty combinations.
And the gem was of such a remarkable water that the like of it
could not have been found in the celebrated Dresden collection.

"Who knows," said the maid, "how long this beautiful ring has
been underground?   And it must have got shoved up somehow,
and then the carrot has grown right through it."

Fräulein Aennchen took the ring off the carrot, and it was
strange how the carrot suddenly slipped through her fingers and
disappeared in the ground.   But neither she nor the maid paid
much heed to this circumstance, being lost in admiration of the
beautiful ring, which the young lady immediately put on the little
finger of the right hand without more ado.   As she did so, she felt
a stinging pain all the way up her finger, from the root to the tip; but
this pain went away again as quickly as it had come.

Of course she told her father, at midday, all about this strange
adventure at the carrot bed, and showed him the beautiful ring
which had been sticking upon the carrot.   She was going to take
it off so that he might examine it better, but felt the same kind of
stinging pain as when she put it on.   And this pain lasted all the
time she was trying to get it off, so that she had to give up trying.
Herr Dapsul scanned the ring upon her finger with the most careful
attention.   He made her stretch her finger out, and describe with
it all sorts of circles in all directions.   After which he fell into a
profound meditation, and went up into his tower without uttering

a syllable. Aennchen heard him giving vent to a very considerable amount of groaning and sighing as he went.

Next morning, when she was chasing the big cock about the yard (he was bent on all manner of mischief, and was skirmishing particularly with the pigeons), Herr Dapsul began lamenting so fearfully down from the tower through the speaking trumpet that she cried up to him through her closed hand, "Oh papa dear, what are you making such a terrible howling for? The fowls are all going out of their wits."

Herr Dapsul hailed down to her through the speaking trumpet, saying, "Anna, my daughter Anna, come up here to me immediately."

Fräulein Aennchen was much astonished at this command, for her papa had never in all his life asked her to go into the tower, but rather had kept the door of it carefully shut. As a result she was conscious of a certain sense of anxiety as she climbed the narrow winding stair, and opened the heavy door which led into its one room. Herr Dapsul von Zabelthau was seated upon a large armchair of singular form, surrounded by curious instruments and dusty books. Before him was a kind of stand, upon which there was a paper stretched in a frame, with a number of lines drawn upon it. He had on a tall pointed cap, a wide mantle of grey calimanco, and on his chin a long white beard, so that he had quite the appearance of a magician. On account of his false beard Aennchen didn't know him a bit just at first, and looked curiously about to see if her father were hidden away in some corner; but when she saw that the man with the beard on was really papa, she laughed most heartily, and asked if it was Yule-time, and he was going to act Father Christmas.

Paying no heed to this enquiry, Herr Dapsul von Zabelthau took a small tool of iron in his hand, touched Aennchen's forehead with it, and then stroked it along her right arm several times, from the armpit to the tip of the little finger. While this was going on, she had to sit in the armchair which he had quitted, and to lay the finger which had the ring upon it on the paper which was in the frame, in such a position that the topaz touched the central point where all the lines came together. Yellow rays immediately shot out from the topaz all round, colouring the paper all over with deep yellow light. Then the lines went flickering and crackling up and down, and the little figures which were on the ring seemed to be jumping merrily about all over the paper. Herr Dapsul, without taking his eyes from the paper, had taken hold of a thin plate of some metal, which he held up high over his head with both arms, and was proceeding to press it down upon the paper; but before he could do so his foot slipped on the smooth stone floor, and he fell, anything but softly, upon the sitting portion of his body; while the metal plate, which he had dropped in an instinctive attempt to break his fall, and save damage to his *Os Coccygis*, went clattering down upon the stones. Fräulein Aennchen awoke, with a gentle "Ah!" from a strange dreamy condition in which she had been. Herr Dapsul with some difficulty raised himself, put the grey sugar-loaf cap, which had fallen off, on again, arranged the false beard, and sat down opposite Aennchen upon a pile of folio volumes.

"My daughter," he said, "my daughter Anna; what were your sensations? Describe your thoughts, your feelings? What were the forms seen by the eye of the spirit within your inner being?"

"Ah!" answered Anna, "I was so happy; I never was so happy in all my life. And I thought of Amandus von Nebelstern. And I saw him quite plainly before my eyes, but he was much better-looking than he used to be. He was smoking a pipe of the Virginian tobacco that I sent him, and seemed to be enjoying it tremendously. Then all at once I felt a great appetite for young carrots with sausages; and lo and behold! there the dishes were before me, and I was just going to help myself to some when I woke up from the dream in a moment, with a sort of painful start."

"Amandus von Nebelstern, Virginia canaster, carrots, sausages," quoth Herr Dapsul von Zabelthau to his daughter very reflectively. And he signed to her to stay where she was, for she was preparing to go away.

"Happy is it for you, innocent child," he began, in a tone much sadder than even his usual one, "that you are as yet not initiated into the profounder mysteries of the universe, and are unaware of the threatening perils which surround you. You know nothing of the supernatural science of the sacred cabbala. True, you will never partake of the celestial joy of those wise ones who, having attained the highest step, need never eat or drink except for their pleasure, and are exempt from human necessities. But then, you do not have to endure and suffer the pain of attainment to that step, like your unhappy father, who is still far more liable to attacks of mere human giddiness, to whom that which he laboriously discovers only causes terror and awe, and who is still, from purely earthly necessities, obliged to eat and drink and, in fact, submit to human requirements.

"Learn, my charming child, blessed as you are with absence of knowledge, that the depths of the earth, and the air, water, and fire, are filled with spiritual beings of higher and yet of more restricted nature than mankind. It seems unnecessary, my little unwise one, to explain to you the peculiar nature and characteristics of the gnomes, the salamanders, sylphs and undines; you would not be able to understand them. To give you some slight idea of the danger which you may be undergoing, it is sufficient that I should tell you that these spirits are always striving eagerly to enter into unions with human beings; and as they are well aware that human beings are strongly adverse to those unions, they employ all manner of subtle and crafty artifices to delude those as they have fixed their affections upon. Often it is a twig, a flower, a glass of water, a fire-steel, or something else, in appearance of no importance, which they employ as a means of carrying out their intent. It is true that unions of this sort often turn out exceedingly happily, as in the case of two priests, mentioned by Prince della Mirandola, who spent forty years of the happiest possible wedlock with a spirit of this description. It is true, moreover, that the most renowned sages have been the offspring of such unions between human beings and elementary spirits. Thus, the great Zoroaster was a son of the salamander Oromasis; the great Apollonius, the sage Merlin, the valiant Count of Cleve, and the great cabbalist, Ben-Syra, were the glorious fruits of marriages of this description, and according to Paracelsus the beautiful Melusina was no other than a sylph. But yet the peril of such a union is much too great, for not only do the elemental spirits require of those on whom they confer their favours that the clearest light of the profoundest wisdom shall have arisen and shall shine upon them, but besides this they are extraordinarily touchy and sensitive, and revenge offenses with extreme severity. Thus, it once happened that a sylph who was in union with a philosopher, on an occasion when he was talking with friends about a pretty woman— and perhaps rather too warmly—suddenly allowed her white beautifully formed leg to become visible in the air, as if to convince the friends of her beauty, and then killed the poor philosopher on the spot. But ah! why should I refer to others? Why don't I speak of myself? I am aware that for the last twelve years I have been beloved by a sylph, but she is timorous and coy, and I am tortured by the thought of the danger of fettering her to me more closely by cabbalistic processes, inasmuch as I am still much too dependent on earthly necessities, and consequently lack the necessary degree of wisdom. Every morning I make up my mind to fast, and I succeed in letting breakfast pass without touching any food; but when mid-day comes, oh! Anna, my daughter Anna, you know well that I cannot stop eating."

These latter words Herr Dapsul uttered almost in a howl, while bitter tears rolled down his lean chop-fallen cheeks. He then went on more calmly:

"But I take the greatest of pains to behave towards the elemental spirit who is thus favourably disposed towards me with the utmost refinement of manners, the most exquisite *galanterie*. I never venture to smoke a pipe of tobacco without employing the proper pre-liminary cabbalistic precautions, for I cannot tell whether or not my tender air-spirit may like the brand of the tobacco, and so be annoyed at the defilement of her element. For this reason those who smoke Hunter's mix or Flower of Saxony can never become wise or win the love of a sylph. And I take the same precautions when I cut a hazel twig, pluck a flower, eat a fruit, or strike fire, all my efforts being directed to avoid giving offense to any elementary spirit. And yet—there, you see that nutshell, which I slid upon and, falling over backwards, completely nullified the whole important experiment, which would have revealed to me the whole mystery of the ring? I do not remember that I have eaten ever a nut in this chamber, completely devoted as it is to science (you know now why I have my breakfast on the stairs), and it is all the clearer that some little gnome must have been hidden away in that shell, very likely having come here to prosecute his studies and watch some of my experiments. For the elemental spirits are fond of human science, particularly such kinds of it as the uninitiated vulgar consider to be, if not foolish and superstitious, at all events beyond the powers of the human mind to comprehend, and for that reason style 'dangerous.' Thus, when I accidentally trod upon this little student's head, I suppose he got in a rage, and threw me down. But it is probable that he had a deeper reason for preventing me from finding out the secret of the ring. Anna, my dear Anna, listen to this. I had ascertained that there is a gnome bestowing his favour upon you, and to judge by the ring he must be a gnome of rank and dis-tinction, as well as of superior cultivation. But, my dear Anna, my most beloved little stupid girl, how do you suppose you are going to enter into any kind of union with an elemental spirit without running the most terrible risk? If you had read Cassiodorus Remus you might, of course, reply that, according to his veracious chronicle, the celebrated Magdalena de la Croix, abbess of a convent at Cordova, in Spain, lived for thirty years in the happiest wedlock imaginable with a little gnome, while a similar result followed in the case of a sylph and the young Gertrude, a nun in Kloster Nazareth, near Cologne. But, then, think of the learned pursuits of those ecclesiastical ladies and of your own; what a mighty difference. Instead of reading in learned books you are often employing your time in feeding hens, geese, ducks, and other creatures, which simply molest and annoy all cabbalists; instead of watching the course of the stars, the heavens, you dig in the earth; instead of deciphering the traces of the future in skillfully constructed horoscopes you are churning milk into butter, and putting sauerkraut up to pickle for mean everyday winter use; although, really, I must say that for my own part I should be very sorry to be without such articles of food. Say, is all this likely, in the long run, to content a refined philosophic elemental spirit? And then, oh Anna! it must be through you that the Dapsulheim line must continue, which earthly demand upon your being you cannot in any possible case refuse to obey. Yet, in connection with this ring, you in your instinctive way felt a strange irreflective sense of physical enjoyment. By means of the operation in which I was engaged, I desired and intended to break the power of the ring, and free you entirely from the gnome which is pursuing you. That operation failed, in consequence of the trick played me by the little student in the nutshell. And yet, notwithstanding, I feel inspired by a courage such as I never felt before to do battle with this elemental spirit. You are my child, whom I begot, not indeed with a sylph, salamandress, or other elemental spirit, but of that poor country lady of a fine old family, to whom the god-forgotten neighbours gave the nickname of the 'goat-girl' on account of her idyllic nature. For she used to go out with a flock of pretty little white goats, and pasture them on the green hillocks, I meanwhile blowing a reed-pipe on my tower, a love-stricken young fool, by way of accompaniment. Yes, you are my own child, my flesh and blood, and I mean to rescue you. Here, this magic file shall free you from the pernicious ring."

With this, Herr Dapsul von Zabelthau took up a small file and began filing away with it at the ring. But scarcely had he passed it once or twice backwards and forwards when Fräulein Aennchen cried aloud in pain, "Papa, papa, you're filing my finger off!" And actually there was dark thick blood oozing from under the ring. Seeing this, Herr Dapsul let the file fall upon the floor, sank half fainting into the armchair, and cried, in utter despair, "Oh—oh—oh—oh! It is all over with me! The infuriated gnome may come this very hour and bite my head off unless the sylph saves me.   Oh, Anna, Anna, go—fly!"

As her father's extraordinary talk had long made her wish herself far enough away, she ran downstairs like the wind.

III

Herr Dapsul von Zabelthau had just embraced his daughter with many tears, and was moving off to ascend his tower, where he dreaded every moment the alarming visit of the incensed gnome, when the sound of a horn, loud and clear, made itself heard, and into the courtyard came bounding and curvetting a little cavalier of rather strange appearance.   His yellow horse was not at all large, and was of delicate build, so that the little rider, in spite of his large shapeless head, did not look so dwarfish as might otherwise have been the case, as he sat a considerable height above the horse's head.   But this was attributable to the length of his body, for what of him hung over the saddle in the nature of legs and feet was hardly worth mentioning.   For the rest, the little fellow had on a very rich habit of gold-yellow satin, a fine high cap with a splendid grass-green plume, and riding boots of beautifully polished mahogany colour.   With a resounding "P-r-r-r-r-r!" he reined up before Herr von Zabelthau, and seemed to be going to dismount. But he suddenly slipped under the horse's belly as quick as lightning, and having got to the other side of him, threw himself three times in succession some twelve ells up in the air, turning six somersaults in every ell, and then alighted on his head in the saddle.   Standing on his head there, he galloped backwards, forwards, and sideways in all sorts of extraordinary curves and ups and downs, his feet meanwhile playing trochees, dactyls, pyrrhics, and so on, in the air. When this accomplished gymnast and trick-act rider at length stood still, and politely saluted, there were to be seen on the ground of the courtyard the words, "My most courteous greeting to you and your lady daughter, most highly respected Herr Dapsul von Zabelthau."   These words he had ridden into the ground in handsome Roman uncial letters.   Thereupon, he sprang from his horse, turned three catherine wheels, and said that he was charged by his gracious master, the Herr Baron Porphyrio von Ockerodastes, called "Cordovanspitz," to present his compliments to Herr Dapsul von Zabelthau, and to say, that if the latter had no objection, the Herr Baron proposed to pay him a friendly visit of a day or two, as he was expecting presently to be his nearest neighbour.

Herr Dapsul looked more dead than alive, so pale and motionless did he stand, leaning on his daughter. Scarcely had a half involuntary, "It—will—give—me—much—pleasure," escaped his trembling lips, when the little horseman departed with lightning speed, and similar ceremonies to those with which he had arrived.

"Ah, my daughter!" cried Herr Dapsul, weeping and lamenting, "alas! it is but too certain that this is the gnome come to carry you off, and twist my unfortunate neck. But we will pluck up the very last scrap of courage which we can scrape together. Perhaps it may be still possible to pacify this irritated elemental spirit. We must be as careful in our conduct towards him as ever we can. I will at once read to you, my dear child, a chapter or two of Lactantius or Thomas Aquinas concerning the mode of dealing with elementals, so that you mayn't make some tremendous mistake or other."

But before he could go and get hold of Lactantius or Thomas Aquinas or Knigge's Etiquette book a band was heard close by, sounding very much like the kind of performance which children who are musical enough get up about Christmas-time. And a fine long procession was coming up the street. At the head of it rode some sixty or seventy little cavaliers on little yellow horses, all dressed like the one who had arrived as avant-courier at first, in yellow habits, pointed caps, and boots of polished mahogany. They were followed by a coach of purest crystal, drawn by eight yellow horses, and behind this came well onto forty other less magnificent coaches, some with six horses, some with only four. And there were swarms of pages, running footmen, and other attendants, moving up and down among and around those coaches in brilliant costumes, so that the whole thing formed a sight as charming as uncommon. Herr Dapsul stood sunk in gloomy amazement. Aennchen, who had never dreamed that the world could contain such lovely delightful creatures as these little horses and people, was quite out of her senses with delight, and forgot everything, even to shut her mouth, which she had opened to emit a cry of joy.

The coach and eight drew up before Herr Dapsul. Riders jumped from their horses, pages and attendants came hurrying forward, and the personage who was now lifted down the steps of the coach on their arms was none other than the Herr Baron Porphyrio von Ockerodastes, otherwise known as Cordovanspitz. In figure the Baron could not be compared to the Apollo Belvedere or even the Dying Gladiator. For, besides being scarcely three feet high, one-third of his small body consisted of his too large and broad head, which was adorned by a tremendously long Roman nose and a pair of great round projecting eyes. And as his body was disproportionately long for his height, there was nothing left for his legs and feet to occupy but some four inches or so. This small space was made the most of, however, for the little Baron's feet were the neatest and prettiest little things ever beheld. No doubt they seemed to be scarcely strong enough to support the large, important head. For the Baron's gait was somewhat tottery and uncertain, and he even toppled over altogether pretty frequently, but got up upon his feet immediately, after the manner of a jack-in-the-box. This toppling over resembled some rather eccentric dance step more than anything else one could compare it to. He had on a close-fitting suit of some shining gold fabric, and a headdress, which was almost like a crown, with an enormous plume of green feathers in it.

As soon as the Baron had alighted on the ground, he hastened up to Herr Dapsul von Zabelthau, took hold of both his hands, swung himself up to his neck, and cried out, in a voice wonderfully more powerful than his shortness of stature would have led one to expect, "Oh, my Dapsul von Zabelthau, my most beloved father!" He then lowered himself down from Herr Dapsul's neck with the same deftness with which he had climbed up to it, sprang, or rather slung himself, to Fräulein Aennchen, took that hand of hers which had the ring on it, covered it with loud resounding kisses, and cried out in the same almost thundering voice as before, "Oh, my loveliest Fräulein Anna von Zabelthau, my most beloved bride-elect!"

He then clapped his hands, and immediately that noisy clattering childlike band struck up, and over a hundred little fellows, who had got off their horses and out of the carriages, danced as the avant-courier had done, sometimes on their heads, sometimes on their feet, in the prettiest possible trochees, spondees, iambics, pyrrhics, anapaests, tribachs, bacchi, antibacchi, choriambs, and dactyls, so that it was a joy to behold them. But as this was going on, Fräulein Aennchen recovered from the terrible fright which the little Baron's speech to her had put her in, and entered into several important and necessary economic questions and considerations. "How is it possible," she asked herself, "that these little beings can find room in this place of ours? Would it hold even their servants if they were to be put to sleep in the big barn? Then what could I do with the nobles who came in the coaches, and of course expect to be put into fine bedrooms, with soft beds, as they're accustomed to be? And even if the two plough horses were to go out of the stable, and I were to be so hard-hearted as to turn the old lame chestnut out into the grass field, would there be anything like room enough for all those little beasts of horses that this nasty ugly Baron has brought? And just the same with the one and forty coaches. But the worst of all comes after that. Oh, my gracious! is the whole year's provender anything like enough to keep all these little creatures going for even a couple of days?"

This last was the climax. She saw in her mind's eye everything eaten up—all the new vegetables, the sheep, the poultry, the salt meat—nay, the very beet brandy gone. And this brought salt tears to her eyes. She thought she caught the Baron making a sort of wicked impudent face at her, and that gave her courage to say to him (while his people were keeping up their dancing with might and main), in the plainest language possible, that however flattering his visit might be to her father, it was impossible to think of such a thing as its lasting more than a couple of hours or so, as there was neither room nor anything else for the proper reception and entertainment of such a grand gentleman and such a numerous retinue. But little Cordovanspitz immediately looked as marvellously sweet and tender as any marzipan tart, pressing with closed eyes Fräulein Aennchen's hand (which was rather rough, and not particularly white) to his lips, as he assured her that the last thing he should think of was causing the dear papa and his lovely daughter the slightest inconvenience. He said he had brought everything in the kitchen and cellar department with him, and as for the lodging, he needed nothing but a little bit of ground with the open air above it, where his people could put up his ordinary travelling palace, which would accommodate him, his whole retinue, and the animals pertaining to them.

Fräulein Aennchen was so delighted with these words of the Baron Porphyrio von Ockerodastes that, to show that she wasn't grudging a little bit of hospitality, she was going to offer him the little fritter cakes she had made for the last consecration day, and a small glass of brandy, unless he would have preferred double bitters, which the maid had brought from the town and recommended as strengthening to the stomach. But at this moment Cordovanspitz announced that he had chosen the kitchen garden as the site of his palace, and Aennchen's happiness was gone. While the Baron's retainers, in celebration of their lord's arrival at Dapsulheim, continued their Olympic games, sometimes butting with their big heads at each other's stomachs, knocking each other over backwards, sometimes springing up in the air again, playing at skittles, being themselves in turn skittles, balls, and players, and so forth, Baron Porphyrio von Ockerodastes got into a very deep and interesting conversation with Herr Dapsul von Zabelthau, which seemed to go on increasing in importance till they went away together hand in hand, and up into the astronomical tower.

Full of alarm and anxiety, Fräulein Aennchen now made haste to her kitchen garden, with the view of trying to save whatever it might be possible to save. The maid-servant was there already, standing staring before her with open mouth, motionless as a person turned like Lot's wife into a pillar of salt. Aennchen at once fell into the same condition beside her. At last they both cried out, making the welkin ring, "Oh, Herr Gemini! What a terrible sort of thing!" For the whole beautiful vegetable garden was turned into a wilderness. Not the trace of a plant in it, it looked like an empty barren.

"No," cried the maid, "there's no other way of accounting for it, these cursed little creatures have done it coming here in their coaches! coaches, ha! as if they were people of quality! Ha! ha! A lot of kobolds, that's what *they* are, trust *me* for that Miss. And if I had a drop of holy water here I'd soon show you what all those fine things of theirs would turn to. But if they come here, the little brutes, I'll bash the heads of them with this spade here." And she flourished this threatening spade over her head, while Anna wept aloud. But at this point, four members of Cordovanspitz's suite came up with such very pleasant ingratiating speeches and such courteous reverences, being such wonderful creatures to behold, at the same time that the maid, instead of attacking them with the spade, let it slowly sink, and Fräulein Aennchen ceased weeping.

They announced themselves as being the four friends who were the most immediately attached to their lord's person, saying that they belonged to four different nationalities (as their dress indicated, symbolically, at all events), and that their names were, respectively, Pan Kapustowicz, from Poland; Herr von Schwartzrettig, from Pomerania; Signor di Broccoli, from Italy; and Monsieur de Rocambolle, from France. They said, moreover, that the builders would come directly, and afford the beautiful lady the gratification of seeing them erect a lovely palace, all of silk, in the shortest possible time.

"What good will the silken palace be to me?" cried Fräulein Aennchen, weeping aloud in her bitter sorrow. "And what do I care abut your Baron Cordovanspitz, now that you have gone and destroyed my beautiful vegetables, wretched creatures that you are. All my happy days are over."

But the polite interlocutors comforted her, and assured her that they had not by any means had the blame of desolating the kitchen garden, and that, moreover, it would very soon be growing green and flourishing in such luxuriance as she had never seen, or anybody else in the world for that matter.

The little building-people arrived, and then there began such a mad, confused dashing back and forth that Fräulein Anna and the maid ran away quite frightened, and took shelter behind some thickets, whence they could see what would happen.

But though they couldn't explain to themselves how things *could* come about as they did, there arose before their eyes, in a few minutes' time, a lofty and magnificent pavilion tent, made of a golden-yellow material and ornamented with many-coloured garlands and plumes, occupying the whole extent of the vegetable garden, so that its guy ropes extended away over the village and into the wood beyond, where they were made fast to sturdy trees.

As soon as this tent was ready, Baron Porphyrio came down with Herr Dapsul from the astronomical tower, after profuse embraces resumed his seat in the coach and eight, and in the same order in which they had made their entry into Dapsulheim, he and his following went into the silken palace, which, when the last of the procession was within it, instantly closed itself up.

Fräulein Aennchen had never seen her papa as he was then. The melancholy which had hitherto always so distressed him had completely disappeared from his countenance. One would really almost have said he smiled. There was a sublimity about his facial expression such as sometimes indicates that some great and unexpected happiness has come upon a person. He led his daughter by the hand in silence into the house, embraced her three times consecutively, and then broke out:

"Fortunate Anna! Thrice happy girl! Fortunate father! Oh, daughter, all sorrow and melancholy, all solicitude and misgiving are over for ever! Yours is a fate such as falls to the lot of few mortals. This Baron Porphyrio von Ockerodastes, otherwise known as Cordovanspitz, is by no means a hostile gnome, although he is descended from one of those elemental spirits who, however, was so fortunate as to purify his nature by the teaching of Oromasis the Salamander. The love of this being was bestowed upon a daughter of the human race, with whom he formed a union, and became founder of the most illustrious family whose name ever adorned a parchment. I have an impression that I told you before, beloved daughter Anna, that the pupil of the great Salamander Oromasis, the noble gnome Tsilmenech (a Chaldean name, which interpreted into our language has a somewhat similar significance to our word 'Thickhead'), bestowed his affection on the celebrated Magdalena de la Croix, abbess of a convent at Cordova in Spain, and lived in happy wedlock with her for nearly thirty years. And a descendant of the sublime family of higher beings which sprung from this union is our dear Baron Porphyrio von Ockerodastes, who has adopted the sobriquet of Cordovanspitz to indicate his ancestral connection with Cordova in Spain, and to distinguish himself by it from a more haughty but less worthy collateral line of the family, which bears the title of 'Saffian.' That a 'spitz' has been added to the 'Cordovan' doubtless possesses its own astrological causes; I have not as yet gone into that subject. Following the example of his illustrious ancestor the gnome Tsilmenech, this splendid Ockerodastes of ours fell in love with you when you were only twelve years of age (Tsilmenech had done precisely the same thing in the case of Magdalena de la Croix). He was fortunate enough at that time to get a small gold ring from you, and now you wear his, so that your betrothal is indissoluble."

"What?" cried Fräulein Aennchen, in fear and amazement. "What? I betrothed to *him*—I to marry that horrible little kobold? Haven't I been engaged for ever so long to Herr Amandus von Nebelstern? No, I never will have that hideous monster of a wizard for a husband. I don't care whether he comes from Cordova or from Saffian."

"There," said Herr Dapsul von Zabelthau more gravely, "there I perceive, to my sorrow and distress, how impossible it is for celestial wisdom to penetrate into your withered mundane mind. You stigmatize this noble, elemental Porphyrio von Ockerodastes as 'horrible' and 'ugly,' probably, I presume, because he is only three feet high, and, with the exception of his head, has very little worth speaking of on his body in the shape of arms, legs, and other appurtenances; and an earthly idiot, such as you probably admire, can't have legs long enough, on account of coattails. Oh, my daughter, in what a terrible misapprehension you are involved! All beauty lies in wisdom, in the thought; and the physical symbol of thought is the head. The more head, the more beauty and wisdom. And if mankind could but cast away all the other members of the body as pernicious articles of luxury tending to evil, they would reach the condition of a perfect ideal of the highest type. Whence come all trouble and difficulty, vexation and annoyance, strife and contention—in short, all the depravities and miseries of humanity—but from the accursed luxury and voluptuousness of the members? Oh, what joy, what peace, what blessedness there would be on earth if the human race could exist without arms or legs, or the nether parts of the body—in short, if we were nothing but busts! Therefore it is a happy idea of the sculptors to represent great statesmen, or celebrated men of science and learning as busts, symbolically indicating the higher nature within them. Wherefore, my daughter Anna, no more of such words as 'ugly and abominable' applied to the noblest of spirits, the grand Porphyrio von Ockerodastes, whose bride-elect you most indubitably are.

"I must just tell you, at the same time, that with his important aid your father will soon attain that highest step of bliss towards which he has so long been striving. Porphyrio von Ockerodastes is in possession of authentic information that I am beloved by the sylph Nehabilah (which in Syriac has very much the signification of our expression 'Peaky nose'), and he has promised to assist me to the utmost of his power to render myself worthy of a union with this higher spiritual nature. I have no doubt whatever, my dear child, that you will be well satisfied with your future stepmother. All I hope is, that a favourable destiny may so order matters that our marriages may both take place at one and the same fortunate hour."

Having thus spoken, Herr Dapsul von Zabelthau, casting a significant glance at his daughter, left the room.

It was a great weight on Aennchen's heart that she remembered having, a great while ago, lost a little gold ring, such as a child might wear, from her finger. So that it really seemed too certain that this abominable little wizard of a creature had her enmeshed in his net, so that she couldn't see how she was ever to get out of it. And thus she fell into the utmost grief and bewilderment. She had to relieve her oppressed heart; and this took place through the medium of a goose-quill, which she seized, and at once wrote off to Herr Amandus von Nebelstern as follows:

My dearest Amandus—

All is over with me completely. I am the most unfortunate creature in the whole world, and I'm sobbing and crying for sheer misery so terribly that the dear dumb animals themselves are sorry for me. And *you'll* be still sorrier than they are, because it's just as great a misfortune for you as it is for me, and you can't help being quite as much distressed about it as I am myself. You know that we love one another as fondly as any two lovers possibly can, and that I am betrothed to you, and that papa was going with us to the church. Very well. All of a sudden a nasty little creature comes here in a coach and eight, with a lot of people and servants, and says I have changed rings with him, and that he and I are engaged. And—just fancy how awful! papa says as well, that I must marry this little wretch, because he belongs to a very grand family. I suppose he very likely does, judging by his following and the splendid dresses they have on. But the creature has such a horrible name that, for that alone if it were for nothing else, I never would marry him. I can't even pronounce the heathenish words of the name; but one of them is Cordovanspitz, and it seems that is the family name. Write and tell me if these Cordovanspitzes really *are* so very great and aristocratic a family—people in the town will be sure to know if they are. And the things papa takes in his head at his time of life I really can't understand; but he wants to marry again, and this nasty Cordovanspitz is going to get him a wife that flies in the air. God protect us! Our servant girl is looking over my shoulder, and says she hasn't much of an opinion of ladies who can fly in the air and swim in the water, and that she'll have to be looking out for another situation, and hopes, for my sake, that my stepmother may break her neck the first time she goes riding through the air to St. Walpurgis. Nice state of things, isn't it? But all my hope is in *you*. For I know you are the person who must and will, and will save me from a great danger. The danger has come, so be quick, and rescue

Your grieved to death, but most true and loving fiancée,

Anna von Zabelthau.

P.S.—Couldn't you call this yellow little Cordovanspitz out? I'm sure you could win. He's feeble on his legs.

What I implore you to do is to put on your things as fast as you can and hasten to

Your most unfortunate and miserable,

But always most faithful fiancée,

Anna von Zabelthau.

IV

Fräulein Aennchen was so miserable and distressed that she felt paralyzed in all her members. She was sitting at the window with folded arms gazing straight before her, heedless of the cackling, crowing, and queaking of the fowls, who couldn't understand why she didn't come and drive them into their roosts as usual, seeing that the twilight was coming on fast. Nay, she sat there with perfect indifference and allowed the maid to carry out this duty, and to hit the big cock (who opposed himself to the state of things and evinced decided resistance to her authority) a good sharp whang with her whip. For the love-pain which was rending her own heart was making her indifferent to the troubles of the dear pupils of her happier hours—those which she devoted to their upbringing, although she had never studied Chesterfield or Knigge, or consulted Madame de Genlis, or any of those other authorities on the mental culture of the young, who know to a hair's-breadth exactly how they ought to be moulded. In this respect she really laid herself open to censure for lack of due seriousness.

All that day Cordovanspitz had not shown himself, but had been shut up in the tower with Herr Dapsul, no doubt assisting in the carrying on of important operations. But now Fräulein Aennchen caught sight of the little creature coming tottering across the court-yard in the glowing light of the setting sun. And it struck her that he looked more hideous in that yellow habit of his than ever before. The ridiculous manner in which he went wavering about, jumping here and there, seeming to topple over every minute and then pick himself up again (at which anybody else would have died of laughing), only caused her the bitterer distress. Indeed, she at last held her hands in front of her eyes, so that she mightn't so much as see the little horrid creature at all. Suddenly she felt something tugging at her dress, and cried "Down, Feldmann!" thinking it was the dachshund. But it was not the dog; and what Fräulein Aennchen saw when she took her hands from her eyes was the Herr Baron Porphyrio von Ockerodastes, who hoisted himself into her lap with extraordinary agility, and clasped both his arms about her. She screamed aloud with fear and disgust, and started up from her chair. But Cordovanspitz kept clinging on to her neck, and instantly became so wonderfully heavy that he seemed to weigh a ton at least, and he dragged the unfortunate Aennchen back again into her chair. Having got her there, however, he slid down out of her lap, sank on one knee as gracefully as possible, and as prettily as his weakness in the direction of equilibrium permitted, and said, in a clear voice—rather peculiar, but by no means unpleasing: "Adored Anna von Zabelthau, most glorious of ladies, most choice of brides-elect; no anger, I implore, no anger, no anger. I know you think my people laid waste your beautiful vegetable garden to put up my palace. Oh, powers of the universe, if you could but look into this little body of mine which throbs with magnanimity and love; if you could but detect all the cardinal virtues which are collected in my breast, under this yellow satin habit. Oh, how guiltless I am of the shameful cruelty which you attribute to me! How could a beneficent prince treat in such a way his very own subjects. But hold—hold! What are words, phrases? You must see with your own eyes, my betrothed, the splendours which attend you. You must come with me at once. I will lead you to my palace, where a joyful people await the arrival of her who is beloved by their lord."

It may be imagined how terrified Fräulein Aennchen was at this proposition of Cordovanspitz's, and how hard she tried to avoid going so much as a single step with the little monster. But he continued to describe the extraordinary beauty and the marvellous richness of the vegetable garden which was his palace, in such eloquent and persuasive language, that at last she thought she would just have a peep into the tent, as that couldn't do her much harm. The little creature, in his joy and delight, turned at least twelve catherine wheels in succession, and then took her hand with much courtesy, and led her through the garden to the silken palace.

With a loud "Ah!" Fräulein Aennchen stood riveted to the ground with delight when the curtains of the entrance drew apart, displaying a vegetable garden stretching away further than the eye could reach, of such marvellous beauty and luxuriance as was never seen in the loveliest dreams. Here there was growing and flourishing everything in the nature of cabbage and greens, roots and salads, peas and beans, in such a shimmer of light, and in such luxuriance that it is impossible to describe it. A band of pipes, drums and cymbals sounded louder, and the four gentlemen whose acquaintance she had previously made, viz. Herr von Schwartzrettig, Monsieur de Rocambolle, Signor di Broccoli and Pan Kapustowicz, approached with many ceremonious reverences.

"My chamberlains," said Porphyrio von Ockerodastes, smiling; and preceded by them, he conducted Fräulein Aennchen between the double ranks of the bodyguard of Red English Carrots to the center of the plain, where stood a splendid throne. Around this throne were assembled the grandees of the realm; the Lettuce Princes with the Bean Princesses, the Dukes of Cucumber with the Prince of Melon at their head, the Cabbage Minister, the General Officer of Onions and Carrots, the Colewort ladies and so on, all in the gala dresses of their rank and station. And amid them moved up and down well on to a hundred of the prettiest and most delightful Lavender and Fennel pages, diffusing sweet perfume. When Ockerodastes had ascended the throne with Fräulein Aennchen, Chief Court-Marshal Turnip waved his long wand of office, and immediately the band stopped playing, and the multitude listened in reverential silence as Ockerodastes raised his voice and said, in solemn accents, "My faithful and beloved subjects, you see by my side the noble Fräulein Anna von Zabelthau, whom I have chosen to be my consort. Rich in beauty and virtues, she has long watched over you with the eye of maternal affection, preparing soft and succulent beds for you, caring for you, and tending you with ceaseless ardour. She will ever be a true and befitting mother of this realm. Wherefore I call upon you to evince and give expression to the dutiful approval, and the duly regulated rejoicing at the favour and benefit which I am graciously about to confer upon you."

At a signal given by Chief Court-Marshal Turnip there arose the shout of a thousand voices, the Bulb Artillery fired their pieces, and the band of the Carrot Guard played the celebrated National Anthem—

> Salad and lettuce, and parsley so green.

It was a grand, a sublime moment, which drew tears from the eyes of the grandees, particularly from those of the Colewort ladies. Fräulein Aennchen, too, nearly lost all her self-control when she noticed that little Ockerodastes had a crown on his head all sparkling with diamonds, and a golden sceptre in his hand.

"Ah!" she cried clapping her hands. "Oh, Gemini! You seem to be something much grander than we thought, my dear Herr von Cordovanspitz."

"My adored Anna," he replied, "the stars compelled me to appear before your father under an assumed name. You must be told, dearest girl, that I am one of the mightiest of kings, and rule over a realm whose boundaries are not discoverable, as it has been omitted to lay them down in the maps. Oh, sweetest Anna, he who offers you his hand and crown is Daucus Carota the First, King of the Vegetables. All the vegetable princes are my vassals, save that the King of Beans reigns for one single day in every year, in conformity to an ancient usage."

"Then I am to be a queen, am I?" cried Fräulein Aennchen, overjoyed. "And all this great splendid vegetable garden is to be mine?"

King Daucus assured her that of course it was to be so, and added that he and she would jointly rule over all the vegetables in the world. She had never dreamed of any thing of the kind, and thought little Cordovanspitz wasn't at all as nasty-looking as he used to be now that he was transformed into King Daucus Carota the First; the crown and sceptre were very becoming to him, and the kingly mantle as well. When she reckoned his delightful manners into the bargain, and the property this marriage would bring her, she felt certain that there wasn't a country lady in all the world who could have made a better match than she, who found herself betrothed to a king before she knew where she was. So she was delighted beyond measure, and asked her royal fiancé whether she could not take up her abode in the palace then and there, and be married next day. But King Daucus answered that eagerly as he longed for the time when he might call her his own, certain constellations compelled him to postpone that happiness a little longer. And that Herr Dapsul von Zabelthau, moreover, must be kept in ignorance of his son-in-law's royal station, because otherwise the operations necessary for bringing about the desired union with the sylph Nehabilah might be unsuccessful. Besides, he said, he had promised that both the weddings should take place on the same day. So Fräulein Aennchen had to take a solemn vow not to mention one syllable to Herr Dapsul of what had been happening to her. She therefore left the silken palace amid long and loud rejoicings of the people, who were in raptures with her beauty as well as with her affability and gracious condescension of manners and behaviour.

In her dreams she once more beheld the realms of the charming King Daucus, and was lapped in Elysium.

The letter which she had sent to Herr Amandus von Nebelstern had made a frightful impression on him. It was not long before Fräulein Aennchen received the following answer:

Idol of my Heart, Heavenly Anna—
Daggers—sharp, glowing, poisoned, death-dealing daggers were to me the words of your letter, which pierced my breast through and through. Oh, Anna! *you* to be torn from me. What a thought! I cannot, even now, understand how it was that I did not go mad on the spot and commit some terrible deed. But I fled the face of man, overpowered with rage at my deadly destiny, after dinner—without the game of billiards which I generally play—out into the woods, where I wrung my hands, and called on your name a thousand times. There came on a tremendously heavy rain, and I had on a new cap, red velvet, with a splendid gold tassel (everybody says I never had anything so becoming). The rain was spoiling it, and it was brand-new. But what are caps, what are velvet and gold, to a despairing lover? I strode up and down till I was wet to the skin and chilled to the bone, and had a terrible pain in my stomach. This drove me into a restaurant near, where I got them to make me some excellent mulled wine, and had a pipe of your heavenly Virginia tobacco. I soon felt myself elevated on the wings of a celestial inspiration, took out my pocket-book, and, oh!—wondrous gift of poetry—the love-despair and the stomach-ache both disappeared at once. I shall content myself with writing out for you only the last of these poems; it will inspire you with heavenly hope, as it did myself.

Wrapped in darkest sorrow—
In my heart, extinguished,
No love-tapers burning—
Joy hath no to-morrow.

Ha! the Muse approaches,
Words and rhymes inspiring,
Little verse inscribing,
Joy return apace.

New love-tapers blazing,
All the heart inspiring,
Fare thee well, my sorrow,
Joy thy place doth borrow.

Ay, my sweet Anna, soon shall I, thy champion, hasten to rescue
you from the miscreant who would carry you off from me. So, once
more take comfort, sweetest maid. Bear me ever in thy heart. He
comes; he rescues you; he clasps you to his bosom, which heaves in
tumultuous emotion.

> Your ever faithful
> *Amandus von Nebelstern.*

P.S.—It would be quite impossible for me to call Herr von
Cordovanspitz out. For, oh Anna! every drop of blood drawn from
your Amandus by the weapon of a presumptuous adversary were
glorious poet's blood—ichor of the gods—which never ought to be
shed. The world very properly claims that such a spirit as mine has
it imposed upon it as public duty to take care of itself for the world's
benefit, and preserve itself by every possible means. The sword of the
poet is the word—the song. I will attack my rival with Tyrtæan
battle-songs; strike him to earth with sharp-pointed epigrams; hew
him down with dithyrambics full of lover's fury. Such are the
weapons of a true, genuine poet, powerful to shield him from every
danger. And it is so accoutred that I shall appear, and do battle—
victorious battle—for your hand, oh Anna!

Farewell. I press you once more to my heart. Hope all things
from my love, and, especially, from my heroic courage, which will
shun no danger to set you free from the shameful nets of captivity in
which, to all appearance, you are entangled by a demoniacal monster.

Fräulein Aennchen received this letter at a time when she was
playing a game at "Catch-me-if-you-can" with her royal bride-
groom-elect, King Daucus Carota the First, in the meadow at the
back of the garden, and immensely enjoying it when, as was often
the case, she suddenly ducked down in full career, and the little king
would go shooting right away over her head. Instead of reading
the letter immediately (which she had always done before), she put
it in her pocket unopened, and we shall presently see that it came
too late.

Herr Dapsul could not understand why Fräulein Aennchen had changed her mind so suddenly, and grown quite fond of Herr Porphyrio von Ockerodastes, whom she had so cordially detested before. He consulted the stars on the subject, but as they gave him no satisfactory information, he was obliged to come to the conclusion that human hearts are more mysterious and inscrutable than all the secrets of the universe, and cannot be explained by the constellations. That it was simply the higher nature of the groom that had awakened Aennchen's love, he could not accept, since he was well aware that the little man was completely lacking in physical beauty. If (as the reader knows) the canon of beauty as laid down by Herr Dapsul is very unlike the ideas which young ladies form upon that subject, he did after all possess sufficient knowledge of the world to know that, although the said young women hold that good sense, wit, cleverness and pleasant manners are very agreeable fellow lodgers in a comfortable house, still, a man who can't call himself the possessor of a properly-made, fashionable coat—were he a Shakespeare, a Goethe, a Tieck, or a Jean Paul Richter— would run a decided risk of being beaten out of the field by any sufficiently well-put-together lieutenant of hussars in uniform, if he took it in his head to pay his addresses to one of them. Now in Fräulein Aennchen's case it was a different matter altogether. It was neither good looks nor cleverness that were in question; but it is not exactly every day that a poor country lady becomes a queen in a moment, and accordingly it was not very likely that Herr Dapsul should hit upon the cause which had been operating, particularly as the very stars had left him in the lurch.

As may be supposed, those three, Herr Porphyrio, Herr Dapsul and Fräulein Aennchen, were one heart and one soul. This went so far that Herr Dapsul left his tower oftener than he had ever been known to do before, to chat with his much prized son-in-law on all sorts of agreeable subjects; and not only this, but he now regularly took his breakfast in the house. About this hour, too, Herr Porphyrio was wont to come forth from his silken palace, and eat a good share of Fräulein Aennchen's bread and butter.

"Ah, ah!" she would often whisper softly in his ear, "if papa only knew that you are a real king, dearest Cordovanspitz!"

"Be still, oh heart! Do not melt away in rapture," Daucus Carota the First would say. "Near, near is the joyful day!"

It chanced that the schoolmaster had sent Fräulein Aennchen a present of some of the finest radishes from his garden. She was particularly pleased at this, as Herr Dapsul was very fond of radishes and she could not get anything from the vegetable garden because it was covered by the silk tent. Besides this, it now occurred to her for the first time, that, among all the roots and vegetables she had seen in the palace, radishes were conspicuous by their absence.

So she speedily cleaned them and served them up for her father's breakfast. He had ruthlessly shorn several of them of their leafy crowns, dipped them in salt, and eaten them with much relish, when Cordovanspitz came in.

"Oh, my Ockerodastes," Herr Dapsul called to him, "are you fond of radishes?"

There was still a particularly fine and beautiful radish on the dish. But the moment Cordovanspitz saw it his eyes gleamed with fury, and he cried in a resonant voice:

"What, unworthy duke, do you dare to appear in my presence again, and to force your way, with the coolest of audacity, into a house which is under my protection? Have I not pronounced sentence of perpetual banishment upon you as a pretender to the imperial throne? Away, treasonous vassal; begone from my sight for ever!"

Two little legs had suddenly shot out beneath the radish's large head, and with them he made a spring out of the plate, placed himself close in front of Cordovanspitz, and addressed him as follows:

"Fierce and tyrannical Daucus Carota the First, you have striven in vain to exterminate my race. Has any of your family as large a head as I or my family have? *We* are all gifted with talent, common sense, wisdom, sharpness, cultivated manners: and while *you* loaf about in kitchens and stables, and are of no use as soon as your early youth is gone (so that in very truth it is nothing but the *diable de la jeunesse* that bestows upon you your brief, transitory, little bit of good fortune), *we* enjoy the friendship of, and the intercourse with, people of position, and are greeted with acclamation as soon as ever we lift up our green heads. But I despise you, Daucus Carota. You're nothing but a low, uncultivated, ignorant boor, like all the lot of you. Let's see which of us two is the better man."

With this the Duke of Radish, flourishing a long whip about his head, proceeded, without more ado, to attack the person of King Daucus Carota the First. The latter quickly drew his little sword, and defended himself in the bravest manner. The two little creatures darted about in the room, fighting fiercely, and executing the most wonderful leaps and bounds, till Daucus Carota pressed the Duke of Radish so hard that the latter found himself obliged to make a tremendous jump out of the window and take to the open.

But Daucus Carota—with whose remarkable agility and dexterity the reader is already acquainted—bounded out after him, and followed the Duke of Radish across the field.

Herr Dapsul von Zabelthau had looked on at this terrible encounter rigid and speechless, but he now broke forth into loud and bitter lamentation, crying, "Oh, daughter Anna! oh, my poor unfortunate daughter Anna! Lost—I—you—both of us. All is over with us." With which he left the room, and ascended the astronomical tower as fast as his legs would carry him.

Fräulein Aennchen couldn't understand a bit, or form the very slightest idea what in all the world had set her father into all this boundless misery all of a sudden. The whole thing had caused *her* the greatest pleasure; moreover, her heart was rejoiced that she had had an opportunity of seeing that her future husband was brave, as well as rich and great; for it would be difficult to find any woman in all the world capable of loving a poltroon. And now that she had proof of the bravery of King Daucus Carota the First, it struck her painfully, for the first time, that Herr Amandus von Nebelstern had cried off from fighting him. If she had for a moment hesitated about sacrificing Herr Amandus to King Daucus, she was quite decided on the point now that she had an opportunity of assuring herself of all the excellencies of her future lord. She sat down and wrote the following letter:

My Dear Amandus,

Everything in this world is liable to change. Everything passes away, as the schoolmaster says, and he's quite right. I'm sure *you,* my dear Amandus, are such a learned and wise student that you will agree with the schoolmaster, and not be in the very least surprised that my heart and mind have undergone the least little bit of a change. You may quite believe me when I say that I still like you very well, and I can quite imagine how nice you look in your red velvet cap with the gold tassel. But, with regard to marriage, you know very well, Amandus dear, that, clever as you are, and beautiful as are your verses, you will never, in all your days, be a king, and (don't be frightened, dear) little Herr von Cordovanspitz isn't Herr von Cordovanspitz at all, but a great king, Daucus Carota the First, who reigns over the great vegetable kingdom, and has chosen me to be his queen. Since my dear king has thrown aside his incognito he has grown much nicer-looking, and I see now that papa was quite right when he said that the head was the beauty of the man, and therefore couldn't possibly be big enough. And then, Daucus Carota the First (you see how well I remember the beautiful name and how nicely I write it now that it has got so familiar to me), I was going to say that my little royal husband, that is to be, has such charming and delightful manners that there's no describing them. And what courage, what bravery there is in him! Before my eyes he put to flight the Duke of Radish (and a very disagreeable, unfriendly creature *he* appears to be) and hey, how he did jump after him out of the window! You should just have seen him: I only wish you had! And I don't really think that my Daucus Carota would care about those weapons of yours that you speak about one bit. He seems pretty tough, and I don't believe verses would do him any harm at all, however fine and pointed they might be. So now, dear Amandus, you must just make up your mind to be contented with your lot, like a good fellow, and not be vexed with me that I am going to be a Queen instead of marrying you. Never mind, I shall always be your affectionate friend, and if ever you would like an appointment in the Carrot bodyguard, or (as you don't care so much about fighting as about learning) in the Parsley Academy or the Pumpkin Office, you have but to say the word and your fortune is made. Farewell, and don't be vexed with

> Your former fiancée, but now friend and well-wisher, as well as future Queen,
>
> *Anna von Zabelthau*
> (but soon to be no more von Zabelthau, but simply
> *ANNA.*)

P.S.—You shall always be kept well supplied with the very finest Virginia tobacco, of that you need have no fear. As far as I can see there won't be any smoking at my court, but I shall take care to have a bed or two of Virginia tobacco planted not far from the throne, under my own special care. This will further culture and morality, and my little Daucus will no doubt have a statute specially enacted on the subject.

V

Fräulein Aennchen had just finished her letter to Herr Amandus von Nebelstern, when in came Herr Dapsul von Zabelthau and began, in the bitterest grief and sorrow to say, "O, my daughter Anna, how shamefully we are both deceived and betrayed! This miscreant who made me believe he was Baron Porphyrio von Ockerodastes, known as Cordovanspitz, member of a most illustrious family descended from the mighty gnome Tsilmenech and the noble Abbess of Cordova—this miscreant, I say—learn it and fall down insensible—*is* indeed a gnome, but of the lowest race of gnomes—those who control the vegetable world. The gnome Tsilmenech was of the highest race of all, that, namely, to which the care of the diamonds is committed. Next comes the race which has care of the metals in the realms of the metal-king, and then follow the flower-gnomes, who are lower in position, as depending on the sylphs. But the lowest and most ignoble are the vegetable gnomes, and not only is this deceiver Cordovanspitz a gnome of this caste, but he is actual king of it, and his name is Daucus Carota."

Fräulein Aennchen was far from fainting away, neither was she in the smallest degree frightened; she smiled in the kindliest way at her lamenting papa, and the courteous reader is aware of the reason. But as Herr Dapsul was very much surprised at this, and kept imploring her for Heaven's sake to realize the terrible position in which she was, and to feel the full horror of it, she thought herself at liberty to divulge the secret entrusted to her. She told Herr Dapsul how the so-called Baron von Cordovanspitz had told her his real position long ago, and that since then she had found him altogether so pleasant and delightful that she couldn't wish for a better husband. Moreover, she described all the marvellous beauties of the vegetable kingdom into which King Daucus Carota the First had taken her, not forgetting to extol duly the remarkably delightful manners of the inhabitants of that realm.

Herr Dapsul struck his hands together several times, and wept bitterly over the deceiving wickedness of the Gnome-king, who had been, and still was, employing the most artful means—most dangerous for himself as well—to lure the unfortunate Anna down into his dark, demoniac kingdom. "Glorious," he explained, "glorious and advantageous as may be the union of an elemental spirit with a human being, grand as is the example of this given by the wedlock of the gnome Tsilmenech with Magdalena de la Croix (which is of course the reason why this deceiver Daucus Carota has given himself out as being a descendant of that union), yet the kings and princes of those races are very different. If the salamander kings are only irascible, the sylph kings proud and haughty, the undine queens affectionate and jealous, the gnome kings are fierce, cruel, and deceitful. Merely to revenge themselves on the children of earth, who deprive them of their vassals, they are constantly trying their utmost to lure one of them away, who then wholly lays aside her human nature, and, becoming as shapeless as the gnomes themselves, has to go down into the earth, and is nevermore seen."

Fräulein Aennchen didn't seem disposed to believe what her father was telling her to her dear Daucus's discredit, but began talking again about the marvels of the beautiful vegetable country over which she was expecting so soon to reign as queen.

"Foolish, blinded child," cried Herr Dapsul, "do you not give your father credit for possessing sufficient cabbalistic science to be well aware that what the abominable Daucus Carota made you suppose you saw was all deception and falsehood? No, you don't believe me, and to save you, my only child, I must convince you, and this conviction must be arrived at by most desperate methods. Come with me."

For the second time she had to go up into the astronomical tower with her papa. From a big band-box Herr Dapsul took a quantity of yellow, red, white, and green ribbon, and, with strange ceremonies, he wrapped Fräulein Aennchen up in it from head to foot. He did the same to himself, and then they both went very carefully to the silken palace of Daucus Carota the First. It was close shut, and by her papa's directions, she had to rip a small opening in one of the seams of it with a large pair of scissors, and then peep in at the opening.

Heaven be about us! what did she see? Instead of the beautiful vegetable garden, the carrot guards, the plumed ladies, lavender pages, lettuce princes, and so forth, she found herself looking down into a deep pool which seemed to be full of a colourless, disgusting-looking slime, in which all kinds of horrible creatures from the bowels of the earth were creeping and twining about. There were fat worms slowly writhing about amongst each other, and beetle-like creatures stretching out their short legs and creeping heavily out. On their backs they bore big onions; but these onions had ugly human faces, and kept fleering and leering at each other with bleared yellow eyes, and trying, with their little claws (which were close behind their ears), to catch hold of one another by their long roman noses, and drag each other down into the slime, while long, naked slugs were rolling about in crowds, with repulsive torpidity, stretching their long horns out of their depths. Fräulein Aennchen nearly fainted away at this horrid sight. She held both hands to her face, and ran away as hard as she could.

"You see now, do you not?" said Herr Dapsul, "how this atrocious Daucus Carota has been deceiving you in showing you splendours of brief duration? He dressed his vassals up in gala dresses to delude you with dazzling displays. But now you have seen the kingdom which you want to reign over in undress uniform; and when you become the consort of the frightful Daucus Carota you will have to live for ever in the subterranean realms, and never appear on the surface any more. And if—Oh, oh, what do I see, wretched, most miserable of fathers that I am?"

He suddenly became so excited that she felt certain some fresh misfortune had just come to light, and asked him anxiously what he was lamenting about now. However, he could do nothing for sheer sobbing, but stammer out, "Oh—oh— dau—gh—ter. You look . . . you look . . . " and he dashed precipitously up the stairs of his tower. She ran to her room, looked into the mirror, and started back, terrified almost to death.

And she had reason. As Herr Dapsul was trying to open the eyes of Daucus Carota's intended queen to the danger of gradually losing her pretty figure and good looks, and growing more and more into the semblance of a gnome queen, he suddenly became aware of how far the process had proceeded already. Aennchen's head had got much broader and bigger, and her skin had turned yellow, so that she was quite ugly enough already. And though vanity was not one of her failings, she was woman enough to know that to grow ugly is the greatest and most frightful misfortune which can happen here below. How often had she thought how delightful it would be when she would drive, as queen, to church in the coach and eight, with the crown on her head, in satins and velvets, with diamonds, and gold chains, and rings, seated beside her royal husband, setting all the women, the schoolmaster's wife included, into amazement of admiration, and most likely, in fact, no doubt, instilling a proper sense of respect even into the minds of the pompous lord and lady of the manor themselves. Ay, indeed, how often had she been lapped in these and other such eccentric dreams, and visions of the future!—Fräulein Aennchen burst into long and bitter weeping.

"Anna, my daughter Anna," cried Herr Dapsul down through the speaking trumpet; "come up here to me immediately!"

She found him dressed very much like a miner. He spoke in a tone of decision and resolution, saying, "When need is the sorest, help is often nearest. I have ascertained that Daucus Carota will not leave his palace today, and most probably not till noon of tomorrow. He has assembled the princes of his house, the ministers, and other people of consequence to hold a council on the subject of the next crop of winter cabbage. The sitting is important, and it may be prolonged so much that we may not have any cabbage at all next winter. I mean to take advantage of this opportunity, while he is so occupied with his official affairs that he won't be able to attend to my proceedings, to prepare a weapon with which I may perhaps attack this shameful gnome, and prevail over him, so that he will be compelled to withdraw, and set you at liberty. While I am at work, look uninterruptedly at the palace through this glass and tell me instantly if anybody comes out, or even looks out of it."

She did as she was directed, but the tent remained closed, although she often heard (notwithstanding that Herr Dapsul was making a tremendous hammering on plates of metal a few paces behind her), a wild confused crying and screaming, apparently coming from the tent, and also distinct sounds of slapping, as if ears were being well boxed. She told Herr Dapsul this, and he was delighted, saying that the more they quarrelled in there the less they were likely to know what was being prepared for their destruction.

Fräulein Aennchen was much surprised when she found that Herr Dapsul had hammered out and made several most lovely kitchen pots and stew pans of copper. As an expert in such matters, she observed that the tinning of them was done in a most superior style, so that her papa must have paid careful heed to the duties legally enjoined on coppersmiths. She begged to be allowed to take these nice pots and pans down to the kitchen, and use them there. But Herr Dapsul smiled a mysterious smile, and merely said:

"All in good time, my daughter Anna. Just you go downstairs, my beloved child, and wait quietly till you see what happens to-morrow."

He gave a melancholy smile, and that infused a little hope and confidence into his luckless daughter.

Next day, as dinner-time came on, Herr Dapsul brought down his pots and pans, and betook himself to the kitchen, telling his daughter and the maid to go away and leave him by himself, as *he* was going to cook the dinner. He particularly enjoined Fräulein Aennchen to be as kind and pleasant with Cordovanspitz as ever she could, when he came in—as he was pretty sure to do.

Cordovanspitz—or rather, King Daucus Carota the First—did come in very soon, and if he had borne himself like an ardent lover on previous occasions, he far outdid himself on this. Aennchen noticed, to her terror, that she had grown so small by this time, that Daucus had no difficulty in getting up into her lap to caress and kiss her; and the wretched girl had to submit to this, notwithstanding her disgust with the horrid little monster. Presently Herr Dapsul came in, and said:

"Oh, my dear Porphyrio von Ockerodastes, won't you come into the kitchen with my daughter and me, and see what beautiful order your future bride has got everything in there?"

Aennchen had never seen the malicious look upon her father's face before, which it wore when he took little Daucus by the arm, and almost forced him from the sitting-room to the kitchen. At a sign from her father she went there after them.

Her heart swelled within her when she saw the fire burning so merrily, the glowing coals, the beautiful copper pots and pans. As Herr Dapsul drew Cordovanspitz closer to the fireplace, the hissing and bubbling in the pots grew louder and louder, and at last changed into whimpering and groaning. And out of one of the pots came voices, crying, "Oh Daucus Carota! Oh King, rescue your faithful vassals! Rescue us poor carrots! Cut up, thrown into despicable water; rubbed over with salt and butter to our torture, we suffer indescribable woe, whereof a number of noble young parsleys are partakers with us!"

And out of the pans came the plaint: "Oh Daucus Carota! Oh King! Rescue your faithful vassals—rescue us poor carrots. We are roasting in hell—and they put so little water with us, that our direful thirst forces us to drink our own heart's blood!"

And from another of the pots came: "Oh Daucus Carota! Oh King! Rescue your faithful vassals—rescue us poor carrots. A horrible cook eviscerated us, and stuffed our insides full of egg, cream, and butter, so that our minds are in utter confusion, and we don't know ourselves what we are thinking about!"

And out of all the pots and pans came howling at once a general chorus of "Oh Daucus Carota! Mighty King! Rescue us, thy faithful vassals—rescue us poor carrots!"

On this, Cordovanspitz gave a loud croaking cry of "Cursed, infernal, stupid humbug and nonsense!" sprang with his usual agility on to the kitchen range, looked into one of the pots, and suddenly popped down into it bodily. Herr Dapsul sprang forward and tried to clap on the pot lid, with a triumphant cry of "A Prisoner!" But with the speed of a spiral spring Cordovanspitz came bounding up out of the pot, and gave Herr Dapsul two or three ringing slaps on the face, crying "Meddling idiot of an old cabbalist, you shall pay for this! Come out, my lads, one and all!"

Then there came swarming out of all the pots and pans hundreds and hundreds of little creatures about the length of one's finger, and they attached themselves firmly all over Herr Dapsul's body, threw him down backwards into an enormous dish, and there dished him up, pouring the hot juice out of the pots and pans over him, and bestrewing him with chopped egg, mace, and grated breadcrumbs. Having done this, Daucus Carota darted out of the window, his people after him.

Fräulein Aennchen sank down in terror beside the dish whereon her poor papa lay, served up in this manner as if for table. She supposed he was dead, as he gave not the faintest sign of life.

She began to lament: "Ah, poor papa—you're dead now, and there's nobody to save me from this diabolical Daucus!" But Herr Dapsul opened his eyes, sprang up from the dish with renewed energy, and cried in a terrible voice, such as she had never heard him make use of before, "Ah accursed Daucus Carota, I am not at the end of my resources yet. You shall soon see what a meddling old idiot of a cabbalist can do."

Aennchen had to set to work and clean him with the kitchen broom of all the chopped egg, mace, and grated breadcrumbs; and then he seized a copper pot, crammed it on his head by way of a helmet, took a frying pan in his left hand, and a long iron kitchen ladle in his right, and thus armed and accoutred, he darted out into the open. Fräulein Aennchen saw him running as hard as he could towards Cordovanspitz's tent, and yet never moving from the same spot. At this her senses left her.

When she came to herself, Herr Dapsul had disappeared, and she got terribly anxious when evening came, and night, and even the next morning, without his making his appearance. She could not but dread the very worst.

VI

Fräulein Aennchen was sitting in her room in the deepest sorrow, when the door opened, and who should come in but Herr Amandus von Nebelstern. All shame and contrition, she shed a flood of tears, and in the most weeping accents addressed him as follows: "Oh, my darling Amandus, pray forgive what I wrote to you in my blinded state! I was bewitched, and I am so still, no doubt. I am yellow, and I'm hideous, may God pity me! But my heart is true to you, and I am not going to marry any king at all."

"My dear girl," said Amandus, "I really don't see what you have to complain of. I consider you one of the luckiest women in the world."

"Oh, don't mock at me," she cried. "I am punished severely enough for my absurd vanity in wishing to be a queen."

"Really and truly, my dear girl," said Amandus, "I can't make you out one bit. To tell you the real truth, your last letter drove me stark, staring mad. I first thrashed my servant boy, then my poodle, smashed several glasses—and you know a student who's breathing out threatenings and slaughter in that sort of way isn't to be trifled with. But when I got a little calmer I made up my mind to come here as quickly as I could, and see with my own eyes how, why, and to whom I had lost my intended bride. Love makes no distinction of class or station, and I made up my mind that I would make this King Daucus Carota give a proper account of himself, and ask him if this tale about his marrying you was mere brag, or if he really meant it—but everything here is different from what I expected. As I was passing near the grand tent yonder, King Daucus Carota came out of it, and I soon found that I had before me the most charming prince I ever saw—at the same time he happens to be the first I ever did see; but that's nothing. For, just fancy, my dear girl, he immediately detected the sublime poet in me, praised my poems (which he has never read) above measure, and offered to appoint me Poet Laureate in his service. Now a position of that sort has long been the fairest goal of my warmest wishes, so I accepted his offer with a thousandfold delight. Oh, my dear girl, with what an enthusiasm of inspiration will I chant your praises! A poet can love queens and princesses: or rather, it is really a part of his simple duty to choose a person of that exalted station to be the lady of his heart. And if he *does* get a little silly on the subject, that circumstance of itself gives rise to that divine frenzy without which no poetry is possible, and no one ought to feel any surprise at a poet's perhaps somewhat extravagant proceedings. Remember the great Tasso, who must have had a considerable bee in his bonnet when in love with the Princess Leonore d'Este. Yes, my dear girl, as you are going to be a queen so soon, you will always be the lady of my heart, and I will extol you to the stars in the sublimest and most celestial verses."

"What, you have seen him, the wicked kobold?" Fräulein Aennchen broke out in the deepest amazement. "And he has—"

But at that moment in came the little gnomish King himself, and said, in the tenderest accents, "Oh, my sweet, darling fiancée! Idol of my heart! Do not suppose for a moment that I am in the least degree annoyed with the little piece of rather unseemly conduct which Herr Dapsul von Zabelthau was guilty of. Oh, no—and indeed it has led to the more rapid fulfilment of my hopes; so that the solemn ceremony of our marriage will actually be celebrated tomorrow. You will be pleased to find that I have appointed Herr Amandus von Nebelstern our Poet Laureate, and I wish him to favour us at once with a specimen of his talents, and recite one of his poems. But let us go out under the trees, for I love the open air: and I will lie in your lap, while you, my most beloved bride-elect, may scratch my head a little while he is singing—for I am fond of having my head scratched in such circumstances."

Fräulein Aennchen, turned to stone with horror and alarm, made no resistance to this proposal. Daucus Carota, out under the trees, laid himself in her lap, she scratched his head, and Herr Amandus, accompanying himself on the guitar, began the first of twelve dozen songs which he had composed and written out in a thick book.

It is a matter of regret that in the Chronicle of Dapsulheim (from which all this history is taken), these songs have not been inserted, it being merely stated that the country folk who were passing, stopped on their way, and anxiously inquired who could be in such terrible pain in Herr Dapsul's wood, that he was crying and screaming out in such a style.

Daucus Carota, in Aennchen's lap, twisted and writhed, and groaned and whined more and more lamentably, as if he had a violent pain in his stomach. Moreover, Fräulein Aennchen fancied she observed, to her great amazement, that Cordovanspitz was growing smaller and smaller as the song went on. At last Herr Amandus sung the following sublime effusion (which is preserved in the Chronicle):

> Gladly sings the Bard, enraptured,
> Breath of blossoms, bright dream-visions,
> Moving thro' roseate spaces in Heaven,
> Blessed and beautiful, whither away?
> 'Whither away?' oh, question of questions—
> Towards that 'Whither,' the Bard is borne onward,
> Caring for nought but to love, to believe.
> Moving through roseate heavenly spaces,
> Towards this 'Whither,' where'er it may be,
> Singeth the bard, in a tumult of rapture,
> Ever becoming a radiant em——

At this point, Daucus Carota uttered a loud croaking cry, and, now dwindled into a little, little carrot, slipped down from Aennchen's lap, and into the ground, leaving no trace behind. Upon which, the great gray fungus which had grown in the nighttime beside the grassy bank, shot up and up. This fungus was nothing less than Herr Dapsul von Zabelthau's gray felt hat, and he himself was under it; he fell stormily on Amandus's breast, crying out in the utmost ecstasy, "Oh, my dearest, best, most beloved Herr Amandus von Nebelstern, with that mighty song of conjuration you have beaten all my cabbalistic science out of the field? What the profoundest magical art, the utmost daring of the philosopher fighting for his very existence, could not accomplish, your verses achieved, passing into the frame of the deceitful Daucus Carota like the deadliest poison, so that he would have perished of stomach-ache, in spite of his gnomish nature, if he had not made off into his kingdom.

"My daughter Anna is delivered—I am delivered from the horrible charm which held me spellbound here in the shape of a nasty fungus, at the risk of being hewn to pieces by my own daughter's hands; for the good soul hacks them all down with her spade, unless their edible character is unmistakable, as in the case of the mushrooms. Thanks, my most heartfelt thanks, and I have no doubt your intentions as regards my daughter have undergone no change. I am sorry to say she has lost her good looks, through the machinations of that inimical gnome; but you are too much of a philosopher to—"

"Oh, dearest papa," cried Aennchen, overjoyed, "just look there! The silken palace is gone! The abominable monster is off and away with all his tribe of salad-princes, cucumber-ministers, and Lord knows what all!" And she ran away to the vegetable garden, delighted, Herr Dapsul following as fast as he could. Herr Amandus went behind them, muttering to himself, "I'm sure I don't know quite what to make of all this. But this I maintain, that that ugly little carrot creature is a vile, prosaic lubber, and none of your poetical kings, or my sublime lay wouldn't have given him the stomach-ache, and sent him scuttling into the ground."

As Fräulein Aennchen was standing in the vegetable garden, where there wasn't the trace of a green blade to be seen, she suddenly felt a sharp pain in the finger which had on the fateful ring. At the same time a cry of piercing sorrow sounded from the ground, and the tip of a carrot peeped out. Guided by her inspiration she quickly took the ring off (it came quite easily this time), stuck it on the carrot, and the latter disappeared while the cry of sorrow ceased. But, oh, wonder of wonders! all at once Fräulein Aennchen was as pretty as ever, well-proportioned, and as fair and white as a country lady can be expected to be. She and her father rejoiced greatly, while Amandus stood puzzled, not knowing what to make of it all.

Fräulein Aennchen took the spade from the maid, who had come running up, and flourished it in the air with a joyful shout of "Now let's set to work," in doing which she was unfortunate enough to deal Herr Amandus such a thwack on the head with it (just at the place where the Sensorium Commune is supposed to be situated) that he fell down as if dead.

Aennchen threw the murderous weapon far from her, cast herself down beside her beloved, and broke out into the most despairing lamentations, while the maid poured the contents of a watering pot over him, and Herr Dapsul quickly ascended the astronomic tower to consult the stars with as little delay as possible as to whether Herr Amandus was dead or not. But it was not long before the latter opened his eyes again, jumped to his legs, clasped Fräulein Aennchen in his arms, and cried, with all the rapture of affection, "Now, my best and dearest Anna, we are one another again."

The very remarkable, scarcely credible effect of this occurrence on the two lovers very soon made itself perceptible. Fräulein Aennchen took a dislike to touching a spade, and she did really reign like a queen over the vegetable world, inasmuch as, though taking care that her vassals were properly supervised and attended to, she set no hand to the work herself, but entrusted it to maids in whom she had confidence.

Herr Amandus, for his part, saw now that everything he had ever written in the shape of verses was wretched, miserable trash, and, burying himself in the works of the real poets, both of ancient and modern times, his being was soon so filled with a beneficent enthusiasm that no room was left for any consideration of himself. He arrived at the conviction that a real poem has got to be something other than a confused jumble of words shaken together under the influence of a crude, jejune delirium, and threw all his own (so-called) poetry, of which he had had such a tremendous opinion, into the fire, becoming once more quite the sensible young gentleman, clear and open in heart and mind, which he had been originally.

And one morning Herr Dapsul did actually come down from his astronomical tower to go to church with Fräulein Aennchen and Herr Amandus von Nebelstern on the occasion of their marriage.

They led an exceedingly happy wedded life. But as to whether Herr Dapsul's union with the Sylph Nehabilah ever actually came to anything the Chronicle of Dapsulheim is silent.

A CATALOG OF SELECTED
DOVER BOOKS
IN ALL FIELDS OF INTEREST

A CATALOG OF SELECTED DOVER
BOOKS IN ALL FIELDS OF INTEREST

CONCERNING THE SPIRITUAL IN ART, Wassily Kandinsky. Pioneering work by father of abstract art. Thoughts on color theory, nature of art. Analysis of earlier masters. 12 illustrations. 80pp. of text. 5⅜ x 8½. 0-486-23411-8

CELTIC ART: The Methods of Construction, George Bain. Simple geometric techniques for making Celtic interlacements, spirals, Kells-type initials, animals, humans, etc. Over 500 illustrations. 160pp. 9 x 12. (Available in U.S. only.) 0-486-22923-8

AN ATLAS OF ANATOMY FOR ARTISTS, Fritz Schider. Most thorough reference work on art anatomy in the world. Hundreds of illustrations, including selections from works by Vesalius, Leonardo, Goya, Ingres, Michelangelo, others. 593 illustrations. 192pp. 7⅛ x 10¼. 0-486-20241-0

CELTIC HAND STROKE-BY-STROKE (Irish Half-Uncial from "The Book of Kells"): An Arthur Baker Calligraphy Manual, Arthur Baker. Complete guide to creating each letter of the alphabet in distinctive Celtic manner. Covers hand position, strokes, pens, inks, paper, more. Illustrated. 48pp. 8¼ x 11. 0-486-24336-2

EASY ORIGAMI, John Montroll. Charming collection of 32 projects (hat, cup, pelican, piano, swan, many more) specially designed for the novice origami hobbyist. Clearly illustrated easy-to-follow instructions insure that even beginning papercrafters will achieve successful results. 48pp. 8¼ x 11. 0-486-27298-2

BLOOMINGDALE'S ILLUSTRATED 1886 CATALOG: Fashions, Dry Goods and Housewares, Bloomingdale Brothers. Famed merchants' extremely rare catalog depicting about 1,700 products: clothing, housewares, firearms, dry goods, jewelry, more. Invaluable for dating, identifying vintage items. Also, copyright-free graphics for artists, designers. Co-published with Henry Ford Museum & Greenfield Village. 160pp. 8¼ x 11. 0-486-25780-0

THE ART OF WORLDLY WISDOM, Baltasar Gracian. "Think with the few and speak with the many," "Friends are a second existence," and "Be able to forget" are among this 1637 volume's 300 pithy maxims. A perfect source of mental and spiritual refreshment, it can be opened at random and appreciated either in brief or at length. 128pp. 5⅜ x 8½. 0-486-44034-6

JOHNSON'S DICTIONARY: A Modern Selection, Samuel Johnson (E. L. McAdam and George Milne, eds.). This modern version reduces the original 1755 edition's 2,300 pages of definitions and literary examples to a more manageable length, retaining the verbal pleasure and historical curiosity of the original. 480pp. 5³⁄₁₆ x 8¼. 0-486-44089-3

ADVENTURES OF HUCKLEBERRY FINN, Mark Twain, Illustrated by E. W. Kemble. A work of eternal richness and complexity, a source of ongoing critical debate, and a literary landmark, Twain's 1885 masterpiece about a barefoot boy's journey of self-discovery has enthralled readers around the world. This handsome clothbound reproduction of the first edition features all 174 of the original black-and-white illustrations. 368pp. 5⅜ x 8½. 0-486-44322-1

CATALOG OF DOVER BOOKS

LIGHT AND SHADE: A Classic Approach to Three-Dimensional Drawing, Mrs. Mary P. Merrifield. Handy reference clearly demonstrates principles of light and shade by revealing effects of common daylight, sunshine, and candle or artificial light on geometrical solids. 13 plates. 64pp. 5⅜ x 8½. 0-486-44143-1

ASTROLOGY AND ASTRONOMY: A Pictorial Archive of Signs and Symbols, Ernst and Johanna Lehner. Treasure trove of stories, lore, and myth, accompanied by more than 300 rare illustrations of planets, the Milky Way, signs of the zodiac, comets, meteors, and other astronomical phenomena. 192pp. 8⅜ x 11.
0-486-43981-X

JEWELRY MAKING: Techniques for Metal, Tim McCreight. Easy-to-follow instructions and carefully executed illustrations describe tools and techniques, use of gems and enamels, wire inlay, casting, and other topics. 72 line illustrations and diagrams. 176pp. 8¼ x 10⅞. 0-486-44043-5

MAKING BIRDHOUSES: Easy and Advanced Projects, Gladstone Califf. Easy-to-follow instructions include diagrams for everything from a one-room house for bluebirds to a forty-two-room structure for purple martins. 56 plates; 4 figures. 80pp. 8¾ x 6⅜. 0-486-44183-0

LITTLE BOOK OF LOG CABINS: How to Build and Furnish Them, William S. Wicks. Handy how-to manual, with instructions and illustrations for building cabins in the Adirondack style, fireplaces, stairways, furniture, beamed ceilings, and more. 102 line drawings. 96pp. 8¾ x 6⅜. 0-486-44259-4

THE SEASONS OF AMERICA PAST, Eric Sloane. From "sugaring time" and strawberry picking to Indian summer and fall harvest, a whole year's activities described in charming prose and enhanced with 79 of the author's own illustrations. 160pp. 8¼ x 11. 0-486-44220-9

THE METROPOLIS OF TOMORROW, Hugh Ferriss. Generous, prophetic vision of the metropolis of the future, as perceived in 1929. Powerful illustrations of towering structures, wide avenues, and rooftop parks—all features in many of today's modern cities. 59 illustrations. 144pp. 8¼ x 11. 0-486-43727-2

THE PATH TO ROME, Hilaire Belloc. This 1902 memoir abounds in lively vignettes from a vanished time, recounting a pilgrimage on foot across the Alps and Apennines in order to "see all Europe which the Christian Faith has saved." 77 of the author's original line drawings complement his sparkling prose. 272pp. 5⅜ x 8½.
0-486-44001-X

THE HISTORY OF RASSELAS: Prince of Abissinia, Samuel Johnson. Distinguished English writer attacks eighteenth-century optimism and man's unrealistic estimates of what life has to offer. 112pp. 5⅜ x 8½. 0-486-44094-X

A VOYAGE TO ARCTURUS, David Lindsay. A brilliant flight of pure fancy, where wild creatures crowd the fantastic landscape and demented torturers dominate victims with their bizarre mental powers. 272pp. 5⅜ x 8½. 0-486-44198-9

Paperbound unless otherwise indicated. Available at your book dealer, online at **www.doverpublications.com**, or by writing to Dept. GI, Dover Publications, Inc., 31 East 2nd Street, Mineola, NY 11501. For current price information or for free catalogs (please indicate field of interest), write to Dover Publications or log on to **www.doverpublications.com** and see every Dover book in print. Dover publishes more than 500 books each year on science, elementary and advanced mathematics, biology, music, art, literary history, social sciences, and other areas.

ON RESERVE FOR:

Hum 220-F08
Ger 391 512

DATE DUE